The Collected Supernatural and Weird Fiction of Edgar Allan Poe Volume 2

The Collected Supernatural and Weird Fiction of Edgar Allan Poe Volume 2

Including Two Novelettes
"The Gold-Bug," and "The Murders in the Rue Morgue," Twenty-Eight Short Stories, One Prose "Eureka" and Eleven Poems of the Strange and Unusual

Edgar Allan Poe

LEONAUR

The Collected
Supernatural and Weird
Fiction of
Edgar Allan Poe
Volume 2
Including Two Novelettes "The Gold-Bug," and "The Murders in the Rue Morgue,"
Twenty-Eight Short Stories, One Prose "Eureka" and Eleven Poems
of the Strange and Unusual
by Edgar Allan Poe

FIRST EDITION

Leonaur is an imprint
of Oakpast Ltd

ISBN: 978-1-78282-180-9 (hardcover)
ISBN:978-1-78282-181-6 (softcover)

http://www.leonaur.com

Publisher's Notes

Contents

Introduction

By John Buchan

Last year a selection of Emerson's writings was issued in this series, and it seems desirable to follow it with a collection of the best work of that American writer who, morally and intellectually, was Emerson's extreme antitype. There could be no harsher contrast than between the careers of the two men. One came early to recognition, and lived his simple, blameless, prosperous life amid the plaudits of the world. The other died young after a career of bitter drudgery, and left little behind him but a legacy of hate. In Edgar Allan Poe genius burned with no "hard, gem-like flame," but with a murky intensity that scandalised his contemporaries. In the orderly *bourgeois* world of young America he moved like a panther among polar-bears. No nation least of all a young, self-satisfied nation likes to be told that it is "one vast perambulating humbug," and he spoke his opinions equally plainly of his colleagues in literature.

The natural result followed. Every species of literary vulture battened on his reputation, the scandals of his life were magnified, and his genius was hidden by a cloud of vulgar abuse. No man was less, fortunate in his epoch and his country. He found an America, middle-class, prosaic, still half Puritan and indomitably respectable, and he ran his head against the stone walls which hemmed him in. He wrote his great stories for starvation wages, since the taste which could value them had largely to be created. Had he lived today, we can well imagine that a more cosmopolitan America would have made him a hero almost beyond his deserts. Had he fared less hardly at the world's hands, there might have been no gall in his pen and fewer dark places in his life.

His posthumous reward has been great, for to no other American writer has it been given to exercise so profound an influence at once on English and French literature. For myself, I should rank him, in the hierarchy of American prose, below Hawthorne, who seems to me to have combined a profounder moral insight with an equal sense of form and an equal imaginative force; but certainly, save for Hawthorne, he has no rival.

The tragic story of his life has been often written: one of the best short biographies is that by Professor Harrison of Virginia, which is prefixed to the recent *Virginia Edition* of his works. He was born in 1809, the same year which gave to the world Tennyson, Gladstone, Lincoln, Darwin, Mendelssohn, and Chopin. It is part of the irony of his fate that Boston, the city which he hated like the plague, should have had the honour of giving him birth. He came of good stock, originally from Ulster; his parents were on the stage, and lived a roving, unhappy, impecunious life, both dying shortly after he was born. He was adopted by an elderly Scotsman called Allan, a merchant in Richmond, Virginia; and till his adopted father's second marriage regarded himself, and was regarded by others, as his heir. He spent some years at school in England, where he imbibed the romance of an older country, and then went at an early age to the University of Virginia.

He did not greatly distinguish himself there in scholarship, but became noted as a Ion vivant and an athlete. He next went to the famous West Point Academy, and afterwards, Allan having died without leaving him anything, turned to journalism as a profession. For the rest of his days he was tied to the drudgery of the pen, and wrote for his bread tales, poems, reviews, essays, any kind of work, much of it strangely bad, but some of an excellence which no contemporary could claim. He made many enemies, and his wild neurotic nature kept him always in a state of white-heat, a fury either of affection or dislike. He took to drink and drugs, though he was never an ordinary drunkard, seeking a stimulant or a narcotic to relieve the misery of his daily life. His end was as tragic and strange as his life. Passing through Baltimore, he seems to have been drinking in a tavern, where he was drugged by some electioneering roughs and carried round in their custody to the different voting-booths. He never recovered from the treatment, and a few days later died in hospital.

To most people Poe is best known as a poet, and the poems which have the widest vogue are unfortunately his worst productions. *The Raven* was, in his own words, to be composed of "equal proportions of Beauty and Quaintness intermingled with Melancholy." The result was a parody of his peculiar qualities, and the parody, as in the similar case of *The Bells*, has been accepted for the original. That sinister fowl has stood between him and the highest kind of poetic fame. "The vagueness of exaltation," he wrote, "aroused by a sweet air (which should be strictly indefinite and never too strongly suggestive) is precisely what we should aim at in poetry." It is a narrow definition, but in his small body of verse he repeatedly reaches the ideal. *To Helen, The City in the Sea, The Haunted Palace, To One in Paradise, The Sleeper, For Annie, Annabel Lee*, and even beautiful nonsense like *Ulalume*, have all the strange haunting sweetness of music.

On his own definition Poe is a master-singer, and on any definition he is a true lyric poet. But his real medium was prose, for, apart from gifts of style and melody, he had in the highest degree the constructive imagination which can reproduce a realm of fancy with the minute realism of everyday life. He reveals all around us the shadowy domain of the back-world, and behind our smug complacency the shrieking horror of the unknown. There is no humour in him, none of that wise detachment which makes *Wandering Willie's* Tale immortal, for every nerve, as he writes, quivers at the terrors he is conjuring. To this imaginative intensity he added a style of singular flexibility and grace. He has, to be sure, appalling lapses into the banal, but at his best he has a store of apt and jewelled words in which to clothe his recondite thoughts.

It is this combination which endeared him to Théophile

Gautier and his school, and gave him Baudelaire and Mallarmé as his translators. But style and imagination, if left alone, might have landed him in an unprofitable mysticism. What gives him his unique power is the mathematical accuracy of his mind. All his life he had a passion for cryptographs, and maintained that human ingenuity could create no cipher which human ingenuity could not unravel. His mind worked on data with the most logical precision, and he once startled Dickens by predicting the whole plot of *Barnaby Rudge* from the material furnished in the earlier chapters. Hence in all his tales there is a clear sequence of cause and effect which gives them an imaginative coherence and verisimilitude.

Without this gift his fancy would have lost itself in vague flights and barren splendours. The conjunction of such very different talents gives him a right to a high place among the masters of the short story, in his own genre perhaps to the highest place, for I know no French imitator who can produce the haunting sense of fate which we get from *The Fall of the House of Usher*, or the devilish horror of *The Cask of Amontillado*. How admirable, too, are his mystifications, *The Murders in the Rue Morgue* or *The Gold-Bug*. Sometimes, as in *Berenice*, his "mortuary turn of mind" carries him too far for serious art; but he makes amends in tales like *The Narrative of A. Gordon Pym*, where his imagination works soberly and convincingly among realities.

It is a fascinating but barren game which critics sometimes indulge in to discuss which is the best short story in the world. If I were put on oath I should decide for Scott's *Wandering Willie's Tale*, and give the second place to Mr. Kipling's *Man who would be King*. But such a classification, like the Cambridge Senior Wranglership, is captious and unintelligent. A more sensible form of the game is to create a small first-class, say of a dozen. Here it is possible to get something nearer a general agreement. Most people would give one place to Scott (*Wandering Willie's Tale*); one to Stevenson (*Thrawn Janet*, perhaps); one to Hawthorne (the choice is large); one place each to Tourgeniev, Balzac, Guy de Maupassant, Daudet, Anatole France, and Mr. Kipling. In the remaining three I should include Mr. Joseph Conrad's *Youth*, and the two other places I should leave to Poe. The truth seems to be that while Poe wrote nothing that wholly transcends his rivals in his own sphere, he wrote more stories that reach the level of the very best. He deserves two places in a roll of honour where the others have only one.

In an excellent recent essay Mr. Hamilton W. Mabie discusses Poe's place in American literature, and finds in his complete aloofness from vulgar ideals, his exquisite craftsmanship, and his devotion to an austere art for its own sake the example which was especially needed by his generation. He sought above all things distinction, and to a nation which was apt to content itself with the gods of the market-place he preached in his strange way a wholesome lesson. "The final justification of a democracy lies in its ability to clear the way for superiority." The democracy which suffered under his lash is at last beginning to realise the superiority of its critic. So far he is the one great surprise of American letters. A shrewd observer, after the Revolution, might have predicted Longfellow and Emerson and Holmes and Hawthorne, but it would have passed the wit of man to foretell Poe.

J. B.

Berenice

Dicebant mihi sodales, si sepulchrum amicae visitarem, curas meas aliquantulum fore levatas.—Ebn Zaiat.

Misery is manifold. The wretchedness of earth is multiform. Overreaching the wide horizon as the rainbow, its hues are as various as the hues of that arch—as distinct too, yet as intimately blended. Overreaching the wide horizon as the rainbow! How is it that from beauty I have derived a type of unloveliness?—from the covenant of peace, a simile of sorrow? But as, in ethics, evil is a consequence of good, so, in fact, out of joy is sorrow born. Either the memory of past bliss is the anguish of today, or the agonies which *are*, have their origin in the ecstasies which *might have been*.

My baptismal name is Egaeus; that of my family I will not mention. Yet there are no towers in the land more time-honored than my gloomy, gray, hereditary halls. Our line has been called a race of visionaries; and in many striking particulars—in the character of the family mansion—in the frescos of the chief saloon—in the tapestries of the dormitories—in the chiselling of some buttresses in the armory—but more especially in the gallery of antique paintings—in the fashion of the library chamber—and, lastly, in the very peculiar nature of the library's contents—there is more than sufficient evidence to warrant the belief.

The recollections of my earliest years are connected with that chamber, and with its volumes—of which latter I will say no more. Here died my mother. Herein was I born. But it is mere idleness to say that I had not lived before—that the soul has no previous existence. You deny it?—let us not argue the matter. Convinced myself, I seek not to convince. There is, however, a remembrance of aerial forms—of spiritual and meaning eyes—of sounds, musical yet sad—a remembrance which will not be excluded; a memory like a shadow—vague, variable, indefinite, unsteady; and like a shadow, too, in the impossibility of my getting rid of it while the sunlight of my reason shall exist.

In that chamber was I born. Thus awaking from the long night of what seemed, but was not, nonentity, at once into the very regions of fairy land—into a palace of imagination—into the wild dominions of monastic thought and erudition—it is not singular that I gazed around me with a startled and ardent eye—that I loitered away my boyhood in books, and dissipated my youth in reverie; but it *is* singular that as years rolled away, and the noon of manhood found me still in the mansion of my fathers—it *is* wonderful what stagnation there fell upon the springs of my life—wonderful how total an inversion took place in the character of my commonest thought. The realities of the world affected me as visions, and as visions only, while the wild ideas of the land of dreams became, in turn, not the material of my every-day existence, but in very deed that existence utterly and solely in itself.

******

Berenice and I were cousins, and we grew up together in my paternal halls. Yet differently we grew—I, ill of health, and buried in gloom—she, agile, graceful, and overflowing with energy; hers, the ramble on the hill-side—mine the studies of the cloister; I, living within my own heart, and addicted, body and soul, to the most intense and painful meditation—she, roaming carelessly through life, with no thought of the shadows in her path, or the silent flight of the raven-winged hours. Berenice!—I call upon her name—Berenice!—and from the gray ruins of memory a thousand tumultuous recollections are startled at the sound! Ah, vividly is her image before me now, as in the early days of her light-heartedness and joy!

Oh, gorgeous yet fantastic beauty! Oh, sylph amid the shrubberies of Arnheim! Oh, Naiad among its fountains! And then—then all is mystery and terror, and a tale which should not be told. Disease—a fatal disease, fell like the *simoon* upon her frame; and, even while I gazed upon her, the spirit of change swept over her, pervading her mind, her habits, and her character, and, in a manner the most subtle and terrible, disturbing even the identity of her person! Alas! the destroyer came and went!—and the victim—where is she? I knew her not—or knew her no longer as Berenice.

Among the numerous train of maladies superinduced by that fatal and primary one which effected a revolution of so horrible a kind in the moral and physical being of my cousin, may be mentioned as the most distressing and obstinate in its nature, a species of epilepsy not unfrequently terminating in *trance* itself—trance very nearly resembling positive dissolution, and from which her manner of recovery was in most instances, startlingly abrupt. In the meantime my own disease—for I have been told that I should call it by no other appellation—my own disease, then, grew rapidly upon me, and assumed finally a monomaniac character of a novel and extraordinary form—hourly and momently gaining vigour—and at length obtaining over me the most incomprehensible ascendancy.

This monomania, if I must so term it, consisted in a morbid irritability of those properties of the mind in metaphysical science termed the *attentive*. It is more than probable that I am not understood; but I fear, indeed, that it is in no manner possible to convey to the mind of the merely general reader, an adequate idea of that nervous *intensity of interest* with which, in my case, the powers of meditation (not to speak technically) busied and buried themselves, in the contemplation of even the most ordinary objects of the universe.

To muse for long unwearied hours, with my attention riveted to some frivolous device on the margin, or in the typography of a book; to become absorbed, for the better part of a summer's day, in a quaint shadow falling aslant upon the tapestry or upon the floor; to lose myself, for an entire night, in watching the steady flame of a lamp, or the embers of a fire; to dream away whole days over the perfume of a flower; to repeat, monotonously, some common word, until the sound, by dint of frequent repetition, ceased to convey any idea whatever to the mind; to lose all sense of motion or physical existence, by means of absolute bodily quiescence long and obstinately persevered in: such were a few of the most common and least pernicious vagaries induced by a condition of the mental faculties, not, indeed, altogether unparalleled, but certainly bidding defiance to anything like analysis or explanation.

Yet let me not be misapprehended. The undue, earnest, and morbid attention thus excited by objects in their own nature frivolous, must not be confounded in character with that ruminating propensity common to all mankind, and more especially indulged in by persons of ardent imagination. It was not even, as might be at first supposed, an extreme condition, or exaggeration of such propensity, but primarily and essentially distinct and different. In the one instance, the dreamer, or enthusiast, being interested by an object usually *not* frivolous, imperceptibly loses sight of this object in a wilderness of deductions and suggestions issuing therefrom, until, at the conclusion of a day dream *often replete with luxury*, he finds the *incitamentum*, or first cause of his musings, entirely vanished and forgotten.

In my case, the primary object was *invariably frivolous*, although assuming, through the medium of my distempered vision, a refracted and unreal importance. Few deductions, if any, were made; and those few pertinaciously returning in upon the original object as a centre. The meditations were *never* pleasurable; and, at the termination of the reverie, the first cause, so far from being out of sight, had attained that supernaturally exaggerated interest which was the prevailing feature of the disease. In a word, the powers of mind more particularly exercised were, with me, as I have said before, the *attentive*, and are, with the day-dreamer, the *speculative*.

My books, at this epoch, if they did not actually serve to irritate the disorder, partook, it will be perceived, largely, in their imaginative and inconsequential nature, of the characteristic qualities of the disorder itself. I well remember, among others, the treatise of the noble Italian, Coelius Secundus Curio, *De Amplitudine Beati Regni Dei;* St. Austin's great work, the *City of God*; and Tertullian's *De Carne Christi*, in which the paradoxical sentence "*Mortuus est Dei filius; credible est quia ineptum est: et sepultus resurrexit; certum est quia impossibile est,*" occupied my undivided time, for many weeks of laborious and fruitless investigation.

Thus it will appear that, shaken from its balance only by trivial things, my reason bore resemblance to that ocean-crag spoken of by Ptolemy Hephestion, which steadily resisting the attacks of human violence, and the fiercer fury of the waters and the winds, trembled only to the touch of the flower called Asphodel. And although, to a careless thinker, it might appear a matter beyond doubt, that the alteration produced by her unhappy malady, in the *moral* condition of Berenice, would afford me many objects for the exercise of that intense and abnormal meditation whose nature I have been at some trouble in explaining, yet such was not in any degree the case.

In the lucid intervals of my infirmity, her calamity, indeed, gave me pain, and, taking deeply to heart that total wreck of her fair and gentle life, I did not fail to ponder, frequently and bitterly, upon the wonder-working means by which so strange a revolution had been so suddenly brought to pass. But these reflections partook not of the idiosyncrasy of my disease, and were such as would have occurred, under similar circumstances, to the ordinary mass of mankind. True to its own character, my disorder revelled in the less important but more startling changes wrought in the *physical* frame of Berenice—in the singular and most appalling distortion of her personal identity.

During the brightest days of her unparalleled beauty, most surely I had never loved her. In the strange anomaly of my existence, feelings with me, *had never been* of the heart, and my passions *always were* of the mind. Through the gray of the early morning—among the trellised shadows of the forest at noon-day—and in the silence of my library at night—she had flitted by my eyes, and I had seen her—not as the living and breathing Berenice, but as the Berenice of a dream; not as a being of the earth, earthy, but as the abstraction of such a being; not as a thing to admire, but to analyze; not as an object of love, but as the theme of the most abstruse although desultory speculation. And *now*—now I shuddered in her presence, and grew pale at her approach; yet, bitterly lamenting her fallen and desolate condition, I called to mind that she had loved me long, and, in an evil moment, I spoke to her of marriage.

And at length the period of our nuptials was approaching, when, upon an afternoon in the winter of the year—one of those unseasonably warm, calm, and misty days which are the nurse of the beautiful Halcyon[1],—I sat, (and sat, as I thought, alone,) in the inner apartment of the library. But, uplifting my eyes, I saw that Berenice stood before me.

Was it my own excited imagination—or the misty influence of the atmosphere—or the uncertain twilight of the chamber—or the gray draperies which fell around her figure—that caused in it so vacillating and indistinct an outline? I could not tell. She spoke no word; and I—not for worlds could I have uttered a syllable. An icy chill ran through my frame; a sense of insufferable anxiety oppressed me; a consuming curiosity pervaded my soul; and sinking back upon the chair, I remained for some time breathless and motionless, with my eyes riveted upon her person. Alas! its emaciation was excessive, and not one vestige of the former being lurked in any single line of the contour. My burning glances at length fell upon the face.

The forehead was high, and very pale, and singularly placid; and the once jetty hair fell partially over it, and overshadowed the hollow temples with innumerable ringlets, now of a vivid yellow, and jarring discordantly, in their fantastic character, with the reigning melancholy of the countenance. The eyes were lifeless, and lustreless, and seemingly pupilless, and I shrank involun-

1. For as Jove, during the winter season, gives twice seven days of warmth, men have called this element and temperate time the nurse of the beautiful Halcyon—*Simonides*

tarily from their glassy stare to the contemplation of the thin and shrunken lips. They parted; and in a smile of peculiar meaning, *the teeth* of the changed Berenice disclosed themselves slowly to my view. Would to God that I had never beheld them, or that, having done so, I had died!

******

The shutting of a door disturbed me, and, looking up, I found that my cousin had departed from the chamber. But from the disordered chamber of my brain, had not, alas! departed, and would not be driven away, the white and ghastly *spectrum* of the teeth. Not a speck on their surface—not a shade on their enamel—not an indenture in their edges—but what that period of her smile had sufficed to brand in upon my memory. I saw them *now* even more unequivocally than I beheld them *then*. The teeth!—the teeth!—they were here, and there, and everywhere, and visibly and palpably before me; long, narrow, and excessively white, with the pale lips writhing about them, as in the very moment of their first terrible development. Then came the full fury of my *monomania*, and I struggled in vain against its strange and irresistible influence. In the multiplied objects of the external world I had no thoughts but for the teeth. For these I longed with a phrenzied desire.

All other matters and all different interests became absorbed in their single contemplation. They—they alone were present to the mental eye, and they, in their sole individuality, became the essence of my mental life. I held them in every light. I turned them in every attitude. I surveyed their characteristics. I dwelt upon their peculiarities. I pondered upon their conformation. I mused upon the alteration in their nature. I shuddered as I assigned to them in imagination a sensitive and sentient power, and even when unassisted by the lips, a capability of moral expression.

Of Mademoiselle Salle it has been well said, "*Que tous ses pas etaient des sentiments*," and of Berenice I more seriously believed *que toutes ses dents etaient des idees. Des idees!*—ah here was the idiotic thought that destroyed me! *Des idees!*—ah *therefore* it was that I coveted them so madly! I felt that their possession could alone ever restore me to peace, in giving me back to reason.

And the evening closed in upon me thus—and then the darkness came, and tarried, and went—and the day again dawned—and the mists of a second night were now gathering around—and still I sat motionless in that solitary room—and still I sat buried in meditation—and still the *phantasma* of the teeth maintained its terrible ascendancy, as, with the most vivid hideous distinctness, it floated about amid the changing lights and shadows of the chamber. At length there broke in upon my dreams a cry as of horror and dismay; and thereunto, after a pause, succeeded the sound of troubled voices, intermingled with many low moanings of sorrow or of pain. I arose from my seat, and throwing open one of the doors of the library, saw standing out in the ante-chamber a servant maiden, all in tears, who told me that Berenice was—no more! She had been seized with epilepsy in the early morning, and now, at the closing in of the night, the grave was ready for its tenant, and all the preparations for the burial were completed.

******

I found myself sitting in the library, and again sitting there alone. It seemed that I had newly awakened from a confused and exciting dream. I knew that it was now midnight, and I was well aware, that since the setting of the sun, Berenice had been interred. But of that dreary period which intervened I had no positive, at least no definite comprehension. Yet its memory was replete with horror—horror more horrible from being vague, and terror more terrible from ambiguity. It was a fearful page in the record my existence, written all over with dim, and hideous, and unintelligible recollections. I strived to decipher them, but in vain; while ever and anon, like the spirit of a departed sound, the shrill and piercing shriek of a female voice seemed to be ringing in my ears. I had done a deed—what was it? I asked myself the question aloud, and the whispering echoes of the chamber answered me,—"*What was it?*"

On the table beside me burned a lamp, and near it lay a little box. It was of no remarkable character, and I had seen it frequently before, for it was the property of the family physician; but how came it *there*, upon my table, and why did I shudder in regarding it? These things were in no manner to be accounted for, and my eyes at length dropped to the open pages of a book, and to a sentence underscored therein. The words were the singular but simple ones of the poet Ebn Zaiat:—"*Dicebant mihi sodales si sepulchrum amicae visitarem, curas meas aliquantulum fore levatas.*" Why then, as I perused them, did the hairs of my head erect themselves on end, and the blood of my body become congealed within my veins?

There came a light tap at the library door—and, pale as the tenant of a tomb, a menial entered upon tiptoe. His looks were wild with terror, and he spoke to me in a voice tremulous, husky, and very low. What said he?—some broken sentences I heard. He told of a wild cry disturbing the silence of the night—of the gathering together of the household—of a search in the direction of the sound; and then his tones grew thrillingly distinct as he whispered me of a violated grave—of a disfigured body enshrouded, yet still breathing—still palpitating—*still alive*!

He pointed to garments;—they were muddy and clotted with gore. I spoke not, and he took me gently by the hand: it was indented with the impress of human nails. He directed my attention to some object against the wall. I looked at it for some minutes: it was a spade. With a shriek I bounded to the table, and grasped the box that lay upon it. But I could not force it open; and in my tremor, it slipped from my hands, and fell heavily, and burst into pieces; and from it, with a rattling sound, there rolled out some instruments of dental surgery, intermingled with thirty-two small, white and ivory-looking substances that were scattered to and fro about the floor.

A Descent into the Maelström

The ways of God in Nature, as in Providence, are not as our ways; nor are the models that we frame any way commensurate to the vastness, profundity, and unsearchableness of His works, which have a depth in them greater than the well of Democritus.

Joseph Glanville.

We had now reached the summit of the loftiest crag. For some minutes the old man seemed too much exhausted to speak.

"Not long ago," said he at length, "and I could have guided you on this route as well as the youngest of my sons; but, about three years past, there happened to me an event such as never happened before to mortal man—or at least such as no man ever survived to tell of—and the six hours of deadly terror which I then endured have broken me up body and soul. You suppose me a *very* old man—but I am not. It took less than a single day to change these hairs from a jetty black to white, to weaken my limbs, and to unstring my nerves, so that I tremble at the least exertion, and am frightened at a shadow. Do you know I can scarcely look over this little cliff without getting giddy?"

The "little cliff," upon whose edge he had so carelessly thrown himself down to rest that the weightier portion of his body hung over it, while he was only kept from falling by the tenure of his elbow on its extreme and slippery edge—this "little cliff" arose, a sheer unobstructed precipice of black shining rock, some fifteen or sixteen hundred feet from the world of crags beneath us. Nothing would have tempted me to within half-a-dozen yards of its brink. In truth so deeply was I excited by the perilous position of my companion, that I fell at full length upon the ground, clung to the shrubs around me, and dared not even glance upward at the sky—while I struggled in vain to divest myself of the idea that the very foundations of the mountain were in danger from the fury of the winds. It was long before I could reason myself into sufficient courage to sit up and look out into the distance.

"You must get over these fancies," said the guide, "for I have brought you here that you might have the best possible view of the scene of that event I mentioned—and to tell you the whole story with the spot just under your eye."

"We are now," he continued in that particularising manner which distinguished him—"we are now close upon the Norwegian coast—in the sixty-eighth degree of latitude—in the great province of Nordland—and in the dreary district of Lofoden. The mountain upon whose top we sit is Helseggen, the Cloudy. Now raise yourself up a little higher—hold on to the grass if you feel giddy—so—and look out, beyond the belt of vapour beneath us, into the sea."

I looked dizzily, and beheld a wide expanse of ocean, whose waters wore so inky a hue as to bring at once to my mind the Nubian geographer's account of the *Mare Tenebrarum*. A panorama more deplorably desolate no human imagination can conceive. To the right and left as far as the eye could reach, there lay outstretched, like ramparts of the world, lines of horridly black and beetling cliff, whose character of gloom was but the more forcibly illustrated by the surf which reared high up against it its white and ghastly crest, howling and shrieking for ever. Just opposite the promontory upon whose apex we were placed, and at a distance of some five or six miles out at sea, there was visible a small, bleak-looking island; or, more properly, its position was discernible through the wilderness of surge in which it was enveloped. About two miles nearer the land arose another of smaller size, hideously craggy and barren, and encompassed at various intervals by a cluster of dark rocks.

The appearance of the ocean, in the space between the more

distant island and the shore, had something very unusual about it. Although at the time so strong a gale was blowing landward that a brig in the remote offing lay to under a double-reefed trysail, and constantly plunged her whole hull out of sight, still there was here nothing like a regular swell, but only a short, quick, angry cross dashing of water in every direction—as well in the teeth of the wind as otherwise. Of foam there was little except in the immediate vicinity of the rocks.

"The island in the distance," resumed the old man, "is called by the Norwegians Vurrgh. The one midway is Moskoe. That a mile to the northward is Ambaaren. Yonder are Islesen, Hotholm, Keildhelm, Suarven. and Buckholm. Farther off—between Moskoe and Vurrgh—are Otterholm, Flimen, Sandflesen, and Stockholm. These are the true names of the places—but why it has been thought necessary to name them at all, is more than cither you or I can understand. Do you hear anything? Do you see any change in the water?"

We had now been about ten minutes upon the top of Helseggen, to which we had ascended from the interior of Lofoden, so that we had caught no glimpse of the sea until it had burst upon us from the summit. As the old man spoke, I became aware of a loud and gradually increasing sound, like the moaning of a vast herd of buffaloes upon an American prairie; and at the same moment I perceived that what seamen term the *chopping* character of the ocean beneath us, was rapidly changing into a current which set to the eastward.

Even while I gazed this current acquired a monstrous velocity. Each moment added to its speed—to its headlong impetuosity. In five minutes the whole sea as far as Vurrgh was lashed into ungovernable fury; but it was between Moskoe and the coast that the main uproar held its sway. Here the vast bed of the waters, seamed and scarred into a thousand conflicting channels, burst suddenly into frenzied convulsion—heaving, boiling, hissing,—gyrating in gigantic and innumerable vortices, and all whirling and plunging on to the eastward with a rapidity which water never elsewhere assumes except in precipitous descents.

In a few minutes more, there came over the scene another radical alteration. The general surface grew somewhat more smooth, and the whirlpools one by one disappeared, while prodigious streaks of foam became apparent where none had been seen before. These streaks, at length, spreading out to a great distance, and entering into combination, took unto themselves the gyratory motion of the subsided vortices, and seemed to form the germ of another more vast. Suddenly—very suddenly—this assumed a distinct and definite existence in a circle of more than a mile in diameter. The edge of the whirl was represented by a broad belt of gleaming spray; but no particle of this slipped into the mouth of the terrific funnel, whose interior, as far as the eye could fathom it, was a smooth, shining, and jet-black wall of water, inclined to the horizon at an angle of some forty-five degrees, speeding dizzily round and round with a swaying and sweltering motion, and sending forth to the winds an appalling voice, half-shriek, half-roar, such as not even the mighty cataract of Niagara ever lifts up in its agony to Heaven.

The mountain trembled to its very base, and the rock rocked. I threw myself upon my face, and clung to the scant herbage in an excess of nervous agitation.

"This," said I at length, to the old man—"this can be nothing else than the great whirlpool of the *Maelström*."

"So it is sometimes termed," said he. "We Norwegians call it the *Moskoe-ström*, from the island of Moskoe in the midway."

The ordinary accounts of this vortex had by no means prepared me for what I saw. That of Jonas Ramus, which is perhaps the most circumstantial of any, cannot impart the faintest conception either of the magnificence, or of the horror of the scene or of the wild bewildering sense of *the novel* which confounds the beholder. I am not sure from what point of view the writer in question surveyed it, nor at what time; but it could neither have been from the summit of Helseggen, nor during a storm. There are some passages of his description, nevertheless, which may be quoted for their details, although their effect is exceedingly feeble in conveying an impression of the spectacle.

"Between Lofoden and Moskoe," he says, "the depth of the water is between thirty-five and forty fathoms; but on the other side, toward Ver (Vurrgh) this depth decreases so as not to afford a convenient passage for a vessel, without the risk of splitting on the rocks, which happens even in the calmest weather. When it is flood, the stream runs up the country between Lofoden and Moskoe with a boisterous rapidity, but the roar of its impetuous ebb to the sea is scarce equalled by the loudest and most dreadful cataracts—the noise being heard several leagues off, and the vortices or pits are of such an extent and depth, that if a ship comes within its attraction it is inevitably absorbed and carried down to the bottom, and there beat to pieces against the rocks, and when the water relaxes the fragments thereof are thrown up again.

"But these intervals of tranquillity are only at the turn of the ebb and flood, and in calm weather, and last but a quarter of an hour, its violence gradually returning. When the stream is most boisterous, and its fury heightened by a storm, it is dangerous to come within a Norway mile of it. Boats, yachts, and ships have been carried away by not guarding against it before they were within its reach. It likewise happens frequently that whales come too near the stream, and are overpowered by its violence, and then it is impossible to describe their howlings and bellowings in their fruitless struggles to disengage themselves. A bear once, attempting to swim from Lofoden to Moskoe, was caught by the stream and borne down, while he roared terribly, so as to be heard on shore.

"Large stocks of firs and pine trees, after being absorbed by the current, rise again broken and torn to such a degree as if bristles grew upon them. This plainly shows the bottom to consist of craggy rocks, among which they are whirled to and fro. This stream is regulated by the flux and reflux of the sea—it being constantly high and low water every six hours. In the year 1645, early in the morning of *Sexagesima* Sunday, it raged with such noise and impetuosity that the very stones of the houses on the coast fell to the ground."

In regard to the depth of the water, I could not see how this could have been ascertained at all in the immediate vicinity of the vortex. The "forty fathoms" must have reference only to portions of the channel close Upon the shore either of Moskoe or Lofoden. The depth in the centre of the *Moskoe-ström* must be immeasurably greater; and no better proof of this fact is necessary than can be obtained from even the sidelong glance into the abyss of the whirl which may be had from the highest crag of Helseggen. Looking down from this pinnacle upon the howling Phlegethon below, I could not help smiling at the simplicity with which the honest Jonas Ramus records, as a matter difficult of belief, the anecdotes of the whales and the bears; for it appeared to me, in fact, a self-evident thing that the largest ship of the line in existence coming within the influence of that deadly attraction could resist it as little as a feather the hurricane, and must disappear bodily and at once.

The attempts to account for the phenomenon—some of which I remember seemed to me sufficiently plausible in perusal—now wore a very different and unsatisfactory aspect. The idea generally received is that this, as well as three smaller vortices among the Ferroe Islands:

> Have no other cause than the collision of waves rising and falling at flux and reflux against a ridge of rocks and shelves, which confines the water so that it precipitates itself like a cataract; and thus the higher the flood rises the deeper must the fall be, and the natural result of all is a whirlpool or vortex, the prodigious suction of which is sufficiently known by lesser experiments.—These are the words of the *Encyclopaedia Britannica*.

Kircher and others imagine that in the centre of the channel of the *Maelström* is an abyss penetrating the globe, and issuing in some very remote part—the Gulf of Bothnia being somewhat decidedly named in one instance. This opinion, idle in itself, was the one to which, as I gazed, my imagination most readily assented; and, mentioning it to the guide, I was rather surprised to hear him say that, although it was the view almost universally entertained of the subject by the Norwegians, it nevertheless was not his own. As to the former notion he confessed his inability to comprehend it; and here I agreed with him—for, however conclusive on paper, it becomes altogether unintelligible, and even absurd, amid the thunder of the abyss.

"You have had a good look at the whirl now," said the old man, "and if you will creep round this crag so as to get in its lee, and deaden the roar of the water I will tell you a story that will convince you I ought to know something of the *Moskoe-ström*."

I placed myself as desired, and he proceeded.

"Myself and my two brothers once owned a schooner-rigged smack of about seventy tons burthen, with which we were in the habit of fishing among the islands beyond Moskoe, nearly to Vurrgh. In all violent eddies at sea there is good fishing at proper opportunities if one has only the courage to attempt it, but among the whole of the Lofoden coastmen, we three were the only ones who made a regular business of going out to the islands, as I tell you. The usual grounds are a great way lower down to the southward. There fish can be got at all hours, without much risk, and therefore these places are preferred. The choice spots over here among the rocks, however, not only yield the finest variety, but in far greater abundance, so that we often got in a single day what the more timid of the craft could not scrape together in a week. In fact, we made it a matter of desperate speculation—the risk of life standing instead of labour, and courage answering for capital.

"We kept the smack in a cove about five miles higher up the coast than this; and it was our practice, in fine weather, to take advantage of the fifteen minutes' slack to push across the main channel of the *Moskoe-ström*, far above the pool, and then drop down upon anchorage somewhere near Otterholm, or Sandflesen, where the eddies are not so violent as elsewhere. Here we used to remain until nearly time for slack-water again, when we weighed and made for home. We never set out upon this expedition without a steady side wind for going and coming—one that we felt sure would not fail us before our return—and we seldom made a miscalculation upon this point. Twice during six years we were forced to stay all night at anchor on account of a dead calm, which is a rare thing indeed just about here; and once we had to remain on the grounds nearly a week, starving to death, owing to a gale which blew up shortly after our arrival, and made the channel too boisterous to be thought of.

"Upon this occasion we should have been driven out to sea in spite of everything (for the whirlpools threw us round and round so violently that at length we fouled our anchor and dragged it) if it had not been that we drifted into one of the innumerable cross currents—here today and gone tomorrow—which drove us under the lee of Flimen, where, by good luck, we brought up.

"I could not tell you the twentieth part of the difficulties we encountered 'on the grounds'—it is a bad spot to be in, even in good weather—but we made shift always to run the gauntlet of the *Moskoe-ström* itself without accident; although at times my heart has been in my mouth when we happened to be a minute or so behind or before the slack. The wind sometimes was not as strong as we thought it at starting, and then we made rather less way than we could wish, while the current rendered the smack unmanageable. My eldest brother had a son eighteen years old, and I had two stout boys of my own. These would have been of great assistance at such times in using the sweeps, as well as afterward in fishing, but somehow, although we ran the risk ourselves, we had not the heart to let the young ones get into the danger—for, after all is said and done, it *was* a horrible danger, and that is the truth.

"It is now within a few days of three years since what I am going to tell you occurred. It was on the tenth day of July 18—, a day which the people of this part of the world will never forget—for it was one in which blew the most terrible hurricane that ever came out of the heavens; and yet all the morning, and indeed until late in the afternoon, there was a gentle and steady breeze from the south-west, while the sun shone brightly, so that the oldest seaman among us could not have foreseen what was to follow.

"The three of us—my two brothers and myself—had crossed over to the islands about 2 o'clock p.m., and had soon nearly loaded the smack with fine fish, which, we all remarked, were more plentiful that day than we had ever known them. It was just seven *by my watch* when we weighed and started for home, so as to make the worst of the *Ström* at slack water, which we knew would be at eight.

"We set out with a fresh wind on our starboard quarter, and for some time spanked along at a great rate, never dreaming of danger, for indeed we saw not the slightest reason to apprehend it. All at once we were taken aback by a breeze from over Helseggen. This was most unusual—something that had never happened to us before—and I began to feel a little uneasy without exactly knowing why. We put the boat on the wind, but could make no headway at all for the eddies, and I was put upon the point of proposing to return to the anchorage, when, looking astern, we saw the whole horizon covered with a singular copper-coloured cloud that rose with the most amazing velocity.

"In the meantime the breeze that had headed us off fell away, and we were dead becalmed, drifting about in every direction. This state of things, however, did not last long enough to give us time to think about it. In less than a minute the storm was upon us—in less than two the sky was entirely overcast—and what with this and the driving spray it became suddenly so dark that we could not see each other in the smack.

"Such a hurricane as then blew it is folly to attempt describing. The oldest seaman in Norway never experienced anything like it. We had let our sails go by the run before it cleverly took us but, at the first puff, both our masts went by the board as if they had been sawed off—the mainmast taking with it my youngest brother, who had lashed himself to it for safety.

"Our boat was the lightest feather of a thing that ever sat upon water. It had a complete flush deck, with only a small hatch near the bow, and this hatch it had always been our custom to batten down when about to cross the *Ström* by way of precaution against the chopping seas. But for this circumstance we should have foundered at once—for we lay entirely buried for some moments. How my elder brother escaped destruction I cannot say, for I never had an opportunity of ascertaining. For my part, as soon as I had let the foresail run, I threw myself flat on deck, with my feet against the narrow gunwale of the bow, and with my hands grasping a ring-bolt near the foot of the foremast. It was mere instinct that prompted me to do this—which was undoubtedly the very best thing I could have done—for I was too much flurried to think.

"For some moments we were completely deluged, as I say, and all this time I held my breath, and clung to the bolt. When I could stand it no longer I raised myself upon my knees, still keeping hold with my hands, and thus got my head clear. Presently our little boat gave herself a shake, just as a dog does in coming out of the water, and thus rid herself in some measure of the seas. I was now trying to get the better of the stupor that had come over me, and to collect my senses so as to see what was to be done; when I felt somebody grasp my arm. It was my elder brother, and my heart leaped for joy, for I had made sure that he was overboard but the next moment all this joy was turned into horror for he put his mouth close to my ear, and screamed out the word '*Moskoe-ström!*'

"No one ever will know what my feelings were at that moment. I shook from head to foot, as if I had had the most violent fit of the ague. I knew what he meant by that one word well enough—I knew what he wished to make me understand. With the wind that now drove us on we were bound for the whirl of the *Ström*, and nothing could save us!

"You perceive that in crossing the *Ström* channel, we always went a long way up above the whirl, even in the calmest weather, and then had to wait and watch carefully for the slack—but now we were driving right upon the pool itself, and in such a hurricane as this! 'To be sure,' I thought, 'we shall get there just about the slack—there is some little hope in that'—but in the next moment I cursed myself for being so great a fool as to dream of hope at all. I knew very well that we were doomed had we been ten times a ninety-gun ship.

"By this time the first fury of the tempest had spent itself, or perhaps we did not feel it so much as we scudded before it, but at all events the seas, which at first had been kept down by the wind and lay flat and frothing now got up into absolute mountains. A singular change, too, had come over the heavens. Around in every direction it was still as black as pitch, but nearly overhead there burst out, all at once a circular rift of clear sky—as clear as I ever saw, and of a deep bright blue and through it there blazed forth the full moon with a lustre that I never before knew her to wear. She lit up everything about us with the greatest distinctness—but, O God, what a scene it was to light up!

"I now made one or two attempts to speak to my brother—but, in some manner which I could not understand, the din had so increased that I could not make him hear a single word, although I screamed at the top of my voice in his ear. Presently he shook his head, looking as pale as death, and held up one of his fingers as if to say '*listen!*'

"At first I could not make out what he meant—but soon a hideous thought flashed upon me. I dragged my watch from its fob. It was not going. I glanced at its face by the moonlight, and then burst into tears as I flung it far away into the ocean. *It had run down at seven o'clock! We were behind, the time of the slack, and the whirl of the Ström was in full fury!*

"When a boat is well built, properly trimmed, and not deep laden, the waves in a strong gale, when she is going large, seem always to slip from beneath her—which appears very strange to a landsman—and this is what is called *riding*, in sea-phrase. Well, so far we had ridden the swells very cleverly, but presently a gigantic sea happened to take us right under the counter, and bore us with it as it rose—up—up—as if into the sky. I would not have believed that any wave could rise so high. And then down we came with a sweep, a slide, and a plunge, that made me feel sick and dizzy, as if I was falling from some lofty mountain-top in a dream. But while we were up I had thrown a quick glance around—and that one glance was all sufficient. I saw our exact position in an instant. The *Moskoe-ström* whirlpool was about a quarter of a mile dead ahead—but no more like the every-day *Moskoe-ström*, than the whirl as you now see it is like a mill-race. If I had not known where we were, and what we had to expect, I should not have recognised the place at all. As it was, I involuntarily closed my eyes in horror, The lids clenched themselves together as if in a spasm.

"It could not have been more than two minutes afterward until we suddenly felt the waves subside, and were enveloped in foam. The boat made a sharp half turn to larboard, and then shot off in its new direction like a thunderbolt. At the same moment the roaring noise of the water was completely drowned in a kind of shrill shriek—such a sound as you might imagine given out by the waste-pipes of many thousand steam-vessels letting off their steam all together. We were now in the belt of surf that always surrounds the whirl; and I thought of course that another moment would plunge us into the abyss—down which we could only see indistinctly on account of the amazing velocity with which we were borne along. The boat did not seem to sink into the water at all, but to skim like an air-bubble upon the surface of the surge. Her starboard side was next the whirl, and on the larboard arose the world of ocean we had left. It stood like a huge writhing wall between us and the horizon.

"It may appear strange, but now, when we were in the very jaws of the gulf, I felt more composed than when we were only approaching it. Having made up my mind to hope no more, I got rid of a great deal of that terror which unmanned me at first. I suppose it was despair that strung my nerves.

"It may look like boasting—but what I tell you is truth—I began to reflect how magnificent a thing it was to die in such a manner, and how foolish it was in me to think of so paltry a consideration as my own individual life in view of so wonderful a manifestation of God's power. I do believe that I blushed with shame when this idea crossed my mind. After a little while I became possessed with the keenest curiosity about the whirl itself. I positively felt a *wish* to explore its depths, even at the sacrifice I was going to make; and my principal grief was that I should never be able to tell my old companions on shore about the mysteries I should see. These, no doubt, were singular fancies to occupy a man's mind in such extremity, and I have often thought since that the revolutions of the boat around the pool might have rendered me a little light-headed.

"There was another circumstance which tended to restore my self-possession, and this was the cessation of the wind, which could not reach us in our present situation—for, as you saw yourself, the belt of surf is considerably lower than the general bed of the ocean, and this latter now towered above us, a high, black, mountainous ridge. If you have never been at sea in a heavy gale you can form no idea of the confusion of mind occasioned by the wind and spray together. They blind, deafen, and strangle you, and take away all power of action or reflection. But we were now, in a great measure, rid of these annoyances—just as death-condemned felons in prison are allowed petty indulgences, forbidden them while their doom is yet uncertain.

"How often we made the circuit of the belt it is impossible to say. We careered round and round for perhaps an hour, flying rather than floating, getting gradually more and more into the middle of the surge, and then nearer and nearer to its horrible inner edge. All this time I had never let go of the ring-bolt. My brother was at the stern, holding on to a small empty water-cask which had been securely lashed under the coop of the counter, and was the only thing on deck that had not been swept overboard when the gale first took us.

"As we approached the brink of the pit he let go his hold upon this, and made for the ring, from which, in the agony of his terror, he endeavoured to force my hands, as it was not large enough to afford us both a secure grasp. I never felt deeper grief than when I saw him attempt this act—although I knew he was a madman when he did it—a raving maniac through sheer fright. I did not care, however, to contest the point with him. I knew it could make no difference whether either of us held on at all, so I let him have the bolt, and went astern to the cask. This there was no great difficulty in doing, for the smack flew round steadily enough, and upon an even keel, only swaying to and fro with the immense sweeps and swelters of the whirl. Scarcely had I secured myself in my new position when we gave a wild lurch to starboard, and rushed headlong into the abyss. I muttered a hurried prayer to God, and thought all was over.

"As I felt the sickening sweep of the descent I had instinctively tightened my hold upon the barrel, and closed my eyes. For some seconds I dared not open them, while I expected instant destruction, and wondered that I was not already in my death-struggles with the water. But moment after moment elapsed. I still lived. The sense of falling had ceased; and the motion of the vessel seemed much as it had been before while in the belt of foam, with the exception that she now lay more along. I took courage, and looked once again upon the scene.

"Never shall I forget the sensations of awe, horror, and admiration with which I gazed about me. The boat appeared to be hanging, as if by magic, midway down, upon the interior surface of a funnel vast in circumference, prodigious in depth, and whose perfectly smooth sides might have been mistaken for ebony but for the bewildering rapidity with which they spun around, and for the gleaming and ghastly radiance they shot forth, as the rays of the full moon, from that circular rift amid the clouds which I have already described, streamed in a flood of golden glory along the black walls, and far away down into the inmost recesses of the abyss.

"At first I was too much confused to observe anything accurately. The general burst of terrific grandeur was all that I beheld. When I recovered myself a little, however, my gaze fell instinctively downward. In this direction I was able to obtain an unobstructed view from the manner in which the smack hung on the inclined surface of the pool. She was quite upon an even keel—that is to say, her deck lay in a plane parallel with that of the water—but this latter sloped at an angle of more than forty-five degrees, so that we seemed to be lying upon our beam-ends. I could not help observing, nevertheless, that I had scarcely more difficulty in maintaining my hold and footing in this situation than if we had been upon a dead level, and this, I suppose, was owing to the speed at which we revolved.

"The rays of the moon seemed to search the very bottom of the profound gulf; but still I could make out nothing distinctly, on account of a thick mist in which everything there was enveloped, and over which there hung a magnificent rainbow, like that narrow and tottering bridge which Mussulmen say is the only pathway between Time and Eternity. This mist or spray was no doubt occasioned by the clashing of the great walls of the funnel as they all met together at the bottom, but the yell that went up to the Heavens from out of that mist I dare not attempt to describe.

"Our first slide into the abyss itself, from the belt of foam above, had carried us a great distance down the slope, but our farther descent was by no means proportionate. Round and round we swept—not with any uniform movement—but in dizzying swings and jerks, that sent us sometimes only a few hundred yards—sometimes nearly the complete circuit of the whirl. Our progress downward at each revolution was slow but very perceptible.

"Looking about me upon the wide waste of liquid ebony on which we were thus borne, I perceived that our boat was not the only object in the embrace of the whirl. Both above and below us were visible fragments of vessels, large masses of building timber and trunks of trees, with many smaller articles, such as pieces of house furniture, broken boxes, barrels, and staves. I have already described the unnatural curiosity which had taken the place of my original terrors. It appeared to grow upon me as I drew nearer and nearer to my dreadful doom. I now began to watch, with a strange interest, the numerous things that floated in our company.

"I *must* have been delirious, for I even sought *amusement* in speculating upon the relative velocities of their several descents toward the foam below. 'This fir-tree,' I found myself at one time saying, 'will certainly be the next thing that takes the awful plunge and disappears,' and then I was disappointed to find that the wreck of a Dutch merchant ship overtook it and went down before. At length, after making several guesses of this nature, and being deceived in all, this fact—the fact of my invariable miscalculation—set me upon a train of reflection that made my limbs again tremble, and my heart beat heavily once more.

"It was not a new terror that thus affected me, but the dawn of a more exciting *hope*. This hope arose partly from memory, and partly from present observation. I called to mind the great variety of buoyant matter that strewed the coast of Lofoden, having been absorbed and then thrown forth by the *Moskoe-ström*. By far the greater number of the articles were shattered in the most extraordinary way—so chafed and roughened as to have the appearance of being stuck full of splinters—but then I distinctly recollected that there were some of them which were not disfigured at all. Now I could not account for this difference except by supposing that the roughened fragments were the only ones which had been *completely absorbed*—that the others had entered the whirl at so late a period of the tide, or, for some reason, had descended so slowly after entering, that they did not reach the bottom before the turn of the flood came, or of the ebb, as the case might be. I conceived it possible, in either instance, that they might thus be whirled up again to the level of the ocean, without undergoing the fate of those which had been drawn in more early, or absorbed more rapidly.

"I made also three important observations. The first was that, as a general rule, the larger the bodies were the more rapid their descent; the second, that, between two masses of equal extent, the one spherical and the other *of any other shape*, the superiority in speed of descent was with the sphere; the third, that, between two masses of equal size, the one cylindrical and the other of any other shape, the cylinder was absorbed the more slowly. Since my escape I have had several conversations on this subject with an old schoolmaster of the district, and it was from him that I learned the use of the words 'cylinder' and 'sphere.' He explained to me—although I have forgotten the explanation—how what I observed was in fact the natural consequence of the forms of the floating fragments, and showed me how it happened that a cylinder swimming in a vortex offered more resistance to its suction, and was drawn in with greater difficulty than an equally bulky body of any form whatever.[1]

"There was one startling circumstance which went a great way in enforcing these observations and rendering me anxious to turn them to account, and this was that at every revolution we passed something like a barrel, or else the yard or the mast of a vessel, while many of these things which had been on our level when I first opened my eyes upon the wonders of the whirlpool were now high up above us, and seemed to have moved but little from their original station.

"I no longer hesitated what to do. I resolved to lash myself securely to the water-cask upon which I now held, to cut it loose from the counter, and to throw myself with it into the water. I attracted my brother's attention by signs, pointed to the floating barrels that came near us, and did everything in my power to make him understand what I was about to do. I thought at length that he comprehended my design, but, whether this was the case or not, he shook his head despairingly, and refused to move from his station by the ring-bolt. It was impossible to reach him, the emergency admitted of no delay, and so, with a bitter struggle, I resigned him to his fate, fastened myself to the cask by means of the lashings which secured it to the counter, and precipitated myself with it into the sea without another moment's hesitation.

"The result was precisely what I had hoped it might be. As it is myself who now tell you this tale—as you see that I *did* escape—and as you are already in possession of the mode in which this escape was effected, and must therefore anticipate all that I have further to say, I will bring my story quickly to conclusion.

1. See Archimedes, *De Incidentibus in Fluido, lib.* 2.

It might have been an hour or thereabout after my quitting the smack, when, having descended to a vast distance beneath me, it made three or four wild gyrations in rapid succession, and, bearing my loved brother with it, plunged headlong at once and for ever into the chaos of foam below. The barrel to which I was attached sunk very little farther than half the distance between the bottom of the gulf and the spot at which I leaped overboard, before a great change took place in the character of the whirlpool. The slope of the sides of the vast funnel became momently less and less steep. The gyrations of the whirl grew gradually less and less violent.

"By degrees the froth and the rainbow disappeared, and the bottom of the gulf seemed slowly to uprise. The sky was clear, the winds had gone down, and the full moon was setting radiantly in the west, when I found myself on the surface of the ocean, in full view of the shores of Lofoden, and above the spot where the pool of the *Moskoe-ström had been*. It was the hour of the slack—but the sea still heaved in mountainous waves from the effects of the hurricane. I was borne violently into the channel of the *Ström*, and in a few minutes was hurried down the coast into the 'grounds' of the fishermen. A boat picked me up, exhausted from fatigue and (now that the danger was removed) speechless from the memory of its horror. Those who drew me on board were my old mates and daily companions, but they knew me no more than they would have known a traveller from the spirit land.

"My hair, which had been raven-black the day before, was as white as you see it now. They say, too, that the whole expression of my countenance had changed. I told them my story—they did not believe it. I now tell it to *you*, and I can scarcely expect you to put more faith in it than did the merry fishermen of Lofoden."

Ligeia

And the will therein lieth, which dieth not. Who knoweth the mysteries of the will, with its vigor? For God is but a great will pervading all things by nature of its intentness. Man doth not yield himself to the angels, nor unto death utterly, save only through the weakness of his feeble will.—Joseph Glanvill.

I cannot, for my soul, remember how, when, or even precisely where, I first became acquainted with the lady Ligeia. Long years have since elapsed, and my memory is feeble through much suffering. Or, perhaps, I cannot now bring these points to mind, because, in truth, the character of my beloved, her rare learning, her singular yet placid cast of beauty, and the thrilling and enthralling eloquence of her low musical language, made their way into my heart by paces so steadily and stealthily progressive that they have been unnoticed and unknown. Yet I believe that I met her first and most frequently in some large, old, decaying city near the Rhine.

Of her family—I have surely heard her speak. That it is of a remotely ancient date cannot be doubted. Ligeia! Ligeia! in studies of a nature more than all else adapted to deaden impressions of the outward world, it is by that sweet word alone—by Ligeia—that I bring before mine eyes in fancy the image of her who is no more. And now, while I write, a recollection flashes upon me that I have *never known* the paternal name of her who was my friend and my betrothed, and who became the partner of my studies, and finally the wife of my bosom.

Was it a playful charge on the part of my Ligeia? or was it a test of my strength of affection, that I should institute no inquiries upon this point? or was it rather a caprice of my own—a wildly romantic offering on the shrine of the most passionate devotion? I but indistinctly recall the fact itself—what wonder that I have utterly forgotten the circumstances which originated or attended it? And, indeed, if ever that spirit which is entitled *Romance*—if ever she, the wan and the misty-winged *Ashtophet* of idolatrous Egypt, presided, as they tell, over marriages ill-omened, then most surely she presided over mine.

There is one dear topic, however, on which my memory falls me not. It is the *person* of Ligeia. In stature she was tall, somewhat slender, and, in her latter days, even emaciated. I would in vain attempt to portray the majesty, the quiet ease, of her demeanour, or the incomprehensible lightness and elasticity of her footfall. She came and departed as a shadow. I was never made aware of her entrance into my closed study save by the dear music of her low sweet voice, as she placed her marble hand upon my shoulder. In beauty of face no maiden ever equalled her.

It was the radiance of an opium-dream—an airy and spirit-lifting vision more wildly divine than the phantasies which hovered vision about the slumbering souls of the daughters of Delos. Yet her features were not of that regular mould which we have been falsely taught to worship in the classical labours of the heathen. "There is no exquisite beauty," says Bacon, Lord Verulam, speaking truly of all the forms and *genera* of beauty, "without some *strangeness* in the proportion." Yet, although I saw that the features of Ligeia were not of a classic regularity—although I perceived that her loveliness was indeed "exquisite," and felt that there was much of "strangeness" pervading it, yet I have tried in vain to detect the irregularity and to trace home my own perception of "the strange."

I examined the contour of the lofty and pale forehead—it was faultless—how cold indeed that word when applied to a majesty so divine!—the skin rivalling the purest ivory, the commanding extent and repose, the gentle prominence of the regions above the temples; and then the raven-black, the glossy, the luxuriant and naturally-curling tresses, setting forth the full force of the Homeric epithet, "*hyacinthine!*" I looked at the delicate outlines of the nose—and nowhere but in the graceful medallions of the Hebrews had I beheld a similar perfection. There were the same luxurious smoothness of surface, the same scarcely perceptible tendency to the aquiline, the same harmoniously curved nostrils speaking the free spirit. I regarded the sweet mouth.

Here was indeed the triumph of all things heavenly—the magnificent turn of the short upper lip—the soft, voluptuous slumber of the under—the dimples which sported, and the colour which spoke—the teeth glancing back, with a brilliancy almost startling, every ray of the holy light which fell upon them in her serene and placid, yet most exultingly radiant of all smiles. I scrutinized the formation of the chin—and here, too, I found the gentleness of breadth, the softness and the majesty, the fullness and the spirituality, of the Greek—the contour which the god Apollo revealed but in a dream, to Cleomenes, the son of the Athenian. And then I peered into the large eyes of Ligeia.

For eyes we have no models in the remotely antique. It might have been, too, that in these eyes of my beloved lay the secret to which Lord Verulam alludes. They were, I must believe, far larger than the ordinary eyes of our own race. They were even fuller than the fullest of the gazelle eyes of the tribe of the valley of Nourjahad. Yet it was only at intervals—in moments of intense excitement—that this peculiarity became more than slightly noticeable in Ligeia. And at such moments was her beauty—in my heated fancy thus it appeared perhaps—the beauty of beings either above or apart from the earth—the beauty of the fabulous *houri* of the Turk. The hue of the orbs was the most brilliant of black, and, far over them, hung jetty lashes of great length. The brows, slightly irregular in outline, had the same tint.

The "strangeness," however, which I found in the eyes, was of a nature distinct from the formation, or the colour, or the brilliancy of the features, and must, after all, be referred to the *expression*. Ah, word of no meaning! behind whose vast latitude of mere sound we entrench our ignorance of so much of the spiritual. The expression of the eyes of Ligeia! How for long hours have I pondered upon it! How have I, through the whole of a midsummer night, struggled to fathom it! What was it—that something more profound than the well of Democritus—which lay far within the pupils of my beloved? What was it? I was possessed with a passion to discover. Those eyes! those large, those shining, those divine orbs! they became to me twin stars of Leda, and I to them devoutest of astrologers.

There is no point, among the many incomprehensible anomalies of the science of mind, more thrillingly exciting than the fact—never, I believe, noticed in the schools—that, in our endeavours to recall to memory something long forgotten, we often find ourselves *upon the very verge of remembrance,* without being able, in the end, to remember. And thus how frequently, in my intense scrutiny of Ligeia's eyes, have I felt approaching the full knowledge of their expression—felt it approaching—yet not quite be mine—and so at length entirely depart! And (strange, oh strangest mystery of all!) I found, in the commonest objects of the universe, a circle of analogies to that expression.

I mean to say that, subsequently to the period when Ligeia's beauty passed into my spirit, there dwelling as in a shrine, I derived, from many existences in the material world, a sentiment such as I felt always aroused within me by her large and luminous orbs. Yet not the more could I define that sentiment, or analyze, or even steadily view it. I recognized it, let me repeat, sometimes in the survey of a rapidly-growing vine—in the contemplation of a moth, a butterfly, a chrysalis, a stream of running water. I have felt it in the ocean; in the falling of a meteor. I have felt it in the glances of unusually aged people.

And there are one or two stars in heaven—(one especially, a star of the sixth magnitude, double and changeable, to be found near the large star in Lyra) in a telescopic scrutiny of which I have been made aware of the feeling. I have been filled with it by certain sounds from stringed instruments, and not unfrequently by passages from books. Among innumerable other instances, I well remember something in a volume of Joseph Glanvill, which (perhaps merely from its quaintness—who shall say?) never failed to inspire me with the sentiment;—

> And the will therein lieth, which dieth not. Who knoweth the mysteries of the will, with its vigour? For God is but a great will pervading all things by nature of its intentness. Man doth not yield him to the angels, nor unto death utterly, save only through the weakness of his feeble will.

Length of years, and subsequent reflection, have enabled me to trace, indeed, some remote connection between this passage in the English moralist and a portion of the character of Ligeia. An *intensity* in thought, action, or speech, was possibly, in her, a result, or at least an index, of that gigantic volition which, during our long intercourse, failed to give other and more immediate evidence of its existence. Of all the women whom I have ever known, she, the outwardly calm, the ever-placid Ligeia, was the most violently a prey to the tumultuous vultures of stern passion. And of such passion I could form no estimate, save by the miraculous expansion of those eyes which at once so delighted and appalled me—by the almost magical melody, modulation, distinctness and placidity of her very low voice—and by the fierce energy (rendered doubly effective by contrast with her manner of utterance) of the wild words which she habitually uttered.

I have spoken of the learning of Ligeia: it was immense—such as I have never known in woman. In the classical tongues was she deeply proficient, and as far as my own acquaintance extended in regard to the modern dialects of Europe, I have never known her at fault. Indeed upon any theme of the most admired, because simply the most abstruse of the boasted erudition of the academy, have I *ever* found Ligeia at fault? How singularly—how thrillingly, this one point in the nature of my wife has forced itself, at this late period only, upon my attention! I said her knowledge was such as I have never known in woman—but where breathes the man who has traversed, and successfully, *all* the wide areas of moral, physical, and mathematical science?

I saw not then what I now clearly perceive, that the acquisitions of Ligeia were gigantic, were astounding; yet I was sufficiently aware of her infinite supremacy to resign myself, with a child-like confidence, to her guidance through the chaotic world of metaphysical investigation at which I was most busily occupied during the earlier years of our marriage. With how vast a triumph—with how vivid a delight—with how much of all that is ethereal in hope—did I *feel*, as she bent over me in studies but little sought—but less known—that delicious *vista* by slow degrees expanding before me, down whose long, gorgeous, and all untrodden path, I might at length pass onward to the goal of a wisdom too divinely precious not to be forbidden!

How poignant, then, must have been the grief with which, after some years, I beheld my well-grounded expectations take wings to themselves and fly away! Without Ligeia I was but as a child groping benighted. Her presence, her readings alone, rendered vividly luminous the many mysteries of the transcendentalism in which we were immersed. Wanting the radiant lustre of her eyes, letters, lambent and golden, grew duller than Saturnian lead. And now those eyes shone less and less frequently upon the pages over which I pored. Ligeia grew ill. The wild eyes blazed with a too—too glorious effulgence; the pale fingers became of the transparent waxen hue of the grave, and the blue veins upon the lofty forehead swelled and sank impetuously with the tides of the gentle emotion.

I saw that she must die—and I struggled desperately in spirit with the grim Azrael. And the struggles of the passionate wife were, to my astonishment, even more energetic than my own. There had been much in her stern nature to impress me with the belief that, to her, death would have come without its terrors;—but not so. Words are impotent to convey any just idea of the fierceness of resistance with which she wrestled with the Shadow. I groaned in anguish at the pitiable spectacle. I would have soothed—I would have reasoned; but, in the intensity of her wild desire for life,—for life—*but* for life—solace and reason were the uttermost folly.

Yet not until the last instance, amid the most convulsive writhings of her fierce spirit, was shaken the external placidity of her demeanour. Her voice grew more gentle—grew more low—yet I would not wish to dwell upon the wild meaning of the quietly uttered words. My brain reeled as I hearkened entranced, to a melody more than mortal—to assumptions and aspirations which mortality had never before known.

That she loved me I should not have doubted; and I might have been easily aware that, in a bosom such as hers, love would have reigned no ordinary passion. But in death only, was I fully impressed with the strength of her affection. For long hours, detaining my hand, would she pour out before me the overflowing of a heart whose more than passionate devotion amounted to idolatry. How had I deserved to be so blessed by such confessions?—how had I deserved to be so cursed with the removal of my beloved in the hour of her making them.

But upon this subject I cannot bear to dilate. Let me say only, that in Ligeia's more than womanly abandonment to a love, alas! all unmerited, all unworthily bestowed, I at length recognized the principle of her longing with so wildly earnest a desire for the life which was now fleeing so rapidly away. It is this wild longing—it is this eager vehemence of desire for life—*but* for life—that I have no power to portray—no utterance capable of expressing.

At high noon of the night in which she departed, beckoning me, peremptorily, to her side, she bade me repeat certain verses composed by herself not many days before. I obeyed her.—They were these:—

Lo! 'tis a gala night
Within the lonesome latter years!
An angel throng, bewinged, bedight
In veils, and drowned in tears,
Sit in a theatre, to see
A play of hopes and fears,
While the orchestra breathes fitfully

The music of the spheres.

Mimes, in the form of God on high,
Mutter and mumble low,
And hither and thither fly;
Mere puppets they, who come and go
At bidding of vast formless things
That shift the scenery to and fro,
Flapping from out their Condor wings
Invisible Wo!

That motley drama!—oh, be sure
It shall not be forgot!
With its Phantom chased forever more,
By a crowd that seize it not,
Through a circle that ever returneth in
To the self-same spot,
And much of Madness and more of Sin
And Horror the soul of the plot.

But see, amid the mimic rout,
A crawling shape intrude!
A blood-red thing that writhes from out
The scenic solitude!
It writhes!—it writhes!—with mortal pangs
The mimes become its food,
And the seraphs sob at vermin fangs
In human gore imbued.

Out—out are the lights—out all!
And over each quivering form,
The curtain, a funeral pall,
Comes down with the rush of a storm,
And the angels, all pallid and wan,
Uprising, unveiling, affirm
That the play is the tragedy, "Man,"
And its hero the Conqueror Worm.

"O God!" half shrieked Ligeia, leaping to her feet and extending her arms aloft with a spasmodic movement, as I made an end of these lines—"O God! O Divine Father!—shall these things be undeviatingly so?—shall this Conqueror be not once conquered? Are we not part and parcel in Thee? Who—who knoweth the mysteries of the will with its vigour? Man doth not yield him to the angels, nor unto death utterly, save only through the weakness of his feeble will."

And now, as if exhausted with emotion, she suffered her white arms to fall, and returned solemnly to her bed of death. And as she breathed her last sighs, there came mingled with them a low murmur from her lips. I bent to them my ear and distinguished, again, the concluding words of the passage in Glanvill—

> Man doth not yield him to the angels, nor unto death utterly, save only through the weakness of his feeble will.

She died;—and I, crushed into the very dust with sorrow, could no longer endure the lonely desolation of my dwelling in the dim and decaying city by the Rhine. I had no lack of what the world calls wealth. Ligeia had brought me far more, very far more than ordinarily falls to the lot of mortals. After a few months, therefore, of weary and aimless wandering, I purchased, and put in some repair, an abbey, which I shall not name, in one of the wildest and least frequented portions of fair England. The gloomy and dreary grandeur of the building, the almost savage aspect of the domain, the many melancholy and time-honoured memories connected with both, had much in unison with the feelings of utter abandonment which had driven me into that remote and unsocial region of the country.

Yet although the external abbey, with its verdant decay hanging about it, suffered but little alteration, I gave way, with a child-like perversity, and perchance with a faint hope of alleviating my sorrows, to a display of more than regal magnificence within.—For such follies, even in childhood, I had imbibed a taste and now they came back to me as if in the dotage of grief. Alas, I feel how much even of incipient madness might have been discovered in the gorgeous and fantastic draperies, in the solemn carvings of Egypt, in the wild cornices and furniture, in the Bedlam patterns of the carpets of tufted gold! I had become a bounden slave in the trammels of opium, and my labours and my orders had taken a colouring from my dreams. But these absurdities must not pause to detail. Let me speak only of that one chamber, ever accursed, whither in a moment of mental alienation, I led from the altar as my bride—as the successor of the unforgotten Ligeia—the fair-haired and blue-eyed Lady Rowena Trevanion, of Tremaine.

There is no individual portion of the architecture and decoration of that bridal chamber which is not now visibly before me. Where were the souls of the haughty family of the bride, when, through thirst of gold, they permitted to pass the threshold of an apartment so bedecked, a maiden and a daughter so beloved? I have said that I minutely remember the details of the chamber—yet I am sadly forgetful on topics of deep moment—and here there was no system, no keeping, in the fantastic display, to take hold upon the memory. The room lay in a high turret of the castellated abbey, was pentagonal in shape, and of capacious size. Occupying the whole southern face of the pentagon was the sole window—an immense sheet of unbroken glass from Venice—a single pane, and tinted of a leaden hue, so that the rays of either the sun or moon, passing through it, fell with a ghastly lustre on the objects within.

Over the upper portion of this huge window, extended the trellis-work of an aged vine, which clambered up the massy walls of the turret. The ceiling, of gloomy-looking oak, was excessively lofty, vaulted, and elaborately fretted with the wildest and most grotesque specimens of a semi-Gothic, semi-Druidical device. From out the most central recess of this melancholy vaulting, depended, by a single chain of gold with long links, a huge censer of the same metal, Saracenic in pattern, and with many perforations so contrived that there writhed in and out of them, as if endued with a serpent vitality, a continual succession of parti-coloured fires.

Some few ottomans and golden candelabra, of Eastern figure, were in various stations about—and there was the couch, too—

bridal couch—of an Indian model, and low, and sculptured of solid ebony, with a pall-like canopy above. In each of the angles of the chamber stood on end a gigantic sarcophagus of black granite, from the tombs of the kings over against Luxor, with their aged lids full of immemorial sculpture.

But in the draping of the apartment lay, alas! the chief phantasy of all. The lofty walls, gigantic in height—even unproportionably so—were hung from summit to foot, in vast folds, with a heavy and massive-looking tapestry—tapestry of a material which was found alike as a carpet on the floor, as a covering for the ottomans and the ebony bed, as a canopy for the bed, and as the gorgeous volutes of the curtains which partially shaded the window. The material was the richest cloth of gold. It was spotted all over, at irregular intervals, with arabesque figures, about a foot in diameter, and wrought upon the cloth in patterns of the most jetty black. But these figures partook of the true character of the arabesque only when regarded from a single point of view.

By a contrivance now common, and indeed traceable to a very remote period of antiquity, they were made changeable in aspect. To one entering the room, they bore the appearance of simple monstrosities; but upon a farther advance, this appearance gradually departed; and step by step, as the visitor moved his station in the chamber, he saw himself surrounded by an endless succession of the ghastly forms which belong to the superstition of the Norman, or arise in the guilty slumbers of the monk. The phantasmagoric effect was vastly heightened by the artificial introduction of a strong continual current of wind behind the draperies—giving a hideous and uneasy animation to the whole.

In halls such as these—in a bridal chamber such as this—I passed, with the Lady of Tremaine, the unhallowed hours of the first month of our marriage—passed them with but little disquietude. That my wife dreaded the fierce moodiness of my temper—that she shunned me and loved me but little—I could not help perceiving; but it gave me rather pleasure than otherwise.

I loathed her with a hatred belonging more to demon than to man. My memory flew back, (oh, with what intensity of regret!) to Ligeia, the beloved, the august, the beautiful, the entombed. I revelled in recollections of her purity, of her wisdom, of her lofty, her ethereal nature, of her passionate, her idolatrous love. Now, then, did my spirit fully and freely burn with more than all the fires of her own.

In the excitement of my opium dreams (for I was habitually fettered in the shackles of the drug) I would call aloud upon her name, during the silence of the night, or among the sheltered recesses of the glens by day, as if, through the wild eagerness, the solemn passion, the consuming ardour of my longing for the departed, I could restore her to the pathway she had abandoned—ah, *could* it be forever?—upon the earth.

About the commencement of the second month of the marriage, the Lady Rowena was attacked with sudden illness, from which her recovery was slow. The fever which consumed her rendered her nights uneasy; and in her perturbed state of half-slumber, she spoke of sounds, and of motions, in and about the chamber of the turret, which I concluded had no origin save in the distemper of her fancy, or perhaps in the phantasmagoric influences of the chamber itself. She became at length convalescent—finally well. Yet but a brief period elapsed, ere a second more violent disorder again threw her upon a bed of suffering; and from this attack her frame, at all times feeble, never altogether recovered.

Her illnesses were, after this epoch, of alarming character, and of more alarming recurrence, defying alike the knowledge and the great exertions of her physicians. With the increase of the chronic disease which had thus, apparently, taken too sure hold upon her constitution to be eradicated by human means, I could not fall to observe a similar increase in the nervous irritation of her temperament, and in her excitability by trivial causes of fear. She spoke again, and now more frequently and pertinaciously, of the sounds—of the slight sounds—and of the unusual motions among the tapestries, to which she had formerly alluded.

One night, near the closing in of September, she pressed this distressing subject with more than usual emphasis upon my attention. She had just awakened from an unquiet slumber, and I had been watching, with feelings half of anxiety, half of vague terror, the workings of her emaciated countenance. I sat by the side of her ebony bed, upon one of the ottomans of India. She partly arose, and spoke, in an earnest low whisper, of sounds which she *then* heard, but which I could not hear—of motions which she *then* saw, but which I could not perceive. The wind was rushing hurriedly behind the tapestries, and I wished to show her (what, let me confess it, I could not *all* believe) that those almost inarticulate breathings, and those very gentle variations of the figures upon the wall, were but the natural effects of that customary rushing of the wind.

But a deadly pallor, overspreading her face, had proved to me that my exertions to reassure her would be fruitless. She appeared to be fainting, and no attendants were within call. I remembered where was deposited a decanter of light wine which had been ordered by her physicians, and hastened across the chamber to procure it. But, as I stepped beneath the light of the censer, two circumstances of a startling nature attracted my attention. I had felt that some palpable although invisible object had passed lightly by my person; and I saw that there lay upon the golden carpet, in the very middle of the rich lustre thrown from the censer, a shadow—a faint, indefinite shadow of angelic aspect—such as might be fancied for the shadow of a shade. But I was wild with the excitement of an immoderate dose of opium, and heeded these things but little, nor spoke of them to Rowena.

Having found the wine, I recrossed the chamber, and poured out a gobletful, which I held to the lips of the fainting lady. She had now partially recovered, however, and took the vessel herself, while I sank upon an ottoman near me, with my eyes fastened upon her person. It was then that I became distinctly aware of a gentle footfall upon the carpet, and near the couch; and in a second thereafter, as Rowena was in the act of raising the wine to her lips, I saw, or may have dreamed that I saw, fall within the goblet, as if from some invisible spring in the atmosphere of the room, three or four large drops of a brilliant and ruby coloured fluid. If this I saw—not so Rowena. She swallowed the wine unhesitatingly, and I forbore to speak to her of a circumstance which must, after all, I considered, have been but the suggestion of a vivid imagination, rendered morbidly active by the terror of the lady, by the opium, and by the hour.

Yet I cannot conceal it from my own perception that, immediately subsequent to the fall of the ruby-drops, a rapid change for the worse took place in the disorder of my wife; so that, on the third subsequent night, the hands of her menials prepared her for the tomb, and on the fourth, I sat alone, with her shrouded body, in that fantastic chamber which had received her as my bride.—Wild visions, opium-engendered, flitted, shadow-like, before me. I gazed with unquiet eye upon the sarcophagi in the angles of the room, upon the varying figures of the drapery, and upon the writhing of the parti-coloured fires in the censer overhead.

My eyes then fell, as I called to mind the circumstances of a former night, to the spot beneath the glare of the censer where I had seen the faint traces of the shadow. It was there, however, no longer; and breathing with greater freedom, I turned my glances to the pallid and rigid figure upon the bed. Then rushed upon me a thousand memories of Ligeia—and then came back upon my heart, with the turbulent violence of a flood, the whole of that unutterable woe with which I had regarded *her* thus enshrouded. The night waned; and still, with a bosom full of bitter thoughts of the one only and supremely beloved, I remained gazing upon the body of Rowena.

It might have been midnight, or perhaps earlier, or later, for I had taken no note of time, when a sob, low, gentle, but very distinct, startled me from my reverie.—I *felt* that it came from the bed of ebony—the bed of death. I listened in an agony of superstitious terror—but there was no repetition of the sound. I strained my vision to detect any motion in the corpse—but there was not the slightest perceptible. Yet I could not have been deceived. I *had* heard the noise, however faint, and my soul was awakened within me. I resolutely and perseveringly kept my attention riveted upon the body. Many minutes elapsed before any circumstance occurred tending to throw light upon the mystery.

At length it became evident that a slight, a very feeble, and barely noticeable tinge of colour had flushed up within the cheeks, and along the sunken small veins of the eyelids. Through a species of unutterable horror and awe, for which the language of mortality has no sufficiently energetic expression, I felt my heart cease to beat, my limbs grow rigid where I sat. Yet a sense of duty finally operated to restore my self-possession. I could no longer doubt that we had been precipitate in our preparations—that Rowena still lived. It was necessary that some immediate exertion be made; yet turret was altogether apart from the portion of the abbey tenanted by the servants—there were none within call—I had no means of summoning them to my aid without leaving the room for many minutes—and this I could not venture to do. I therefore struggled alone in my endeavours to call back the spirit ill hovering.

In a short period it was certain, however, that a relapse had taken place; the colour disappeared from both eyelid and cheek, leaving a wanness even more than that of marble; the lips became doubly shrivelled and pinched up in the ghastly expression of death; a repulsive clamminess and coldness overspread rapidly the surface of the body; and all the usual rigorous illness immediately supervened. I fell back with a shudder upon the couch from which I had been so startlingly aroused, and again gave myself up to passionate waking visions of Ligeia.

An hour thus elapsed when (could it be possible?) I was a second time aware of some vague sound issuing from the region of the bed. I listened—in extremity of horror. The sound came again—it was a sigh. Rushing to the corpse, I saw—distinctly saw—a tremor upon the lips. In a minute afterward they relaxed, disclosing a bright line of the pearly teeth. Amazement now struggled in my bosom with the profound awe which had hitherto reigned there alone. I felt that my vision grew dim, that my reason wandered; and it was only by a violent effort that I at length succeeded in nerving myself to the task which duty thus once more had pointed out.

There was now a partial glow upon the forehead and upon the cheek and throat; a perceptible warmth pervaded the whole frame; there was even a slight pulsation at the heart. The lady *lived*; and with redoubled ardour I betook myself to the task of restoration. I chafed and bathed the temples and the hands, and used every exertion which experience, and no little medical reading, could suggest. But in vain. Suddenly, the colour fled, the pulsation ceased, the lips resumed the expression of the dead, and, in an instant afterward, the whole body took upon itself the icy chilliness, the livid hue, the intense rigidity, the sunken outline, and all the loathsome peculiarities of that which has been, for many days, a tenant of the tomb.

And again I sunk into visions of Ligeia—and again, (what marvel that I shudder while I write,) *again* there reached my ears a low sob from the region of the ebony bed. But why shall I minutely detail the unspeakable horrors of that night? Why shall I pause to relate how, time after time, until near the period of the gray dawn, this hideous drama of revivification was repeated; how each terrific relapse was only into a sterner and apparently more irredeemable death; how each agony wore the aspect of a struggle with some invisible foe; and how each struggle was succeeded by I know not what of wild change in the personal appearance of the corpse? Let me hurry to a conclusion.

The greater part of the fearful night had worn away, and she who had been dead, once again stirred—and now more vigorously than hitherto, although arousing from a dissolution more appalling in its utter hopelessness than any. I had long ceased to struggle or to move, and remained sitting rigidly upon the ottoman, a helpless prey to a whirl of violent emotions, of which extreme awe was perhaps the least terrible, the least consuming.

The corpse, I repeat, stirred, and now more vigorously than

before. The hues of life flushed up with unwonted energy into the countenance—the limbs relaxed—and, save that the eyelids were yet pressed heavily together, and that the bandages and draperies of the grave still imparted their charnel character to the figure, I might have dreamed that Rowena had indeed shaken off, utterly, the fetters of Death. But if this idea was not, even then, altogether adopted, I could at least doubt no longer, when, arising from the bed, tottering, with feeble steps, with closed eyes, and with the manner of one bewildered in a dream, the thing that was enshrouded advanced boldly and palpably into the middle of the apartment.

I trembled not—I stirred not—for a crowd of unutterable fancies connected with the air, the stature, the demeanour of the figure, rushing hurriedly through my brain, had paralyzed—had chilled me into stone. I stirred not—but gazed upon the apparition. There was a mad disorder in my thoughts—a tumult unappeasable. Could it, indeed, be the *living* Rowena who confronted me? Could it indeed be Rowena *at all*—the fair-haired, the blue-eyed Lady Rowena Trevanion of Tremaine? Why, why should I doubt it? The bandage lay heavily about the mouth—but then might it not be the mouth of the breathing Lady of Tremaine? And the cheeks—there were the roses as in her noon of life—yes, these might indeed be the fair cheeks of the living Lady of Tremaine. And the chin, with its dimples, as in health, might it not be hers?—but *had she then grown taller since her malady?*

What inexpressible madness seized me with that thought? One bound, and I had reached her feet! Shrinking from my touch, she let fall from her head, unloosened, the ghastly cerements which had confined it, and there streamed forth, into the rushing atmosphere of the chamber, huge masses of long and dishevelled hair; *it was blacker than the raven wings of the midnight!* And now slowly opened the eyes of the figure which stood before me. "Here then, at least," I shrieked aloud, "can I never—can I never be mistaken—these are the full, and the black, and the wild eyes—of my lost love—of the lady—of the *Lady Ligeia.*"

Lionizing

——— *all people went*
Upon their ten toes in wild wonderment.
—Bishop Hall's Satires.

I am—that is to say I *was*—a great man; but I am neither the author of Junius nor the man in the mask; for my name, I believe, is Robert Jones, and I was born somewhere in the city of Fum-Fudge.

The first action of my life was the taking hold of my nose with both hands. My mother saw this and called me a genius: my father wept for joy and presented me with a treatise on Nosology. This I mastered before I was breeched.

I now began to feel my way in the science, and soon came to understand that, provided a man had a nose sufficiently conspicuous he might, by merely following it, arrive at a Lionship. But my attention was not confined to theories alone. Every morning I gave my proboscis a couple of pulls and swallowed a half dozen of drams.

When I came of age my father asked me, one day, If I would step with him into his study.

"My son," said he, when we were seated, "what is the chief end of your existence?"

"My father," I answered, "it is the study of Nosology."

"And what, Robert," he inquired, "is Nosology?"

"Sir," I said, "it is the Science of Noses."

"And can you tell me," he demanded, "what is the meaning of a nose?"

"A nose, my father;" I replied, greatly softened, "has been variously defined by about a thousand different authors." (Here I pulled out my watch.) "It is now noon or thereabouts—we shall have time enough to get through with them all before midnight. To commence then:—The nose, according to Bartholinus, is that protuberance—that bump—that excrescence—that—"

"Will do, Robert," interrupted the good old gentleman. "I am thunderstruck at the extent of your information—I am positively—upon my soul." (Here he closed his eyes and placed his hand upon his heart.) "Come here!" (Here he took me by the arm.) "Your education may now be considered as finished—it is high time you should scuffle for yourself—and you cannot do a better thing than merely follow your nose—so—so—so—" (Here he kicked me down stairs and out of the door)—"so get out of my house, and God bless you!"

As I felt within me the *divine* afflatus, I considered this accident rather fortunate than otherwise. I resolved to be guided by the paternal advice. I determined to follow my nose. I gave it a pull or two upon the spot, and wrote a pamphlet on Nosology forthwith.

All Fum-Fudge was in an uproar.

"Wonderful genius!" said the *Quarterly*.

"Superb physiologist!" said the *Westminster*.

"Clever fellow!" said the *Foreign*.

"Fine writer!" said the *Edinburgh*.

"Profound thinker!" said the *Dublin*.

"Great man!" said *Bentley*.

"Divine soul!" said *Fraser*.

"One of us!" said *Blackwood*.

"Who can he be?" said Mrs. Bas-Bleu.

"What can he be?" said big Miss Bas-Bleu.

"Where can he be?" said little Miss Bas-Bleu.—But I paid these people no attention whatever—I just stepped into the shop of an artist.

The Duchess of Bless-my-Soul was sitting for her portrait; the Marquis of So-and-So was holding the duchess' poodle; the

Earl of This-and-That was flirting with her salts; and his Royal Highness of Touch-me-Not was leaning upon the back of her chair.

I approached the artist and turned up my nose.

"Oh, beautiful!" sighed her Grace.

"Oh my!" lisped the marquis.

"Oh, shocking!" groaned the earl.

"Oh, abominable!" growled his Royal Highness.

"What will you take for it?" asked the artist.

"For his nose!" shouted her Grace.

"A thousand pounds," said I, sitting down.

"A thousand pounds?" inquired the artist, musingly.

"A thousand pounds," said I.

"Beautiful!" said he, entranced.

"A thousand pounds," said I.

"Do you warrant it?" he asked, turning the nose to the light.

"I do," said I, blowing it well.

"Is it quite original?" he inquired; touching it with reverence.

"Humph!" said I, twisting it to one side.

"Has no copy been taken?" he demanded, surveying it through a microscope.

"None," said I, turning it up.

"*Admirable!*" he ejaculated, thrown quite off his guard by the beauty of the manoeuvre.

"A thousand pounds," said I.

"A thousand pounds?" said he.

"Precisely," said I.

"A thousand *pounds?*" said he.

"Just so," said I.

"You shall have them," said he. "What a piece of *virtu!*" So he drew me a check upon the spot, and took a sketch of my nose. I engaged rooms in Jermyn street, and sent her Majesty the ninety-ninth edition of the "Nosology," with a portrait of the proboscis.—That sad little rake, the Prince of Wales, invited me to dinner.

We were all lions and *recherchés*.

There was a modern Platonist. He quoted Porphyry, Iamblicus, Plotinus, Proclus, Hierocles, Maximus Tyrius, and Syrianus.

There was a human-perfectibility man. He quoted Turgôt, Price, Priestly, Condorcêt, De Staël, and the *Ambitious Student in Ill Health*.

There was Sir Positive Paradox. He observed that all fools were philosophers, and that all philosophers were fools.

There was Æstheticus Ethix. He spoke of fire, unity, and atoms; bi-part and pre-existent soul; affinity and discord; primitive intelligence and homöomeria.

There was Theologos Theology. He talked of Eusebius and Arianus; heresy and the Council of Nice; Puseyism and consubstantialism; Homousios and Homouioisios.

There was Fricassée from the Rocher de Cancale. He mentioned Muriton of red tongue; cauliflowers with *velouté* sauce; veal *à la* St. Menehoult; marinade *à la* St. Florentin; and orange jellies *en mosaïques*.

There was Bibulus O'Bumper. He touched upon Latour and Markbrünnen; upon Mousseux and Chambertin; upon Richbourg and St. George; upon Haubrion, Leonville, and Medoc; upon Barac and Preignac; upon Grâve, upon Sauterne, upon Lafitte, and upon St. Peray. He shook his head at Clos de Vougeot, and told, with his eyes shut, the difference between Sherry and Amontillado.

There was Signor Tintontintino from Florence. He discoursed of Cimabué, Arpino, Carpaccio, and Argostino—of the gloom of Caravaggio, of the amenity of Albano, of the colors of Titian, of the *frows* of Rubens, and of the waggeries of Jan Steen.

There was the President of the Fum-Fudge University. He was of opinion that the moon was called Bendis in Thrace, Bubastis in Egypt, Dian in Rome, and Artemis in Greece. There was a Grand Turk from Stamboul. He could not help thinking that the angels were horses, cocks, and bulls; that somebody in the sixth heaven had seventy thousand heads; and that the earth was supported by a sky-blue cow with an incalculable number of green horns.

There was Delphinus Polyglott. He told us what had become of the eighty-three lost tragedies of Æschylus; of the fifty-four orations of Isæus; of the three hundred and ninety-one speeches of Lysias; of the hundred and eighty treatises of Theophrastus; of the eighth book of the conic sections of Apollonius; of Pindar's hymns and dithyrambics; and of the five and forty tragedies of Homer Junior.

There was Ferdinand Fitz-Fossillus Feltspar. He informed us all about internal fires and tertiary formations; about *äeriforms*, fluidiforms, and solidiforms; about quartz and marl; about schist and schorl; about gypsum and trap; about talc and calc; about blende and horn-blende; about mica-slate and pudding-stone; about cyanite and lepidolite; about hematite and tremolite; about antimony and calcedony; about manganese and whatever you please.

There was myself. I spoke of myself;—of myself, of myself, of myself;—of Nosology, of my pamphlet, and of myself. I turned up my nose, and I spoke of myself.

"Marvellous clever man!" said the prince.

"Superb!" said his guests:—and next morning her Grace of Bless-my-Soul paid me a visit.

"Will you go to Almack's, pretty creature?" she said, tapping me under the chin.

"Upon honor," said I.

"Nose and all?" she asked.

"As I live," I replied.

"Here then is a card, my life. Shall I say you *will* be there?"

"Dear duchess, with all my heart."

"Pshaw, no!—but with all your nose?"

"Every bit of it, my love," said I: so I gave it a twist or two, and found myself at Almack's. The rooms were crowded to suffocation.

"He is coming!" said somebody on the staircase.

"He is coming!" said somebody farther up.

"He is coming!" said somebody farther still.

"He is come!" exclaimed the duchess. "He is come, the little love!"—and, seizing me firmly by both hands, she kissed me thrice upon the nose. A marked sensation immediately ensued.

"*Diavolo!*" cried Count Capricornutti.

"*Dios guarda!*" muttered Don Stiletto.

"*Mille tonnerres!*" ejaculated the Prince de Grenouille.

"*Tousand teufel!*" growled the Elector of Bluddennuff.

It was not to be borne. I grew angry. I turned short upon Bluddennuff.

"Sir!" said I to him, "you are a baboon."

"Sir," he replied, after a pause, "*Donner und Blitzen!*"

This was all that could be desired. We exchanged cards. At Chalk-Farm, the next morning, I shot off his nose—and then called upon my friends.

"*Bête!*" said the first.

"Fool!" said the second.

"Dolt!" said the third.

"Ass!" said the fourth.

"Ninny!" said the fifth.

"Noodle!" said the sixth.

"Be off!" said the seventh.

At all this I felt mortified, and so called upon my father.

"Father," I asked, "what is the chief end of my existence?"

"My son," he replied, "it is still the study of Nosology; but in hitting the Elector upon the nose you have overshot your mark. You have a fine nose, it is true; but then Bluddennuff has none. You are damned, and he has become the hero of the day. I grant you that in Fum-Fudge the greatness of a lion is in proportion to the size of his proboscis—but, good heavens! there is no competing with a lion who has no proboscis at all."

Mellonta Tauta

On Board Balloon "Skylark"
April, 1, 2848

Now, my dear friend—now, for your sins, you are to suffer the infliction of a long gossiping letter. I tell you distinctly that I am going to punish you for all your impertinences by being as tedious, as discursive, as incoherent and as unsatisfactory as possible. Besides, here I am, cooped up in a dirty balloon, with some one or two hundred of the *canaille*, all bound on a *pleasure* excursion, (what a funny idea some people have of pleasure!) and I have no prospect of touching *terra firma* for a month at least. Nobody to talk to. Nothing to do. When one has nothing to do, then is the time to correspond with ones friends. You perceive, then, why it is that I write you this letter—it is on account of my *ennui* and your sins.

Get ready your spectacles and make up your mind to be annoyed. I mean to write at you every day during this odious voyage.

Heigho! when will any *invention* visit the human *pericranium*? Are we forever to be doomed to the thousand inconveniences of the balloon? Will *nobody* contrive a more expeditious mode of progress? The jog-trot movement, to my thinking, is little less than positive torture. Upon my word we have not made more than a hundred miles the hour since leaving home! The very birds beat us—at least some of them. I assure you that I do not exaggerate at all. Our motion, no doubt, seems slower than it actually is—this on account of our having no objects about us by which to estimate our velocity, and on account of our going with the wind. To be sure, whenever we meet a balloon we have a chance of perceiving our rate, and then, I admit, things do not appear so very bad. Accustomed as I am to this mode of travelling, I cannot get over a kind of giddiness whenever a balloon passes us in a current directly overhead.

It always seems to me like an immense bird of prey about to pounce upon us and carry us off in its claws. One went over us this morning about sunrise, and so nearly overhead that its drag-rope actually brushed the network suspending our car, and caused us very serious apprehension. Our captain said that if the material of the bag had been the trumpery varnished "silk" of five hundred or a thousand years ago, we should inevitably have been damaged. This silk, as he explained it to me, was a fabric composed of the entrails of a species of earth-worm. The worm was carefully fed on mulberries—kind of fruit resembling a water-melon—and, when sufficiently fat, was crushed in a mill. The paste thus arising was called *papyrus* in its primary state, and went through a variety of processes until it finally became "silk." Singular to relate, it was once much admired as an article of *female dress!* Balloons were also very generally constructed from it.

A better kind of material, it appears, was subsequently found in the down surrounding the seed-vessels of a plant vulgarly called *euphorbium*, and at that time botanically termed milk-weed. This latter kind of silk was designated as silk-buckingham, on account of its superior durability, and was usually prepared for use by being varnished with a solution of gum caoutchouc—a substance which in some respects must have resembled the *gutta percha* now in common use. This caoutchouc was occasionally called Indian rubber or rubber of twist, and was no doubt one of the numerous *fungi*. Never tell me again that I am not at heart an antiquarian.

Talking of drag-ropes—our own, it seems, has this moment knocked a man overboard from one of the small magnetic propellers that swarm in ocean below us—a boat of about six thousand tons, and, from all accounts, shamefully crowded. These diminutive barques should be prohibited from carrying more than a definite number of passengers. The man, of course, was not permitted to get on board again, and was soon out of sight, he and his life-preserver. I rejoice, my dear friend, that we live in an age so enlightened that no such a thing as an individual is supposed to exist. It is the mass for which the true humanity cares.

By-the-by, talking of humanity, do you know that our immortal Wiggins is not so original in his views of the social condition and so forth, as his contemporaries are inclined to suppose? Pundit assures me that the same ideas were put nearly in the same way, about a thousand years ago, by an Irish philosopher called Furrier, on account of his keeping a retail shop for cat peltries and other furs. Pundit *knows*, you know; there can be no mistake about it. How very wonderfully do we see verified every day, the profound observation of the Hindoo Aries Tottle (as quoted by Pundit)—"Thus must we say that, not once or twice, or a few times, but with almost infinite repetitions, the same opinions come round in a circle among men."

April 2nd.—Spoke today the magnetic cutter in charge of the middle section of floating telegraph wires. I learn that when this species of telegraph was first put into operation by Horse, it was considered quite impossible to convey the wires over sea, but now we are at a loss to comprehend where the difficulty lay! So wags the world. *Tempora mutantur*—excuse me for quoting the Etruscan. What *would* we do without the Atlantic telegraph? (Pundit says Atlantic was the ancient adjective.) We lay to a few minutes to ask the cutter some questions, and learned, among other glorious news, that civil war is raging in Africa, while the plague is doing its good work beautifully both in Yurope and Ayesher. Is it not truly remarkable that, before the magnificent light shed upon philosophy by humanity, the world was accustomed to regard war and pestilence as calamities? Do you know that prayers were actually offered up in the ancient temples to the end that these *evils* (!) might not be visited upon mankind? Is it not really difficult to comprehend upon what principle of interest our forefathers acted? Were they so blind as not to perceive that the destruction of a myriad of individuals is only so much positive advantage to the mass!

April 3rd.—It is really a very fine amusement to ascend the rope-ladder leading to the summit of the balloon-bag, and thence survey the surrounding world. From the car below you know the prospect is not so comprehensive—you can see little vertically. But seated here (where I write this) in the luxuriously-cushioned open *piazza* of the summit, one can see everything that is going on in all directions. Just now there is quite a crowd of balloons in sight, and they present a very animated appearance, while the air is resonant with the hum of so many millions of human voices. I have heard it asserted that when Yellow or (Pundit *will* have it) Violet, who is supposed to have been the first aeronaut, maintained the practicability of traversing the atmosphere in all directions, by merely ascending or descending until a favorable current was attained, he was scarcely hearkened to at all by his contemporaries, who looked upon him as merely an ingenious sort of madman, because the philosophers (?) of the day declared the thing impossible. Really now it does seem to me *quite* unaccountable how any thing so obviously feasible could have escaped the sagacity of the ancient *savans.*

But in all ages the great obstacles to advancement in Art have been opposed by the so-called men of science. To be sure, *our* men of science are not quite so bigoted as those of old:—oh, I have something so queer to tell you on this topic. Do you know that it is not more than a thousand years ago since the metaphysicians consented to relieve the people of the singular fancy that there existed but *two possible roads for the attainment of Truth!* Believe it if you can! It appears that long, long ago, in the night of Time, there lived a Turkish philosopher (or Hindoo possibly) called Aries Tottle. This person introduced, or at all events propagated what was termed the deductive or *à priori* mode of investigation. He started with what he maintained to be *axioms* or "self-evident truths," and thence proceeded "logically" to results.

His greatest disciples were one Neuclid, and one Cant. Well, Aries Tottle flourished supreme until advent of one Hog, surnamed the "Ettrick Shepherd," who preached an entirely different system, which he called the *à posteriori* or *in*-ductive. His plan referred altogether to Sensation. He proceeded by observing, analyzing, and classifying facts—*instantiae naturae,* as they were affectedly called—into general laws. Aries Tottle's mode, in a word, was based on *noumena*; Hog's on *phenomena*. Well, so great was the admiration excited by this latter system that, at its first introduction, Aries Tottle fell into disrepute; but finally he recovered ground and was permitted to divide the realm of Truth with his more modern rival. The *savans* now maintained the Aristotelian and *Baconian* roads were the sole possible avenues to knowledge. "Baconian," you must know, was an adjective invented as equivalent to Hog-ian and more euphonious and dignified.

Now, my dear friend, I do assure you, most positively, that I represent this matter fairly, on the soundest authority and you can easily understand how a notion so absurd on its very face must have operated to retard the progress of all true knowledge—which makes its advances almost invariably by intuitive bounds. The ancient idea confined investigations to *crawling*; and for hundreds of years so great was the infatuation about Hog especially, that a virtual end was put to all thinking, properly so called. No man dared utter a truth to which he felt himself indebted to his *soul* alone. It mattered not whether the truth was even *demonstrably* a truth, for the bullet-headed *savans* of the time regarded only *the road* by which he had attained it. They would not even *look* at the end. "Let us see the means," they cried, "the means!" If, upon investigation of the means, it was found to come under neither the category Aries (that is to say Ram) nor under the category Hog, why then the *savans* went no farther, but pronounced the "theorist" a fool, and would have nothing to do with him or his truth.

Now, it cannot be maintained, even, that by the crawling system the greatest amount of truth would be attained in any long series of ages, for the repression of *imagination* was an evil not to be compensated for by any superior *certainty* in the ancient modes of investigation. The error of these Jurmains, these Vrinch, these Inglitch, and these Amriccans (the latter, by the way, were our own immediate progenitors), was an error quite analogous with that of the wiseacre who fancies that he must necessarily see an object the better the more closely he holds it to his eyes. These people blinded themselves by details. When they proceeded Hoggishly, their "facts" were by no means always facts—a matter of little consequence had it not been for assuming that they were facts and must be facts because they appeared to be such.

When they proceeded on the path of the Ram, their course was scarcely as straight as a ram's horn, for they *never had* an axiom which was an axiom at all. They must have been very blind not to see this, even in their own day; for even in their own day many of the long "established" axioms had been rejected. For example—"*Ex nihilo nihil fit*"; "a body cannot act where it is not"; "there cannot exist antipodes"; "darkness cannot come out of light"—all these, and a dozen other similar propositions, formerly admitted without hesitation as axioms, were, even at the period of which I speak, seen to be untenable. How absurd in these people, then, to persist in putting faith in "axioms" as immutable bases of Truth!

But even out of the mouths of their soundest reasoners it is easy to demonstrate the futility, the impalpability of their axioms in general. Who *was* the soundest of their logicians? Let me see! I will go and ask Pundit and be back in a minute. . . . Ah, here we have it! Here is a book written nearly a thousand years ago and lately translated from the Inglitch—which, by the way, appears to have been the rudiment of the Amriccan. Pundit says it is decidedly the cleverest ancient work on its topic, Logic. The author (who was much thought of in his day) was one Miller, or Mill; and we find it recorded of him, as a point of some importance, that he had a mill-horse called Bentham. But let us glance at the treatise!

Ah!—"Ability or inability to conceive," says Mr. Mill, very properly, "is in no case to be received as a criterion of axiomatic truth." What *modern* in his senses would ever think of disputing this truism? The only wonder with us must be, how it happened that Mr. Mill conceived it necessary even to hint at any thing so obvious. So far good—but let us turn over another paper. What have we here?—"Contradictories cannot both be true—that is, cannot co-exist in nature." Here Mr. Mill means, for example, that a tree must be either a tree or not a tree—that it cannot be at the same time a tree and not a tree. Very well; but I ask him *why*. His reply is this—and never pretends to be any thing else than this—"Because it is impossible to conceive that contradictories can both be true." But this is no answer at all, by his own showing, for has he not just admitted as a truism that "ability or inability to conceive is *in no case* to be received as a criterion of axiomatic truth."

Now I do not complain of these ancients so much because their logic is, by their own showing, utterly baseless, worthless and fantastic altogether, as because of their pompous and imbecile proscription of all *other* roads of Truth, of all *other* means for its attainment than the two preposterous paths—the one of creeping and the one of crawling—to which they have dared to confine the soul that loves nothing so well as to *soar*.

By the by, my dear friend, do you not think it would have puzzled these ancient dogmaticians to have determined by *which* of their two roads it was that the most important and most sublime of *all* their truths was, in effect, attained? I mean the truth of Gravitation. Newton owed it to Kepler. Kepler admitted that his three laws were guessed at—these three laws of all laws which led the great Inglitch mathematician to his principle, the basis of all physical principle—to go behind which we must enter the Kingdom of Metaphysics. Kepler guessed—that is to say *imagined*. He was essentially a "theorist"—that word now of so much sanctity, formerly an epithet of contempt. Would it not have puzzled these old moles too, to have explained by which of the two "roads" a cryptographist unriddles a cryptograph of more than usual secrecy, or by which of the two roads Champollion directed mankind to those enduring and almost innumerable truths which resulted from his deciphering the Hieroglyphics.

One word more on this topic and I will be done boring you. Is it not *passing* strange that, with their eternal prattling about *roads* to Truth, these bigoted people missed what we now so clearly perceive to be the great highway—that of Consistency? Does it not seem singular how they should have failed to deduce from the works of God the vital fact that a perfect consistency *must* be an absolute truth! How plain has been our progress since the late announcement of this proposition! Investigation has been taken out of the hands of the ground-moles and given, as a task, to the true and only true thinkers, the men of ardent imagination. These latter *theorise*. Can you not fancy the shout of scorn with which my words would be received by our progenitors were it possible for them to be now looking over my shoulder? These men, I say, *theorise*; and their theories are simply corrected, reduced, systematized—cleared, little by little, of their dross of inconsistency—until, finally, a perfect consistency stands apparent which even the most stolid admit, because it *is* a consistency, to be an absolute and an unquestionable *truth*.

April 4th.—The new gas is doing wonders, in conjunction with the new improvement with *gutta percha*. How very safe, commodious, manageable, and in every respect convenient are our modern balloons! Here is an immense one approaching us at the rate of at least a hundred and fifty miles an hour. It seems to be crowded with people—perhaps there are three or four hundred passengers—and yet it soars to an elevation of nearly a mile, looking down upon poor us with sovereign contempt. Still a hundred or even two hundred miles an hour is slow travelling after all. *Do* you remember our flight on the railroad across the Kanadaw continent?—fully three hundred miles the hour—*that* was travelling. Nothing to be seen though—nothing to be done but flirt, feast and dance in the magnificent saloons.

Do you remember what an odd sensation was experienced when, by chance, we caught a glimpse of external objects while the cars were in full flight? Everything seemed unique—in one mass. For my part, I cannot say but that I preferred the travelling by the slow train of a hundred miles the hour. Here we were permitted to have glass windows—even to have them open—and something like a distinct view of the country was attainable. . . . Pundit says that *the route* for the great Kanadaw railroad must have been in some measure marked out about nine hundred years ago! In fact, he goes so far as to assert that actual traces of a road are still discernible—traces referable to a period quite as remote as that mentioned.

The track, it appears was *double* only; ours, you know, has twelve paths; and three or four new ones are in preparation. The ancient rails were very slight, and placed so close together as to be, according to modern notions, quite frivolous, if not dangerous in the extreme. The present width of track—fifty feet—is considered, indeed, scarcely secure enough. For my part, I make no doubt that a track of some sort *must* have existed in very remote times, as Pundit asserts; for nothing can be clearer, to my mind, than that, at some period—not less than seven centuries ago, certainly—the Northern and Southern Kanadaw continents were *united*; the Kanawdians, then, would have been driven, by necessity, to a great railroad across the continent.

April 5th.—I am almost devoured by *ennui*. Pundit is the only conversible person on board; and he, poor soul! can speak of nothing but antiquities. He has been occupied all the day in the attempt to convince me that the ancient Americans *governed themselves!*—did ever anybody hear of such an absurdity?—that they existed in a sort of every-man-for-himself confederacy, after the fashion of the "prairie dogs" that we read of in fable. He says that they started with the queerest idea conceivable, *viz*: that all men are born free and equal—this in the very teeth of the laws of *gradation* so visibly impressed upon all things both in the moral and physical universe. Every man "voted," as they called it—that is to say meddled with public affairs—until at length, it was discovered that what is everybody's business is nobody's, and that the "Republic" (so the absurd thing was called) was without a government at all.

It is related, however, that the first circumstance which disturbed, very particularly, the self-complacency of the philosophers who constructed this "Republic," was the startling discovery that universal suffrage gave opportunity for fraudulent schemes, by means of which any desired number of votes might at any time be polled, without the possibility of prevention or even detection, by any party which should be merely villainous enough not to be ashamed of the fraud. A little reflection upon this discovery sufficed to render evident the consequences, which were that rascality *must* predominate—in a word, that a republican government *could* never be any thing but a rascally one. While the philosophers, however, were busied in blushing at their stupidity in not having foreseen these inevitable evils, and intent upon the invention of new theories, the matter was put to an abrupt issue by a fellow of the name of *Mob*, who took every thing into his own hands and set up a despotism, in comparison with which those of the fabulous Zeros and Hellofagabaluses were respectable and delectable.

This Mob (a foreigner, by-the-by), is said to have been the most odious of all men that ever encumbered the earth. He was a giant in stature—insolent, rapacious, filthy, had the gall of a bullock with the heart of a hyena and the brains of a peacock. He died, at length, by dint of his own energies, which exhausted him. Nevertheless, he had his uses, as every thing has, however vile, and taught mankind a lesson which to this day it is in no danger of forgetting—never to run directly contrary to the natural analogies. As for Republicanism, no analogy could be found for it upon the face of the earth—unless we except the case of the "prairie dogs," an exception which seems to demonstrate, if anything, that democracy is a very admirable form of government—for dogs.

April 6th.—Last night had a fine view of Alpha Lyrae, whose disk, through our captain's spy-glass, subtends an angle of half a degree, looking very much as our sun does to the naked eye on a misty day. Alpha Lyrae, although so very much larger than our sun, by the by, resembles him closely as regards its spots, its atmosphere, and in many other particulars. It is only within the last century, Pundit tells me, that the binary relation existing between these two orbs began even to be suspected. The evident motion of our system in the heavens was (strange to say!) referred to an orbit about a prodigious star in the centre of the galaxy.

About this star, or at all events about a centre of gravity common to all the globes of the Milky Way and supposed to be near Alcyone in the Pleiades, every one of these globes was declared to be revolving, our own performing the circuit in a period of 117,000,000 of years! *We*, with our present lights, our vast telescopic improvements, and so forth, of course find it difficult to comprehend *the ground* of an idea such as this. Its first propagator was one Mudler. He was led, we must presume, to this wild hypothesis by mere analogy in the first instance; but, this being the case, he should have at least adhered to analogy in its development. A great central orb *was*, in fact, suggested; so far Mudler was consistent. This central orb, however, dynamically, should have been greater than all its surrounding orbs taken together. The question might then have been asked—"Why do we not see it?"—*we*, especially, who occupy the mid region of the cluster—the very locality near which, at least, must be situated this inconceivable central sun.

The astronomer, perhaps, at this point, took refuge in the suggestion of non-luminosity; and here analogy was suddenly let fall. But even admitting the central orb non-luminous, how did he manage to explain its failure to be rendered visible by the incalculable host of glorious suns glaring in all directions about it? No doubt what he finally maintained was merely a centre of gravity common to all the revolving orbs—but here again analogy must have been let fall. Our system revolves, it is true, about a common centre of gravity, but it does this in connection with and in consequence of a material sun whose mass more than counterbalances the rest of the system.

The mathematical circle is a curve composed of an infinity of straight lines; but this idea of the circle—this idea of it which, in regard to all earthly geometry, we consider as merely the mathematical, in contradistinction from the practical, idea—is, in sober fact, the *practical* conception which alone we have any right to entertain in respect to those Titanic circles with which we have to deal, at least in fancy, when we suppose our system, with its fellows, revolving about a point in the centre of the galaxy. Let the most vigorous of human imaginations but attempt to take a single step toward the comprehension of a circuit so unutterable! I would scarcely be paradoxical to say that a flash of lightning itself, travelling *forever* upon the circumference of this inconceivable circle, would still *forever* be travelling in a straight line.

That the path of our sun along such a circumference—that the direction of our system in such an orbit—would, to any human perception, deviate in the slightest degree from a straight line even in a million of years, is a proposition not to be entertained; and yet these ancient astronomers were absolutely cajoled, it appears, into believing that a decisive curvature had become apparent during the brief period of their astronomical history—during the mere point—during the utter nothingness of two or three thousand years! How incomprehensible, that considerations such as this did not at once indicate to them the true state of affairs—that of the binary revolution of our sun and Alpha Lyrae around a common centre of gravity!

April 7th.—Continued last night our astronomical amusements. Had a fine view of the five Neptunian asteroids, and watched with much interest the putting up of a huge impost on a couple of lintels in the new temple at Daphnis in the moon. It was amusing to think that creatures so diminutive as the lunarians, and bearing so little resemblance to humanity, yet evinced a mechanical ingenuity so much superior to our own. One finds it difficult, too, to conceive the vast masses which these people handle so easily, to be as light as our own reason tells us they actually are.

April 8th.—*Eureka!* Pundit is in his glory. A balloon from

Kanadaw spoke us today and threw on board several late papers; they contain some exceedingly curious information relative to Kanawdian or rather American antiquities. You know, I presume, that laborers have for some months been employed in preparing the ground for a new fountain at Paradise, the emperor's principal pleasure garden. Paradise, it appears, has been, *literally* speaking, an island time out of mind—that is to say, its northern boundary was always (as far back as any record extends) a rivulet, or rather a very narrow arm of the sea.

This arm was gradually widened until it attained its present breadth—a mile. The whole length of the island is nine miles; the breadth varies materially. The entire area (so Pundit says) was, about eight hundred years ago, densely packed with houses, some of them twenty stories high; land (for some most unaccountable reason) being considered as especially precious just in this vicinity. The disastrous earthquake, however, of the year 2050, so totally uprooted and overwhelmed the town (for it was almost too large to be called a village) that the most indefatigable of our antiquarians have never yet been able to obtain from the site any sufficient data (in the shape of coins, medals or inscriptions) wherewith to build up even the ghost of a theory concerning the manners, customs, &c., &c., &c., of the aboriginal inhabitants.

Nearly all that we have hitherto known of them is, that they were a portion of the Knickerbocker tribe of savages infesting the continent at its first discovery by Recorder Riker, a knight of the Golden Fleece. They were by no means uncivilised, however, but cultivated various arts and even sciences after a fashion of their own. It is related of them that they were acute in many respects, but were oddly afflicted with monomania for building what, in the ancient African, was denominated "churches"—a kind of *pagoda* instituted for the worship of two idols that went by the names of Wealth and Fashion.

In the end, it is said, the island became, nine tenths of it, church. The women, too, it appears, were oddly deformed by a natural protuberance of the region just below the small of the back—although, most unaccountably, this deformity was looked upon altogether in the light of a beauty. One or two pictures of these singular women have in fact, been miraculously preserved. They look very odd, *very*—like something between a turkey-cock and a dromedary.

Well, these few details are nearly all that have descended to us respecting the ancient Knickerbockers. It seems, however, that while digging in the centre of the emperors garden, (which, you know, covers the whole island), some of the workmen unearthed a cubical and evidently chiseled block of granite, weighing several hundred pounds. It was in good preservation, having received, apparently, little injury from the convulsion which entombed it. On one of its surfaces was a marble slab with (only think of it!) *an inscription—a legible inscription.* Pundit is in ecstasies.

Upon detaching the slab, a cavity appeared, containing a leaden box filled with various coins, a long scroll of names, several documents which appear to resemble newspapers, with other matters of intense interest to the antiquarian! There can be no doubt that all these are genuine American relics belonging to the tribe called Knickerbocker. The papers thrown on board our balloon are filled with facsimiles of the coins, MSS., typography, &c., &c. I copy for your amusement the Knickerbocker inscription on the marble slab:—

This Corner Stone of a Monument to
The Memory of
GEORGE WASHINGTON
Was Laid With Appropriate Ceremonies
on the
19th Day of October, 1847
The anniversary of the surrender of
Lord Cornwallis
to General Washington at Yorktown
A. D. 1781
Under the Auspices of the
Washington Monument Association of
the city of New York

This, as I give it, is a *verbatim* translation done by Pundit himself, so there *can* be no mistake about it. From the few words thus preserved, we glean several important items of knowledge, not the least interesting of which is the fact that a thousand years ago *actual* monuments had fallen into disuse—as was all very proper—the people contenting themselves, as we do now, with a mere indication of the design to erect a monument at some future time; a corner-stone being cautiously laid by itself "solitary and alone" (excuse me for quoting the great American poet Benton!), as a guarantee of the magnanimous *intention*. We ascertain, too, very distinctly, from this admirable inscription, the how as well as the where and the what, of the great surrender in question.

As to the *where*, it was Yorktown (wherever that was), and as to the *what*, it was General Cornwallis (no doubt some wealthy dealer in corn). *He* was surrendered. The inscription commemorates the surrender of—what? why, "of Lord Cornwallis." The only question is what could the savages wish him surrendered for. But when we remember that these savages were undoubtedly cannibals, we are led to the conclusion that they intended him for sausage. As to the *how* of the surrender, no language can be more explicit. Lord Cornwallis was surrendered (for sausage) "under the auspices of the Washington Monument Association"—no doubt a charitable institution for the depositing of corner-stones.—But, Heaven bless me! what is the matter? Ah, I see—the balloon has collapsed, and we shall have a tumble into the sea. I have, therefore, only time enough to add that, from a hasty inspection of the facsimiles of newspapers, &c., &c., I find that *the* great men in those days among the Americans, were one John, a smith, and one Zacchary, a tailor.

Goodbye, until I see you again. Whether you ever get this letter or not is point of little importance, as I write altogether for my own amusement. I shall cork the MS. up in a bottle, however, and throw it into the sea.

Yours everlastingly, Pundita.

Metzengerstein

Pestis eram vivus—moriens tua mors ero.

—Martin Luther

Horror and fatality have been stalking abroad in all ages. Why then give a date to this story I have to tell? Let it suffice to say, that at the period of which I speak, there existed, in the interior of Hungary, a settled although hidden belief in the doctrines of the Metempsychosis. Of the doctrines themselves—that is, of their falsity, or of their probability—I say nothing. I assert, however, that much of our incredulity—as La Bruyère says of all our unhappiness "*vient de ne pouvoir être seuls.*"[1]

But there are some points in the Hungarian superstition which were fast verging to absurdity. They—the Hungarians—differed very essentially from their Eastern authorities. For example, "*The soul,*" said the former—I give the words of an acute and intelligent Parisian—"*ne demeure qu'un seul fois dans un corps sensible: au reste—un cheval, un chien, un homme même, n'est que la ressemblance peu tangible de ces animaux.*"

The families of Berlifitzing and Metzengerstein had been at variance for centuries. Never before were two houses so illustrious, mutually embittered by hostility so deadly. The origin of this enmity seems to be found in the words of an ancient prophecy—

1. Mercier, in *L'an deux mille quatre cents quarante*, seriously maintains the doctrines of the metempsychosis, and J. D'Israeli says that "no system is so simple and so little repugnant to the understanding." Colonel Ethan Allen, the "Green Mountain Boy," is also said to have been a serious metempsychosist.

> A lofty name shall have a fearful fall when, as the rider over his horse, the mortality of Metzengerstein shall triumph over the immortality of Berlifitzing.

To be sure the words themselves had little or no meaning. But more trivial causes have given rise—and that no long while ago—to consequences equally eventful. Besides, the estates, which were contiguous, had long exercised a rival influence in the affairs of a busy government. Moreover, near neighbors are seldom friends; and the inhabitants of the Castle Berlifitzing might look, from their lofty buttresses, into the very windows of the palace Metzengerstein. Least of all had the more than feudal magnificence, thus discovered, a tendency to allay the irritable feelings of the less ancient and less wealthy Berlifitzings. What wonder then, that the words, however silly, of that prediction, should have succeeded in setting and keeping at variance two families already predisposed to quarrel by every instigation of hereditary jealousy? The prophecy seemed to imply—if it implied anything—a final triumph on the part of the already more powerful house; and was of course remembered with the more bitter animosity by the weaker and less influential.

Wilhelm, Count Berlifitzing, although loftily descended, was, at the epoch of this narrative, an infirm and doting old man, remarkable for nothing but an inordinate and inveterate personal antipathy to the family of his rival, and so passionate a love of horses, and of hunting, that neither bodily infirmity, great age, nor mental incapacity, prevented his daily participation in the dangers of the chase.

Frederick, Baron Metzengerstein, was, on the other hand, not yet of age. His father, the Minister G—, died young. His mother, the Lady Mary, followed him quickly after. Frederick was, at that time, in his fifteenth year. In a city, fifteen years are no long period—a child may be still a child in his third lustrum: but in a wilderness—in so magnificent a wilderness as that old principality, fifteen years have a far deeper meaning.

From some peculiar circumstances attending the administration of his father, the young baron, at the decease of the former, entered immediately upon his vast possessions. Such estates were seldom held before by a nobleman of Hungary. His castles were without number. The chief in point of splendour and extent was the "Palace Metzengerstein." The boundary line of his dominions was never clearly defined; but his principal park embraced a circuit of fifty miles.

Upon the succession of a proprietor so young, with a character so well known, to a fortune so unparalleled, little speculation was afloat in regard to his probable course of conduct. And, indeed, for the space of three days, the behaviour of the heir out-Heroded Herod, and fairly surpassed the expectations of his most enthusiastic admirers. Shameful debaucheries—flagrant treacheries—unheard-of atrocities—gave his trembling vassals quickly to understand that no servile submission on their part—no punctilios of conscience on his own—were thenceforward to prove any security against the remorseless fangs of a petty Caligula. On the night of the fourth day, the stables of the castle Berlifitzing were discovered to be on fire; and the unanimous opinion of the neighbourhood added the crime of the incendiary to the already hideous list of the baron's misdemeanours and enormities.

But during the tumult occasioned by this occurrence, the young nobleman himself sat apparently buried in meditation, in a vast and desolate upper apartment of the family palace of Metzengerstein. The rich although faded tapestry hangings which swung gloomily upon the walls, represented the shadowy and majestic forms of a thousand illustrious ancestors. *Here*, rich-ermined priests, and pontifical dignitaries, familiarly seated with the autocrat and the sovereign, put a veto on the wishes of a temporal king, or restrained with the fiat of papal supremacy the rebellious sceptre of the Arch-enemy. *There*, the dark, tall statures of the Princes Metzengerstein—their muscular war-coursers plunging over the carcasses of fallen foes—startled the steadiest nerves with their vigorous expression; and *here*, again, the voluptuous and swan-like figures of the dames of days gone by, floated away in the mazes of an unreal dance to the strains of imaginary melody.

But as the baron listened, or affected to listen, to the gradually increasing uproar in the stables of Berlifitzing—or perhaps pondered upon some more novel, some more decided act of audacity—his eyes became unwittingly riveted to the figure of an enormous, and unnaturally coloured horse, represented in the tapestry as belonging to a Saracen ancestor of the family of his rival. The horse itself, in the foreground of the design, stood motionless and statue-like—while farther back, its discomfited rider perished by the dagger of a Metzengerstein.

On Frederick's lip arose a fiendish expression, as he became aware of the direction which his glance had, without his consciousness, assumed. Yet he did not remove it. On the contrary, he could by no means account for the overwhelming anxiety which appeared falling like a pall upon his senses. It was with difficulty that he reconciled his dreamy and incoherent feelings with the certainty of being awake. The longer he gazed the more absorbing became the spell—the more impossible did it appear that he could ever withdraw his glance from the fascination of that tapestry. But the tumult without becoming suddenly more violent, with a compulsory exertion he diverted his attention to the glare of ruddy light thrown full by the flaming stables upon the windows of the apartment.

The action, however, was but momentary, his gaze returned mechanically to the wall. To his extreme horror and astonishment, the head of the gigantic steed had, in the meantime, altered its position. The neck of the animal, before arched, as if in compassion, over the prostrate body of its lord, was now extended, at full length, in the direction of the baron. The eyes, before invisible, now wore an energetic and human expression, while they gleamed with a fiery and unusual red; and the distended lips of the apparently enraged horse left in full view his gigantic and disgusting teeth.

Stupefied with terror, the young nobleman tottered to the door. As he threw it open, a flash of red light, streaming far into the chamber, flung his shadow with a clear outline against the quivering tapestry, and he shuddered to perceive that shadow—as he staggered awhile upon the threshold—assuming the exact position, and precisely filling up the contour, of the relentless and triumphant murderer of the Saracen Berlifitzing.

To lighten the depression of his spirits, the baron hurried into the open air. At the principal gate of the palace he encountered three equerries. With much difficulty, and at the imminent peril of their lives, they were restraining the convulsive plunges of a gigantic and fiery-coloured horse.

"Whose horse? Where did you get him?" demanded the youth, in a querulous and husky tone of voice, as he became instantly aware that the mysterious steed in the tapestried chamber was the very counterpart of the furious animal before his eyes.

"He is your own property, sire," replied one of the equerries, "at least he is claimed by no other owner. We caught him flying, all smoking and foaming with rage, from the burning stables of the Castle Berlifitzing. Supposing him to have belonged to the old count's stud of foreign horses, we led him back as an estray. But the grooms there disclaim any title to the creature; which is strange, since he bears evident marks of having made a narrow escape from the flames.

"The letters W. V. B. are also branded very distinctly on his forehead," interrupted a second equerry, "I supposed them, of course, to be the initials of Wilhelm Von Berlifitzing—but all at the castle are positive in denying any knowledge of the horse."

"Extremely singular!" said the young baron, with a musing air, and apparently unconscious of the meaning of his words. "He is, as you say, a remarkable horse—a prodigious horse! although, as you very justly observe, of a suspicious and untractable character, let him be mine, however," he added, after a pause, "perhaps a rider like Frederick of Metzengerstein, may tame even the devil from the stables of Berlifitzing."

"You are mistaken, my lord; the horse, as I think we mentioned, is *not* from the stables of the count. If such had been the case, we know our duty better than to bring him into the presence of a noble of your family."

"True!" observed the baron, dryly, and at that instant a page of the bedchamber came from the palace with a heightened colour, and a precipitate step. He whispered into his master's ear an account of the sudden disappearance of a small portion of the tapestry, in an apartment which he designated; entering, at the same time, into particulars of a minute and circumstantial character; but from the low tone of voice in which these latter were communicated, nothing escaped to gratify the excited curiosity of the equerries.

The young Frederick, during the conference, seemed agitated by a variety of emotions. He soon, however, recovered his composure, and an expression of determined malignancy settled upon his countenance, as he gave peremptory orders that a certain chamber should be immediately locked up, and the key placed in his own possession.

"Have you heard of the unhappy death of the old hunter Berlifitzing?" said one of his vassals to the baron, as, after the departure of the page, the huge steed which that nobleman had adopted as his own, plunged and curvetted, with redoubled fury, down the long avenue which extended from the *château* to the stables of Metzengerstein.

"No!" said the baron, turning abruptly toward the speaker, "dead! say you?"

"It is indeed true, my lord; and, to a noble of your name, will be, I imagine, no unwelcome intelligence."

A rapid smile shot over the countenance of the listener. "How died he?"

"In his rash exertions to rescue a favourite portion of his hunting stud, he has himself perished miserably in the flames."

"I-n-d-e-e-d-!" ejaculated the baron, as if slowly and deliberately impressed with the truth of some exciting idea.

"Indeed;" repeated the vassal.

"Shocking!" said the youth, calmly, and turned quietly into the *château*.

From this date a marked alteration took place in the outward demeanour of the dissolute young Baron Frederick Von Metzengerstein. Indeed, his behaviour disappointed every expectation, and proved little in accordance with the views of many a manoeuvring mamma; while his habits and manner, still less than formerly, offered any thing congenial with those of the neighbouring aristocracy. He was never to be seen beyond the limits of his own domain, and, in this wide and social world, was utterly companionless—unless, indeed, that unnatural, impetuous, and fiery-coloured horse, which he henceforward continually bestrode, had any mysterious right to the title of his friend.

Numerous invitations on the part of the neighbourhood for a long time, however, periodically came in. "Will the baron honour our festivals with his presence?" "Will the baron join us in a hunting of the boar?"—"Metzengerstein does not hunt;" "Metzengerstein will not attend," were the haughty and laconic answers.

These repeated insults were not to be endured by an imperious nobility. Such invitations became less cordial—less frequent—in time they ceased altogether. The widow of the unfortunate Count Berlifitzing was even heard to express a hope "that the baron might be at home when he did not wish to be at home, since he disdained the company of his equals; and ride when he did not wish to ride, since he preferred the society of a horse." This to be sure was a very silly explosion of hereditary pique; and merely proved how singularly unmeaning our sayings are apt to become, when we desire to be unusually energetic.

The charitable, nevertheless, attributed the alteration in the conduct of the young nobleman to the natural sorrow of a son for the untimely loss of his parents—forgetting, however, his atrocious and reckless behaviour during the short period immediately succeeding that bereavement. Some there were, indeed, who suggested a too haughty idea of self-consequence and dignity. Others again (among them may be mentioned the family physician) did not hesitate in speaking of morbid melancholy, and hereditary ill-health; while dark hints, of a more equivocal nature, were current among the multitude.

Indeed, the Baron's perverse attachment to his lately-acquired charger—an attachment which seemed to attain new strength from every fresh example of the animal's ferocious and demon-like propensities—at length became, in the eyes of all reasonable men, a hideous and unnatural fervour. In the glare of noon—at the dead hour of night—in sickness or in health—in calm or in tempest—the young Metzengerstein seemed riveted to the saddle of that colossal horse, whose intractable audacities so well accorded with his own spirit.

There were circumstances, moreover, which coupled with late events, gave an unearthly and portentous character to the mania of the rider, and to the capabilities of the steed. The space passed over in a single leap had been accurately measured, and was found to exceed, by an astounding difference, the wildest expectations of the most imaginative. The baron, besides, had no particular *name* for the animal, although all the rest in his collection were distinguished by characteristic appellations. His stable, too, was appointed at a distance from the rest; and with regard to grooming and other necessary offices, none but the owner in person had ventured to officiate, or even to enter the enclosure of that particular stall.

It was also to be observed, that although the three grooms, who had caught the steed as he fled from the conflagration at Berlifitzing, had succeeded in arresting his course, by means of a chain-bridle and noose—yet no one of the three could with any certainty affirm that he had, during that dangerous struggle, or at any period thereafter, actually placed his hand upon the body of the beast. Instances of peculiar intelligence in the demeanour of a noble and high-spirited horse are not to be supposed capable of exciting unreasonable attention—especially among men who, daily trained to the labours of the chase, might appear well acquainted with the sagacity of a horse—but there were certain circumstances which intruded themselves per force upon the most sceptical and phlegmatic; and it is said there were times when the animal caused the gaping crowd who stood around to recoil in horror from the deep and impressive meaning of his terrible stamp—times when the young Metzengerstein turned pale and shrunk away from the rapid and searching expression of his earnest and human-looking eye.

Among all the retinue of the baron, however, none were found to doubt the ardour of that extraordinary affection which existed on the part of the young nobleman for the fiery qualities of his horse; at least, none but an insignificant and misshapen little page, whose deformities were in everybody's way, and whose opinions were of the least possible importance. He—if his ideas are worth mentioning at all—had the effrontery to assert that his master never vaulted into the saddle without an unaccountable and almost imperceptible shudder, and that, upon his return from every long-continued and habitual ride, an expression of triumphant malignity distorted every muscle in his countenance.

One tempestuous night, Metzengerstein, awaking from a heavy slumber, descended like a maniac from his chamber, and, mounting in hot haste, bounded away into the mazes of the forest. An occurrence so common attracted no particular attention, but his return was looked for with intense anxiety on the part of his domestics, when, after some hours' absence, the stupendous and magnificent battlements of the Chateau Metzengerstein, were discovered crackling and rocking to their very foundation, under the influence of a dense and livid mass of ungovernable fire.

As the flames, when first seen, had already made so terrible a progress that all efforts to save any portion of the building were evidently futile, the astonished neighbourhood stood idly around in silent and pathetic wonder. But a new and fearful object soon riveted the attention of the multitude, and proved how much more intense is the excitement wrought in the feelings of a crowd by the contemplation of human agony, than that brought about by the most appalling spectacles of inanimate matter.

Up the long avenue of aged oaks which led from the forest to the main entrance of the Château Metzengerstein, a steed, bearing an unbonneted and disordered rider, was seen leaping with an impetuosity which outstripped the very Demon of the

Tempest.

The career of the horseman was indisputably, on his own part, uncontrollable. The agony of his countenance, the convulsive struggle of his frame, gave evidence of superhuman exertion: but no sound, save a solitary shriek, escaped from his lacerated lips, which were bitten through and through in the intensity of terror. One instant, and the clattering of hoofs resounded sharply and shrilly above the roaring of the flames and the shrieking of the winds—another, and, clearing at a single plunge the gateway and the moat, the steed bounded far up the tottering staircases of the palace, and, with its rider, disappeared amid the whirlwind of chaotic fire.

The fury of the tempest immediately died away, and a dead calm sullenly succeeded. A white flame still enveloped the building like a shroud, and, streaming far away into the quiet atmosphere, shot forth a glare of preternatural light; while a cloud of smoke settled heavily over the battlements in the distinct colossal figure of—*a horse.*

Morella

Αυτο καθ' αυτο μεθ' αυτου, μονο ειδες αιει ου.
Itself, by itself, solely, one everlasting, and single.
—Plato: *Sympos.*

With a feeling of deep yet most singular affection I regarded my friend Morella. Thrown by accident into her society many years ago, my soul from our first meeting, burned with fires it had never before known; but the fires were not of Eros, and bitter and tormenting to my spirit was the gradual conviction that I could in no manner define their unusual meaning or regulate their vague intensity. Yet we met; and fate bound us together at the altar, and I never spoke of passion nor thought of love. She, however, shunned society, and, attaching herself to me alone rendered me happy. It is a happiness to wonder; it is a happiness to dream.

Morella's erudition was profound. As I hope to live, her talents were of no common order—her powers of mind were gigantic. I felt this, and, in many matters, became her pupil. I soon, however, found that, perhaps on account of her Presburg education, she placed before me a number of those mystical writings which are usually considered the mere dross of the early German literature. These, for what reason I could not imagine, were her favourite and constant study—and that in process of time they became my own, should be attributed to the simple but effectual influence of habit and example.

In all this, if I err not, my reason had little to do. My convictions, or I forget myself, were in no manner acted upon by the ideal, nor was any tincture of the mysticism which I read to be discovered, unless I am greatly mistaken, either in my deeds or in my thoughts. Persuaded of this, I abandoned myself implicitly to the guidance of my wife, and entered with an unflinching heart into the intricacies of her studies. And then—then, when poring over forbidden pages, I felt a forbidden spirit enkindling within me—would Morella place her cold hand upon my own, and rake up from the ashes of a dead philosophy some low, singular words, whose strange meaning burned themselves in upon my memory. And then, hour after hour, would I linger by her side, and dwell upon the music of her voice, until at length its melody was tainted with terror, and there fell a shadow upon my soul, and I grew pale, and shuddered inwardly at those too unearthly tones. And thus, joy suddenly faded into horror, and the most beautiful became the most hideous, as Hinnon became Ge-Henna.

It is unnecessary to state the exact character of those disquisitions which, growing out of the volumes I have mentioned, formed, for so long a time, almost the sole conversation of Morella and myself. By the learned in what might be termed theological morality they will be readily conceived, and by the unlearned they would, at all events, be little understood. The wild Pantheism of Fichte; the modified *Παλιγγενεσια* Paliggenedia of the Pythagoreans; and, above all, the doctrines of *Identity* as urged by Schelling, were generally the points of discussion presenting the most of beauty to the imaginative Morella. That identity which is termed personal, Mr. Locke, I think, truly defines to consist in the saneness of rational being. And since by person we understand an intelligent essence having reason, and since there is a consciousness which always accompanies thinking, it is this which makes us all to be that which we call *ourselves*—thereby distinguishing us from other beings that think, and giving us our personal identity. But the *principium indivduationis*—the notion of that identity *which at death is or is not lost forever*—was to me, at all times, a consideration of intense interest; not more from the perplexing and exciting nature of its consequences, than from the marked and agitated manner in which Morella mentioned them.

But, indeed, the time had now arrived when the mystery of my wife's manner oppressed me as a spell. I could no longer bear the touch of her wan fingers, nor the low tone of her musical language, nor the lustre of her melancholy eyes. And she knew all this, but did not upbraid; she seemed conscious of my weakness or my folly, and, smiling, called it fate. She seemed also conscious of a cause, to me unknown, for the gradual alienation of my regard; but she gave me no hint or token of its nature. Yet was she woman, and pined away daily. In time the crimson spot settled steadily upon the cheek, and the blue veins upon the pale forehead became prominent; and one instant my nature melted into pity, but in, next I met the glance of her meaning eyes, and then my soul sickened and became giddy with the giddiness of one who gazes downward into some dreary and unfathomable abyss.

Shall I then say that I longed with an earnest and consuming desire for the moment of Morella's decease? I did; but the fragile spirit clung to its tenement of clay for many days, for many weeks and irksome months, until my tortured nerves obtained the mastery over my mind, and I grew furious through delay, and, with the heart of a fiend, cursed the days and the hours and the bitter moments, which seemed to lengthen and lengthen as her gentle life declined, like shadows in the dying of the day.

But one autumnal evening, when the winds lay still in heaven, Morella called me to her bedside. There was a dim mist over all the earth, and a warm glow upon the waters, and amid the rich October leaves of the forest, a rainbow from the firmament had surely fallen.

"It is a day of days," she said, as I approached; "a day of all days either to live or die. It is a fair day for the sons of earth and life—ah, more fair for the daughters of heaven and death!"

I kissed her forehead, and she continued:

"I am dying, yet shall I live."

"Morella!"

"The days have never been when thou couldst love me—but her whom in life thou didst abhor, in death thou shalt adore."

"Morella!"

"I repeat I am dying. But within me is a pledge of that affection—ah, how little!—which thou didst feel for me, Morella. And when my spirit departs shall the child live—thy child and mine, Morella's. But thy days shall be days of sorrow—that sorrow which is the most lasting of impressions, as the cypress is the most enduring of trees. For the hours of thy happiness are over and joy is not gathered twice in a life, as the roses of Paestum twice in a year. Thou shalt no longer, then, play the Teian with time, but, being ignorant of the myrtle and the vine, thou shalt bear about with thee thy shroud on the earth, as do the Moslemin at Mecca."

"Morella!" I cried, "Morella! how knowest thou this?" but she turned away her face upon the pillow and a slight tremor coming over her limbs, she thus died, and I heard her voice no more.

Yet, as she had foretold, her child, to which in dying she had given birth, which breathed not until the mother breathed no more, her child, a daughter, lived. And she grew strangely in stature and intellect, and was the perfect resemblance of her who had departed, and I loved her with a love more fervent than I had believed it possible to feel for any denizen of earth.

But, ere long the heaven of this pure affection became darkened, and gloom, and horror, and grief swept over it in clouds. I said the child grew strangely in stature and intelligence. Strange, indeed, was her rapid increase in bodily size, but terrible, oh! terrible were the tumultuous thoughts which crowded upon me while watching the development of her mental being. Could it be otherwise, when I daily discovered in the conceptions of the child the adult powers and faculties of the woman? when the lessons of experience fell from the lips of infancy? and when the wisdom or the passions of maturity I found hourly gleaming from its full and speculative eye?

When, I say, all this became evident to my appalled senses,

when I could no longer hide it from my soul, nor throw it off from those perceptions which trembled to receive it, is it to be wondered at that suspicions, of a nature fearful and exciting, crept in upon my spirit, or that my thoughts fell back aghast upon the wild tales and thrilling theories of the entombed Morella? I snatched from the scrutiny of the world a being whom destiny compelled me to adore, and in the rigorous seclusion of my home, watched with an agonising anxiety over all which concerned the beloved.

And as years rolled away, and I gazed day after day upon her holy, and mild, and eloquent face, and poured over her maturing form, day after day did I discover new points of resemblance in the child to her mother, the melancholy and the dead. And hourly grew darker these shadows of similitude, and more full, and more definite, and more perplexing, and more hideously terrible in their aspect. For that her smile was like her mother's I could bear; but then I shuddered at its too perfect *identity*—that her eyes were like Morella's I could endure; but then they, too, often looked down into the depths of my soul with Morella's own intense and bewildering meaning. And in the contour of the high forehead, and in the ringlets of the silken hair, and in the wan fingers which buried themselves therein, and in the sad musical tones of her speech, and above all—oh, above all, in the phrases and expressions of the dead on the lips of the loved and the living, I found food for consuming thought and horror—for a worm that *would* not die.

Thus passed away two *lustra* of her life, and as yet my daughter remained nameless upon the earth. "My child," and "my love," were the designations usually prompted by a father's affection, and the rigid seclusion of her days precluded all other intercourse. Morella's name died with her at her death. Of the mother I had never spoken to the daughter—it was impossible to speak. Indeed, during the brief period of her existence, the latter had received no impressions from the outward world, save such as might have been afforded by the narrow limits of her privacy. But at length the ceremony of baptism presented to my mind, in its unnerved and agitated condition, a present deliverance from the terrors of my destiny.

And at the baptismal font I hesitated for a name. And many titles of the wise and beautiful, of old and modern times, of my own and foreign lands, came thronging to my lips, with many, many fair titles of the gentle, and the happy, and the good. What prompted me then to disturb the memory of the buried dead? What demon urged me to breathe that sound, which in its very recollection was wont to make ebb the purple blood in torrents from the temples to the heart? What fiend spoke from the recesses of my soul, when amid those dim aisles, and in the silence of the night, I whispered within the ears of the holy man the syllables—Morella? What more than fiend convulsed the features of my child, and overspread them with hues of death, as starting at that scarcely audible sound, she turned her glassy eyes from the earth to heaven, and falling prostrate on the black slabs of our ancestral vault, responded—"I am here!"

Distinct, coldly, calmly distinct, fell those few simple sounds within my ear, and thence like molten lead rolled hissingly into my brain. Years—years may pass away, but the memory of that epoch never. Nor was I indeed ignorant of the flowers and the vine—but the hemlock and the cypress overshadowed me night and day. And I kept no reckoning of time or place, and the stars of my fate faded from heaven, and therefore the earth grew dark, and its figures passed by me like flitting shadows, and among them all I beheld only—Morella. The winds of the firmament breathed but one sound within my ears, and the ripples upon the sea murmured evermore—Morella. But she died; and with my own hands I bore her to the tomb; and I laughed with a long and bitter laugh as I found no traces of the first in the channel where I laid the second.—Morella.

Mystification

A.k.a. *Von Jung*

Slid, if these be your "passados" and "montantes,"
I'll have none o' them. —Ned Knowles.

The Baron Ritzner Von Jung was a noble Hungarian family, every member of which (at least as far back into antiquity as any certain records extend) was more or less remarkable for talent of some description—the majority for that species of *grotesquerie* in conception of which Tieck, a scion of the house, has given a vivid, although by no means the most vivid exemplifications. My acquaintance with Ritzner commenced at the magnificent Château Jung, into which a train of droll adventures, not to be made public, threw me during the summer months of the year 18—. Here it was that I obtained a place in his regard, and here, with somewhat more difficulty, a partial insight into his mental conformation. In later days this insight grew more clear, as the intimacy which had at first permitted it became more close; and when, after three years separation, we met at G——, I knew all that it was necessary to know of the character of the Baron Ritzner von Jung.

I remember the buzz of curiosity which his advent excited within the college precincts on the night of the twenty-fifth of June. I remember still more distinctly, that while he was pronounced by all parties at first sight "the most remarkable man in the world," no person made any attempt at accounting for his opinion. That he was *unique* appeared so undeniable, that it was deemed impertinent to inquire wherein the uniquity consisted.

But, letting this matter pass for the present, I will merely observe that, from the first moment of his setting foot within the limits of the university, he began to exercise over the habits, manners, persons, purses, and propensities of the whole community which surrounded him, an influence the most extensive and despotic, yet at the same time the most indefinite and altogether unaccountable. Thus the brief period of his residence at the university forms an era in its annals, and is characterised by all classes of people appertaining to it or its dependencies as "that very extraordinary epoch forming the domination of the Baron Ritzner von Jung."

Upon his advent to G——n, he sought me out in my apartments. He was then of no particular age, by which I mean that it was impossible to form a guess respecting his age by any data personally afforded. He might have been fifteen or fifty, and *was* twenty-one years and seven months. He was by no means a handsome man—perhaps the reverse. The contour of his face was somewhat angular and harsh. His forehead was lofty and very fair; his nose a snub; his eyes large, heavy, glassy, and meaningless. About the mouth there was more to be observed. The lips were gently protruded, and rested the one upon the other, after such a fashion that it is impossible to conceive any, even the most complex, combination of human features, conveying so entirely, and so singly, the idea of unmitigated gravity, solemnity and repose.

It will be perceived, no doubt, from what I have already said, that the baron was one of those human anomalies now and then to be found, who make the science of *mystification* the study and the business of their lives. For this science a peculiar turn of mind gave him instinctively the cue, while his physical appearance afforded him unusual facilities for carrying his prospects into effect. I firmly believe that no student at G——n, during that renowned epoch so quaintly termed the domination of the Baron Ritzner von Jung, ever rightly entered into the mystery which overshadowed his character.

I truly think that no person at the university, with the exception of myself, ever suspected him to be capable of a joke, verbal or practical:—the old bull-dog at the garden-gate would sooner have been accused,—the ghost of Heraclitus,—or the wig of the Emeritus Professor of Theology. This, too, when it was evident that the most egregious and unpardonable of all conceivable tricks, whimsicalities and buffooneries were brought about, if not directly by him, at least plainly through his intermediate agency or connivance. The beauty, if I may so call it, of his art *mystifique*, lay in that consummate ability (resulting from an almost intuitive knowledge of human nature, and a most wonderful self-possession,) by means of which he never failed to make it appear that the drolleries he was occupied in bringing to a point, arose partly in spite, and partly in consequence of the laudable efforts he was making for their prevention, and for the preservation of the good order and dignity of Alma Mater.

The deep, the poignant, the overwhelming mortification, which upon each such failure of his praise worthy endeavors, would suffuse every lineament of his countenance, left not the slightest room for doubt of his sincerity in the bosoms of even his most skeptical companions. The adroitness, too, was no less worthy of observation by which he contrived to shift the sense of the grotesque from the creator to the created—from his own person to the absurdities to which he had given rise. In no instance before that of which I speak, have I known the habitual mystific escape the natural consequence of his manoeuvres—an attachment of the ludicrous to his own character and person. Continually enveloped in an atmosphere of whim, my friend appeared to live only for the severities of society; and not even his own household have for a moment associated other ideas than those of the rigid and august with the memory of the Baron Ritzner von Jung.

During the epoch of his residence at G——n it really appeared that the demon of the *dolce far niente* lay like an incubus upon the university. Nothing, at least, was done beyond eating and drinking and making merry. The apartments of the students were converted into so many pot-houses, and there was no pot-house of them all more famous or more frequented than that of the baron. Our carousals here were many, and boisterous, and long, and never unfruitful of events.

Upon one occasion we had protracted our sitting until nearly daybreak, and an unusual quantity of wine had been drunk. The company consisted of seven or eight individuals besides the Baron and myself. Most of these were young men of wealth, of high connection, of great family pride, and all alive with an exaggerated sense of honor. They abounded in the most ultra German opinions respecting the *duello*. To these Quixotic notions some recent Parisian publications, backed by three or four desperate and fatal encounters at G——n, had given new vigour and impulse; and thus the conversation, during the greater part of the night, had run wild upon the all—engrossing topic of the times.

The baron, who had been unusually silent and abstracted in the earlier portion of the evening, at length seemed to be aroused from his apathy, took a leading part in the discourse, and dwelt upon the benefits, and more especially upon the beauties, of the received code of etiquette in passages of arms with an ardor, an eloquence, an impressiveness, and an affectionateness of manner, which elicited the warmest enthusiasm from his hearers in general, and absolutely staggered even myself, who well knew him to be at heart a ridiculer of those very points for which he contended, and especially to hold the entire *fanfaronade* of duelling etiquette in the sovereign contempt which it deserves.

Looking around me during a pause in the baron's discourse (of which my readers may gather some faint idea when I say that it bore resemblance to the fervid, chanting, monotonous, yet musical sermonic manner of Coleridge), I perceived symptoms of even more than the general interest in the countenance of one of the party. This gentleman, whom I shall call Hermann, was an original in every respect—except, perhaps, in the single particular that he was a very great fool. He contrived to bear, however, among a particular set at the university, a reputation for deep metaphysical thinking, and, I believe, for some logical talent.

As a duellist he had acquired great renown, even at G——n. I forget the precise number of victims who had fallen at his hands; but they were many. He was a man of courage undoubtedly. But it was upon his minute acquaintance with the etiquette of the *duello*, and the *nicety* of his sense of honour, that he most especially prided himself. These things were a hobby which he rode to the death. To Ritzner, ever upon the lookout for the grotesque, his peculiarities had for a long time past afforded food for mystification. Of this, however, I was not aware; although, in the present instance, I saw clearly that something of a whimsical nature was upon the *tapis* with my friend, and that Hermann was its especial object.

As the former proceeded in his discourse, or rather monologue I perceived the excitement of the latter momently increasing. At length he spoke; offering some objection to a point insisted upon by R., and giving his reasons in detail. To these the baron replied at length (still maintaining his exaggerated tone of sentiment) and concluding, in what I thought very bad taste, with a sarcasm and a sneer. The hobby of Hermann now took the bit in his teeth. This I could discern by the studied hair-splitting *farrago* of his rejoinder.

His last words I distinctly remember. "Your opinions, allow me to say, Baron von Jung, although in the main correct, are, in many nice points, discreditable to yourself and to the university of which you are a member. In a few respects they are even unworthy of serious refutation. I would say more than this, sir, were it not for the fear of giving you offence (here the speaker smiled blandly), I would say, sir, that your opinions are not the opinions to be expected from a gentleman."

As Hermann completed this equivocal sentence, all eyes were turned upon the baron. He became pale, then excessively red; then, dropping his pocket-handkerchief, stooped to recover it, when I caught a glimpse of his countenance, while it could be seen by no one else at the table. It was radiant with the quizzical expression which was its natural character, but which I had never seen it assume except when we were alone together, and when he unbent himself freely. In an instant afterward he stood erect, confronting Hermann; and so total an alteration of countenance in so short a period I certainly never saw before. For a moment I even fancied that I had misconceived him, and that he was in sober earnest. He appeared to be stifling with passion, and his face was cadaverously white. For a short time he remained silent, apparently striving to master his emotion. Having at length seemingly succeeded, he reached a decanter which stood near him, saying as he held it firmly clenched—

"The language you have thought proper to employ, Mynheer Hermann, in addressing yourself to me, is objectionable in so many particulars, that I have neither temper nor time for specification. That my opinions, however, are not the opinions to be expected from a gentleman, is an observation so directly offensive as to allow me but one line of conduct. Some courtesy, nevertheless, is due to the presence of this company, and to yourself, at this moment, as my guest. You will pardon me, therefore, if, upon this consideration, I deviate slightly from the general usage among gentlemen in similar cases of personal affront.

"You will forgive me for the moderate tax I shall make upon your imagination, and endeavor to consider, for an instant, the reflection of your person in yonder mirror as the living Mynheer Hermann himself. This being done, there will be no difficulty whatever. I shall discharge this decanter of wine at your image in yonder mirror, and thus fulfil all the spirit, if not the exact letter, of resentment for your insult, while the necessity of physical violence to your real person will be obviated."

With these words he hurled the decanter, full of wine, against the mirror which hung directly opposite Hermann; striking the reflection of his person with great precision, and of course shattering the glass into fragments. The whole company at once started to their feet, and, with the exception of myself and Ritzner, took their departure. As Hermann went out, the baron whispered me that I should follow him and make an offer of my services. To this I agreed; not knowing precisely what to make of so ridiculous a piece of business.

The duellist accepted my aid with his stiff and *ultra recherché* air, and, taking my arm, led me to his apartment. I could hardly forbear laughing in his face while he proceeded to discuss, with the profoundest gravity, what he termed "the refinedly peculiar character" of the insult he had received. After a tiresome harangue in his ordinary style, he took down from his book shelves a number of musty volumes on the subject of the *duello*, and entertained me for a long time with their contents; reading aloud, and commenting earnestly as he read. I can just remember the titles of some of the works. There were the *Ordonnance of Philip le Bel on Single Combat*; the *Theatre of Honour*, by Favyn, and a treatise *On the Permission of Duels*, by Andiguier.

He displayed, also, with much pomposity, Brantome's *Memoirs of Duels*,—published at Cologne, 1666, in the types of Elzevir—a precious and unique vellum-paper volume, with a fine margin, and bound by Derôme. But he requested my attention particularly, and with an air of mysterious sagacity, to a thick *octavo*, written in barbarous Latin by one Hedelin, a Frenchman, and having the quaint title, *Duelli Lex Scripta, et non; aliterque*. From this he read me one of the drollest chapters in the world concerning *Injuriae per applicationem, per constructionem, et per se*, about half of which, he averred, was strictly applicable to his own "refinedly peculiar" case, although not one syllable of the whole matter could I understand for the life of me. Having finished the chapter, he closed the book, and demanded what I thought necessary to be done. I replied that I had entire confidence in his superior delicacy of feeling, and would abide by what he proposed. With this answer he seemed flattered, and sat down to write a note to the baron. It ran thus:

> Sir,—My friend, M. P.-, will hand you this note. I find it incumbent upon me to request, at your earliest convenience, an explanation of this evening's occurrences at your chambers. In the event of your declining this request, Mr. P. will be happy to arrange, with any friend whom you may appoint, the steps preliminary to a meeting.

With sentiments of perfect respect,
Your most humble servant,
Johann Herman.
To the Baron Ritzner von Jung,
August 18th, 18—

Not knowing what better to do, I called upon Ritzner with this epistle. He bowed as I presented it; then, with a grave countenance, motioned me to a seat. Having perused the *cartel*, he wrote the following reply, which I carried to Hermann.

Sir,—Through our common friend, Mr. P., I have received your note of this evening. Upon due reflection I frankly admit the propriety of the explanation you suggest. This being admitted, I still find great difficulty, (owing to the *refinedly peculiar* nature of our disagreement, and of the personal affront offered on my part,) in so wording what I have to say by way of apology, as to meet all the minute exigencies, and all the variable shadows, of the case. I have great reliance, however, on that extreme delicacy of discrimination, in matters appertaining to the rules of etiquette, for which you have been so long and so pre-eminently distinguished. With perfect certainty, therefore, of being comprehended, I beg leave, in lieu of offering any sentiments of my own, to refer you to the opinions of Sieur Hedelin, as set forth in the ninth paragraph of the chapter of "*Injuriae per applicationem, per constructionem, et per se,*" in his *Duelli Lex scripta, et non; aliterque*. The nicety of your discernment in all the matters here treated, will be sufficient, I am assured, to convince you *that the mere circumstance of me referring you* to this admirable passage, ought to satisfy your request, as a man of honor, for explanation.

With sentiments of profound respect,
Your most obedient servant,
Von Jung.

The Herr Johann Hermann
August 18th, 18—

Hermann commenced the perusal of this epistle with a scowl, which, however, was converted into a smile of the most ludicrous self-complacency as he came to the rigmarole about *Injuriae per applicationem, per constructionem, et per se.* Having finished reading, he begged me, with the blandest of all possible smiles, to be seated, while he made reference to the treatise in question. Turning to the passage specified, he read it with great care to himself, then closed the book, and desired me, in my character of confidential acquaintance, to express to the Baron von Jung his exalted sense of his chivalrous behavior, and, in that of second, to assure him that the explanation offered was of the fullest, the most honorable, and the most unequivocally satisfactory nature.

Somewhat amazed at all this, I made my retreat to the Baron. He seemed to receive Hermann's amicable letter as a matter of course, and after a few words of general conversation, went to an inner room and brought out the everlasting treatise *Duelli Lex scripta, et non; aliterque.* He handed me the volume and asked me to look over some portion of it. I did so, but to little purpose, not being able to gather the least particle of meaning. He then took the book himself, and read me a chapter aloud. To my surprise, what he read proved to be a most horribly absurd account of a duel between two baboons.

He now explained the mystery; showing that the volume, as it appeared *prima facie,* was written upon the plan of the nonsense verses of Du Bartas; that is to say, the language was ingeniously framed so as to present to the ear all the outward signs of intelligibility, and even of profundity, while in fact not a shadow of meaning existed. The key to the whole was found in leaving out every second and third word alternately, when there appeared a series of ludicrous quizzes upon a single combat as practised in modern times.

The baron afterwards informed me that he had purposely thrown the treatise in Hermann's way two or three weeks before the adventure, and that he was satisfied, from the general tenor of his conversation, that he had studied it with the deepest attention, and firmly believed it to be a work of unusual merit. Upon this hint he proceeded. Hermann would have died a thousand deaths rather than acknowledge his inability to understand anything and everything in the universe that had ever been written about the *duello*.

Shadow—A Parable

Yea, though I walk through the valley of the Shadow:
—Psalm of David.

Ye who read are still among the living; but I who write shall have long since gone my way into the region of shadows. For indeed strange things shall happen, and secret things be known, and many centuries shall pass away, ere these memorials be seen of men. And, when seen, there will be some to disbelieve, and some to doubt, and yet a few who will find much to ponder upon in the characters here graven with a stylus of iron.

The year had been a year of terror, and of feelings more intense than terror for which there is no name upon the earth. For many prodigies and signs had taken place, and far and wide, over sea and land, the black wings of the Pestilence were spread abroad. To those, nevertheless, cunning in the stars, it was not unknown that the heavens wore an aspect of ill; and to me, the Greek Oinos, among others, it was evident that now had arrived the alternation of that seven hundred and ninety-fourth year when, at the entrance of Aries, the planet Jupiter is conjoined with the red ring of the terrible Saturnus. The peculiar spirit of the skies, if I mistake not greatly, made itself manifest, not only in the physical orb of the earth, but in the souls, imaginations, and meditations of mankind.

Over some flasks of the red Chian wine, within the walls of a noble hall, in a dim city called Ptolemais, we sat, at night, a company of seven. And to our chamber there was no entrance save by a lofty door of brass: and the door was fashioned by the artisan Corinnos, and, being of rare workmanship, was fastened from within. Black draperies, likewise, in the gloomy room, shut out from our view the moon, the lurid stars, and the peopleless streets—but the boding and the memory of Evil they would not be so excluded. There were things around us and about of which I can render no distinct account—things material and spiritual—heaviness in the atmosphere—a sense of suffocation—anxiety—and, above all, that terrible state of existence which the nervous experience when the senses are keenly living and awake, and meanwhile the powers of thought lie dormant.

A dead weight hung upon us. It hung upon our limbs—upon the household furniture—upon the goblets from which we drank; and all things were depressed, and borne down thereby—all things save only the flames of the seven lamps which illumined our revel. Uprearing themselves in tall slender lines of light, they thus remained burning all pallid and motionless; and in the mirror which their lustre formed upon the round table of ebony at which we sat, each of us there assembled beheld the pallor of his own countenance, and the unquiet glare in the downcast eyes of his companions. Yet we laughed and were merry in our proper way—which was hysterical; and sang the songs of Anacreon—which are madness; and drank deeply—although the purple wine reminded us of blood. For there was yet another tenant of our chamber in the person of young Zoilus. Dead, and at full length he lay, enshrouded; the genius and the demon of the scene.

Alas! he bore no portion in our mirth, save that his countenance, distorted with the plague, and his eyes, in which Death had but half extinguished the fire of the pestilence, seemed to take such interest in our merriment as the dead may haply take in the merriment of those who are to die. But although I, Oinos, felt that the eyes of the departed were upon me, still I forced myself not to perceive the bitterness of their expression, and gazing down steadily into the depths of the ebony mirror, sang with a loud and sonorous voice the songs of the son of Teios. But gradually my songs they ceased, and their echoes, rolling afar off among the sable draperies of the chamber, became weak, and undistinguishable, and so faded away.

And lo! from among those sable draperies where the sounds of the song departed, there came forth a dark and undefined shadow—a shadow such as the moon, when low in heaven, might fashion from the figure of a man: but it was the shadow neither of man nor of God, nor of any familiar thing. And quivering awhile among the draperies of the room, it at length rested in full view upon the surface of the door of brass. But the shadow was vague, and formless, and indefinite, and was the shadow neither of man nor of God—neither God of Greece, nor God of Chaldaea, nor any Egyptian God.

And the shadow rested upon the brazen doorway, and under the arch of the entablature of the door, and moved not, nor spoke any word, but there became stationary and remained. And the door whereupon the shadow rested was, if I remember aright, over against the feet of the young Zoilus enshrouded. But we, the seven there assembled, having seen the shadow as it came out from among the draperies, dared not steadily behold it, but cast down our eyes, and gazed continually into the depths of the mirror of ebony. And at length I, Oinos, speaking some low words, demanded of the shadow its dwelling and its appellation. And the shadow answered, "I am *Shadow*, and my dwelling is near to the Catacombs of Ptolemais, and hard by those dim plains of Helusion which border upon the foul Charonian canal."

And then did we, the seven, start from our seats in horror, and stand trembling, and shuddering, and aghast, for the tones in the voice of the shadow were not the tones of any one being, but of a multitude of beings, and, varying in their cadences from syllable to syllable fell duskly upon our ears in the well-remembered and familiar accents of many thousand departed friends.

Silence—A Fable

'Ευδουσιν ορεων κορυφαι τε και φαραγγες
Πρωονες τε και χαραδραι. —ALCMAN.

The mountain pinnacles slumber; valleys, crags and caves are silent.

"Listen to *me*," said the demon as he placed his hand upon my head. "The region of which I speak is a dreary region in Libya, by the borders of the river Zaire. And there is no quiet there, nor silence.

"The waters of the river have a saffron and sickly hue; and they flow not onwards to the sea, but palpitate forever and forever beneath the red eye of the sun with a tumultuous and convulsive motion. For many miles on either side of the river's oozy bed is a pale desert of gigantic water-lilies. They sigh one unto the other in that solitude, and stretch towards the heaven their long and ghastly necks, and nod to and fro their everlasting heads. And there is an indistinct murmur which cometh out from among them like the rushing of subterrene water. And they sigh one unto the other.

"But there is a boundary to their realm—the boundary of the dark, horrible, lofty forest. There, like the waves about the Hebrides, the low underwood is agitated continually. But there is no wind throughout the heaven. And the tall primeval trees rock eternally hither and thither with a crashing and mighty sound. And from their high summits, one by one, drop everlasting dews. And at the roots strange poisonous flowers lie writhing in perturbed slumber. And overhead, with a rustling and loud noise, the gray clouds rush westwardly forever, until they roll, a cataract, over the fiery wall of the horizon. But there is no wind throughout the heaven. And by the shores of the river Zaire there is neither quiet nor silence.

"It was night, and the rain fell; and falling, it was rain, but, having fallen, it was blood. And I stood in the morass among the tall and the rain fell upon my head—and the lilies sighed one unto the other in the solemnity of their desolation.

"And, all at once, the moon arose through the thin ghastly mist, and was crimson in colour. And mine eyes fell upon a huge gray rock which stood by the shore of the river, and was lighted by the light of the moon. And the rock was gray, and ghastly, and tall,—and the rock was gray. Upon its front were characters engraven in the stone; and I walked through the morass of water-lilies, until I came close unto the shore, that I might read the characters upon the stone. But I could not decipher them. And I was going back into the morass, when the moon shone with a fuller red, and I turned and looked again upon the rock, and upon the characters;—and the characters were *desolation.*

"And I looked upwards, and there stood a man upon the summit of the rock; and I hid myself among the water-lilies that I might discover the actions of the man. And the man was tall and stately in form, and was wrapped up from his shoulders to his feet in the toga of old Rome. And the outlines of his figure were indistinct—but his features were the features of a deity; for the mantle of the night, and of the mist, and of the moon, and of the dew, had left uncovered the features of his face. And his brow was lofty with thought, and his eye wild with care; and, in the few furrows upon his cheek I read the fables of sorrow, and weariness, and disgust with mankind, and a longing after solitude.

"And the man sat upon the rock, and leaned his head upon his hand, and looked out upon the desolation. He looked down into the low unquiet shrubbery, and up into the tall primeval trees, and up higher at the rustling heaven, and into the crimson moon. And I lay close within shelter of the lilies, and observed the actions of the man. And the man trembled in the solitude;—

but the night waned, and he sat upon the rock.

"And the man turned his attention from the heaven, and looked out upon the dreary River Zaire, and upon the yellow ghastly waters, and upon the pale legions of the water-lilies. And the man listened to the sighs of the water-lilies, and to the murmur that came up from among them. And I lay close within my covert and observed the actions of the man. And the man trembled in the solitude;—but the night waned and he sat upon the rock.

"Then I went down into the recesses of the morass, and waded afar in among the wilderness of the lilies, and called unto the hippopotami which dwelt among the fens in the recesses of the morass. And the hippopotami heard my call, and came, with the behemoth, unto the foot of the rock, and roared loudly and fearfully beneath the moon. And I lay close within my covert and observed the actions of the man. And the man trembled in the solitude;—but the night waned and he sat upon the rock.

"Then I cursed the elements with the curse of tumult; and a frightful tempest gathered in the heaven where, before, there had been no wind. And the heaven became livid with the violence of the tempest—and the rain beat upon the head of the man—and the floods of the river came down—and the river was tormented into foam—and the water-lilies shrieked within their beds—and the forest crumbled before the wind—and the thunder rolled—and the lightning fell—and the rock rocked to its foundation. And I lay close within my covert and observed the actions of the man. And the man trembled in the solitude;—but the night waned and he sat upon the rock.

"Then I grew angry and cursed, with the curse of *silence*, the river, and the lilies, and the wind, and the forest, and the heaven, and the thunder, and the sighs of the water-lilies. And they became accursed, and *were still.* And the moon ceased to totter up its pathway to heaven—and the thunder died away—and the lightning did not flash—and the clouds hung motionless—and the waters sunk to their level and remained—and the trees ceased to rock—and the water-lilies sighed no more—and the murmur was heard no longer from among them, nor any shadow of sound throughout the vast illimitable desert. And I looked upon the characters of the rock, and they were changed;—and the characters were *silence.*

"And mine eyes fell upon the countenance of the man, and his countenance was wan with terror. And, hurriedly, he raised his head from his hand, and stood forth upon the rock and listened. But there was no voice throughout the vast illimitable desert, and the characters upon the rock were *silence.* And the man shuddered, and turned his face away, and fled afar off, in haste, so that I beheld him no more."

★★★★★★

Now there are fine tales in the volumes of the *Magi*—in the iron-bound, melancholy volumes of the *Magi.* Therein, I say, are glorious histories of the Heaven, and of the Earth, and of the mighty sea—and of the *genii* that over-ruled the sea, and the earth, and the lofty heaven. There was much lore too in the sayings which were said by the Sybils; and holy, holy things were heard of old by the dim leaves that trembled around Dodona—but, as *Allah* liveth, that fable which the demon told me as he sat by my side in the shadow of the tomb, I hold to be the most wonderful of all! And as the demon made an end of his story, he fell back within the cavity of the tomb and laughed. And I could not laugh with the demon, and he cursed me because I could not laugh. And the lynx which dwelleth forever in the tomb, came out therefrom, and lay down at the feet of the demon, and looked at him steadily in the face.

The Angel of the Odd

An Extravaganza

It was a chilly November afternoon. I had just consummated an unusually hearty dinner, of which the dyspeptic *truffe* formed not the least important item, and was sitting alone in the dining-room, with my feet upon the fender, and at my elbow a small table which I had rolled up to the fire, and upon which were some apologies for dessert, with some miscellaneous bottles of wine, spirit and *liqueur*. In the morning I had been reading Glover's *Leonidas*, Wilkie's *Epigoniad*, Lamartine's *Pilgrimage*, Barlow's *Columbiad*, Tuckermann's *Sicily*, and Griswold's *Curiosities*; I am willing to confess, therefore, that I now felt a little stupid. I made effort to arouse myself by aid of frequent *Lafite*, and, all failing, I betook myself to a stray newspaper in despair. Having carefully perused the column of "houses to let," and the column of "dogs lost," and then the two columns of "wives and apprentices runaway," I attacked with great resolution the editorial matter, and, reading it from beginning to end without understanding a syllable, conceived the possibility of its being Chinese, and so re-read it from the end to the beginning, but with no more satisfactory result. I was about throwing away, in disgust, . . .

This folio of four pages, happy work
Which not even critics criticise,

. . . when I felt my attention somewhat aroused by the paragraph which follows:

The avenues to death are numerous and strange. A Lon-

> don paper mentions the decease of a person from a singular cause. He was playing at 'puff the dart,' which is played with a long needle inserted in some worsted, and blown at a target through a tin tube. He placed the needle at the wrong end of the tube, and drawing his breath strongly to puff the dart forward with force, drew the needle into his throat. It entered the lungs, and in a few days killed him.

Upon seeing this I fell into a great rage, without exactly knowing why. "This thing," I exclaimed, "is a contemptible falsehood—a poor hoax—the lees of the invention of some pitiable penny-a-liner—of some wretched concoctor of accidents in Cocaigne. These fellows, knowing the extravagant gullibility of the age, set their wits to work in the imagination of improbable possibilities—of odd accidents, as they term them; but to a reflecting intellect (like mine," I added, in parenthesis, putting my forefinger unconsciously to the side of my nose,) "to a contemplative understanding such as I myself possess, it seems evident at once that the marvelous increase of late in these 'odd accidents' is by far the oddest accident of all. For my own part, I intend to believe nothing henceforward that has anything of the 'singular' about it."

"*Mein Gott*, den, vat a vool you bees for dat!" replied one of the most remarkable voices I ever heard. At first I took it for a rumbling in my ears—such as a man sometimes experiences when getting very drunk—but, upon second thought, I considered the sound as more nearly resembling that which proceeds from an empty barrel beaten with a big stick; and, in fact, this I should have concluded it to be, but for the articulation of the syllables and words. I am by no means naturally nervous, and the very few glasses of *Lafite* which I had sipped served to embolden me no little, so that I felt nothing of trepidation, but merely uplifted my eyes with a leisurely movement, and looked carefully around the room for the intruder. I could not, however, perceive any one at all.

"Humph!" resumed the voice, as I continued my survey, "you mus pe so dronk as *de* pig, den, for not zee me as I zit here at your zide."

Hereupon I bethought me of looking immediately before my nose, and there, sure enough, confronting me at the table sat a personage nondescript, although not altogether indescribable. His body was a wine-pipe, or a rum-puncheon, or something of that character, and had a truly Falstaffian air. In its nether extremity were inserted two kegs, which seemed to answer all the purposes of legs. For arms there dangled from the upper portion of the carcass two tolerably long bottles, with the necks outward for hands. All the head that I saw the monster possessed of was one of those Hessian canteens which resemble a large snuff-box with a hole in the middle of the lid. This canteen (with a funnel on its top, like a cavalier cap slouched over the eyes) was set on edge upon the puncheon, with the hole toward myself; and through this hole, which seemed puckered up like the mouth of a very precise old maid, the creature was emitting certain rumbling and grumbling noises which he evidently intended for intelligible talk.

"I zay," said he, "you mos pe dronk as *de* pig, vor zit dare and not zee me zit ere; and I zay, doo, you mos pe pigger vool as *de* goose, vor to dispelief vat iz print in de print. 'Tiz *de* troof—dat it iz—eberry vord ob it."

"Who are you, pray?" said I, with much dignity, although somewhat puzzled; "how did you get here? and what is it you are talking about?"

"Az vor ow I com'd ere," replied the figure, "dat iz none of your pizzness; and as vor vat I be talking apout, I be talk apout vat I tink proper; and as vor who I be, vy dat is de very ting I com'd here for to let you zee for yourzelf."

"You are a drunken vagabond," said I, "and I shall ring the bell and order my footman to kick you into the street."

"He! he! he!" said the fellow, "hu! hu! hu! dat you can't do."

"Can't do!" said I, "what do you mean?—I can't do what?"

"Ring *de* pell;" he replied, attempting a grin with his little villainous mouth.

Upon this I made an effort to get up, in order to put my

threat into execution; but the ruffian just reached across the table very deliberately, and hitting me a tap on the forehead with the neck of one of the long bottles, knocked me back into the arm-chair from which I had half arisen. I was utterly astounded; and, for a moment, was quite at a loss what to do. In the meantime, he continued his talk.

"You zee," said he, "it iz te bess vor zit still; and now you shall know who I pe. Look at me! zee! I am te *Angel ov te Odd*."

"And odd enough, too," I ventured to reply; "but I was always under the impression that an angel had wings."

"Te wing!" he cried, highly incensed, "vat I pe do *mit* te wing? *Mein Gott!* do you take me vor a shicken?"

"No—oh no!" I replied, much alarmed, "you are no chicken—certainly not."

"Well, den, zit still and pehabe yourself, or I'll rap you again mid me vist. It iz te shicken ab te wing, und te owl ab te wing, und te imp ab te wing, und te head-teuffel ab te wing. Te angel ab *not* te wing, and I am te *Angel ov te Odd*."

"And your business with me at present is—is"—

"My pizzness!" ejaculated the thing, "vy vat a low bred buppy you mos pe vor to ask a gentleman *und* an angel apout his pizziness!"

This language was rather more than I could bear, even from an angel; so, plucking up courage, I seized a salt-cellar which lay within reach, and hurled it at the head of the intruder. Either he dodged, however, or my aim was inaccurate; for all I accomplished was the demolition of the crystal which protected the dial of the clock upon the mantel-piece. As for the angel, he evinced his sense of my assault by giving me two or three hard consecutive raps upon the forehead as before. These reduced me at once to submission, and I am almost ashamed to confess that either through pain or vexation, there came a few tears into my eyes.

"*Mein Gott!*" said the Angel of the Odd, apparently much softened at my distress; "*mein Gott*, te man is eder ferry dronk or ferry zorry. You mos not trink it so strong—you mos put te water in te wine. Here, trink dis, like a goot veller, und don't gry now—don't!"

Hereupon the Angel of the Odd replenished my goblet (which was about a third full of Port) with a colorless fluid that he poured from one of his hand bottles. I observed that these bottles had labels about their necks, and that these labels were inscribed "*Kirschenwasser*."

The considerate kindness of the angel mollified me in no little measure; and, aided by the water with which he diluted my Port more than once, I at length regained sufficient temper to listen to his very extraordinary discourse. I cannot pretend to recount all that he told me, but I gleaned from what he said that he was the genius who presided over the *contretemps* of mankind, and whose business it was to bring about the *odd accidents* which are continually astonishing the skeptic. Once or twice, upon my venturing to express my total incredulity in respect to his pretensions, he grew very angry indeed, so that at length I considered it the wiser policy to say nothing at all, and let him have his own way.

He talked on, therefore, at great length, while I merely leaned back in my chair with my eyes shut, and amused myself with munching raisins and filliping the stems about the room. But, by-and-by, the angel suddenly construed this behavior of mine into contempt. He arose in a terrible passion, slouched his funnel down over his eyes, swore a vast oath, uttered a threat of some character which I did not precisely comprehend, and finally made me a low bow and departed, wishing me, in the language of the archbishop in *Gil-Blas*, "*beaucoup de bonheur et un peu plus de bon sens*."

His departure afforded me relief. The *very* few glasses of *Lafite* that I had sipped had the effect of rendering me drowsy, and I felt inclined to take a nap of some fifteen or twenty minutes, as is my custom after dinner. At six I had an appointment of consequence, which it was quite indispensable that I should keep. The policy of insurance for my dwelling house had expired the day before; and, some dispute having arisen, it was agreed that, at six, I should meet the board of directors of the company and settle the terms of a renewal. Glancing upward at the clock on the mantel-piece, (for I felt too drowsy to take out my watch), I had the pleasure to find that I had still twenty-five minutes to spare. It was half past five; I could easily walk to the insurance office in five minutes; and my usual siestas had never been known to exceed five and twenty. I felt sufficiently safe, therefore, and composed myself to my slumbers forthwith.

Having completed them to my satisfaction, I again looked toward the time-piece and was half inclined to believe in the possibility of odd accidents when I found that, instead of my ordinary fifteen or twenty minutes, I had been dozing only three; for it still wanted seven and twenty of the appointed hour. I betook myself again to my nap, and at length a second time awoke, when, to my utter amazement, it *still* wanted twenty-seven minutes of six. I jumped up to examine the clock, and found that it had ceased running. My watch informed me that it was half past seven; and, of course, having slept two hours, I was too late for my appointment.

"It will make no difference," I said: "I can call at the office in the morning and apologise; in the meantime what can be the matter with the clock?" Upon examining it I discovered that one of the raisin stems which I had been filliping about the room during the discourse of the Angel of the Odd, had flown through the fractured crystal, and lodging, singularly enough, in the key-hole, with an end projecting outward, had thus arrested the revolution of the minute hand.

"Ah!" said I, "I see how it is. This thing speaks for itself. A natural accident, such as *will* happen now and then!"

I gave the matter no further consideration, and at my usual hour retired to bed. Here, having placed a candle upon a reading stand at the bed head, and having made an attempt to peruse some pages of the *Omnipresence of the Deity*, I unfortunately fell asleep in less than twenty seconds, leaving the light burning as it was.

My dreams were terrifically disturbed by visions of the Angel of the Odd. Methought he stood at the foot of the couch, drew aside the curtains, and, in the hollow, detestable tones of a rum puncheon, menaced me with the bitterest vengeance for the contempt with which I had treated him. He concluded a long harangue by taking off his funnel-cap, inserting the tube into my gullet, and thus deluging me with an ocean of *Kirschenwässer*, which he poured, in a continuous flood, from one of the long necked bottles that stood him instead of an arm.

My agony was at length insufferable, and I awoke just in time to perceive that a rat had ran off with the lighted candle from the stand, but *not* in season to prevent his making his escape with it through the hole. Very soon, a strong suffocating odor assailed my nostrils; the house, I clearly perceived, was on fire. In a few minutes the blaze broke forth with violence, and in an incredibly brief period the entire building was wrapped in flames. All egress from my chamber, except through a window, was cut off. The crowd, however, quickly procured and raised a long ladder.

By means of this I was descending rapidly, and in apparent safety, when a huge hog, about whose rotund stomach, and indeed about whose whole air and physiognomy, there was something which reminded me of the Angel of the Odd,—when this hog, I say, which hitherto had been quietly slumbering in the mud, took it suddenly into his head that his left shoulder needed scratching, and could find no more convenient rubbing-post than that afforded by the foot of the ladder. In an instant I was precipitated and had the misfortune to fracture my arm.

This accident, with the loss of my insurance, and with the more serious loss of my hair, the whole of which had been singed off by the fire, predisposed me to serious impressions, so that, finally, I made up my mind to take a wife. There was a rich widow disconsolate for the loss of her seventh husband, and to her wounded spirit I offered the balm of my vows. She yielded a reluctant consent to my prayers. I knelt at her feet in gratitude and adoration. She blushed and bowed her luxuriant tresses into close contact with those supplied me, temporarily, by Grandjean. I know not how the entanglement took place, but so it was. I arose with a shining pate, wigless; she in disdain and wrath, half buried in alien hair. Thus ended my hopes of the widow by an accident which could not have been anticipated, to be sure, but which the natural sequence of events had brought about.

Without despairing, however, I undertook the siege of a less implacable heart. The fates were again propitious for a brief period; but again a trivial incident interfered. Meeting my betrothed in an avenue thronged with the *élite* of the city, I was hastening to greet her with one of my best considered bows, when a small particle of some foreign matter, lodging in the corner of my eye, rendered me, for the moment, completely blind. Before I could recover my sight, the lady of my love had disappeared—irreparably affronted at what she chose to consider my premeditated rudeness in passing her by ungreeted.

While I stood bewildered at the suddenness of this accident, (which might have happened, nevertheless, to any one under the sun), and while I still continued incapable of sight, I was accosted by the Angel of the Odd, who proffered me his aid with a civility which I had no reason to expect. He examined my disordered eye with much gentleness and skill, informed me that I had a drop in it, and (whatever a "drop" was) took it out, and afforded me relief.

I now considered it high time to die, (since fortune had so determined to persecute me,) and accordingly made my way to the nearest river. Here, divesting myself of my clothes, (for there is no reason why we cannot die as we were born), I threw myself headlong into the current; the sole witness of my fate being a solitary crow that had been seduced into the eating of brandy-saturated corn, and so had staggered away from his fellows. No sooner had I entered the water than this bird took it into its head to fly away with the most indispensable portion of my apparel. Postponing, therefore, for the present, my suicidal design, I just slipped my nether extremities into the sleeves of my coat, and betook myself to a pursuit of the felon with all the nimbleness which the case required and its circumstances would admit.

But my evil destiny attended me still. As I ran at full speed, with my nose up in the atmosphere, and intent only upon the purloiner of my property, I suddenly perceived that my feet rested no longer upon *terra-firma*; the fact is, I had thrown myself over a precipice, and should inevitably have been dashed to pieces but for my good fortune in grasping the end of a long guide-rope, which depended from a passing balloon.

As soon as I sufficiently recovered my senses to comprehend the terrific predicament in which I stood or rather hung, I exerted all the power of my lungs to make that predicament known to the æronaut overhead. But for a long time I exerted myself in vain. Either the fool could not, or the villain would not perceive me. Meantime the machine rapidly soared, while my strength even more rapidly failed. I was soon upon the point of resigning myself to my fate, and dropping quietly into the sea, when my spirits were suddenly revived by hearing a hollow voice from above, which seemed to be lazily humming an opera air. Looking up, I perceived the Angel of the Odd. He was leaning with his arms folded, over the rim of the car; and with a pipe in his mouth, at which he puffed leisurely, seemed to be upon excellent terms with himself and the universe. I was too much exhausted to speak, so I merely regarded him with an imploring air.

For several minutes, although he looked me full in the face, he said nothing. At length removing carefully his meerschaum from the right to the left corner of his mouth, he condescended to speak.

"Who pe you," he asked, "und what der teuffel you pe do dare?"

To this piece of impudence, cruelty and affectation, I could reply only by ejaculating the monosyllable "Help!"

"Elp!" echoed the ruffian—"not I. Dare iz te pottle—elp yourself, *und* pe tam'd!"

With these words he let fall a heavy bottle of *Kirschenwasser* which, dropping precisely upon the crown of my head, caused me to imagine that my brains were entirely knocked out. Impressed with this idea, I was about to relinquish my hold and give up the ghost with a good grace, when I was arrested by the cry of the angel, who bade me hold on.

"Old on!" he said; "don't pe in te urry—don't. Will you pe take *de* odder pottle, or ave you pe got zober yet and come to your zenzes?"

I made haste, hereupon, to nod my head twice—once in the negative, meaning thereby that I would prefer not taking the other bottle at present—and once in the affirmative, intending thus to imply that I *was* sober and *had* positively come to my senses. By these means I somewhat softened the angel.

"Und you pelief, ten," he inquired, "at te last? You pelief, ten, in te possibilty of te odd?"

I again nodded my head in assent.

"Und you ave pelief in *me, te Angel of te Odd?*"

I nodded again.

"Und you acknowledge tat you pe te blind dronk and te vool?"

I nodded once more.

"Put your right hand into your left hand preeches pocket, ten, in token ov your vull zubmizzion unto *te Angel ov te Odd*."

This thing, for very obvious reasons, I found it quite impossible to do. In the first place, my left arm had been broken in my fall from the ladder, and, therefore, had I let go my hold with the right hand, I must have let go altogether. In the second place, I could have no breeches until I came across the crow. I was therefore obliged, much to my regret, to shake my head in the negative—intending thus to give the angel to understand that I found it inconvenient, just at that moment, to comply with his very reasonable demand! No sooner, however, had I ceased shaking my head than—

"Go to *der* teuffel, ten!" roared the Angel of the Odd.

In pronouncing these words, he drew a sharp knife across the guide-rope by which I was suspended, and as we then happened to be precisely over my own house, (which, during my peregrinations, had been handsomely rebuilt,) it so occurred that I tumbled headlong down the ample chimney and alit upon the dining-room hearth.

Upon coming to my senses, (for the fall had very thoroughly stunned me,) I found it about four o'clock in the morning. I lay outstretched where I had fallen from the balloon. My head grovelled in the ashes of an extinguished fire, while my feet reposed upon the wreck of a small table, overthrown, and amid the fragments of a miscellaneous dessert, intermingled with a newspaper, some broken glass and shattered bottles, and an empty jug of the Schiedam *Kirschenwasser*. Thus revenged himself the Angel of the Odd.

The Assignation

A.k.a. The Visionary

Stay for me there! I will not fail.
To meet thee in that hollow vale.
(Exequy on the death of his wife, by Henry King, Bishop of Chichester.)

Ill-fated and mysterious man!—bewildered in the brilliancy of thine own imagination, and fallen in the flames of thine own youth! Again in fancy I behold thee! Once more thy form hath risen before me!—not—oh not as thou art—in the cold valley and shadow—but as thou *shouldst be*—squandering away a life of magnificent meditation in that city of dim visions, thine own Venice—which is a star-beloved Elysium of the sea, and the wide windows of whose Palladian palaces look down with a deep and bitter meaning upon the secrets of her silent waters. Yes! I repeat it—as thou *shouldst be*. There are surely other worlds than this—other thoughts than the thoughts of the multitude—other speculations than the speculations of the sophist. Who then shall call thy conduct into question? who blame thee for thy visionary hours, or denounce those occupations as a wasting away of life, which were but the overflowings of thine everlasting energies?

It was at Venice, beneath the covered archway there called the *Ponte di Sospiri*, that I met for the third or fourth time the person of whom I speak. It is with a confused recollection that I bring to mind the circumstances of that meeting. Yet I remember—ah! how should I forget?—the deep midnight, the Bridge of Sighs, the beauty of woman, and the Genius of Romance that stalked up and down the narrow canal.

It was a night of unusual gloom. The great clock of the *piazza* had sounded the fifth hour of the Italian evening. The square of the Campanile lay silent and deserted, and the lights in the old Ducal Palace were dying fast away. I was returning home from the *piazetta*, by way of the Grand Canal. But as my *gondola* arrived opposite the mouth of the canal San Marco, a female voice from its recesses broke suddenly upon the night, in one wild, hysterical, and long continued shriek. Startled at the sound, I sprang upon my feet: while the *gondolier*, letting slip his single oar, lost it in the pitchy darkness beyond a chance of recovery, and we were consequently left to the guidance of the current which here sets from the greater into the smaller channel. Like some huge and sable-feathered condor, we were slowly drifting down towards the Bridge of Sighs, when a thousand *flambeaux* flashing from the windows, and down the staircases of the Ducal Palace, turned all at once that deep gloom into a livid and preternatural day.

A child, slipping from the arms of its own mother, had fallen from an upper window of the lofty structure into the deep and dim canal. The quiet waters had closed placidly over their victim; and, although my own *gondola* was the only one in sight, many a stout swimmer, already in the stream, was seeking in vain upon the surface, the treasure which was to be found, alas! only within the abyss. Upon the broad black marble flagstones at the entrance of the palace, and a few steps above the water, stood a figure which none who then saw can have ever since forgotten. It was the Marchesa Aphrodite—the adoration of all Venice—the gayest of the gay—the most lovely where all were beautiful—but still the young wife of the old and intriguing Mentoni, and the mother of that fair child, her first and only one, who now, deep beneath the murky water, was thinking in bitterness of heart upon her sweet caresses, and exhausting its little life in struggles to call upon her name.

She stood alone. Her small, bare, and silvery feet gleamed in the black mirror of marble beneath her. Her hair, not as yet more than half loosened for the night from its ball-room array, clustered, amid a shower of diamonds, round and round her classical head, in curls like those of the young hyacinth. A snowy-white and gauze-like drapery seemed to be nearly the sole covering to her delicate form; but the midsummer and midnight air was hot, sullen, and still, and no motion in the statue-like form itself, stirred even the folds of that raiment of very vapour which hung around it as the heavy marble hangs around the Niobe.

Yet—strange to say!—her large lustrous eyes were not turned downwards upon that grave wherein her brightest hope lay buried—but riveted in a widely different direction! The prison of the Old Republic is, I think, the stateliest building in all Venice—but how could that lady gaze so fixedly upon it, when beneath her lay stifling her only child? Yon dark, gloomy niche, too, yawns right opposite her chamber window—what, then, *could* there be in its shadows—in its architecture—in its ivy-wreathed and solemn cornices—that the Marchesa di Mentoni had not wondered at a thousand times before? Nonsense!—Who does not remember that, at such a time as this, the eye, like a shattered mirror, multiplies the images of its sorrow, and sees in innumerable far-off places, the woe which is close at hand?

Many steps above the *marchesa*, and within the arch of the water-gate, stood, in full dress, the Satyr-like figure of Mentoni himself. He was occasionally occupied in thrumming a guitar, and seemed *ennuyé* to the very death, as at intervals he gave directions for the recovery of his child. Stupefied and aghast, I had myself no power to move from the upright position I had assumed upon first hearing the shriek, and must have presented to the eyes of the agitated group a spectral and ominous appearance, as with pale countenance and rigid limbs, I floated down among them in that funereal *gondola*.

All efforts proved in vain. Many of the most energetic in the search were relaxing their exertions, and yielding to a gloomy sorrow. There seemed but little hope for the child; (how much less than for the mother!) but now, from the interior of that dark niche which has been already mentioned as forming a part of the Old Republican prison, and as fronting the lattice of the *marchesa*, a figure muffled in a cloak, stepped out within reach of the light, and, pausing a moment upon the verge of the giddy descent, plunged headlong into the canal. As, in an instant afterwards, he stood with the still living and breathing child within his grasp, upon the marble flagstones by the side of the *marchesa*, his cloak, heavy with the drenching water, became unfastened, and, falling in folds about his feet, discovered to the wonder-stricken spectators the graceful person of a very young man, with the sound of whose name the greater part of Europe was then ringing.

No word spoke the deliverer. But the *marchesa!* She will now receive her child—she will press it to her heart—she will cling to its little form, and smother it with her caresses. Alas! *another's* arms have taken it from the stranger—*another's* arms have taken it away, and borne it afar off, unnoticed, into the palace! And the *marchesa!* Her lip—her beautiful lip trembles: tears are gathering in her eyes—those eyes which, like Pliny's acanthus, are "soft and almost liquid." Yes! tears are gathering in those eyes—and see! the entire woman thrills throughout the soul, and the statue has started into life! The pallor of the marble countenance, the swelling of the marble bosom, the very purity of the marble feet, we behold suddenly flushed over with a tide of ungovernable crimson; and a slight shudder quivers about her delicate frame, as a gentle air at Napoli about the rich silver lilies in the grass.

Why *should* that lady blush! To this demand there is no answer—except that, having left, in the eager haste and terror of a mother's heart, the privacy of her own *boudoir*, she has neglected to enthral her tiny feet in their slippers, and utterly forgotten to throw over her Venetian shoulders that drapery which is their due. What other possible reason could there have been for her so blushing?—for the glance of those wild appealing eyes? for the unusual tumult of that throbbing bosom?—for the convulsive pressure of that trembling hand?—that hand which fell, as Mentoni turned into the palace, accidentally, upon the hand of the stranger. What reason could there have been for the low—the singularly low tone of those unmeaning words which the lady uttered hurriedly in bidding him *adieu*? "Thou hast conquered," she said, or the murmurs of the water deceived me; "thou hast conquered—one hour after sunrise—we shall meet—so let it be!"

******

The tumult had subsided, the lights had died away within the palace, and the stranger, whom I now recognized, stood alone upon the flags. He shook with inconceivable agitation, and his eye glanced around in search of a *gondola*. I could not do less than offer him the service of my own; and he accepted the civility. Having obtained an oar at the water-gate, we proceeded together to his residence, while he rapidly recovered his self-possession, and spoke of our former slight acquaintance in terms of great apparent cordiality.

There are some subjects upon which I take pleasure in being minute. The person of the stranger—let me call him by this title, who to all the world was still a stranger—the person of the stranger is one of these subjects. In height he might have been below rather than above the medium size: although there were moments of intense passion when his frame actually *expanded* and belied the assertion. The light, almost slender symmetry of his figure, promised more of that ready activity which he evinced at the Bridge of Sighs, than of that Herculean strength which he has been known to wield without an effort, upon occasions of more dangerous emergency.

With the mouth and chin of a deity—singular, wild, full, liquid eyes, whose shadows varied from pure hazel to intense and brilliant jet—and a profusion of curling, black hair, from which a forehead of unusual breadth gleamed forth at intervals all light and ivory—his were features than which I have seen none more classically regular, except, perhaps, the marble ones of the Emperor Commodus. Yet his countenance was, nevertheless, one of those which all men have seen at some period of their lives, and have never afterwards seen again. It had no peculiar—it had no settled predominant expression to be fastened upon the memory; a countenance seen and instantly forgotten—but forgotten with a vague and never-ceasing desire of recalling it to mind. Not that the spirit of each rapid passion failed, at any time, to throw its own distinct image upon the mirror of that face—but that the mirror, mirror-like, retained no vestige of the passion, when the passion had departed.

Upon leaving him on the night of our adventure, he solicited me, in what I thought an urgent manner, to call upon him *very* early the next morning. Shortly after sunrise, I found myself accordingly at his *palazzo*, one of those huge structures of gloomy, yet fantastic pomp, which tower above the waters of the Grand Canal in the vicinity of the Rialto. I was shown up a broad winding staircase of mosaics, into an apartment whose unparalleled splendour burst through the opening door with an actual glare, making me blind and dizzy with luxuriousness.

I knew my acquaintance to be wealthy. Report had spoken of his possessions in terms which I had even ventured to call terms of ridiculous exaggeration. But as I gazed about me, I could not bring myself to believe that the wealth of any subject in Europe could have supplied the princely magnificence which burned and blazed around.

Although, as I say, the sun had arisen, yet the room was still brilliantly lighted up. I judge from this circumstance, as well as from an air of exhaustion in the countenance of my friend, that he had not retired to bed during the whole of the preceding night. In the architecture and embellishments of the chamber, the evident design had been to dazzle and astound. Little attention had been paid to the *decora* of what is technically called *keeping*, or to the proprieties of nationality. The eye wandered from object to object, and rested upon none—neither the *grotesques* of the Greek painters, nor the sculptures of the best Italian days, nor the huge carvings of untutored Egypt.

Rich draperies in every part of the room trembled to the vibration of low, melancholy music, whose origin was not to be discovered. The senses were oppressed by mingled and conflicting perfumes, reeking up from strange convolute censers, together with multitudinous flaring and flickering tongues of emerald and violet fire. The rays of the newly risen sun poured in upon the whole, through windows, formed each of a single pane of crimson-tinted glass. Glancing to and fro, in a thousand reflections, from curtains which rolled from their cornices like cataracts of molten silver, the beams of natural glory mingled at length fitfully with the artificial light, and lay weltering in subdued masses upon a carpet of rich, liquid-looking cloth of Chili gold.

"Ha! ha! ha!—ha! ha! ha!"—laughed the proprietor, motioning me to a seat as I entered the room, and throwing himself back at full-length upon an ottoman. "I see," said he, perceiving that I could not immediately reconcile myself to the *bienséance* of so singular a welcome—"I see you are astonished at my apartment—at my statues—my pictures—my originality of conception in architecture and upholstery! absolutely drunk, eh, with my magnificence? But pardon me, my dear sir, (here his tone of voice dropped to the very spirit of cordiality,) pardon me for my uncharitable laughter. You appeared so *utterly* astonished. Besides, some things are so completely ludicrous, that a man *must* laugh or die.

"To die laughing, must be the most glorious of all glorious deaths! Sir Thomas More—a very fine man was Sir Thomas More—Sir Thomas More died laughing, you remember. Also in the *Absurdities* of Ravisius Textor, there is a long list of characters who came to the same magnificent end. Do you know, however," continued he musingly, "that at Sparta (which is now Palæ; ochori,) at Sparta, I say, to the west of the citadel, among a chaos of scarcely visible ruins, is a kind of *socle*, upon which are still legible the letters *ΛΑΞΜ.* They are undoubtedly part of *ΓΕΛΑΞΜΑ.* . Now, at Sparta were a thousand temples and shrines to a thousand different divinities. How exceedingly strange that the altar of Laughter should have survived all the others! But in the present instance," he resumed, with a singular alteration of voice and manner, "I have no right to be merry at your expense.

You might well have been amazed. Europe cannot produce anything so fine as this, my little regal cabinet. My other apartments are by no means of the same order—mere *ultras* of fashionable insipidity. This is better than fashion—is it not? Yet this has but to be seen to become the rage—that is, with those who could afford it at the cost of their entire patrimony. I have guarded, however, against any such profanation. With one exception, you are the only human being besides myself and my *valet*, who has been admitted within the mysteries of these imperial precincts, since they have been bedizened as you see!"

I bowed in acknowledgment—for the overpowering sense of splendour and perfume, and music, together with the unexpected eccentricity of his address and manner, prevented me from expressing, in words, my appreciation of what I might have construed into a compliment.

"Here," he resumed, arising and leaning on my arm as he sauntered around the apartment, "here are paintings from the Greeks to Cimabue, and from Cimabue to the present hour. Many are chosen, as you see, with little deference to the opinions of Virtu. They are all, however, fitting tapestry for a chamber such as this. Here, too, are some *chefs d'œuvres* of the unknown great; and here, unfinished designs by men, celebrated in their day, whose very names the perspicacity of the academies has left to silence and to me. What think you," said he, turning abruptly as he spoke—"what think you of this Madonna della Pieta?"

"It is Guido's own!" I said, with all the enthusiasm of my nature, for I had been poring intently over its surpassing loveliness. "It is Guido's own!—how *could* you have obtained it?—she is undoubtedly in painting what the Venus is in sculpture."

"Ha!" said he thoughtfully, "the Venus—the beautiful Venus?—the Venus of the Medici?—she of the diminutive head and the gilded hair? Part of the left arm (here his voice dropped so as to be heard with difficulty,) and all the right, are restorations; and in the coquetry of that right arm lies, I think, the quintessence of all affectation. Give *me* the Canova! The Apollo, too, is a copy—there can be no doubt of it—blind fool that I am, who cannot behold the boasted inspiration of the Apollo! I cannot help—pity me!—I cannot help preferring the Antinous. Was it not Socrates who said that the statuary found his statue in the block of marble? Then Michael Angelo was by no means original in his couplet—

Non ha l'ottimo artista alcun concetto
Che un marmo solo in se non circunscriva."

It has been, or should be remarked, that, in the manner of the true gentleman, we are always aware of a difference from the bearing of the vulgar, without being at once precisely able to determine in what such difference consists. Allowing the remark to have applied in its full force to the outward demeanour of my acquaintance, I felt it, on that eventful morning, still more fully applicable to his moral temperament and character. Nor can I better define that peculiarity of spirit which seemed to place him so essentially apart from all other human beings, than by calling it a *habit* of intense and continual thought, pervading even his most trivial actions—intruding upon his moments of dalliance—and interweaving itself with his very flashes of merriment—like adders which writhe from out the eyes of the grinning masks in the cornices around the temples of Persepolis.

I could not help, however, repeatedly observing, through the mingled tone of levity and solemnity with which he rapidly descanted upon matters of little importance, a certain air of trepidation—a degree of nervous *unction* in action and in speech—an unquiet excitability of manner which appeared to me at all times unaccountable, and upon some occasions even filled me with alarm. Frequently, too, pausing in the middle of a sentence whose commencement he had apparently forgotten, he seemed to be listening in the deepest attention, as if either in momentary expectation of a visitor, or to sounds which must have had existence in his imagination alone.

It was during one of these reveries or pauses of apparent abstraction, that, in turning over a page of the poet and scholar Politian's beautiful tragedy *The Orfeo*, (the first native Italian tragedy,) which lay near me upon an ottoman, I discovered a passage underlined in pencil. It was a passage towards the end of the third act—a passage of the most heart-stirring excitement—a passage which, although tainted with impurity, no man shall read without a thrill of novel emotion—no woman without a sigh. The whole page was blotted with fresh tears; and, upon the opposite interleaf, were the following English lines, written in a hand so very different from the peculiar characters of my acquaintance, that I had some difficulty in recognising it as his own:—

Thou wast that all to me, love,
For which my soul did pine—
A green isle in the sea, love,
A fountain and a shrine,
All wreathed with fairy fruits and flowers;
And all the flowers were mine.

Ah, dream too bright to last!
Ah, starry Hope, that didst arise
But to be overcast!
A voice from out the Future cries,
"Onward!"—but o'er the Past
(Dim gulf!) my spirit hovering lies,
Mute—motionless—aghast!

For alas! alas! with me
The light of life is o'er.
"No more—no more—no more,"
(Such language holds the solemn sea
To the sands upon the shore,)
Shall bloom the thunder-blasted tree,
Or the stricken eagle soar!

Now all my hours are trances;
And all my nightly dreams
Are where the dark eye glances,
And where thy footstep gleams,
In what ethereal dances,
By what Italian streams.

Alas! for that accursed time
They bore thee o'er the billow,
From Love to titled age and crime,
And an unholy pillow!—
From me, and from our misty clime,
Where weeps the silver willow!

That these lines were written in English—a language with which I had not believed their author acquainted—afforded me little matter for surprise. I was too well aware of the extent of his acquirements, and of the singular pleasure he took in concealing them from observation, to be astonished at any similar discovery; but the place of date, I must confess, occasioned me no little amazement. It had been originally written *London*, and afterwards carefully overscored—not, however, so effectually as to conceal the word from a scrutinizing eye. I say, this occasioned me no little amazement; for I well remember that, in a former conversation with a friend, I particularly inquired if he had at any time met in London the Marchesa di Mentoni, (who for some years previous to her marriage had resided in that city,) when his answer, if I mistake not, gave me to understand that he had never visited the metropolis of Great Britain. I might as well here mention, that I have more than once heard, (without, of course, giving credit to a report involving so many improbabilities,) that the person of whom I speak, was not only by birth, but in education, an *Englishman*.

******

"There is one painting," said he, without being aware of my notice of the tragedy—"there is still one painting which you have not seen." And throwing aside a drapery, he discovered a full-length portrait of the Marchesa Aphrodite.

Human art could have done no more in the delineation of her superhuman beauty. The same ethereal figure which stood before me the preceding night upon the steps of the Ducal Palace, stood before me once again. But in the expression of the countenance, which was beaming all over with smiles, there still lurked (incomprehensible anomaly!) that fitful stain of melancholy which will ever be found inseparable from the perfection of the beautiful. Her right arm lay folded over her bosom. With her left she pointed downward to a curiously fashioned vase. One small, fairy foot, alone visible, barely touched the earth; and, scarcely discernible in the brilliant atmosphere which seemed to encircle and enshrine her loveliness, floated a pair of the most delicately imagined wings. My glance fell from the painting to the figure of my friend, and the vigorous words of Chapman's *Bussy D'Ambois,* quivered instinctively upon my lips:

He is up
There like a Roman statue! He will stand
Till Death hath made him marble!

"Come," he said at length, turning towards a table of richly enamelled and massive silver, upon which were a few goblets fantastically stained, together with two large Etruscan vases, fashioned in the same extraordinary model as that in the foreground of the portrait, and filled with what I supposed to be *Johannisberger.* "Come," he said, abruptly, "let us drink! It is early—but let us drink. It is *indeed* early," he continued, musingly, as a cherub with a heavy golden hammer made the apartment ring with the first hour after sunrise: "It is *indeed* early—but what matters it? let us drink! Let us pour out an offering to yon solemn sun which these gaudy lamps and censers are so eager to subdue!" And, having made me pledge him in a bumper, he swallowed in rapid succession several goblets of the wine.

"To dream," he continued, resuming the tone of his desultory conversation, as he held up to the rich light of a censer one of the magnificent vases—"to dream has been the business of my life. I have therefore framed for myself, as you see, a bower of dreams. In the heart of Venice could I have erected a better? You behold around you, it is true, a medley of architectural embellishments. The chastity of Ionia is offended by antediluvian devices, and the sphinxes of Egypt are outstretched upon carpets of gold. Yet the effect is incongruous to the timid alone. Proprieties of place, and especially of time, are the bugbears which terrify mankind from the contemplation of the magnificent.

Once I was myself a *decorist*; but that sublimation of folly has palled upon my soul. All this is now the fitter for my purpose. Like these arabesque censers, my spirit is writhing in fire, and the delirium of this scene is fashioning me for the wilder visions of that land of real dreams whither I am now rapidly departing." He here paused abruptly, bent his head to his bosom, and seemed to listen to a sound which I could not hear. At length, erecting his frame, he looked upwards, and ejaculated the lines of the Bishop of Chichester:

Stay for me there! I will not fail
To meet thee in that hollow vale.

In the next instant, confessing the power of the wine, he threw himself at full-length upon an ottoman.

A quick step was now heard upon the staircase, and a loud knock at the door rapidly succeeded. I was hastening to anticipate a second disturbance, when a page of Mentoni's household burst into the room, and faltered out, in a voice choking with emotion, the incoherent words, "My mistress!—my mistress!—Poisoned!—poisoned! Oh, beautiful—oh, beautiful Aphrodite!"

Bewildered, I flew to the ottoman, and endeavoured to arouse the sleeper to a sense of the startling intelligence. But his limbs were rigid—his lips were livid—his lately beaming eyes were riveted in *death*. I staggered back towards the table—my hand fell upon a cracked and blackened goblet—and a consciousness of the entire and terrible truth flashed suddenly over my soul.

The Balloon-Hoax

(Astounding news by express, *via* Norfolk!—The Atlantic crossed in three days! Signal triumph of Mr. Monck Mason's flying machine!—Arrival at Sullivan's Island, near Charlestown, S.C., of Mr. Mason, Mr. Robert Holland, Mr. Henson, Mr. Harrison Ainsworth, and four others, in the steering balloon, "Victoria," after a passage of seventy-five hours from land to land! Full particulars of the voyage!

The subjoined *jeu d'esprit* with the preceding heading in magnificent capitals, well interspersed with notes of admiration, was originally published, as matter of fact, in the *New York Sun,* a daily newspaper, and therein fully subserved the purpose of creating indigestible aliment for the *quidnuncs* during the few hours intervening between a couple of the Charleston mails. The rush for the "sole paper which had the news," was something beyond even the prodigious; and, in fact, if (as some assert) the "Victoria" *did* not absolutely accomplish the voyage recorded, it will be difficult to assign a reason why she *should* not have accomplished it.)

The great problem is at length solved! The air, as well as the earth and the ocean, has been subdued by science, and will become a common and convenient highway for mankind. *The Atlantic has been actually crossed in a balloon!* and this too without difficulty—without any great apparent danger—with thorough control of the machine—and in the inconceivably brief period of seventy-five hours from shore to shore! By the energy of an agent at Charleston, S.C., we are enabled to be the first to furnish the public with a detailed account of this most extraordinary voyage, which was performed between Saturday, the 6th instant, at 11, a.m., and 2, p.m., on Tuesday, the 9th instant, by Sir Everard Bringhurst; Mr. Osborne, a nephew of Lord Bentinck's; Mr. Monck Mason and Mr. Robert Holland, the well-known aeronauts; Mr. Harrison Ainsworth, author of *Jack Sheppard*, &c.; and Mr. Henson, the projector of the late unsuccessful flying machine—with two seamen from Woolwich—in all, eight persons.

The particulars furnished below may be relied on as authentic and accurate in every respect, as, with a slight exception, they are copied *verbatim* from the joint diaries of Mr. Monck Mason and Mr. Harrison Ainsworth, to whose politeness our agent is also indebted for much verbal information respecting the balloon itself, its construction, and other matters of interest. The only alteration in the MS. received, has been made for the purpose of throwing the hurried account of our agent, Mr. Forsyth, into a connected and intelligible form.

THE BALLOON.

Two very decided failures, of late—those of Mr. Henson and Sir George Cayley—had much weakened the public interest in the subject of aerial navigation. Mr. Henson's scheme (which at first was considered very feasible even by men of science,) was founded upon the principle of an inclined plane, started from an eminence by an extrinsic force, applied and continued by the revolution of impinging vanes, in form and number resembling the vanes of a windmill. But, in all the experiments made with models at the Adelaide Gallery, it was found that the operation of these fans not only did not propel the machine, but actually impeded its flight.

The only propelling force it ever exhibited, was the mere *impetus* acquired from the descent of the inclined plane;

and this *impetus* carried the machine farther when the vanes were at rest, than when they were in motion—a fact which sufficiently demonstrates their inutility; and in the absence of the propelling, which was also the *sustaining* power, the whole fabric would necessarily descend. This consideration led Sir George Cayley to think only of adapting a propeller to some machine having of itself an independent power of support—in a word, to a balloon; the idea, however, being novel, or original, with Sir George, only so far as regards the mode of its application to practice. He exhibited a model of his invention at the Polytechnic Institution. The propelling principle, or power, was here, also, applied to interrupted surfaces, or vanes, put in revolution. These vanes were four in number, but were found entirely ineffectual in moving the balloon, or in aiding its ascending power. The whole project was thus a complete failure.

It was at this juncture that Mr. Monck Mason (whose voyage from Dover to Weilburg in the balloon, "Nassau," occasioned so much excitement in 1837,) conceived the idea of employing the principle of the Archimedean screw for the purpose of propulsion through the air—rightly attributing the failure of Mr. Henson's scheme, and of Sir George Cayley's, to the interruption of surface in the independent vanes. He made the first public experiment at Willis's Rooms, but afterward removed his model to the Adelaide Gallery.

Like Sir George Cayley's balloon, his own was an ellipsoid. Its length was thirteen feet six inches—height, six feet eight inches. It contained about three hundred and twenty cubic feet of gas, which, if pure hydrogen, would support twenty-one pounds upon its first inflation, before the gas has time to deteriorate or escape. The weight of the whole machine and apparatus was seventeen pounds—leaving about four pounds to spare. Beneath the centre of the balloon, was a frame of light wood, about nine feet long, and rigged on to the balloon itself with a network in the customary manner. From this framework was suspended a wicker basket or car.

The screw consists of an axis of hollow brass tube, eighteen inches in length, through which, upon a semi-spiral inclined at fifteen degrees, pass a series of steel wire radii, two feet long, and thus projecting a foot on either side. These radii are connected at the outer extremities by two bands of flattened wire—the whole in this manner forming the framework of the screw, which is completed by a covering of oiled silk cut into gores, and tightened so as to present a tolerably uniform surface.

At each end of its axis this screw is supported by pillars of hollow brass tube descending from the hoop. In the lower ends of these tubes are holes in which the pivots of the axis revolve. From the end of the axis which is next the car, proceeds a shaft of steel, connecting the screw with the pinion of a piece of spring machinery fixed in the car. By the operation of this spring, the screw is made to revolve with great rapidity, communicating a progressive motion to the whole. By means of the rudder, the machine was readily turned in any direction. The spring was of great power, compared with its dimensions, being capable of raising forty-five pounds upon a barrel of four inches diameter, after the first turn, and gradually increasing as it was wound up.

It weighed, altogether, eight pounds six ounces. The rudder was a light frame of cane covered with silk, shaped somewhat like a battle-door, and was about three feet long, and at the widest, one foot. Its weight was about two ounces. It could be turned *flat*, and directed upwards or downwards, as well as to the right or left; and thus enabled the aeronaut to transfer the resistance of the air which in an inclined position it must generate in its passage, to any side upon which he might desire to act; thus determining the balloon in the opposite direction.

This model (which, through want of time, we have necessarily described in an imperfect manner,) was put in action at the Adelaide Gallery, where it accomplished a velocity of five miles per hour; although, strange to say, it excited very little interest in comparison with the previous complex machine of Mr. Henson—so resolute is the world to despise anything which carries with it an air of simplicity. To accomplish the great desideratum of aerial navigation, it was very generally supposed that some exceedingly complicated application must be made of some unusually profound principle in dynamics.

So well satisfied, however, was Mr. Mason of the ultimate success of his invention, that he determined to construct immediately, if possible, a balloon of sufficient capacity to test the question by a voyage of some extent—the original design being to cross the British Channel, as before, in the Nassau balloon. To carry out his views, he solicited and obtained the patronage of Sir Everard Bringhurst and Mr. Osborne, two gentlemen well known for scientific acquirement, and especially for the interest they have exhibited in the progress of aerostation. The project, at the desire of Mr. Osborne, was kept a profound secret from the public—the only persons entrusted with the design being those actually engaged in the construction of the machine, which was built (under the superintendence of Mr. Mason, Mr. Holland, Sir Everard Bringhurst, and Mr. Osborne,) at the seat of the latter gentleman near Penstruthal, in Wales.

Mr. Henson, accompanied by his friend Mr. Ainsworth, was admitted to a private view of the balloon, on Saturday last—when the two gentlemen made final arrangements to be included in the adventure. We are not informed for what reason the two seamen were also included in the party—but, in the course of a day or two, we shall put our readers in possession of the minutest particulars respecting this extraordinary voyage.

The balloon is composed of silk, varnished with the liquid gum *caoutchouc*. It is of vast dimensions, containing more than 40,000 cubic feet of gas; but as coal gas was employed in place of the more expensive and inconvenient hydrogen, the supporting power of the machine, when fully inflated, and immediately after inflation, is not more than about 2500 pounds. The coal gas is not only much less costly, but is easily procured and managed.

For its introduction into common use for purposes of aerostation, we are indebted to Mr. Charles Green. Up to his discovery, the process of inflation was not only exceedingly expensive, but uncertain. Two, and even three days, have frequently been wasted in futile attempts to procure a sufficiency of hydrogen to fill a balloon, from which it had great tendency to escape, owing to its extreme subtlety, and its affinity for the surrounding atmosphere. In a balloon sufficiently perfect to retain its contents of coal-gas unaltered, in quantity or amount, for six months, an equal quantity of hydrogen could not be maintained in equal purity for six weeks.

The supporting power being estimated at 2500 pounds, and the united weights of the party amounting only to about 1200, there was left a surplus of 1300, of which again 1200 was exhausted by ballast, arranged in bags of different sizes, with their respective weights marked upon them—by cordage, barometers, telescopes, barrels containing provision for a fortnight, water-casks, cloaks, carpet-bags, and various other indispensable matters, including a coffee-warmer, contrived for warming coffee by means of slack-lime, so as to dispense altogether with fire, if it should be judged prudent to do so.

All these articles, with the exception of the ballast, and a few trifles, were suspended from the hoop overhead. The car is much smaller and lighter, in proportion, than the one appended to the model. It is formed of a light wicker, and is wonderfully strong, for so frail looking a machine.

Its rim is about four feet deep. The rudder is also very much larger, in proportion, than that of the model; and the screw is considerably smaller. The balloon is furnished besides with a grapnel, and a guide-rope; which latter is of the most indispensable importance. A few words, in explanation, will here be necessary for such of our readers as are not conversant with the details of aerostation.

As soon as the balloon quits the earth, it is subjected to the influence of many circumstances tending to create a difference in its weight; augmenting or diminishing its ascending power. For example, there may be a deposition of dew upon the silk, to the extent, even, of several hundred pounds; ballast has then to be thrown out, or the machine may descend. This ballast being discarded, and a clear sunshine evaporating the dew, and at the same time expanding the gas in the silk, the whole will again rapidly ascend. To check this ascent, the only recourse is, (or rather *was*, until Mr. Green's invention of the guide-rope,) the permission of the escape of gas from the valve; but, in the loss of gas, is a proportionate general loss of ascending power; so that, in a comparatively brief period, the best-constructed balloon must necessarily exhaust all its resources, and come to the earth. This was the great obstacle to voyages of length.

The guide-rope remedies the difficulty in the simplest manner conceivable. It is merely a very long rope which is suffered to trail from the car, and the effect of which is to prevent the balloon from changing its level in any material degree. If, for example, there should be a deposition of moisture upon the silk, and the machine begins to descend in consequence, there will be no necessity for discharging ballast to remedy the increase of weight, for it is remedied, or counteracted, in an exactly just proportion, by the deposit on the ground of just so much of the end of the rope as is necessary.

If, on the other hand, any circumstances should cause undue levity, and consequent ascent, this levity is immediately counteracted by the additional weight of rope upraised from the earth. Thus, the balloon can neither ascend or descend, except within very narrow limits, and its resources, either in gas or ballast, remain comparatively unimpaired. When passing over an expanse of water, it becomes necessary to employ small kegs of copper or wood, filled with liquid ballast of a lighter nature than water. These float, and serve all the purposes of a mere rope on land. Another most important office of the guide-rope, is to point out the *direction* of the balloon.

The rope *drags*, either on land or sea, while the balloon is free; the latter, consequently, is always in advance, when any progress whatever is made: a comparison, therefore, by means of the compass, of the relative positions of the two objects, will always indicate the *course*. In the same way, the angle formed by the rope with the vertical axis of the machine, indicates the *velocity*. When there is *no* angle—in other words, when the rope hangs perpendicularly, the whole apparatus is stationary; but the larger the angle, that is to say, the farther the balloon precedes the end of the rope, the greater the velocity; and the converse.

As the original design was to cross the British Channel, and alight as near Paris as possible, the voyagers had taken the precaution to prepare themselves with passports directed to all parts of the Continent, specifying the nature of the expedition, as in the case of the Nassau voyage, and entitling the adventurers to exemption from the usual formalities of office: unexpected events, however, rendered these passports superfluous.

The inflation was commenced very quietly at daybreak, on Saturday morning, the 6th instant, in the Court-Yard of Weal-Vor House, Mr. Osborne's seat, about a mile from Penstruthal, in North Wales; and at 7 minutes past 11, every thing being ready for departure, the balloon was set free, rising gently but steadily, in a direction nearly South; no use being made, for the first half hour, of either the screw or the rudder. We proceed now with the journal, as transcribed by Mr. Forsyth from the joint MSS. of Mr. Monck Mason, and Mr. Ainsworth. The body of the journal, as given, is in the hand-writing of Mr. Mason, and a P. S. is appended, each day, by Mr. Ainsworth, who has in preparation, and will shortly give the public a more minute, and no doubt, a thrillingly interesting account of the voyage.

THE JOURNAL.

Saturday, April the 6th.—Every preparation likely to embarrass us, having been made over night, we commenced the inflation this morning at daybreak; but owing to a thick fog, which encumbered the folds of the silk and rendered it unmanageable, we did not get through before nearly eleven o'clock. Cut loose, then, in high spirits, and rose gently but steadily, with a light breeze at North, which bore us in the direction of the British Channel. Found the ascending force greater than we had expected; and as we arose higher and so got clear of the cliffs, and more in the sun's rays, our ascent became very rapid. I did not wish, however, to lose gas at so early a period of the adventure, and so concluded to ascend for the present.

We soon ran out our guide-rope; but even when we had raised it clear of the earth, we still went up very rapidly. The balloon was unusually steady, and looked beautifully. In about ten minutes after starting, the barometer indicated an altitude of 15,000 feet. The weather was remarkably fine, and the view of the subjacent country—a most romantic one when seen from any point,—was now especially sublime. The numerous deep gorges presented the appearance of lakes, on account of the dense vapours with which they were filled, and the pinnacles and crags to the South East, piled in inextricable confusion, resembling nothing so much as the giant cities of eastern fable.

We were rapidly approaching the mountains in the South; but our elevation was more than sufficient to enable us to pass them in safety. In a few minutes we soared over them in fine style; and Mr. Ainsworth, with the seamen, was surprised at their apparent want of altitude when viewed from the car, the tendency of great elevation in a balloon being to reduce inequalities of the surface below, to nearly a dead level. At half-past eleven still proceeding nearly South, we obtained our first view of the Bristol Channel; and, in fifteen minutes afterward, the line of breakers on the coast appeared immediately beneath us, and we were fairly out at sea.

We now resolved to let off enough gas to bring our guide-rope, with the buoys affixed, into the water. This was immediately done, and we commenced a gradual descent. In about twenty minutes our first buoy dipped, and at the touch of the second soon afterwards, we remained stationary as to elevation. We were all now anxious to test the efficiency of the rudder and screw, and we put them both into requisition forthwith, for the purpose of altering our direction more to the eastward, and in a line for Paris. By means of the rudder we instantly effected the necessary change of direction, and our course was brought nearly at right angles to that of the wind; when we set in motion the spring of the screw, and were rejoiced to find it propel us readily as desired.

Upon this we gave nine hearty cheers, and dropped in the sea a bottle, enclosing a slip of parchment with a brief account of the principle of the invention. Hardly, however, had we done with our rejoicings, when an unforeseen accident occurred which discouraged us in no little degree. The steel rod connecting the spring with the propeller was suddenly jerked out of place, at the car end, (by a swaying of the car through some movement of one of the two seamen we had taken up,) and in an instant hung dangling out of reach, from the pivot of the axis of the screw. While we were endeavouring to regain it, our attention being completely absorbed, we became involved in a strong current of wind from the East, which bore us, with rapidly increasing force, towards the Atlantic. We soon found ourselves driving out to sea at the rate of not less, certainly, than fifty or sixty miles an hour, so that we came up with Cape Clear, at some forty miles to our North, before we had secured the rod, and had time to think what we were about.

It was now that Mr. Ainsworth made an extraordinary, but to my fancy, a by no means unreasonable or chimerical proposition, in which he was instantly seconded by Mr. Holland—*viz.*: that we should take advantage of the strong gale which bore us on, and in place of beating back to Paris, make an attempt to reach the coast of North America. After slight reflection I gave a willing assent to this bold proposition, which (strange to say) met with objection from the two seamen only. As the stronger party, however, we overruled their fears, and kept resolutely upon our course. We steered due west; but as the trailing of the buoys materially impeded our progress, and we had the balloon abundantly at command, either for ascent or descent, we first threw out fifty pounds of ballast, and then wound up (by means of a windlass) so much of the rope as brought it quite clear of the sea.

We perceived the effect of this manoeuvre immediately, in a vastly increased rate of progress; and, as the gale freshened, we flew with a velocity nearly inconceivable; the guide-rope flying out behind the car, like a streamer from a vessel. It is needless to say that a very short time sufficed us to lose sight of the coast. We passed over innumerable vessels of all kinds, a few of which were endeavouring to beat up, but the most of them lying to. We occasioned the greatest excitement on board all—an excitement greatly relished by ourselves, and especially by our two men, who, now under the influence of a dram of Geneva, seemed resolved to give all scruple, or fear, to the wind.

Many of the vessels fired signal guns; and in all we were

saluted with loud cheers (which we heard with surprising distinctness) and the waving of caps and handkerchiefs. We kept on in this manner throughout the day, with no material incident, and, as the shades of night closed around us, we made a rough estimate of the distance traversed. It could not have been less than five hundred miles, and was probably much more. The propeller was kept in constant operation, and, no doubt, aided our progress materially.

As the sun went down, the gale freshened into an absolute hurricane, and the ocean beneath was clearly visible on account of its phosphorescence. The wind was from the East all night, and gave us the brightest omen of success. We suffered no little from cold, and the dampness of the atmosphere was most unpleasant; but the ample space in the car enabled us to lie down, and by means of cloaks and a few blankets, we did sufficiently well.

P.S. (*by Mr. Ainsworth.*) The last nine hours have been unquestionably the most exciting of my life. I can conceive nothing more sublimating than the strange peril and novelty of an adventure such as this. May God grant that we succeed! I ask not success for mere safety to my insignificant person, but for the sake of human knowledge and—for the vastness of the triumph. And yet the feat is only so evidently feasible that the sole wonder is why men have scrupled to attempt it before. One single gale such as now befriends us—let such a tempest whirl forward a balloon for four or five days (these gales often last longer) and the voyager will be easily borne, in that period, from coast to coast.

In view of such a gale the broad Atlantic becomes a mere lake. I am more struck, just now, with the supreme silence which reigns in the sea beneath us, notwithstanding its agitation, than with any other phenomenon presenting itself. The waters give up no voice to the heavens. The immense flaming ocean writhes and is tortured uncomplainingly. The mountainous surges suggest the idea of innumerable dumb gigantic fiends struggling in impotent agony. In a night such as is this to me, a man *lives*—lives a whole century of ordinary life—nor would I forego this rapturous delight for that of a whole century of ordinary existence.

Sunday, the seventh. (Mr. Mason's MS.) This morning the gale, by 10, had subsided to an eight or nine—knot breeze, (for a vessel at sea,) and bears us, perhaps, thirty miles per hour, or more. It has veered, however, very considerably to the north; and now, at sundown, we are holding our course due west, principally by the screw and rudder, which answer their purposes to admiration. I regard the project as thoroughly successful, and the easy navigation of the air in any direction (not exactly in the teeth of a gale) as no longer problematical. We could not have made head against the strong wind of yesterday; but, by ascending, we might have got out of its influence, if requisite.
Against a pretty stiff breeze, I feel convinced, we can make our way with the propeller. At noon, today, ascended to an elevation of nearly 25,000 feet, by discharging ballast. Did this to search for a more direct current, but found none so favorable as the one we are now in. We have an abundance of gas to take us across this small pond, even should the voyage last three weeks. I have not the slightest fear for the result. The difficulty has been strangely exaggerated and misapprehended. I can choose my current, and should I find *all* currents against me, I can make very tolerable headway with the propeller. We have had no incidents worth recording. The night promises fair.

P.S. (*By Mr. Ainsworth.*) I have little to record, except the fact (to me quite a surprising one) that, at an elevation equal to that of Cotopaxi, I experienced neither very intense cold, nor headache, nor difficulty of breathing; neither, I find, did Mr. Mason, nor Mr. Holland, nor Sir Everard. Mr. Osborne complained of constriction of the chest—but this soon wore off. We have flown at a great rate during the day, and we must be more than half way across the Atlantic. We have passed over some twenty or thirty vessels of various kinds, and all seem to be delightfully astonished. Crossing the ocean in a balloon is not so difficult a feat after all. *Omne ignotum pro magnifico. Mem:* at 25,000 feet elevation the sky appears nearly black, and the stars are distinctly visible; while the sea does not seem convex (as one might suppose) but absolutely and most unequivocally *concave.*[1]

Monday, the 8th. (*Mr. Mason's MS.*) This morning we had again some little trouble with the rod of the propeller, which must be entirely remodelled, for fear of serious accident—I mean the steel rod—not the vanes. The latter could not be improved. The wind has been blowing steadily and strongly from the north-east all day and so far fortune seems bent upon favouring us. Just before day, we were all somewhat alarmed at some odd noises and concussions in the balloon, accompanied with the apparent rapid subsidence of the whole machine. These phenomena were occasioned by the expansion of the gas, through increase of heat in the atmosphere, and the consequent disruption of the minute particles of ice with which the network had become encrusted during the night. Threw

1. *Note.*—Mr. Ainsworth has not attempted to account for this phenomenon, which, however, is quite susceptible of explanation. A line dropped from an elevation of 25,000 feet, perpendicularly to the surface of the earth (or sea), would form the perpendicular of a right-angled triangle, of which the base would extend from the right angle to the horizon, and the hypotenuse from the horizon to the balloon. But the 25,000 feet of altitude is little or nothing, in comparison with the extent of the prospect. In other words, the base and hypotenuse of the supposed triangle would be so long when compared with the perpendicular, that the two former may be regarded as nearly parallel. In this manner the horizon of the aeronaut would appear to be *on a level* with the car. But, as the point immediately beneath him seems, and is, at a great distance below him, it seems, of course, also, at a great distance below the horizon. Hence the impression of *concavity*; and this impression must remain, until the elevation shall bear so great a proportion to the extent of prospect, that the apparent parallelism of the base and hypotenuse disappears—when the earth's real convexity must become apparent.

down several bottles to the vessels below. Saw one of them picked up by a large ship—seemingly one of the New York line packets. Endeavoured to make out her name, but could not be sure of it. Mr. Osborne's telescope made it out something like *Atalanta*. It is now twelve at night, and we are still going nearly west, at a rapid pace. The sea is peculiarly phosphorescent.

P.S. (*By Mr. Ainsworth.*) It is now two a.m., and nearly calm, as well as I can judge—but it is very difficult to determine this point, since we move *with* the air so completely. I have not slept since quitting Wheal-Vor, but can stand it no longer, and must take a nap. We cannot be far from the American coast.

Tuesday, the 9th. (Mr. Ainsworth's MS.) *One, p.m. We are in full view of the low coast of South Carolina.* The great problem is accomplished. We have crossed the Atlantic—fairly and *easily* crossed it in a balloon! God be praised! Who shall say that anything is impossible hereafter?

The journal here ceases. Some particulars of the descent were communicated, however, by Mr. Ainsworth to Mr. Forsyth. It was nearly dead calm when the voyagers first came in view of the coast, which was immediately recognized by both the seamen, and by Mr. Osborne. The latter gentleman having acquaintances at Fort Moultrie, it was immediately resolved to descend in its vicinity. The balloon was brought over the beach (the tide being out and the sand hard, smooth, and admirably adapted for a descent,) and the grapnel let go, which took firm hold at once. The inhabitants of the island, and of the fort, thronged out, of course, to see the balloon; but it was with the greatest difficulty that any one could be made to credit the actual voyage—*the crossing of the Atlantic.*

The grapnel caught at two p.m., precisely; and thus the whole voyage was completed in seventy-five hours; or rather less, counting from shore to shore. No serious accident occurred. No real danger was at any time apprehended. The balloon was exhausted and secured without trouble; and when the MS. from which this narrative is compiled was despatched from Charleston, the party were still at Fort Moultrie. Their farther intentions were not ascertained; but we can safely promise our readers some additional information either on Monday or in the course of the next day, at farthest.

This is unquestionably the most stupendous, the most interesting, and the most important undertaking, ever accomplished or even attempted by man. What magnificent events may ensue, it would be useless now to think of determining.

The Cask of Amontillado

The thousand injuries of Fortunato I had borne as I best could, but when he ventured upon insult, I vowed revenge. You, who so well know the nature of my soul, will not suppose, however, that I gave utterance to a threat. *At length* I would be avenged; this was a point definitely settled—but the very definiteness with which it was resolved precluded the idea of risk. I must not only punish, but punish with impunity. A wrong is unredressed when retribution overtakes its redresser. It is equally unredressed when the avenger fails to make himself felt as such to him who has done the wrong.

It must be understood that neither by word nor deed had I given Fortunato cause to doubt my good will. I continued, as was my wont, to smile in his face, and he did not perceive that my smile now was at the thought of his immolation.

He had a weak point—this Fortunato—although in other regards he was a man to be respected and even feared. He prided himself on his connoisseurship in wine. Few Italians have the true *virtuoso* spirit. For the most part their enthusiasm is adopted to suit the time and opportunity to practise imposture upon the British and Austrian *millionaires*. In painting and gemmary Fortunate, like his countrymen, was a quack, but in the matter of old wines he was sincere. In this respect I did not differ from him materially; I was skilful in the Italian vintages myself, and bought largely whenever I could.

It was about dusk, one evening during the supreme madness of the carnival season, that I encountered my friend. He accosted me with excessive warmth, for he had been drinking much. The man wore motley. He had on a tight-fitting parti-striped dress, and his head was surmounted by the conical cap and bells. I was so pleased to see him, that I thought I should never have done wringing his hand.

I said to him—"My dear Fortunato, you are luckily met. How remarkably well you are looking today! But I have received a pipe of what passes for Amontillado, and I have my doubts."

"How?" said he, "Amontillado? A pipe? Impossible? And in the middle of the carnival?"

"I have my doubts," I replied; "and I was silly enough to pay the full Amontillado price without consulting you in the matter. You were not to be found, and I was fearful of losing a bargain,"

"Amontillado!"

"I have my doubts."

"Amontillado!"

"And I must satisfy them."

"Amontillado!"

"As you are engaged, I am on my way to Luchesi. If any one has a critical turn, it is he. He will tell me—"

"Luchesi cannot tell Amontillado from Sherry."

"And yet some fools will have it that his taste is a match for your own."

"Come, let us go."

"Whither?"

"To your vaults."

"My friend, no; I will not impose upon your good nature. I perceive you have an engagement. Luchesi—"

"I have no engagement come."

"My friend, no. It is not the engagement, but the severe cold with which I perceive you are afflicted. The vaults are insufferably damp. They are encrusted with nitre."

"Let us go, nevertheless. The cold is merely nothing. Amontillado! You have been imposed upon; and as for Luchesi, he cannot distinguish Sherry from Amontillado."

Thus speaking, Fortunate possessed himself of my arm. Putting on a mask of black silk, and drawing a *roquelaure* closely about my person, I suffered him to hurry me to my *palazzo.*

There were no attendants at home; they had absconded to make merry in honour of the time. I had told them that I should not return until the morning, and had given them explicit orders not to stir from the house. These orders were sufficient, I well knew, to insure their immediate disappearance, one and all, as soon as my back was turned.

I took from their sconces two *flambeaux*, and giving one to Fortunate, bowed him through several suites of rooms to the archway that led into the vaults. I passed down a long and winding staircase, requesting him to be cautious as he followed. We came at length to the foot of the descent, and stood together on the damp ground of the catacombs of the Montresors.

The gait of my friend was unsteady, and the bells upon his cap jingled as he strode.

"The pipe," said he.

"It is farther on," said I; "but observe the white web-work which gleams from these cavern walls."

He turned towards me, and looked into my eyes with two filmy orbs that distilled the rheum of intoxication.

"Nitre?" he asked, at length.

"Nitre," I replied. "How long have you had that cough?"

"Ugh! ugh! ugh!—ugh! ugh! ugh!—ugh! ugh! ugh!—ugh! ugh! ugh!—ugh! ugh! ugh!"

My poor friend found it impossible to reply for many minutes.

"It is nothing," he said, at last.

"Come," I said, with decision, "we will go back; your health is precious. You are rich, respected, admired, beloved; you are happy, as once I was. You are a man to be missed. For me it is no matter. We will go back; you will be ill, and I cannot be responsible. Besides, there is Luchesi—"

"Enough," he said; "the cough is a mere nothing; it will not kill me. I shall not die of a cough."

"True—true," replied I; "and, indeed, I had no intention of alarming you unnecessarily—but you should use all proper caution. A draught of this Medoc will defend us from the damps."

Here I knocked off the neck of a bottle which I drew from a long row of its fellows that lay upon the mould.

"Drink," I said, presenting him the wine.

He raised it to his lips with a leer. He paused and nodded to me familiarly, while his bells jingled.

"I drink," he said, "to the buried that repose around us."

"And I to your long life."

He again took my arm, and we proceeded.

"These vaults," he said, "are extensive."

"The Montresors," I replied, "were a great and numerous family."

"I forget your arms."

"A huge human foot *d'or*, in a field azure; the foot crushes a serpent rampant whose fangs are imbedded in the heel."

"And the motto?"

"*Nemo me imfune lacessit.*"

"Good!" he said.

The wine sparkled in his eyes and the bells jingled. My own fancy grew warm with the Medoc. We had passed through walls of piled bones, with casks and puncheons intermingling, into the inmost recesses of the catacombs. I paused again, and this time I made bold to seize Fortunato by an arm above the elbow.

"The nitre!" I said: "see, it increases. It hangs like moss upon the vaults. We are below the river's bed. The drops of moisture trickle among the bones. Come, we will go back ere it is too late. Your cough—"

"It is nothing," he said; "let us go on. But first, another draught of the Medoc."

I broke and reached him a *flaçon* of De Grâve. He emptied it at a breath. His eyes flashed with a fierce light. He laughed and threw the bottle upwards with a gesticulation I did not understand.

I looked at him in surprise. He repeated the movement—a

grotesque one.

"You do not comprehend?" he said.

"Not I," I replied.

"Then you are not of the brotherhood?"

"How?"

"You are not of the masons."

"Yes, yes," I said, "yes, yes."

"You? Impossible! A mason?"

"A mason," I replied.

"A sign," he said.

"It is this," I answered, producing a trowel from beneath the folds of my *roquelaure*.

"You jest," he exclaimed, recoiling a few paces. "But let us proceed to the Amontillado."

"Be it so," I said, replacing the tool beneath the cloak, and again offering him my arm. He leaned upon it heavily. We continued our route in search of the Amontillado. We passed through a range of low arches, descended, passed on, and descending again, arrived at a deep crypt, in which the foulness of the air caused our *flambeaux* rather to glow than flame.

At the most remote end of the crypt there appeared another less spacious. Its walls had been lined with human remains piled to the vault overhead, in the fashion of the great catacombs of Paris. Three sides of this interior crypt were still ornamented in this manner. From the fourth the bones had been thrown down, and lay promiscuously upon the earth, forming at one point a mound of some size. Within the wall thus exposed by the displacing of the bones, we perceived a still interior recess, in depth about four feet, in width three, in height six or seven. It seemed to have been constructed for no especial use within itself, but formed merely the interval between two of the colossal supports of the roof of the catacombs, and was backed by one of their circumscribing walls of solid granite.

It was in vain that Fortunate, uplifting his dull torch, endeavoured to pry into the depths of the recess. Its termination the feeble light did not enable us to see.

"Proceed," I said; "herein is the Amontillado. As for Luchesi—"

"He is an ignoramus," interrupted my friend, as he stepped unsteadily forward, while I followed immediately at his heels. In an instant he had reached the extremity of the niche, and finding his progress arrested by the rock, stood stupidly bewildered. A moment more and I had fettered him to the granite. In its surface were two iron staples, distant from each other about two feet, horizontally. From one of these depended a short chain, from the other a padlock. Throwing the links about his waist, it was but the work of a few seconds to secure it. He was too much astounded to resist. Withdrawing the key I stepped back from the recess.

"Pass your hand," I said, "over the wall; you cannot help feeling the nitre. Indeed it is *very* damp. Once more let me *implore* you to return. No? Then I must positively leave you. But I must first render you all the attentions in my power."

"The Amontillado!" ejaculated my friend, not yet recovered from his astonishment.

"True," I replied; "the Amontillado."

As I said these words I busied myself among the pile of bones of which I have before spoken. Throwing them aside, I soon uncovered a quantity of building stone and mortar. With these materials and with the aid of my trowel, I began vigorously to wall up the entrance of the niche.

I had scarcely laid the first tier of the masonry when I discovered that the intoxication of Fortunato had in a great measure worn off. The earliest indication I had of this was a low moaning cry from the depth of the recess. It was *not* the cry of a drunken man. There was then a long and obstinate silence. I laid the second tier, and the third, and the fourth; and then I heard the furious vibrations of the chain. The noise lasted for several minutes, during which, that I might hearken to it with the more satisfaction, I ceased my labours and sat down upon the bones. When at last the clanking subsided, I resumed the trowel, and finished without interruption the fifth, the sixth, and the seventh tier.

The wall was now nearly upon a level with my breast. I again paused, and holding the *flambeaux* over the mason-work, threw a few feeble rays upon the figure within.

A succession of loud and shrill screams, bursting suddenly from the throat of the chained form, seemed to thrust me violently back. For a brief moment I hesitated—I trembled. Unsheathing my rapier, I began to grope with it about the recess; but the thought of an instant reassured me. I placed my hand upon the solid fabric of the catacombs, and felt satisfied. I reapproached the wall. I replied to the yells of him who clamoured. I re-echoed—I aided—I surpassed them in volume and in strength. I did this, and the clamourer grew still.

It was now midnight, and my task was drawing to a close. I had completed the eighth, the ninth, and the tenth tier. I had finished a portion of the last and the eleventh; there remained but a single stone to be fitted and plastered in. I struggled with its weight; I placed it partially in its destined position. But now there came from out the niche a low laugh that erected the hairs upon my head. It was succeeded by a sad voice, which I had difficulty in recognising as that of the noble Fortunato. The voice said—

"Ha! ha! ha!—he! he!—a very good joke indeed—an excellent jest. We will have many a rich laugh about it at the *palazzo*—he! he! He!—over our wine—he! he! he!"

"The Amontillado!" I said.

"He! he! he!—he! he! he!—yes, the Amontillado. But is it not getting late? Will not they be awaiting us at the *palazzo*, the Lady Fortunato and the rest? Let us be gone."

"Yes," I said, "let us be gone."

"*For the love of God, Montresor!*"

"Yes," I said, "for the love of God!"

But to these words I hearkened in vain for a reply. I grew impatient. I called aloud—

"Fortunato!"

No answer. I called again—

"Fortunato!"

No answer still. I thrust a torch through the remaining aperture and let it fall within. There came forth in return only a jingling of the bells. My heart grew sick—on account of the dampness of the catacombs. I hastened to make an end of my labour. I forced the last stone into its position; I plastered it up. Against the new masonry I re-erected the old rampart of bones. For the half of a century no mortal has disturbed them.

In pace requiescat!

The Colloquy of Monos and Una

Μελλοντα ταυτα.
These; things are in the future.

—Sophocles—Antig:

Una. "Born again?"

Monos. Yes, fairest and best beloved Una, "born again." These were the words upon whose mystical meaning I had so long pondered, rejecting the explanations of the priesthood, until Death himself resolved for me the secret.

Una. Death!

Monos. How strangely, sweet Una, you echo my words! I observe, too, a vacillation in your step—a joyous inquietude in your eyes. You are confused and oppressed by the majestic novelty of the Life Eternal. Yes, it was of Death I spoke. And here how singularly sounds that word which of old was wont to bring terror to all hearts—throwing a mildew upon all pleasures!

Una. Ah, Death, the spectre which sate at all feasts! How often, Monos, did we lose ourselves in speculations upon its nature! How mysteriously did it act as a check to human bliss—saying unto it "thus far, and no farther!" That earnest mutual love, my own Monos, which burned within our bosoms—how vainly did we flatter ourselves, feeling happy in its first upspringing, that our happiness would strengthen with its strength! Alas! as it grew, so grew in our hearts the dread of that evil hour which was hurrying to separate us forever! Thus, in time, it became painful to love. Hate would have been mercy then.

Monos. Speak not here of these griefs, dear Una—mine, mine, forever now!

Una. But the memory of past sorrow—is it not present joy? I have much to say yet of the things which have been. Above all, I burn to know the incidents of your own passage through the dark Valley and Shadow.

Monos. And when did the radiant Una ask anything of her Monos in vain? I will be minute in relating all—but at what point shall the weird narrative begin?

Una. At what point?

Monos. You have said.

Una. Monos, I comprehend you. In Death we have both learned the propensity of man to define the indefinable. I will not say, then, commence with the moment of life's cessation—but commence with that sad, sad instant when, the fever having abandoned you, you sank into a breathless and motionless torpor, and I pressed down your pallid eyelids with the passionate fingers of love.

Monos. One word first, my Una, in regard to man's general condition at this epoch. You will remember that one or two of the wise among our forefathers—wise in fact, although not in the world's esteem—had ventured to doubt the propriety of the term "improvement," as applied to the progress of our civilization. There were periods in each of the five or six centuries immediately preceding our dissolution, when arose some vigorous intellect, boldly contending for those principles whose truth appears now, to our disenfranchised reason, so utterly obvious—principles which should have taught our race to submit to the guidance of the natural laws, rather than attempt their control.

At long intervals some masterminds appeared, looking upon each advance in practical science as a retro-gradation in the true utility. Occasionally the poetic intellect—that intellect which we now feel to have been the most exalted of all—since those truths which to us were of the most enduring importance could only be reached by that *analogy* which speaks in proof tones to the imagination alone and to the unaided reason bears no weight—occasionally did this poetic intellect proceed a step farther in the evolving of the vague idea of the philosophic, and find in the mystic parable that tells of the tree of knowledge, and of its forbidden fruit, death-producing, a distinct intimation that knowledge was not meet for man in the infant condition of his soul.

And these men—the poets—living and perishing amid the scorn of the "utilitarians"—of rough pedants, who arrogated to themselves a title which could have been properly applied only to the scorned—these men, the poets, pondered piningly, yet not unwisely, upon the ancient days when our wants were not more simple than our enjoyments were keen—days when *mirth* was a word unknown, so solemnly deep-toned was happiness—holy, august and blissful days, when blue rivers ran undammed, between hills unhewn, into far forest solitudes, primeval, odorous, and unexplored.

Yet these noble exceptions from the general misrule served but to strengthen it by opposition. Alas! we had fallen upon the most evil of all our evil days. The great "movement"—that was the cant term—went on: a diseased commotion, moral and physical. Art—the Arts—arose supreme, and, once enthroned, cast chains upon the intellect which had elevated them to power. Man, because he could not but acknowledge the majesty of Nature, fell into childish exultation at his acquired and still-increasing dominion over her elements. Even while he stalked a God in his own fancy, an infantine imbecility came over him. As might be supposed from the origin of his disorder, he grew infected with system, and with abstraction. He enwrapped himself in generalities.

Among other odd ideas, that of universal equality gained ground; and in the face of analogy and of God—in despite of the loud warning voice of the laws of *gradation* so visibly pervading all things in Earth an Heaven—wild attempts at an omniprevalent Democracy were made. Yet this evil sprang necessarily from the leading evil, Knowledge. Man could not both know and succumb. Meantime huge smoking cities arose, innumerable. Green leaves shrank before the hot breath of furnaces. The fair face of Nature was deformed as with the ravages of some loathsome disease. And methinks, sweet Una, even our slumbering sense of the forced and of the far-fetched might have arrested us here.

But now it appears that we had worked out our own destruction in the perversion of our *taste*, or rather in the blind neglect of its culture in the schools. For, in truth, it was at this crisis that taste alone—that faculty which, holding a middle position between the pure intellect and the moral sense, could never safely have been disregarded—it was now that taste alone could have led us gently back to Beauty, to Nature, and to Life. But alas for the pure contemplative spirit and majestic intuition of Plato! Alas for the which he justly regarded as an all-sufficient education for the soul! Alas for him and for it!—since both were most desperately needed when both were most entirely forgotten or despised.[1]

Pascal, a philosopher whom we both love, has said, how truly!—"*que tout notre raisonnement se réduit à céder au sentiment*;" and it is not impossible that the sentiment of the natural, had time permitted it, would have regained its old ascendancy over the harsh mathematical reason of the schools. But this thing was not to be. Prematurely induced by intemperance of knowledge the old age of the world drew on. This the mass of mankind saw not, or, living lustily although unhappily, affected not to see. But, for myself, the Earth's records had taught me to look for widest ruin as the price of highest civilization.

---

1. "It will be hard to discover a better (method of education) than that which the experience of so many ages has already discovered; and this may be summed up as consisting in gymnastics for the body, and music for the soul."—Repub. lib. 2. "For this reason is a musical education most essential ; since it causes rhythm and harmony to penetrate most intimately into the soul, taking the strongest hold upon it, filling it with beauty and making the man beautifully-minded. . . . . He will praise and admire *the beautiful*; will receive it with joy into his soul, will feed upon it, and *assimilate his own condition with it*."—*Ibid*. lib. 3. Music μουσικη had, however, among the Athenians, a far more comprehensive signification than with us. It included not only the harmonics of time and of tune, but the poetic diction, sentiment and creation each in its widest sense. The study of *music* was with them, in fact, the general cultivation of the taste—of that which recognizes the beautiful—in contra-distinction, from reason, which deals only with the true.

I had imbibed a prescience of our Fate from comparison of China the simple and enduring, with Assyria the architect, with Egypt the astrologer, with Nubia, more crafty than either, the turbulent mother of all Arts. In history [2] of these regions I met with a ray from the Future. The individual artificialities of the three latter were local diseases of the Earth, and in their individual overthrows we had seen local remedies applied; but for the infected world at large I could anticipate no regeneration save in death. That man, as a race, should not become extinct, I saw that he must be "born again."

And now it was, fairest and dearest, that we wrapped our spirits, daily, in dreams. Now it was that, in twilight, we discoursed of the days to come, when the Art-scarred surface of the Earth, having undergone that purification [3] which alone could efface its rectangular obscenities, should clothe itself anew in the verdure and the mountain-slopes and the smiling waters of Paradise, and be rendered at length a fit dwelling-place for man:—for man the Death purged—for man to whose now exalted intellect there should be poison in knowledge no more—for the redeemed, regenerated, blissful, and now immortal, but still for the *material*, man.

Una. Well do I remember these conversations, dear Monos; but the epoch of the fiery overthrow was not so near at hand as we believed, and as the corruption you indicate did surely warrant us in believing. Men lived; and died individually. You yourself sickened, and passed into the grave; and thither your constant Una speedily followed you. And though the century which has since elapsed, and whose conclusion brings us thus together once more, tortured our slumbering senses with no impatience of duration, yet, my Monos, it was a century still.

Monos. Say, rather, a point in the vague infinity. Unquestionably, it was in the Earth's dotage that I died. Wearied at heart with anxieties which had their origin in the general turmoil

2. History, from *ἱστορειν*, to contemplate.

3. the word "purification" seems here to be used with reference to its root in Greek *πυρ*, fire

and decay, I succumbed to the fierce fever. After some few days of pain, and many of dreamy delirium replete with ecstasy, the manifestations of which you mistook for pain, while I longed but was impotent to undeceive you—after some days there came upon me, as you have said, a breathless and motionless torpor; and this was termed *Death* by those who stood around me.

Words are vague things. My condition did not deprive me of sentience. It appeared to me not greatly dissimilar to the extreme quiescence of him, who, having slumbered long and profoundly, lying motionless and fully prostrate in a midsummer noon, begins to steal slowly back into consciousness, through the mere sufficiency of his sleep, and without being awakened by external disturbances.

I breathed no longer. The pulses were still. The heart had ceased to beat. Volition had not departed, but was powerless. The senses were unusually active, although eccentrically so—assuming often each other's functions at random. The taste and the smell were inextricably confounded, and became one sentiment, abnormal and intense. The rose-water with which your tenderness had moistened my lips to the last, affected me with sweet fancies of flowers—fantastic flowers, far more lovely than any of the old Earth, but whose prototypes we have here blooming around us. The eyelids, transparent and bloodless, offered no complete impediment to vision. As volition was in abeyance, the balls could not roll in their sockets but all objects within the range of the visual hemisphere were seen with more or less distinctness; the rays which fell upon the external retina, or into the corner of the eye, producing a more vivid effect than those which struck the front or interior surface.

Yet, in the former instance, this effect was so far anomalous that I appreciated it only as *sound*—sound sweet or discordant as the matters presenting themselves at my side were light or dark in shade—curved or angular in outline. The hearing, at the same time, although excited in degree, was not irregular in action—estimating real sounds with an extravagance of precision, not less than of sensibility. Touch had undergone a modification more peculiar. Its impressions were tardily received, but pertinaciously retained, and resulted always in the highest physical pleasure. Thus the pressure of your sweet fingers upon my eyelids, at first only recognised through vision, at length, long after their removal, filled my whole being with a sensual delight immeasurable. I say with a sensual delight.

All my perceptions were purely sensual. The materials furnished the passive brain by the senses were not in the least degree wrought into shape by the deceased understanding. Of pain there was some little; of pleasure there was much; but of moral pain or pleasure none at all. Thus your wild sobs floated into my ear with all their mournful cadences, and were appreciated in their every variation of sad tone; but they were soft musical sounds and no more; they conveyed to the extinct reason no intimation of the sorrows which gave them birth; while the large and constant tears which fell upon my face, telling the bystanders of a heart which broke, thrilled every fibre of my frame with ecstasy alone. And this was in truth the *Death* of which these bystanders spoke reverently, in low whispers—you, sweet Una, gaspingly, with loud cries.

They attired me for the coffin—three or four dark figures which flitted busily to and fro. As these crossed the direct line of my vision they affected me as *forms*; but upon passing to my side their images impressed me with the idea of shrieks, groans, and other dismal expressions of terror, of horror, or of woe. You alone, habited in a white robe, passed in all directions musically about me.

The day waned; and, as its light faded away, I became possessed by a vague uneasiness—an anxiety such as the sleeper feels when sad real sounds fall continuously within his ear—low distant bell-tones, solemn, at long but equal intervals, and mingling with melancholy dreams. Night arrived; and with its shadows a heavy discomfort. It oppressed my limbs with the oppression of some dull weight, and was palpable. There was also a moaning sound, not unlike the distant reverberation of surf, but more continuous, which, beginning with the first twilight, had grown in strength with the darkness. Suddenly lights were brought into the room, and this reverberation became forthwith interrupted into frequent unequal bursts of the same sound, but less dreary and less distinct. The ponderous oppression was in a great measure relieved; and, issuing from the flame of each lamp, (for there were many,) there flowed unbrokenly into my ears a strain of melodious monotone.

And when now, dear Una, approaching the bed upon which I lay outstretched, you sat gently by my side, breathing odour from your sweet lips, and pressing them upon my brow, there arose tremulously within my bosom, and mingling with the merely physical sensations which circumstances had called forth, a something akin to sentiment itself—a feeling that, half appreciating, half responded to your earnest love and sorrow; but this feeling took no root in the pulseless heart, and seemed indeed rather a shadow than a reality, and faded quickly away, first into extreme quiescence, and then into a purely sensual pleasure as before.

And now, from the wreck and the chaos of the usual senses, there appeared to have arisen within me a sixth, all perfect. In its exercise I found a wild delight—yet a delight still physical, inasmuch as the understanding had in it no part. Motion in the animal frame had fully ceased. No muscle quivered; no nerve thrilled; no artery throbbed. But there seemed to have sprung up in the brain, *that* of which no words could convey to the merely human intelligence even an indistinct conception. Let me term it a mental pendulous pulsation. It was the moral embodiment of man's abstract idea of *Time*. By the absolute equalization of this movement—or of such as this—had the cycles of the firmamental orbs themselves, been adjusted.

By its aid I measured the irregularities of the clock upon the mantel, and of the watches of the attendants. Their tickings came sonorously to my ears. The slightest deviations from the true proportion—and these deviations were omni-prevalent—affected me just as violations of abstract truth were wont, on earth, to affect the moral sense. Although no two of the time-pieces in the chamber struck the individual seconds accurately together, yet I had no difficulty in holding steadily in mind the tones, and the respective momentary errors of each. And this—this keen, perfect, self-existing sentiment of *duration*—this sentiment existing (as man could not possibly have conceived it to exist) independently of any succession of events—this idea—this sixth sense, upspringing from the ashes of the rest, was the first obvious and certain step of the intemporal soul upon the threshold of the temporal Eternity.

It was midnight; and you still sat by my side. All others had departed from the chamber of *Death*. They had deposited me in the coffin. The lamps burned flickeringly; for this I knew by the tremulousness of the monotonous strains. But, suddenly these strains diminished in distinctness and in volume. Finally they ceased. The perfume in my nostrils died away. Forms affected my vision no longer. The oppression of the *Darkness* uplifted itself from my bosom. A dull shock like that of electricity pervaded my frame, and was followed by total loss of the idea of contact. All of what man has termed sense was merged in the sole consciousness of entity, and in the one abiding sentiment of duration. The mortal body had been at length stricken with the hand of the deadly *Decay*.

Yet had not all of sentience departed; for the consciousness and the sentiment remaining supplied some of its functions by a lethargic intuition. I appreciated the direful change now in operation upon the flesh, and, as the dreamer is sometimes aware of the bodily presence of one who leans over him, so, sweet Una, I still dully felt that you sat by my side. So, too, when the noon of the second day came, I was not unconscious of those movements which displaced you from my side, which confined me within the coffin, which deposited me within the hearse, which bore me to the grave, which lowered me within it, which heaped heavily the mould upon me, and which thus left me, in blackness and corruption, to my sad and solemn slumbers with the worm.

And here, in the prison-house which has few secrets to disclose, there rolled away days and weeks and months; and the soul watched narrowly each second as it flew, and, without effort, took record of its flight—without effort and without object.

A year passed. The consciousness of *being* had grown hourly more indistinct, and that of mere *locality* had, in great measure, usurped its position. The idea of entity was becoming merged in that of *place*. The narrow space immediately surrounding what had been the body, was now growing to be the body itself. At length, as often happens to the sleeper (by sleep and its world alone is *Death* imaged)—at length, as sometimes happened on Earth to the deep slumberer, when some flitting light half startled him into awaking, yet left him half enveloped in dreams—so to me, in the strict embrace of the *Shadow* came *that* light which alone might have had power to startle—the light of enduring *Love*. Men toiled at the grave in which I lay darkling. They upthrew the damp earth. Upon my mouldering bones there descended the coffin of Una.

And now again all was void. That nebulous light had been extinguished. That feeble thrill had vibrated itself into quiescence. Many *lustra* had supervened. Dust had returned to dust. The worm had food no more. The sense of being had at length utterly departed, and there reigned in its stead—instead of all things—dominant and perpetual—the autocrats *Place* and *Time*. For *that* which *was not*—for that which had no form—for that which had no thought—for that which had no sentience—for that which was soulless, yet of which matter formed no portion—for all this nothingness, yet for all this immortality, the grave was still a home, and the corrosive hours, co-mates.

The Conversation of Eiros and Charmion

Πυρ σοι προσοισω.

I will bring fire to thee.

—Euripides—Androm:

EIROS.

Why do you call me Eiros?

CHARMION

So henceforward will you always be called. You must forget too, *my* earthly name, and speak to me as Charmion.

EIROS.

This is indeed no dream!

CHARMION.

Dreams are with us no more;—but of these mysteries *anon*. I rejoice to see you looking life-like and rational. The film of the shadow has already passed from off your eyes. Be of heart and fear nothing. Your allotted days of stupor have expired and, to-morrow, I will myself induct you into the full joys and wonders of your novel existence.

EIROS.

True—I feel no stupor—none at all. The wild sickness and the terrible darkness have left me, and I hear no longer that mad, rushing, horrible sound, like the "voice of many waters." Yet my senses are bewildered, Charmion, with the keenness of their perception of the *new*.

CHARMION.

A few days will remove all this;—but I fully understand you, and feel for you. It is now ten earthly years since I underwent what you undergo—yet the remembrance of it hangs by me still. You have now suffered all of pain, however, which you will suffer in Aidenn.

EIROS.

In Aidenn?

CHARMION.

In Aidenn.

EIROS.

Oh God!—pity me, Charmion!—I am overburthened with the majesty of all things—of the unknown now known—of the speculative Future merged in the august and certain Present.

CHARMION.

Grapple not now with such thoughts. Tomorrow we will speak of this. Your mind wavers, and its agitation will find relief in the exercise of simple memories. Look not around, nor forward—but back. I am burning with anxiety to hear the details of that stupendous event which threw you among us. Tell me of it. Let us converse of familiar things, in the old familiar language of the world which has so fearfully perished.

EIROS.

Most fearfully, fearfully!—this is indeed no dream.

CHARMION.

Dreams are no more. Was I much mourned, my Eiros?

EIROS.

Mourned, Charmion?—oh deeply. To that last hour of all, there hung a cloud of intense gloom and devout sorrow over your household.

CHARMION.

And that last hour—speak of it. Remember that, beyond the naked fact of the catastrophe itself, I know nothing. When, coming out from among mankind, I passed into Night through the Grave—at that period, if I remember aright, the calamity which overwhelmed you was utterly unanticipated.

But, indeed, I knew little of the speculative philosophy of the day.

EIROS.

The individual calamity was as you say entirely unanticipated; but analogous misfortunes had been long a subject of discussion with astronomers. I need scarce tell you, my friend, that, even when you left us, men had agreed to understand those passages in the most holy writings which speak of the final destruction of all things by fire, as having reference to the orb of the earth alone. But in regard to the immediate agency of the ruin, speculation had been at fault from that epoch in astronomical knowledge in which the comets were divested of the terrors of flame. The very moderate density of these bodies had been well established. They had been observed to pass among the satellites of Jupiter, without bringing about any sensible alteration either in the masses or in the orbits of these secondary planets.

We had long regarded the wanderers as vapory creations of inconceivable tenuity, and as altogether incapable of doing injury to our substantial globe, even in the event of contact. But contact was not in any degree dreaded; for the elements of all the comets were accurately known. That among *them* we should look for the agency of the threatened fiery destruction had been for many years considered an inadmissible idea. But wonders and wild fancies had been, of late days, strangely rife among mankind; and, although it was only with a few of the ignorant that actual apprehension prevailed, upon the announcement by astronomers of a *new* comet, yet this announcement was generally received with I know not what of agitation and mistrust.

The elements of the strange orb were immediately calculated, and it was at once conceded by all observers, that its path, at perihelion, would bring it into very close proximity with the earth. There were two or three astronomers, of secondary note, who resolutely maintained that a contact was inevitable. I cannot very well express to you the effect of this intelligence upon the people. For a few short days they would not believe an assertion which their intellect so long employed among worldly considerations could not in any manner grasp. But the truth of a vitally important fact soon makes its way into the understanding of even the most stolid.

Finally, all men saw that astronomical knowledge lied not, and they awaited the comet. Its approach was not, at first, seemingly rapid; nor was its appearance of very unusual character. It was of a dull red, and had little perceptible train. For seven or eight days we saw no material increase in its apparent diameter, and but a partial alteration in its colour. Meantime, the ordinary affairs of men were discarded and all interests absorbed in a growing discussion, instituted by the philosophic, in respect to the cometary nature. Even the grossly ignorant aroused their sluggish capacities to such considerations. The learned now gave their intellect—their soul—to no such points as the allaying of fear, or to the sustenance of loved theory. They sought—they panted for right views. They groaned for perfected knowledge. *Truth* arose in the purity of her strength and exceeding majesty, and the wise bowed down and adored.

That material injury to our globe or to its inhabitants would result from the apprehended contact, was an opinion which hourly lost ground among the wise; and the wise were now freely permitted to rule the reason and the fancy of the crowd. It was demonstrated, that the density of the comet's *nucleus* was far less than that of our rarest gas; and the harmless passage of a similar visitor among the satellites of Jupiter was a point strongly insisted upon, and which served greatly to allay terror. Theologists with an earnestness fear-enkindled, dwelt upon the biblical prophecies, and expounded them to the people with a directness and simplicity of which no previous instance had been known.

That the final destruction of the earth must be brought about by the agency of fire, was urged with a spirit that enforced every where conviction; and that the comets were of no fiery nature (as all men now knew) was a truth which relieved all, in a great measure, from the apprehension of the great calamity foretold. It is noticeable that the popular prejudices and vulgar errors in regard to pestilences and wars—errors which were wont to prevail upon every appearance of a comet—were now altogether unknown. As if by some sudden convulsive exertion, reason had at once hurled superstition from her throne. The feeblest intellect had derived vigour from excessive interest.

What minor evils might arise from the contact were points of elaborate question. The learned spoke of slight geological disturbances, of probable alterations in climate, and consequently in vegetation, of possible magnetic and electric influences. Many held that no visible or perceptible effect would in any manner be produced. While such discussions were going on, their subject gradually approached, growing larger in apparent diameter, and of a more brilliant lustre. Mankind grew paler as it came. All human operations were suspended.

There was an epoch in the course of the general sentiment when the comet had attained, at length, a size surpassing that of any previously recorded visitation. The people now, dismissing any lingering hope that the astronomers were wrong, experienced all the certainty of evil. The chimerical aspect of their terror was gone. The hearts of the stoutest of our race beat violently within their bosoms. A very few days sufficed, however, to merge even such feelings in sentiments more unendurable We could no longer apply to the strange orb any *accustomed* thoughts. Its *historical* attributes had disappeared. It oppressed us with a hideous *novelty* of emotion. We saw it not as an astronomical phenomenon in the heavens, but as an incubus upon our hearts, and a shadow upon our brains. It had taken, with inconceivable rapidity, the character of a gigantic mantle of rare flame, extending from horizon to horizon.

Yet a day, and men breathed with greater freedom. It was clear that we were already within the influence of the comet; yet we lived. We even felt an unusual elasticity of frame and vivacity of mind. The exceeding tenuity of the object of our dread was apparent; for all heavenly objects were plainly visible through it. Meantime, our vegetation had perceptibly altered; and we gained faith, from this predicted circumstance, in the foresight of the wise. A wild luxuriance of foliage, utterly unknown before, burst out upon every vegetable thing.

Yet another day—and the evil was not altogether upon us.

It was now evident that its nucleus would first reach us. A wild change had come over all men; and the first sense of *pain* was the wild signal for general lamentation and horror. This first sense of pain lay in a rigorous constriction of the breast and lungs, and an insufferable dryness of the skin. It could not be denied that our atmosphere was radically affected; the conformation of this atmosphere and the possible modifications to which it might be subjected, were now the topics of discussion. The result of investigation sent an electric thrill of the intensest terror through the universal heart of man.

It had been long known that the air which encircled us was a compound of oxygen and nitrogen gases, in the proportion of twenty-one measures of oxygen, and seventy-nine of nitrogen in every one hundred of the atmosphere. Oxygen, which was the principle of combustion, and the vehicle of heat, was absolutely necessary to the support of animal life, and was the most powerful and energetic agent in nature. Nitrogen, on the contrary, was incapable of supporting either animal life or flame. An unnatural excess of oxygen would result, it had been ascertained in just such an elevation of the animal spirits as we had latterly experienced. It was the pursuit, the extension of the idea, which had engendered awe. What would be the result of *a total extraction of the nitrogen?* A combustion irresistible, all-devouring, omni-prevalent, immediate;—the entire fulfilment, in all their minute and terrible details, of the fiery and horror-inspiring denunciations of the prophecies of the Holy Book.

Why need I paint, Charmion, the now disenchained frenzy of mankind? That tenuity in the comet which had previously inspired us with hope, was now the source of the bitterness of despair. In its impalpable gaseous character we clearly perceived the consummation of Fate. Meantime a day again passed—bearing away with it the last shadow of Hope. We gasped in the rapid modification of the air. The red blood bounded tumultuously through its strict channels. A furious delirium possessed all men; and, with arms rigidly outstretched towards the threatening heavens, they trembled and shrieked aloud. But the nucleus of the destroyer was now upon us;—even here in Aidenn, I shudder while I speak.

Let me be brief—brief as the ruin that overwhelmed. For a moment there was a wild lurid light alone, visiting and penetrating all things. Then—let us bow down Charmion, before the excessive majesty of the great God!—then, there came a shouting and pervading sound, as if from the mouth itself of *Him*; while the whole incumbent mass of ether in which we existed, burst at once into a species of intense flame, for whose surpassing brilliancy and all-fervid heat even the angels in the high Heaven of pure knowledge have no name. Thus ended all.

The Devil in the Belfry

What o'clock is it?—Old Saying.

Everybody knows, in a general way, that the finest place in the world is—or, alas, *was*—the Dutch borough of Vondervotteimittiss. Yet as it lies some distance from any of the main roads, being in a somewhat out-of-the-way situation, there are perhaps very few of my readers who have ever paid it a visit. For the benefit of those who have *not*, therefore, it will be only proper that I should enter into some account of it. And this is indeed the more necessary, as with the hope of enlisting public sympathy in behalf of the inhabitants, I design here to give a history of the calamitous events which have so lately occurred within its limits. No one who knows me will doubt that the duty thus self-imposed will be executed to the best of my ability, with all that rigid impartiality, all that cautious examination into facts, and diligent collation of authorities, which should ever distinguish him who aspires to the title of historian.

By the united aid of medals, manuscripts, and inscriptions, I am enabled to say, positively, that the borough of Vondervotteimittiss has existed, from its origin, in precisely the same condition which it at present preserves. Of the date of this origin, however, I grieve that I can only speak with that species of indefinite definiteness which mathematicians are, at times, forced to put up with in certain algebraic formulae. The date, I may thus say, in regard to the remoteness of its antiquity, cannot be less than any assignable quantity whatsoever.

Touching the derivation of the name Vondervotteimittiss, I confess myself, with sorrow, equally at fault. Among a multitude of opinions upon this delicate point—some acute, some learned, some sufficiently the reverse—I am able to select nothing which ought to be considered satisfactory. Perhaps the idea of Grogswigg—nearly coincident with that of Kroutaplenttey—is to be cautiously preferred.—It runs:—

"*Vondervotteimittis—Vonder, lege Donder—Votteimittis, quasi und Bleitziz—Bleitziz obsol:—pro Blitzen.*"

This derivative, to say the truth, is still countenanced by some traces of the electric fluid evident on the summit of the steeple of the House of the Town-Council. I do not choose, however, to commit myself on a theme of such importance, and must refer the reader desirous of information to the "*Oratiunculae de Rebus Praeter-Veteris,*" of Dundergutz. See, also, Blunderbuzzard *De Derivationibus*, pp. 27 to 5010, Folio, Gothic edit., Red and Black character, Catch-word and No Cipher; wherein consult, also, marginal notes in the autograph of Stuffundpuff, with the Sub-Commentaries of Gruntundguzzell.

Notwithstanding the obscurity which thus envelops the date of the foundation of Vondervotteimittis, and the derivation of its name, there can be no doubt, as I said before, that it has always existed as we find it at this epoch. The oldest man in the borough can remember not the slightest difference in the appearance of any portion of it; and, indeed, the very suggestion of such a possibility is considered an insult. The site of the village is in a perfectly circular valley, about a quarter of a mile in circumference, and entirely surrounded by gentle hills, over whose summit the people have never yet ventured to pass. For this they assign the very good reason that they do not believe there is anything at all on the other side.

Round the skirts of the valley (which is quite level, and paved throughout with flat tiles), extends a continuous row of sixty little houses. These, having their backs on the hills, must look, of course, to the centre of the plain, which is just sixty yards from the front door of each dwelling. Every house has a small garden before it, with a circular path, a sun-dial, and twenty-four cabbages. The buildings themselves are so precisely alike, that one can in no manner be distinguished from the other. Owing to the vast antiquity, the style of architecture is somewhat odd, but it is not for that reason the less strikingly picturesque. They are fashioned of hard-burned little bricks, red, with black ends, so that the walls look like a chess-board upon a great scale.

The gables are turned to the front, and there are cornices, as big as all the rest of the house, over the eaves and over the main doors. The windows are narrow and deep, with very tiny panes and a great deal of sash. On the roof is a vast quantity of tiles with long curly ears. The woodwork, throughout, is of a dark hue and there is much carving about it, with but a trifling variety of pattern for, time out of mind, the carvers of Vondervotteimittiss have never been able to carve more than two objects—a time-piece and a cabbage. But these they do exceedingly well, and intersperse them, with singular ingenuity, wherever they find room for the chisel.

The dwellings are as much alike inside as out, and the furniture is all upon one plan. The floors are of square tiles, the chairs and tables of black-looking wood with thin crooked legs and puppy feet. The mantelpieces are wide and high, and have not only time-pieces and cabbages sculptured over the front, but a real time-piece, which makes a prodigious ticking, on the top in the middle, with a flower-pot containing a cabbage standing on each extremity by way of outrider. Between each cabbage and the time-piece, again, is a little China man having a large stomach with a great round hole in it, through which is seen the dial-plate of a watch.

The fireplaces are large and deep, with fierce crooked-looking fire-dogs. There is constantly a rousing fire, and a huge pot over it, full of *sauerkraut* and pork, to which the good woman of the house is always busy in attending. She is a little fat old lady, with blue eyes and a red face, and wears a huge cap like a sugar-loaf, ornamented with purple and yellow ribbons. Her dress is of orange-coloured linsey-woolsey, made very full behind and very short in the waist—and indeed very short in other respects, not reaching below the middle of her leg.

This is somewhat thick, and so are her ankles, but she has a fine pair of green stockings to cover them. Her shoes—of pink leather—are fastened each with a bunch of yellow ribbons puckered up in the shape of a cabbage. In her left hand she has a little heavy Dutch watch; in her right she wields a ladle for the *sauerkraut* and pork. By her side there stands a fat tabby cat, with a gilt toy-repeater tied to its tail, which "the boys" have there fastened by way of a quiz.

The boys themselves are, all three of them, in the garden attending the pig. They are each two feet in height. They have three-cornered cocked hats, purple waistcoats reaching down to their thighs, buckskin knee-breeches, red stockings, heavy shoes with big silver buckles, long *surtout* coats with large buttons of mother-of-pearl. Each, too, has a pipe in his mouth, and a little dumpy watch in his right hand. He takes a puff and a look, and then a look and a puff. The pig—which is corpulent and lazy—is occupied now in picking up the stray leaves that fall from the cabbages, and now in giving a kick behind at the gilt repeater, which the urchins have also tied to *his* tail in order to make him look as handsome as the cat.

Right at the front door, in a high-backed leather-bottomed armed chair, with crooked legs and puppy feet like the tables, is seated the old man of the house himself. He is an exceedingly puffy little old gentleman, with big circular eyes and a huge double chin. His dress resembles that of the boys—and I need say nothing farther about it. All the difference is, that his pipe is somewhat bigger than theirs and he can make a greater smoke. Like them, he has a watch, but he carries his watch in his pocket. To say the truth, he has something of more importance than a watch to attend to—and what that is, I shall presently explain. He sits with his right leg upon his left knee, wears a grave countenance, and always keeps one of his eyes, at least, resolutely bent upon a certain remarkable object in the centre of the plain.

This object is situated in the steeple of the House of the Town Council. The Town Council are all very little, round, oily, intelligent men, with big saucer eyes and fat double chins, and have their coats much longer and their shoe-buckles much bigger than the ordinary inhabitants of Vondervotteimittiss. Since my sojourn in the borough, they have had several special meetings, and have adopted these three important resolutions:

"That it is wrong to alter the good old course of things:"

"That there is nothing tolerable out of Vondervotteimittiss:" and—

"That we will stick by our clocks and our cabbages."

Above the session-room of the Council is the steeple, and in the steeple is the belfry, where exists, and has existed time out of mind, the pride and wonder of the village—the great clock of the borough of Vondervotteimittiss. And this is the object to which the eyes of the old gentlemen are turned who sit in the leather-bottomed armchairs.

The great clock has seven faces—one in each of the seven sides of the steeple—so that it can be readily seen from all quarters. Its faces are large and white, and its hands heavy and black. There is a belfry-man whose sole duty is to attend to it; but this duty is the most perfect of sinecures—for the clock of Vondervotteimittis was never yet known to have anything the matter with it. Until lately, the bare supposition of such a thing was considered heretical. From the remotest period of antiquity to which the archives have reference, the hours have been regularly struck by the big bell. And, indeed the case was just the same with all the other clocks and watches in the borough. Never was such a place for keeping the true time. When the large clapper thought proper to say "Twelve o'clock!" all its obedient followers opened their throats simultaneously, and responded like a very echo. In short, the good *burghers* were fond of their *sauerkraut*, but then they were proud of their clocks.

All people who hold sinecure offices are held in more or less respect, and as the belfry—man of Vondervotteimittiss has the most perfect of sinecures, he is the most perfectly respected of any man in the world. He is the chief dignitary of the borough, and the very pigs look up to him with a sentiment of reverence.

His coat-tail is *very* far longer—his pipe, his shoe—buckles, his eyes, and his stomach, *very* far bigger—than those of any other old gentleman in the village; and as to his chin, it is not only double, but triple.

I have thus painted the happy estate of Vondervotteimittiss: alas, that so fair a picture should ever experience a reverse!

There has been long a saying among the wisest inhabitants, that "no good can come from over the hills"; and it really seemed that the words had in them something of the spirit of prophecy. It wanted five minutes of noon, on the day before yesterday, when there appeared a very odd-looking object on the summit of the ridge of the eastward. Such an occurrence, of course, attracted universal attention, and every little old gentleman who sat in a leather-bottomed arm-chair turned one of his eyes with a stare of dismay upon the phenomenon, still keeping the other upon the clock in the steeple.

By the time that it wanted only three minutes to noon, the droll object in question was perceived to be a very diminutive foreign-looking young man. He descended the hills at a great rate, so that everybody had soon a good look at him. He was really the most finicky little personage that had ever been seen in Vondervotteimittiss. His countenance was of a dark snuff-color, and he had a long hooked nose, pea eyes, a wide mouth, and an excellent set of teeth, which latter he seemed anxious of displaying, as he was grinning from ear to ear. What with *mustachios* and whiskers, there was none of the rest of his face to be seen. His head was uncovered, and his hair neatly done up in *papillotes*. His dress was a tight-fitting swallow-tailed black coat (from one of whose pockets dangled a vast length of white handkerchief), black kerseymere knee-breeches, black stockings, and stumpy-looking pumps, with huge bunches of black satin ribbon for bows.

Under one arm he carried a huge *chapeau-de-bras*, and under the other a fiddle nearly five times as big as himself. In his left hand was a gold snuff-box, from which, as he capered down the hill, cutting all manner of fantastic steps, he took snuff incessantly with an air of the greatest possible self-satisfaction. God bless me!—here was a sight for the honest *burghers* of Vondervotteimittiss!

To speak plainly, the fellow had, in spite of his grinning, an audacious and sinister kind of face; and as he curvetted right into the village, the old stumpy appearance of his pumps excited no little suspicion; and many a *burgher* who beheld him that day would have given a trifle for a peep beneath the white cambric handkerchief which hung so obtrusively from the pocket of his swallow-tailed coat. But what mainly occasioned a righteous indignation was, that the scoundrelly popinjay, while he cut a *fandango* here, and a whirligig there, did not seem to have the remotest idea in the world of such a thing as *keeping time* in his steps.

The good people of the borough had scarcely a chance, however, to get their eyes thoroughly open, when, just as it wanted half a minute of noon, the rascal bounced, as I say, right into the midst of them; gave a *chassez* here, and a *balancez* there; and then, after a *pirouette* and a *pas-de-zephyr*, pigeon-winged himself right up into the belfry of the House of the Town Council, where the wonder-stricken belfry-man sat smoking in a state of dignity and dismay. But the little chap seized him at once by the nose; gave it a swing and a pull; clapped the big *chapeau de-bras* upon his head; knocked it down over his eyes and mouth; and then, lifting up the big fiddle, beat him with it so long and so soundly, that what with the belfry-man being so fat, and the fiddle being so hollow, you would have sworn that there was a regiment of double-bass drummers all beating the devil's tattoo up in the belfry of the steeple of Vondervotteimittiss.

There is no knowing to what desperate act of vengeance this unprincipled attack might have aroused the inhabitants, but for the important fact that it now wanted only half a second of noon. The bell was about to strike, and it was a matter of absolute and pre-eminent necessity that everybody should look well at his watch. It was evident, however, that just at this moment the fellow in the steeple was doing something that he had no business to do with the clock. But as it now began to strike, nobody had any time to attend to his manoeuvres, for they had all to count the strokes of the bell as it sounded.

"One!" said the clock.

"*Von!*" echoed every little old gentleman in every leather-bottomed arm-chair in Vondervotteimittiss. "*Von!*" said his watch also; "*von!*" said the watch of his *vrow*; and "*von!*" said the watches of the boys, and the little gilt repeaters on the tails of the cat and pig.

"Two!" continued the big bell; and

"*Doo!*" repeated all the repeaters.

"Three! Four! Five! Six! Seven! Eight! Nine! Ten!" said the bell.

"*Dree! Vour! Fibe! Sax! Seben! Aight! Noin! Den!*" answered the others.

"Eleven!" said the big one.

"*Eleben!*" assented the little ones.

"Twelve!" said the bell.

"*Dvelf!*" they replied perfectly satisfied, and dropping their voices.

"Und *dvelf* it is!" said all the little old gentlemen, putting up their watches. But the big bell had not done with them yet.

"Thirteen!" said he.

"*Der Teufel!*" gasped the little old gentlemen, turning pale, dropping their pipes, and putting down all their right legs from over their left knees.

"*Der Teufel!*" groaned they, "*Dirteen! Dirteen!!—Mein Gott,* it is *Dirteen* o'clock!!"

Why attempt to describe the terrible scene which ensued? All Vondervotteimittiss flew at once into a lamentable state of uproar.

"*Vot is cum'd to mein pelly?*" roared all the boys—"I've been ongry for *dis* hour!"

"*Vot is com'd to mein kraut?*" screamed all the *vrows*, "It has been done to rags for this hour!"

"*Vot is cum'd to mein pipe?*" swore all the little old gentlemen,

"*Donder* and *Blitzen*; it has been smoked out for *dis* hour!"—and they filled them up again in a great rage, and sinking back in their armchairs, puffed away so fast and so fiercely that the whole valley was immediately filled with impenetrable smoke.

Meantime the cabbages all turned very red in the face, and it seemed as if old Nick himself had taken possession of every thing in the shape of a timepiece. The clocks carved upon the furniture took to dancing as if bewitched, while those upon the mantel-pieces could scarcely contain themselves for fury, and kept such a continual striking of thirteen, and such a frisking and wriggling of their pendulums as was really horrible to see. But, worse than all, neither the cats nor the pigs could put up any longer with the behaviour of the little repeaters tied to their tails, and resented it by scampering all over the place, scratching and poking, and squeaking and screeching, and caterwauling and squalling, and flying into the faces, and running under the petticoats of the people, and creating altogether the most abominable din and confusion which it is possible for a reasonable person to conceive.

And to make matters still more distressing, the rascally little scape-grace in the steeple was evidently exerting himself to the utmost. Every now and then one might catch a glimpse of the scoundrel through the smoke. There he sat in the belfry upon the belfry-man, who was lying flat upon his back. In his teeth the villain held the bell-rope, which he kept jerking about with his head, raising such a clatter that my ears ring again even to think of it. On his lap lay the big fiddle, at which he was scraping, out of all time and tune, with both hands, making a great show, the nincompoop! of playing "Judy O'Flannagan and Paddy O'Rafferty."

Affairs being thus miserably situated, I left the place in disgust, and now appeal for aid to all lovers of correct time and fine *kraut*. Let us proceed in a body to the borough, and restore the ancient order of things in Vondervotteimittiss by ejecting that little fellow from the steeple.

The Duc de l'Omelette

And stepped at once into a cooler clime.—Cowper

Keats fell by a criticism. Who was it died of "The Andromache"? [1] Ignoble souls!—De l'Omelette perished of an ortolan. *L'histoire en est brève.* Assist me, Spirit of Apicius!

A golden cage bore the little winged wanderer, enamored, melting, indolent, to the *Chaussée D'Antin,* from its home in far Peru. From its queenly possessor La Bellissima, to the Duc de l'Omelette, six peers of the empire conveyed the happy bird.

That night the *duc* was to sup alone. In the privacy of his bureau he reclined languidly on that ottoman for which he sacrificed his loyalty in outbidding his king—the notorious ottoman of Cadet.

He buries his face in the pillow. The clock strikes! Unable to restrain his feelings, His Grace swallows an olive. At this moment the door gently opens to the sound of soft music, and lo! the most delicate of birds is before the most enamored of men! But what inexpressible dismay now overshadows the countenance of the *duc?*—"*Horreur!—chien! Baptiste!—l'oiseau! ah, bon Dieu! cet oiseau modeste que tu as déshabillé de ses plumes, et que tu as servi sans papier!*" It is superfluous to say more:—the *duc* expired in a paroxysm of disgust.

"Ha! ha! ha!" said His Grace on the third day after his decease.

"He! he! he!" replied the Devil faintly, drawing himself up

1. Montfleury. The author of the *Parnasse Réformé* makes him speak in Hades:—"*L'homme donc qui voudrait savoir ce don't je suis mort, qui'l ne demande pas si'l fût de fievre ou de podagre ou d'autre chose mais qui'l entende que ce fût de L'Andromache.*"

with an air of hauteur.

"Why, surely you are not serious," retorted De l'Omelette. "I have sinned—*c'est vrai*—but, my good sir, consider!—you have no actual intention of putting such—such barbarous threats into execution."

"No *what?*" said His Majesty—"come, sir, strip!"

"Strip, indeed! very pretty i' faith! no, sir, I shall *not* strip. Who are you, pray, that I, Duc de l'Omelette, Prince de Foie-Gras, just come of age, author of the 'Mazurkiad,' and Member of the Academy, should divest myself at your bidding of the sweetest pantaloons ever made by Bourdon, the daintiest *robe-de-chambre* ever put together by Rombert—to say nothing of the taking my hair out of paper—not to mention the trouble I should have in drawing off my gloves?"

"Who am I?—ah, true! I am Baal-Zebub, Prince of the Fly. I took thee, just now, from a rose-wood coffin inlaid with ivory. Thou wast curiously scented, and labelled as per invoice. Belial sent thee,—my Inspector of Cemeteries. The pantaloons, which thou sayest were made by Bourdon, are an excellent pair of linen drawers, and thy *robe-de-chambre* is a shroud of no scanty dimensions."

"Sir!" replied the *duc*, "I am not to be insulted with impunity!—Sir! I shall take the earliest opportunity of avenging this insult!—Sir! you shall hear from me! in the meantime *au revoir!*"—and the *duc* was bowing himself out of the Satanic presence, when he was interrupted and brought back by a gentleman in waiting. Hereupon His Grace rubbed his eyes, yawned, shrugged his shoulders, reflected. Having become satisfied of his identity, he took a bird's eye view of his whereabouts.

The apartment was superb. Even De l'Omelette pronounced it *bien comme il faut*. It was not its length nor its breadth,—but its height—ah, that was appalling!—There was no ceiling—certainly none—but a dense whirling mass of fiery-colored clouds. His Grace's brain reeled as he glanced upward. From above, hung a chain of an unknown blood-red metal—its upper end lost, like the city of Boston, *parmi les nues*. From its nether extremity swung a large cresset. The *duc* knew it to be a ruby; but from it there poured a light so intense, so still, so terrible, Persia never worshipped such—Gheber never imagined such—Mussulman never dreamed of such when, drugged with opium, he has tottered to a bed of poppies, his back to the flowers, and his face to the God Apollo. The *duc* muttered a slight oath, decidedly approbatory.

The corners of the room were rounded into niches. Three of these were filled with statues of gigantic proportions. Their beauty was Grecian, their deformity Egyptian, their *tout ensemble* French. In the fourth niche the statue was veiled; it was *not* colossal. But then there was a taper ankle, a sandaled foot. De l'Omelette pressed his hand upon his heart, closed his eyes, raised them, and caught his Satanic Majesty—in a blush.

But the paintings!—Kupris! Astarte! Astoreth!—a thousand and the same! And Rafaelle has beheld them! Yes, Rafaelle has been here, for did he not paint the—? and was he not consequently damned? The paintings—the paintings! O luxury! O love!—who, gazing on those forbidden beauties, shall have eyes for the dainty devices of the golden frames that besprinkled, like stars, the hyacinth and the porphyry walls?

But the *duc's* heart is fainting within him. He is not, however, as you suppose, dizzy with magnificence, nor drunk with the ecstatic breath of those innumerable censers. *C'est vrai que de toutes ces choses il a pense beaucoup—mais!* The Duc de l'Omelette is terror-stricken; for, through the lurid vista which a single uncurtained window is affording, lo! gleams the most ghastly of all fires!

Le pauvre duc! He could not help imagining that the glorious, the voluptuous, the never-dying melodies which pervaded that hall, as they passed filtered and transmuted through the alchemy of the enchanted window-panes, were the wailings and the howlings of the hopeless and the damned! And there, too!—there!—upon the ottoman!—who could *he* be?—he, the *petitmaître*—no, the Deity—who sat as if carved in marble, *et qui sourit*, with his pale countenance, *si amérement?*

Mais il faut agir—that is to say, a Frenchman never faints outright. Besides, His Grace hated a scene—De l'Omelette is himself again. There were some foils upon a table—some points also. The *duc* had studied under B——*; il avait tué ses six hommes.* Now, then, *il peut s'échapper.* He measures two points, and, with a grace inimitable, offers His Majesty the choice. *Horreur!* His Majesty does not fence!

Mais il joue!—how happy a thought!—but His Grace had always an excellent memory. He had dipped in the *Diable* of Abbé Gualtier. Therein it is said "*que le Diable n'ose pas refuser un jeu d'écarte.*"

But the chances—the chances! True—desperate: but scarcely more desperate than the *duc.* Besides, was he not in the secret?—had he not skimmed over Père Le Brun?—was he not a member of the *Club Vingt-un?* "*Si je perds,*" said he, "*je serai deux fois perdu*—I shall be doubly dammed—*voilà tout!* (Here his Grace shrugged his shoulders.) *Si je gagne, je reviendrai a mes ortolans—que les cartes soient préparées!*"

His Grace was all care, all attention—His Majesty all confidence. A spectator would have thought of Francis and Charles. His Grace thought of his game. His Majesty did not think; he shuffled. The *duc* cut.

The cards were dealt. The trump is turned—it is—it is—the king! No—it was the queen. His Majesty cursed her masculine *habiliments.* De l'Omelette placed his hand upon his heart.

They play. The *duc* counts. The hand is out. His Majesty counts heavily, smiles, and is taking wine. The *duc* slips a card.

"*C'est à vous à faire,*" said His Majesty, cutting. His Grace bowed, dealt, and arose from the table *en presentant le roi.*

His Majesty looked chagrined.

Had Alexander not been Alexander, he would have been Diogenes; and the *duc* assured his antagonist in taking leave, "*que s'il n'eût été De l'Omelette il n'aurait point d'objection d'être le Diable.*"

The Fall of the House of Usher

Son cœur est un luth suspendu;
Sitôt qu'on le touche il résonne.

De Béranger.

During the whole of a dull, dark, and soundless day in the autumn of the year, when the clouds hung oppressively low in the heavens, I had been passing alone, on horseback, through a singularly dreary tract of country, and at length found myself, as the shades of evening drew on, within view of the melancholy House of Usher. I know not how it was—but, with the first glimpse of the building, a sense of insufferable gloom pervaded my spirit. I say insufferable; for the feeling was unrelieved by any of that half-pleasurable, because poetic, sentiment, with which the mind usually receives even the sternest natural images of the desolate or terrible.

I looked upon the scene before me—upon the mere house, and the simple landscape features of the domain—upon the bleak walls upon the vacant eye-like windows—upon a few rank sedges—and upon a few white trunks of decayed trees—with an utter depression of soul which I can compare to no earthly sensation more properly than to the after-dream of the reveller upon opium—the bitter lapse into every-day life—the hideous dropping of the veil. There was an iciness, a sinking, a sickening of the heart—an unredeemed dreariness of thought which no goading of the imagination could torture into aught of the sublime. What was it—I paused to think—what was it that so unnerved me in the contemplation of the House of Usher?

It was a mystery all insoluble; nor could I grapple with the shadowy fancies that crowded upon me as I pondered. I was forced to fall back upon the unsatisfactory conclusion, that while, beyond doubt, there *are* combinations of very simple natural objects which have the power of thus affecting us, still the analysis of this power lies among considerations beyond our depth. It was possible, I reflected, that a mere different arrangement of the particulars of the scene, of the details of the picture, would be sufficient to modify, or perhaps to annihilate its capacity for sorrowful impression; and, acting upon this idea, I reined my horse to the precipitous brink of a black and lurid tarn that lay in unruffled lustre by the dwelling, and gazed down—but with a shudder more thrilling than before—upon the remodelled and inverted images of the grey sedge, and the ghastly tree-stems, and the vacant and eye-like windows.

Nevertheless, in this mansion of gloom I now proposed to myself a sojourn of some weeks. Its proprietor, Roderick Usher, had been one of my boon companions in boyhood, but many years had elapsed since our last meeting. A letter, however, had lately reached me in a distant part of the country—a letter from him—which, in its wildly importunate nature, had admitted of no other than a personal reply. The MS. gave evidence of nervous agitation. The writer spoke of acute bodily illness—of a mental disorder which oppressed him—and of an earnest desire to see me, as his best, and indeed his only personal friend, with a view of attempting, by the cheerfulness of my society, some alleviation of his malady. It was the manner in which all this, and much more, was said—it was the apparent *heart* that went with his request—which allowed me no room for hesitation, and I accordingly obeyed forthwith what I still considered a very singular summons.

Although, as boys, we had been even intimate associates, yet I really knew little of my friend. His reserve had been always excessive and habitual. I was aware, however, that his very ancient family had been noted, time out of mind, for a peculiar sensibility of temperament, displaying itself through long ages in many works of exalted art, and manifested of late in repeated deeds of munificent yet unobtrusive charity, as well as in a passionate devotion to the intricacies, perhaps even more than to the orthodox and easily-recognisable beauties of musical science. I had learned, too, the very remarkable fact that the stem of the Usher race, all time-honoured as it was, had put forth at no period any enduring branch; in other words, that the entire family lay in the direct line of descent, and had always, with very trifling and very temporary variation, so lain.

It was this deficiency, I considered, while running over in thought the perfect keeping of the character of the premises with the accredited character of the people, and while speculating upon the possible influence which the one, in the long lapse of centuries, might have exercised upon the other—it was this deficiency perhaps of collateral issue, and the consequent undeviating transmission from sire to son of the patrimony with the name, which had at length so identified the two as to merge the original title of the estate in the quaint and equivocal appellation of the "House of Usher"—an appellation which seemed to include, in the minds of the peasantry who used it, both the family and the family mansion.

I have said that the sole effect of my somewhat childish experiment—that of looking down within the tarn—had been to deepen the first singular impression. There can be no doubt that the consciousness of the rapid increase of my superstition—for why should I not so term it?—served mainly to accelerate the increase itself. Such, I have long known, is the paradoxical law of all sentiments having terror as a basis; and it might have been for this reason only that, when I again uplifted my eyes to the house itself from its image in the pool, there grew in my mind a strange fancy—a fancy so ridiculous indeed that I but mention it to show the vivid force of the sensations which oppressed me.

I had so worked upon my imagination as really to believe that about the whole mansion and domain there hung an atmosphere peculiar to themselves and their immediate vicinity—an atmosphere which had no affinity with the air of heaven but which had reeked up from the decayed trees, and the grey wall, and the silent tarn—a pestilent and mystic vapour, dull, sluggish, faintly discernible, and leaden-hued.

Shaking off from my spirit what *must* have been a dream, I scanned more narrowly the real aspect of the building. Its principal feature seemed to be that of an excessive antiquity. The discoloration of ages had been great. Minute fungi overspread the whole exterior, hanging in a fine tangled web-work from the eaves. Yet all this was apart from any extraordinary dilapidation. No portion of the masonry had fallen, and there appeared to be a wild inconsistency between its still perfect adaptation of parts and the crumbling condition of the individual stones. In this there was much that reminded me of the specious totality of old woodwork which has rotted for long years in some neglected vault with no disturbance from the breath of the external air. Beyond this indication of extensive decay, however, the fabric gave little token of instability. Perhaps the eye of a scrutinising observer might have discovered a barely perceptible fissure, which, extending from the roof of the building in front, made its way down the wall in a zigzag direction, until it became lost in the sullen waters of the tarn.

Noticing these things, I rode over a short causeway to the house. A servant in waiting took my horse, and I entered the Gothic archway of the hall. A valet, of stealthy step, thence conducted me in silence through many dark and intricate passages in my progress to the *studio* of his master. Much that I encountered on the way contributed, I know not how, to heighten the vague sentiments of which I have already spoken. While the objects around me—while the carvings of the ceilings, the sombre tapestries of the walls, the ebon blackness of the floors, and the phantasmagoric armorial trophies which rattled as I strode, were but matters to which, or to such as which, I had been accustomed from my infancy—while I hesitated not to acknowledge how familiar was all this—I still wondered to find how unfamiliar were the fancies which ordinary images were stirring up. On one of the staircases I met the physician of the family. His countenance, I thought, wore a mingled expression of low cunning and perplexity. He accosted me with trepidation and passed on. The valet now threw open a door and ushered me into the presence of his master.

The room in which I found myself was very large and lofty. The windows were long, narrow, and pointed, and at so vast a distance from the black oaken floor as to be altogether inaccessible from within. Feeble gleams of encrimsoned light made their way through the trellised panes, and served to render sufficiently distinct the more prominent objects around; the eye, however, struggled in vain to reach the remoter angles of the chamber, or the recesses of the vaulted and fretted ceiling. Dark draperies hung upon the walls. The general furniture was profuse, comfortless, antique, and tattered. Many books and musical instruments lay scattered about, but failed to give any vitality to the scene. I felt that I breathed an atmosphere of sorrow. An air of stern, deep, and irredeemable gloom hung over and pervaded all.

Upon my entrance, Usher arose from a sofa on which he had been lying at full length, and greeted me with a vivacious warmth which had much in it, I at first thought, of an overdone cordiality—of the constrained effort of the *ennuyé* man of the world. A glance, however, at his countenance convinced me of his perfect sincerity. We sat down; and for some moments, while he spoke not, I gazed upon him with a feeling half of pity, half of awe. Surely, man had never before so terribly altered, in so brief a period, as had Roderick Usher! It was with difficulty that I could bring myself to admit the identity of the wan being before me with the companion of my early boyhood.

Yet the character of his face had been at all times remarkable. A cadaverousness of complexion; an eye large, liquid, and luminous beyond comparison; lips somewhat thin and very pallid, but of a surpassingly beautiful curve; a nose of a delicate Hebrew model, but with a breadth of nostril unusual in similar formations; a finely moulded chin, speaking, in its want of prominence, of a want of moral energy; hair of a more than web-like softness and tenuity; these features, with an inordinate expansion above the regions of the temple, made up altogether a countenance not easily to be forgotten. And now in the mere exaggeration of the prevailing character of these features, and of the expression they were wont to convey, lay so much of change that I doubted to whom I spoke. The now ghastly pallor of the skin, and the now miraculous lustre of the eye, above all things startled and even awed me. The silken hair, too, had been suffered to grow all unheeded, and as, in its wild gossamer texture, it floated rather than fell about the face, I could not, even with effort, connect its Arabesque expression with any idea of simple humanity.

In the manner of my friend I was at once struck with an incoherence—an inconsistency; and I soon found this to arise from a series of feeble and futile struggles to overcome an habitual trepidancy—an excessive nervous agitation. For something of this nature I had indeed been prepared, no less by his letter than by reminiscences of certain boyish traits, and by conclusions deduced from his peculiar physical conformation and temperament. His action was alternately vivacious and sullen. His voice varied rapidly from a tremulous indecision (when the animal spirits seemed utterly in abeyance) to that species of energetic concision—that abrupt, weighty, unhurried, and hollow-sounding enunciation—that leaden, self-balanced and perfectly modulated guttural utterance which may be observed in the lost drunkard, or the irreclaimable eater of opium, during the periods of his most intense excitement.

It was thus that he spoke of the object of my visit, of his earnest desire to see me, and of the solace he expected me to afford him. He entered at some length into what he conceived to be the nature of his malady. It was, he said, a constitutional and a family evil, and one for which he despaired to find a remedy—a mere nervous affection, he immediately added, which would undoubtedly soon pass off. It displayed itself in a host of unnatural sensations. Some of these, as he detailed them, interested and bewildered me; although perhaps the terms and the general manner of the narration had their weight. He suffered much from a morbid acuteness of the senses; the most insipid food was alone endurable; he could wear only garments of certain texture; the odours of all flowers were oppressive; his eyes were tortured by even a faint light; and there were but peculiar sounds, and these from stringed instruments, which did not inspire him with horror.

To an anomalous species of terror I found him a bounden slave. "I shall perish," said he, "I *must* perish in this deplorable folly. Thus, thus, and not otherwise, shall I be lost. I dread the events of the future, not in themselves, but in their results. I shudder at the thought of any, even the most trivial incident, which may operate upon this intolerable agitation of soul. I have indeed no abhorrence of danger, except in its absolute effect—in terror. In this unnerved—in this pitiable condition—I feel that the period will sooner or later arrive when I must abandon life and reason together in some struggle with the grim phantasm, FEAR."

I learned, moreover, at intervals, and through broken and equivocal hints, another singular feature of his mental condition. He was enchained by certain superstitious impressions in regard to the dwelling which he tenanted, and whence, for many years, he had never ventured forth—in regard to an influence whose supposititious force was conveyed in terms too shadowy here to be re-stated an influence which some peculiarities in the mere form and substance of his family mansion, had, by dint of long sufferance, he said, obtained over his spirit—an effect which the *physique* of the grey walls and turrets, and of the dim tarn into which they all looked down, had at length brought about upon the *morale* of his existence.

He admitted, however, although with hesitation, that much of the peculiar gloom which thus afflicted him could be traced to a more natural and far more palpable origin—to the severe and long-continued illness—indeed to the evidently approaching dissolution—of a tenderly beloved sister—his sole companion for long years—his last and only relative on earth. "Her decease," he said, with a bitterness which I can never forget, "would leave him (him the hopeless and the frail) the last of the ancient race of the Ushers." While he spoke, the lady Madeline (for so was she called) passed slowly through a remote portion of the apartment, and, without having noticed my presence, disappeared. I regarded her with an utter astonishment not unmingled with dread—and yet I found it impossible to account for such feelings.

A sensation of stupor oppressed me as my eyes followed her retreating steps. When a door at length closed upon her, my glance sought instinctively and eagerly the countenance of the brother—but he had buried his face in his hands, and I could only perceive that a far more than ordinary wanness had overspread the emaciated fingers through which trickled many passionate tears.

The disease of the lady Madeline had long baffled the skill of her physicians. A settled apathy, a gradual wasting away of the person, and frequent although transient affections of a partially cataleptical character, were the unusual diagnosis. Hitherto she had steadily borne up against the pressure of her malady, and had not betaken herself finally to bed; but, on the closing in of the evening of my arrival at the house, she succumbed (as her brother told me at night with inexpressible agitation) to the prostrating power of the destroyer; and I learned that the glimpse I had obtained of her person would thus probably be the last I should obtain—that the lady, at least while living, would be seen by me no more.

For several days ensuing her name was unmentioned by either Usher or myself and during this period I was busied in earnest endeavours to alleviate the melancholy of my friend. We painted and read together, or I listened, as if in a dream, to the wild improvisations of his speaking guitar. And thus, as a closer and still closer intimacy admitted me more unreservedly into the recesses of his spirit, the more bitterly did I perceive the futility of all attempts at cheering a mind from which darkness, as if an inherent positive quality, poured forth upon all objects of the moral and physical universe in one unceasing radiation of gloom.

I shall ever bear about me a memory of the many solemn hours I thus spent alone with the master of the House of Usher. Yet I should fail in any attempt to convey an idea of the exact character of the studies, or of the occupations in which he involved me or led me the way. An excited and highly distempered ideality threw a sulphurous lustre over all. His long improvised dirges will ring forever in my ears. Among other things, I hold painfully in mind a certain singular perversion and amplification of the wild air of the last waltz of Von Weber. From the paintings over which his elaborate fancy brooded, and which grew, touch by touch, into vaguenesses at which I shuddered the more thrillingly, because I shuddered knowing not why;—from these paintings (vivid as their images now are before me) I would in vain endeavour to educe more than a small portion which should lie within the compass of merely written words.

By the utter simplicity, by the nakedness of his designs, he arrested and overawed attention. If ever mortal painted an idea that mortal was Roderick Usher. For me at least—in the circumstances then surrounding me—there arose out of the pure abstractions which the hypochondriac contrived to throw upon his canvas an intensity of intolerable awe, no shadow of which felt I ever yet in the contemplation of the certainly glowing yet too concrete reveries of Fuseli.

One of the phantasmagoric conceptions of my friend, partaking not so rigidly of the spirit of abstraction, may be shadowed forth, although feebly, in words. A small picture presented the interior of an immensely long and rectangular vault or tunnel, with low walls, smooth, white, and without interruption or device. Certain accessory points of the design served well to convey the idea that this excavation lay at an exceeding depth below the surface of the earth. No outlet was observed in any portion of its vast extent, and no torch, or other artificial source of light, was discernible, yet a flood of intense rays rolled throughout, and bathed the whole in a ghastly and inappropriate splendour.

I have just spoken of that morbid condition of the auditory

nerve which rendered all music intolerable to the sufferer, with the exception of certain effects of stringed instruments. It was perhaps the narrow limits to which he thus confined himself upon the guitar which gave birth, in great measure, to the fantastic character of his performances. But the fervid *facility* of his *impromptus* could not be so accounted for. They must have been and were, in the notes, as well as in the words of his wild fantasias (for he not unfrequently accompanied himself with rhymed-verbal improvisations), the result of that intense mental collectedness and concentration to which I have previously alluded as observable only in particular moments of the highest artificial excitement. The words of one of these rhapsodies I have easily remembered. I was perhaps the more forcibly impressed with it as he gave it, because, in the under or mystic current of its meaning, I fancied that I perceived, and for the first time, a full consciousness on the part of Usher, of the tottering of his lofty reason upon her throne. The verses, which were entitled *The Haunted Palace*, ran very nearly, if not accurately,

thus:

1

In the greenest of our valleys,
By good angels tenanted,
Once a fair and stately palace—
Radiant palace—reared its head.
In the monarch Thought's dominion—
It stood there!
Never seraph spread a pinion
Over fabric half so fair.

2

Banners yellow, glorious, golden,
On its roof did float and flow;
(This—all this—was in the olden
Time long ago)
And every gentle air that dallied,
In that sweet day,
Along the ramparts plumed and pallid,

A winged odour went away.

3

Wanderers in that happy valley
Through two luminous windows saw
Spirits moving musically
To a lute's well-tuned law,
Round about a throne, where sitting
(Porphyrogene!)
In state his glory well befitting,
The ruler of the realm was seen.

4

And all with pearl and ruby glowing
Was the fair palace door,
Through which came flowing, flowing, flowing,
And sparkling evermore,
A troop of Echoes whose sweet duty
Was but to sing,
In voices of surpassing beauty,
The wit and wisdom of their king.

5

But evil things, in robes of sorrow,
Assailed the monarch's high estate;
(Ah, let us mourn, for never morrow
Shall dawn upon him, desolate!)
And, round about his home, the glory
That blushed and bloomed
Is but a dim-remembered story
Of the old time entombed.

6

And travellers now within that valley,
Through the red-litten windows, see
Vast forms that move fantastically
To a discordant melody;
While, like a rapid ghastly river,
Through the pale door,

A hideous throng rush out for ever,
And laugh—but smile no more.

I well remember that suggestions arising from this ballad led us into a train of thought wherein there became manifest an opinion of Usher's, which I mention not so much on account of its novelty (for other men[1] have thought thus), as on account of the pertinacity with which he maintained it. This opinion, in its general form, was that of the sentience of all vegetable things. But, in his disordered fancy, the idea had assumed a more daring character, and trespassed, under certain conditions, upon the kingdom of inorganisation. I lack words to express the full extent, or the earnest *abandon* of his persuasion. The belief, however, was connected (as I have previously hinted) with the grey stones of the home of his forefathers.

The conditions of the sentience had been here, he imagined, fulfilled in the method of collocation of these stones—in the order of their arrangement, as well as in that of the many *fungi* which overspread them, and of the decayed trees which stood around—above all, in the long undisturbed endurance of this arrangement, and in its reduplication in the still waters of the tarn. Its evidence—the evidence of the sentience—was to be seen, he said (and I here started as he spoke), in the gradual yet certain condensation of an atmosphere of their own about the waters and the walls. The result was discoverable, he added, in that silent yet importunate and terrible influence which for centuries had moulded the destinies of his family, and which made *him* what I now saw him—what he was. Such opinions need no comment, and I will make none.

Our books—the books which for years had formed no small portion of the mental existence of the invalid—were, as might be supposed, in strict keeping with this character of phantasm. We pored together over such works as the *Ververt et Chartreuse of Gresset; The Belphegor of Machiavelli; The Heaven and Hell of Swedenborg; The Subterranean Voyage of Nicholas Klimm by Holberg; The*

1. Watson, Dr. Percival, Spallanzani, and especially the Bishop of Llandaff—See *Chemical Essays*, vol. v.

Chiromancy of Robert Flud, of Jean D'Indaginé, and of De la Chambre; The Journey into the Blue Distance of Tieck; and *The City of the Sun of Campanella.* One favourite volume was a small *octavo* edition of the *Directorium Inquisitorum*, by the Dominican Eymeric de Gironne; and there were passages in Pomponius Mela, about the old African Satyrs and Œgipans, over which Usher would sit dreaming for hours. His chief delight, however, was found in the perusal of an exceedingly rare and curious book in *quarto* Gothic—the manual of a forgotten church—the *Vigiliae Mortuorum secundum Chorum Ecclesiae Maguntinae.*

I could not help thinking of the wild ritual of this work, and of its probable influence upon the hypochondriac, when, one evening, having informed me abruptly that the lady Madeline was no more, he stated his intention of preserving her corpse for a fortnight (previously to its final interment), in one of the numerous vaults within the main walls of the building. The worldly reason, however, assigned for this singular proceeding was one which I did not feel at liberty to dispute. The brother had been led to his resolution (so he told me) by consideration of the unusual character of the malady of the deceased, of certain obtrusive and eager inquiries on the part of her medical man, and of the remote and exposed situation of the burial-ground of the family. I will not deny that when I called to mind the sinister countenance of the person whom I met upon the staircase on the day of my arrival at the house, I had no desire to oppose what I regarded as at best but a harmless and by no means an unnatural precaution.

At the request of Usher, I personally aided him in the arrangements for the temporary entombment. The body having been encoffined, we two alone bore it to its rest. The vault in which we placed it (and which had been so long unopened that our torches, half smothered in its oppressive atmosphere, gave us little opportunity for investigation) was small, damp, and entirely without means of admission for light, lying at great depth immediately beneath that portion of the building in which was my own sleeping apartment. It had been used apparently in remote feudal times for the worst purposes of a donjon-keep, and in later days as a place of deposit for powder or some other highly combustible substance, as a portion of its floor, and the whole interior of a long archway through which we reached it, were carefully sheathed with copper. The door, of massive iron, had been also similarly protected. Its immense weight caused an unusually sharp grating sound as it moved upon its hinges.

Having deposited our mournful burden upon tressels within this region of horror, we partially turned aside the yet unscrewed lid of the coffin and looked upon the face of the tenant. A striking similitude between the brother and sister now first arrested my attention, and Usher, divining perhaps my thoughts, murmured out some few words from which I learned that the deceased and himself had been twins, and that sympathies of a scarcely intelligible nature had always existed between them. Our glances, however, rested not long upon the dead—for we could not regard her unawed. The disease which had thus entombed the lady in the maturity of youth had left, as usual in all maladies of a strictly cataleptical character, the mockery of a faint blush upon the bosom and the face, and that suspiciously lingering smile upon the lip which is so terrible in death. We replaced and screwed down the lid, and having secured the door of iron, made our way with toil into the scarcely less gloomy apartments of the upper portion of the house.

And now, some days of bitter grief having elapsed, an observable change came over the features of the mental disorder of my friend. His ordinary manner had vanished. His ordinary occupations were neglected or forgotten. He roamed from chamber to chamber with hurried, unequal, and objectless step. The pallor of his countenance had assumed if possible a more ghastly hue—but the luminousness of his eye had utterly gone out. The once occasional huskiness of his tone was heard no more, and a tremulous quaver, as if of extreme terror, habitually characterised his utterance. There were times indeed when I thought his unceasingly agitated mind was labouring with some oppressive secret, to divulge which he struggled for the necessary courage.

At times again I was obliged to resolve all into the mere inexplicable vagaries of madness, for I beheld him gazing upon vacancy for long hours in an attitude of the profoundest attention, as if listening to some imaginary sound. It was no wonder that his condition terrified—that it infected me. I felt creeping upon me, by slow yet certain degrees, the wild influences of his own fantastic yet impressive superstitions.

It was especially upon retiring to bed late in the night of the seventh or eighth day after the placing of the lady Madeline within the donjon that I experienced the full power of such feelings. Sleep came not near my couch—while the hours waned and waned away. I struggled to reason off the nervousness which had dominion over me. I endeavoured to believe that much if not all of what I felt was due to the bewildering influence of the gloomy furniture of the room—of the dark and tattered draperies which, tortured into motion by the breath of a rising tempest, swayed fitfully to and fro upon the walls, and rustled uneasily about the decorations of the bed. But my efforts were fruitless. An irrepressible tremor gradually pervaded my frame, and at length there sat upon my very heart an incubus of utterly causeless alarm.

Shaking this off with a gasp and a struggle I uplifted myself upon the pillows, and peering earnestly within the intense darkness of the chamber, hearkened—I know not why, except that an instinctive spirit prompted me—to certain low and indefinite sounds which came, through the pauses of the storm, at long intervals, I knew not whence. Overpowered by an intense sentiment of horror, unaccountable yet unendurable, I threw on my clothes with haste (for I felt that I should sleep no more during the night), and endeavoured to arouse myself from the pitiable condition into which I had fallen, by pacing rapidly to and fro through the apartment.

I had taken but few turns in this manner, when a light step on an adjoining staircase arrested my attention. I presently recognised it as that of Usher. In an instant afterward he rapped with a gentle touch at my door, and entered, bearing a lamp.

His countenance was as usual cadaverously wan—but, moreover, there was a species of mad hilarity in his eyes—an evidently restrained *hysteria* in his whole demeanour. His air appalled me—but anything was preferable to the solitude which I had so long endured, and I even welcomed his presence as a relief.

"And you have not seen it?" he said abruptly, after having stared about him for some moments in silence—"you have not then seen it?—but, stay! you shall." Thus speaking, and having carefully shaded his lamp, he hurried to one of the casements, and threw it freely open to the storm.

The impetuous fury of the entering gust nearly lifted us from our feet. It was indeed a tempestuous yet sternly beautiful night, and one wildly singular in its terror and its beauty. A whirlwind had apparently collected its force in our vicinity, for there were frequent and violent alterations in the direction of the wind, and the exceeding density of the clouds (which hung so low as to press upon the turrets of the house) did not prevent our perceiving the life-like velocity with which they flew careering from all points against each other without passing away into the distance.

I say that even their exceeding density did not prevent our perceiving this—yet we had no glimpse of the moon or stars—nor was there any flashing forth of the lightning. But the under surfaces of the huge masses of agitated vapour, as well as all terrestrial objects immediately around us, were glowing in the unnatural light of a faintly luminous and distinctly visible gaseous exhalation which hung about and enshrouded the mansion.

"You must not—you shall not behold this!" said I, shudderingly, to Usher, as I led him with a gentle violence from the window to a seat. "These appearances which bewilder you are merely electrical phenomena not uncommon, or it may be that they have their ghastly origin in the rank miasma of the tarn. Let us close this casement; the air is chilling and dangerous to your frame. Here is one of your favourite romances. I will read, and you shall listen; and so we will pass away this terrible night together."

The antique volume which I had taken up was the *Mad Trist* of Sir Launcelot Canning, but I had called it a favourite of Usher's more in sad jest than in earnest; for in truth, there is little in its uncouth and unimaginative prolixity which could have had interest for the lofty and spiritual ideality of my friend. It was, however, the only book immediately at hand, and I indulged a vague hope that the excitement which now agitated the hypochondriac might find relief (for the history of mental disorder is full of similar anomalies) even in the extremeness of the folly which I should read. Could I have judged, indeed, by the wild overstrained air of vivacity with which he hearkened, or apparently hearkened, to the words of the tale, I might well have congratulated myself upon the success of my design.

I had arrived at that well-known portion of the story where Ethelred, the hero of the Trist, having sought in vain for peaceable admission into the dwelling of the hermit, proceeds to make good an entrance by force. Here, it will be remembered, the words of the narrative run thus:

> And Ethelred, who was by nature of a doughty heart, and who was now mighty withal, on account of the powerfulness of the wine which he had drunken, waited no longer to hold parley with the hermit, who in sooth was of an obstinate and maliceful turn, but feeling the rain upon his shoulders, and fearing the rising of the tempest, uplifted his mace outright, and with blows made quickly room in the plankings of the door for his gauntleted hand; and now pulling therewith sturdily, he so cracked and ripped, and tore all asunder, that the noise of the dry and hollow-sounding wood alarummed and reverberated throughout the forest.

At the termination of this sentence I started, and for a moment paused, for it appeared to me (although I at once concluded that my excited fancy had deceived me) that from some very remote portion of the mansion there came indistinctly to my ears what might have been, in its exact similarity of character, the echo (but a stifled and dull one certainly) of the very cracking and ripping sound which Sir Launcelot had so particularly described. It was beyond doubt the coincidence alone which had arrested my attention; for amid the rattling of the sashes of the casements, and the ordinary commingled noises of the still increasing storm, the sound in itself had nothing surely which should have interested or disturbed me. I continued the story:

> But the good champion Ethelred, now entering within the door, was sore enraged and amazed to perceive no signal of the maliceful hermit; but in the stead thereof, a dragon of a scaly and prodigious demeanour, and of a fiery tongue, which sate in guard before a palace of gold, with a floor of silver; and upon the wall there hung a shield of shining brass with this legend enwritten—
>
> *Who entereth herein, a conqueror hath bin;*
> *Who slayeth the dragon, the shield he shall win.*
>
> And Ethelred uplifted his mace, and struck upon the head of the dragon, which fell before him, and gave up his pesty breath, with a shriek so horrid and harsh, and withal so piercing, that Ethelred had fain to close his ears with his hands against the dreadful noise of it, the like whereof was never before heard.

Here again I paused abruptly, and now with a feeling of wild amazement—for there could be no doubt whatever that in this instance I did actually hear (although from what direction it proceeded I found it impossible to say) a low and apparently distant, but harsh, protracted, and most unusual screaming or grating sound—the exact counterpart of what my fancy had already conjured up for the dragon's unnatural shriek as described by the romancer.

Oppressed, as I certainly was upon the occurrence of this second and most extraordinary coincidence, by a thousand conflicting sensations, in which wonder and extreme terror were predominant, I still retained sufficient presence of mind to avoid exciting by any observation the sensitive nervousness of my companion. I was by no means certain that he had noticed the sounds in question, although, assuredly, a strange alteration had during the last few minutes taken place in his demeanour. From a position fronting my own, he had gradually brought round his chair, so as to sit with his face to the door of the chamber; and thus I could but partially perceive his features, although I saw that his lips trembled as if he were murmuring inaudibly. His head had dropped upon his breast, yet I knew that he was not asleep, from the wide and rigid opening of the eye as I caught a glance of it in profile. The motion of his body too was at variance with this idea,—for he rocked from side to side with a gentle yet constant and uniform sway. Having rapidly taken notice of all this, I resumed the narrative of Sir Launcelot, which thus proceeded:

> And now, the champion having escaped from the terrible fury of the dragon, bethinking himself of the brazen shield, and of the breaking up of the enchantment which was upon it, removed the carcase from out of the way before him, and approached valorously over the silver pavement of the castle to where the shield was upon the wall; which in sooth tarried not for his full coming, but fell down at his feet upon the silver floor with a mighty great and terrible ringing sound.

No sooner had these syllables passed my lips, than—as if a shield of brass had indeed at the moment fallen heavily upon a floor of silver—I became aware of a distinct, hollow, metallic, and clangorous, yet apparently muffled, reverberation. Completely unnerved, I leaped to my feet, but the measured rocking movement of Usher was undisturbed. I rushed to the chair in which he sat. His eyes were bent fixedly before him, and throughout his whole countenance there reigned a stony rigidity. But, as I placed my hand upon his shoulder, there came a strong shudder over his whole person; a sickly smile quivered about his lips, and I saw that he spoke in a low, hurried, and gibbering murmur, as if unconscious of my presence. Bending closely over him, I at length drank in the hideous import of his words.

"Not hear it?—yes, I hear it, and *have* heard it. Long—long—long—many minutes, many hours, many days, have I heard it—yet I dared not—oh, pity me, miserable wretch that I am!—I dared not—I *dared* not speak! *We have put her living in the tomb!* Said I not that my senses were acute? I *now* tell you that I heard her first feeble movements in the hollow coffin. I heard them—many, many days ago—yet I dared not—*I dared not speak!* And now—tonight—Ethelred—ha! ha!—the breaking of the hermit's door, and the death-cry of the dragon, and the clangour of the shield!—say, rather, the rending of her coffin, and the grating of the iron hinges of her prison, and her struggles within the coppered archway of the vault. O whither shall I fly? Will she not be here *anon?* Is she not hurrying to upbraid me for my haste? Have I not heard her footstep on the stair? Do I not distinguish that heavy and horrible beating of her heart? Madman!" Here he sprang furiously to his feet, and shrieked out his syllables, as if in the effort he were giving up his soul—"*Madman! I tell you that she now stands without the door!*"

As if in the superhuman energy of his utterance there had been found the potency of a spell—the huge antique panels to which the speaker pointed, threw slowly back, upon the instant, their ponderous and ebony jaws. It was the work of the rushing gust—but then without those doors there *did* stand the lofty and enshrouded figure of the lady Madeline of Usher. There was blood upon her white robes, and the evidence of some bitter struggle upon every portion of her emaciated frame. For a moment she remained trembling and reeling to and fro upon the threshold—then, with a low moaning cry, fell heavily inward upon the person of her brother, and in her violent and now final death-agonies, bore him to the floor a corpse, and a victim to the terrors he had anticipated.

From that chamber and from that mansion I fled aghast. The storm was still abroad in all its wrath as I found myself crossing the old causeway. Suddenly there shot along the path a wild light, and I turned to see whence a gleam so unusual could have issued, for the vast house and its shadows were alone behind me. The radiance was that of the full, setting, and blood-red moon, which now shone vividly through that once barely-discernible fissure, of which I have before spoken as extending from the roof of the building in a zigzag direction to the base. While I gazed, this fissure rapidly widened; there came a fierce breath of the whirlwind; the entire orb of the satellite burst at once upon my sight; my brain reeled as I saw the mighty walls rushing asunder; there was a long tumultuous shouting sound like the voice of a thousand waters, and the deep and dark tarn at my feet closed sullenly and silently over the fragments of the "*House of Usher.*"

The Facts in the Case of M. Valdemar

Of course I shall not pretend to consider it any matter for wonder, that the extraordinary case of M. Valdemar has excited discussion. It would have been a miracle had it not—especially under the circumstances. Through the desire of all parties concerned, to keep the affair from the public, at least for the present, or until we had farther opportunities for investigation—through our endeavors to effect this—a garbled or exaggerated account made its way into society, and became the source of many unpleasant misrepresentations, and, very naturally, of a great deal of disbelief.

It is now rendered necessary that I give the *facts*—as far as I comprehend them myself. They are, succinctly, these:

My attention, for the last three years, had been repeatedly drawn to the subject of mesmerism; and, about nine months ago it occurred to me, quite suddenly, that in the series of experiments made hitherto, there had been a very remarkable and most unaccountable omission:—no person had as yet been mesmerized *in articulo mortis*. It remained to be seen, first, whether, in such condition, there existed in the patient any susceptibility to the magnetic influence; secondly, whether, if any existed, it was impaired or increased by the condition; thirdly, to what extent, or for how long a period, the encroachments of death might be arrested by the process. There were other points to be ascertained, but these most excited my curiosity—the last in especial, from the immensely important character of its consequences.

In looking around me for some subject by whose means I might test these particulars, I was brought to think of my friend, M. Ernest Valdemar, the well-known compiler of the *Bibliotheca Forensica*, and author (under the *nom de plume* of Issachar Marx) of the Polish versions of *Wallenstein* and *Gargantua*. M. Valdemar, who has resided principally at Harlaem, N.Y., since the year 1839, is (or was) particularly noticeable for the extreme spareness of his person—his lower limbs much resembling those of John Randolph; and, also, for the whiteness of his whiskers, in violent contrast to the blackness of his hair—the latter, in consequence, being very generally mistaken for a wig. His temperament was markedly nervous, and rendered him a good subject for mesmeric experiment. On two or three occasions I had put him to sleep with little difficulty, but was disappointed in other results which his peculiar constitution had naturally led me to anticipate. His will was at no period positively, or thoroughly, under my control, and in regard to *clairvoyance*, I could accomplish with him nothing to be relied upon. I always attributed my failure at these points to the disordered state of his health. For some months previous to my becoming acquainted with him, his physicians had declared him in a confirmed phthisis. It was his custom, indeed, to speak calmly of his approaching dissolution, as of a matter neither to be avoided nor regretted.

When the ideas to which I have alluded first occurred to me, it was of course very natural that I should think of M. Valdemar. I knew the steady philosophy of the man too well to apprehend any scruples from *him*; and he had no relatives in America who would be likely to interfere. I spoke to him frankly upon the subject; and, to my surprise, his interest seemed vividly excited. I say to my surprise, for, although he had always yielded his person freely to my experiments, he had never before given me any tokens of sympathy with what I did. His disease was of that character which would admit of exact calculation in respect to the epoch of its termination in death; and it was finally arranged between us that he would send for me about twenty-four hours before the period announced by his physicians as that of his decease.

It is now rather more than seven months since I received, from M. Valdemar himself, the subjoined note:

> My Dear P—,
> You may as well come *now*. D—— and F—— are agreed that I cannot hold out beyond tomorrow midnight; and I think they have hit the time very nearly.
>
> Valdemar

I received this note within half an hour after it was written, and in fifteen minutes more I was in the dying man's chamber. I had not seen him for ten days, and was appalled by the fearful alteration which the brief interval had wrought in him. His face wore a leaden hue; the eyes were utterly lustreless; and the emaciation was so extreme that the skin had been broken through by the cheek-bones. His expectoration was excessive. The pulse was barely perceptible. He retained, nevertheless, in a very remarkable manner, both his mental power and a certain degree of physical strength. He spoke with distinctness—took some palliative medicines without aid—and, when I entered the room, was occupied in penciling memoranda in a pocket-book. He was propped up in the bed by pillows. Doctors D—— and F—— were in attendance.

After pressing Valdemar's hand, I took these gentlemen aside, and obtained from them a minute account of the patient's condition. The left lung had been for eighteen months in a semi-osseous or cartilaginous state, and was, of course, entirely useless for all purposes of vitality. The right, in its upper portion, was also partially, if not thoroughly, ossified, while the lower region was merely a mass of purulent tubercles, running one into another. Several extensive perforations existed; and, at one point, permanent adhesion to the ribs had taken place. These appearances in the right lobe were of comparatively recent date. The ossification had proceeded with very unusual rapidity; no sign of it had been discovered a month before, and the adhesion had only been observed during the three previous days.

Independently of the phthisis, the patient was suspected of aneurism of the aorta; but on this point the osseous symptoms rendered an exact diagnosis impossible. It was the opinion of both physicians that M. Valdemar would die about midnight on the morrow (Sunday). It was then seven o'clock on Saturday evening.

On quitting the invalid's bedside to hold conversation with myself, Doctors D—— and F—— had bidden him a final farewell. It had not been their intention to return; but, at my request, they agreed to look in upon the patient about ten the next night.

When they had gone, I spoke freely with M. Valdemar on the subject of his approaching dissolution, as well as, more particularly, of the experiment proposed. He still professed himself quite willing and even anxious to have it made, and urged me to commence it at once. A male and a female nurse were in attendance; but I did not feel myself altogether at liberty to engage in a task of this character with no more reliable witnesses than these people, in case of sudden accident, might prove. I therefore postponed operations until about eight the next night, when the arrival of a medical student with whom I had some acquaintance, (Mr. Theodore L—l,) relieved me from farther embarrassment. It had been my design, originally, to wait for the physicians; but I was induced to proceed, first, by the urgent entreaties of M. Valdemar, and secondly, by my conviction that I had not a moment to lose, as he was evidently sinking fast.

Mr. L—l was so kind as to accede to my desire that he would take notes of all that occurred, and it is from his memoranda that what I now have to relate is, for the most part, either condensed or copied *verbatim*.

It wanted about five minutes of eight when, taking the patient's hand, I begged him to state, as distinctly as he could, to Mr. L—l, whether he (M. Valdemar) was entirely willing that I should make the experiment of mesmerizing him in his then condition.

He replied feebly, yet quite audibly, "Yes, I wish to be. I fear you have mesmerised"—adding immediately afterwards, "deferred it too long."

While he spoke thus, I commenced the passes which I had already found most effectual in subduing him. He was evidently influenced with the first lateral stroke of my hand across his forehead; but although I exerted all my powers, no further perceptible effect was induced until some minutes after ten o'clock, when Doctors D— and F— called, according to appointment. I explained to them, in a few words, what I designed, and as they opposed no objection, saying that the patient was already in the death agony, I proceeded without hesitation—exchanging, however, the lateral passes for downward ones, and directing my gaze entirely into the right eye of the sufferer.

By this time his pulse was imperceptible and his breathing was stertorous, and at intervals of half a minute.

This condition was nearly unaltered for a quarter of an hour. At the expiration of this period, however, a natural although a very deep sigh escaped the bosom of the dying man, and the stertorous breathing ceased—that is to say, its stertorousness was no longer apparent; the intervals were undiminished. The patient's extremities were of an icy coldness.

At five minutes before eleven I perceived unequivocal signs of the mesmeric influence. The glassy roll of the eye was changed for that expression of uneasy *inward* examination which is never seen except in cases of sleep-waking, and which it is quite impossible to mistake. With a few rapid lateral passes I made the lids quiver, as in incipient sleep, and with a few more I closed them altogether. I was not satisfied, however, with this, but continued the manipulations vigorously, and with the fullest exertion of the will, until I had completely stiffened the limbs of the slumberer, after placing them in a seemingly easy position. The legs were at full length; the arms were nearly so, and reposed on the bed at a moderate distance from the loin. The head was very slightly elevated.

When I had accomplished this, it was fully midnight, and I requested the gentlemen present to examine M. Valdemar's condition. After a few experiments, they admitted him to be an unusually perfect state of mesmeric trance. The curiosity of both the physicians was greatly excited. Dr. D—— resolved at once to remain with the patient all night, while Dr. F—— took leave with a promise to return at daybreak. Mr. L—l and the nurses remained.

We left M. Valdemar entirely undisturbed until about three o'clock in the morning, when I approached him and found him in precisely the same condition as when Dr. F—went away—that is to say, he lay in the same position; the pulse was imperceptible; the breathing was gentle (scarcely noticeable, unless through the application of a mirror to the lips); the eyes were closed naturally; and the limbs were as rigid and as cold as marble. Still, the general appearance was certainly not that of death.

As I approached M. Valdemar I made a kind of half effort to influence his right arm into pursuit of my own, as I passed the latter gently to and fro above his person. In such experiments with this patient, I had never perfectly succeeded before, and assuredly I had little thought of succeeding now; but to my astonishment, his arm very readily, although feebly, followed every direction I assigned it with mine. I determined to hazard a few words of conversation.

"M. Valdemar," I said, "are you asleep?" He made no answer, but I perceived a tremor about the lips, and was thus induced to repeat the question, again and again. At its third repetition, his whole frame was agitated by a very slight shivering; the eyelids unclosed themselves so far as to display a white line of the ball; the lips moved sluggishly, and from between them, in a barely audible whisper, issued the words:

"Yes;—asleep now. Do not wake me!—let me die so!"

I here felt the limbs and found them as rigid as ever. The right arm, as before, obeyed the direction of my hand. I questioned the sleep-waker again:

"Do you still feel pain in the breast, M. Valdemar?"

The answer now was immediate, but even less audible than before:

"No pain—I am dying."

I did not think it advisable to disturb him farther just then, and nothing more was said or done until the arrival of Dr. F—, who came a little before sunrise, and expressed unbounded astonishment at finding the patient still alive. After feeling the pulse and applying a mirror to the lips, he requested me to speak to the sleep-waker again. I did so, saying:

"M. Valdemar, do you still sleep?"

As before, some minutes elapsed ere a reply was made; and during the interval the dying man seemed to be collecting his energies to speak. At my fourth repetition of the question, he said very faintly, almost inaudibly:

"Yes; still asleep—dying."

It was now the opinion, or rather the wish, of the physicians, that M. Valdemar should be suffered to remain undisturbed in his present apparently tranquil condition, until death should supervene—and this, it was generally agreed, must now take place within a few minutes. I concluded, however, to speak to him once more, and merely repeated my previous question.

While I spoke, there came a marked change over the countenance of the sleep-waker. The eyes rolled themselves slowly open, the pupils disappearing upwardly; the skin generally assumed a cadaverous hue, resembling not so much parchment as white paper; and the circular hectic spots which, hitherto, had been strongly defined in the centre of each cheek, *went out* at once. I use this expression, because the suddenness of their departure put me in mind of nothing so much as the extinguishment of a candle by a puff of the breath. The upper lip, at the same time, writhed itself away from the teeth, which it had previously covered completely; while the lower jaw fell with an audible jerk, leaving the mouth widely extended, and disclosing in full view the swollen and blackened tongue. I presume that no member of the party then present had been unaccustomed to death-bed horrors; but so hideous beyond conception was the appearance of M. Valdemar at this moment, that there was a general shrinking back from the region of the bed.

I now feel that I have reached a point of this narrative at which every reader will be startled into positive disbelief. It is my business, however, simply to proceed.

There was no longer the faintest sign of vitality in M. Valdemar; and concluding him to be dead, we were consigning him to the charge of the nurses, when a strong vibratory motion was observable in the tongue. This continued for perhaps a minute. At the expiration of this period, there issued from the distended and motionless jaws a voice—such as it would be madness in me to attempt describing. There are, indeed, two or three epithets which might be considered as applicable to it in part; I might say, for example, that the sound was harsh, and broken and hollow; but the hideous whole is indescribable, for the simple reason that no similar sounds have ever jarred upon the ear of humanity.

There were two particulars, nevertheless, which I thought then, and still think, might fairly be stated as characteristic of the intonation—as well adapted to convey some idea of its unearthly peculiarity. In the first place, the voice seemed to reach our ears—at least mine—from a vast distance, or from some deep cavern within the earth. In the second place, it impressed me (I fear, indeed, that it will be impossible to make myself comprehended) as gelatinous or glutinous matters impress the sense of touch.

I have spoken both of "sound" and of "voice." I mean to say that the sound was one of distinct—of even wonderfully, thrillingly distinct—syllabification. M. Valdemar *spoke*—obviously in reply to the question I had propounded to him a few minutes before. I had asked him, it will be remembered, if he still slept. He now said:

"Yes;—no;—I *have been* sleeping—and now—now—*I am dead*."

No person present even affected to deny, or attempted to repress, the unutterable, shuddering horror which these few words, thus uttered, were so well calculated to convey. Mr. L—l (the student) swooned. The nurses immediately left the chamber, and could not be induced to return. My own impressions I would not pretend to render intelligible to the reader. For nearly an hour, we busied ourselves, silently—without the utterance of a word—in endeavors to revive Mr. L—l. When he came to himself, we addressed ourselves again to an investigation of M. Valdemar's condition.

It remained in all respects as I have last described it, with the exception that the mirror no longer afforded evidence of respiration. An attempt to draw blood from the arm failed. I should mention, too, that this limb was no farther subject to my will. I endeavored in vain to make it follow the direction of my hand. The only real indication, indeed, of the mesmeric influence, was now found in the vibratory movement of the tongue, whenever I addressed M. Valdemar a question. He seemed to be making an effort to reply, but had no longer sufficient volition. To queries put to him by any other person than myself he seemed utterly insensible—although I endeavored to place each member of the company in mesmeric *rapport* with him. I believe that I have now related all that is necessary to an understanding of the sleep-waker's state at this epoch. Other nurses were procured; and at ten o'clock I left the house in company with the two physicians and Mr. L—l.

In the afternoon we all called again to see the patient. His condition remained precisely the same. We had now some discussion as to the propriety and feasibility of awakening him; but we had little difficulty in agreeing that no good purpose would be served by so doing. It was evident that, so far, death (or what is usually termed death) had been arrested by the mesmeric process. It seemed clear to us all that to awaken M. Valdemar would be merely to insure his instant, or at least his speedy dissolution.

From this period until the close of last week—*an interval of nearly seven months*—we continued to make daily calls at M. Valdemar's house, accompanied, now and then, by medical and other friends. All this time the sleeper-waker remained *exactly* as I have last described him. The nurses' attentions were continual.

It was on Friday last that we finally resolved to make the

experiment of awakening or attempting to awaken him; and it is the (perhaps) unfortunate result of this latter experiment which has given rise to so much discussion in private circles—to so much of what I cannot help thinking unwarranted popular feeling.

For the purpose of relieving M.Valdemar from the mesmeric trance, I made use of the customary passes. These, for a time, were unsuccessful. The first indication of revival was afforded by a partial descent of the iris. It was observed, as especially remarkable, that this lowering of the pupil was accompanied by the profuse out-flowing of a yellowish ichor (from beneath the lids) of a pungent and highly offensive odor.

It was now suggested that I should attempt to influence the patient's arm, as heretofore. I made the attempt and failed. Dr. F—then intimated a desire to have me put a question. I did so, as follows:

"M. Valdemar, can you explain to us what are your feelings or wishes now?"

There was an instant return of the hectic circles on the cheeks; the tongue quivered, or rather rolled violently in the mouth (although the jaws and lips remained rigid as before;) and at length the same hideous voice which I have already described, broke forth:

"For God's sake!—quick!—quick!—put me to sleep—or, quick!—waken me!—quick!—*I say to you that I am dead!*"

I was thoroughly unnerved, and for an instant remained undecided what to do. At first I made an endeavor to re-compose the patient; but, failing in this through total abeyance of the will, I retraced my steps and as earnestly struggled to awaken him. In this attempt I soon saw that I should be successful—or at least I soon fancied that my success would be complete—and I am sure that all in the room were prepared to see the patient awaken.

For what really occurred, however, it is quite impossible that any human being could have been prepared.

As I rapidly made the mesmeric passes, amid ejaculations of "dead! dead!" absolutely *bursting* from the tongue and not from the lips of the sufferer, his whole frame at once—within the space of a single minute, or even less, shrunk—crumbled—absolutely *rotted* away beneath my hands. Upon the bed, before that whole company, there lay a nearly liquid mass of loathsome—of detestable putridity.

The Gold-Bug

What ho! what ho! this fellow is dancing mad!
He hath been bitten by the Tarantula.

All in the Wrong.

Many years ago I contracted an intimacy with a Mr. William Legrand. He was of an ancient Huguenot family, and had once been wealthy; but a series of misfortunes had reduced him to want. To avoid the mortification consequent upon his disasters, he left New Orleans, the city of his forefathers, and took up his residence at Sullivan's Island, near Charleston, South Carolina.

This island is a very singular one. It consists of little else than the sea sand, and is about three miles long. Its breadth at no point exceeds a quarter of a mile. It is separated from the mainland by a scarcely perceptible creek, oozing its way through a wilderness of reeds and slime, a favourite resort of the marsh-hen. The vegetation, as might be supposed, is scant, or at least dwarfish. No trees of any magnitude are to be seen. Near the western extremity, where Fort Moultrie stands, and where are some miserable frame buildings, tenanted, during summer, by the fugitives from Charleston dust and fever, may be found, indeed, the bristly palmetto; but the whole island, with the exception of this western point, and a line of hard, white beach on the sea coast, is covered with a dense undergrowth of the sweet myrtle, so much prized by the horticulturists of England. The shrub here often attains the height of fifteen or twenty feet, and forms an almost impenetrable coppice, burthening the air with its fragrance.

In the inmost recesses of this coppice, not far from the eastern or more remote end of the island, Legrand had built himself a small hut, which he occupied when I first, by mere accident, made his acquaintance. This soon ripened into friendship—for there was much in the recluse to excite interest and esteem. I found him well educated, with unusual powers of mind, but infected with misanthropy, and subject to perverse moods of alternate enthusiasm and melancholy. He had with him many books, but rarely employed them. His chief amusements were gunning and fishing, or sauntering along the beach and through the myrtles, in quest of shells or entomological specimens;—his collection of the latter might have been envied by a Swammerdamm.

In these excursions he was usually accompanied by an old negro, called Jupiter, who had been manumitted before the reverses of the family, but who could be induced, neither by threats nor by promises, to abandon what he considered his right of attendance upon the footsteps of his young "Massa Will." It is not improbable that the relatives of Legrand, conceiving him to be somewhat unsettled in intellect, had contrived to instil this obstinacy into Jupiter, with a view to the supervision and guardianship of the wanderer.

The winters in the latitude of Sullivan's Island are seldom very severe, and in the fall of the year it is a rare event indeed when a fire is considered necessary. About the middle of October, 18—, there occurred, however, a day of remarkable chilliness. Just before sunset I scrambled my way through the evergreens to the hut of my friend, whom I had not visited for several weeks—my residence being at that time in Charleston, a distance of nine miles from the island, while the facilities of passage and re-passage were very far behind those of the present day. Upon reaching the hut I rapped, as was my custom, and getting no reply, sought for the key where I knew it was secreted, unlocked the door and went in. A fine fire was blazing upon the hearth. It was a novelty, and by no means an ungrateful one. I threw off an overcoat, took an armchair by the crackling logs, and awaited patiently the arrival of my hosts.

Soon after dark they arrived, and gave me a most cordial welcome. Jupiter, grinning from ear to ear, bustled about to prepare some marsh-hens for supper. Legrand was in one of his fits—how else shall I term them?—of enthusiasm. He had found an unknown bivalve, forming a new genus, and, more than this, he had hunted down and secured, with Jupiter's assistance, a *scarabæus* which he believed to be totally new, but in respect to which he wished to have my opinion on the morrow.

"And why not tonight?" I asked, rubbing my hands over the blaze, and wishing the whole tribe of *scarabæi* at the devil.

"Ah, if I had only known you were here!" said Legrand, "but it's so long since I saw you; and how could I foresee that you would pay me a visit this very night of all others? As I was coming home I met Lieutenant G——, from the fort, and, very foolishly, I lent him the bug; so it will be impossible for you to see it until the morning. Stay here tonight, and I will send Jup down for it at sunrise. It is the loveliest thing in creation!"

"What!—sunrise?"

"Nonsense! no!—the bug. It is of a brilliant gold colour—about the size of a large hickory-nut—with two jet black spots near one extremity of the back, and another, somewhat longer, at the other. The *antennæ* are—"

"Dey aint *no* tin in him, Massa Will, I keep a tellin on you," here interrupted Jupiter; "de bug is a goole-bug, solid, ebery bit of him, inside and all, sep him wing—neber feel half so hebby a bug in my life."

"Well, suppose it is, Jup," replied Legrand, somewhat more earnestly, it seemed to me, than the case demanded, "is that any reason for your letting the birds burn? The colour—" here he turned to me—"is really almost enough to warrant Jupiter's idea. You never saw a more brilliant metallic lustre than the scales emit—but of this you cannot judge till tomorrow. In the meantime I can give you some idea of the shape." Saying this, he seated himself at a small table, on which were a pen and ink, but no paper. He looked for some in a drawer, but found none.

"Never mind," said he at length, "this will answer;" and he

drew from his waistcoat pocket a scrap of what I took to be very dirty foolscap, and made upon it a rough drawing with the pen. While he did this, I retained my seat by the fire, for I was still chilly. When the design was complete, he handed it to me without rising. As I received it, a loud growl was heard, succeeded by a scratching at the door. Jupiter opened it, and a large Newfoundland, belonging to Legrand, rushed in, leaped upon my shoulders, and loaded me with caresses; for I had shown him much attention during previous visits. When his gambols were over, I looked at the paper, and, to speak the truth, found myself not a little puzzled at what my friend had depicted.

"Well!" I said, after contemplating it for some minutes, "this is a strange *scarabcæus*, I must confess: new to me: never saw anything like it before—unless it was a skull, or a death's-head—which it more nearly resembles than anything else that has come under *my* observation."

"A death's-head!" echoed Legrand—"Oh—yes—well, it has something of that appearance upon paper, no doubt. The two upper black spots look like eyes, eh? and the longer one at the bottom like a mouth—and then the shape of the whole is oval."

"Perhaps so," said I; "but, Legrand, I fear you are no artist. I must wait until I see the beetle itself, if I am to form any idea of its personal appearance."

"Well. I don't know," said he, a little nettled. "I draw tolerably—*should* do it at least—have had good masters, and flatter myself that I am not quite a blockhead."

"But, my dear fellow, you are joking then," said I; "this is a very passable *skull*—indeed, I may say that it is a very *excellent* skull, according to the vulgar notions about such specimens of physiology—and your *scarabæus* must be the queerest *scarabæus* in the world if it resembles it. Why, we may get up a very thrilling bit of superstition upon this hint. I presume you will call the bug *scarabæus caput hominis*, or something of that kind—there are many similar titles in the Natural Histories. But where are the *antennæ* you spoke of?"

"The *antennæ!*" said Legrand, who seemed to be getting unaccountably warm upon the subject; "I am sure you must see the *antennaæ*. I made them as distinct as they are in the original insect, and I presume that is sufficient."

"Well, well," I said, "perhaps you have—still I don't see them;" and I handed him the paper without additional remark, not wishing to ruffle his temper; but I was much surprised at the turn affairs had taken; his ill-humour puzzled me and, as for the drawing of the beetle, there were positively *no antennæ* visible, and the whole *did* bear a very close resemblance to the ordinary cuts of a death's-head.

He received the paper very peevishly, and was about to crumple it, apparently to throw it in the fire, when a casual glance at the design seemed suddenly to rivet his attention. In an instant his face grew violently red—in another as excessively pale. For some minutes he continued to scrutinise the drawing minutely where he sat. At length he arose, took a candle from the table, and proceeded to seat himself upon a sea-chest in the farthest corner of the room. Here again he made an anxious examination oi the paper; turning it in all directions. He said nothing, however, and his conduct greatly astonished me; yet I thought it prudent not to exacerbate the growing moodiness of his temper by any comment.

Presently he took from his coat pocket a wallet, placed the paper carefully in it, and deposited both in a writing-desk, which he locked. He now grew more composed in his demeanour; but his original air of enthusiasm had quite disappeared. Yet he seemed not so much sulky as abstracted. As the evening wore away he became more and more absorbed in reverie, from which no sallies of mine could arouse him. It had been my intention to pass the night at the hut, as I had frequently done before, but, seeing my host in this mood, I deemed it proper to take leave. He did not press me to remain, but, as I departed, he shook my hand with even more than his usual cordiality.

It was about a month after this (and during the interval I had seen nothing of Legrand) when I received a visit, at Charleston, from his man, Jupiter. I had never seen the good old negro look so dispirited, and I feared that some serious disaster had befallen my friend.

"Well, Jup," said I, "what is the matter now?—how is your master?"

"Why, to speak de troof, massa, him not so berry well as mought be."

"Not well! I am truly sorry to hear it. What does he complain of?"

"Dar! dat's it!—him nebber plain of notin—but him berry sick for all dat."

"*Very* sick, Jupiter!—why didn't you say so at once? Is he confined to bed?"

"No dat he aint!—he aint find nowhar—dat's just whar de shoe pinch—my mind is got to be berry hebby bout poor Massa Will."

"Jupiter, I should like to understand what it is you are talking about. You say your master is sick. Hasn't he told you what ails him?"

"Why, massa, taint worf while for to git mad about de matter—Massa Will say noffin at all aint de matter wid him—but den what make him go about looking dis here way, wid he head down and he soldiers up, and as white as a gose? And den he keep a syphon all de time —"

"Keeps a what, Jupiter?"

"Keeps a syphon wid de figgurs on de slate—de queerest figgurs I ebber did see. Ise gittin to be skeered, I tell you. Hab for to keep mighty tight eye pon him noovers. Todder day he gib me slip fore de sun up, and was gone de whole ob de blessed day. I had a big stick ready cut for to gib him deuced good beating when he did come—but Ise sich a fool dat I hadn't de heart arter all he look so berry poorly."

"Eh?—what?—ah yes!—upon the whole I think you had better not be too severe with the poor fellow—don't flog him, Jupiter—he can't very well stand it—but can you form no idea of what has occasioned this illness, or rather this change of conduct? Has anything unpleasant happened since I saw you?"

"No, massa, dey aint bin noffin on pleasant *since* den—'twas *fore* den I'm feared—'twas de berry day you was dare."

"How? what do you mean?"

"Why, massa, I mean de bug—dare now."

"The what?"

"De bug—I'm berry sartain dat Massa Will bin bit somewhere bout de head by dat goole-bug."

"And what cause have you, Jupiter, for such a supposition?"

"Claws enuff, massa, and mouff too. I nebber did see sich a deuced bug—he kick and he bite ebery ting what cum near him. Massa Will cotch him fuss, but had for to let him go gin mighty quick, I tell you—den was de time he must ha got de bite. I didn't like de look ob de bug mouff, myself, no how, so I wouldn't take hold ob him wid my finger, but I cotch him wid a piece ob paper dat I found. I rap him up in de paper and stuff piece ob it in he mouff—dat was de way."

"And you think, then, that your master was really bitten by the beetle, and that the bite made him sick?"

"I don't tink noffin about it—I nose it. What make him dream bout de goole so much, if taint cause he bit by de goole-bug? Ise heerd bout dem goole-bugs fore dis."

"But how do you know he dreams about gold?"

"How I know? why, cause he talk about it in he sleep—dat's how I nose."

"Well, Jup, perhaps you are right; but to what fortunate circumstance am I to attribute the honour of a visit from you today?"

"What de matter, massa?"

"Did you bring any message from Mr. Legrand?"

"No, massa, I bring dis here pissel;" and here Jupiter handed me a note which ran thus:

My Dear ——

Why have I not seen you for so long a time? I hope you have not been so foolish as to take offence at any little *brusquerie* of mine; but no, that is improbable.

Since I saw you I have had great cause for anxiety. I have something to tell you, yet scarcely know how to tell it, or whether I should tell it at all.

I have not been quite well for some days past, and poor old Jup annoys me, almost beyond endurance, by his well-meant attentions. Would you believe it?—he had prepared a huge stick, the other day, with which to chastise me for giving him the slip, and spending the day, *solus*, among the hills on the mainland. I verily believe that my ill looks alone saved me a flogging.

I have made no addition to my cabinet since we met.

If you can, in any way, make it convenient, come over with Jupiter. *Do* come. I wish to see you *tonight*, upon business of importance. I assure you that it is of the *highest* importance,—Ever yours,

William Legrand.

There was something in the tone of this note which gave me great uneasiness. Its whole style differed materially from that of Legrand. What could he be dreaming of? What new crotchet possessed his excitable brain? What "business of the highest importance" could *he* possibly have to transact? Jupiter's account of him boded no good. I dreaded lest the continued pressure of misfortune had, at length, fairly unsettled the reason of my friend. Without a moment's hesitation, therefore, I prepared to accompany the negro.

Upon reaching the wharf, I noticed a scythe and three spades, all apparently new, lying in the bottom of the boat in which we were to embark.

"What is the meaning of all this, Jup?" I inquired.

"Him syfe, massa, and spade."

"Very true; but what are they doing here?"

"Him de syfe and de spade what Massa Will sis pon my buying for him in de town, and de debbil's own lot of money I had to gib for em."

"But what, in the name of all that is mysterious, is your 'Massa Will' going to do with scythes and spades?"

"Dat's more dan *I* know, and debbil take me if I don't blieve 'tis more dan he know too. But it's all cum ob de bug."

Finding that no satisfaction was to be obtained of Jupiter, whose whole intellect seemed to be absorbed by "de bug," I now stepped into the boat and made sail. With a fair and strong breeze we soon ran into the little cove to the northward of Fort Moultrie, and a walk of some two miles brought us to the hut. It was about three in the afternoon when we arrived. Legrand had been awaiting us in eager expectation. He grasped my hand with a nervous *empressement* which alarmed me and strengthened the suspicions already entertained. His countenance was pale even to ghastliness, and his deep-set eyes glared with unnatural lustre. After some inquiries respecting his health, I asked him, not knowing what better to say, if he had yet obtained the *scarabæus* from Lieutenant G—— .

"Oh, yes," he replied, colouring violently, "I got it from him the next morning. Nothing should tempt me to part with that *scarabæus*. Do you know that Jupiter is quite right about it!"

"In what way?" I asked, with a sad foreboding at heart.

"In supposing it to be a bug of *real gold*." He said this with an air of profound seriousness, and I felt inexpressibly shocked.

"This bug is to make my fortune," he continued, with a triumphant smile, "to reinstate me in my family possessions. Is it any wonder, then, that I prize it? Since Fortune has thought fit to bestow it upon me, I have only to use it properly and I shall arrive at the gold of which it is the index. Jupiter, bring me that *scarabæus!*"

"What! de bug, massa? I'd rudder not go fer trubble dat bug—you mus git him for your own self."

Hereupon Legrand arose, with a grave and stately air, and brought me the beetle from a glass case in which it was enclosed. It was a beautiful *scarabæus*, and, at that time, unknown to naturalists—of course a great prize in a scientific point of view. There were two round black spots near one extremity of the back, and a long one near the other. The scales were exceedingly hard and glossy, with all the appearance of burnished gold. The weight of the insect was very remarkable, and, taking all things into consideration, I could hardly blame Jupiter for his opinion respecting it; but what to make of Legrand's concordance with that opinion, I could not, for the life of me, tell.

"I sent for you," said he, in a grandiloquent tone, when I had completed my examination of the beetle, "I sent for you, that I might have your counsel and assistance in furthering the views of Fate and of the bug—"

"My dear Legrand," I cried, interrupting him, "you are certainly unwell, and had better use some little precautions. You shall go to bed, and I will remain with you a few days, until you get over this. You are feverish and—"

"Feel my pulse," said he.

I felt it, and, to say the truth, found not the slightest indication of fever.

"But you may be ill and yet have no fever. Allow me this once to prescribe for you. In the first place, go to bed. In the next—"

"You are mistaken," he interposed; "I am as well as I can expect to be under the excitement which I suffer. If you really wish me well, you will relieve this excitement."

"And how is this to be done ?"

"Very easily. Jupiter and myself are going upon an expedition into the hills, upon the mainland, and, in this expedition, we shall need the aid of some person in whom we can confide. You are the only one we can trust. Whether we succeed or fail, the excitement which you now perceive in me will be equally allayed."

"I am anxious to oblige you in any way," I replied; "but do you mean to say that this infernal beetle has any connection with your expedition into the hills?"

"It has."

"Then, Legrand, I can become a party to no such absurd proceeding."

"I am sorry—very sorry—for we shall have to try it by ourselves."

"Try it by yourselves! The man is surely mad!—but stay!—how long do you propose to be absent?"

"Probably all night. We shall start immediately, and be back, at all events by sunrise."

"And will you promise me upon your honour, that when this freak of yours is over, and the bug business (good God!)' settled to your satisfaction, you will then return home and follow my advice implicitly, as that of your physician?"

"Yes; I promise; and now let us be off, for we have no time to lose."

With a heavy heart I accompanied my friend. We started about four o'clock—Legrand, Jupiter, the dog, and myself. Jupiter had with him the scythe and spades—the whole of which he insisted upon carrying—more through fear, it seemed to me, of trusting either of the implements within reach of his master, than from any excess of industry or complaisance. His demeanour was dogged in the extreme, and "dat deuced bug" were the sole words which escaped his lips during the journey. For my own part, I had charge of a couple of dark lanterns, while Legrand contented himself with the *scarabæus*, which he carried attached to the end of a bit of whip-cord; twirling it to and fro, with the air of a conjuror, as he went.

When I observed this last plain evidence of my friend's aberration of mind I could scarcely refrain from tears. I thought it best, however, to humour his fancy, at least for the present, or until I could adopt some more energetic measures with a chance of success. In the meantime I endeavoured, but all in vain, to sound him in regard to the object of the expedition. Having succeeded in inducing me to accompany him, he seemed unwilling to hold conversation upon any topic of minor importance, and to all my questions vouchsafed no other reply than "We shall see!"

We crossed the creek at the head of the island by means of a skiff, and, ascending the high grounds on the shore of the mainland, proceeded in a north-westerly direction, through a tract of country excessively wild and desolate, where no trace of a human footstep was to be seen. Legrand led the way with decision; pausing only for an instant, here and there, to consult what appeared to be certain landmarks of his own contrivance upon a former occasion.

In this manner we journeyed for about two hours, and the sun was just setting when we entered a region infinitely more dreary than any yet seen. It was a species of tableland, near the summit of an almost inaccessible hill, densely wooded from base to pinnacle, and interspersed with huge crags that appeared to lie loosely upon the soil, and in many cases were prevented from precipitating themselves into the valleys below, merely by the support of the trees against which they reclined. Deep ravines, in various directions, gave an air of still sterner solemnity to the scene.

The natural platform to which we had clambered was thickly overgrown with brambles, through which we soon discovered that it would have been impossible to force our way but for the scythe; and Jupiter, by direction of his master, proceeded to clear for us a path to the foot of an enormously tall tulip-tree, which stood, with some eight or ten oaks, upon the level, and far surpassed them all, and all other trees which I had then ever seen, in the beauty of its foliage and form, in the wide spread of its branches, and in the general majesty of its appearance. When we reached this tree, Legrand turned to Jupiter, and asked him if he thought he could climb it. The old man seemed a little staggered by the question, and for some moments made no reply. At length he approached the huge trunk, walked slowly around it, and examined it with minute attention. When he had completed his scrutiny, he merely said,

"Yes, massa, Jup climb any tree he ebber see in he life."

"Then up with you as soon as possible, for it will soon be too dark to see what we are about."

"How far mus go up, massa?" inquired Jupiter.

"Get up the main trunk first, and then I will tell you which way to go—and here—stop! take this beetle with you."

"De bug, Massa Will!—de goole-bug" cried the negro, drawing back in dismay—"what for mus tote bug way up de tree?—

d—n if I do!"

"If you are afraid, Jup, a great big negro like you, to take hold of a harmless little dead beetle, why you can carry it up by this string—but if you do not take it up with you in some way, I shall be under the necessity of breaking your head with this shovel."

"What de matter now, massa?" said Jup, evidently shamed into compliance; "always want for to raise fuss wid old nigger. Was only funnin any how. *Me* feered de bug! what I keer for de bug?" Here he took cautiously hold of the extreme end of the string, and, maintaining the insect as far from his person as circumstances would permit, prepared to ascend the tree.

In youth, the tulip-tree, or *Liriodendron tulipiferum*, the most magnificent of American foresters, has a trunk peculiarly smooth, and often rises to a great height without lateral branches; but, in its riper age, the bark becomes gnarled and uneven, while many short limbs make their appearance on the stem. Thus the difficulty of ascension, in the present case, lay more in semblance than in reality. Embracing the huge cylinder, as closely as possible, with his arms and knees, seizing with his hands some projections, and resting his naked toes upon others, Jupiter, after one or two narrow escapes from falling, at length wriggled himself into the first great fork, and seemed to consider the whole business as virtually accomplished. The *risk* of the achievement was, in fact, now over, although the climber was some sixty or seventy feet from the ground.

"Which way mus go now, Massa Will" he asked.

"Keep up the largest branch—the one on this side," said Legrand. The negro obeyed him promptly, and apparently with but little trouble; ascending higher and higher, until no glimpse of his squat figure could be obtained through the dense foliage which enveloped it. Presently his voice was heard in a sort of halloo.

"How much f udder is got for go?"

"How high up are you?" asked Legrand.

"Ebber so fur," replied the negro; "can see de sky fru de top ob de tree."

"Never mind the sky, but attend to what I say. Look down the trunk and count the limbs below you on this side. How many limbs have you passed?"

"One, two, tree, four, fibe—I done pass fibe big limb, massa, pon dis side."

"Then go one limb higher."

In a few minutes the voice was heard again, announcing that the seventh limb was attained.

"Now, Jup," cried Legrand, evidently much excited, "I want you to work your way out upon that limb as far as you can. If you see anything strange, let me know."

By this time what little doubt I might have entertained of my poor friend's insanity was put finally at rest. I had no alternative but to conclude him stricken with lunacy, and I became seriously anxious about getting him home. While I was pondering upon what was best to be done, Jupiter's voice was again heard.

"Mos feerd for to ventur pon dis limb berry far—tis dead limb putty much all de way."

"Did you say it was a *dead* limb, Jupiter?" cried Legrand in a quavering voice.

"Yes, massa, him dead as de door-nail—done up for sartain—done departed dis here life."

"What in the name of heaven shall I do?" asked Legrand, seemingly in the greatest distress.

"Do!" said I, glad of an opportunity to interpose a word, "why come home and go to bed. Come now!—that's a fine fellow. It's getting late, and, besides, you remember your promise."

"Jupiter," cried he, without heeding me in the least, "do you hear me?"

"Yes, Massa Will, hear you ebber so plain."

"Try the wood well, then, with your knife, and see if you think it *very* rotten."

"Him rotten, massa, sure miff," replied the negro in a few moments, "but not so berry rotten as mought be. Mought ventur out leetle way pon de limb by myself, dat's true."

"By yourself!—What do you mean?"

"Why, I mean de bug. 'Tis *berry* hebby bug. Spose I drop him down fuss, and den de limb won't break wid just de weight ob one nigger."

"You infernal scoundrel!" cried Legrand, apparently much relieved, "what do you mean by telling me such nonsense as that? As sure as you drop that beetle I'll break your neck. Look here, Jupiter, do you hear me?"

"Yes, massa, needn't hollo at poor nigger dat style."

"Well! now listen!—if you will venture out on the limb as far as you think safe, and not let go the beetle. I'll make you a present of a silver dollar as soon as you get down."

"I'm gwine, Massa Will—deed I is," replied the negro very promptly—"mos out to the eend now."

"*Out to the end!*" here fairly screamed Legrand, "do you say you are out to the end of that limb?"

"Soon be to de eend, massa,—o-o-o-o-oh! Lor-gol- a-marcy! what *is* dis here pon de tree?"

"Well," cried Legrand, highly delighted, "what is it?"

"Why, taint nuffin but a skull—somebody bin lef him head up de tree, and de crows done gobble ebery bit ob de meat off."

"A skull, you say!—very well!—how is it fastened to the limb? what holds it on?"

"Sure nuff, massa; mus look. Why dis berry curous sarcumstance, pon my word—dare's a great big nail in de skull, what fastens ob it on to de tree."

"Well now, Jupiter, do exactly as I tell you—do you hear?"

"Yes, massa."

"Pay attention, then!—find the left eye of the skull."

"Hum! hoo! dat's good! why dare aint no eye lef at all."

"Curse your stupidity! do you know your right hand from your left?"

"Yes, I nose dat—nose all bout dat—tis my lef hand what I chops de wood wid."

"To be sure! you are left-handed; and your left eye is on the same side as your left hand. Now, I suppose, you can find the left eye of the skull, or the place where the left eye has been. Have you found it?"

Here was a long pause. At length the negro asked,

"Is de lef eye of de skull pon de same side as de lef hand of de skull, too?—cause de skull aint got not a bit ob a hand at all—nebber mind! I got de lef eye now—here de lef eye! what mus do wid it?"

"Let the beetle drop through it, as far as the string will reach—but be careful and not let go your hold of the string."

"All dat done, Massa Will; mighty easy ting for to put de bug fru de hole—look out for him dare below!"

During this colloquy no portion of Jupiter's person could be seen; but the beetle, which he had suffered to descend, was now visible at the end of the string, and glistened, like a globe of burnished gold, in the last rays of the setting sun, some of which still faintly illumined the eminence upon which we stood. The *scarabæus* hung quite clear of any branches, and, if allowed to fall, would have fallen at our feet. Legrand immediately took the scythe, and cleared with it a circular space, three or four yards in diameter, just beneath the insect, and, having accomplished this, ordered Jupiter to let go the string and come down from the tree.

Driving a peg, with great nicety, into the ground, at the precise spot where the beetle fell, my friend now produced from his pocket a tape-measure. Fastening one end of this at that point of the trunk of the tree which was nearest the peg, he unrolled it till it reached the peg, and thence farther unrolled it, in the direction already established by the two points of the tree and the peg, for the distance of fifty feet—Jupiter clearing away the brambles with the scythe. At the spot thus attained a second peg was driven, and about this, as a centre, a rude circle, about four feet in diameter, described. Taking now a spade himself, and giving one to Jupiter and one to me, Legrand begged us to set about digging as quickly as possible.

To speak the truth, I had no especial relish for such amusement at any time, and, at that particular moment, would most willingly have declined it; for the night was coming on, and I felt much fatigued with the exercise already taken; but I saw no mode of escape, and was fearful of disturbing my poor friend's equanimity by a refusal. Could I have depended, indeed, upon Jupiter's aid, I would have had no hesitation in attempting to get the lunatic home by force; but I was too well assured of the old negro's disposition, to hope that he would assist me, under any circumstances, in a personal contest with his master.

I made no doubt that the latter had been infected with some of the innumerable Southern superstitions about money buried, and that his fantasy had received confirmation by the finding of the *scarabæus*, or, perhaps, by Jupiter's obstinacy in maintaining it to be "a bug of real gold." A mind disposed to lunacy would readily be led away by such suggestions—especially if chiming in with favourite preconceived ideas and then I called to mind the poor fellow's speech about the beetle's being "the index of his fortune." Upon the whole, I was sadly vexed and puzzled, but, at length, I concluded to make a virtue of necessity—to dig with a goodwill, and thus the sooner to convince the visionary, by ocular demonstration, of the fallacy of the opinions he entertained.

The lanterns having been lit, we all fell to work with a zeal worthy a more rational cause; and, as the glare fell upon our persons and implements, I could not help thinking how picturesque a group we composed, and how strange and suspicious our labours must have appeared to any interloper who, by chance, might have stumbled upon our whereabouts.

We dug very steadily for two hours. Little was said; and our chief embarrassment lay in the yelpings of the dog, who took exceeding interest in our proceedings. He at length became so obstreperous, that we grew fearful of his giving the alarm to some stragglers in the vicinity 3 or, rather, this was the apprehension of Legrand;—for myself, I should have rejoiced at any interruption which might have enabled me to get the wanderer home. The noise was, at length, very effectually silenced by Jupiter, who, getting out of the hole with a dogged air of deliberation, tied the brute's mouth up with one of his suspenders, and then returned, with a grave chuckle, to his task.

When the time mentioned had expired, we had reached a depth of five feet, and yet no signs of any treasure became manifest. A general pause ensued, and I began to hope that the farce was at an end. Legrand, however, although evidently much disconcerted, wiped his brow thoughtfully and recommenced. We had excavated the entire circle of four feet diameter, and now we slightly enlarged the limit, and went to the farther depth of two feet. Still nothing appeared. The gold-seeker, whom I sincerely pitied, at length clambered from the pit, with the bitterest disappointment imprinted upon every feature, and proceeded, slowly and reluctantly, to put on his coat, which he had thrown off at the beginning of his labour. In the meantime I made no remark. Jupiter, at a signal from his master, began to gather up his tools. This done, and the dog having been unmuzzled, we turned in profound silence towards home.

We had taken, perhaps, a dozen steps in this direction, when, with a loud oath, Legrand strode up to Jupiter, and seized him by the collar. The astonished negro opened his eyes and mouth to the fullest extent, let fall the spades, and fell upon his knees.

"You scoundrel," said Legrand, hissing out the syllables from between his clenched teeth—"you infernal black villain!—speak, I tell you!—answer me this instant, without prevarication!—which which is your left eye?"

"Oh, my golly, Massa Will! aint dis here my lef eye for sartain?" roared the terrified Jupiter, placing his hand upon his right organ of vision, and holding it there with a desperate pertinacity, as if in immediate dread of his master's attempt at a gouge.

"I thought so!—I knew it! hurrah!" vociferated Legrand, letting the negro go, and executing a series of curvets and caracoles, much to the astonishment of his valet, who, arising from his knees, looked, mutely, from his master to myself, and then from myself to his master.

"Come! we must go back," said the latter; "the game's not up yet;" and he again led the way to the tulip-tree.

"Jupiter," said he, when he reached its foot, "come here! was the skull nailed to the limb with the face outwards, or with the face to the limb?"

"De face was out, massa, so dat de crows could get at de eyes good, widout any trouble."

"Well, then, was it this eye or that through which you dropped the beetle?" here Legrand touched each of Jupiter's eyes.

"'Twas dis eye, massa—de lef eye jis as you tell me," and here it was his right eye that the negro indicated.

"That will do—we must try it again."

Here my friend, about whose madness I now saw, or fancied that I saw, certain indications of method, removed the peg which marked the spot where the beetle fell, to a spot about three inches to the westward of its former position. Taking, now, the tape-measure from the nearest point of the trunk to the peg, as before, and continuing the extension in a straight line to the distance of fifty feet, a spot was indicated, removed by several yards from the point at which we had been digging.

Around the new position a circle, somewhat larger than in the former instance, was now described, and we again set to work with the spades. I was dreadfully weary, but scarcely understanding what had occasioned the change in my thoughts, I felt no longer any great aversion from the labour imposed. I had become most unaccountably interested—nay, even excited. Perhaps there was something, amid all the extravagant demeanour of Legrand—some air of forethought, or of deliberation, which impressed me. I dug eagerly, and now and then caught myself actually looking, with something that very much resembled expectation, for the fancied treasure, the vision of which had demented my unfortunate companion.

At a period when such vagaries of thought most fully possessed me, and when we had been at work perhaps an hour and a half, we were again interrupted by the violent howlings of the dog. His uneasiness, in the first instance, had been, evidently, but the result of playfulness or caprice, but he now assumed a bitter and serious tone. Upon Jupiter's again attempting to muzzle him, he made furious resistance, and, leaping into the hole, tore up the mould frantically with his claws. In a few seconds he had uncovered a mass of human bones, forming two complete skeletons, intermingled with several buttons of metal, and what appeared to be the dust of decayed woollen. One or two strokes of a spade upturned the blade of a large Spanish knife, and, as we dug farther, three or four loose pieces of gold and silver coin came to light.

At the sight of these the joy of Jupiter could scarcely be restrained, but the countenance of his master wore an air of extreme disappointment. He urged us, however, to continue our exertions, and the words were hardly uttered when I stumbled and fell forward, having caught the toe of my boot in a large ring of iron that lay half-buried in the loose earth.

We now worked in earnest, and never did I pass ten minutes of more intense excitement. During this interval we had fairly unearthed an oblong chest of wood, which, from its perfect preservation and wonderful hardness, had plainly been subjected to some mineralising process—perhaps that of the bichloride of mercury. This box was three feet and a half long, three feet broad, and two and a half feet deep. It was firmly secured by bands of wrought iron, riveted, and forming a kind of open trellis-work over the whole. On each side of the chest, near the top, were three rings of iron—six in all—by means of which a firm hold could be obtained by six persons.

Our utmost united endeavours served only to disturb the coffer very slightly in its bed. We at once saw the impossibility of removing so great a weight. Luckily, the sole fastenings of the lid consisted of two sliding bolts. These we drew back—trembling and panting with anxiety. In an instant, a treasure of incalculable value lay gleaming before us. As the rays of the lanterns fell within the pit, there flashed upwards a glow and a glare, from a confused heap of gold and of jewels, that absolutely dazzled our eyes.

I shall not pretend to describe the feelings with which I gazed. Amazement was, of course, predominant. Legrand appeared exhausted with excitement, and spoke very few words. Jupiter's countenance wore, for some minutes, as deadly a pallor as it is possible, in the nature of things, for any negro's visage to assume. He seemed stupefied—thunderstricken. Presently he fell upon his knees in the pit, and, burying his naked arms up to the elbows in gold, let them there remain, as if enjoying the luxury of a bath. At length, with a deep sigh, he exclaimed, as if in a soliloquy,

"And dis all cum ob de goole-bug! de putty goole-bug! de poor little goole-bug, what I boosed in dat sabage kind ob style! Aint you shamed ob yourself, nigger?—answer me dat!"

It became necessary, at last, that I should arouse both master and valet to the expediency of removing the treasure. It was growing late, and it behoved us to make exertion, that we might get everything housed be fore daylight. It was difficult to say what should be done, and much time was spent in deliberation—so confused were the ideas of all. We, finally, lightened the box by removing two-thirds of its contents, when we were enabled, with some trouble, to raise it from the hole. The articles taken out were deposited among the brambles, and the dog left to guard them, with strict orders from Jupiter neither, upon any pretence, to stir from the spot, nor to open his mouth until our return.

We then hurriedly made for home with the chest; reaching the hut in safety, but after excessive toil, at one o'clock in the morning. Worn out as we were, it was not in human nature to do more immediately. We rested until two, and had supper; starting for the hills immediately afterwards, armed with three stout sacks, which, by good luck, were upon the premises. A little before four we arrived at the pit, divided the remainder of the booty, as equally as might be, among us, and, leaving the holes unfilled, again set out for the hut, at which, for the second time, we deposited our golden burthens, just as the first faint streaks of the dawn gleamed from over the tree-tops in the East.

We were now thoroughly broken down; but the intense excitement of the time denied us repose. After an unquiet slumber of some three or four hours' duration, we arose, as if by preconcert, to make examination of our treasure.

The chest had been full to the brim, and we spent the whole day, and the greater part of the next night, in a scrutiny of its contents. There had been nothing like order or arrangement. Everything had been heaped in promiscuously. Having assorted all with care, we found ourselves possessed of even vaster wealth than we had at first supposed. In coin there was rather more than four hundred and fifty thousand dollars—estimating the value of the pieces, as accurately as we could, by the tables of the period. There was not a particle of silver. All was gold of antique date and of great variety—French, Spanish, and German money, with a few English guineas, and some counters, of which we had never seen specimens before. There were several very large and heavy coins, so worn that we could make nothing of their inscriptions.

There was no American money. The value of the jewels we found more difficulty in estimating. There were diamonds—some of them exceedingly large and fine—a hundred and ten in all, and not one of them small; eighteen rubies of remarkable brilliancy; three hundred and ten emeralds, all very beautiful; and twenty-one sapphires, with an opal. These stones had all been broken from their settings and thrown loose in the chest The settings themselves, which we picked out from among the other gold, appeared to have been beaten up with hammers, as if to prevent identification. Besides all this, there was a vast quantity of solid gold ornaments;—nearly two hundred massive finger and ear rings; rich chains—thirty of these, if I remember; eighty-three very large and heavy crucifixes; five gold censers of great value; a prodigious golden punch-bowl, ornamented with richly chased vine-leaves and Bacchanalian figures; with two sword-handles exquisitely embossed, and many other smaller articles which I cannot recollect.

The weight of these valuables exceeded three hundred and fifty pounds *avoirdupois*; and in this estimate I have not included one hundred and ninety-seven superb gold watches; three of the number being worth each five hundred dollars, if one. Many of them were very old, and as time-keepers valueless; the works having suffered more or less, from corrosion—but all were richly jewelled and in cases of great worth. We estimated the entire contents of the chest, that night, at a million and a half of dollars; and, upon the subsequent disposal of the trinkets and jewels (a few being retained for our own use), it was found that we had greatly undervalued the treasure.

When, at length, we had concluded our examination, and the intense excitement of the time had in some measure subsided, Legrand, who saw that I was dying with impatience for a solution of this most extraordinary riddle, entered into a full detail of all the circumstances connected with it.

"You remember," said he, "the night when I handed you the rough sketch I had made of the *scarabæus*. You recollect also, that I became quite vexed at you for insisting that my drawing resembled a death's-head. When you first made this assertion I thought you were jesting; but afterwards I called to mind the peculiar spots on the. back of the insect, and admitted to myself that your remark had some little foundation in fact. Still, the sneer at my graphic powers irritated me—for I am considered a good artist—and, therefore, when you handed me the scrap of parchment, I was about to crumple it up and throw it angrily into the fire."

"The scrap of paper, you mean," said I.

"No; it had much of the appearance of paper, and at first I supposed it to be such, but when I came to draw upon it, I discovered it, at once, to be a piece of very thin parchment. It was quite dirty, you remember. Well, as I was in the very act of crumpling it up, my glance fell upon the sketch at which you had been looking, and you may imagine my astonishment when I perceived, in fact, the figure of a death's-head just where, it seemed to me, I had made the drawing of the beetle. For a moment I was too much amazed to think with accuracy. I knew that my design was very different in detail from this—although there was a certain similarity in general outline.

"Presently I took a candle, and seating myself at the other end of the room, proceeded to scrutinise the parchment more closely. Upon turning it over, I saw my own sketch upon the reverse, just as I had made it. My first idea, now, was mere surprise at the really remarkable similarity of outline—at the singular coincidence involved in the fact, that unknown to me, there should have been a skull upon the other side of the parchment, immediately beneath my figure of the *scarabæus*, and that this skull, not only in outline, but in size, should so closely resemble my drawing. I say the singularity of this coincidence absolutely stupefied me for a time. This is the usual effect of such coincidences. The mind struggles to establish a connection—a sequence of cause and effect—and, being unable to do so, suffers a species of temporary paralysis.

"But when I recovered from this stupor, there dawned upon me gradually a conviction which startled me even far more than the coincidence. I began distinctly, positively, to remember that there had been *no* drawing upon the parchment when I made my sketch of the *scarabæus*. I became perfectly certain of this; for I recollected turning up first one side and then the other, in search of the cleanest spot. Had the skull been then there, of course I could not have failed to notice it. Here was indeed a mystery which I felt it impossible to explain; but, even at that early moment, there seemed to glimmer, faintly, within the most remote and secret chambers of my intellect, a glowworm-like conception of that truth which last night's adventure brought to so magnificent a demonstration. I arose at once, and putting the parchment securely away, dismissed all farther reflection until I should be alone.

"When you had gone, and when Jupiter was fast asleep, I betook myself to a more methodical investigation of the affair. In the first place I considered the manner in which the parchment had come into my possession. The spot where we discovered the *scarabæus* was on the coast of the mainland, about a mile eastward of the island, and but a short distance above high-water mark. Upon my taking hold of it, it gave me a sharp bite, which caused me to let it drop. Jupiter, with his accustomed caution, before seizing the insect, which had flown towards him, looked about him for a leaf, or something of that nature, by which to take hold of it.

"It was at this moment that his eyes, and mine also, fell upon the scrap of parchment, which I then supposed to be paper. It was lying half buried in the sand, a corner sticking up. Near the spot where we found it, I observed the remnants of the hull of what appeared to have been a ship's long-boat. The wreck seemed to have been there for a very great while; for the resemblance to boat timbers could scarcely be traced.

"Well, Jupiter picked up the parchment, wrapped the beetle in it, and gave it to me. Soon afterwards we turned to go home, and on the way met Lieutenant G——. I showed him the insect, and he begged me to let him take it to the fort. Upon my consenting, he thrust it forthwith into his waistcoat pocket, without the parchment in which it had been wrapped, and which I had continued to hold in my hand during his inspection. Perhaps he dreaded my changing my mind, and thought it best to make sure of the prize at once—you know how enthusiastic he is on all subjects connected with Natural History. At the same time, without being conscious of it, I must have deposited the parchment in my own pocket.

"You remember that when I went to the table, for the purpose of making a sketch of the beetle, I found no paper where it was usually kept. I looked in the drawer, and found none there. I searched my pockets, hoping to find an old letter, when my hand fell upon the parchment. I thus detail the precise mode in which it came into my possession: for the circumstances impressed me with peculiar force.

"No doubt you will think me fanciful—but I had already established a kind of *connection*. I had put together two links of a great chain. There was a boat lying upon a sea-coast, and not far from the boat was a parchment—*not a paper*—with a skull depicted upon it. You will, of course, ask 'Where is the connection?' I reply that the skull, or death's-head, is the well-known emblem of the pirate. The flag of the death's-head is hoisted in all engagements.

"I have said that the scrap was parchment, and not paper. Parchment is durable—almost imperishable. Matters of little moment are rarely consigned to parchment; since, for the mere ordinary purposes of drawing or writing, it is not nearly so well adapted as paper. This reflection suggested some meaning—some relevancy—in the death's-head. I did not fail to observe, also, the *form* of the parchment. Although one of its corners had been, by some accident, destroyed, it could be seen that the original form was oblong. It was just such a slip, indeed, as might have been chosen for a memorandum—for a record of something to be long remembered and carefully preserved."

"But," I interposed, "you say that the skull was *not* upon the parchment when you made the drawing of the beetle. How then do you trace any connection between the boat and the skull—since this latter, according to your own admission, must have been designed (God only knows how or by whom) at some period subsequent to your sketching the *scarabæus*?"

"Ah, hereupon turns the whole mystery; although the secret, at this point, I had comparatively little difficulty in solving. My steps were sure, and could afford but a single result. I reasoned, for example, thus: When I drew the *scarabæus*, there was no skull apparent upon the parchment. When I had completed the drawing I gave it to you, and observed you narrowly until you returned it. *You*, therefore, did not design the skull, and no one else was present to do it. Then it was not done by human agency. And nevertheless it was done.

"At this stage of my reflections I endeavoured to remember, and *did* remember, with entire distinctness, every incident which occurred about the period in question. The weather was chilly (oh rare and happy accident !), and a fire was blazing upon the hearth. I was heated with exercise and sat near the table. You, however, had drawn a chair close to the chimney. Just as I placed the parchment in your hand, and as you were in the act of inspecting it, Wolf, the Newfoundland, entered, and leaped upon your shoulders. With your left hand you caressed him and kept him off, while your right, holding the parchment, was permitted to fall listlessly between your knees, and in close proximity to the fire.

"At one moment I thought the blaze had caught it, and was about to caution you, but, before I could speak, you had withdrawn it, and were engaged in its examination. When I considered all these particulars, I doubted not for a moment that *heat* had been the agent in bringing to light, upon the parchment, the skull which I saw designed upon it. You are well aware that chemical preparations exist, and have existed time out of mind, by means of which it is possible to write upon either paper or vellum, so that the characters shall become visible only when subjected to the action of fire. Zaffre, digested in *aqua regia*, and diluted with four times its weight of water, is sometimes employed; a green tint results. The *regulus* of cobalt, dissolved in spirit of nitre, gives a red. These colours disappear at longer or shorter intervals after the material written upon cools, but again become apparent upon the reapplication of heat.

"I now scrutinised the death's-head with care. Its outer edges—the edges of the drawing nearest the edge of the vellum—were far more *distinct* than the others. It was clear that the action of the caloric had been imperfect or unequal. I immediately kindled a fire, and subjected every portion of the parchment to a glowing heat. At first, the only effect was the strengthening of the faint lines in the skull; but, upon persevering in the experiment, there became visible, at the corner of the slip, diagonally opposite to the spot in which the death's-head was delineated, the figure of what I at first supposed to be a goat. A closer scrutiny, however, satisfied me that it was intended for a kid."

"Ha! ha!" said I, "to be sure I have no right to laugh at you—a million and a half of money is too serious a matter for mirth—but you are not about to establish a third link in your chain—you will not find any especial connection between your pirates and a goat—pirates, you know, have nothing to do with goats; they appertain to the farming interest."

"But I have said that the figure was *not* that of a goat."

"Well, a kid then—pretty much the same thing."

"Pretty much, but not altogether," said Legrand, "You may have heard of one *Captain* Kidd. I at once looked upon the figure of the animal as a kind of punning or hieroglyphical signature. I say signature; because its position upon the vellum suggested this idea. The death's-head at the corner diagonally opposite had, in the same manner, the air of a stamp, or seal. But I was sorely put out by the absence of all else—of the body to my imagined instrument—of the text for my context."

"I presume you expected to find a letter between the stamp and the signature."

"Something of that kind. The fact is, I felt irresistibly impressed with a presentiment of some vast good fortune impending. I can scarcely say why. Perhaps, after all, it was rather a desire than an actual belief; but do you know that Jupiter's silly words, about the bug being of solid gold, had a remarkable effect upon my fancy? And then the series of accidents and coincidences—these were so *very* extraordinary. Do you observe how mere an accident it was that these events should have occurred upon the *sole* day of all the year in which it has been, or may be, sufficiently cool for fire, and that without the fire, or without the intervention of the dog at the precise moment in which he appeared, I should never have become aware of the death's-head, and so never the possessor of the treasure?"

"But proceed—I am all impatience."

"Well; you have heard, of course, the many stories current—the thousand vague rumours afloat about money buried, somewhere upon the Atlantic coast, by Kidd and his associates. These rumours must have had some foundation in fact. And that the rumours have existed so long and so continuous, could have resulted, it appeared to me, only from the circumstance of the buried treasure still remaining *entombed*. Had Kidd concealed his plunder for a time, and afterwards reclaimed it, the rumours would scarcely have reached us in their present unvarying form. You will observe that the stories told are all about money-seekers, not about money-finders.

"Had the pirate recovered his money, there the affair would have dropped. It seemed to me that some accident—say the loss of a memorandum indicating its locality—had deprived him of the means of recovering it, and that this accident had become known to his followers, who otherwise might never have heard that treasure had been concealed at all, and who, busying themselves in vain, because unguided attempts, to regain it, had given first birth, and then universal currency, to the reports which are now so common. Have you ever heard of any important treasure being unearthed along the coast?"

"Never."

"But that Kidd's accumulations were immense is well known. I took it for granted, therefore, that the earth still held them; and you will scarcely be surprised when I tell you that I felt a hope, nearly amounting to certainty, that the parchment so strangely found, involved a lost record of the place of deposit."

"But how did you proceed?"

"I held the vellum again to the fire, after increasing the heat; but nothing appeared. I now thought it possible that the coating of dirt might have something to do with the failure; so I carefully rinsed the parchment by pouring warm water over it, and, having done this, I placed it in a tin pan, with the skull downwards, and put the pan upon a furnace of lighted charcoal. In a few minutes, the pan having become thoroughly heated, I removed the slip, and, to my inexpressible joy, found it spotted, in several places, with what appeared to be figures arranged in lines. Again I placed it in the pan, and suffered it to remain another minute, Upon taking it off, the whole was just as you see it now." Here Legrand, having re-heated the parchment, submitted it to my inspection. The following characters were rudely traced, in a red tint, between the death's-head and the goat:

53‡‡†305))6*;4826)4‡.)4‡);806*;48†8¶60))85;1‡(;:‡*8†8
3(88)5*†;46(;88*96*?;8)*‡(;485);5*†2:*‡(;4956*2(5*—4)8¶
8*;4069285);)6†8)4‡‡;1(‡9;48081;8:8‡1;48†85;4)485†52880
6*81(‡9;48;(88;4(‡?34;48)4‡;161;:188;‡?;

"But," said I, returning him the slip, "I am as much in the dark as ever. Were all the jewels of Golconda awaiting me upon my solution of this enigma, I am quite sure that I should be unable to earn them."

"And yet," said Legrand, "the solution is by no means so difficult as you might be led to imagine from the first hasty inspection of the characters. These characters, as any one might readily guess, form a cipher—that is to say, they convey a meaning: but then, from what is known of Kidd, I could not suppose him capable of constructing any of the more abstruse cryptographs, I made up my mind, at once, that this was of a simple species—such, however, as would appear, to the crude intellect of the sailor, absolutely insoluble without the key."

"And you really solved it?"

"Readily; I have solved others of an abstruseness ten thousand times greater. Circumstances, and a certain bias of mind, have led me to take interest in such riddles, and it may well be doubted whether human ingenuity can construct an enigma of the kind which human ingenuity may not, by proper application, resolve. In fact, having once established connected and legible characters, I scarcely gave a thought to the mere difficulty of developing their import.

"In the present case—indeed in all cases of secret writing—the first question regards the *language* of the cipher; for the principles of solution, so far, especially, as the more simple ciphers are concerned, depend upon, and are varied by, the genius of the particular idiom. In general, there is no alternative but experiment (directed by probabilities) of every tongue known to him who attempts the solution, until the true one be attained. But, with the cipher now before us, all difficulty was removed by the signature. The pun upon the word 'Kidd' is appreciable in no other language than the English. But for this consideration I should have begun my attempts with the Spanish and French, as the tongues in which a secret of this kind would most naturally have been written by a pirate of the Spanish main. As it was, I assumed the cryptograph to be English.

"You observe there are no divisions between the words. Had there been divisions, the task would have been comparatively easy. In such case I should have commenced with a collation and analysis of the shorter words, and had a word of a single letter occurred, as is most likely (*a* or *I*, for example), I should have considered the solution as assured. But, there being no division, my first step was to ascertain the predominant letters, as well as the least frequent. Counting all, I constructed a table thus:

Of the character 8	there are	33.
;	"	26.
4	"	19.
‡)	"	16.
*	"	13.
5	"	12.
6	"	11.
†1	"	8.
0	"	6.
92	"	5.
:3	"	4.
?	"	3.
¶	"	2.
—.	"	1.

"Now, in English, the letter which most frequently occurs is *e*. Afterwards, the succession runs thus: *a o i d h n r s t u y c f g l m w b k p q x z*. E predominates so remarkably that an individual sentence of any length is rarely seen, in which it is not the prevailing character.

"Here, then, we have, in the very beginning, the groundwork for something more than a mere guess. The general use which may be made of the table is obvious—but in this particular cipher we shall only very partially require its aid. As our predominant character is 8, we will commence by assuming it as the *e* of the natural alphabet. To verify the supposition, let us observe if the 8 be seen often in couples—for e is doubled with great frequency in English in such words, for example, as 'meet,' 'fleet,' 'speed,' 'seen,' 'been,' 'agree,' etc. In the present instance we see it doubled no less than five times, although the cryptograph is brief,

"Let us assume 8 then, as *e*. Now, of all *words* in the language, 'the' is most usual; let us see, therefore, whether there are not repetitions of any three characters, in the same order of collocation, the last of them being 8. If we discover repetitions of such letters, so arranged, they will most probably represent the word 'the.' Upon inspection, we find no less than seven such arrangements, the characters being ;48. We may, therefore, assume that ; represents *t* 4 represents *h*, and 8 represents *e* the last being now well confirmed. Thus a great step has been taken.

"But, having established a single word, we are enabled to establish a vastly important point; that is to say, several commencements and terminations of other words. Let us refer, for example, to the last instance but one, in which the combination ;48 occurs—not far from the end of the cipher. We know that the; immediately ensuing is the commencement of a word, and, of the six characters succeeding this 'the,' we are cognisant of no less than five. Let us set these characters down, thus, by the letters we know them to represent, leaving a space for the unknown—

t eeth.

"Here we are enabled, at once, to discard the '*th*,' as forming no portion of the word commencing with the first *t*; since, by experiment of the entire alphabet for a letter adapted to the vacancy, we perceive that no word can be formed of which this *th* can be a part. We are thus narrowed into

t ee,

and, going through the alphabet, if necessary, as before, we arrive at the word 'tree,' as the sole possible reading. We thus gain another letter, *r*, represented by (, with the words 'the tree' in juxtaposition.

"Looking beyond these words, for a short distance, we again see the combination ;48, and employ it by way of *termination* to what immediately precedes. We have thus this arrangement:

the tree ;4(‡?34 the,

or, substituting the natural letters, where known, it reads thus:

the tree thr‡?3h the.

"Now, if, in place of the unknown characters, we leave blank spaces, or substitute dots, we read thus:

the tree thr .h the,

when the word '*through*' makes itself evident at once. But this discovery gives us three new letters, *o, u* and *g*, represented by ‡ ? and 3.

"Looking now, narrowly, through the cipher for combinations of known characters, we find, not very far from the beginning, this arrangement,

83(88, or egree,

which, plainly, is the conclusion of the word 'degree,' and gives us another letter, *d*, represented by †.

"Four letters beyond the word 'degree,' we perceive the combination

;48(;88.

"Translating the known characters, and representing the unknown by dots, as before, we read thus:

th rtee,

an arrangement immediately suggestive of the word 'thirteen,' and again furnishing us with two new characters *i* and *n*, represented by 6 and *.

"Referring, now, to the beginning of the cryptograph, we find the combination

53‡‡†.

"Translating, as before, we obtain

. good,

which assures us that the first letter is *A*, and that the first two words are 'A good.'

"It is now time that we arrange our key, as far as discovered, in a tabular form, to avoid confusion. It will stand thus:

5	represents	a
†	"	d
8	"	e
3	"	g
4	"	h
6	"	i
*	"	n
‡	"	o
(	"	r
;	"	t

"We have, therefore, no less than ten of the most important letters represented, and it will be unnecessary to proceed with the details of the solution. I have said enough to convince you that ciphers of this nature are readily soluble, and to give you some insight into the rationale of their development. But be assured that the specimen before us appertains to the very simplest species of cryptograph. It now only remains to give you the full translation of the characters upon the parchment, as unriddled. Here it is:

> A good glass in the bishop's hostel in the devil's seat forty-one degrees and thirteen minutes northeast and by north main branch seventh limb east side shoot from the left eye of the death's-head a bee line from the tree through the shot fifty feet out.

"But," said I, "the enigma seems still in as bad a condition as ever. How is it possible to extort a meaning from all this jargon about 'devil's seats,' 'death's-heads,' and 'bishop's hotels?'"

"I confess," replied Legrand, "that the matter still wears a serious aspect, when regarded with a casual glance. My first endeavour was to divide the sentence into the natural division intended by the cryptographist."

"You mean to punctuate it?"

"Something of that kind."

"But how was it possible to effect this?"

"I reflected that it had been a *point* with the writer to run his words together without division, so as to increase the difficulty of solution. Now, a not over-acute man, in pursuing such an object, would be nearly certain to overdo the matter. When, in the course of his composition, he arrived at a break in his subject which would naturally require a pause, or a point, he would be exceedingly apt to run his characters, at this place, more than usually close together. If you will observe the MS. in the present instance you will easily detect five such cases of unusual crowding. Acting upon this hint, I made the division thus:

> A good glass in the bishop's hostel in the devil's seat—forty-one degrees and thirteen minutes—northeast and by north—main branch seventh limb east side—shoot from the left eye of the death's-head—a bee line from the tree through the shot fifty feet out.

"Even this division," said I, "leaves me still in the dark."

"It left me also in the dark," replied Legrand, "for a few days; during which I made diligent inquiry, in the neighbourhood of Sullivan's Island, for any building which went by the name of the 'Bishop's Hotel;' for, of course, I dropped the obsolete word 'hostel.' Gaining no information on the subject, I was on the point of extending my sphere of search, and proceeding in a more systematic manner, when, one morning, it entered into my head, quite suddenly, that this 'Bishop's Hostel' might have some reference to an old family, of the name of Bessop, which, time out of mind, had held possession of an ancient manor-house, about four miles to the northward of the Island. I accordingly went over to the plantation, and re-instituted my inquiries among the older negroes of the place. At length one of the most aged of the women said that she had heard of such a place as *Bessop's Castle*, and thought that she could guide me to it, but that it was not a castle, nor a tavern, but a high rock.

"I offered to pay her well for her trouble, and, after some demur, she consented to accompany me to the spot. We found it without much difficulty, when, dismissing her, I proceeded to examine the place. The 'castle' consisted of an irregular assemblage of cliffs and rocks—one of the latter being quite remarkable for its height as well as for its insulated and artificial appearance. I clambered to its apex, and then felt much at a loss as to what should be next done.

"While I was busied in reflection, my eyes fell upon a narrow ledge in the eastern face of the rock, perhaps a yard below the summit upon which I stood. This ledge projected about eighteen inches, and was not more than a foot wide, while a niche in the cliff just above it gave it a rude resemblance to one of the hollow-backed chairs used by our ancestors. I made no doubt that here was the 'devil's seat' alluded to in the MS., and now I seemed to grasp the full secret of the riddle.

"The 'good glass,' I knew, could have reference to nothing but a telescope; for the word 'glass' is rarely employed in any other sense by seamen. Now here, I at once saw, was a telescope to be used, and a definite point of view, *admitting no variation*, from which to use it. Nor did I hesitate to believe that the phrases, 'forty-one degrees and thirteen minutes,' and 'northeast and by north,' were intended as directions for the levelling of the glass. Greatly excited by these discoveries, I hurried home, procured a telescope, and returned to the rock.

"I let myself down to the ledge, and found that it was impossible to retain a seat upon it except in one particular position. This fact confirmed my preconceived idea. I proceeded to use the glass. Of course, the 'forty-one degrees and thirteen minutes' could allude to nothing but elevation above the visible horizon, since the horizontal direction was clearly indicated by the words, 'northeast and by north.' This latter direction I at once established by means of a pocket-compass; then, pointing the glass as nearly at an angle of forty one degrees of elevation as I could do it by guess, I moved it cautiously up or down, until my attention was arrested by a circular rift or opening in the foliage of a large tree that overtopped its fellows in the distance. In the centre of this rift I perceived a white spot, but could not, at first, distinguish what it was. Adjusting the focus of the telescope, I again looked, and now made it out to be a human skull.

"Upon this discovery I was so sanguine as to consider the enigma solved; for the phrase 'main branch, seventh limb, east side,' could refer only to the position of the skull upon the tree, while 'shoot from the left eye of the death's head,' admitted also of but one interpretation, in regard to a search for buried treasure. I perceived that the design was to drop a bullet from the left eye of the skull, and that a bee-line, or, in other words, a straight line, drawn from the nearest point of the trunk through 'the shot' (or the spot where the bullet fell), and thence extended to a distance of fifty feet, would indicate a definite point—and beneath this point I thought it at least *possible* that a deposit of value lay concealed."

"All this," I said, "is exceedingly clear, and, although ingenious, still simple and explicit. When you left the Bishop's Hotel, what then?"

"Why, having carefully taken the bearings of the tree, I turned homewards. The instant that I left the ' devil's seat,' however, the circular rift vanished; nor could I get a glimpse of it afterwards, turn as I would. What seems to me the chief ingenuity in this whole business is the fact (for repeated experiment has convinced me it is a fact) that the circular opening in question is visible from no other attainable point of view than that afforded by the narrow ledge upon the face of the rock.

"In this expedition to the 'Bishop's Hotel' I had been attended by Jupiter, who had no doubt observed for some weeks past the abstraction of my demeanour, and took especial care not to leave me alone. But on the next day, getting up very early, I contrived to give him the slip, and went into the hills in search of the tree. After much toil I found it. When I came home at night my valet proposed to give me a flogging. With the rest of the adventure I believe you are as well acquainted as myself."

"I suppose," said I, "you missed the spot, in the first attempt at digging, through Jupiter's stupidity in letting the bug fall through the right instead of through the left eye of the skull."

"Precisely. This mistake made a difference of about two inches and a half in the 'shot'—that is to say, in the position of the peg nearest the tree; and had the treasure been *beneath* the 'shot,' the error would have been of little moment; but the 'shot,' together with the nearest point of the tree, were merely two points for the establishment of a line of direction; of course the error, how ever trivial in the beginning, increased as we proceeded with the line, and, by the time we had gone fifty feet, threw us quite off the scent. But for my deep-seated impressions that treasure was here somewhere actually buried, we might have had all our labour in vain."

"But your grandiloquence, and your conduct in swinging the beetle—how excessively odd! I was sure you were mad. And why did you insist upon letting fall the bug, instead of a bullet, from the skull?"

"Why, to be frank, I felt somewhat annoyed by your evident suspicions touching my sanity, and so resolved to punish you quietly, in my own way, by a little bit of sober mystification. For this reason I swung the beetle, and for this reason I let it fall from the tree. An observation of yours about its great weight suggested the latter idea."

"Yes, I perceive; and now there is only one point which puzzles me. What are we to make of the skeletons found in the hole?"

"That is a question I am no more able to answer than yourself. There seems, however, only one plausible way of accounting for them—and yet it is dreadful to believe in such atrocity as my suggestion would imply. It is clear that Kidd—if Kidd indeed secreted this treasure, which I doubt not—it is clear that he must have had assistance in the labour. But this labour concluded, he may have thought it expedient to remove all participants in his secret. Perhaps a couple of blows with a mattock were sufficient, while his coadjutors were busy in the pit: perhaps it required a dozen—who shall tell?"

The Imp of the Perverse

In the consideration of the faculties and impulses—of the *prima mobilia* of the human soul, the phrenologists have failed to make room for a propensity which, although obviously existing as a radical, primitive, irreducible sentiment, has been equally overlooked by all the moralists who have preceded them. In the pure arrogance of the reason, we have all overlooked it. We have suffered its existence to escape our senses, solely through want of belief—of faith;—whether it be faith in Revelation, or faith in the *Kabbala*. The idea of it has never occurred to us, simply because of its supererogation. We saw no need of the impulse—for the propensity. We could not perceive its necessity. We could not understand, that is to say, we could not have understood, had the notion of this *primum mobile* ever obtruded itself;—we could not have understood in what manner it might be made to further the objects of humanity, either temporal or eternal.

It cannot be denied that phrenology and, in great measure, all metaphysicianism have been concocted *à priori*. The intellectual or logical man, rather than the understanding or observant man, set himself to imagine designs—to dictate purposes to God. Having thus fathomed, to his satisfaction, the intentions of Jehovah, out of these intentions he built his innumerable systems of mind. In the matter of phrenology, for example, we first determined, naturally enough, that it was the design of the Deity that man should eat. We then assigned to man an organ of alimentiveness, and this organ is the scourge with which the Deity compels man, will-I nill-I, into eating.

Secondly, having settled it to be God's will that man should continue his species, we discovered an organ of amativeness, forthwith. And so with combativeness, with ideality, with causality, with constructiveness,—so, in short, with every organ, whether representing a propensity, a moral sentiment, or a faculty of the pure intellect. And in these arrangements of the *principia* of human action, the Spurzheimites, whether right or wrong, in part, or upon the whole, have but followed, in principle, the footsteps of their predecessors: deducing and establishing every thing from the preconceived destiny of man, and upon the ground of the objects of his Creator.

It would have been wiser, it would have been safer, to classify (if classify we must) upon the basis of what man usually or occasionally did, and was always occasionally doing, rather than upon the basis of what we took it for granted the Deity intended him to do. If we cannot comprehend God in his visible works, how then in his inconceivable thoughts, that call the works into being? If we cannot understand him in his objective creatures, how then in his substantive moods and phases of creation?

Induction, *à posteriori*, would have brought phrenology to admit, as an innate and primitive principle of human action, a paradoxical something, which we may call *perverseness*, for want of a more characteristic term. In the sense I intend, it is, in fact, a mobile without motive, a motive not *motivirt*. Through its promptings we act without comprehensible object; or, if this shall be understood as a contradiction in terms, we may so far modify the proposition as to say, that through its promptings we act, for the reason that we should *not*. In theory, no reason can be more unreasonable, but, in fact, there is none more strong. With certain minds, under certain conditions, it becomes absolutely irresistible.

I am not more certain that I breathe, than that the assurance of the wrong or error of any action is often the one unconquerable *force* which impels us, and alone impels us to its prosecution. Nor will this overwhelming tendency to do wrong for the wrong's sake, admit of analysis, or resolution into ulterior elements. It is a radical, a primitive impulse—elementary. It will be said, I am aware, that when we persist in acts because we feel we should *not* persist in them, our conduct is but a modification of that which ordinarily springs from the *combativeness* of phrenology. But a glance will show the fallacy of this idea. The phrenological combativeness has for its essence, the necessity of self-defence. It is our safeguard against injury. Its principle regards our well-being; and thus the desire to be well is excited simultaneously with its development. It follows, that the desire to be well must be excited simultaneously with any principle which shall be merely a modification of combativeness, but in the case of that something which I term *perverseness*, the desire to be well is not only not aroused, but a strongly antagonistical sentiment exists.

An appeal to one's own heart is, after all, the best reply to the sophistry just noticed. No one who trustingly consults and thoroughly questions his own soul, will be disposed to deny the entire radicalness of the propensity in question. It is not more incomprehensible than distinctive. There lives no man who at some period has not been tormented, for example, by an earnest desire to tantalize a listener by circumlocution. The speaker is aware that he displeases; he has every intention to please, he is usually curt, precise, and clear, the most laconic and luminous language is struggling for utterance upon his tongue, it is only with difficulty that he restrains himself from giving it flow; he dreads and deprecates the anger of him whom he addresses; yet, the thought strikes him, that by certain involutions and parentheses this anger may be engendered. That single thought is enough. The impulse increases to a wish, the wish to a desire, the desire to an uncontrollable longing, and the longing (to the deep regret and mortification of the speaker, and in defiance of all consequences) is indulged.

We have a task before us which must be speedily performed. We know that it will be ruinous to make delay. The most important crisis of our life calls, trumpet-tongued, for immediate energy and action. We glow, we are consumed with eagerness to commence the work, with the anticipation of whose glorious result our whole souls are on fire. It must, it shall be undertaken today, and yet we put it off until tomorrow, and why? There is no answer, except that we feel *perverse*, using the word with no comprehension of the principle. Tomorrow arrives, and with it a more impatient anxiety to do our duty, but with this very increase of anxiety arrives, also, a nameless, a positively fearful, because unfathomable, craving for delay.

This craving gathers strength as the moments fly. The last hour for action is at hand. We tremble with the violence of the conflict within us,—of the definite with the indefinite—of the substance with the shadow. But, if the contest have proceeded thus far, it is the shadow which prevails,—we struggle in vain. The clock strikes, and is the knell of our welfare. At the same time, it is the chanticleer—note to the ghost that has so long overawed us. It flies—it disappears—we are free. The old energy returns. We will labor *now*. Alas, it is *too late!*

We stand upon the brink of a precipice. We peer into the abyss—we grow sick and dizzy. Our first impulse is to shrink from the danger. Unaccountably we remain. By slow degrees our sickness and dizziness and horror become merged in a cloud of unnamable feeling. By gradations, still more imperceptible, this cloud assumes shape, as did the vapor from the bottle out of which arose the genius in the *Arabian Nights*. But out of this *our* cloud upon the precipice's edge, there grows into palpability, a shape, far more terrible than any genius or any demon of a tale, and yet it is but a thought, although a fearful one, and one which chills the very marrow of our bones with the fierceness of the delight of its horror. It is merely the idea of what would be our sensations during the sweeping precipitancy of a fall from such a height. And this fall—this rushing annihilation—for the very reason that it involves that one most ghastly and loathsome of all the most ghastly and loathsome images of death and suffering which have ever presented themselves to our imagination—for this very cause do we now the most vividly desire it.

And because our reason violently deters us from the brink,

therefore do we the most impetuously approach it. There is no passion in nature so demoniacally impatient, as that of him who, shuddering upon the edge of a precipice, thus meditates a plunge. To indulge, for a moment, in any attempt at *thought*, is to be inevitably lost; for reflection but urges us to forbear, and *therefore* it is, I say, that we *cannot*. If there be no friendly arm to check us, or if we fail in a sudden effort to prostrate ourselves backward from the abyss, we plunge, and are destroyed.

Examine these similar actions as we will, we shall find them resulting solely from the spirit of the *perverse*. We perpetrate them because we feel that we should *not*. Beyond or behind this there is no intelligible principle; and we might, indeed, deem this perverseness a direct instigation of the Arch-Fiend, were it not occasionally known to operate in furtherance of good.

I have said thus much, that in some measure I may answer your question, that I may explain to you why I am here, that I may assign to you something that shall have at least the faint aspect of a cause for my wearing these fetters, and for my tenanting this cell of the condemned. Had I not been thus prolix, you might either have misunderstood me altogether, or, with the rabble, have fancied me mad. As it is, you will easily perceive that I am one of the many uncounted victims of the Imp of the Perverse.

It is impossible that any deed could have been wrought with a more thorough deliberation. For weeks, for months, I pondered upon the means of the murder. I rejected a thousand schemes, because their accomplishment involved a *chance* of detection. At length, in reading some French memoirs, I found an account of a nearly fatal illness that occurred to Madame Pilau, through the agency of a candle accidentally poisoned. The idea struck my fancy at once. I knew my victim's habit of reading in bed. I knew, too, that his apartment was narrow and ill-ventilated. But I need not vex you with impertinent details. I need not describe the easy artifices by which I substituted, in his bedroom candlestand, a wax-light of my own making for the one which I there found. The next morning he was discovered dead in his bed, and the coroner's verdict was—"Death by the visitation of God."

Having inherited his estate, all went well with me for years. The idea of detection never once entered my brain. Of the remains of the fatal taper I had myself carefully disposed. I had left no shadow of a clew by which it would be possible to convict, or even to suspect me of the crime. It is inconceivable how rich a sentiment of satisfaction arose in my bosom as I reflected upon my absolute security. For a very long period of time I was accustomed to revel in this sentiment. It afforded me more real delight than all the mere worldly advantages accruing from my sin. But there arrived at length an epoch, from which the pleasurable feeling grew, by scarcely perceptible gradations, into a haunting and harassing thought. It harassed because it haunted. I could scarcely get rid of it for an instant. It is quite a common thing to be thus annoyed with the ringing in our ears, or rather in our memories, of the burthen of some ordinary song, or some unimpressive snatches from an opera. Nor will we be the less tormented if the song in itself be good, or the opera air meritorious. In this manner, at last, I would perpetually catch myself pondering upon my security, and repeating, in a low undertone, the phrase, "I am safe."

One day, whilst sauntering along the streets, I arrested myself in the act of murmuring, half aloud, these customary syllables. In a fit of petulance, I remodelled them thus; "I am safe—I am safe—yes—if I be not fool enough to make open confession!"

No sooner had I spoken these words, than I felt an icy chill creep to my heart. I had had some experience in these fits of perversity, (whose nature I have been at some trouble to explain), and I remembered well that in no instance I had successfully resisted their attacks. And now my own casual self-suggestion that I might possibly be fool enough to confess the murder of which I had been guilty, confronted me, as if the very ghost of him whom I had murdered—and beckoned me on to death.

At first, I made an effort to shake off this nightmare of the soul. I walked vigorously—faster—still faster—at length I ran. I felt a maddening desire to shriek aloud. Every succeeding wave of thought overwhelmed me with new terror, for, alas! I well, too well understood that to *think*, in my situation, was to be lost. I still quickened my pace. I bounded like a madman through the crowded thoroughfares. At length, the populace took the alarm, and pursued me. I felt *then* the consummation of my fate. Could I have torn out my tongue, I would have done it, but a rough voice resounded in my ears—a rougher grasp seized me by the shoulder. I turned—I gasped for breath. For a moment I experienced all the pangs of suffocation; I became blind, and deaf, and giddy; and then some invisible fiend, I thought, struck me with his broad palm upon the back. The long imprisoned secret burst forth from my soul.

They say that I spoke with a distinct enunciation, but with marked emphasis and passionate hurry, as if in dread of interruption before concluding the brief, but pregnant sentences that consigned me to the hangman and to hell.

Having related all that was necessary for the fullest judicial conviction, I fell prostrate in a swoon.

But why shall I say more? Today I wear these chains, and am *here!* Tomorrow I shall be fetterless!—*but where?*

The Island of the Fay

Nullus enim locus sine genio est.—*Servius.*

"*La musique*," says Marmontel, in those *Contes Moraux* [1] which in all our translations, we have insisted upon calling *Moral Tales*, as if in mockery of their spirit—"*la musique est le seul des talents qui jouissent de lui-même; tous les autres veulent des temoins.*" He here confounds the pleasure derivable from sweet sounds with the capacity for creating them. No more than any other talent, is that for music susceptible of complete enjoyment, where there is no second party to appreciate its exercise. And it is only in common with other *talents* that it produces *effects* which may be fully enjoyed in solitude. The idea which the *raconteur* has either failed to entertain clearly, or has sacrificed in its expression to his national love of *point*, is, doubtless, the very tenable one that the higher order of music is the most thoroughly estimated when we are exclusively alone. The proposition, in this form, will be admitted at once by those who love the lyre for its own sake, and for its spiritual uses.

But there is one pleasure still within the reach of fallen mortality and perhaps only one—which owes even more than does music to the accessory sentiment of seclusion. I mean the happiness experienced in the contemplation of natural scenery. In truth, the man who would behold aright the glory of God upon earth must in solitude behold that glory. To me, at least, the presence—not of human life only, but of life in any other

1. Moraux is here derived from *moeurs*, and its meaning is "*fashionable*," or, more strictly, "of manners."

form than that of the green things which grow upon the soil and are voiceless—is a stain upon the landscape—is at war with the genius of the scene.

I love, indeed, to regard the dark valleys, and the gray rocks, and the waters that silently smile, and the forests that sigh in uneasy slumbers, and the proud watchful mountains that look down upon all,—I love to regard these as themselves but the colossal members of one vast animate and sentient whole—a whole whose form (that of the sphere) is the most perfect and most inclusive of all; whose path is among associate planets; whose meek handmaiden is the moon, whose mediate sovereign is the sun; whose life is eternity, whose thought is that of a God; whose enjoyment is knowledge; whose destinies are lost in immensity, whose cognizance of ourselves is akin with our own cognisance of the *animalculae* which infest the brain—a being which we, in consequence, regard as purely inanimate and material much in the same manner as these *animalculae* must thus regard us.

Our telescopes and our mathematical investigations assure us on every hand—notwithstanding the cant of the more ignorant of the priesthood—that space, and therefore that bulk, is an important consideration in the eyes of the Almighty. The cycles in which the stars move are those best adapted for the evolution, without collision, of the greatest possible number of bodies. The forms of those bodies are accurately such as, within a given surface, to include the greatest possible amount of matter;—while the surfaces themselves are so disposed as to accommodate a denser population than could be accommodated on the same surfaces otherwise arranged. Nor is it any argument against bulk being an object with God, that space itself is infinite; for there may be an infinity of matter to fill it.

And since we see clearly that the endowment of matter with vitality is a principle—indeed, as far as our judgments extend, the *leading* principle in the operations of Deity,—it is scarcely logical to imagine it confined to the regions of the minute, where we daily trace it, and not extending to those of the august. As we find cycle within cycle without end,—yet all revolving around one far-distant centre which is the God-head, may we not analogically suppose in the same manner, life within life, the less within the greater, and all within the Spirit Divine? In short, we are madly erring, through self-esteem, in believing man, in either his temporal or future destinies, to be of more moment in the universe than that vast "clod of the valley" which he tills and contemns, and to which he denies a soul for no more profound reason than that he does not behold it in operation. [2]

These fancies, and such as these, have always given to my meditations among the mountains and the forests, by the rivers and the ocean, a tinge of what the everyday world would not fail to term fantastic. My wanderings amid such scenes have been many, and far-searching, and often solitary; and the interest with which I have strayed through many a dim, deep valley, or gazed into the reflected Heaven of many a bright lake, has been an interest greatly deepened by the thought that I have strayed and gazed alone. What flippant Frenchman[3] was it who said in allusion to the well-known work of Zimmerman, that, "*la solitude est une belle chose; mais il faut quelqu'un pour vous dire que la solitude est une belle chose?*" The epigram cannot be gainsayed; but the necessity is a thing that does not exist.

It was during one of my lonely journeyings, amid a far distant region of mountain locked within mountain, and sad rivers and melancholy tarn writhing or sleeping within all—that I chanced upon a certain rivulet and island. I came upon them suddenly in the leafy June, and threw myself upon the turf, beneath the branches of an unknown odorous shrub, that I might doze as I contemplated the scene. I felt that thus only should I look upon it—such was the character of phantasm which it wore.

On all sides—save to the west, where the sun was about sinking—arose the verdant walls of the forest. The little river which turned sharply in its course, and was thus immediately lost to sight, seemed to have no exit from its prison, but to be absorbed

2. Speaking of the tides, Pomponius Mela, in his treatise *De Situ Orbis*, says "either the world is a great animal, or" etc.

3. Balzac—in substance—I do not remember the words.

by the deep green foliage of the trees to the east—while in the opposite quarter (so it appeared to me as I lay at length and glanced upward) there poured down noiselessly and continuously into the valley, a rich golden and crimson waterfall from the sunset fountains of the sky.

About midway in the short vista which my dreamy vision took in, one small circular island, profusely verdured, reposed upon the bosom of the stream.

So blended bank and shadow there
That each seemed pendulous in air—

So mirror-like was the glassy water, that it was scarcely possible to say at what point upon the slope of the emerald turf its crystal dominion began.

My position enabled me to include in a single view both the eastern and western extremities of the islet; and I observed a singularly-marked difference in their aspects. The latter was all one radiant *harem* of garden beauties. It glowed and blushed beneath the eyes of the slant sunlight, and fairly laughed with flowers. The grass was short, springy, sweet-scented, and Asphodel-interspersed. The trees were lithe, mirthful, erect—bright, slender, and graceful,—of eastern figure and foliage, with bark smooth, glossy, and parti-coloured. There seemed a deep sense of life and joy about all; and although no airs blew from out the heavens, yet every thing had motion through the gentle sweepings to and fro of innumerable butterflies, that might have been mistaken for tulips with wings. [4]

The other or eastern end of the isle was whelmed in the blackest shade. A sombre, yet beautiful and peaceful gloom here pervaded all things. The trees were dark in colour, and mournful in form and attitude, wreathing themselves into sad, solemn, and spectral shapes that conveyed ideas of mortal sorrow and untimely death. The grass wore the deep tint of the cypress, and the heads of its blades hung droopingly, and hither and thither among it were many small unsightly hillocks, low and narrow,

4. *Florem putares nare per liquidum aethera.—P. Commire.*

and not very long, that had the aspect of graves, but were not; although over and all about them the rue and the rosemary clambered. The shade of the trees fell heavily upon the water, and seemed to bury itself therein, impregnating the depths of the element with darkness. I fancied that each shadow, as the sun descended lower and lower, separated itself sullenly from the trunk that gave it birth, and thus became absorbed by the stream; while other shadows issued momently from the trees, taking the place of their predecessors thus entombed.

This idea, having once seized upon my fancy, greatly excited it, and I lost myself forthwith in revery. "If ever island were enchanted," said I to myself, "this is it. This is the haunt of the few gentle Fays who remain from the wreck of the race. Are these green tombs theirs?—or do they yield up their sweet lives as mankind yield up their own? In dying, do they not rather waste away mournfully, rendering unto God, little by little, their existence, as these trees render up shadow after shadow, exhausting their substance unto dissolution? What the wasting tree is to the water that imbibes its shade, growing thus blacker by what it preys upon, may not the life of the Fay be to the death which engulfs it?"

As I thus mused, with half-shut eyes, while the sun sank rapidly to rest, and eddying currents careered round and round the island, bearing upon their bosom large, dazzling, white flakes of the bark of the sycamore-flakes which, in their multiform positions upon the water, a quick imagination might have converted into any thing it pleased, while I thus mused, it appeared to me that the form of one of those very Fays about whom I had been pondering made its way slowly into the darkness from out the light at the western end of the island. She stood erect in a singularly fragile canoe, and urged it with the mere phantom of an oar. While within the influence of the lingering sunbeams, her attitude seemed indicative of joy—but sorrow deformed it as she passed within the shade.

Slowly she glided along, and at length rounded the islet and re-entered the region of light. "The revolution which has just been made by the Fay," continued I, musingly, "is the cycle of the brief year of her life. She has floated through her winter and through her summer. She is a year nearer unto Death; for I did not fail to see that, as she came into the shade, her shadow fell from her, and was swallowed up in the dark water, making its blackness more black."

And again the boat appeared and the Fay, but about the attitude of the latter there was more of care and uncertainty and less of elastic joy. She floated again from out the light and into the gloom (which deepened momently) and again her shadow fell from her into the ebony water, and became absorbed into its blackness. And again and again she made the circuit of the island, (while the sun rushed down to his slumbers), and at each issuing into the light there was more sorrow about her person, while it grew feebler and far fainter and more indistinct, and at each passage into the gloom there fell from her a darker shade, which became whelmed in a shadow more black. But at length when the sun had utterly departed, the Fay, now the mere ghost of her former self, went disconsolately with her boat into the region of the ebony flood—and that she issued thence at all I cannot say, for darkness fell over all things and I beheld her magical figure no more.

The Man That Was Used Up

A Tale of the Late Bugaboo and Kickapoo Campaign

Pleurez, pleurez, mes yeux, et fondez vous en eau!
La moitié; de ma vie a mis l'autre au tombeau.

—Corneille.

I cannot just now remember when or where I first made the acquaintance of that truly fine-looking fellow, Brevet Brigadier General John A. B. C. Smith. Some one *did* introduce me to the gentleman, I am sure—at some public meeting, I know very well—held about something of great importance, no doubt—at some place or other, I feel convinced,—whose name I have unaccountably forgotten. The truth is—that the introduction was attended, upon my part, with a degree of anxious embarrassment which operated to prevent any definite impressions of either time or place. I am constitutionally nervous—this, with me, is a family failing, and I can't help it. In especial, the slightest appearance of mystery—of any point I cannot exactly comprehend—puts me at once into a pitiable state of agitation.

There was something, as it were, remarkable—yes, *remarkable*, although this is but a feeble term to express my full meaning—about the entire individuality of the personage in question. He was, perhaps, six feet in height, and of a presence singularly commanding. There was an *air distingué* pervading the whole man, which spoke of high breeding, and hinted at high birth. Upon this topic—the topic of Smith's personal appearance—I have a kind of melancholy satisfaction in being minute. His head of hair would have done honour to a Brutus;—nothing could be more richly flowing, or possess a brighter gloss. It was of a jetty black;—which was also the colour, or more properly the no colour of his unimaginable whiskers.

You perceive I cannot speak of these latter without enthusiasm; it is not too much to say that they were the handsomest pair of whiskers under the sun. At all events, they encircled, and at times partially overshadowed, a mouth utterly unequalled. Here were the most entirely even, and the most brilliantly white of all conceivable teeth. From between them, upon every proper occasion, issued a voice of surpassing clearness, melody, and strength. In the matter of eyes, also, my acquaintance was pre-eminently endowed. Either one of such a pair was worth a couple of the ordinary ocular organs. They were of a deep hazel, exceedingly large and lustrous; and there was perceptible about them, ever and anon, just that amount of interesting obliquity which gives pregnancy to expression.

The bust of the general was unquestionably the finest bust I ever saw. For your life you could not have found a fault with its wonderful proportion. This rare peculiarity set off to great advantage a pair of shoulders which would have called up a blush of conscious inferiority into the countenance of the marble Apollo. I have a passion for fine shoulders, and may say that I never beheld them in perfection before. The arms altogether were admirably modelled. Nor were the lower limbs less superb. These were, indeed, the *ne plus ultra* of good legs.

Every connoisseur in such matters admitted the legs to be good. There was neither too much flesh, nor too little,—neither rudeness nor fragility. I could not imagine a more graceful curve than that of the *os femoris*, and there was just that due gentle prominence in the rear of the *fibula* which goes to the conformation of a properly proportioned calf. I wish to God my young and talented friend Chiponchipino, the sculptor, had but seen the legs of Brevet Brigadier General John A. B. C. Smith.

But although men so absolutely fine-looking are neither as plenty as reasons or blackberries, still I could not bring myself to believe that *the remarkable* something to which I alluded just now,—that the odd air of *je ne sais quoi* which hung about my new acquaintance,—lay altogether, or indeed at all, in the supreme excellence of his bodily endowments. Perhaps it might be traced to the *manner*;—yet here again I could not pretend to be positive. There *was* a primness, not to say stiffness, in his carriage—a degree of measured, and, if I may so express it, of rectangular precision, attending his every movement, which, observed in a more diminutive figure, would have had the least little savour in the world, of affectation, pomposity or constraint, but which noticed in a gentleman of his undoubted dimensions, was readily placed to the account of reserve, *hauteur*—of a commendable sense, in short, of what is due to the dignity of colossal proportion.

The kind friend who presented me to General Smith whispered in my ear some few words of comment upon the man. He was a *remarkable* man—a *very* remarkable man—indeed one of the *most* remarkable men of the age. He was an especial favourite, too, with the ladies—chiefly on account of his high reputation for courage.

"In *that* point he is unrivalled—indeed he is a perfect *desperado*—a down-right fire-eater, and no mistake," said my friend, here dropping his voice excessively low, and thrilling me with the mystery of his tone.

"A downright fire-eater, and *no* mistake. Showed *that*, I should say, to some purpose, in the late tremendous swamp-fight away down South, with the Bugaboo and Kickapoo Indians." (Here my friend opened his eyes to some extent.) "Bless my soul!—blood and thunder, and all that!—*prodigies* of valour!—heard of him of course?—you know he's the man—"

"Man alive, how *do* you do? why, how *are* ye? *very* glad to see ye, indeed!" here interrupted the general himself, seizing my companion by the hand as he drew near, and bowing stiffly, but profoundly, as I was presented. I then thought, (and I think so still,) that I never heard a clearer nor a stronger voice, nor beheld a finer set of teeth: but I *must* say that I was sorry for the interruption just at that moment, as, owing to the whispers and insinuations aforesaid, my interest had been greatly excited in the hero of the Bugaboo and Kickapoo campaign.

However, the delightfully luminous conversation of Brevet Brigadier General John A. B. C. Smith soon completely dissipated this chagrin. My friend leaving us immediately, we had quite a long *tête-à-tête*, and I was not only pleased but *really*—instructed. I never heard a more fluent talker, or a man of greater general information. With becoming modesty, he forbore, nevertheless, to touch upon the theme I had just then most at heart—I mean the mysterious circumstances attending the Bugaboo war—and, on my own part, what I conceive to be a proper sense of delicacy forbade me to broach the subject; although, in truth, I was exceedingly tempted to do so. I perceived, too, that the gallant soldier preferred topics of philosophical interest, and that he delighted, especially, in commenting upon the rapid march of mechanical invention. Indeed, lead him where I would, this was a point to which he invariably came back.

"There is nothing at all like it," he would say; "we are a wonderful people, and live in a wonderful age. Parachutes and railroads—man-traps and spring-guns! Our steam-boats are upon every sea, and the Nassau balloon packet is about to run regular trips (fare either way only twenty pounds sterling) between London and Timbuctoo. And who shall calculate the immense influence upon social life—upon arts—upon commerce—upon literature—which will be the immediate result of the great principles of electro magnetics! Nor, is this all, let me assure you! There is really no end to the march of invention. The most wonderful—the most ingenious—and let me add, Mr.—Mr.—Thompson, I believe, is your name—let me add, I say, the most *useful*—the most truly *useful* mechanical contrivances, are daily springing up like mushrooms, if I may so express myself, or, more figuratively, like—ah—grasshoppers—like grasshoppers, Mr. Thompson—about us and ah—ah—ah—around us!"

Thompson, to be sure, is not my name; but it is needless to say that I left General Smith with a heightened interest in the man, with an exalted opinion of his conversational powers, and a deep sense of the valuable privileges we enjoy in living in this age of mechanical invention. My curiosity, however, had not been altogether satisfied, and I resolved to prosecute immediate inquiry among my acquaintances touching the Brevet Brigadier General himself, and particularly respecting the tremendous events *quorum pars magna fuit*, during the Bugaboo and Kickapoo campaign.

The first opportunity which presented itself, and which (*horresco referens*) I did not in the least scruple to seize, occurred at the Church of the Reverend Doctor Drummummupp, where I found myself established, one Sunday, just at sermon time, not only in the pew, but by the side, of that worthy and communicative little friend of mine, Miss Tabitha T. Thus seated, I congratulated myself, and with much reason, upon the very flattering state of affairs. If any person knew anything about Brevet Brigadier General John A. B. C. Smith, that person, it was clear to me, was Miss Tabitha T. We telegraphed a few signals, and then commenced, *sotto voce*, a brisk *tête-à-tête*.

"Smith!" said she, in reply to my very earnest inquiry; "Smith!—why, not General John A. B. C.? Bless me, I thought you *knew* all about *him!* This is a wonderfully inventive age! Horrid affair that!—a bloody set of wretches, those Kickapoos!—fought like a hero—prodigies of valour—immortal renown. Smith!—Brevet Brigadier General John A. B. C.! why, you know he's the man—"

"Man," here broke in Doctor Drummummupp, at the top of his voice, and with a thump that came near knocking the pulpit about our ears—"*man that is born of a woman hath but a short time to live; he cometh up and is cut down like a flower!*" I started to the extremity of the pew, and perceived by the animated looks of the divine, that the wrath which had nearly proved fatal to the pulpit had been excited by the whispers of the lady and myself. There was no help for it; so I submitted with a good grace, and listened, in all the martyrdom of dignified silence, to the balance of that very capital discourse.

Next evening found me a somewhat late visitor at the

Rantipole theatre, where I felt sure of satisfying my curiosity at once, by merely stepping into the box of those exquisite specimens of affability and omniscience, the Misses Arabella and Miranda Cognoscenti. That fine tragedian, Climax, was doing Iago to a very crowded house, and I experienced some little difficulty in making my wishes understood; especially, as our box was next the slips, and completely overlooked the stage.

"Smith?" said Miss Arabella, as she at length comprehended the purport of my query; "Smith?—why, not General John A. B. C.?"

"Smith?" inquired Miranda, musingly. "God bless me, did you ever behold a finer figure?"

"Never, madam, but *do* tell me—"

"Or so inimitable grace?"

"Never, upon my word!—But pray inform me—"

"Or so just an appreciation of stage effect?"

"Madam!"

"Or a more delicate sense of the true beauties of Shakespeare? Be so good as to look at that leg!"

"The devil!" and I turned again to her sister.

"Smith?" said she, "why, not General John A. B. C.? Horrid affair that, wasn't it?—great wretches, those Bugaboos—savage and so on—but we live in a wonderfully inventive age!—Smith!—O yes! great man!—perfect *desperado*—immortal renown—prodigies of valour! *Never heard!*" (This was given in a scream.) "Bless my soul! why, he's the man—"

> ——*mandragora*
> *Nor all the drowsy syrups of the world*
> *Shall ever medicine thee to that sweet sleep*
> *Which thou owd'st yesterday!*

Here roared our Climax just in my ear, and shaking his fist in my face all the time, in a way that I *couldn't* stand, and I *wouldn't*. I left the Misses Cognoscenti immediately, went behind the scenes forthwith, and gave the beggarly scoundrel such a thrashing as I trust he will remember to the day of his death.

At the *soirée* of the lovely widow, Mrs. Kathleen O'Trump, I was confident that I should meet with no similar disappointment. Accordingly, I was no sooner seated at the card-table, with my pretty hostess for a *vis-à-vis*, than I propounded those questions the solution of which had become a matter so essential to my peace.

"Smith?" said my partner, "why, not General John A. B. C.? Horrid affair that, wasn't it?—diamonds, did you say?—terrible wretches those Kickapoos!—we are playing *whist*, if you please, Mr. Tattle—however, this is the age of invention, most certainly *the* age, one may say—*the* age *par excellence*—speak French?—oh, quite a hero—perfect *desperado*!—*no hearts*, Mr. Tattle? I don't believe it!—immortal renown and all that!—prodigies of valour! *Never heard!!*—why, bless me, he's the man—"

"Mann?—*Captain* Mann?" here screamed some little feminine interloper from the farthest corner of the room. "Are you talking about Captain Mann and the duel?—oh, I *must* hear—do tell—go on, Mrs. O'Trump!—do now go on!" And go on Mrs. O'Trump did—all about a certain Captain Mann, who was either shot or hung, or should have been both shot and hung. Yes! Mrs. O'Trump, she went on, and I—I went off. There was no chance of hearing anything farther that evening in regard to Brevet Brigadier General John A. B. C. Smith.

Still I consoled myself with the reflection that the tide of ill luck would not run against me forever, and so determined to make a bold push for information at the rout of that bewitching little angel, the graceful Mrs. Pirouette.

"Smith?" said Mrs. P., as we twirled about together in a *pas de zephyr*, "Smith?—why, not General John A. B. C.? Dreadful business that of the Bugaboos, wasn't it?—dreadful creatures, those Indians!—*do* turn out your toes! I really am ashamed of you—man of great courage, poor fellow!—but this is a wonderful age for invention—O dear me, I'm out of breath—quite a *desperado*—prodigies of valour—*never heard!!*—can't believe it—I shall have to sit down and enlighten you—Smith! why, he's the man—"

"Man-*Fred*, I tell you!" here bawled out Miss Bas-Bleu, as I led Mrs. Pirouette to a seat. "Did ever anybody hear the like? It's Man-*Fred*, I say, and not at all by any means Man-*Friday*." Here Miss Bas-Bleu beckoned to me in a very peremptory manner; and I was obliged, will I nill I, to leave Mrs. P. for the purpose of deciding a dispute touching the title of a certain poetical drama of Lord Byron's. Although I pronounced, with great promptness, that the true title was Man-*Friday*, and not by any means Man-*Fred*, yet when I returned to seek Mrs. Pirouette she was not to be discovered, and I made my retreat from the house in a very bitter spirit of animosity against the whole race of the Bas-Bleus.

Matters had now assumed a really serious aspect, and I resolved to call at once upon my particular friend, Mr. Theodore Sinivate; for I knew that here at least I should get something like definite information.

"Smith?" said he, in his well-known peculiar way of drawling out his syllables; "Smith?—why, not General John A. B. C.? Savage affair that with the Kickapo-o-o-os, wasn't it? Say! don't you think so?—perfect *despera-a-ado*—great pity, 'pon my honour!—wonderfully inventive age!—pro-o-odigies of valour! By the by, did you ever hear about Captain Ma-a-a-a-n?"

"Captain Mann be d—d!" said I; "please to go on with your story."

"Hem!—oh well!—quite *la même cho-o-ose*, as we say in France. Smith, eh? Brigadier-General John A. B. C.? I say"—(here Mr. S. thought proper to put his finger to the side of his nose)—"I say, you don't mean to insinuate now, really and truly, and conscientiously, that you don't know all about that affair of Smith's, as well as I do, eh? Smith? John A-B-C.? Why, bless me, he's the ma-a-an—"

"*Mr.* Sinivate," said I, imploringly, "*is* he the man in the mask?"

"No-o-o!" said he, looking wise, "nor the man in the mo-o-on."

This reply I considered a pointed and positive insult, and

so left the house at once in high dudgeon, with a firm resolve to call my friend, Mr. Sinivate, to a speedy account for his ungentlemanly conduct and ill-breeding.

In the meantime, however, I had no notion of being thwarted touching the information I desired. There was one resource left me yet. I would go to the fountain-head. I would call forthwith upon the general himself, and demand, in explicit terms, a solution of this abominable piece of mystery. Here, at least, there should be no chance for equivocation. I would be plain, positive, peremptory—as short as pie-crust—as concise as Tacitus or Montesquieu.

It was early when I called, and the general was dressing; but I pleaded urgent business, and was shown at once into his bedroom by an old negro valet, who remained in attendance during my visit. As I entered the chamber, I looked about, of course, for the occupant, but did not immediately perceive him. There was a large and exceedingly odd-looking bundle of something which lay close by my feet on the floor, and, as I was not in the best humour in the world, I gave it a kick out of the way.

"Hem! ahem! rather civil that, I should say!" said the bundle, in one of the smallest, and altogether the funniest little voices, between a squeak and a whistle, that I ever heard in all the days of my existence.

"Ahem! rather civil that, I should observe."

I fairly shouted with terror, and made off, at a tangent, into the farthest extremity of the room.

"God bless me! my dear fellow," here again whistled the bundle, "what—what—what—why, what *is* the matter? I really believe you don't know me at all."

What *could* I say to all this—what *could* I? I staggered into an armchair, and, with staring eyes and open mouth, awaited the solution of the wonder.

"Strange you shouldn't know me though, isn't it?" presently re-squeaked the nondescript, which I now perceived was performing, upon the floor, some inexplicable evolution, very analogous to the drawing on of a stocking. There was only a single leg, however, apparent.

"Strange you shouldn't know me, though, isn't it? Pompey, bring me that leg!" Here Pompey handed the bundle, a very capital cork leg, already dressed, which it screwed on in a trice; and then it stood up before my eyes.

"And a bloody action it *was*," continued the thing, as if in a soliloquy; "but then one mustn't fight with the Bugaboos and Kickapoos, and think of coming off with a mere scratch. Pompey, I'll thank you now for that arm. Thomas" (turning to me) "is decidedly the best hand at a cork leg; but if you should ever want an arm, my dear fellow, you must really let me recommend you to Bishop." Here Pompey screwed on an arm.

"We had rather hot work of it, that you may say. Now, you dog, slip on my shoulders and bosom! Pettitt makes the best shoulders, but for a bosom you will have to go to Ducrow."

"Bosom!" said I.

"Pompey, will you *never* be ready with that wig? Scalping is a rough process after all; but then you can procure such a capital scratch at De L'Orme's."

"Scratch!"

"Now, you nigger, my teeth! For a *good* set of these you had better go to Parmly's at once; high prices, but excellent work. I swallowed some very capital articles, though, when the big Bugaboo rammed me down with the butt end of his rifle."

"Butt end! ram down!! my eye!!"

"O yes, by-the-by, my eye—here, Pompey, you scamp, screw it in ! Those Kickapoos are not so very slow at a gouge; but he's a belied man, that Dr. Williams, after all; you can't imagine how well I see with the eyes of his make."

I now began very clearly to perceive that the object before me was nothing more nor less than my new acquaintance, Brevet Brigadier General John A. B. C. Smith. The manipulations of Pompey had made, I must confess, a very striking difference in the appearance of the personal man. The voice, however, still puzzled me no little; but even this apparent mystery was speedily cleared up.

"Pompey, you black rascal," squeaked the general, "I really do believe you would let me go out without my palate."

Hereupon, the negro, grumbling out an apology, went up to his master, opened his mouth with the knowing air of a horse-jockey, and adjusted therein a somewhat singular-looking machine, in a very dexterous manner, that I could not altogether comprehend. The alteration, however, in the entire expression of the general's countenance was instantaneous and surprising. When he again spoke, his voice had resumed all that rich melody and strength which I had noticed upon our original introduction.

"D—n the vagabonds!" said he, in so clear a tone that I positively started at the change, "D—n the vagabonds! they not only knocked in the roof of my mouth, but took the trouble to cut off at least seven-eighths of my tongue. There isn't Bonfanti's equal, however, in America, for really good articles of this description. I can recommend you to him with confidence," (here the general bowed,) "and assure you that I have the greatest pleasure in so doing."

I acknowledged his kindness in my best manner, and took leave of him at once, with a perfect understanding of the true state of affairs—with a full comprehension of the mystery which had troubled me so long. It was evident. It was a clear case. Brevet Brigadier General John A. B. C. Smith was the man—was *the man that was used up.*

The Murders in the Rue Morgue

What song the Syrens sang, or what name Achilles assumed when he hid himself among women, although puzzling questions, are not beyond all conjecture. Sir Thomas Browne.

The mental features discoursed of as the analytical are, in themselves, but little susceptible of analysis. We appreciate them only in their effects. We know of them, among other things, that they are always to their possessor, when inordinately possessed, a source of the liveliest enjoyment. As the strong man exults in his physical ability, delighting in such exercises as call his muscles into action, so glories the analyst in that moral activity which *disentangles*. He derives pleasure from even the most trivial occupations bringing his talent into play. He is fond of enigmas, of conundrums, of hieroglyphics; exhibiting in his solutions of each a degree of *acumen* which appears to the ordinary apprehension preternatural. His results, brought about by the very soul and essence of method, have, in truth, the whole air of intuition.

The faculty of resolution is possibly much invigorated by mathematical study, and especially by that highest branch of it which, unjustly, and merely on account of its retrograde operations, has been called, as if *par excellence*, analysis. Yet to calculate is not in itself to analyse. A chess-player, for example, does the one without effort at the other. It follows that the game of chess, in its effects upon mental character, is greatly misunderstood. I am not now writing a treatise, but simply prefacing a somewhat peculiar narrative by observations very much at random; I will therefore take occasion to assert that the higher powers of the reflective intellect are more decidedly and more usefully tasked by the unostentatious game of draughts than by all the elaborate frivolity of chess.

In this latter, where the pieces have different and *bizarre* motions, with various and variable values, what is only complex is mistaken (a not unusual error) for what is profound. The *attention* is here called powerfully into play. If it flag for an instant, an oversight is committed, resulting in injury or defeat. The possible moves being not only manifold but involute, the chances of such oversights are multiplied; and in nine cases out of ten it is the more concentrative rather than the more acute player who conquers. In draughts, on the contrary, where the moves are *unique* and have but little variation, the probabilities of inadvertence are diminished, and the mere attention being left comparatively unemployed, what advantages are obtained by either party are obtained by superior *acumen*.

To be less abstract—let us suppose a game of draughts where the pieces are reduced to four kings, and where, of course, no oversight is to be expected. It is obvious that here the victory can be decided (the players being at all equal) only by some *recherché* movement, the result of some strong exertion of the intellect. Deprived of ordinary resources, the analyst throws himself into the spirit of his opponent, identifies himself therewith, and not unfrequently sees thus, at a glance, the sole methods (sometimes indeed absurdly simple ones) by which he may seduce into error or hurry into miscalculation.

Whist has long been noted for its influence upon what is termed the calculating power; and men of the highest order of intellect have been known to take an apparently unaccountable delight in it, while eschewing chess as frivolous. Beyond doubt there is nothing of a similar nature so greatly tasking the faculty of analysis. The best chess-player in Christendom *may* be little more than the best player of chess; but proficiency in whist implies capacity for success in all those more important undertakings where mind struggles with mind. When I say proficiency, I mean that perfection in the game which includes a comprehension of *all* the sources whence legitimate advantage may be derived. These are not only manifold but multiform, and lie frequently among recessed of thought altogether inaccessible to the ordinary understanding.

To observe attentively is to remember distinctly; and, so far, the concentrative chess-player will do very well at whist; while the rules of Hoyle (themselves based upon the mere mechanism of the game) are sufficiently and generally comprehensible. Thus to have a retentive memory, and to proceed by "the book," are points commonly regarded as the sum total of good playing. But it is in matters beyond the limits of mere rule that the skill of the analyst is evinced. He makes, in silence, a host of observations and inferences. So, perhaps, do his companions; and the difference in the extent of the information obtained lies not so much in the validity of the inference as in the quality of the observation.

The necessary knowledge is that of *what* to observe. Our player confines himself not at all; nor, because the game is the object, does he reject deductions from things external to the game. He examines the countenance of his partner, comparing it carefully with that of each of his opponents. He considers the mode of assorting the cards in each hand; often counting trump by trump, and honour by honour, through the glances bestowed by their holders upon each. He notes every variation of face as the play progresses, gathering a fund of thought from the differences in the expression of certainty, of surprise, of triumph, or of chagrin. From the manner of gathering up a trick he judges whether the person taking it can make another in the suit. He recognises what is played through feint, by the air with which it is thrown upon the table.

A casual or inadvertent word; the accidental dropping or turning of a card, with the accompanying anxiety or carelessness in regard to its concealment; the counting of the tricks, with the order of their arrangement; embarrassment, hesitation, eagerness or trepidation—all afford, to his apparently intuitive perception, indications of the true state of affairs. The first two or three rounds having been played, he is in full possession of the contents of each hand, and thenceforward puts down his cards with as absolute a precision of purpose as if the rest of the party had turned outward the faces of their own.

The analytical power should not be confounded with simple ingenuity; for while the analyst is necessarily ingenious, the ingenious man is often remarkably incapable of analysis. The constructive or combining power, by which ingenuity is usually manifested, and to which the phrenologists (I believe erroneously) have assigned a separate organ, supposing it a primitive faculty, has been so frequently seen in those whose intellect bordered otherwise upon idiocy, as to have attracted general observation among writers on morals. Between ingenuity and the analytic ability there exists a difference far greater indeed, than that between the fancy and the imagination, but of a character very strictly analogous. It will be found, in fact, that the ingenious are always fanciful, and the *truly* imaginative never otherwise than analytic.

The narrative which follows will appear to the reader somewhat in the light of a commentary upon the propositions just advanced.

Residing in Paris during the spring and part of the summer of 18—, I there became acquainted with a Monsieur G. Auguste Dupin. This young gentleman was of an excellent indeed of an illustrious family, but, by a variety of untoward events, had been reduced to such poverty that the energy of his character succumbed beneath it, and he ceased to bestir himself in the world, or to care for the retrieval of his fortunes. By courtesy of his creditors, there still remained in his possession a small remnant of his patrimony; and upon the income arising from this, he managed by means of a rigorous economy to procure the necessaries of life, without troubling himself about its superfluities. Books, indeed, were his sole luxuries, and in Paris these are easily obtained.

Our first meeting was at an obscure library in the Rue Montmartre, where the accident of our both being in search of the same very rare and very remarkable volume brought us into closer communion. We saw each other again and again. I was deeply interested in the little family history which he detailed to me with all that candour which a Frenchman indulges whenever mere self is his theme. I was astonished, too, at the vast extent of his reading; and, above all, I felt my soul enkindled within me by the wild fervour, and the vivid freshness of his imagination. Seeking in Paris the objects I then sought, I felt that the society of such a man would be to me a treasure beyond price; and this feeling I frankly confided to him.

It was at length arranged that we should live together during my stay in the city; and as my worldly circumstances were somewhat less embarrassed than his own, I was permitted to be at the expense of renting and furnishing, in a style which suited the rather fantastic gloom of our common temper, a time-eaten and grotesque mansion, long deserted through superstitions into which we did not inquire, and tottering to its fall in a retired and desolate portion of the Faubourg St. Germain.

Had the routine of our life at this place been known to the world, we should have been regarded as madmen—although, perhaps, as madmen of a harmless nature. Our seclusion was perfect. We admitted no visitors. Indeed the locality of our retirement had been carefully kept a secret from my own former associates; and it had been many years since Dupin had ceased to know or be known in Paris. We existed within ourselves alone.

It was a freak of fancy in my friend (for what else shall I call it?) to be enamoured of the Night for her own sake; and into this *bizarrerie*, as into all his others, I quietly fell; giving myself up to his wild whims with a perfect *abandon*. The sable divinity would not herself dwell with us always; but we could counterfeit her presence. At the first dawn of the morning we closed all the massive shutters of our old building; lighting a couple of tapers which, strongly perfumed, threw out only the ghastliest and feeblest of rays. By the aid of these We then busied our souls in dreams—reading, writing, or conversing, until warned by the clock of the advent of the true Darkness. Then we sallied forth into the streets, arm in arm, continuing the topics of the day, or roaming far and wide until a late hour, seeking amid the wild lights and shadows of the populous city that infinity of mental excitement which quiet observation can afford.

At such times I could not help remarking and admiring (although from his rich ideality I had been prepared to expect it) a peculiar analytic ability in Dupin. He seemed, too, to take an eager delight in its exercise—if not exactly in its display—and did not hesitate to confess the pleasure thus derived. He boasted to me, with a low chuckling laugh, that most men, in respect to himself, wore windows in their bosoms, and was wont to follow up such assertions by direct and very startling proofs of his intimate knowledge of my own. His manner at these moments was frigid and abstract; his eyes were vacant in expression; while his voice, usually a rich tenor, rose into a treble which would have sounded petulantly but for the deliberateness and entire distinctness of the enunciation. Observing him in these moods, I often dwelt meditatively upon the old philosophy of the Bi-Part Soul, and amused myself with the fancy of a double Dupin—the creative and the resolvent.

Let it not be supposed from what I have just said that I am detailing any mystery, or penning any romance. What I have described in the Frenchman was merely the result of an excited or perhaps of a diseased intelligence. But of the character of his remarks at the periods in question an example will best convey the idea.

We were strolling one night down a long dirty street, in the vicinity of the Palais Royal. Being both apparently occupied with thought, neither of us had spoken a syllable for fifteen minutes at least. All at once Dupin broke forth with these words:

"He is a very little fellow, that's true, and would do better for the *Théâtre des Variétés*."

"There can be no doubt of that," I replied unwittingly, and not at first observing (so much had I been absorbed in reflection) the extraordinary manner in which the speaker had chimed in with my meditations. In an instant afterwards I recollected myself, and my astonishment was profound.

"Dupin," said I gravely, "this is beyond my comprehension. I do not hesitate to say that I am amazed, and can scarcely credit my senses. How was it possible you should know I was thinking of—?" Here I paused, to ascertain beyond a doubt whether he really knew of whom I thought.

"—of Chantilly," said he; "why do you pause? You were remarking to yourself that his diminutive figure unfitted him for tragedy."

This was precisely what had formed the subject of my reflections. Chantilly was a *quondam* cobbler of the Rue St. Denis, who, becoming stage-mad, had attempted the *rôle* of Xerxes, in Crébillon's tragedy so-called, and been notoriously *pasquinaded* for his pains.

"Tell me, for Heaven's sake," I exclaimed, "the method—if method there is—by which you have been enabled to fathom my soul in this matter." In fact I was even more startled than I would have been willing to express.

"It was the fruiterer," replied my friend, "who brought you to the conclusion that the mender of soles was not of sufficient height for Xerxes *et id genus omne*."

"The fruiterer!—you astonish me—I know no fruiterer whomsoever."

"The man who ran up against you as we entered the street it may have been fifteen minutes ago."

I now remembered that, in fact, a fruiterer, carrying upon his head a large basket of apples, had nearly thrown me down by accident as we passed from the Rue C—— into the thoroughfare where we stood; but what this had to do with Chantilly I could not possibly understand.

There was not a particle of *charlatanerie* about Dupin "I will explain," he said, "and that you may comprehend all clearly, we will first retrace the course of your meditations from the moment in which I spoke to you until that of the *rencontre* with the fruiterer in question. The larger links of the chain run thus—Chantilly, Orion, Dr. Nichols, Epicurus, Stereotomy, the street stones, the fruiterer."

There are few persons who have not at some period of their lives amused themselves in retracing the steps by which particular conclusions of their own minds have been attained. The occupation is often full of interest; and he who attempts it for the first time is astonished by the apparently illimitable distance and incoherence between the starting-point and the goal What then must have been my amazement when I heard the Frenchman speak what he had just spoken, and when I could not help acknowledging that he had spoken the truth. He continued:

"We had been talking of horses, if I remember aright, just before leaving the Rue C——. This was the last subject we discussed. As we crossed into this street, a fruiterer, with a large basket upon his head, brushing quickly past us, thrust you upon a pile of paving-stones collected at a spot where the causeway is undergoing repair. You stepped upon one of the loose fragments, slipped, slightly strained your ankle, appeared vexed or sulky, muttered a few words, turned to look at the pile, and then proceeded in silence. I was not particularly attentive to what you did; but observation has become with me, of late, a species of necessity.

"You kept your eyes upon the ground—glancing, with a petulant expression, at the holes and ruts in the pavement (so that I saw you were still thinking of the stones), until we reached the little alley called Lamartine, which has been paved, by way of experiment, with the overlapping and riveted blocks. Here your countenance brightened up, and, perceiving your lips move, I could not doubt that you murmured the word 'stereotomy,' a term very affectedly applied to this species of pavement, I knew that you could not say to yourself 'stereotomy' without being brought to think of atomies, and thus of the theories of Epicurus; and since, when we discussed this subject not very long ago, I mentioned to you how singularly, yet with how little notice, the vague guesses of that noble Greek had met with confirmation in the late nebular cosmogony, I felt that you could not avoid casting your eyes upward to the great *nebula* in Orion, and

I certainly expected that you would do so. You did look up; and I was now assured that I had correctly followed your steps, But in that bitter *tirade* upon Chantilly, which appeared in yesterday's *Musée*, the satirist, making some disgraceful allusions to the cobbler's change of name upon assuming the buskin, quoted a Latin line about which we have often conversed. I mean the line

Perdidit antiquum litera prima sonum.

I had told you that this was in reference to Orion, formerly written Urion; and from certain pungencies connected with this explanation I was aware that you could not have forgotten it. It was clear, therefore, that you would not fail to combine the two ideas of Orion and Chantilly. That you did combine them I saw by the character of the smile which passed over your lips. You thought of the poor cobbler's immolation. So far you had been stooping in your gait, but now I saw you draw yourself up to your full height. I was then sure that you reflected upon the diminutive figure of Chantilly. At this point I interrupted your meditations to remark that as, in fact, he *was* a very little fellow that Chantilly, he would do better at the *Théâtre des Variétés*."

Not long after this we were looking over an evening edition of the *Gazette des Tribunaux*, when the following paragraphs arrested our attention.

> EXTRAORDINARY MURDERS.—This morning about three o'clock the inhabitants of the Quartier St. Roch were aroused from sleep by a succession of terrific shrieks, issuing, apparently, from the fourth storey of a house in the Rue Morgue, known to be in the sole occupancy of one Madame L'Espanaye, and her daughter, Mademoiselle Camille L'Espanaye. After some delay, occasioned by a fruitless attempt to procure admission in the usual manner, the gateway was broken in with a crowbar, and eight or ten of the neighbours entered, accompanied by two *gendarmes*. By this time the cries had ceased, but as the party rushed up the first flight of stairs, two or more rough voices in angry contention were distinguished, and seemed to proceed from the upper part of the house. As

the second landing was reached these sounds also had ceased, and everything remained perfectly quiet. The party spread themselves and hurried from room to room. Upon arriving at a large back chamber in the fourth storey (the door of which, being found locked with the key inside, was forced open), a spectacle presented itself which struck every one present not less with horror than with astonishment.

The apartment was in the wildest disorder, the furniture broken and thrown about in all directions. There was only one bedstead, and from this the bed had been removed and thrown into the middle of the floor. On a chair lay a razor besmeared with blood. On the hearth were two or three long and thick tresses of grey human hair, also dabbled in blood, and seeming to have been pulled out by the roots. Upon the floor were found four *napoleons*, an earring of topaz, three large silver spoons, three smaller of *métal d'Alger*, and two bags containing nearly four thousand *francs* in gold. The drawers of a *bureau* which stood in one corner were open, and had been apparently rifled, although many articles still remained in them. A small iron safe was discovered under the *bed* (not under the bedstead). It was open, with the key still in the door. It had no contents beyond a few old letters and other papers of little consequence.

Of Madame L'Espanaye no traces were here seen, but an unusual quantity of soot being observed in the fireplace, a search was made in the chimney, and (horrible to relate !) the corpse of the daughter, head downward, was dragged therefrom, it having been thus forced up the narrow aperture for a considerable distance. The body was quite warm. Upon examining it many excoriations were perceived, no doubt occasioned by the violence with which it had been thrust up and disengaged. Upon the face were many severe scratches, and upon the throat, dark bruises and deep indentations of finger nails, as if the deceased had been throttled to death.

After a thorough investigation of every portion of the house, without further discovery, the party made its way into a small paved yard in the rear of the building, where lay the corpse of the old lady, with her throat so entirely cut that, upon an attempt to raise her, the head fell off. The body as well as the head was fearfully mutilated, the former so much so as scarcely to retain any semblance of humanity.

To this horrible mystery there is not as yet, we believe, the slightest clue.

The next day's paper had these additional particulars.

The Tragedy in the Rue Morgue.—Many individuals have been examined in relation to this most extraordinary and frightful affair" (the word "*affaire* "has not yet in France that levity of import which it conveys with us),"but nothing whatever has transpired to throw light upon it. We give below all the material testimony elicited.

Pauline Dubourg, laundress, deposes that she has known both the deceased for three years, having washed for them during that period.The old lady and her daughter seemed on good terms—very affectionate towards each other. They were excellent pay. Could not speak in regard to their mode or means of living. Believed that Madame L. told fortunes for a living.Was reputed to have money put by. Never met any persons in the house when she called for the clothes or took them home.Was sure that they had no servant in employ.There appeared to be no furniture in any part of the building except in the fourth storey.

Pierre Moreau, tobacconist, deposes that he has been in the habit of selling small quantities of tobacco and snuff to Madame L'Espanaye for nearly four years. Was born in the neighbourhood, and has always resided there.The deceased and her daughter had occupied the house in which the corpses were found for more than six years. It was formerly occupied by a jeweller, who underlet the upper rooms to various persons. The house was the property of Madame L. She became dissatisfied with the abuse of the premises by her tenant, and moved into them herself, refusing to let any portion. The old lady was childish. Witness had seen the daughter some five or six times during the six years. The two lived an exceedingly retired life—were reputed to have money. Had heard it said among the neighbours that Madame L. told fortunes—did not believe it. Had never seen any person enter the door except the old lady and her daughter, a porter once or twice, and a physician some eight or ten times.

Many other persons, neighbours, gave evidence to the same effect. No one was spoken of as frequenting the house. It was not known whether there were any living connections of Madame L. and her daughter. The shutters of the front windows were seldom opened. Those in the rear were always closed with the exception of the large back room, fourth storey. The house was a good house, not very old.

Isidore Muset, gendarme, deposes that he was called to the house about three o'clock in the morning, and found some twenty or thirty persons at the gateway endeavouring to gain admittance. Forced it open at length with a bayonet—not with a crowbar. Had but little difficulty in getting it open on account of its being a double or folding gate, and bolted neither at bottom nor top. The shrieks were continued until the gate was forced, and then suddenly ceased. They seemed to be screams of some person (or persons) in great agony, were loud and drawn out, not short and quick. Witness led the way up stairs. Upon reaching the first landing, heard two voices in loud and angry contention—the one a gruff voice, the other much shriller—a very strange voice. Could distinguish some words of the former, which was that of a Frenchman. Was positive that it was not a woman's voice. Could distinguish the words '*sacre*' and '*diable*.' The shrill voice was that of a foreigner. Could not be sure whether it was the voice of a man or of a woman. Could not make out what was said, but believed the language to be Spanish. The state of the room and of the bodies was described by this witness as we described them yesterday.

Henri Duval, a neighbour, and by trade a silversmith, deposes that he was one of the party who first entered the house. Corroborates the testimony of Muset in general. As soon as they forced an entrance, they reclosed the door to keep out the crowd, which collected very fast, notwithstanding the lateness of the hour. The shrill voice, this witness thinks, was that of an Italian. Was certain it was not French. Could not be sure that it was a man's voice. It might have been a woman's. Was not acquainted with the Italian language. Could not distinguish the words, but was convinced by the intonation that the speaker was an Italian. Knew Madame L. and her daughter. Had conversed with both frequently. Was sure that the shrill voice was not that of either of the deceased.

—— *Odenheimer, restaurateur*. This witness volunteered his testimony. Not speaking French, was examined through an interpreter. Is a native of Amsterdam. Was passing the house at the time of the shrieks. They lasted for several minutes—probably ten. They were long and loud—very awful and distressing. Was one of those who entered the building. Corroborated the previous evidence in every respect but one. Was sure that the shrill voice was that of a man—of a Frenchman. Could not distinguish the words uttered. They were loud and quick—unequal—spoken apparently in fear as well as in anger. The voice was harsh—not so much shrill as harsh. Could not call it a shrill voice. The gruff voice said repeatedly '*sacre*,' '*diable*,' and once '*mon Dieu*.'

Jules Mignaud, banker, of the firm of Mignaud et Fils, Rue Deloraine.—Is the elder Mignaud. Madame L'Espanaye had some property. Had opened an account with his banking house in the spring of the year—(eight years previously). Made frequent deposits in small sums. Had checked for nothing until the third day before her death, when she took out in person the sum of 4000 *francs*. This sum was paid in gold, and a clerk sent home with the money.

Adolphe Lebon, clerk to Mignaud et Fils, deposes that on the day in question, about noon, he accompanied Madame L'Espanaye to her residence with the 4000 *francs* put up in two bags. Upon the door being opened, Mademoiselle L. appeared and took from his hands one of the bags, while the old lady relieved him of the other. He then bowed and departed. Did not see any person in the street at the time. It is a bye-street—very lonely.

William Bird, tailor, deposes that he was one of the party who entered the house. Is an Englishman. Has lived in Paris two years. Was one of the first to ascend the stairs. Heard the voices in contention. The gruff voice was that of a Frenchman. Could make out several words, but cannot now remember all. Heard distinctly '*sacre*' and '*mon Dieu*.' There was a sound at the moment as if of several persons struggling—a scraping and scuffling sound. The shrill voice was very loud—louder than the gruff one. Is sure that it was not the voice of an Englishman. Appeared to be that of a German. Might have been a woman's voice. Does not understand German.

Four of the above-named witnesses, being recalled, deposed that the door of the chamber in which was found the body of Mademoiselle L. was locked on the inside when the party reached it. Everything was perfectly silent—no groans or noises of any kind. Upon forcing the door no person was seen. The windows, both of the back and front room, were down and firmly fastened from within. A door between the two rooms was closed, but not locked. The door leading from the front room into the passage was locked, with the key on the inside. A small room in the front of the house, on the fourth storey, at the head of the passage, was open, the door being ajar. This room was crowded with old beds, boxes, and so forth. These were carefully removed and searched.

There was not an inch of any portion of the house which was not carefully searched. Sweeps were sent up and down the chimneys. The house was a four storey one, with garrets (*mansardes*). A trap-door on the roof was nailed down very securely—did not appear to have been opened for years. The time elapsing between the hearing of the voices in contention and the breaking open of the room door was variously stated by the witnesses. Some made it as short as three minutes—some as long as five. The door was opened with difficulty.

Alfonzo Garcio, undertaker, deposes that he resides in the Rue Morgue. Is a native of Spain. Was one of the party who entered the house. Did not proceed up stairs. Is nervous, and was apprehensive of the consequences of agitation. Heard the voices in contention. The gruff voice was that of a Frenchman. Could not distinguish what was said. The shrill voice was that of an Englishman—is sure of this. Does not understand the English language, but judges by the intonation.

Alberto Montani, confectioner, deposes that he was among the first to ascend the stairs. Heard the voices in question. The gruff voice was that of a Frenchman. Distinguished several words. The speaker appeared to be expostulating. Could not make out the words of the shrill voice. Spoke quick and unevenly. Thinks it the voice of a Russian. Corroborates the general testimony. Is an Italian. Never conversed with a native of Russia.

Several witnesses, recalled, here testified that the chimneys of all the rooms on the fourth storey were too narrow to admit the passage of a human being. By 'sweeps' were meant cylindrical sweeping-brushes, such as are employed by those who clean chimneys. These brushes were passed up and down every flue in the house. There is no back passage by which any one could have descended while the party proceeded up stairs. The body of Mademoiselle L'Espanaye was so firmly wedged in the chimney that it could not be got down until four or five of the party united their strength.

Paul Dumas, physician, deposes that he was called to view the bodies about daybreak. They were both then lying on the sacking of the bedstead in the chamber where Mademoiselle L. was found. The corpse of the young lady was much bruised and excoriated. The fact that it had been thrust up the chimney would sufficiently account for these appearances. The throat was greatly chafed. There were several deep scratches just below the chin, together with a series of livid spots which were evidently the impression of fingers. The face was fearfully discoloured, and the eyeballs protruded.

The tongue had been partially bitten through. A large bruise was discovered upon the pit of the stomach, produced apparently by the pressure of a knee. In the opinion of M. Dumas, Mademoiselle L'Espanaye had been throttled to death by some person or persons unknown. The corpse of the mother was horribly mutilated. All the bones of the right leg and arm were more or less shattered. The left *tibia* much splintered, as well as all the ribs of the left side. Whole body dreadfully bruised and discoloured. It was not possible to say how the injuries had been inflicted. A heavy club of wood, or a broad bar of iron—a chair—any large, heavy, and obtuse weapon would have produced such results if wielded by the hands of a very powerful man. No woman could have inflicted the blows with any weapon. The head of the deceased, when seen by witness, was entirely separated from the body, and was also greatly shattered. The throat had evidently been cut with some very sharp instrument—probably with a razor.

Alexandre Etienne, surgeon, was called with M. Dumas

to view the bodies. Corroborated the testimony, and the opinions of M. Dumas.

Nothing further of importance was elicited, although several other persons were examined. A murder so mysterious, and so perplexing in all its particulars, was never before committed in Paris—if indeed a murder has been committed at all. The police are entirely at fault—an unusual occurrence in affairs of this nature. There is not, however, the shadow of a clue apparent.

The evening edition of the paper stated that the greatest excitement still continued in the Quartier St. Roch—that the premises in question had been carefully researched, and fresh examinations of witnesses instituted, but all to no purpose. A postscript, however, mentioned that Adolphe Lebon had been arrested and imprisoned—although nothing appeared to criminate him beyond the facts already detailed.

Dupin seemed singularly interested in the progress of this affair—at least so I judged from his manner, for he made no comments. It was only after the announcement that Lebon had been imprisoned that he asked me my opinion respecting the murders.

I could merely agree with all Paris in considering them an insoluble mystery. I saw no means by which it would be possible to trace the murderer.

"We must not judge of the means," said Dupin, "by this shell of an examination. The Parisian police, so much extolled for *acumen*, are cunning, but no more. There is no method in their proceedings, beyond the method of the moment. They make a vast parade of measures; but, not unfrequently, these are so ill-adapted to the objects proposed as to put us in mind of Monsieur Jourdain's calling for his *robe-de-chambre—pour mieux entendre la musique*. The results attained by them are not unfrequently surprising, but for the most part are brought about by simple diligence and activity. When these qualities are unavailing, their schemes fail. Vidocq, for example, was a good guesser, and a persevering man. But, without educated thought, he erred continually by the very intensity of his investigations. He impaired his vision by holding the object too close.

"He might see, perhaps, one or two points with unusual clearness, but in so doing, he necessarily lost sight of the matter as a whole. Thus there is such a thing as being too profound. Truth is not always in a well. In fact, as regards the more important knowledge, I do believe that she is invariably superficial. The depth lies in the valleys where we seek her, and not upon the mountaintop where she is found. The modes and sources of this kind of error are well typified in the contemplation of the heavenly bodies.

"To look at a star by glances—to view it in a side-long way, by turning towards it the exterior portions of the *retina* (more susceptible of feeble impressions of light than the interior), is to behold the star distinctly—is to have the best appreciation of its lustre—a lustre which grows dim just in proportion as we turn our vision *fully* upon it. A greater number of rays actually fall upon the eye in the latter case, but in the former there is the more refined capacity for comprehension. By undue profundity we perplex and enfeeble thought; and it is possible to make even Venus herself vanish from the firmament by a scrutiny too sustained, too concentrated, or too direct.

"As for these murders, let us enter into some examinations for ourselves before we make up an opinion respecting them. An inquiry will afford us amusement" (I thought this an odd term so applied, but said nothing), "and besides, Lebon once rendered me a service for which I am not ungrateful. We will go and see the premises with our own eyes. I know G——, the *prefect* of police, and shall have no difficulty in obtaining the necessary permission."

The permission was obtained, and we proceeded at once to the Rue Morgue. This is one of those miserable thoroughfares which intervene between the Rue Richelieu and the Rue St. Roch. It was late in the afternoon when we reached it, as this quarter is at a great distance from that in which we resided. The house was readily found; for there were still many persons gazing up at the closed shutters, with an objectless curiosity, from the opposite side of the way. It was an ordinary Parisian house, with a gateway, on one side of which was a glazed watch-box, with a sliding panel in the window, indicating a *loge du concierge*. Before going in we walked up the street, turned down an alley, and then, again turning, passed in the rear of the building—Dupin, meanwhile, examining the whole neighbourhood, as well as the house, with a minuteness of attention for which I could see no possible object.

Retracing our steps, we came again to the front of the dwelling, rang, and, having shown our credentials, were admitted by the agents in charge. We went upstairs—into the chamber where the body of Mademoiselle L'Espanaye had been found, and where both the deceased still lay. The disorders of the room had, as usual, been suffered to exist. I saw nothing beyond what had been stated in the *Gazette des Tribunaux*. Dupin scrutinised everything—not excepting the bodies of the victims. We then went into the other rooms, and into the yard; a *gendarme* accompanying us throughout. The examination occupied us until dark, when we took our departure. On our way home my companion stepped in for a moment at the office of one of the daily papers.

I have said that the whims of my friend were manifold, and that *Je les ménageais*—for this phrase there is no English equivalent. It was his humour now to decline all conversation on the subject of the murder, until about noon the next day. He then asked me suddenly, if I had observed anything *peculiar* at the scene of the atrocity.

There was something in his manner of emphasising the word "peculiar," which caused me to shudder, without knowing why.

"No, nothing *peculiar*," I said; "nothing more, at least, than we both saw stated in the paper."

"The *Gazette*," he replied, "has not entered, I fear, into the unusual horror of the thing. But dismiss the idle opinions of this print. It appears to me that this mystery is considered insoluble for the very reason which should cause it to be regarded as easy of solution I mean for the *outré* character of its features. The police are confounded by the seeming absence of motive—not for the murder itself, but for the atrocity of the murder. They are puzzled, too, by the seeming impossibility of reconciling the voices heard in contention, with the facts that no one was discovered upstairs but the assassinated Mademoiselle L'Espanaye, and that there were no means of egress without the notice of the party ascending. The wild disorder of the room; the corpse thrust, with the head downward, up the chimney; the frightful mutilation of the body of the old lady; these considerations, with those just mentioned, and others which I need not mention, have sufficed to paralyse the powers, by putting completely at fault the boasted *acumen* of the government agents.

"They have fallen into the gross but common error of confounding the unusual with the abstruse. But it is by these deviations from the plane of the ordinary that reason feels its way, if at all, in its search for the true. In investigations such as we are now pursuing it should not be so much asked 'what has occurred,' as 'what has occurred that has never occurred before.' In fact, the facility with which I shall arrive, or have arrived at the solution of this mystery, is in the direct ratio of its apparent insolubility in the eyes of the police."

I stared at the speaker in mute astonishment.

"I am now awaiting," continued he, looking towards the door of our apartment—"I am now awaiting a person who, although perhaps not the perpetrator of these butcheries, must have been in some measure implicated in their perpetration. Of the worst portion of the crimes committed, it is probable that he is innocent. I hope that I am right in this supposition; for upon it I build my expectation of reading the entire riddle. I look for the man here—in this room—every moment. It is true that he may not arrive; but the probability is that he will. Should he come, it will be necessary to detain him. Here are pistols; and we both know how to use them when occasion demands their, use."

I took the pistols, scarcely knowing what I did, or believing what I heard, while Dupin went on, very much as if in a soliloquy. I have already spoken of his abstract manner at such times. His discourse was addressed to myself; but his voice, although by no means loud, had that intonation which is commonly employed in speaking to some one at a great distance. His eves, vacant in expression, regarded only the wall.

"That the voices heard in contention," he said, "by the party upon the stairs, were not the voices of the women themselves, was fully proved by the evidence. This relieves us of all doubt upon the question whether the old lady could have first destroyed the daughter, and afterwards have committed suicide. I speak of this point chiefly for the sake of method; for the strength of Madame L'Espanaye would have been utterly unequal to the task of thrusting her daughter's corpse up the chimney as it was found and the nature of the wounds upon her own person entirely precludes the idea of self-destruction. Murder, then, has been committed by some third party; and the voices of this third party were those heard in contention. Let me now advert—not to the whole testimony respecting these voices—but to what was *peculiar* in that testimony. Did you observe anything peculiar about it?"

I remarked that, while all the witnesses agreed in supposing the gruff voice to be that of a Frenchman, there was much disagreement in regard to the shrill, or, as one individual termed it, the harsh voice.

"That was the evidence itself," said Dupin, "but it was not the peculiarity of the evidence. You have observed nothing distinctive. Yet there *was* something to be observed. The witnesses, as you remark, agreed about the gruff voice; they were here unanimous. But in regard to the shrill voice, the peculiarity is—not that they disagreed—but that, while an Italian, an Englishman, a Spaniard, a Hollander, and a Frenchman attempted to describe it, each one spoke of it as that *of a foreigner*. Each is sure that it was not the voice of one of his own countrymen. Each likens it—not to the voice of an individual of any nation with whose language he is conversant—but the converse. The Frenchman supposes it the voice of a Spaniard, and 'might have distinguished some words *had he been acquainted with the Spanish.'* The Dutchman maintains it to have been that of a Frenchman; but we find it stated that '*not understanding French this witness was examined through an interpreter.*' The Englishman thinks it the voice of a German, and '*does not understand German.*'

"The Spaniard 'is sure' that it was that of an Englishman, but 'judges by the intonation' altogether, '*as he has no knowledge of the English.*' The Italian believes it the voice of a Russian, but '*has never conversed with a native of Russia.*' A second Frenchman differs, moreover, with the first, and is positive that the voice was that of an Italian; but, *not being cognisant of that tongue*, is, like the Spaniard, 'convinced by the intonation.' Now, how strangely unusual must that voice have really been, about which such testimony as this *could* have been elicited!—in whose *tones*, even, denizens of the five great divisions of Europe could recognise nothing familiar! You will say that it might have been the voice of an Asiatic—of an African. Neither Asiatics nor Africans abound in Paris; but, without denying the inference, I will now merely call your attention to three points The voice is termed by one witness 'harsh rather than shrill.' It is represented by two others to have been 'quick and *unequal.*' No words—no sounds resembling words—were by any witness mentioned as distinguishable.

"I know not," continued Dupin, "what impression I may have made, so far, upon your own understanding, but I do not hesitate to say that legitimate deductions even from this portion of the testimony—the portion respecting the gruff and shrill voices—are in themselves sufficient to engender a suspicion which should give direction to all further progress in the investigation of the mystery. I said 'legitimate deductions,' but my meaning is not thus fully expressed. I designed to imply that the deductions are the *sole* proper ones, and that the suspicion arises *inevitably* from them as the single result. What the suspicion is, however, I will not say just yet. I merely wish you to bear in mind that, with myself, it was sufficiently forcible to give a definite form—a certain tendency—to my inquiries in the chamber.

"Let us now transport ourselves, in fancy, to this chamber.

What shall we first seek here? The means of egress employed by the murderers. It is not too much so say that neither of us believe in preternatural events. Madame and Mademoiselle L'Espanaye were not destroyed by spirits. The doers of the deed were material and escaped materially. Then how? Fortunately there is but one mode of reasoning upon the point, and that mode *must* lead us to a definite decision. Let us examine, each by each, the possible means of egress. It is clear that the assassins were in the room where Mademoiselle L'Espanaye was found, or at least in the room adjoining, when the party ascended the stairs. It is then only from these two apartments that we have to seek issues.

"The police have laid bare the floors, the ceilings, and the masonry of the walls in every direction. No *secret* issues could have escaped their vigilance. But, not trusting to *their* eyes, I examined with my own, There were, then, *no* secret issues. Both doors leading from the rooms into the passage were securely locked, with the keys inside. Let us turn to the chimneys. These, although of ordinary width for some eight or ten feet above the hearths, will not admit, throughout their extent, the body of a large cat. The impossibility of egress, by means already stated, being thus absolute, we are reduced to the windows. Through those of the front room no one could have escaped without notice from the crowd in the street. The murderers *must* have passed, then, through those of the back room. Now, brought to this conclusion in so unequivocal a manner as we are, it is not our part, as reasoners, to reject it on account of apparent impossibilities. It is only left for us to prove that these apparent 'impossibilities' are, in reality, not such.

"There are two windows in the chamber. One of them is unobstructed by furniture, and is wholly visible. The lower portion of the other is hidden from view by the head of the unwieldy bedstead which is thrust close up against it. The former was found securely fastened from within. It resisted the utmost force of those who endeavoured to raise it. A large gimlet-hole had been pierced in its frame to the left, and a very stout nail was found fitted therein, nearly to the head. Upon examining the other window a similar nail was seen similarly fitted in it; and a vigorous attempt to raise this sash failed also. The police were now entirely satisfied that egress had not been in these directions. And, *therefore*, it was thought a matter of supererogation to withdraw the nails and open the windows.

"My own examination was somewhat more particular, and was so for the reason I have just given—because here it was, I knew, that all apparent impossibilities *must* be proved to be not such in reality.

"I proceeded to think thus—a *posteriori*. The murderers *did* escape from one of these windows. This being so, they could not have re-fastened the sashes from the inside, as they were found fastened—the consideration which put a stop, through its obviousness, to the scrutiny of the police in this quarter. Yet the sashes *were* fastened. They *must*, then, have the power of fastening themselves. There was no escape from this conclusion. I stepped to the unobstructed casement, withdrew the nail with some difficulty, and attempted to raise the sash. It resisted all my efforts, as I had anticipated. A concealed spring must, I now knew, exist; and this corroboration of my idea convinced me that my premises, at least, were correct, however mysterious still appeared the circumstances attending the nails. A careful search soon brought to light the hidden spring. I pressed it, and, satisfied with the discovery, forbore to upraise the sash.

"I now replaced the nail and regarded it attentively. A person passing out through this window might have reclosed it, and the spring would have caught; but the nail could not have been replaced. The conclusion was plain, and again narrowed in the field of my investigations. The assassins *must* have escaped through the other window. Supposing, then, the springs upon each sash to be the same, as was probable, there *must* be found a difference between the nails, or at least between the modes of their fixture. Getting upon the sacking of the bedstead, I looked over the headboard minutely at the second casement. Passing my hand down behind the board, I readily discovered and pressed the spring, which was, as I had supposed, identical in character with its neighbour. I now looked at the nail. It was as stout as the other, and apparently fitted in the same manner driven in nearly up to the head.

"You will say that I was puzzled; but if you think so you must have misunderstood the nature of the inductions. To use a sporting phrase, I had not been once 'at fault.' The scent had never for an instant been lost. There was no flaw in any link of the chain. I had traced the secret to its ultimate result; and that result was *the nail.* It had, I say, in every respect the appearance of its fellow in the other window; but this fact was an absolute nullity (conclusive as it might seem to be) when compared with the consideration that here at this point terminated the clue. 'There *must* be something wrong,' I said, 'about the nail.' I touched it, and the head, with about a quarter of an inch of the shank, came off in my fingers.

"The rest of the shank was in the gimlet-hole, where it had been broken off. The fracture was an old one (for its edges were incrusted with rust), and had apparently been accomplished by the blow of a hammer, which had partially imbedded in the top of the bottom sash the head portion of the nail. I now carefully replaced this head portion in the indentation whence I had taken it, and the resemblance to a perfect nail was complete—the fissure was invisible. Pressing the spring, I gently raised the sash for a few inches; the head went up with it, remaining firm in its bed. I closed the window, and the semblance of the whole nail was again perfect.

"The riddle, so far, was now unriddled. The assassin had escaped through the window which looked upon the bed. Dropping of its own accord upon his exit (or perhaps purposely closed), it had become fastened by the spring; and it was the retention of this spring which had been mistaken by the police for that of the nail,—further inquiry being thus considered unnecessary.

"The next question is that of the mode of descent. Upon this point I had been satisfied in my walk with you around the building. About five feet and a-half from the casement in question there runs a lightning-rod. From this rod it would have been impossible for anyone to reach the window itself, to say nothing of entering it. I observed, however, that the shutters of the fourth storey were of the peculiar kind called by Parisian carpenters *ferrades*—a kind rarely employed at the present day, but frequently seen upon very old mansions at Lyons and Bordeaux. They are in the form of an ordinary door (a single, not a folding door), except that the lower half is latticed or worked in open trellis, thus affording an excellent hold for the hands. In the present instance these shutters are fully three feet and a-half broad.

"When we saw them from the rear of the house they were both about half-open—that is to say, they stood off at right angles from the wall. It is probable that the police, as well as myself, examined the back of the tenement; but if so, in looking at these *ferrades* in the line of their breadth (as they must have done), they did not perceive this great breadth itself, or, at all events, failed to take it into due consideration. In fact, having once satisfied themselves that no egress could have been made in this quarter, they would naturally bestow here a very cursory examination. It was clear to me, however, that the shutter belonging to the window at the head of the bed would, if swung fully back to the wall, reach to within two feet of the lightning-rod. It was also evident that by exertion of a very unusual degree of activity and courage an entrance into the window from the rod might have been thus effected.

"By reaching to the distance of two feet and a half (we now suppose the shutter open to its whole extent) a robber might have taken a firm grasp upon the trelliswork. Letting go, then, his hold upon the rod, placing his feet securely against the wall, and springing boldly from it, he might have swung the shutter so as to close it, and, if we imagine the window open at the time, might even have swung himself into the room.

"I wish you to bear especially in mind that I have spoken of a *very* unusual degree of activity as requisite to success in so hazardous and so difficult a feat. It is my design to show you, first, that the thing might possibly have been accomplished; but, secondly and *chiefly*, I wish to impress upon your understanding the *very extraordinary*, the almost preternatural, character of that agility which could have accomplished it.

"You will say, no doubt, using the language of the law, that 'to make out my case,' I should rather undervalue than insist upon a full estimation of the activity required in this matter. This may be the practice in law, but it is not the usage of reason. My ultimate object is only the truth. My immediate purpose is to lead you to place in juxtaposition that *very unusual* activity of which I have just spoken with that *very peculiar* shrill (or harsh) and *unequal* voice, about whose nationality no two persons could be found to agree, and in whose utterance no syllabification could be detected."

At these words a vague and half-formed conception of the meaning of Dupin flitted over my mind. I seemed to be upon the verge of comprehension, without power to comprehend, as men at times find themselves upon the brink of remembrance, without being able in the end to remember. My friend went on with his discourse.

"You will see," he said, "that I have shifted the question from the mode of egress to that of ingress. It was my design to convey the idea that both were effected in the same manner at the same point. Let us now revert to the interior of the room. Let us survey the appearances here. The drawers of the bureau, it is said, had been rifled, although many articles of apparel still remained within them. The conclusion here is absurd. It is a mere guess—a very silly one—and no more. How are we to know that the articles found in the drawers were not all these drawers had originally contained? Madame L'Espanaye and her daughter lived an exceedingly retired life—saw no company—seldom went out—had little use for numerous changes of habiliment.

"Those found were at least of as good quality as any likely to be possessed by these ladies. If a thief had taken any, why did he not take the best—why did he not take all? In a word, why did he abandon four thousand *francs* in gold to encumber himself with a bundle of linen? The gold *was* abandoned. Nearly the whole sum mentioned by Monsieur Mignaud, the banker, was discovered in bags upon the floor. I wish you, therefore, to discard from your thoughts the blundering idea of *motive*, engendered in the brains of the police by that portion of the evidence which speaks of money delivered at the door of the house. Coincidences ten times as remarkable as this (the delivery of the money, and murder committed within three days upon the party receiving it), happen to all of us every hour of our lives, without attracting even momentary notice.

"Coincidences, in general, are great stumbling-blocks in the way of that class of thinkers who have been educated to know nothing of the theory of probabilities——that theory to which the most glorious objects of human research are indebted for the most glorious of illustration. In the present instance, had the gold been gone, the fact of its delivery three days before would have formed something more than a coincidence. It would have been corroborative of this idea of motive. But, under the real circumstances of the case, if we are to suppose gold the motive of this outrage, we must also imagine the perpetrator so vacillating an idiot as to have abandoned his gold and his motive together.

"Keeping now steadily in mind the points to which I have drawn your attention—that peculiar voice, that unusual agility, and that startling absence of motive in a murder so singularly atrocious as this let us glance at the butchery itself. Here is a woman strangled to death by manual strength, and thrust up a chimney, head downward. Ordinary assassins employ no such modes of murder as this. Least of all do they thus dispose of the murdered. In the manner of thrusting the corpse up the chimney, you will admit that there was something excessively *outré*—something altogether irreconcilable with our common notions of human action, even when we suppose the actors the most depraved of men. Think, too, how great must have been that strength which could have thrust the body *up* such an aperture so forcibly that the united vigour of several persons was found barely sufficient to drag it *down!*

"Turn, now, to other indications of the employment of a vigour most marvellous. On the hearth were thick tresses—very thick tresses—of grey human hair. These had been torn out by the roots. You are aware of the great force necessary in tearing thus from the head even twenty or thirty hairs together. You saw the locks in question as well as myself. Their roots (a hideous sight) were clotted with fragments of the flesh of the scalp—sure token of the prodigious power which had been exerted in uprooting perhaps half-a-million of hairs at a time. The throat of the old lady was not merely cut, but the head absolutely severed from the body—the instrument was a mere razor. I wish you also to look at the *brutal* ferocity of these deeds.

"Of the bruises upon the body of Madame L'Espanaye I do not speak. Monsieur Dumas, and his worthy coadjutor, Monsieur Etienne, have pronounced that they were inflicted by some obtuse instrument; and so far these gentlemen are very correct. The obtuse instrument was clearly the stone pavement in the yard upon which the victim had fallen from the window which looked in upon the bed. This idea, however simple it may now seem, escaped the police for the same reason that the breadth of the shutters escaped them—because, by the affair of the nails, their perceptions had been hermetically sealed against the possibility of the windows having ever been opened at all.

"If, now, in addition to all these things, you have properly reflected upon the odd disorder of the chamber, we have gone so far as to combine the ideas of an agility astounding, a strength superhuman, a ferocity brutal, a butchery without motive, a *grotesquerie* in horror absolutely alien from humanity, and a voice foreign in tone to the ears of men of many nations, and devoid of all distinct or intelligible syllabification. What result, then, has ensued? What impression have I made upon your fancy?"

I felt a creeping of the flesh as Dupin asked me the question. "A madman," I said, "has done this deed—some raving maniac escaped from a neighbouring *maison de santé*."

"In some respects," he replied, "your idea is not irrelevant;

but the voices of madmen, even in their wildest paroxysms, are never found to tally with that peculiar voice heard upon the stairs. Madmen are of some nation, and their language, however incoherent in its words, has always the coherence of syllabification. Besides, the hair of a madman is not such as I now hold in my hand, I disentangled this little tuft from the rigidly clutched fingers of Madame L'Espanaye. Tell me what you can make of it?"

"Dupin!" I said, completely unnerved, "this hair is most unusual—this is no *human* hair."

"I have not asserted that it is," said he; "but, before we decide this point, I wish you to glance at the little sketch I have here traced upon this paper. It is a *facsimile* drawing of what has been described in one portion of the testimony as 'dark bruises, and deep indentations of finger nails,' upon the throat of Mademoiselle L'Espanaye, and in another (by Messrs. Dumas and Etienne), as a 'series of livid spots evidently the impression of fingers.'

"You will perceive," continued my friend, spreading out the paper upon the table before us, "that this drawing gives the idea of a firm and fixed hold. There is no *slipping* apparent. Each finger has retained—possibly until the death of the victim—the fearful grasp by which it originally embedded itself. Attempt, now, to place all your fingers, at the same time, in the respective impressions as you see them."

I made the attempt in vain.

"We are possibly not giving this matter a fair trial," he said. "The paper is spread out upon a plane surface; but the human throat is cylindrical. Here is a billet of wood, the circumference of which is about that of the throat. Wrap the drawing around it, and try the experiment again."

I did so; but the difficulty was even more obvious than before. "This," I said, "is the mark of no human hand."

"Read now," replied Dupin, "this passage from Cuvier."

It was a minute anatomical and generally descriptive account of the large fulvous Orang-utan of the East Indian Islands. The gigantic stature, the prodigious strength and activity, the wild ferocity, and the imitative propensities of these *mammalia* are sufficiently well known to all. I understood the full horrors of the murder at once.

"The description of the digits," said I, as I made an end of reading, "is in exact accordance with this drawing. I see that no animal but an Orang-utan, of the species here mentioned, could have impressed the indentations as you have traced them. This tuft of tawny hair, too, is identical in character with that of the beast of Cuvier. But I cannot possibly comprehend the particulars of this frightful mystery. Besides, there were *two* voices heard in contention, and one of them was unquestionably the voice of a Frenchman."

"True; and you will remember an expression attributed almost unanimously, by the evidence, to this voice,—the expression '*Mon Dieu!*' This, under the circumstances, has been justly characterised by one of the witnesses (Montani, the confectioner) as an expression of remonstrance or expostulation. Upon these two words, therefore, I have mainly built my hopes of a full solution of the riddle. A Frenchman was cognisant of the murder. It is possible—indeed it is far more than probable—that he was innocent of all participation in the bloody transactions which took place. The Orang-utan may have escaped from him. He may have traced it to the chamber; but, under the agitating circumstances which ensued, he could never have recaptured it. It is still at large.

"I will not pursue these guesses—for I have no right to call them more—since the shades of reflection upon which they are based are scarcely of sufficient depth to be appreciable by my own intellect, and since I could not pretend to make them intelligible to the understanding of another. We will call them guesses, then, and speak of them as such. If the Frenchman in question is indeed, as I suppose, innocent of this atrocity, this advertisement which I left last night upon our return home at the office of *Le Monde* (a paper devoted to the shipping interest, and much sought by sailors) will bring him to our residence."

He handed me a paper, and I read thus:

> Caught.—In the Bois de Boulogne, early in the morning of the —— inst. (the morning of the murder), a very large, tawny Orang-utan of the Bornese species. The owner (who is ascertained to be a sailor, belonging to a Maltese vessel) may have the animal again, upon identifying it satisfactorily, and paying a few charges arising from its capture and keeping. Call at No. —, Rue ——, Faubourg St. Germain—*au troisieme*.

"How was it possible," I asked, "that you should know the man to be a sailor, and belonging to a Maltese vessel?"

"I do *not* know it," said Dupin. "I am not *sure* of it. Here, however, is a small piece of ribbon, which from its form, and from its greasy appearance, has evidently been used in tying the hair in one of those long *queues* of which sailors are so fond. Moreover, this knot is one which few besides sailors can tie, and is peculiar to the Maltese. I picked the ribbon up at the foot of the lightning-rod. It could not have belonged to either of the deceased. Now if, after all, I am wrong in my induction from this ribbon, that the Frenchman was a sailor belonging to a Maltese vessel, still I can have done no harm in saying what I did in the advertisement.

"If I am in error, he will merely suppose that I have been misled by some circumstance into which he will not take the trouble to inquire. But if I am right, a great point is gained. Cognisant, although innocent, of the murder, the Frenchman will naturally hesitate about replying to the advertisement—about demanding the Orang-utan. He will reason thus:—'I am innocent; I am poor; my Orang-utan is of great value—to one in my circumstances a fortune of itself—why should I lose it through idle apprehensions of danger? Here it is within my grasp. It was found in the Bois de Boulogne—at a vast distance from the scene of that butchery. How can it ever be suspected that a brute beast should have done the deed? The police are at fault—they have failed to procure the slightest clue. Should they even trace the animal, it would be impossible to prove me cognisant of the murder, or to implicate me in guilt on account of that cognisance.

"Above all, *I am known.* The advertiser designates me as the possessor of the beast. I am not sure to what limit his knowledge may extend. Should I avoid claiming a property of so great value, which it is known that I possess, I will render the animal at least liable to suspicion. It is not my policy to attract attention either to myself or to the beast. I will answer the advertisement, get the Orang-utan, and keep it close until this matter has blown over."

At this moment we heard a step upon the stairs.

"Be ready," said Dupin, "with your pistols, but neither use them nor show them until at a signal from myself."

The front door of the house had been left open, and the visitor had entered without ringing, and advanced several steps upon the staircase. Now, however, he seemed to hesitate. Presently we heard him descending. Dupin was moving quickly to the door, when we again heard him coming up. He did not turn back a second time, but stepped up with decision, and rapped at the door of our chamber.

"Come in," said Dupin, in a cheerful and hearty tone.

A man entered. He was a sailor, evidently—a tall, stout, and muscular-looking person, with a certain daredevil expression of countenance, not altogether unprepossessing. His face, greatly sunburnt, was more than half hidden by whisker and *mustachio*. He had with him a huge oaken cudgel, but appeared to be otherwise unarmed. He bowed awkwardly, and bade us "good evening" in French accents, which, although somewhat Neufchatelish, were still sufficiently indicative of a Parisian origin.

"Sit down, my friend," said Dupin. "I suppose you have called about the Orang-utan. Upon my word I almost envy you the possession of him; a remarkably fine, and no doubt a very valuable animal. How old do you suppose him to be?"

The sailor drew a long breath, with the air of a man relieved of some intolerable burden, and then replied in an assured tone:

"I have no way of telling—but he can't be more than four or

five years old. Have you got him here?"

"Oh no; we had no conveniences for keeping him here. He is at a livery stable in the Rue Dubourg, just by. You can get him in the morning. Of course you are prepared to identify the property?"

"To be sure I am, sir."

"I shall be sorry to part with him," said Dupin.

"I don't mean that you should be at all this trouble for nothing, sir," said the man. "Couldn't expect it. Am very willing to pay a reward for the finding of the animal—that is to say, anything in reason."

"Well," replied my friend, "that is all very fair, to be sure. Let me think!—what should I have? Oh! I will tell you. My reward shall be this. You shall give me all the information in your power about these murders in the Rue Morgue."

Dupin said the last words in a very low tone, and very quietly. Just as quietly, too, he walked towards the door, locked it, and put the key in his pocket. He then drew a pistol from his bosom and placed it, without the least flurry, upon the table.

The sailor's face flushed up as if he were struggling with suffocation. He started to his feet and grasped his cudgel; but the next moment he fell back into his seat, trembling violently, and with the countenance of death itself. He spoke not a word. I pitied him from the bottom of my heart.

"My friend," said Dupin in a kind tone, "you are alarming yourself unnecessarily—you are indeed. We mean you no harm whatever. I pledge you the honour of a gentleman, and of a Frenchman, that we intend you no injury. I perfectly well know that you are innocent of the atrocities in the Rue Morgue. It will not do, however, to deny that you are in some measure implicated in them. From what I have already said, you must know that I have had means of information about this matter—means of which you could never have dreamed. Now the thing stands thus. You have done nothing which you could have avoided—nothing, certainly, which renders you culpable. You were not even guilty of robbery, when you might have robbed with impunity. You have nothing to conceal. You have no reason for concealment. On the other hand, you are bound by every principle of honour to confess all you know. An innocent man is now imprisoned, charged with that crime of which you can point out the perpetrator."

The sailor had recovered his presence of mind, in a great measure, while Dupin uttered these words; but his original boldness of bearing was all gone.

"So help me God," said he, after a brief pause, "I *will* tell you all I know about this affair;—but I do not expect you to believe one-half I say—I would be a fool indeed if I did. Still I *am* innocent, and I will make a clean breast if I die for it."

What he stated was in substance this. He had lately made a voyage to the Indian Archipelago. A party, of which he formed one, landed at Borneo, and passed into the interior on an excursion of pleasure. Himself and a companion had captured the Orang-utan. This companion dying, the animal fell into his own exclusive possession. After great trouble, occasioned by the intractable ferocity of his captive during the home voyage, he at length succeeded in lodging it safely at his own residence in Paris, where, not to attract towards himself the unpleasant curiosity of his neighbours, he kept it carefully secluded until such time as it should recover from a wound in the foot received from a splinter on board ship. His ultimate design was to sell it.

Returning home from some sailor's frolic on the night, or rather in the morning of the murder, he found the beast occupying his own bedroom, into which it had broken from a closet adjoining, where it had been, as was thought, securely confined. Razor in hand, and fully lathered, it was sitting before a looking-glass attempting the operation of shaving, in which it had no doubt previously watched its master through the key-hole of the closet. Terrified at the sight of so dangerous a weapon in the possession of an animal so ferocious and so well able to use it, the man, for some moments, was at a loss what to do. He had been accustomed, however, to quiet the creature, even in its fiercest moods, by the use of a whip, and to this he now resorted. Upon sight of it, the Orang-utan sprang at once through the door of the chamber, down the stairs, and thence through a window, unfortunately open, into the street.

The Frenchman followed in despair; the ape, razor still in hand, occasionally stopping to look back and gesticulate at its pursuer, until the latter had nearly come up with it. It then again made off. In this manner chase continued for a long time. The streets were profoundly quiet, as it was nearly three o'clock in the morning. In passing down an alley in the rear of the Rue Morgue, the fugitive's attention was arrested by a light gleaming from the open window of Madame L'Espanaye's chamber, in the fourth storey of her house. Rushing to the building, it perceived the lightning-rod, clambered up with inconceivable agility, grasped the shutter, which was thrown fully back against the wall, and, by its means, swung itself directly upon the headboard of the bed. The whole feat did not occupy a minute. The shutter was kicked open again by the Orang-utan, as it entered the room.

The sailor, in the meantime, was both rejoiced and perplexed. He had strong hopes of now recapturing the brute, as it could scarcely escape from the trap into which it had ventured except by the rod, where it might be intercepted as it came down. On the other hand, there was much cause for anxiety as to what it might do in the house. This latter reflection urged the man still to follow the fugitive. A lightning-rod is ascended without difficulty, especially by a sailor; but when he had arrived as high as the window, which lay far to his left, his career was stopped; the most that he could accomplish was to reach over so as to obtain a glimpse of the interior of the room. At this glimpse he nearly fell from his hold through excess of horror. Now it was that those hideous shrieks arose upon the night which had startled from slumber the inmates of the Rue Morgue.

Madame L'Espanaye and her daughter, habited in their night-clothes, had apparently been occupied in arranging some papers in the iron chest already mentioned, which had been wheeled into the middle of the room. It was open, and its contents lay beside it on the floor. The victims must have been sitting with their backs towards the window; and, from the time elapsing between the ingress of the beast and the screams, it seems probable that it was not immediately perceived. The flapping to of the shutter would naturally have been attributed to the wind.

As the sailor looked in, the gigantic animal had seized Madame L'Espanaye by the hair (which was loose, as she had been combing it), and was flourishing the razor about her face in imitation of the motions of a barber. The daughter lay prostrate and motionless; she had swooned. The screams and struggles of the old lady (during which the hair was torn from her head) had the effect of changing the probably pacific purposes of the Orang-utan into those of wrath. With one determined sweep of its muscular arm it nearly severed her head from her body. The sight of blood inflamed its anger into frenzy. Gnashing its teeth and flashing fire from its eyes, it flew upon the body of the girl, and imbedded its fearful talons in her throat, retaining its grasp until she expired.

Its wandering and wild glances fell at this moment upon the head of the bed, over which the face of its master, rigid with horror, was just discernible. The fury of the beast, which no doubt bore still in mind the dreaded whip, was instantly converted into fear. Conscious of having deserved punishment, it seemed desirous of concealing its bloody deeds, and skipped about the chamber in an agony of nervous agitation, throwing down and beaking the furniture as it moved, and dragging the bed from the bedstead. In conclusion, it seized first the corpse of the daughter and thrust it up the chimney, as it was found; then that of the old lady, which it immediately hurled through the window headlong.

As the ape approached the casement with its mutilated burden, the sailor shrank aghast to the rod, and, rather gliding than clambering down it, hurried at once home—dreading the consequences of the butchery, and gladly abandoning, in his terror, all solicitude about the fate of the Orang-utan. The words heard by the party upon the staircase were the Frenchman's exclamations of horror and affright, commingled with the fiendish jabberings of the brute.

I have scarcely anything to add. The Orang-utan must have escaped from the chamber by the rod, just before the breaking of the door. It must have closed the window as it passed through it. It was subsequently caught by the owner himself, who obtained for it a very large sum at the *Jardin des Plantes*. Lebon was instantly released, upon our narration of the circumstances (with some comments from Dupin) at the *bureau* of the Prefect of Police. This functionary, however well disposed to my friend, could not altogether conceal his chagrin at the turn which affairs had taken, and was fain to indulge in a sarcasm or two about the propriety of every person minding his own business.

"Let him talk," said Dupin, who had not thought it necessary to reply. "Let him discourse; it will ease his conscience. I am satisfied with having defeated him in his own castle. Nevertheless, that he failed in the solution of this mystery is by no means that matter for wonder which he supposes it; for, in truth, our friend the *prefect* is somewhat too cunning to be profound. In his wisdom is no *stamen*. It is all head and no body, like the pictures of the Goddess Laverna,—or, at best, all head and shoulders, like a codfish. But he is a good creature after all. I like him especially for one masterstroke of cant, by which he has attained his reputation for ingenuity. I mean the way he has '*de nier ce qui est, et d'expliquer ce qui* n'est pas.'"[1]

---

1. Rousseau—Nouvelle Héloïse.

The Oval Portrait

The *château* into which my valet had ventured to make forcible entrance, rather than permit me, in my desperately wounded condition, to pass a night in the open air, was one of those piles of commingled gloom and grandeur which have so long frowned among the Appennines, not less in fact than in the fancy of Mrs. Radcliffe. To all appearance it had been temporarily and very lately abandoned. We established ourselves in one of the smallest and least sumptuously furnished apartments. It lay in a remote turret of the building. Its decorations were rich, yet tattered and antique. Its walls were hung with tapestry and bedecked with manifold and multiform armorial trophies, together with an unusually great number of very spirited modern paintings in frames of rich golden arabesque.

In these paintings, which depended from the walls not only in their main surfaces, but in very many nooks which the bizarre architecture of the *château* rendered necessary—in these paintings my incipient delirium, perhaps, had caused me to take deep interest; so that I bade Pedro to close the heavy shutters of the room—since it was already night—to light the tongues of a tall candelabrum which stood by the head of my bed—and to throw open far and wide the fringed curtains of black velvet which enveloped the bed itself. I wished all this done that I might resign myself, if not to sleep, at least alternately to the contemplation of these pictures, and the perusal of a small volume which had been found upon the pillow, and which purported to criticise and describe them.

Long—long I read—and devoutly, devotedly I gazed. Rapidly and gloriously the hours flew by and the deep midnight came. The position of the candelabrum displeased me, and outreaching my hand with difficulty, rather than disturb my slumbering valet, I placed it so as to throw its rays more fully upon the book.

But the action produced an effect altogether unanticipated. The rays of the numerous candles (for there were many) now fell within a niche of the room which had hitherto been thrown into deep shade by one of the bed-posts. I thus saw in vivid light a picture all unnoticed before. It was the portrait of a young girl just ripening into womanhood. I glanced at the painting hurriedly, and then closed my eyes. Why I did this was not at first apparent even to my own perception. But while my lids remained thus shut, I ran over in my mind my reason for so shutting them. It was an impulsive movement to gain time for thought—to make sure that my vision had not deceived me—to calm and subdue my fancy for a more sober and more certain gaze. In a very few moments I again looked fixedly at the painting.

That I now saw aright I could not and would not doubt; for the first flashing of the candles upon that canvas had seemed to dissipate the dreamy stupor which was stealing over my senses, and to startle me at once into waking life.

The portrait, I have already said, was that of a young girl. It was a mere head and shoulders, done in what is technically termed a *vignette* manner; much in the style of the favorite heads of Sully. The arms, the bosom, and even the ends of the radiant hair melted imperceptibly into the vague yet deep shadow which formed the back-ground of the whole. The frame was oval, richly gilded and filigreed in *Moresque*. As a thing of art nothing could be more admirable than the painting itself.

But it could have been neither the execution of the work, nor the immortal beauty of the countenance, which had so suddenly and so vehemently moved me. Least of all, could it have been that my fancy, shaken from its half slumber, had mistaken the head for that of a living person. I saw at once that the peculiarities of the design, of the *vignetting*, and of the frame, must have instantly dispelled such idea—must have prevented even its momentary entertainment. Thinking earnestly upon these points, I remained, for an hour perhaps, half sitting, half reclining, with my vision riveted upon the portrait. At length, satisfied with the true secret of its effect, I fell back within the bed. I had found the spell of the picture in an absolute *life-likeliness* of expression, which, at first startling, finally confounded, subdued, and appalled me. With deep and reverent awe I replaced the candelabrum in its former position. The cause of my deep agitation being thus shut from view, I sought eagerly the volume which discussed the paintings and their histories. Turning to the number which designated the oval portrait, I there read the vague and quaint words which follow:

> She was a maiden of rarest beauty, and not more lovely than full of glee. And evil was the hour when she saw, and loved, and wedded the painter. He, passionate, studious, austere, and having already a bride in his art; she a maiden of rarest beauty, and not more lovely than full of glee; all light and smiles, and frolicsome as the young fawn; loving and cherishing all things; hating only the art which was her rival; dreading only the pallet and brushes and other untoward instruments which deprived her of the countenance of her lover. It was thus a terrible thing for this lady to hear the painter speak of his desire to portray even his young bride.
>
> But she was humble and obedient, and sat meekly for many weeks in the dark, high turret-chamber where the light dripped upon the pale canvas only from overhead. But he, the painter, took glory in his work, which went on from hour to hour, and from day to day. And he was a passionate, and wild, and moody man, who became lost in reveries; so that he would not see that the light which fell so ghastly in that lone turret withered the health and the spirits of his bride, who pined visibly to all but him.
>
> Yet she smiled on and still on, uncomplainingly, because she saw that the painter (who had high renown) took a

fervid and burning pleasure in his task, and wrought day and night to depict her who so loved him, yet who grew daily more dispirited and weak. And in sooth some who beheld the portrait spoke of its resemblance in low words, as of a mighty marvel, and a proof not less of the power of the painter than of his deep love for her whom he depicted so surpassingly well.

But at length, as the labour drew nearer to its conclusion, there were admitted none into the turret; for the painter had grown wild with the ardour of his work, and turned his eyes from canvas merely, even to regard the countenance of his wife. And he *would* not see that the tints which he spread upon the canvas were drawn from the cheeks of her who sate beside him. And when many weeks had passed, and but little remained to do, save one brush upon the mouth and one tint upon the eye, the spirit of the lady again flickered up as the flame within the socket of the lamp.

And then the brush was given, and then the tint was placed; and, for one moment, the painter stood entranced before the work which he had wrought; but in the next, while he yet gazed, he grew tremulous and very pallid, and aghast, and crying with a loud voice, 'This is indeed *Life* itself!' turned suddenly to regard his beloved:—She was dead!

The Premature Burial

There are certain themes of which the interest is all-absorbing, but which are too entirely horrible for the purposes of legitimate fiction. These the mere romanticist must eschew, if he do not wish to offend or to disgust. They are with propriety handled only when the severity and majesty of truth sanctify and sustain them. We thrill, for example, with the most intense of "pleasurable pain" over the accounts of the Passage of the Beresina, of the Earthquake at Lisbon, of the Plague at London, of the Massacre of St. Bartholomew, or of the stifling of the hundred and twenty-three prisoners in the Black Hole at Calcutta. But in these accounts it is the fact—it is the reality—it is the history which excites. As inventions, we should regard them with simple abhorrence.

I have mentioned some few of the more prominent and august calamities on record; but in these it is the extent, not less than the character of the calamity, which so vividly impresses the fancy. I need not remind the reader that, from the long and weird catalogue of human miseries, I might have selected many individual instances more replete with essential suffering than any of these vast generalities of disaster. The true wretchedness, indeed—the ultimate woe—is particular, not diffuse. That the ghastly extremes of agony are endured by man the unit, and never by man the mass—for this let us thank a merciful God!

To be buried while alive is beyond question the most terrific of these extremes which has ever fallen to the lot of mere mortality. That it has frequently, very frequently, so fallen, will scarcely be denied by those who think. The boundaries which divide life from death are at best shadowy and vague. Who shall say where the one ends and where the other begins? We know that there are diseases in which occur total cessations of all the apparent functions of vitality and yet in which these cessations are merely suspensions, properly so called. They are only temporary pauses in the incomprehensible mechanism. A certain period elapses, and some unseen mysterious principle again sets in motion the magic pinions and the wizard wheels. The silver cord was not for ever loosed, nor the golden bowl irreparably broken. But where meantime was the soul?

Apart, however, from the inevitable conclusion, *a priori*, that such causes must produce such effects that the well-known occurrence of such cases of suspended animation must naturally give rise now and then to premature interments—apart from this consideration, we have the direct testimony of medical and ordinary experience to prove that a vast number of such interments have actually taken place. I might refer at once, if necessary, to a hundred well authenticated instances. One of very remarkable character, and of which the circumstances may be fresh in the memory of some of my readers, occurred not very long ago in the neighbouring city of Baltimore, where it occasioned a painful, intense, and widely-extended excitement. The wife of one of the most respectable citizens—a lawyer of eminence and a member of Congress—was seized with a sudden and unaccountable illness, which completely baffled the skill of her physicians.

After much suffering she died, or was supposed to die. No one suspected, indeed, or had reason to suspect, that she was not actually dead. She presented all the ordinary appearances of death. The face assumed the usual pinched and sunken outline. The lips were of the usual marble pallor. The eyes were lustreless. There was no warmth. Pulsation had ceased. For three days the body was preserved unburied, during which it had acquired a stony rigidity. The funeral, in short, was hastened, on account of the rapid advance of what was supposed to be decomposition.

The lady was deposited in her family vault, which for three subsequent years was undisturbed. At the expiration of this term it was opened for the reception of a sarcophagus;—but, alas! how fearful a shock awaited the husband, who personally threw open the door. As its portals swung outwardly back, some white-apparelled object fell rattling within his arms. It was the skeleton of his wife in her yet unmouldered shroud.

A careful investigation rendered it evident that she had revived within two days after her entombment—that her struggles within the coffin had caused it to fall from a ledge or shelf to the floor, where it was so broken as to permit her escape. A lamp which had been accidentally left full of oil within the tomb was found empty; it might have been exhausted, however, by evaporation. On the uppermost of the steps which led down into the dread chamber was a large fragment of the coffin, with which it seemed that she had endeavoured to arrest attention by striking the iron door. While thus occupied she probably swooned, or possibly died, through sheer terror; and, in falling, her shroud became entangled in some iron-work which projected interiorly. Thus she remained, and thus she rotted, erect.

In the year 1810, a case of living inhumation happened in France, attended with circumstances which go far to warrant the assertion that truth is indeed stranger than fiction. The heroine of the story was a Mademoiselle Victorine Latourcade, a young girl of illustrious family, of wealth, and of great personal beauty. Among her numerous suitors was Julien Bossuet, a poor *littérateur*, or journalist, of Paris. His talents and general amiability had recommended him to the notice of the heiress, by whom he seems to have been truly beloved; but her pride of birth decided her finally to reject him, and to wed a Monsieur Renelle, a banker, and a diplomatist of some eminence.

After marriage, however, this gentleman neglected, and perhaps even more positively ill-treated her. Having passed with him some wretched years, she died,—at least her condition so closely resembled death as to deceive every one who saw her. She was buried—not in a vault—but in an ordinary grave in the village of her nativity. Filled with despair, and still inflamed by the memory of a profound attachment, the lover journeys from the capital to the remote province in which the village lies, with the romantic purpose of disinterring the corpse and possessing himself of its luxuriant tresses. He reaches the grave. At midnight he unearths the coffin, opens it, and is in the act of detaching the hair, when he is arrested by the unclosing of the beloved eyes. In fact the lady had been buried alive. Vitality had not altogether departed; and she was aroused by the caresses of her lover from the lethargy which had been mistaken for death. He bore her frantically to his lodgings in the village. He employed certain powerful restoratives suggested by no little medical learning.

In fine, she revived. She recognised her preserver. She remained with him until by slow degrees she fully recovered her original health. Her woman's heart was not adamant, and this last lesson of love sufficed to soften it. She bestowed it upon Bossuet. She returned no more to her husband, but concealing from him her resurrection, fled with her lover to America. Twenty years afterwards the two returned to France, in the persuasion that time had so greatly altered the lady's appearance that her friends would be unable to recognise her. They were mistaken, however; for at the first meeting Monsieur Renelle did actually recognise and make claim to his wife. This claim she resisted; and a judicial tribunal sustained her in her resistance, deciding that the peculiar circumstances, with the long lapse of years, had extinguished, not only equitably but legally, the authority of the husband.

The *Chirurgical Journal* of Leipsic—a periodical of high authority and merit, which some American bookseller would do well to translate and republish—records in a late number a very distressing event of the character in question.

An officer of artillery, a man of gigantic stature and of robust health, being thrown from an unmanageable horse, received a very severe contusion upon the head, which rendered him insensible at once; the skull was slightly fractured, but no immediate danger was apprehended. Trepanning was accomplished successfully, He was bled, and many other of the ordinary means of relief were adopted. Gradually, however, he fell into a more and more hopeless state of stupor, and, finally, it was thought that he died.

The weather was warm, and he was buried with indecent haste in one of the public cemeteries. His funeral took place on Thursday. On the Sunday following the grounds of the cemetery were as usual much thronged with visitors; and about noon an intense excitement was created by the declaration of a peasant that, while sitting upon the grave of the officer, he had distinctly felt a commotion of the earth, as if occasioned by some one struggling beneath. At first little attention was paid to the man's asseveration; but his evident terror, and the dogged obstinacy with which he persisted in his story, had at length their natural effect upon the crowd. Spades were hurriedly procured, and the grave, which was shamefully shallow, was in a few minutes so far thrown open that the head of its occupant appeared. He was then seemingly dead, but he sat nearly erect within his coffin, the lid of which, in his furious struggles, he had partially uplifted.

He was forthwith conveyed to the nearest hospital, and there pronounced to be still living, although in an asphyctic condition. After some hours he revived, recognised individuals of his acquaintance, and in broken sentences spoke of his agonies in the grave.

From what he related it was clear that he must have been conscious of life for more than an hour, while inhumed, before lapsing into insensibility. The grave was carelessly and loosely filled with an exceedingly porous soil, and thus some air was necessarily admitted. He heard the footsteps of the crowd overhead, and endeavoured to make himself heard in turn. It was the tumult within the grounds of the cemetery, he said, which appeared to awaken him from a deep sleep, but no sooner was he awake than he became fully aware of the awful horrors of his position.

This patient, it is recorded, was doing well, and seemed to be in a fair way of ultimate recovery, but fell a victim to the quackeries of medical experiment. The galvanic battery was applied, and he suddenly expired in one of those ecstatic paroxysms which occasionally it superinduces.

The mention of the galvanic battery, nevertheless, recalls to my memory a well-known and very extraordinary case in point, where its action proved the means of restoring to animation a young attorney of London, who had been interred for two days. This occurred in 1831, and created at the time a very profound sensation wherever it was made the subject of converse.

The patient, Mr. Edward Stapleton, had died apparently of typhus fever, accompanied with some anomalous symptoms which had excited the curiosity of his medical attendants. Upon his seeming decease his friends were requested to sanction a *post-mortem* examination, but declined to permit it. As often happens when such refusals are made, the practitioners resolved to disinter the body and dissect it at leisure in private. Arrangements were easily effected with some of the numerous corps of body-snatchers with which London abounds; and upon the third night after the funeral, the supposed corpse was unearthed from a grave eight feet deep, and deposited in the operating chamber of one of the private hospitals.

An incision of some extent had been actually made in the abdomen, when the fresh and undecayed appearance of the subject suggested an application of the battery. One experiment succeeded another, and the customary effects supervened, with nothing to characterise them in any respect except upon one or two occasions a more than ordinary degree of life-likeness in the convulsive action.

It grew late. The day was about to dawn, and it was thought expedient at length to proceed at once to the dissection. A student, however, was especially desirous of testing a theory of his own, and insisted upon applying the battery to one of the pectoral muscles. A rough gash was made, and a wire hastily brought in contact, when the patient with a hurried but quite unconvulsive movement, arose from the table, stepped into the middle of the floor, gazed about him uneasily for a few seconds, and then spoke. What he said was unintelligible; but the words were uttered; the syllabification was distinct. Having spoken, he fell heavily to the floor.

For some moments all were paralysed with awe—but the urgency of the case soon restored them to their presence of mind. It was seen that Mr. Stapleton was alive, although in a swoon. Upon exhibition of ether he revived and was rapidly restored to health, and to the society of his friends—from whom, however, all knowledge of his resuscitation was withheld, until a relapse was no longer to be apprehended. Their wonder—their rapturous astonishment—may be conceived.

The most thrilling peculiarity of this incident, nevertheless, is involved in what Mr. S. himself asserts. He declares that at no period was he altogether insensible—that, dully and confusedly, he was aware of everything which happened to him, from the moment in which he was pronounced *dead* by his physicians, to that in which he fell swooning to the floor of the hospital. "I am alive," were the uncomprehended words which, upon recognising the locality of the dissecting-room, he had endeavoured in his extremity to utter.

It were an easy matter to multiply such histories as these, but I forbear, for, indeed, we have no need of such to establish the fact that premature interments occur. When we reflect how very rarely, from the nature of the case, we have it in our power to detect them, we must admit that they may *frequently* occur without our cognisance. Scarcely, in truth, is a graveyard encroached upon for any purpose, to any great extent, that skeletons are not found in postures which suggest the most fearful of suspicions.

Fearful indeed the suspicion, but more fearful the doom! It may be asserted, without hesitation, that no event is so terribly well adapted to inspire the supremeness of bodily and of mental distress as is burial before death. The unendurable oppression of the lungs—the stifling fumes of the damp earth—the clinging to the death garments—the rigid embrace of the narrow house—the blackness of the absolute night—the silence like a sea that overwhelms—the unseen but palpable presence of the conqueror worm—these things, with thoughts of the air and grass above, with memory of dear friends who would fly to save us if but informed of our fate, and with consciousness that of this fate they can *never* be informed—that our hopeless portion is that of the really dead—these considerations, I say, carry into the heart which still palpitates a degree of appalling and intolerable horror from which the most daring imagination must recoil.

We know of nothing so agonising upon earth we can dream of nothing half so hideous in the realms of the nethermost hell; and thus all narratives upon this topic have an interest so profound; an interest, nevertheless, which, through the sacred awe of the topic itself, very properly and very peculiarly depends upon our conviction of the *truth* of the matter narrated. What I have now to tell is of my own actual knowledge—of my own positive and personal experience.

For several years I have been subject to attacks of the singular disorder which physicians have agreed to term catalepsy in default of a more definitive title. Although both the immediate and the predisposing causes, and even the actual diagnosis of this disease, are still mysterious, its obvious and apparent character is sufficiently well understood. Its variations seem to be chiefly of degree. Sometimes the patient lies for a day only, or even for a shorter period, in a species of exaggerated lethargy. He is senseless and externally motionless, but the pulsation of the heart is still faintly perceptible; some traces of warmth remain; a slight colour lingers within the centre of the cheek; and upon application of a mirror to the lips we can detect a torpid, unequal, and vacillating action of the lungs.

Then again the duration of the trance is for weeks—even for months; while the closest scrutiny, and the most rigorous medical tests, fail to establish any material distinction between the state of the sufferer and what we conceive of absolute death. Very usually he is saved from premature interment solely by the knowledge of his friends that he has been previously subject to catalepsy, by the consequent suspicion excited, and, above all, by the non-appearance of decay. The advances of the malady are, luckily, gradual. The first manifestations, although marked, are unequivocal. The fits grow successively more and more distinctive, and endure each for a longer term than the preceding. In this lies the principal security from inhumation. The unfortunate whose *first* attack should be of the extreme character which is occasionally seen would almost inevitably be consigned alive to the tomb.

My own case differed in no important particular from those mentioned in medical books. Sometimes, with out any apparent cause, I sank, little by little, into a condition of semi-syncope or half-swoon; and in this condition, without pain, without ability to stir, or, strictly speaking, to think, but with a dull lethargic consciousness of life and of the presence of those who surrounded my bed, I remained, until the crisis of the disease restored me, suddenly, to perfect sensation. At other times I was quickly and impetuously smitten. I grew sick, and numb, and chilly, and dizzy, and so fell prostrate at once. Then for weeks all was void, and black, and silent, and Nothing became the universe. Total annihilation could be no more. From these latter attacks I awoke, however, with a gradation slow in proportion to the suddenness of the seizure. Just as the day dawns to the friendless and houseless beggar who roams the street throughout the long desolate winter night—just so tardily—just so wearily—just so cheerily came back the light of the soul to me.

Apart from the tendency to trance, however, my general health appeared to be good; nor could I perceive that it was at all affected by the one prevalent malady—unless, indeed, an idiosyncrasy in my ordinary *sleep* may be looked upon as superinduced. Upon awaking from slumber, I could never gain at once thorough possession of my senses, and always remained for many minutes in much bewilderment and perplexity; the mental faculties in general, but the memory in especial, being in a condition of absolute abeyance.

In all that I endured there was no physical suffering, but of moral distress an infinitude. My fancy grew charnel. I talked "of worms, of tombs, and epitaphs." I was lost in reveries of death, and the idea of premature burial held continual possession of my brain. The ghastly danger to which I was subjected haunted me day and night. In the former, the torture of meditation was excessive—in the latter, supreme. When the grim darkness overspread the earth, then, with very horror of thought, I shook—shook as the quivering plumes upon the hearse. When nature could endure wakefulness no longer, it was with a struggle that I consented to sleep—for I shuddered to reflect that upon awaking I might find myself the tenant of a grave. And when, finally, I sank into slumber, it was only to rush at once into a world of phantasms, above which, with vast, sable, overshadowing wings, hovered predominant the one sepulchral idea.

From the innumerable images of gloom which thus oppressed me in dreams, I select for record but a solitary vision. Methought I was immersed in a cataleptic trance of more than usual duration and profundity. Suddenly there came an icy hand upon my forehead, and an impatient gibbering voice whispered the word "arise!" within my ear.

I sat erect. The darkness was total. I could not see the figure of him who had aroused me. I could call to mind neither the period at which I had fallen into the trance, nor the locality in which I then lay. While I remained motionless, and busied in endeavours to collect my thoughts, the cold hand grasped me fiercely by the wrist, shaking it petulantly, while the gibbering voice said again:

"Arise! did I not bid thee arise?"

"And who," I demanded, "art thou?"

"I have no name in the regions which I inhabit," replied the voice, mournfully; "I was mortal, but am fiend I was merciless, but am pitiful. Thou dost feel that I shudder. My teeth chatter as I speak, yet it is not with the chilliness of the night—of the night without end. But this hideousness is insufferable. How canst *thou* tranquilly sleep? I cannot rest for the cry of these great agonies. These sights are more than I can bear. Get thee up! Come with me into the outer night, and let me unfold to thee the graves. Is not this a spectacle of woe!—Behold!"

I looked; and the unseen figure, which still grasped me by the wrist, had caused to be thrown open the graves of all mankind, and from each issued the faint phosphoric radiance of decay, so that I could see into the innermost recesses, and there view the shrouded bodies in their sad and solemn slumbers with the worm. But, alas! the real sleepers were fewer by many millions than those who slumbered not at all; and there was a feeble struggling; and there was a general sad unrest; and from out the depths of the countless pits there came a melancholy rustling from the garments of the buried; and of those who seemed tranquilly to repose I saw that a vast number had changed, in a greater or less degree, the rigid and uneasy position in which they had originally been entombed. And the voice again said to me as I gazed:

"Is it not—O, is it *not* a pitiful sight?" But before I could find word to reply, the figure had ceased to grasp my wrist, the phosphoric lights expired, and the graves were closed with a sudden violence, while from out them arose a tumult of despairing cries, saying again, "Is it not—O, God! is it *not* a very pitiful sight?"

Phantasies such as these presenting themselves at night extended their terrific influence far into my waking hours. My nerves became thoroughly unstrung, and I fell a prey to perpetual horror. I hesitated to ride, or to walk, or to indulge in any exercise that would carry me from home. In fact, I no longer dared trust myself out of the immediate presence of those who were aware of my proneness to catalepsy, lest, falling into one of my usual fits, I should be buried before my real condition could be ascertained. I doubted the care, the fidelity of my dearest friends. I dreaded that, in some trance of more than customary duration, they might be prevailed upon to regard me as irrecoverable.

I even went so far as to fear that, as I occasioned much trouble, they might be glad to consider any very protracted attack as sufficient excuse for getting rid of me altogether. It was in vain they endeavoured to reassure me by the most solemn promises. I exacted the most sacred oaths that under no circumstances they would bury me until decomposition had so materially advanced as to render further preservation impossible; and even then my mortal terrors would listen to no reason, would accept no consolation. I entered into a series of elaborate precautions. Among other things, I had the family vault so remodelled as to admit of being readily opened from within. The slightest pressure upon a long lever that extended far into the tomb would cause the iron portals to fly back.

There were arrangements also for the free admission of air and light, and convenient receptacles for food and water, within immediate reach of the coffin intended for my reception. This coffin was warmly and softly padded, and was provided with a lid, fashioned upon the principle of the vault-door, with the addition of springs so contrived that the feeblest movement of the body would be sufficient to set it at liberty. Besides all this, there was suspended from the roof of the tomb a large bell, the rope of which, it was designed, should extend through a hole in the coffin, and so be fastened to one of the hands of the corpse. But, alas! what avails the vigilance against the destiny of man? Not even these well-contrived securities sufficed to save from the uttermost agonies of living inhumation a wretch to these agonies foredoomed!

There arrived an epoch—as often before there had arrived—in which I found myself emerging from total unconsciousness into the first feeble and indefinite sense of existence. Slowly—with a tortoise gradation—approached the faint grey dawn of the psychal day. A torpid uneasiness. An apathetic endurance of dull pain. No care—no hope—no effort. Then, after long interval, a ringing in the ears; then, after a lapse still longer, a pricking or tingling sensation in the extremities; then a seemingly eternal period of pleasurable quiescence, during which the awakening feelings are struggling into thought; then a brief re-sinking into nonentity; then a sudden recovery.

At length the slight quivering of an eyelid, and immediately thereupon an electric shock of a terror, deadly and indefinite, which sends the blood in torrents from the temples to the heart. And now the first positive effort to think. And now the first endeavour to remember. And now a partial and evanescent success. And now the memory has so far regained its dominion that, in some measure, I am cognisant of my state. I feel that I am not awaking from ordinary sleep. I recollect that I have been subject to catalepsy. And now, at last, as if by the rush of an ocean, my shuddering spirit is overwhelmed by the one grim danger—by the one spectral and ever-prevalent idea.

For some minutes after this fancy possessed me, I remained without motion. And why? I could not summon courage to move. I dared not make the effort which was to satisfy me of my fate; and yet there was something at my heart which whispered me *it was sure*. Despair—such as no other species of wretchedness ever calls into being—despair alone urged me after long irresolution to uplift the heavy lids of my eyes. I uplifted them. It was dark—all dark. I knew that the fit was over. I knew that the crisis of my disorder had long passed. I knew that I had now fully recovered the use of my visual faculties—and yet it was dark—all dark—the intense and utter raylessness of the night that endureth for evermore.

I endeavoured to shriek, and my lips and my parched tongue moved convulsively together in the attempt—but no voice issued from the cavernous lungs, which, oppressed as if by the weight of some incumbent mountain, gasped and palpitated, with the heart, at every elaborate and struggling inspiration.

The movement of the jaws in this effort to cry aloud showed me that they were bound up, as is usual with the dead. I felt too that I lay upon some hard substance; and by something similar my sides were also closely compressed. So far I had not ventured to stir any of my limbs—but now I violently threw up my arms, which had been lying at length with the wrists crossed. They struck a solid wooden substance which extended above my person at an elevation of not more than six inches from my face. I could no longer doubt that I reposed within a coffin at last.

And now amid all my infinite miseries came sweetly the

cherub hope—for I thought of my precautions. I writhed and made spasmodic exertions to force open the lid; it would not move. I felt my wrists for the bellrope; it was not to be found. And now the comforter fled for ever, and a still sterner despair reigned triumphant; for I could not help perceiving the absence of the paddings which I had so carefully prepared; and then too there came suddenly to my nostrils the strong peculiar odour of moist earth. The conclusion was irresistible. I was *not* within the vault. I had fallen into a trance while absent from home—while among strangers—when or how I could not remember; and it was they who had buried me as a dog—nailed up in some common coffin—and thrust deep, deep, and for ever, into some ordinary and nameless *grave*.

As this awful conviction forced itself thus into the innermost chambers of my soul, I once again struggled to cry aloud; and in this second endeavour I succeeded. A long, wild, and continuous shriek, or yell of agony resounded through the realms of the subterrene night.

"Hillo! hillo, there!" said a gruff voice, in reply.

"What the devil's the matter now?" said a second.

"Get out o' that!" said a third.

"What do you mean by yowling in that ere kind of style like a cattymount?" said a fourth; and hereupon I was seized and shaken without ceremony for several minutes by a junto of very rough-looking individuals. They did not arouse me from my slumber—for I was wide awake when I screamed—but they restored me to the full possession of my memory.

This adventure occurred near Richmond, in Virginia. Accompanied by a friend I had proceeded upon a gunning expedition some miles down the banks of James River. Night approached, and we were overtaken by a storm. The cabin of a small sloop lying at anchor in the stream, and laden with garden mould, afforded us the only available shelter. We made the best of it, and passed the night on board. I slept in one of the only two berths in the vessel—and the berths of a sloop of sixty or seventy tons need scarcely be described. That which I occupied had no bedding of any kind. Its extreme width was eighteen inches.

The distance of its bottom from the deck overhead was precisely the same. I found it a matter of exceeding difficulty to squeeze myself in. Nevertheless, I slept soundly; and the whole of my vision—for it was no dream, and no nightmare—arose naturally from the circumstances of my position—from my ordinary bias of thought, and from the difficulty, to which I have alluded, of collecting my senses, and especially of regaining my memory for a long time after awaking from slumber. The men who shook me were the crew of the sloop and some labourers engaged to unload it. From the load itself came the earthy smell. The bandage about the jaws was a silk handkerchief in which I had bound up my head in default of my customary nightcap.

The tortures endured, however, were indubitably quite equal for the time to those of actual sepulture. They were fearfully—they were inconceivably hideous; but out of evil proceeded good, for their very excess wrought in my spirit an inevitable revulsion. My soul acquired tone—acquired temper. I went abroad. I took vigorous exercise. I breathed the free air of heaven. I thought upon other subjects than death. I discarded my medical books. *Buchan* I burned. I read no *Night Thoughts*—no fustian about churchyards—no bugaboo tales—*such as this.* In short I became a new man and lived a man's life. From that memorable night I dismissed for ever my charnel apprehensions, and with them vanished the cataleptic disorder, of which perhaps they had been less the consequence than the cause.

There are moments when, even to the sober eye of reason, the world of our sad humanity may assume the semblance of a hell; but the imagination of man is no Carathis to explore with impunity its every cavern. Alas! the grim legion of sepulchral terrors cannot be regarded as altogether fanciful; but, like the demons in whose company Afrasiab made his voyage down the Oxus, they must sleep or they will devour us—they must be suffered to slumber or we perish.

The Purloined Letter

Nil sapientiae odiosius acumine nimio.—Seneca.

At Paris, just after dark one gusty evening in the autumn of 18—, I was enjoying the twofold luxury of meditation and a *meerschaum*, in company with my friend C. Auguste Dupin, in his little back library, or book-closet, *au troisième, No. 33, Rue Dunôt, Faubourg St. Germain*. For one hour at least we had maintained a profound silence; while each, to any casual observer, might have seemed intently and exclusively occupied with the curling eddies of smoke that oppressed the atmosphere of the chamber. For myself, however, I was mentally discussing certain topics which had formed matter for conversation between us at an earlier period of the evening; I mean the affair of the Rue Morgue, and the mystery attending the murder of Marie Rogêt. I looked upon it, therefore, as something of a coincidence, when the door of our apartment was thrown open and admitted our old acquaintance, Monsieur G——, the *prefect* of the Parisian police.

We gave him a hearty welcome; for there was nearly half as much of the entertaining as of the contemptible about the man, and we had not seen him for several years. We had been sitting in the dark, and Dupin now arose for the purpose of lighting a lamp, but sat down again, without doing so, upon G.'s saying that he had called to consult us, or rather to ask the opinion of my friend, about some official business which had occasioned a great deal of trouble.

"If it is any point requiring reflection," observed Dupin, as he forbore to enkindle the wick, "we shall examine it to better purpose in the dark."

"That is another of your odd notions," said the *Prefect*, who had a fashion of calling every thing "odd" that was beyond his comprehension, and thus lived amid an absolute legion of "oddities."

"Very true," said Dupin, as he supplied his visitor with a pipe, and rolled towards him a comfortable chair.

"And what is the difficulty now?" I asked. "Nothing more in the assassination way, I hope?"

"Oh no; nothing of that nature. The fact is, the business is *very* simple indeed, and I make no doubt that we can manage it sufficiently well ourselves; but then I thought Dupin would like to hear the details of it, because it is so excessively *odd*."

"Simple and odd," said Dupin.

"Why, yes; and not exactly that, either. The fact is, we have all been a good deal puzzled because the affair *is* so simple, and yet baffles us altogether."

"Perhaps it is the very simplicity of the thing which puts you at fault," said my friend.

"What nonsense you *do* talk!" replied the *prefect*, laughing heartily.

"Perhaps the mystery is a little *too* plain," said Dupin.

"Oh, good heavens! who ever heard of such an idea?"

"A little too self-evident."

"Ha! ha! ha—ha! ha! ha!—ho! ho! ho!" roared our visitor, profoundly amused, "oh, Dupin, you will be the death of me yet!"

"And what, after all, *is* the matter on hand?" I asked.

"Why, I will tell you," replied the *prefect*, as he gave a long, steady and contemplative puff, and settled himself in his chair. "I will tell you in a few words; but, before I begin, let me caution you that this is an affair demanding the greatest secrecy, and that I should most probably lose the position I now hold, were it known that I confided it to anyone."

"Proceed," said I.

"Or not," said Dupin.

"Well, then; I have received personal information, from a very high quarter, that a certain document of the last importance, has been purloined from the royal apartments. The individual who purloined it is known; this beyond a doubt; he was seen to take it. It is known, also, that it still remains in his possession."

"How is this known?" asked Dupin.

"It is clearly inferred," replied the *prefect*, "from the nature of the document, and from the non-appearance of certain results which would at once arise from its passing *out* of the robber's possession—that is to say, from his employing it as he must design in the end to employ it."

"Be a little more explicit," I said.

"Well, I may venture so far as to say that the paper gives its holder a certain power in a certain quarter where such power is immensely valuable." The *prefect* was fond of the cant of diplomacy.

"Still I do not quite understand," said Dupin.

"No? Well; the disclosure of the document to a third person, who shall be nameless, would bring in question the honour of a personage of most exalted station; and this fact gives the holder of the document an ascendancy over the illustrious personage whose honour and peace are so jeopardized."

"But this ascendancy," I interposed, "would depend upon the robber's knowledge of the loser's knowledge of the robber. Who would dare—"

"The thief," said G., "is the Minister D—, who dares all things, those unbecoming as well as those becoming a man. The method of the theft was not less ingenious than bold. The document in question—a letter, to be frank—had been received by the personage robbed while alone in the royal *boudoir*. During its perusal she was suddenly interrupted by the entrance of the other exalted personage from whom especially it was her wish to conceal it. After a hurried and vain endeavour to thrust it in a drawer, she was forced to place it, open as it was, upon a table. The address, however, was uppermost, and, the contents thus unexposed, the letter escaped notice.

"At this juncture enters the Minister D—. His lynx eye immediately perceives the paper, recognises the handwriting of the address, observes the confusion of the personage addressed, and fathoms her secret. After some business transactions, hurried through in his ordinary manner, he produces a letter somewhat similar to the one in question, opens it, pretends to read it, and then places it in close juxtaposition to the other. Again he converses, for some fifteen minutes, upon the public affairs. At length, in taking leave, he takes also from the table the letter to which he had no claim. Its rightful owner saw, but, of course, dared not call attention to the act, in the presence of the third personage who stood at her elbow. The minister decamped; leaving his own letter—one of no importance—upon the table."

"Here, then," said Dupin to me, "you have precisely what you demand to make the ascendancy complete—the robber's knowledge of the loser's knowledge of the robber."

"Yes," replied the *prefect*; "and the power thus attained has, for some months past, been wielded, for political purposes, to a very dangerous extent. The personage robbed is more thoroughly convinced, every day, of the necessity of reclaiming her letter. But this, of course, cannot be done openly. In fine, driven to despair, she has committed the matter to me."

"Than whom," said Dupin, amid a perfect whirlwind of smoke, "no more sagacious agent could, I suppose, be desired, or even imagined."

"You flatter me," replied the *prefect*; "but it is possible that some such opinion may have been entertained."

"It is clear," said I, "as you observe, that the letter is still in possession of the minister; since it is this possession, and not any employment of the letter, which bestows the power. With the employment the power departs."

"True," said G.; "and upon this conviction I proceeded. My first care was to make thorough search of the minister's hotel; and here my chief embarrassment lay in the necessity of searching without his knowledge. Beyond all things, I have been warned of the danger which would result from giving him reason to suspect our design."

"But," said I, "you are quite *au fait* in these investigations. The Parisian police have done this thing often before."

"O yes; and for this reason I did not despair. The habits of the minister gave me, too, a great advantage. He is frequently absent from home all night. His servants are by no means numerous. They sleep at a distance from their master's apartment, and, being chiefly Neapolitans, are readily made drunk. I have keys, as you know, with which I can open any chamber or cabinet in Paris. For three months a night has not passed, during the greater part of which I have not been engaged, personally, in ransacking the D— Hotel. My honour is interested, and, to mention a great secret, the reward is enormous. So I did not abandon the search until I had become fully satisfied that the thief is a more astute man than myself. I fancy that I have investigated every nook and corner of the premises in which it is possible that the paper can be concealed."

"But is it not possible," I suggested, "that although the letter may be in possession of the minister, as it unquestionably is, he may have concealed it elsewhere than upon his own premises?"

"This is barely possible," said Dupin. "The present peculiar condition of affairs at court, and especially of those intrigues in which D— is known to be involved, would render the instant availability of the document—its susceptibility of being produced at a moment's notice—a point of nearly equal importance with its possession."

"Its susceptibility of being produced?" said I.

"That is to say, of being *destroyed*," said Dupin.

"True," I observed; "the paper is clearly then upon the premises. As for its being upon the person of the minister, we may consider that as out of the question."

"Entirely," said the *prefect*. "He has been twice waylaid, as if by footpads, and his person rigorously searched under my own inspection."

"You might have spared yourself this trouble," said Dupin.

"D—, I presume, is not altogether a fool, and, if not, must have anticipated these waylayings, as a matter of course."

"Not *altogether* a fool," said G., "but then he's a poet, which I take to be only one remove from a fool."

"True," said Dupin, after a long and thoughtful whiff from his *meerschaum*, "although I have been guilty of certain doggerel myself."

"Suppose you detail," said I, "the particulars of your search."

"Why the fact is, we took our time, and we searched *everywhere*. I have had long experience in these affairs. I took the entire building, room by room; devoting the nights of a whole week to each. We examined, first, the furniture of each apartment. We opened every possible drawer; and I presume you know that, to a properly trained police agent, such a thing as a secret drawer is impossible. Any man is a dolt who permits a '*secret*' drawer to escape him in a search of this kind. The thing is so plain. There is a certain amount of bulk—of space—to be accounted for in every cabinet. Then we have accurate rules. The fiftieth part of a line could not escape us. After the cabinets we took the chairs. The cushions we probed with the fine long needles you have seen me employ. From the tables we removed the tops."

"Why so?"

"Sometimes the top of a table, or other similarly arranged piece of furniture, is removed by the person wishing to conceal an article; then the leg is excavated, the article deposited within the cavity, and the top replaced. The bottoms and tops of bed-posts are employed in the same way."

"But could not the cavity be detected by sounding?" I asked.

"By no means, if, when the article is deposited, a sufficient wadding of cotton be placed around it. Besides, in our case, we were obliged to proceed without noise."

"But you could not have removed—you could not have taken to pieces *all* articles of furniture in which it would have been possible to make a deposit in the manner you mention. A letter may be compressed into a thin spiral roll, not differing much in shape or bulk from a large knitting-needle, and in this form it might be inserted into the rung of a chair, for example. You did not take to pieces all the chairs?"

"Certainly not; but we did better—we examined the rungs of every chair in the hotel, and, indeed the jointings of every description of furniture, by the aid of a most powerful microscope. Had there been any traces of recent disturbance we should not have failed to detect it instantly. A single grain of gimlet-dust, for example, would have been as obvious as an apple. Any disorder in the gluing—any unusual gaping in the joints—would have sufficed to insure detection."

"I presume you looked to the mirrors, between the boards and the plates, and you probed the beds and the bedclothes, as well as the curtains and carpets."

"That of course; and when we had absolutely completed every particle of the furniture in this way, then we examined the house itself. We divided its entire surface into compartments, which we numbered, so that none might be missed; then we scrutinized each individual square inch throughout the premises, including the two houses immediately adjoining, with the microscope, as before."

"The two houses adjoining!" I exclaimed; "you must have had a great deal of trouble."

"We had; but the reward offered is prodigious!"

"You include the *grounds* about the houses?"

"All the grounds are paved with brick. They gave us comparatively little trouble. We examined the moss between the bricks, and found it undisturbed."

"You looked among D—'s papers, of course, and into the books of the library?"

"Certainly; we opened every package and parcel; we not only opened every book, but we turned over every leaf in each volume, not contenting ourselves with a mere shake, according to the fashion of some of our police officers. We also measured the thickness of every book-cover, with the most accurate admeasurement, and applied to each the most jealous scrutiny of the microscope. Had any of the bindings been recently meddled with, it would have been utterly impossible that the fact should have escaped observation. Some five or six volumes, just from the hands of the binder, we carefully probed, longitudinally, with the needles."

"You explored the floors beneath the carpets?"

"Beyond doubt. We removed every carpet, and examined the boards with the microscope."

"And the paper on the walls?"

"Yes."

"You looked into the cellars?"

"We did."

"Then," I said, "you have been making a miscalculation, and the letter is *not* upon the premises, as you suppose."

"I fear you are right there," said the *prefect*. "And now, Dupin, what would you advise me to do?"

"To make a thorough re-search of the premises."

"That is absolutely needless," replied G—. "I am not more sure that I breathe than I am that the letter is not at the hotel."

"I have no better advice to give you," said Dupin. "You have, of course, an accurate description of the letter?"

"Oh yes!"—And here the *prefect*, producing a memorandum-book proceeded to read aloud a minute account of the internal, and especially of the external appearance of the missing document. Soon after finishing the perusal of this description, he took his departure, more entirely depressed in spirits than I had ever known the good gentleman before. In about a month afterwards he paid us another visit, and found us occupied very nearly as before. He took a pipe and a chair and entered into some ordinary conversation. At length I said,—

"Well, but G—, what of the purloined letter? I presume you have at last made up your mind that there is no such thing as overreaching the minister?"

"Confound him, say I—yes; I made the re-examination, however, as Dupin suggested—but it was all labour lost, as I knew it would be."

"How much was the reward offered, did you say?" asked Dupin.

"Why, a very great deal—a *very* liberal reward—I don't like to say how much, precisely; but one thing I *will* say, that I wouldn't mind giving my individual check for fifty thousand *francs* to any one who could obtain me that letter. The fact is, it is becoming of more and more importance every day; and the reward has been lately doubled. If it were trebled, however, I could do no more than I have done."

"Why, yes," said Dupin, drawlingly, between the whiffs of his meerschaum, "I really—think, G—, you have not exerted yourself—to the utmost in this matter. You might—do a little more, I think, eh?"

"How?—in what way?'

"Why—puff, puff—you might—puff, puff—employ counsel in the matter, eh?—puff, puff, puff. Do you remember the story they tell of Abernethy?"

"No; hang Abernethy!"

"To be sure! hang him and welcome. But, once upon a time, a certain rich miser conceived the design of spunging upon this Abernethy for a medical opinion. Getting up, for this purpose, an ordinary conversation in a private company, he insinuated his case to the physician, as that of an imaginary individual.

"'We will suppose,' said the miser, 'that his symptoms are such and such; now, doctor, what would *you* have directed him to take?'

"'Take!' said Abernethy, 'why, take *advice*, to be sure.'"

"But," said the *prefect*, a little discomposed, "I am *perfectly* willing to take advice, and to pay for it. I would *really* give fifty thousand *francs* to anyone who would aid me in the matter."

"In that case," replied Dupin, opening a drawer, and producing a cheque-book, "you may as well fill me up a cheque for the amount mentioned. When you have signed it, I will hand you the letter."

I was astounded. The *prefect* appeared absolutely thunder-stricken. For some minutes he remained speechless and motionless, looking incredulously at my friend with open mouth, and eyes that seemed starting from their sockets; then, apparently recovering himself in some measure, he seized a pen, and after several pauses and vacant stares, finally filled up and signed a check for fifty thousand *francs*, and handed it across the table to Dupin. The latter examined it carefully and deposited it in his pocket-book; then, unlocking an *escritoire*, took thence a letter and gave it to the *prefect*. This functionary grasped it in a perfect agony of joy, opened it with a trembling hand, cast a rapid glance at its contents, and then, scrambling and struggling to the door, rushed at length unceremoniously from the room and from the house, without having uttered a syllable since Dupin had requested him to fill up the cheque.

When he had gone, my friend entered into some explanations.

"The Parisian police," he said, "are exceedingly able in their way. They are persevering, ingenious, cunning, and thoroughly versed in the knowledge which their duties seem chiefly to demand. Thus, when G— detailed to us his mode of searching the premises at the Hotel D—, I felt entire confidence in his having made a satisfactory investigation—so far as his labours extended."

"So far as his labours extended?" said I.

"Yes," said Dupin. "The measures adopted were not only the best of their kind, but carried out to absolute perfection. Had the letter been deposited within the range of their search, these fellows would, beyond a question, have found it."

I merely laughed—but he seemed quite serious in all that he said.

"The measures, then," he continued, "were good in their kind, and well executed; their defect lay in their being inapplicable to the case, and to the man. A certain set of highly ingenious resources are, with the *prefect*, a sort of Procrustean bed, to which he forcibly adapts his designs. But he perpetually errs by being too deep or too shallow, for the matter in hand; and many a schoolboy is a better reasoner than he. I knew one about eight years of age, whose success at guessing in the game of 'even and odd' attracted universal admiration. This game is simple, and is played with marbles. One player holds in his hand a number of these toys, and demands of another whether that number is even or odd. If the guess is right, the guesser wins one; if wrong, he loses one. The boy to whom I allude won all the marbles of the school. Of course he had some principle of guessing; and this lay in mere observation and admeasurement of the astuteness of his opponents. For example, an arrant simpleton is his opponent, and, holding up his closed hand, asks, 'are they even or odd?'

"Our schoolboy replies, 'odd,' and loses; but upon the second trial he wins, for he then says to himself, 'the simpleton had them even upon the first trial, and his amount of cunning is just sufficient to make him have them odd upon the second; I will therefore guess odd;'—he guesses odd, and wins. Now, with a simpleton a degree above the first, he would have reasoned thus: 'This fellow finds that in the first instance I guessed odd, and, in the second, he will propose to himself, upon the first impulse, a simple variation from even to odd, as did the first simpleton; but then a second thought will suggest that this is too simple a variation, and finally he will decide upon putting it even as before. I will therefore guess even;'—he guesses even, and wins. Now this mode of reasoning in the schoolboy, whom his fellows termed 'lucky,'—what, in its last analysis, is it?"

"It is merely," I said, "an identification of the reasoner's intellect with that of his opponent."

"It is," said Dupin; "and, upon inquiring of the boy by what means he effected the *thorough* identification in which his success consisted, I received answer as follows: 'When I wish to find out how wise, or how stupid, or how good, or how wicked is anyone, or what are his thoughts at the moment, I fashion the expression of my face, as accurately as possible, in accordance with the expression of his, and then wait to see what thoughts or sentiments arise in my mind or heart, as if to match or correspond with the expression.' This response of the schoolboy lies at the bottom of all the spurious profundity which has been attributed to Rochefoucault, to La Bougive, to Machiavelli, and to Campanella."

"And the identification," I said, "of the reasoner's intellect with that of his opponent, depends, if I understand you aright, upon the accuracy with which the opponent's intellect is admeasured."

"For its practical value it depends upon this," replied Dupin; "and the *prefect* and his *cohort* fail so frequently, first, by default of this identification, and, secondly, by ill-admeasurement, or rather through non-admeasurement, of the intellect with which they are engaged. They consider only their *own* ideas of ingenuity; and, in searching for anything hidden, advert only to the modes in which *they* would have hidden it. They are right in this much—that their own ingenuity is a faithful representative of that of *the mass;* but when the cunning of the individual felon is diverse in character from their own, the felon foils them, of course. This always happens when it is above their own, and very usually when it is below. They have no variation of principle in their investigations; at best, when urged by some unusual emergency—by some extraordinary reward—they extend or exaggerate their old modes of *practice*, without touching their principles.

"What, for example, in this case of D—, has been done to vary the principle of action? What is all this boring, and probing, and sounding, and scrutinizing with the microscope and dividing the surface of the building into registered square inches—what is it all but an exaggeration *of the application* of the one principle or set of principles of search, which are based upon the one set of notions regarding human ingenuity, to which the *prefect*, in the long routine of his duty, has been accustomed? Do you not see he has taken it for granted that *all* men proceed to conceal a letter,—not exactly in a gimlet hole bored in a chair-leg—but, at least, in some out-of-the-way hole or corner suggested by the same tenor of thought which would urge a man to secrete a letter in a gimlet-hole bored in a chair-leg? And do you not see also, that such *recherchés* nooks for concealment are adapted only for ordinary occasions, and would be adopted only by ordinary intellects; for, in all cases of concealment, a disposal of the article concealed—a disposal of it in this *recherché* manner,—is, in the very first instance, presumable and presumed; and thus its discovery depends, not at all upon the acumen, but altogether upon the mere care, patience, and determination of the seekers; and where the case is of importance—or, what amounts to the same thing in the political eyes, when the reward is of magnitude,—the qualities in question have *never* been known to fail.

"You will now understand what I meant in suggesting that, had the purloined letter been hidden anywhere within the limits of the *prefect's* examination—in other words, had the principle of its concealment been comprehended within the principles of the *prefect*—its discovery would have been a matter altogether beyond question. This functionary, however, has been thoroughly mystified; and the remote source of his defeat lies in the supposition that the minister is a fool, because he has acquired renown as a poet. All fools are poets; this the *prefect* feels; and he is merely guilty of a *non distributio medii* in thence inferring that all poets are fools."

"But is this really the poet?" I asked. "There are two brothers, I know; and both have attained reputation in letters. The minister I believe has written learnedly on the Differential Calculus. He is a mathematician, and no poet."

"You are mistaken; I know him well; he is both. As poet *and* mathematician, he would reason well; as mere mathematician, he could not have reasoned at all, and thus would have been at the mercy of the *prefect*."

"You surprise me," I said, "by these opinions, which have been contradicted by the voice of the world. You do not mean to set at naught the well-digested idea of centuries. The mathematical reason has long been regarded as *the* reason *par excellence*."

"'*Il y a à parièr*,'" replied Dupin, quoting from Chamfort, "'*que toute idée publique, toute convention reçue est une sottise, car elle a convenue au plus grand nombre.*' The mathematicians, I grant you, have done their best to promulgate the popular error to which you allude, and which is none the less an error for its promulgation as truth. With an art worthy a better cause, for example, they have insinuated the term 'analysis' into application to algebra. The French are the originators of this particular deception; but if a term is of any importance—if words derive any value from applicability—then 'analysis' conveys 'algebra' about as much as, in Latin, '*ambitus*' implies 'ambition,' '*religio*' 'religion,' or '*homines honesti*,' a set of *honourable* men."

"You have a quarrel on hand, I see," said I, "with some of the algebraists of Paris; but proceed."

"I dispute the availability, and thus the value, of that reason which is cultivated in any especial form other than the abstractly logical. I dispute, in particular, the reason educed by mathematical study. The mathematics are the science of form and quantity; mathematical reasoning is merely logic applied to observation upon form and quantity. The great error lies in supposing that even the truths of what is called *pure* algebra, are abstract or general truths. And this error is so egregious that I am confounded at the universality with which it has been received. Mathematical axioms are *not* axioms of general truth. What is true of *relation*—of form and quantity—is often grossly false in regard to morals, for example. In this latter science it is very usually *un*-true that the aggregated parts are equal to the whole. In chemistry also the axiom fails.

"In the consideration of motive it fails; for two motives, each of a given value, have not, necessarily, a value when united, equal to the sum of their values apart. There are numerous other mathematical truths which are only truths within the limits of *relation*. But the mathematician argues, from his *finite truths*, through habit, as if they were of an absolutely general applicability—as the world indeed imagines them to be. Bryant, in his very learned 'Mythology,' mentions an analogous source of error, when he says that 'although the Pagan fables are not believed, yet we forget ourselves continually, and make inferences from them as existing realities.'

"With the algebraists, however, who are Pagans themselves,

the 'Pagan fables' *are* believed, and the inferences are made, not so much through lapse of memory, as through an unaccountable addling of the brains. In short, I never yet encountered the mere mathematician who could be trusted out of equal roots, or one who did not clandestinely hold it as a point of his faith that x^2+px was absolutely and unconditionally equal to q. Say to one of these gentlemen, by way of experiment, if you please, that you believe occasions may occur where x^2+px is *not* altogether equal to q, and, having made him understand what you mean, get out of his reach as speedily as convenient, for, beyond doubt, he will endeavour to knock you down.

"I mean to say," continued Dupin, while I merely laughed at his last observations, "that if the minister had been no more than a mathematician, the *prefect* would have been under no necessity of giving me this check. I know him, however, as both mathematician and poet, and my measures were adapted to his capacity, with reference to the circumstances by which he was surrounded. I knew him as a courtier, too, and as a bold *intriguant*. Such a man, I considered, could not fail to be aware of the ordinary policial modes of action. He could not have failed to anticipate—and events have proved that he did not fail to anticipate—the waylayings to which he was subjected. He must have foreseen, I reflected, the secret investigations of his premises.

"His frequent absences from home at night, which were hailed by the *prefect* as certain aids to his success, I regarded only as *ruses*, to afford opportunity for thorough search to the police, and thus the sooner to impress them with the conviction to which G—, in fact, did finally arrive—the conviction that the letter was not upon the premises. I felt, also, that the whole train of thought, which I was at some pains in detailing to you just now, concerning the invariable principle of policial action in searches for articles concealed—I felt that this whole train of thought would necessarily pass through the mind of the minister. It would imperatively lead him to despise all the ordinary *nooks* of concealment. *He* could not, I reflected, be so weak as not to see that the most intricate and remote recess of his hotel would be as open as his commonest closets to the eyes, to the probes, to the gimlets, and to the microscopes of the *prefect.*

"I saw, in fine, that he would be driven, as a matter of course, to *simplicity*, if not deliberately induced to it as a matter of choice. You will remember, perhaps, how desperately the *prefect* laughed when I suggested, upon our first interview, that it was just possible this mystery troubled him so much on account of its being so *very* self-evident."

"Yes," said I, "I remember his merriment well. I really thought he would have fallen into convulsions."

"The material world," continued Dupin, "abounds with very strict analogies to the immaterial; and thus some colour of truth has been given to the rhetorical dogma, that metaphor, or simile, may be made to strengthen an argument, as well as to embellish a description. The principle of the *vis inertiæ*, for example, seems to be identical in physics and metaphysics. It is not more true in the former, that a large body is with more difficulty set in motion than a smaller one, and that its subsequent *momentum* is commensurate with this difficulty, than it is, in the latter, that intellects of the vaster capacity, while more forcible, more constant, and more eventful in their movements than those of inferior grade, are yet the less readily moved, and more embarrassed and full of hesitation in the first few steps of their progress. Again: have you ever noticed which of the street signs, over the shop-doors, are the most attractive of attention?"

"I have never given the matter a thought," I said.

"There is a game of puzzles," he resumed, "which is played upon a map. One party playing requires another to find a given word—the name of town, river, state or empire—any word, in short, upon the motley and perplexed surface of the chart. A novice in the game generally seeks to embarrass his opponents by giving them the most minutely lettered names; but the adept selects such words as stretch, in large characters, from one end of the chart to the other. These, like the over-largely lettered signs and placards of the street, escape observation by dint of being excessively obvious; and here the physical oversight is precisely analogous with the moral inapprehension by which the intellect suffers to pass unnoticed those considerations which are too obtrusively and too palpably self-evident. But this is a point, it appears, somewhat above or beneath the understanding of the *prefect*. He never once thought it probable, or possible, that the minister had deposited the letter immediately beneath the nose of the whole world, by way of best preventing any portion of that world from perceiving it.

"But the more I reflected upon the daring, dashing, and discriminating ingenuity of D—; upon the fact that the document must always have been *at hand*, if he intended to use it to good purpose; and upon the decisive evidence, obtained by the *prefect*, that it was not hidden within the limits of that dignitary's ordinary search—the more satisfied I became that, to conceal this letter, the minister had resorted to the comprehensive and sagacious expedient of not attempting to conceal it at all.

"Full of these ideas, I prepared myself with a pair of green spectacles, and called one fine morning, quite by accident, at the ministerial hotel. I found D— at home, yawning, lounging, and dawdling, as usual, and pretending to be in the last extremity of *ennui*. He is, perhaps, the most really energetic human being now alive—but that is only when nobody sees him.

"To be even with him, I complained of my weak eyes, and lamented the necessity of the spectacles, under cover of which I cautiously and thoroughly surveyed the whole apartment, while seemingly intent only upon the conversation of my host.

"I paid especial attention to a large writing-table near which he sat, and upon which lay confusedly, some miscellaneous letters and other papers, with one or two musical instruments and a few books. Here, however, after a long and very deliberate scrutiny, I saw nothing to excite particular suspicion.

"At length my eyes, in going the circuit of the room, fell upon a trumpery filigree card-rack of pasteboard, that hung dangling by a dirty blue ribbon, from a little brass knob just beneath the middle of the mantel-piece. In this rack, which had three or four compartments, were five or six visiting cards and a solitary letter. This last was much soiled and crumpled. It was torn nearly in two, across the middle—as if a design, in the first instance, to tear it entirely up as worthless, had been altered, or stayed, in the second. It had a large black seal, bearing the D— cipher *very* conspicuously, and was addressed, in a diminutive female hand, to D—, the minister, himself. It was thrust carelessly, and even, as it seemed, contemptuously, into one of the uppermost divisions of the rack.

"No sooner had I glanced at this letter, than I concluded it to be that of which I was in search. To be sure, it was, to all appearance, radically different from the one of which the *prefect* had read us so minute a description. Here the seal was large and black, with the D— cipher; there it was small and red, with the ducal arms of the S— family. Here, the address, to the minister, diminutive and feminine; there the superscription, to a certain royal personage, was markedly bold and decided; the size alone formed a point of correspondence.

"But, then, the *radicalness* of these differences, which was excessive; the dirt; the soiled and torn condition of the paper, so inconsistent with the *true* methodical habits of D—, and so suggestive of a design to delude the beholder into an idea of the worthlessness of the document; these things, together with the hyper-obtrusive situation of this document, full in the view of every visitor, and thus exactly in accordance with the conclusions to which I had previously arrived; these things, I say, were strongly corroborative of suspicion, in one who came with the intention to suspect.

"I protracted my visit as long as possible, and, while I maintained a most animated discussion with the minister upon a topic which I knew well had never failed to interest and excite him, I kept my attention really riveted upon the letter. In this examination, I committed to memory its external appearance and arrangement in the rack; and also fell, at length, upon a discovery which set at rest whatever trivial doubt I might have entertained. In scrutinizing the edges of the paper, I observed them to be more *chafed* than seemed necessary.

"They presented the *broken* appearance which is manifested when a stiff paper, having been once folded and pressed with a folder, is refolded in a reversed direction, in the same creases or edges which had formed the original fold. This discovery was sufficient. It was clear to me that the letter had been turned, as a glove, inside out, re-directed, and re-sealed. I bade the minister good morning, and took my departure at once, leaving a gold snuff-box upon the table.

"The next morning I called for the snuff-box, when we resumed, quite eagerly, the conversation of the preceding day. While thus engaged, however, a loud report, as if of a pistol, was heard immediately beneath the windows of the hotel, and was succeeded by a series of fearful screams, and the shoutings of a terrified mob. D— rushed to a casement, threw it open, and looked out. In the meantime, I stepped to the card-rack, took the letter, put it in my pocket, and replaced it by a *facsimile*, (so far as regards externals,) which I had carefully prepared at my lodgings—imitating the D— cipher, very readily, by means of a seal formed of bread.

"The disturbance in the street had been occasioned by the frantic behaviour of a man with a musket. He had fired it among a crowd of women and children. It proved, however, to have been without ball, and the fellow was suffered to go his way as a lunatic or a drunkard. When he had gone, D— came from the window, whither I had followed him immediately upon securing the object in view. Soon afterwards I bade him farewell. The pretended lunatic was a man in my own pay."

"But what purpose had you," I asked, "in replacing the letter by a *facsimile*? Would it not have been better, at the first visit, to have seized it openly, and departed?"

"D—," replied Dupin, "is a desperate man, and a man of nerve. His hotel, too, is not without attendants devoted to his interests. Had I made the wild attempt you suggest, I might never have left the ministerial presence alive. The good people of Paris might have heard of me no more. But I had an object apart from these considerations. You know my political prepossessions. In this matter, I act as a partisan of the lady concerned. For eighteen months the minister has had her in his power. She has now him in hers—since, being unaware that the letter is not in his possession, he will proceed with his exactions as if it was.

"Thus will he inevitably commit himself, at once, to his political destruction. His downfall, too, will not be more precipitate than awkward. It is all very well to talk about the *facilis descensus Averni;* but in all kinds of climbing, as Catalani said of singing, it is far more easy to get up than to come down. In the present instance I have no sympathy—at least no pity—for him who descends. He is that *monstrum horrendum*, an unprincipled man of genius. I confess, however, that I should like very well to know the precise character of his thoughts, when, being defied by her whom the *prefect* terms 'a certain personage' he is reduced to opening the letter which I left for him in the card-rack."

"How? did you put anything particular in it?"

"Why—it did not seem altogether right to leave the interior blank—that would have been insulting. D—, at Vienna once, did me an evil turn, which I told him, quite good-humouredly, that I should remember. So, as I knew he would feel some curiosity in regard to the identity of the person who had outwitted him, I thought it a pity not to give him a clue. He is well acquainted with my MS., and I just copied into the middle of the blank sheet the words—

— — Un dessein si funeste,
S'il n'est digne d'Atrée, est digne de Thyeste.
They are to be found in Crébillon's 'Atrée.'"

The System of Doctor Tarr and Professor Fether

During the autumn of 18—, while on a tour through the extreme southern provinces of France, my route led me within a few miles of a certain *Maison de Santè* or private Mad-house, about which I had heard much in Paris from my medical friends. As I had never visited a place of the kind, I thought the opportunity too good to be lost; and so proposed to my travelling companion (a gentleman with whom I had made casual acquaintance a few days before) that we should turn aside for an hour or so and look through the establishment. To this he objected—pleading haste in the first place, and in the second, a very usual horror at the sight of a lunatic. He begged me, however, not to let any mere courtesy towards himself interfere with the gratification of my curiosity, and said that he would ride on leisurely, so that I might overtake him during the day, or at all events during the next.

As he bade me goodbye, I bethought me that there might be some difficulty in obtaining access to the premises, and mentioned my fears on this point. He replied that, in fact, unless I had personal knowledge of the superintendent, Monsieur Maillard. or some credential in the way of a letter, a difficulty might be found to exist, as the regulations of these private madhouses were more rigid than the public hospital laws. For himself, he added, he had some years since made the acquaintance of Maillard, and would so far assist me as to ride up to the door and introduce me, although his feelings on the subject of lunacy would not permit of his entering the house.

I thanked him, and turning from the main-road we entered a grass-grown by-path, which, in half-an-hour, nearly lost itself in a dense forest closing the base of a mountain. Through this dank and gloomy wood we rode some two miles, when the *Maison de Santt* came in view. It was a fantastic *château*, much dilapidated, and indeed scarcely tenantable through age and neglect. Its aspect inspired me with absolute dread, and, checking my horse, I half resolved to turn back. I soon, however, grew ashamed of my weakness and proceeded.

As we rode up to the gateway, I perceived it slightly open, and the visage of a man peering through. In an instant afterward, this man came forth, accosted my companion by name, shook him cordially by the hand, and begged him to alight. It was Monsieur Maillard himself. He was a portly, fine-looking gentleman of the old school, with a polished manner, and a certain air of gravity, dignity, and authority, which was very impressive.

My friend having presented me, mentioned my desire to inspect the establishment, and received Monsieur Maillard's assurance that he would show me all attention, now took leave, and I saw him no more.

When he had gone, the superintendent ushered me into a small and exceedingly neat parlour, containing among other indications of refined taste, many books, drawings, pots of flowers, and musical instruments. A cheerful fire blazed upon the hearth. At a piano, singing an aria from Bellini, sat a young and very beautiful woman, who, at my entrance, paused in her song, and received me with graceful courtesy. Her voice was low, and her whole manner subdued I thought, too, that I perceived the traces of sorrow in her countenance, which was excessively, although to my taste, not unpleasingly pale. She was attired in deep mourning, and excited in my bosom a feeling of mingled respect, interest, and admiration.

I had heard, at Paris, that the institution of Monsieur Maillard was managed upon what is vulgarly termed the "system of soothing"—that all punishments were avoided—that even confinement was seldom resorted to—that the patients, while secretly watched, were left much apparent liberty, and that most of them were permitted to roam about the house and grounds in the ordinary apparel of persons in right mind.

Keeping these impressions in view, I was cautious in what I said before the young lady, for I could not be sure that she was sane; and in fact there was a certain restless brilliancy about her eyes which half led me to imagine she was not. I confined my remarks, therefore, to general topics, and to such as I thought would not be displeasing or exciting even to a lunatic. She replied in a perfectly rational manner to all that I said, and even her original observations were marked with the soundest good sense; but a long acquaintance with the metaphysics of *mania* had taught me to put no faith in such evidence of sanity, and I continued to practise, throughout the interview, the caution with which I commenced it.

Presently a smart footman in livery brought in a tray with fruit, wine, and other refreshments, of which I partook, the lady soon afterwards leaving the room. As she departed I turned my eyes in an inquiring manner towards my host.

"No," he said, "oh, no—a member of my family—my niece, and a most accomplished woman."

"I beg a thousand pardons for the suspicion," I replied, "but of course you will know how to excuse me. The excellent administration of your affairs here is well understood in Paris, and I thought it just possible, you know—"

"Yes, yes—say no more—or rather it is myself who should thank you for the commendable prudence you have displayed. We seldom find so much of forethought in young men, and, more than once, some unhappy *contretemps* has occurred in consequence of thoughtlessness on the part of our visitors. While my former system was in operation and my patients were permitted the privilege of roaming to and fro at will, they were often aroused to a dangerous frenzy by injudicious persons who called to inspect the house. Hence I was obliged to enforce a rigid system of exclusion; and none obtained access to the premises upon whose discretion I could not rely."

"While your *former* system was in operation!" I said, repeating his words—"do I understand you then, to say that the 'soothing system' of which I have heard so much, is no longer in force?"

"It is now," he replied, "several weeks since we have concluded to renounce it for ever."

"Indeed! you astonish me!"

"We found it, sir," he said with a sigh, "absolutely necessary to return to the old usages. The *danger* of the soothing system was at all times appalling, and its advantages have been much over-rated. I believe, sir, that in this house it has been given a fair trial, if ever in any. We did everything that rational humanity could suggest. I am sorry that you could not have paid us a visit at an earlier period, that you might have judged for yourself. But I presume you are conversant with the soothing practice—with its details."

"Not altogether. What I have heard has been at third or fourth hand."

"I may state the system then, in general terms, as one in which the patients were *ménagés* humoured. We contradicted no fancies which entered the brains of the mad. On the contrary, we not only indulged but encouraged them; and many of our most permanent cures have been thus effected. There is no argument which so touches the feeble reason of the madman as the *reductio ad absurdum*. We have had men, for example, who fancied themselves chickens. The cure was, to insist upon the thing as a fact—to accuse the patient of stupidity in not sufficiently perceiving it to be a fact—and thus to refuse him any other diet for a week than that which properly appertains to a chicken. In this manner a little corn and gravel were made to perform wonders."

"But was this species of acquiescence all?"

"By no means. We put much faith in amusements of a simple kind, such as music, dancing, gymnastic exercises generally, cards, certain classes of books, and so forth. We affected to treat each individual as if for some ordinary physical disorder, and the word 'lunacy' was never employed. A great point was to set each lunatic to guard the actions of all the others. To repose confidence in the understanding or discretion of a madman is to gain him body and soul. In this way we were enabled to dispense with an expensive body of keepers."

"And you had no punishments of any kind?"

"None."

"And you never confined your patients?"

"Very rarely. Now and then, the malady of some individual growing to a crisis, or taking a sudden turn of fury, we conveyed him to a secret cell, lest his disorder should infect the rest, and there kept him until we could dismiss him to his friends; for with the raging maniac we have nothing to do. He is usually removed to the public hospitals."

"And you have now changed all this—and you think for the better?"

"Decidedly. The system had its disadvantages, and even its dangers. It is now, happily, exploded throughout all the *Maison de Santè* of France."

"I am very much surprised," I said, "at what you tell me; for I made sure that, at this moment, no other method of treatment for mania existed in any portion of the country."

"You are young yet, my friend," replied my host, "but the time will arrive when you will learn to judge for yourself of what is going on in the world, without trusting to the gossip of others:—Believe nothing you hear, and only one half that you see. Now, about our *Maison de Santè*, it is clear that some ignoramus has misled you. After dinner, however, when you have sufficiently recovered from the fatigue of your ride, I will be happy to take you over the house, and introduce to you a system which, in my opinion, and in that of everyone who has witnessed its operation, is incomparably the most effectual as yet devised."

"Your own?" I inquired—"one of your own invention?"

"I am proud," he replied, "to acknowledge that it is—at least in some measure."

In this manner I conversed with Monsieur Maillard for an hour or two, during which he showed me the gardens and conservatories of the place.

"I cannot let you see my patients," he said, "just at present. To a sensitive mind there is always more or less of the shocking in such exhibitions; and I do not wish to spoil your appetite tor dinner. We will dine. I can give you some veal *à la Sainte Ménéhould*, with cauliflowers in *velouté* sauce—after that a glass of *Clos Vougeot*—then your nerves will be sufficiently steadied."

At six dinner was announced; and my host conducted me into a large *salle à manger*, where a very numerous company were assembled—twenty-five or thirty in all. They were, apparently, people of rank—certainly of high breeding—although their habiliments, I thought, were extravagantly rich, partaking somewhat too much of the ostentatious finery of the *vieille cour*. I noticed that at least two-thirds of these guests were ladies; and some of the latter were by no means accoutred in what a Parisian would consider good taste at the present day. Many females, for example, whose age could not have been less than seventy, were bedecked with a profusion of jewelry, such as rings, bracelets, and ear-rings, and wore their bosoms and arms shamefully bare. I observed, too, that very few of the dresses were well made—or, at least, that very few of them fitted the wearers.

In looking about I discovered the interesting girl to whom Monsieur Maillard had presented me in the little parlour; but my surprise was great to see her wearing a hoop and farthingale, with high-heeled shoes, and a dirty cap of Brussels lace, so much too large for her that it gave her face a ridiculously diminutive expression. When I had first seen her she was attired, most becomingly, in deep mourning. There was an air of oddity, in short, about the dress of the whole party, which, at first, caused me to recur to my original idea of the "soothing system," and to fancy that Monsieur Maillard had been willing to deceive me until after dinner, that I might experience no uncomfortable feelings during the repast at finding myself dining with lunatics; but I remembered having been informed in Paris that the southern provincialists were a peculiarly eccentric people, with a vast number of antiquated notions; and then, too, upon conversing with several members of the company, my apprehensions were immediately and fully dispelled.

The dining-room itself, although perhaps sufficiently comfortable and of good dimensions, had nothing too much of elegance about it. For example, the floor was uncarpeted; in France, however, a carpet is frequently dispensed with. The windows, too, were without curtains; the shutters, being shut, were securely fastened with iron bars, applied diagonally, after the fashion of our ordinary shop-shutters. The apartment, I observed, formed in itself a wing of the *château*, and thus the windows were on three sides of the parallelogram—the door being at the other. There were no less than ten windows in all.

The table was superbly set out. It was loaded with plate, and more than loaded with delicacies. The profusion was absolutely barbaric. There were meats enough to have feasted the Anakim. Never in all my life had I witnessed so lavish, so wasteful, an expenditure of the good things of life. There seemed very little taste, however, in the arrangements; and my eyes, accustomed to quiet lights, were sadly offended by the prodigious glare of a multitude of wax candles which, in silver *candelabra*, were deposited upon the table and all about the room, wherever it was possible to find a place. There were several active servants in attendance; and upon a large table at the farther end of the apartment were seated seven or eight people with fiddles, fifes, trombones, and a drum. These fellows annoyed me very much at intervals during the repast, by an infinite variety of noises, which were intended for music, and which appeared to afford much entertainment to all present with the execration of myself.

Upon the whole, I could not help thinking that there was much of the *bizarre* about everything I saw but then the world is made up of all kinds of persons, with all modes of thought, and all sorts of conventional customs. I had travelled, too, so much as to be quite an adept in the *nil admirari*; so I took my seat very coolly at the right hand of my host, and having an excellent appetite, did justice to the good cheer set before me.

The conversation in the meantime was spirited and general.

The ladies, as usual, talked a great deal. I soon found that nearly all the company were well educated; and my host was a world of good-humoured anecdote in himself. He seemed quite willing to speak of his position as superintendent of a *Maison de Santé;* and, indeed, the topic of lunacy was, much to my surprise, a favourite one with all present. A great many amusing stories were told having reference to the whims of the patients.

"We had a fellow here once," said a fat little gentleman, who sat at my right—"a fellow that fancied himself a tea-pot; and, by the way, is it not especially singular how often this particular crotchet has entered the brain of the lunatic? There is scarcely an insane asylum in France which cannot supply a human teapot. *Our* gentleman was a Britannia-ware teapot, and was careful to polish himself every morning with buckskin and whiting."

"And then," said a tall man, just opposite, "we had here, not long ago, a person who had taken it into his head that he was a donkey—which, allegorically speaking, you will say, was quite true. He was a troublesome patient; and we had much ado to keep him within bounds. For a long time he would eat nothing but thistles; but of this idea we soon cured him by insisting upon his eating nothing else. Then he was perpetually kicking out his heels—so—so—"

"Mr. De Kock! I will thank you to behave yourself!" here interrupted an old lady, who sat next to the speaker. "Please keep your feet to yourself! You have spoiled my brocade! Is it necessary, pray, to illustrate a remark in so practical a style? Our friend, here, can surely comprehend you without all this. Upon my word, you are nearly as great a donkey as the poor unfortunate imagined himself. Your acting is very natural, as I live."

"*Mille pardons! Ma'mselle!*" replied Monsieur De Kock, thus addressed—"a thousand pardons! I had no intention of offending. Ma'mselle Laplace—Monsieur De Kock will do himself the honour of taking wine with you."

Here Monsieur De Kock bowed low, kissed his hand with much ceremony, and took wine with Ma'mselle Laplace.

"Allow me, *mon ami*" now said Monsieur Maillard, addressing myself, "allow me to send you a morsel of this veal *à la Ste. Ménéhould*—you will find it particularly fine."

At this instant three sturdy waiters had just succeeded in depositing safely upon the table an enormous dish, or trencher, containing what I supposed to be the "*monstrum, horrendum, informe, ingens, cui lumen ademptum.*" A closer scrutiny assured me, however, that it was only a small calf roasted whole, and set upon its knees, with an apple in its mouth, as is the English fashion of dressing a hare.

"Thank you, no," I replied; "to say the truth, I am not particularly partial to veal *à la Ste.*—what is it?—for I do not find that it altogether agrees with me. I will change my plate, however, and try some of the rabbit."

There were several side-dishes on the table containing what appeared to be the ordinary French rabbit—a very delicious *morceau*, which I can recommend.

"Pierre," cried the host, "change this gentleman's plate, and give him a side-piece of this rabbit *au-chat.*"

"This what?"

"This rabbit *au-chat.*"

"Why, thank you—upon second thoughts, no. I will just help myself to some of the ham."

There is no knowing what one eats, thought I to myself, at the tables of these people of the province. I will have none of their rabbit *au-chat* and for the matter of that, none of their *cat-au-rabbit* either.

"And then," said a cadaverous-looking personage, near the foot of the table, taking up the thread of the conversation where it had been broken off—"and then, among other oddities, we had a patient once upon a time who very pertinaciously maintained himself to be a Cordova cheese, and went about with a knife in his hand soliciting his friends to try a small slice from the middle of his leg."

"He was a great fool, beyond doubt," interposed someone, "but not to be compared with a certain individual whom we all know, with the exception of this strange gentleman. I mean the man who took himself for a bottle of champagne, and always went off with a pop and a fizz, in this fashion."

Here the speaker, very rudely, as I thought, put his right thumb in his left cheek, withdrew it with a sound resembling the popping of a cork, and then, by a dexterous movement of the tongue upon the teeth, created a sharp hissing and fizzing which lasted for several minutes, in imitation of the frothing of champagne. This behaviour, I saw plainly, was not very pleasing to Monsieur Maillard; but that gentleman said nothing, and the conversation was resumed by a very lean little man in a big wig.

"And then there was an ignoramus," said he, "who mistook himself for a frog; which, by the way, he resembled in no little degree. I wish you could have seen him, sir,"—here the speaker addressed myself—"it would have done your heart good to see the natural airs that he put on. Sir, if that man was *not* a frog, I can only observe that it is a pity he was not. His croak thus—o-o-o-o-gh—o-o-o-o-gh! was the finest note in the world—B flat; and when he put his elbows upon the table thus—after taking a glass or two of wine—and distended his mouth thus, and rolled up his eyes thus, and winked them with excessive rapidity thus, why then, sir, I take it upon myself to say positively, that you would have been lost in admiration of the genius of the man."

"I have no doubt of it," I said.

"And then," said somebody else, "then there was Petit Gaillard, who thought himself a pinch of snuff, and was truly distressed because he could not take himself between his own finger and thumb."

"And then there was Jules Desoulières, who was a very singular genius indeed, and went mad with the idea that he was a pumpkin. He persecuted the cook to make him up into pies—a thing which the cook indignantly refused to do. For my part, I am by no means sure that a pumpkin pie *à la Desoulières* would not have been very capital eating indeed!"

"You astonish me!" said I; and I looked inquisitively at Monsieur Maillard.

"Ha! ha! ha!" said that gentleman—"he! he! he!—hi! hi! hi!—ho! ho! ho!—hu! hu! hu!—very good indeed!—You must not be astonished, *mon ami*; our friend here is a wit—a *drôle*—you must not understand him to the letter."

"And then," said some other one of the party, "then there was Bouffon le Grand—another extraordinary personage in his way. He grew deranged through love, and fancied himself possessed of two heads. One of these he maintained to be the head of Cicero; the other he imagined a composite one, being Demosthenes from the top of the forehead to the mouth, and Lord Brougham from the mouth to the chin. It is not impossible that he was wrong; but he would have convinced you of his being in the right; for he was a man of great eloquence. He had an absolute passion for oratory, and could not refrain from display. For example, he used to leap upon the dinner-table thus, and—and—"

Here a friend, at the side of the speaker, put a hand upon his shoulder, and whispered a few words in his ear; upon which he ceased talking with great suddenness, and sank back within his chair.

"And then," said the friend who had whispered, "there was Boullard, the tee-totum. I call him the tee-totum, because, in fact, he was seized with the droll, but not altogether irrational crotchet that he had been converted into a tee-totum. You would have roared with laughter to see him spin. He would turn round upon one heel by the hour, in this manner—so—"

Here the friend whom he had just interrupted by a whisper, performed an exactly similar office for himself.

"But then," cried an old lady, at the top of her voice, "your Monsieur Boullard was a madman, and a very silly madman at best; for who, allow me to ask you, ever heard of a human tee-totum? The thing is absurd Madame Joyeuse was a more sensible person, as you know. She had a crotchet, but it was instinct with common sense, and gave pleasure to all who had the honour of her acquaintance. She found, upon mature deliberation, that by some accident she had been turned into a chicken-cock; but, as such, she behaved with propriety. She flapped her wings with prodigious effect—so—so—so—and as for her crow, it was delicious! Cock-a-doodle-doo!—cock-a-doodle-doo—cock-a-doodle-de-doo-doo-do-o-o-o-o-o-o!"

"Madame Joyeuse, I will thank you to behave yourself!" here interrupted our host, very angrily. "You can either conduct yourself as a lady should do, or you can quit the table forthwith—take your choice."

The lady (whom I was much astonished to hear addressed as Madame Joyeuse, after the description of Madame Joyeuse she had just given) blushed up to the eyebrows, and seemed exceedingly abashed at the reproof. She hung down her head, and said not a syllable in reply. But another and younger lady resumed the theme. It was my beautiful girl of the little parlour!

"Oh, Madame Joyeuse *was* a fool!" she exclaimed; "but there was really much sound sense, after all, in the opinion of Eugenie Salsafette. She was a very beautiful and painfully modest young lady, who thought the ordinary mode of habiliment indecent, and wished to dress herself, always, by getting outside, instead of inside of her clothes. It is a thing very easily done, after all. You have only to do so—and then so—so—so—and then so—so—so and then—"

"*Mon Dieu!* Ma'mselle Salsafette!" here cried a dozen voices at once. "What *are* you about?—forbear!—that is sufficient!—we see, very plainly, how it is done!—hold! hold!" and several persons were already leaping from their seats to withhold Ma'mselle Salsafette from putting herself upon a par with the Medicean Venus, when the point was very effectually and suddenly accomplished by a series of loud screams, or yells, from some portion of the main body of the *château*.

My nerves were very much affected indeed by these yells; but the rest of the company I really pitied. I never saw any set of reasonable people so thoroughly frightened in my life. They all grew as pale as so many corpses, and, shrinking within their seats, sat quivering and gibbering with terror, and listening for a repetition of the sound. It came again—louder and seemingly nearer—and then a third time *very* loud, and then a fourth time with a vigour evidently diminished. At this apparent dying away of the noise, the spirits of the company were immediately regained, and all was life and anecdote as before. I now ventured to inquire the cause of the disturbance.

"A mere *bagatelle*," said Monsieur Maillard. "We are used to these things, and care really very little about them. The lunatics, every now and then, get up a howl in concert; one starting another, as is sometimes the case with a bevy of dogs at night. It occasionally happens, however, that the *concerto* yells are succeeded by a simultaneous effort at breaking loose; when, of course, some little danger is to be apprehended."

"And how many have you in charge?"

"At present we have not more than ten altogether."

"Principally females, I presume?"

"Oh, no—every one of them men, and stout fellows, too, I can tell you."

"Indeed! I have always understood that the majority of lunatics were of the gentler sex."

"It is generally so, but not always. Some time ago there were about twenty-seven patients here, and of that number no less than eighteen were women; but, lately, matters have changed very much, as you see."

"Yes—have changed very much, as you see," here interrupted the gentleman who had broken the shins of Ma'mselle Laplace.

"Yes—have changed very much, as you see!" chimed in the whole company at once.

"Hold your tongues, every one of you!" said my host, in a great rage. Whereupon the whole company maintained a dead silence for nearly a minute. As for one lady, she obeyed Monsieur Maillard to the letter, and thrusting out her tongue, which was an excessively long one, held it very resignedly, with both hands, until the end of the entertainment.

"And this gentlewoman," said I, to Monsieur Maillard, bending over and addressing him in a whisper—"this good lady who has just spoken, and who gives us the cock-a-doodle-de-doo—she, I presume, is harmless—quite harmless, eh?"

"Harmless!" ejaculated he, in unfeigned surprise, "why—why, what can you mean?"

"Only slightly touched?" said I, touching my head. " I take it for granted that she is not particularly—not dangerously affected, eh?"

"*Mon Dieu!* what is it you imagine? This lady, my particular old friend, Madame Joyeuse, is as absolutely sane as myself. She has her little eccentricities, to be sure—but then, you know, all old women—all *very* old women are more or less eccentric!"

"To be sure," said I—"to be sure—and then the rest of these ladies and gentlemen—"

"Are my friends and keepers," interrupted Monsieur Maillard, drawing himself up with *hauteur*— "my very good friends and assistants."

"What! all of them?" I asked—"the women and all?"

"Assuredly," he said—"we could not do at all without the women; they are the best lunatic nurses in the world; they have a way of their own, you know; their bright eyes have a marvellous effect— something like the fascination of the snake, you know."

"To be sure," said I—"to be sure! They behave a little odd, eh?—they are a little *queer*, eh?—don't you think so?"

"Odd!—queer!—why, do you *really* think so? We are not very prudish, to be sure, here in the South—do pretty much as we please—enjoy life, and all that sort of thing, you know—"

"To be sure," said I; "to be sure."

"And then, perhaps, this *Clos de Vougeot* is a little heady, you know—a little *strong*—you understand, eh?"

"To be sure," said I; "to be sure. By-the-by, *monsieur*, did I understand you to say that the system you have adopted, in place of the celebrated soothing system, was one of very rigorous severity?"

"By no means. Our confinement is necessarily close; but the treatment—the medical treatment, I mean—is rather agreeable to the patients than otherwise."

"And the new system is one of your own invention?"

"Not altogether. Some portions of it are referable to Professor Tarr, of whom you have necessarily heard, and, again, there are modifications in my plan which I am happy to acknowledge as belonging of right to the celebrated Fether, with whom, if I mistake not, you have the honour of an intimate acquaintance."

"I am quite ashamed to confess," I replied, "that I have never even heard the name of either gentleman before."

"Good heavens!" ejaculated my host, drawing back his chair abruptly, and uplifting his hands. "I surely do not hear you aright! You did not intend to say, eh? that you had never *heard* either of the learned Doctor Tarr, or of the celebrated Professor Fether?"

"I am forced to acknowledge my ignorance," I replied; "but the truth should be held inviolate above all things. Nevertheless, I feel humbled to the dust, not to be acquainted with the works of these, no doubt, extraordinary men. I will seek out their writings forthwith, and peruse them with deliberate care. Monsieur Maillard, you have really—I must confess it—you have *really*—made me ashamed of myself!"

And this was the fact.

"Say no more, my good young friend," he said kindly, pressing my hand—"join me now in a glass of *Sauterne*."

We drank. The company followed our example, without stint. They chatted—they jested—they laughed—they perpetrated a thousand absurdities—the fiddles shrieked—the drum row-de-dowed—the trombones bellowed like so many brazen bulls of Phalaris—and the whole scene, growing gradually worse and worse as the wines gained the ascendency, became at length a sort of Pandemonium *in petto*. In the meantime, Monsieur Maillard and myself, with some bottles of *Sauterne* and *Clos Vougeot* between us, continued our conversation at the top of the voice. A word spoken in an ordinary key stood no more chance of being heard than the voice of a fish from the bottom of Niagara Falls.

"And, sir," said I, screaming in his ear, "you mentioned something before dinner about the danger incurred in the old system of soothing. How is that?"

"Yes," he replied, "there was occasionally very great danger indeed. There is no accounting for the caprices of madmen; and, in my opinion, as well as in that of Dr. Tarr and Professor Fether, it is *never* safe to permit them to run at large unattended. A lunatic may be 'soothed,' as it is called, for a time, but in the end he is very apt to become obstreperous. His cunning, too, is proverbial and great. If he has a project in view, he conceals his design with a marvellous wisdom; and the dexterity with which he counterfeits sanity, presents to the metaphysician one of the most singular problems in the study of mind. When a madman appears *thoroughly* sane, indeed, it is high time to put him in a strait jacket."

"But the *danger*, my dear sir, of which you were speaking—in your own experience—during your control of this house—have you had practical reason to think liberty hazardous in the case of a lunatic?"

"Here?—in my own experience?—why, I may say yes. For example:—no *very* long while ago, a singular circumstance occurred in this very house. The 'soothing system,' you know, was then in operation, and the patients were at large. They behaved remarkably well—especially so—anyone of sense might have known that some devilish scheme was brewing from that particular fact, that the fellows behaved so *remarkably* well. And, sure enough, one fine morning the keepers found themselves pinioned hand and foot, and thrown into the cells, where they were attended, as if *they* were the lunatics, by the lunatics themselves, who had usurped the offices of the keepers."

"You don't tell me so! I never heard of anything so absurd in my life!"

"Fact—it all came to pass by means of a stupid fellow—a lunatic—who by some means had taken it into his head that he had invented a better system of government than any ever heard of before—of lunatic government, I mean. He wished to give his invention a trial, I suppose, and so he persuaded the rest of the patients to join him in a conspiracy for the overthrow of the reigning powers."

"And he really succeeded?"

"No doubt of it. The keepers and kept were soon made to exchange places. Not that exactly either, for the madmen had been free, but the keepers were shut up in cells forthwith, and treated, I am sorry to say, in a very cavalier manner."

"But I presume a counter-revolution was soon effected. This condition of things could not have long existed. The country people in the neighbourhood—visitors coming to see the establishment—would have given the alarm."

"There you are out. The head rebel was too cunning for that. He admitted no visitors at all—with the exception, one day, of a very stupid-looking young gentleman of whom he had no reason to be afraid. He let him in to see the place—just by way of variety—to have a little fun with him. As soon as he had gammoned him sufficiently, he let him out, and sent him about his business."

"And *how* long, then, did the madmen reign?"

"Oh, a very long time, indeed—a month certainly—how much longer I can't precisely say. In the meantime, the lunatics had a jolly season of it—that you may swear. They doffed their own shabby clothes, and made free with the family wardrobe and jewels. The cellars of the *château* were well stocked with wine; and these madmen are just the devils that know how to drink it. They lived well, I can tell you."

"And the treatment—what was the particular species of treatment which the leader of the rebels put into operation?"

"Why, as for that, a madman is not necessarily a fool, as I have already observed; and it is my honest opinion that his treatment was a much better treatment than that which it superseded. It was a very capital system indeed—simple—neat—no trouble at all, in fact it was delicious—it was—"

Here my host's observations were cut short by another series of yells, of the same character as those which had previously disconcerted us. This time, however, they seemed to proceed from persons rapidly approaching.

"Gracious heavens!" I ejaculated—"the lunatics have most undoubtedly broken loose."

"I very much fear it is so," replied Monsieur Maillard, now becoming excessively pale. He had scarcely finished the sentence before loud shouts and imprecations were heard beneath the windows; and immediately afterwards it became evident that some persons outside were endeavouring to gain entrance into the room. The door was beaten with what appeared to be a sledge-hammer, and the shutters were wrenched and shaken with prodigious violence.

A scene of the most terrible confusion ensued. Monsieur Maillard, to my excessive astonishment, threw himself under the sideboard. I had expected more resolution at his hands. The members of the orchestra, who for the last fifteen minutes had been seemingly too much intoxicated to do duty, now sprang all at once to their feet and to their instruments, and, scrambling upon their table, broke out with one accord into "Yankee Doodle," which they performed, if not exactly in tune, at least with an energy superhuman, during the whole of the uproar.

Meantime, upon the main dining-table, among the bottles and glasses, leaped the gentleman who with such difficulty had been restrained from leaping there before. As soon as he fairly settled himself he commenced an oration, which no doubt was a very capital one if it could only have been heard. At the same moment, the man with the tee-totum predilections set himself to spinning around the apartment with immense energy, and with arms outstretched at right angles with his body, so that he had all the air of a tee-totum in fact, and knocked everybody down that happened to get in his way. And now, too, hearing an incredible popping and fizzing of champagne, I discovered at length that it proceeded from the person who performed the bottle of that delicate drink during dinner.

And then, again, the frogman croaked away as if the salvation of his soul depended upon every note that he uttered. And in the midst of all this, the continuous braying of a donkey arose over all. As for my old friend Madame Joyeuse, I really could have wept for the poor lady, she appeared so terribly perplexed. All she did, however, was to stand up in a corner by the fireplace, and sing out incessantly, at the top of her voice, "Cock-a-doodle-de-dooooooh!"

And now came the climax the catastrophe of the drama. As no resistance beyond whooping and yelling and cock-a-doodleing was offered to the encroachments of the party without, the ten windows were very speedily and almost simultaneously broken in. But I shall never forget the emotions of wonder and horror with which I gazed, when, leaping through these windows and down among us *pêle-mêle*, fighting, stamping, scratching, and howling, there rushed a perfect army of what I took to be Chimpanzees, Orang-utans, or big black baboons of the Cape of Good Hope.

I received a terrible beating, after which I rolled under a sofa and lay still. After lying there some fifteen minutes, however, during which time I listened with all my ears to what was going on in the room, I came to some satisfactory *dénouement* of this tragedy. Monsieur Maillard, it appeared, in giving me the account of the lunatic who had excited his fellows to rebellion, had been merely relating his own exploits. This gentleman had, indeed, some two or three years before been the superintendent of the establishment, but grew crazy himself, and so became a patient. This fact was unknown to the travelling companion who introduced me.

The keepers, ten in number, having been suddenly overpowered, were first well tarred, then carefully feathered, and then shut up in underground cells. They had been so imprisoned for more than a month, during which period Monsieur Maillard had generously allowed them not only the tar and feathers (which constituted his "system"), but some bread and abundance of water. The latter was pumped on them daily. At length, one escaping through a sewer gave freedom to all the rest.

The "soothing system," with important modifications, has been resumed at the *château*; yet I cannot help agreeing with

Monsieur Maillard that his own "treatment "was a very capital one of its kind. As he justly observed, it was "simple, neat, and gave no trouble at all—not the least."

I have only to add that, although I have searched every library in Europe for the works of Doctor Tarr and Professor Fether, I have, up to the present day, utterly failed in my endeavours at procuring an edition.

Thou Art the Man

I will now play the Œdipus to the Rattleborough enigma. I will expound to you—as I alone can—the secret of the enginery that effected the Rattleborough miracle—the one, the true, the admitted, the undisputed, the indisputable miracle, which put a definite end to infidelity among the Rattleburghers and converted to the orthodoxy of the *grandames* all the carnal-minded who had ventured to be sceptical before.

This event—which I should be sorry to discuss in a tone of unsuitable levity—occurred in the summer of 18—. Mr. Barnabas Shuttleworthy—one of the wealthiest and most respectable citizens of the borough—had been missing for several days under circumstances which gave rise to suspicion of foul play. Mr. Shuttleworthy had set out from Rattleborough very early one Saturday morning, on horseback, with the avowed intention of proceeding to the city of ——, about fifteen miles distant, and of returning the night of the same day. Two hours after his departure, however, his horse returned without him, and without the saddle-bags which had been strapped on his back at starting. The animal was wounded, too, and covered with mud. These circumstances naturally gave rise to much alarm among the friends of the missing man; and when it was found, on Sunday morning, that he had not yet made his appearance, the whole borough arose *en masse* to go and look for his body.

The foremost and most energetic in instituting this search was the bosom friend of Mr. Shuttleworthy—a Mr. Charles Goodfellow, or, as he was universally called, "Charley Goodfellow," or "Old Charley Goodfellow." Now, whether it is a marvellous coincidence, or whether it is that the name itself has an imperceptible effect upon the character, I have never yet been able to ascertain; but the fact is unquestionable, that there never yet was any person named Charles who was not an open, manly, honest, good-natured, and frank-hearted fellow, with a rich, clear voice, that did you good to hear it, and an eye that looked you always straight in the face, as much as to say: "I have a clear conscience myself, am afraid of no man, and am altogether above doing a mean action." And thus all the hearty, careless, "walking gentlemen" of the stage are very certain to be called Charles.

Now, "Old Charley Goodfellow," although he had been in Rattleborough not longer than six months or thereabouts, and although nobody knew anything about him before he came to settle in the neighbourhood, had experienced no difficulty in the world in making the acquaintance of all the respectable people in the borough. Not a man of them but would have taken his bare word for a thousand at any moment; and as for the women, there is no saying what they would not have done to oblige him. And all this came of his having been christened Charles, and of his possessing, in consequence, that ingenuous face which is proverbially the very "best letter of recommendation."

I have already said that Mr. Shuttleworthy was one of the most respectable and, undoubtedly, he was the most wealthy man in Rattleborough, while "Old Charley Goodfellow" was upon as intimate terms with him as if he had been his own brother. The two old gentlemen were next-door neighbours, and, although Mr. Shuttleworthy seldom, if ever, visited "Old Charley," and never was known to take a meal in his house, still this did not prevent the two friends from being exceedingly intimate, as I have just observed; for "Old Charley" never let a day pass without stepping in three or four times to see how his neighbour came on, and very often he would stay to breakfast or tea, and almost always to dinner, and then the amount of wine that was made way with by the two cronies at a sitting, it would really be a difficult thing to ascertain.

"Old Charleys" favourite beverage was *Château-Margaux*, and it appeared to do Mr. Shuttleworthy's heart good to see the old fellow swallow it, as he did, quart after quart; so that, one day, when the wine was *in* and the wit as a natural consequence, somewhat *out*, he said to his crony, as he slapped him upon the back—"I tell you what it is, 'Old Charley,' you are, by all odds, the heartiest old fellow I ever came across in all my born days; and, since you love to guzzle the wine at that fashion, I'll be darned if I don't have to make thee a present of a big box of the *Château-Margaux*. Od rot me,"—(Mr. Shuttleworthy had a sad habit of swearing, although he seldom went beyond "Od rot me," or "By gosh," or "By the jolly golly,")—"Od rot me," says he, "if I don't send an order to town this very afternoon for a double box of the best that can be got, and I'll make ye a present of it, I will!—ye needn't say a word now—I *will*, I tell ye, and there's an end of it; so look out for it—it will come to hand some of these fine days, precisely when ye are looking for it the least!" I mention this little bit of liberality on the part of Mr. Shuttleworthy, just by way of showing you how *very* intimate an understanding existed between the two friends.

Well, on the Sunday morning in question, when it came to be fairly understood that Mr. Shuttleworthy had met with foul play, I never saw any one so profoundly affected as "Old Charley Goodfellow." When he first heard that the horse had come home without his master, and without his master's saddle-bags, and all bloody from a pistol-shot, that had gone clean through and through the poor animal's chest without quite killing him; when he heard all this, he turned as pale as if the missing man had been his own dear brother or father, and shivered and shook all over as if he had had a fit of the ague.

At first he was too much overpowered with grief to be able to do any thing at all, or to concert upon any plan of action; so that for a long time he endeavoured to dissuade Mr. Shuttleworthy's other friends from making a stir about the matter, thinking it best to wait awhile—say for a week or two, or a month, or two—to see if something wouldn't turn up, or if Mr. Shuttleworthy wouldn't come in the natural way, and explain his reasons for sending his horse on before. I dare say you have often observed this disposition to temporise, or to procrastinate, in people who are labouring under any very poignant sorrow. Their powers of mind seem to be rendered torpid, so that they have a horror of anything like action, and like nothing in the world so well as to lie quietly in bed and "nurse their grief," as the old ladies express it—that is to say, ruminate over the trouble.

The people of Rattleborough had, indeed, so high an opinion of the wisdom and discretion of "Old Charley," that the greater part of them felt disposed to agree with him, and not make a stir in the business "until something should turn up," as the honest old gentleman worded it; and I believe that, after all this would have been the general determination, but for the very suspicious interference of Mr. Shuttleworthy's nephew, a young man of very dissipated habits, and otherwise of rather bad character. This nephew, whose name was Pennifeather, would listen to nothing like reason in the matter of "lying quiet," but insisted upon making immediate search for the "corpse of the murdered man."—This was the expression he employed; and Mr. Goodfellow acutely remarked at the time, that it was "a *singular* expression, to say no more."

This remark of 'Old Charley's,' too, had great effect upon the crowd; and one of the party was heard to ask, very impressively, "how it happened that young Mr. Pennifeather was so intimately cognizant of all the circumstances connected with his wealthy uncle's disappearance, as to feel authorized to assert, distinctly and unequivocally, that his uncle *was* 'a murdered man.'" Hereupon some little squibbing and bickering occurred among various members of the crowd, and especially between "Old Charley" and Mr. Pennifeather—although this latter occurrence was, indeed, by no means a novelty, for no good will had subsisted between the parties for the last three or four months; and matters had even gone so far that Mr. Pennifeather had actually knocked down his uncles friend for some alleged excess of liberty that the latter had taken in the uncle's house, of which the nephew was an inmate. Upon this occasion "Old Charley" is said to have behaved with exemplary moderation and Christian charity. He arose from the blow, adjusted his clothes, and made no attempt at retaliation at all—merely muttering a few words about "taking summary vengeance at the first convenient opportunity,"—a natural and very justifiable ebullition of anger, which meant nothing, however, and, beyond doubt, was no sooner given vent to than forgotten.

However these matters may be (which have no reference to the point now at issue), it is quite certain that the people of Rattleborough, principally through the persuasion of Mr. Pennifeather, came at length to the determination of dispersion over the adjacent country in search of the missing Mr. Shuttleworthy. I say they came to this determination in the first instance. After it had been fully resolved that a search should be made, it was considered almost a matter of course that the seekers should disperse—that is to say, distribute themselves in parties—for the more thorough examination of the region round about. I forget, however, by what ingenious train of reasoning it was that "Old Charley" finally convinced the assembly that this was the most injudicious plan that could be pursued. Convince them, however, he did—all except Mr. Pennifeather, and, in the end, it was arranged that a search should be instituted, carefully and very thoroughly, by the burghers *en masse*, "Old Charley" himself leading the way.

As for the matter of that, there could have been no better pioneer than "Old Charley," whom everybody knew to have the eye of a lynx; but, although he led them into all manner of out-of-the-way holes and corners, by routes that nobody had ever suspected of existing in the neighbourhood, and although the search was incessantly kept up day and night for nearly a week, still no trace of Mr. Shuttleworthy could be discovered. When I say no trace, however, I must not be understood to speak literally, for trace, to some extent, there certainly was. The poor gentleman had been tracked, by his horses shoes (which were peculiar), to a spot about three miles to the east of the borough, on the main road leading to the city.

Here the track made off into a by-path through a piece of woodland—the path coming out again into the main road, and cutting off about half a mile of the regular distance. Following the shoe-marks down this lane, the party came at length to a pool of stagnant water, half hidden by the brambles, to the right of the lane, and opposite this pool all vestige of the track was lost sight of. It appeared, however, that a struggle of some nature had here taken place, and it seemed as if some large and heavy body, much larger and heavier than a man, had been drawn from the by-path to the pool. This latter was carefully dragged twice, but nothing was found; and the party was upon the point of going away, in despair of coming to any result, when Providence suggested to Mr. Goodfellow the expediency of draining the water off altogether.

This project was received with cheers, and many high compliments to "Old Charley" upon his sagacity and consideration. As many of the *burghers* had brought spades with them, supposing that they might possibly be called upon to disinter a corpse, the drain was easily and speedily effected; and no sooner was the bottom visible, than right in the middle of the mud that remained was discovered a black silk velvet waistcoat, which nearly every one present immediately recognized as the property of Mr. Pennifeather. This waistcoat was much torn and stained with blood, and there were several persons among the party who had a distinct remembrance of its having been worn by its owner on the very morning of Mr. Shuttleworthy's departure for the city; while there were others, again, ready to testify upon oath, if required, that Mr. P. did *not* wear the garment in question at any period during the *remainder* of that memorable day, nor could any one be found to say that he had seen it upon Mr. P.'s person at any period at all subsequent to Mr. Shuttleworthy's disappearance.

Matters now wore a very serious aspect for Mr. Pennifeather, and it was observed, as an indubitable confirmation of the suspicions which were excited against him, that he grew exceedingly pale, and when asked what he had to say for himself, was utterly incapable of saying a word. Hereupon, the few friends his riotous mode of living had left him, deserted him at once to a man, and were even more clamorous than his ancient and avowed enemies for his instantaneous arrest. But, on the other hand, the magnanimity of Mr. Goodfellow shone forth with only the more brilliant lustre through contrast.

He made a warm and intensely eloquent defence of Mr. Pennifeather, in which he alluded more than once to his own sincere forgiveness of that wild young gentleman—"the heir of the worthy Mr. Shuttleworthy,"—for the insult which he (the young gentleman) had, no doubt in the heat of passion, thought proper to put upon him (Mr. Goodfellow). "He forgave him for it," he said, "from the very bottom of his heart; and for himself (Mr. Goodfellow), so far from pushing the suspicious circumstances to extremity, which he was sorry to say, really *had* arisen against Mr. Pennifeather, he (Mr. Goodfellow) would make every exertion in his power, would employ all the little eloquence in his possession to—to—to—soften down, as much as he could conscientiously do so, the worst features of this really exceedingly perplexing piece of business."

Mr. Goodfellow went on for some half hour longer in this strain, very much to the credit both of his head and of his heart; but your warm-hearted people are seldom apposite in their observations—they run into all sorts of blunders, *contre-temps* and *mal àpropos-isms*, in the hot-headedness of their zeal to serve a friend—thus, often with the kindest intentions in the world, doing infinitely more to prejudice his cause than to advance it.

So, in the present instance, it turned out with all the eloquence of "Old Charley"; for, although he laboured earnestly in behalf of the suspected, yet it so happened, somehow or other, that every syllable he uttered of which the direct but unwitting tendency was not to exalt the speaker in the good opinion of his audience, had the effect to deepen the suspicion already attached to the individual whose cause he pleaded, and to arouse against him the fury of the mob.

One of the most unaccountable errors committed by the orator was his allusion to the suspected as "the heir of the worthy old gentleman Mr. Shuttleworthy." The people had really never thought of this before. They had only remembered certain threats of disinheritance uttered a year or two previously by the uncle (who had no living relative except the nephew), and they had, therefore, always looked upon this disinheritance as a matter that was settled—so single-minded a race of beings were the Rattleburghers; but the remark of "Old Charley" brought them at once to a consideration of this point, and thus gave them to see the possibility of the threats having been nothing *more* than a threat. And straightway hereupon, arose the natural question of *cui bono?*—a question that tended even more than the waistcoat to fasten the terrible crime upon the young man.

And here, lest I may be misunderstood, permit me to digress for one moment merely to observe that the exceedingly brief and simple Latin phrase which I have employed, is invariably mistranslated and misconceived. "*Cui bono?*" in all the crack novels and elsewhere,—in those of Mrs. Gore, for example, (the author of "Cecil,") a lady who quotes all tongues from the Chaldaean to Chickasaw, and is helped to her learning, "as needed," upon a systematic plan, by Mr. Beckford,—in *all* the crack novels, I say, from those of Bulwer and Dickens to those of Bulwer and Dickens to those of Turnapenny and Ainsworth, the two little Latin words *cui bono* are rendered "to what purpose?" or, (as if *quo bono*,) "to what good." Their true meaning, nevertheless, is "for whose advantage." *Cui*, to whom; *bono*, is it for a benefit.

It is a purely legal phrase, and applicable precisely in cases such as we have now under consideration, where the probability of the doer of a deed hinges upon the probability of the benefit accruing to this individual or to that from the deed's accomplishment. Now in the present instance, the question *cui bono?* very pointedly implicated Mr. Pennifeather. His uncle had threatened him, after making a will in his favour, with disinheritance. But the threat had not been actually kept; the original will, it appeared, had not been altered. *Had* it been altered, the only supposable motive for murder on the part of the suspected would have been the ordinary one of revenge; and even this would have been counteracted by the hope of reinstation into the good graces of the uncle. But the will being unaltered, while the threat to alter remained suspended over the nephew's head, there appears at once the very strongest possible inducement for the atrocity, and so concluded, very sagaciously, the worthy citizens of the borough of Rattle.

Mr. Pennifeather was, accordingly, arrested upon the spot, and the crowd, after some further search, proceeded homeward, having him in custody. On the route, however, another circumstance occurred tending to confirm the suspicion entertained. Mr. Goodfellow, whose zeal led him to be always a little in advance of the party, was seen suddenly to run forward a few paces, stoop, and then apparently to pick up some small object from the grass. Having quickly examined it he was observed, too, to make a sort of half attempt at concealing it in his coat pocket; but this action was noticed, as I say, and consequently prevented, when the object picked up was found to be a Spanish knife which a dozen persons at once recognised as belonging to Mr. Pennifeather. Moreover, his initials were engraved upon the handle. The blade of this knife was open and bloody.

No doubt now remained of the guilt of the nephew, and immediately upon reaching Rattleborough he was taken before a magistrate for examination.

Here matters again took a most unfavourable turn. The prisoner, being questioned as to his whereabouts on the morning of Mr. Shuttleworthy's disappearance, had absolutely the audacity to acknowledge that on that very morning he had been out with his rifle deer-stalking, in the immediate neighbourhood of the pool where the bloodstained waistcoat had been discovered through the sagacity of Mr. Goodfellow.

This latter now came forward, and, with tears in his eyes, asked permission to be examined. He said that a stern sense of the duty he owed his Maker, not less than his fellow-men, would permit him no longer to remain silent. Hitherto, the sincerest affection for the young man (notwithstanding the latter's ill-treatment of himself, Mr. Goodfellow) had induced him to make every hypothesis which imagination could suggest, by way of endeavouring to account for what appeared suspicious in the circumstances that told so seriously against Mr. Pennifeather, but these circumstances were now altogether *too* convincing—*too* damning, he would hesitate no longer—he would tell all he knew, although his heart (Mr. Goodfellow's) should absolutely burst asunder in the effort.

He then went on to state that, on the afternoon of the day previous to Mr. Shuttleworthy's departure for the city, that worthy old gentleman had mentioned to his nephew, in *his* hearing (Mr. Goodfellow's), that his object in going to town on the morrow was to make a deposit of an unusually large sum of money in the "Farmers and Mechanics' Bank," and that, then and there, the said Mr. Shuttleworthy had distinctly avowed to the said nephew his irrevocable determination of rescinding the will originally made, and of cutting him off with a shilling. He (the witness) now solemnly called upon the accused to state whether what he (the witness) had just stated was or was not the truth in every substantial particular. Much to the astonishment of every one present, Mr. Pennifeather frankly admitted that *it was.*

The magistrate now considered it his duty to send a couple of constables to search the chamber of the accused in the house of his uncle. From this search they almost immediately returned with the well-known steel-bound, russet leather pocket-book which the old gentleman had been in the habit of carrying for years. Its valuable contents, however, had been abstracted, and the magistrate in vain endeavoured to extort from the prisoner the use which had been made of them, or the place of their concealment. Indeed, he obstinately denied all knowledge of the matter. The constables, also, discovered, between the bed and sacking of the unhappy man, a shirt and neck-handkerchief both marked with the initials of his name, and both hideously besmeared with the blood of the victim.

At this juncture, it was announced that the horse of the murdered man had just expired in the stable from the effects of the wound he had received, and it was proposed by Mr. Goodfellow that a *post mortem* examination of the beast should be immediately made, with the view, if possible, of discovering the ball. This was accordingly done; and, as if to demonstrate beyond a question the guilt of the accused, Mr. Goodfellow, after considerable searching in the cavity of the chest was enabled to detect and to pull forth a bullet of very extraordinary size, which, upon trial, was found to be exactly adapted to the bore of Mr. Pennifeather's rifle, while it was far too large for that of any other person in the borough or its vicinity.

To render the matter even surer yet, however, this bullet was discovered to have a flaw or seam at right angles to the usual suture, and upon examination, this seam corresponded precisely with an accidental ridge or elevation in a pair of moulds acknowledged by the accused himself to be his own property. Upon finding of this bullet, the examining magistrate refused to listen to any farther testimony, and immediately committed the prisoner for trial-declining resolutely to take any bail in the case, although against this severity Mr. Goodfellow very warmly remonstrated, and offered to become surety in whatever amount might be required.

This generosity on the part of "Old Charley" was only in accordance with the whole tenour of his amiable and chivalrous conduct during the entire period of his sojourn in the borough of Rattle. In the present instance the worthy man was so entirely carried away by the excessive warmth of his sympathy, that he seemed to have quite forgotten, when he offered to go bail for his young friend, that he himself (Mr. Goodfellow) did not possess a single dollar's worth of property upon the face of the earth.

The result of the committal may be readily foreseen. Mr. Pennifeather, amid the loud execrations of all Rattleborough, was brought to trial at the next criminal sessions, when the chain of circumstantial evidence (strengthened as it was by some additional damning facts, which Mr. Goodfellow's sensitive conscientiousness forbade him to withhold from the court) was considered so unbroken and so thoroughly conclusive, that the jury, without leaving their seats, returned an immediate verdict of "*Guilty of murder in the first degree.*" Soon afterward the unhappy wretch received sentence of death, and was remanded to the county jail to await the inexorable vengeance of the law.

In the meantime, the noble behaviour of "Old Charley Goodfellow," had doubly endeared him to the honest citizens of the borough. He became ten times a greater favourite than ever, and, as a natural result of the hospitality with which he was treated, he relaxed, as it were, perforce, the extremely parsimonious habits which his poverty had hitherto impelled him to observe, and very frequently had little *reunions* at his own house, when wit and jollity reigned supreme-dampened a little, *of course*, by the occasional remembrance of the untoward and melancholy fate which impended over the nephew of the late lamented bosom friend of the generous host.

One fine day, this magnanimous old gentleman was agreeably surprised at the receipt of the following letter:-

Charles Goodfellow, Esq., Rattleborough
From H.F.B. & Co.
Chat. Mar. A—No. 1.—6 doz. bottles (½ Gross)

Charles Goodfellow, Esquire.
Dear Sir—In conformity with an order transmitted to our firm about two months since, by our esteemed correspondent, Mr. Barnabus Shuttleworthy, we have the honour of forwarding this morning, to your address, a double box of *Château-Margaux* of the antelope brand, violet seal. Box numbered and marked as per heading.

We remain, sir,

Your most ob'nt ser'ts,

Hoggs, Frogs, Bogs, & Co.

"City of——, June 21, 18—.

P.S.—The box will reach you by wagon, on the day after

your receipt of this letter. Our respects to Mr. Shuttleworthy.

H., F., B., & CO.

The fact is, that Mr. Goodfellow had, since the death of Mr. Shuttleworthy, given over all expectation of ever receiving the promised *Château-Margaux;* and he, therefore, looked upon it *now* as a sort of especial dispensation of Providence in his behalf. He was highly delighted, of course, and in the exuberance of his joy invited a large party of friends to a *petit souper* on the morrow, for the purpose of broaching the good old Mr. Shuttleworthy's present. Not that he *said* anything about "the good old Mr. Shuttleworthy" when he issued the invitations. The fact is, he thought much and concluded to say nothing at all.

He did *not* mention to anyone—if I remember aright—that he had received a *present* of *Château-Margaux*. He merely asked his friends to come and help him drink some, of a remarkable fine quality and rich flavour, that he had ordered up from the city a couple of months ago, and of which he would be in the receipt upon the morrow. I have often puzzled myself to imagine why it was that "Old Charley" came to the conclusion to say nothing about having received the wine from his old friend, but I could never precisely understand his reason for the silence, although he had *some* excellent and very magnanimous reason, no doubt.

The morrow at length arrived, and with it a very large and highly respectable company at Mr. Goodfellow's house. Indeed, half the borough was there,—I myself among the number,—but, much to the vexation of the host, the *Château-Margaux* did not arrive until a late hour, and when the sumptuous supper supplied by "Old Charley" had been done very ample justice by the guests. It came at length, however,—a monstrously big box of it there was, too—and as the whole party were in excessively good humour, it was decided, *nem. con.*, that it should be lifted upon the table and its contents disembowelled forthwith.

No sooner said than done. I lent a helping hand; and, in a trice we had the box upon the table, in the midst of all the bottles and glasses, not a few of which were demolished in the scuffle. "Old Charley," who was pretty much intoxicated, and excessively red in the face, now took a seat, with an air of mock dignity, at the head of the board, and thumped furiously upon it with a decanter, calling upon the company to keep order "during the ceremony of disinterring the treasure."

After some vociferation, quiet was at length fully restored, and, as very often happens in similar cases, a profound and remarkable silence ensued. Being then requested to force open the lid, I complied, of course, "with an infinite deal of pleasure." I inserted a chisel, and giving it a few slight taps with a hammer, the top of the box flew suddenly off, and at the same instant, there sprang up into a sitting position, directly facing the host, the bruised, bloody, and nearly putrid corpse of the murdered Mr. Shuttleworthy himself. It gazed for a few seconds, fixedly and sorrowfully, with its decaying and lack-lustre eyes, full into the countenance of Mr. Goodfellow; uttered slowly, but clearly and impressively, the words—"Thou art the man!" and then, falling over the side of the chest as if thoroughly satisfied, stretched out its limbs quiveringly upon the table.

The scene that ensued is altogether beyond description. The rush for the doors and windows was terrific, and many of the most robust men in the room fainted outright through sheer horror. But after the first wild, shrieking burst of affright, all eyes were directed to Mr. Goodfellow. If I live a thousand years, I can never forget the more than mortal agony which was depicted in that ghastly face of his, so lately rubicund with triumph and wine. For several minutes he sat rigidly as a statue of marble; his eyes seeming, in the intense vacancy of their gaze, to be turned inward and absorbed in the contemplation of his own miserable, murderous soul.

At length their expression appeared to flash suddenly out into the external world, when, with a quick leap, he sprang from his chair, and falling heavily with his head and shoulders upon the table, and in contact with the corpse, poured out rapidly and vehemently a detailed confession of the hideous crime for which

Mr. Pennifeather was then imprisoned and doomed to die.

What he recounted was in substance this:—He followed his victim to the vicinity of the pool; there shot his horse with a pistol; despatched its rider with the butt end; possessed himself of the pocket-book, and, supposing the horse dead, dragged it with great labour to the brambles by the pond. Upon his own beast he slung the corpse of Mr. Shuttleworthy, and thus bore it to a secure place of concealment a long distance off through the woods.

The waistcoat, the knife, the pocket-book, and bullet, had been placed by himself where found, with the view of avenging himself upon Mr. Pennifeather. He had also contrived the discovery of the stained handkerchief and shirt.

Towards the end of the blood-churning recital the words of the guilty wretch faltered and grew hollow. When the record was finally exhausted, he arose, staggered backward from the table, and fell—*dead*.

******

The means by which this happily-timed confession was extorted, although efficient, were simple indeed. Mr. Goodfellow's excess of frankness had disgusted me, and excited my suspicions from the first. I was present when Mr. Pennifeather had struck him, and the fiendish expression which then arose upon his countenance, although momentary, assured me that his threat of vengeance would, if possible, be rigidly fulfilled. I was thus prepared to view the manoeuvring of "Old Charley" in a very different light from that in which it was regarded by the good citizens of Rattleborough. I saw at once that all the criminating discoveries arose, either directly or indirectly, from himself.

But the fact which clearly opened my eyes to the true state of the case, was the affair of the bullet, *found* by Mr. G. in the carcass of the horse. *I* had not forgotten, although the Rattleburghers *had*, that there was a hole where the ball had entered the horse, and another where it *went out*. If it were found in the animal then, after having made its exit, I saw clearly that it must have been deposited by the person who found it. The bloody shirt and handkerchief confirmed the idea suggested by the bullet; for the blood on examination proved to be capital claret, and no more. When I came to think of these things, and also of the late increase of liberality and expenditure on the part of Mr. Goodfellow, I entertained a suspicion which was none the less strong because I kept it altogether to myself.

In the meantime, I instituted a rigorous private search for the corpse of Mr. Shuttleworthy, and, for good reasons, searched in quarters as divergent as possible from those to which Mr. Goodfellow conducted his party. The result was that, after some days, I came across an old dry well, the mouth of which was nearly hidden by brambles; and here, at the bottom, I discovered what I sought.

Now it so happened that I had overheard the colloquy between the two cronies, when Mr. Goodfellow had contrived to cajole his host into the promise of a box of *Châteaux-Margaux*. Upon this hint I acted. I procured a stiff piece of whalebone, thrust it down the throat of the corpse, and deposited the latter in an old wine box-taking care so to double the body up as to double the whalebone with it. In this manner I had to press forcibly upon the lid to keep it down while I secured it with nails; and I anticipated, of course, that as soon as these latter were removed, the top would fly *off* and the body *up*.

Having thus arranged the box, I marked, numbered, and addressed it as already told; and then writing a letter in the name of the wine merchants with whom Mr. Shuttleworthy dealt, I gave instructions to my servant to wheel the box to Mr. Goodfellow's door, in a barrow, at a given signal from myself. For the words which I intended the corpse to speak, I confidently depended upon my ventriloquial abilities; for their effect, I counted upon the conscience of the murderous wretch.

I believe there is nothing more to be explained. Mr. Pennifeather was released upon the spot, inherited the fortune of his uncle, profited by the lessons of experience, turned over a new leaf, and led happily ever afterward a new life.

Eureka

A Prose Poem

With Very Profound Respect,
This Work is Dedicated
To
Alexander Von Humboldt

Preface

To the few who love me and whom I love—to those who feel rather than to those who think—to the dreamers and those who put faith in dreams as in the only realities—I offer this book of truths, not in its character of truth-teller, but for the beauty that abounds in its Truth; constituting it true. To these I present the composition as an art-product alone:—let us say as a romance; or, if I be not urging too lofty a claim, as a poem. What I here propound is true:—therefore it cannot die:—or if by any means it be now trodden down so that it die, it will "rise again to the life everlasting."

Nevertheless it is as a poem only that I wish this work to be judged after I am dead. E. A. P.

Eureka: An Essay on the Material and Spiritual Universe

It is with humility really unassumed—it is with a sentiment even of awe—that I pen the opening sentence of this work: for of all conceivable subjects I approach the reader with the most solemn—the most comprehensive—the most difficult—the most august.

What terms shall I find sufficiently simple in their sublimity—sufficiently sublime in their simplicity—for the mere enunciation of my theme?

I design to speak of the Physical, Metaphysical and Mathematical—of the Material and Spiritual Universe:—of its essence, its origin, its creation, its present condition and its destiny. I shall be so rash, moreover, as to challenge the conclusions, and thus, in effect, to question the sagacity, of many of the greatest and most justly reverenced of men.

In the beginning, let me as distinctly as possible announce—not the theorem which I hope to demonstrate—for, whatever the mathematicians may assert, there is, in this world at least, no such thing as demonstration—but the ruling idea which, throughout this volume, I shall be continually endeavouring to suggest.

My general proposition, then, is this:—In the original unity of the first thing lies the secondary cause of all things, with the germ of their inevitable annihilation.

In illustration of this idea, I propose to take such a survey of the Universe that the mind may be able really to receive and to perceive an individual impression.

He who from the top of Ætna casts his eyes leisurely around, is affected chiefly by the extent and diversity of the scene. Only by a rapid whirling on his heel could he hope to comprehend the panorama in the sublimity of its oneness. But as, on the summit of Ætna, no man has thought of whirling on his heel, so no man has ever taken into his brain the full uniqueness of the prospect; and so, again, whatever considerations lie involved in this uniqueness, have as yet no practical existence for mankind.

I do not know a treatise in which a survey of the Universe—using the word in its most comprehensive and only legitimate acceptation—is taken at all:—and it may be as well here to mention that by the term "Universe," wherever employed without qualification in this essay, I mean to designate the utmost conceivable expanse of space, with all things, spiritual and material, that can he imagined to exist within the compass of that expanse. In speaking of what is ordinarily implied by the expression, "Universe," I shall take a phrase of limitation—"the Universe of stars." Why this distinction is considered necessary, will be seen in the sequel.

But even of treatises on the really limited, although always assumed as the un limited, Universe of stars, I know none in which a survey, even of this limited Universe, is so taken as to warrant deductions from its individuality. The nearest approach to such a work is made in the *Cosmos* of Alexander Von Humboldt. He presents the subject, however, not in its individuality but in its generality. His theme, in its last result, is the law of each portion of the merely physical Universe, as this law is related to the laws of every other portion of this merely physical Universe. His design is simply synoeretical. In a word, he discusses the universality of material relation, and discloses to the eye of philosophy whatever inferences have hitherto lain hidden behind this universality. But however admirable be the succinctness with which he has treated each particular point of his topic, the mere multiplicity of these points occasions, necessarily, an amount of detail, and thus an involution of idea, which preclude all individuality of impression.

It seems to me that, in aiming at this latter effect, and, through it, at the consequences—the conclusions—the suggestions—the speculations—or, if nothing better offer itself, the mere guesses which may result from it—we require something like a mental gyration on the heel. We need so rapid a revolution of all things about the central point of sight that, while the minutiae vanish altogether, even the more conspicuous objects become blended into one. Among the vanishing minutiae, in a survey of this kind, would be all exclusively terrestrial matters. The Earth would be considered in its planetary relations alone. A man, in this view, becomes mankind; mankind a member of the cosmical family of intelligences.

And now, before proceeding to our subject proper, let me beg the reader's attention to an extract or two from a somewhat remarkable letter, which appears to have been found corked in a bottle and floating on the Mare Tenebrarum—an ocean well described by the Nubian geographer, Ptolemy Hephestion, but little frequented in modern days unless by the Transcendentalists and some other divers for crotchets. The date of this letter, I confess, surprises me even more particularly than its contents; for it seems to have been written in the year Two thousand eight hundred and forty-eight. As for the passages I am about to transcribe, they, I fancy, will speak for themselves.

"Do you know, my dear friend," says the writer, addressing, no doubt, a contemporary—"Do you know that it is scarcely more than eight or nine hundred years ago since the metaphysicians first consented to relieve the people of the singular fancy that there exist but two practicable roads to Truth? Believe it if you can! It appears, however, that long, long ago, in the night of Time, there lived a Turkish philosopher called Aries and surnamed Tottle." (Here, possibly, the letter-writer means Aristotle; the best names are wretchedly corrupted in two or three thousand years.)

"The fame of this great man depended mainly upon his demonstration that sneezing is a natural provision, by means of which over-profound thinkers are enabled to expel superfluous ideas through the nose; but he obtained a scarcely less valuable celebrity as the founder, or at all events as the principal propagator, of what was termed the *deductive* or a *priori* philosophy. He started with what he maintained to be axioms, or self-evident truths:—and the now well-understood fact that no truths are self-evident, really does not make in the slightest degree against his speculations:—it was sufficient for his purpose that the truths in question were evident at all. From *axioms* he proceeded, logically, to results. His most illustrious disciples were one Tuclid, a geometrician,"(meaning Euclid) "and one Kant, a Dutchman, the originator of that species of Transcendentalism which, with the change merely of a C for a K, now bears his peculiar name.

"Well, Aries Tottle flourished supreme, until the advent of one Hog, surnamed 'the Ettrick shepherd,' who preached an entirely different system, which he called the a *posteriori* or *induc-*

tive. His plan referred altogether to sensation. He proceeded by observing, analyzing, and classifying facts—*instantiae Naturae*, as they were somewhat affectedly called—and arranging them into general laws. In a word, while the mode of Aries rested on *noumena*, that of Hog depended on *phenomena*; and so great was the admiration excited by this latter system that, at its first introduction, Aries fell into general disrepute.

Finally, however, he recovered ground, and was permitted to divide the empire of Philosophy with his more modern rival:—the savans contenting themselves with proscribing all other competitors, past, present, and to come; putting an end to all controversy on the topic by the promulgation of a Median law, to the effect that the Aristotelian and Baconian roads are, and of right ought to be, the sole possible avenues to knowledge:—'Baconian,' you must know, my dear friend," adds the letter-writer at this point, "was an adjective invented as equivalent to Hog-ian, and at the same time more dignified and euphonious.

"Now I do assure you most positively"—proceeds the epistle—"that I represent these matters fairly; and you can easily understand how restrictions so absurd on their very face must have operated, in those days, to retard the progress of true science, which makes its most important advances—as all history will show—by seemingly intuitive leaps. These ancient ideas confined investigation to crawling; and I need not suggest to you that crawling, among varieties of locomotion, is a very capital thing of its kind;—but because the tortoise is sure of foot, for this reason must we clip the wings of the eagles? For many centuries, so great was the infatuation, about Hog especially, that a virtual stop was put to all thinking, properly so called.

"No man dared utter a truth for which he felt himself indebted to his soul alone. It mattered not whether the truth was even demonstrably such; for the dogmatizing philosophers of that epoch regarded only the road by which it professed to have been attained. The end, with them, was a point of no moment, whatever:—'the means!' they vociferated—'let us look at the means!'—and if, on scrutiny of the means, it was found to come neither under the category Hog, nor under the category Aries (which means ram), why then the savans went no farther, but, calling the thinker a fool and branding him a 'theorist,' would never, thenceforward, have any thing to do either with him or with his truths.

"Now, my dear friend," continues the letter-writer, "it cannot be maintained that by the crawling system, exclusively adopted, men would arrive at the maximum amount of truth, even in any long series of ages; for the repression of imagination was an evil not to be counterbalanced even by absolute certainty in the snail processes. But their certainty was very far from absolute. The error of our progenitors was quite analogous with that of the wiseacre who fancies he must necessarily see an object the more distinctly, the more closely he holds it to his eyes. They blinded themselves, too, with the impalpable, titillating Scotch snuff of detail; and thus the boasted facts of the Hog-ites were by no means always facts—a point of little importance but for the assumption that they always were.

"The vital taint, however, in Baconianism—its most lamentable fount of error—lay in its tendency to throw power and consideration into the hands of merely perceptive men—of those inter-Tritonic minnows, the microscopical savans—the diggers and pedlers of minute facts, for the most part in physical science—facts all of which they retailed at the same price upon the highway; their value depending, it was supposed, simply upon the fact of their fact, without reference to their applicability or inapplicability in the development of those ultimate and only legitimate facts, called law.

"Than the persons"—the letter goes on to say—"than the persons thus suddenly elevated by the Hog-ian philosophy into a station for which they were unfitted—thus transferred from the sculleries into the parlours of science—from its pantries into its pulpits—than these individuals a more intolerant—a more intolerable set of bigots and tyrants never existed on the face of the Earth. Their creed, their text and their sermon were, alike, the one word 'fact'—but, for the most part, even of this one word, they knew not even the meaning. On those who ventured to disturb their facts with the view of putting them in order and to use, the disciples of Hog had no mercy whatever.

"All attempts at generalisation were met at once by the words 'theoretical,' 'theory,' 'theorist'—all thought, to be brief, was very properly resented as a personal affront to themselves. Cultivating the natural sciences to the exclusion of Metaphysics, the Mathematics, and Logic, many of these Bacon-engendered philosophers—one-idead, one-sided and lame of a leg—were more wretchedly helpless—more miserably ignorant, in view of all the comprehensible objects of knowledge, than the veriest unlettered hind who proves that he knows something at least, in admitting that he knows absolutely nothing.

"Nor had our forefathers any better right to talk about certainty, when pursuing, in blind confidence, the *a priori* path of *axioms*, or of the ram. At innumerable points this path was scarcely as straight as a ram's-horn. The simple truth is, that the Aristotelians erected their castles upon a basis far less reliable than air; for no such things as *axioms* ever existed or can possibly exist at all. This they must have been very blind, indeed, not to see, or at least to suspect; for, even in their own day, many of their long-admitted '*axioms*' had been abandoned:—'*ex nihilo nihil fit*,' for example, and a 'thing cannot act where it is not,' and 'there cannot be antipodes,' and 'darkness cannot proceed from light.' These and numerous similar propositions formerly accepted, without hesitation, as *axioms*, or undeniable truths, were, even at the period of which I speak, seen to be altogether untenable:—how absurd in these people, then, to persist in relying upon a basis, as immutable, whose mutability had become so repeatedly manifest!

"But, even through evidence afforded by themselves against themselves, it is easy to convict these *à priori* reasoners of the grossest unreason—it is easy to show the futility—the impalpability of their *axioms* in general. I have now lying before me"—it will be observed that we still proceed with the letter—"I have now lying before me a book printed about a thousand years ago.

Pundit assures me that it is decidedly the cleverest ancient work on its topic, which is *Logic.* The author, who was much esteemed in his day, was one Miller or Mill; and we find it recorded of him, as a point of some importance, that he rode a mill-horse whom he called Jeremy Bentham:—but let us glance at the volume itself!

"Ah!—Ability or inability to conceive,' says Mr. Mill very properly, 'is in no case to be received as a criterion of axiomatic truth.' Now, that this is a palpable truism no one in his senses will deny. Not to admit the proposition, is to insinuate a charge of variability in Truth itself, whose very title is a synonym of the Steadfast. If ability to conceive be taken as a criterion of truth, then a truth to David Hume would very seldom be a truth to Joe; and ninety-nine hundredths of what is undeniable in Heaven would be demonstrable falsity upon Earth. The proposition of Mr. Mill, then, is sustained. I will not grant it to be an *axiom*; and this merely because I am showing that no axioms exist; but, with a distinction which could not have been cavilled at even by Mr. Mill himself, I am ready to grant that, if an *axiom* there be, then the proposition of which we speak has the fullest right to be considered an *axiom*—that no more absolute *axiom* is—and, consequently, that any subsequent proposition which shall conflict with this one primarily advanced, must be either a falsity in itself—that is to say no *axiom*—or, if admitted *axiomatic*, must at once neutralise both itself and its predecessor.

"And now, by the logic of their own propounder, let us proceed to test any one of the *axioms* propounded. Let us give Mr. Mill the fairest of play. We will bring the point to no ordinary issue. We will select for investigation no common-place *axiom*—no *axiom* of what, not the less preposterously because only impliedly, he terms his secondary class—as if a positive truth by definition could be either more or less positively a truth:—we will select, I say, no *axiom* of an unquestionability so questionable as is to be found in Euclid. We will not talk, for example, about such propositions as that two straight lines cannot enclose a space, or that the whole is greater than any one of its parts. We will afford the logician every advantage. We will come at once to a proposition which he regards as the acme of the unquestionable—as the quintessence of *axiomatic* undeniability. Here it is:—'Contradictions cannot both be true—that is, cannot coexist in nature.' Here Mr. Mill means, for instance,—and I give the most forcible instance conceivable—that a tree must be either a tree or not a tree—that it cannot be at the same time a tree and not a tree:—all which is quite reasonable of itself and will answer remarkably well as an *axiom*, until we bring it into collation with an *axiom* insisted upon a few pages before—in other words—words which I have previously employed—until we test it by the logic of its own propounder.

"'A tree,' Mr. Mill asserts, 'must be either a tree or not a tree.' Very well:—and now let me ask him, why. To this little query there is but one response:—I defy any man living to invent a second. The sole answer is this:—'Because we find it impossible to conceive that a tree can be anything else than a tree or not a tree.' This, I repeat, is Mr. Mill's sole answer:—he will not pretend to suggest another:—and yet, by his own showing, his answer is clearly no answer at all; for has he not already required us to admit, as an *axiom*, that ability or inability to conceive is in no case to be taken as a criterion of *axiomatic* truth? Thus all—absolutely his argumentation is at sea without a rudder. Let it not be urged that an exception from the general rule is to be made, in cases where the 'impossibility to conceive' is so peculiarly great as when we are called upon to conceive a tree both a tree and not a tree.

"Let no attempt, I say, be made at urging this sotticism; for, in the first place, there are no degrees of 'impossibility,' and thus no one impossible conception can be more peculiarly impossible than another impossible conception:—in the second place, Mr. Mill himself, no doubt after thorough deliberation, has most distinctly, and most rationally, excluded all opportunity for exception, by the emphasis of his proposition, that, in no case, is ability or inability to conceive, to be taken as a criterion of axiomatic truth:—in the third place, even were exceptions admissible at all, it remains to be shown how any exception is admissible here. That a tree can be both a tree and not a tree, is an idea which the angels, or the devils, may entertain, and which no doubt many an Earthly Bedlamite, or Transcendentalist, does.

"Now I do not quarrel with these ancients," continues the letter-writer, "so much on account of the transparent frivolity of their logic—which, to be plain, was baseless, worthless and fantastic altogether—as on account of their pompous and infatuate proscription of all other roads to truth than the two narrow and crooked paths—the one of creeping and the other of crawling—to which, in their ignorant perversity, they have dared to confine the soul—the soul which loves nothing so well as to soar in those regions of illimitable intuition which are utterly incognisant of 'path.'

"By the bye, my dear friend, is it not an evidence of the mental slavery entailed upon those bigoted people by their Hogs and Rams, that in spite of the eternal prating of their *savans* about roads to truth, none of them fell, even by accident, into what we now so distinctly perceive to be the broadest, the straightest and most available of all mere roads—the great thoroughfare—the majestic highway of the consistent? Is it not wonderful that they should have failed to deduce from the works of God the vitally momentous consideration that a perfect consistency can be nothing but an absolute truth? How plain—how rapid our progress since the late announcement of this proposition! By its means, investigation has been taken out of the hands of the ground-moles, and given as a duty, rather than as a task, to the true—to the only true thinkers—to the generally-educated men of ardent imagination.

"These latter—our Keplers—our Laplaces—'speculate'—'theorise'—these are the terms—can you not fancy the shout of scorn with which they would be received by our progenitors, were it possible for them to be looking over my shoulders as I write? The Keplers, I repeat, speculate—theorize—and their theories are merely corrected—reduced—sifted—cleared, little by little, of their chaff of inconsistency—until at length there stands apparent an unencumbered consistency—a consistency which the most stolid admit—because it is a consistency—to be an absolute and unquestionable truth.

"I have often thought, my friend, that it must have puzzled these dogmaticians of a thousand years ago, to determine, even, by which of their two boasted roads it is that the cryptographist attains the solution of the more complicated ciphers—or by which of them Champollion guided mankind to those important and innumerable truths which, for so many centuries, have lain entombed amid the phonetical hieroglyphics of Egypt. In especial, would it not have given these bigots some trouble to determine by which of their two roads was reached the most momentous and sublime of their truths—the truth—the fact of gravitation? Newton deduced it from the laws of Kepler. Kepler admitted that these laws he guessed—these laws whose investigation disclosed to the greatest of British astronomers that principle, the basis of all (existing) physical principle, in going behind which we enter at once the nebulous kingdom of Metaphysics.

"Yes!—these vital laws Kepler guessed—that it is to say, he imagined them. Had he been asked to point out either the deductive or inductive route by which he attained them, his reply might have been—'I know nothing about routes—but I do know the machinery of the Universe. Here it is. I grasped it with my soul—I reached it through mere dint of intuition.' Alas, poor ignorant old man! Could not any metaphysician have told him that what he called 'intuition' was but the conviction resulting from deductions or inductions of which the processes were so shadowy as to have escaped his consciousness, eluded his reason, or bidden defiance to his capacity of expression? How great a pity it is that some 'moral philosopher' had not enlightened him about all this! How it would have comforted him on his deathbed to know that, instead of having gone intuitively and thus unbecomingly, he had, in fact, proceeded decorously and legitimately—that is to say Hog-ishly, or at least Ram-ishly—into the vast halls where lay gleaming, untended, and hitherto untouched by mortal hand—unseen by mortal eye—the imperishable and priceless secrets of the Universe!

"Yes, Kepler was essentially a theorist; but this title, now of so much sanctity, was, in those ancient days, a designation of supreme contempt. It is only now that men begin to appreciate that divine old man—to sympathize with the prophetical and poetical rhapsody of his ever-memorable words. For my part," continues the unknown correspondent, "I glow with a sacred fire when I even think of them, and feel that I shall never grow weary of their repetition:—in concluding this letter, let me have the real pleasure of transcribing them once again:— 'I care not whether my work be read now or by posterity. I can afford to wait a century for readers when God himself has waited six thousand years for an observer. I triumph. I have stolen the golden secret of the Egyptians. I will indulge my sacred fury.'"

Here end my quotations from this very unaccountable and, perhaps, somewhat impertinent epistle; and perhaps it would be folly to comment, in any respect, upon the chimerical, not to say revolutionary, fancies of the writer—whoever he is—fancies so radically at war with the well-considered and well-settled opinions of this age. Let us proceed, then, to our legitimate thesis, *The Universe.*

This thesis admits a choice between two modes of discussion:—

We may ascend or descend. Beginning at our own point of view—at the Earth on which we stand—we may pass to the other planets of our system—thence to the Sun—thence to our system considered collectively—and thence, through other systems, indefinitely outwards; or, commencing on high at some point as definite as we can make it or conceive it, we may come down to the habitation of man. Usually—that is to say, in ordinary essays on astronomy—the first of these two modes is, with certain reservation, adopted:—this for the obvious reason that astronomical facts, merely, and principles, being the object, that object is best fulfilled in stepping from the known because proximate, gradually onward to the point where all certitude becomes lost in the remote.

For my present purpose, however,—that of enabling the mind to take in, as if from afar and at one glance, a distant conception of the individual Universe—it is clear that a descent to small from great—to the outskirts from the centre (if we could establish a centre)—to the end from the beginning (if we could fancy a beginning) would be the preferable course, but for the difficulty, if not impossibility, of presenting, in this course, to the unastronomical, a picture at all comprehensible in regard to such considerations as are involved in quantity—that is to say, in number, magnitude and distance.

Now, distinctness—intelligibility, at all points, is a primary feature in my general design. On important topics it is better to be a good deal prolix than even a very little obscure. But abstruseness is a quality appertaining to no subject *per se.* All are alike, in facility of comprehension, to him who approaches them by properly graduated steps. It is merely because a stepping-stone, here and there, is heedlessly left unsupplied in our road to the Differential Calculus, that this latter is not altogether as simple a thing as a sonnet by Mr. Solomon Seesaw.

By way of admitting, then, no chance for misapprehension, I think it advisable to proceed as if even the more obvious facts of astronomy were unknown to the reader. In combining the two modes of discussion to which I have referred, I propose to avail myself of the advantages peculiar to each—and very especially of the iteration in detail which will be unavoidable as a consequence of the plan. Commencing with a descent, I shall reserve for the return upwards those indispensable considerations of quantity to which allusion has already been made.

Let us begin, then, at once, with that merest of words, "Infinity." This, like "God," "spirit," and some other expressions of which the equivalents exist in all languages, is by no means the expression of an idea—but of an effort at one. It stands for the possible attempt at an impossible conception. Man needed a term by which to point out the direction of this effort—the cloud behind which lay, forever invisible, the object of this attempt. A word, in fine, was demanded, by means of which one human being might put himself in relation at once with another human being and with a certain tendency of the human intellect. Out of this demand arose the word, "Infinity;" which is thus the representative but of the thought of a thought.

As regards that infinity now considered—the infinity of space—we often hear it said that "its idea is admitted by the mind—is acquiesced in—is entertained—on account of the greater difficulty which attends the conception of a limit." But this is merely one of those phrases by which even profound thinkers, time out of mind, have occasionally taken pleasure in deceiving themselves. The quibble lies concealed in the word "difficulty." "The mind," we are told, "entertains the idea of limitless, through the greater difficulty which it finds in entertaining that of limited, space." Now, were the proposition but fairly put, its absurdity would become transparent at once. Clearly, there is no mere difficulty in the case. The assertion intended, if presented according to its intention and without sophistry, would run thus:—"The mind admits the idea of limitless, through the greater impossibility of entertaining that of limited, space."

It must be immediately seen that this is not a question of two statements between whose respective credibilities—or of two arguments between whose respective validities—the reason is called upon to decide:—it is a matter of two conceptions, directly conflicting, and each avowedly impossible, one of which the intellect is supposed to be capable of entertaining, on account of the greater impossibility of entertaining the other. The choice is not made between two difficulties;—it is merely fancied to be made between two impossibilities. Now of the former, there are degrees,—but of the latter, none:—just as our impertinent letter-writer has already suggested. A task may be more or less difficult; but it is either possible or not possible:—there are no gradations. It might be more difficult to overthrow the Andes than an ant-hill; but it can be no more impossible to annihilate the matter of the one than the matter of the other. A man may jump ten feet with less difficulty than he can jump twenty, but the impossibility of his leaping to the Moon is not a whit less than that of his leaping to the dog-star.

Since all this is undeniable: since the choice of the mind is to be made between impossibilities of conception: since one impossibility cannot be greater than another: and since, thus, one cannot be preferred to another: the philosophers who not only maintain, on the grounds mentioned, man's idea of infinity but, on account of such supposititious idea, infinity itself—are plainly engaged in demonstrating one impossible thing to be possible by showing how it is that some one other thing—is impossible too. This, it will be said, is nonsense; and perhaps it is:—indeed I think it very capital nonsense—but forego all claim to it as nonsense of mine.

The readiest mode, however, of displaying the fallacy of the philosophical argument on this question, is by simply adverting to a fact respecting it which has been hitherto quite overlooked—the fact that the argument alluded to both proves and disproves its own proposition. "The mind is impelled," say the theologians and others, "to admit a first cause, by the superior difficulty it experiences in conceiving cause beyond cause without end." The quibble, as before, lies in the word "difficulty"—but here what is it employed to sustain? A first cause. And what is a first cause? An ultimate termination of causes. And what is an ultimate termination of causes? Finity—the finite. Thus the one quibble, in two processes, by God knows how many philosophers, is made to support now finity and now infinity—could it not be brought to support something besides? As for the quibblers—they, at least, are insupportable. But—to dismiss them:—what they prove in the one case is the identical nothing which they demonstrate in the other.

Of course, no one will suppose that I here contend for the absolute impossibility of *that* which we attempt to convey in the word "Infinity." My purpose is but to show the folly of endeavouring to prove Infinity itself, or even our conception of it, by any such blundering ratiocination as that which is ordinarily employed.

Nevertheless, as an individual, I may be permitted to say that

I *cannot* conceive Infinity, and am convinced that no human being can. A mind not thoroughly self-conscious—not accustomed to the introspective analysis of its own operations—will, it is true, often deceive itself by supposing that it *has* entertained the conception of which we speak. In the effort to entertain it, we proceed step beyond step—we fancy point still beyond point; and so long as we *continue* the effort, it may be said, in fact, that we are *tending* to the formation of the idea designed; while the strength of the impression that we actually form or have formed it, is in the ratio of the period during which we keep up the mental endeavour.

But it is in the act of discontinuing the endeavour—of fulfilling (as we think) the idea—of putting the finishing stroke (as we suppose) to the conception—that we overthrow at once the whole fabric of our fancy by resting upon some one ultimate and therefore definite point. This fact, however, we fail to perceive, on account of the absolute coincidence, in time, between the settling down upon the ultimate point and the act of cessation in thinking.—In attempting, on the other hand, to frame the idea of a *limited* space, we merely converse the processes which involve the impossibility.

We *believe* in a God. We may or may not *believe* in finite or in infinite space; but our belief, in such cases, is more properly designated as *faith*, and is a matter quite distinct from that belief proper—from that *intellectual* belief—which presupposes the mental conception.

The fact is, that, upon the enunciation of any one of that class of terms to which "Infinity" belongs—the class representing *thoughts of thought*—he who has a right to say that he thinks *at all,* feels himself called upon, *not* to entertain a conception, but simply to direct his mental vision toward some given point, in the intellectual firmament, where lies a nebula never to be resolved. To solve it, indeed, he makes no effort; for with a rapid instinct he comprehends, not only the impossibility, but, as regards all human purposes, the *inessentiality*, of its solution. He perceives that the Deity has not *designed* it to be solved. He sees, at once, that it lies *out* of the brain of man, and even *how*, if not exactly *why*, it lies out of it.

There are people, I am aware, who, busying themselves in attempts at the unattainable, acquire very easily, by dint of the jargon they emit, among those thinkers-that-they-think with whom darkness and depth are synonymous, a kind of cuttlefish reputation for profundity; but the finest quality of Thought is its self-cognisance; and, with some little equivocation, it may be said that no fog of the mind can well be greater than that which, extending to the very boundaries of the mental domain, shuts out even these boundaries themselves from comprehension.

It will now be understood that, in using the phrase, "Infinity of Space," I make no call upon the reader to entertain the impossible conception of an *absolute* infinity. I refer simply to the "*utmost conceivable expanse*" of space—a shadowy and fluctuating domain, now shrinking, now swelling, in accordance with the vacillating energies of the imagination.

Hitherto, the Universe of stars has always been considered as coincident with the Universe proper, as I have defined it in the commencement of this discourse. It has been always either directly or indirectly assumed—at least since the dawn of intelligible astronomy—that, were it possible for us to attain any given point in space, we should still find, on all sides of us, an interminable succession of stars. This was the untenable idea of Pascal when making perhaps the most successful attempt ever made, at paraphrasing the conception for which we struggle in the word "Universe."

"It is a sphere," he says, "of which the centre is everywhere, the circumference, nowhere." But although this intended definition is, in fact, no definition of the Universe of *stars*, we may accept it, with some mental reservation, as a definition (rigorous enough for all practical purposes) of the Universe *proper*—that is to say, of the Universe of *space*. This latter, then, let us regard as "*a sphere of which the centre is everywhere, the circumference nowhere*." In fact, while we find it impossible to fancy an end to space, we have no difficulty in picturing to ourselves any one of an infinity of *beginnings*.

As our starting point, then, let us adopt the *Godhead*. Of this Godhead, *in itself*, he alone is not imbecile—he alone is not impious who propounds—nothing. "*Nous ne connaissons rien*," says the Baron de Bielfeld—"*Nous ne connaissons rien de la nature ou de l'essence de Dieu:—pour savoir ce qu'il est, il faut être Dieu même*."—"We know absolutely *nothing* of the nature or essence of God:—in order to comprehend what he is, we should have to be God ourselves."

"*We should have to be God ourselves!*"—With a phrase so startling as this yet ringing in my ears, I nevertheless venture to demand if this our present ignorance of the Deity is an ignorance to which the soul is *everlastingly* condemned.

By *Him*, however—*now*, at least, the Incomprehensible—by Him—assuming him as *Spirit*—that is to say, as *not Matter*—a distinction which, for all intelligible purposes, will stand well instead of a definition—by Him, then, existing as Spirit, let us content ourselves, tonight, with supposing to have been *created*, or made out of nothing, by dint of his volition—at some point of Space which we will take as a centre—at some period into which we do not pretend to inquire, but at all events immensely remote—by Him, then again, let us suppose to have been created—*what?* This is a vitally momentous epoch in our considerations. *What* is it that we are justified—that alone we are justified in supposing to have been, primarily and solely, *created?*

We have attained a point where only *intuition* can aid us:—but now let me recur to the idea which I have already suggested as that alone which we can properly entertain of intuition. It is *but the conviction arising from those inductions or deductions of which the processes are so shadowy as to escape our consciousness, elude our reason, or defy our capacity of expression*. With this understanding, I now assert—that an intuition altogether irresistible, although inexpressible, forces me to the conclusion that what God originally created—that that matter which, by dint of his Volition, he first made from his Spirit, or from nihility, *could* have been nothing but matter in its utmost conceivable state of—what?—

of *simplicity?*

This will be found the sole absolute *assumption* of my discourse. I use the word "assumption" in its ordinary sense; yet I maintain that even this my primary proposition, is very, very far indeed, from being really a mere assumption. Nothing was ever more certainly—no human conclusion was ever, in fact, more regularly—more rigorously *deduced*:—but, alas! the processes lie out of the human analysis—at all events are beyond the utterance of the human tongue.

Let us now endeavour to conceive what Matter must be, when, or if, in its absolute extreme of *simplicity*. Here the reason flies at once to imparticularity—to a particle—to *one* particle—a particle of *one* kind—of *one* character—of *one* nature—of *one* size—of *one* form—a particle, therefore, "*without* form and void"—a particle positively a particle at all points—a particle absolutely unique, individual, undivided, and not indivisible only because He who *created* it, by dint of his Will, can by an infinitely less energetic exercise of the same Will, as a matter of course, divide it.

Oneness, then, is all that I predicate of the originally created Matter; but I propose to show that this *Oneness is a principle abundantly sufficient to account for the constitution, the existing phenomena and the plainly inevitable annihilation of at least the material Universe.*

The willing into being the primordial particle, has completed the act, or more properly the conception, of creation. We now proceed to the ultimate purpose for which we are to suppose the particle created—that is to say, the ultimate purpose so far as our considerations yet enable us to see it—the constitution of the Universe from it, the particle.

This constitution has been effected by *forcing* the originally and therefore normally *one* into the abnormal condition of *many*. An action of this character implies reaction. A diffusion from unity, under the conditions, involves a tendency to return into unity—a tendency ineradicable until satisfied. But on these points I will speak more fully hereafter.

The assumption of absolute unity in the primordial particle includes that of infinite divisibility. Let us conceive the particle, then, to be only not totally exhausted by diffusion into space. From the one particle, as a centre, let us suppose to be irradiated spherically—in all directions—to immeasurable but still to definite distances in the previously vacant space—a certain inexpressibly great yet limited number of unimaginably yet not infinitely minute atoms.

Now, of these atoms, thus diffused, or upon diffusion, what conditions are we permitted—not to assume, but to infer, from consideration as well of their source as of the character of the design apparent in their diffusion? *Unity* being their source, and *difference* from *unity* the character of the design manifested in their diffusion, we are warranted in supposing this character to be at least generally preserved throughout the design, and to form a portion of the design itself:—that is to say, we shall be warranted in conceiving continual differences at all points from the uniquity and simplicity of the origin.

But, for these reasons, shall we be justified in imagining the atoms heterogeneous, dissimilar, unequal, and in equidistant? More explicitly—are we to consider no two atoms as, at their diffusion, of the same nature, or of the same form, or of the same size?—and, after fulfilment of their diffusion into Space, is absolute in equidistance, each from each, to be understood of all of them? In such arrangement, under such conditions, we most easily and immediately comprehend the subsequent most feasible carrying out to completion of any such design as that which I have suggested—the design of variety out of unity—diversity out of sameness—heterogeneity out of homogeneity—complexity out of simplicity—in a word, the utmost possible multiplicity of *relation* out of the emphatically irrelative *one*.

Undoubtedly, therefore, we *should* be warranted in assuming all that has been mentioned, but for the reflection, first, that supererogation is not presumable of any Divine Act; and, secondly, that the object supposed in view, appears as feasible when some of the conditions in question are dispensed with, in the beginning, as when all are understood immediately to exist. I mean to say that some are involved in the rest, or so instantaneous a consequence of them as to make the distinction inappreciable. Difference of *size*, for example, will at once be brought about through the tendency of one atom to a second, in preference to a third, on account of particular in equidistance; which is to be comprehended as *particular in equidistances between centres of quantity, in neighbouring atoms of different form*—a matter not at all interfering with the generally-equable distribution of the atoms.

Difference of kind, too, is easily conceived to be merely a result of differences in size and form, taken more or less conjointly:—in fact, since the *unity* of the particle Proper implies absolute homogeneity, we cannot imagine the atoms, at their diffusion, differing in kind, without imagining, at the same time, a special exercise of the Divine Will, at the emission of each atom, for the purpose of effecting, in each, a change of its essential nature:—so fantastic an idea is the less to be indulged, as the object proposed is seen to be thoroughly attainable without such minute and elaborate interposition.

We perceive, therefore, upon the whole, that it would be supererogatory, and consequently unphilosophical, to predicate of the atoms, in view of their purposes, anything more than *difference of form* at their dispersion, with particular in equidistance after it—all other differences arising at once out of these, in the very first processes of mass-constitution:—We thus establish the Universe on a purely *geometrical* basis. Of course, it is by no means necessary to assume absolute difference, even of form, among *all* the atoms irradiated—any more than absolute particular in equidistance of each from each. We are required to conceive merely that no *neighbouring* atoms are of similar form—no atoms which can ever approximate, until their inevitable reunition at the end.

Although the immediate and perpetual *tendency* of the disunited atoms to return into their normal unity, is implied, as I have said, in their abnormal diffusion; still it is clear that this tendency will be without consequence—a tendency and no more—until the diffusive energy, in ceasing to be exerted, shall leave *it*, the tendency, free to seek its satisfaction. The Divine Act, however, being considered as determinate, and discontinued on fulfilment of the diffusion, we understand, at once, *a reaction*—in other words, a *satisfiable* tendency of the disunited atoms to return into *one*.

But the diffusive energy being withdrawn, and the reaction having commenced in furtherance of the ultimate design—*that of the utmost possible relation*—this design is now in danger of being frustrated, in detail, by reason of that very tendency to return which is to effect its accomplishment in general. *Multiplicity* is the object; but there is nothing to prevent proximate atoms, from lapsing *at once*, through the now satisfiable tendency—*before* the fulfilment of any ends proposed in multiplicity—into absolute oneness among themselves:—there is nothing to impede the aggregation of various *unique* masses, at various points of space:—in other words, nothing to interfere with the accumulation of various masses, each absolutely one.

For the effectual and thorough completion of the general design, we thus see the necessity for a repulsion of limited capacity—a separate *something* which, on withdrawal of the diffusive Volition, shall at the same time allow the approach, and forbid the junction, of the atoms; suffering them infinitely to approximate, while denying them positive contact; in a word, having the power—*up to a certain epoch*—of preventing their *coalition*, but no ability to interfere with their coalescence in any respect *or degree*. The repulsion, already considered as so peculiarly limited in other regards, must be understood, let me repeat, as having power to prevent absolute coalition, *only up to a certain epoch*.

Unless we are to conceive that the appetite for unity among the atoms is doomed to be satisfied *never*;—unless we are to conceive that what had a beginning is to have no end—a conception which cannot *really* be entertained, however much we may talk or dream of entertaining it—we are forced to conclude that the repulsive influence imagined, will, finally—under pressure of the *uni-tendency collectively* applied, but, never and in no degree *until*, on fulfilment of the Divine purposes, such collective application shall be naturally made—yield to a force which, at that ultimate epoch, shall be the superior force precisely to the extent required, and thus permit the universal subsidence into the inevitable, because original and therefore normal, *one*.—The conditions here to be reconciled are difficult indeed:—we cannot even comprehend the possibility of their conciliation;—nevertheless, the apparent impossibility is brilliantly suggestive.

That the repulsive something actually exists, *we see*. Man neither employs, nor knows, a force sufficient to bring two atoms into contact. This is but the well-established proposition of the impenetrability of matter. All experiment proves—all philosophy admits it. The design of the repulsion—the necessity for its existence—I have endeavoured to show; but from all attempt at investigating its nature have religiously abstained; this on account of an intuitive conviction that the principle at issue is strictly spiritual—lies in a recess impervious to our present understanding—lies involved in a consideration of what now—in our human state—is *not* to be considered—in a consideration of *Spirit in itself*. I feel, in a word, that here the God has interposed, and here only, because here and here only the knot demanded the interposition of the God.

In fact, while the tendency of the diffused atoms to return into unity, will be recognised, at once, as the principle of the Newtonian Gravity, what I have spoken of as a repulsive influence prescribing limits to the (immediate) satisfaction of the tendency, will be understood as that which we have been in the practice of designating now as heat, now as magnetism, now as *electricity*; displaying our ignorance of its awful character in the vacillation of the phraseology with which we endeavour to circumscribe it.

Calling it, merely for the moment, electricity, we know that all experimental analysis of electricity has given, as an ultimate result, the principle, or seeming principle, *heterogeneity*. *Only* where things differ is electricity apparent; and it is presumable that they *never* differ where it is not developed at least, if not apparent. Now, this result is in the fullest keeping with that which I have reached unempirically. The design of the repulsive influence I have maintained to be that of preventing immediate unity among the diffused atoms; and these atoms are represented as different each from each. *Difference* is their character—their essentiality—just as *no-difference* was the essentiality of their course.

When we say, then, that an attempt to bring any two of these atoms together would induce an effort, on the part of the repulsive influence, to prevent the contact we may as well use the strictly convertible sentence that an attempt to bring together any two differences will result in a development of electricity. All existing bodies, of course, are composed of these atoms in proximate contact, and are therefore to be considered as mere assemblages of more or fewer differences; and the resistance made by the repulsive spirit, on bringing together any two such assemblages, would be in the ratio of the two sums of the differences in each:—an expression which, when reduced, is equivalent to this:—

The amount of electricity developed on the approximation of two bodies, is proportional to the difference between the respective sums of the atoms of which the bodies are composed. That *no* two bodies are absolutely alike, is a simple corollary from all that has been here said. Electricity, therefore, existing always, is *developed* whenever *any* bodies, but *manifested* only when bodies of appreciable difference, are brought into approximation.

To electricity—so, for the present, continuing to call it—we *may* not be wrong in referring the various physical appearances of light, heat and magnetism; but far less shall we be liable to err in attributing to this strictly spiritual principle the more important phenomena of vitality, consciousness and *thought*. On this topic, however, I need pause here merely to suggest that these phenomena, whether observed generally or in detail, seem to proceed *at least in the ratio of the heterogeneous.*

Discarding now the two equivocal terms, "gravitation" and "electricity," let us adopt the more definite expressions, "*attrac-*

tion" and "*repulsion*." The former is the body; the latter the soul: the one is the material; the other the spiritual, principle of the Universe. *No other principles exist. All* phenomena are referable to one, or to the other, or to both combined. So rigorously is this the case—so thoroughly demonstrable is it that attraction and repulsion are the sole properties through which we perceive the Universe—in other words, by which matter is manifested to mind—that, for all merely argumentative purposes, we are fully justified in assuming that matter exists only as attraction and repulsion—that attraction and repulsion *are* matter:—there being no conceivable case in which we may not employ the term "matter" and the terms "attraction" and "repulsion," taken together, as equivalent, and therefore convertible, expressions in logic.

I said, just now, that what I have described as the tendency of the diffused atoms to return into their original unity, would be understood as the principle of the Newtonian law of gravity: and, in fact, there can be but little difficulty in such an understanding, if we look at the Newtonian gravity in a merely general view, as a force impelling matter to seek matter; that is to say, when we pay no attention to the known *modus operandi* of the Newtonian force. The general coincidence satisfies us; but, upon looking closely, we see, in detail, much that appears in coincident, and much in regard to which no coincidence, at least, is established. For example; the Newtonian gravity, when we think of it in certain moods, does *not* seem to be a tendency to *oneness* at all, but rather a tendency of all bodies in all directions—a phrase apparently expressive of a tendency to diffusion. Here, then, is an *incoincidence*. Again; when we reflect on the mathematical *law* governing the Newtonian tendency, we see clearly that no coincidence has been made good, in respect of the *modus operandi*, at least, between gravitation as known to exist and that seemingly simple and direct tendency which I have assumed.

In fact, I have attained a point at which it will be advisable to strengthen my position by reversing my processes. So far, we have gone on *à priori*, from an abstract consideration of Simplicity, as that quality most likely to have characterized the original action of God. Let us now see whether the established facts of the Newtonian Gravitation may not afford us, *à posteriori,* some legitimate inductions.

What does the Newtonian law declare?—That all bodies attract each other with forces proportional to their quantities of matter and inversely proportional to the squares of their distances. Purposely, I have here given, in the first place, the vulgar version of the law; and I confess that in this, as in most other vulgar versions of great truths, we find little of a suggestive character. Let us now adopt a more philosophical phraseology:—*Every atom, of every body, attracts every other atom, both of its own and of every other body, with a force which varies inversely as the squares of the distances between the attracting and attracted atom.*—Here, indeed, a flood of suggestion bursts upon the mind.

But let us see distinctly what it was that Newton *proved*—according to the grossly irrational definitions of *proof* prescribed by the metaphysical schools. He was forced to content himself with showing how thoroughly the motions of an imaginary Universe, composed of attracting and attracted atoms obedient to the law he announced, coincide with those of the actually existing Universe so far as it comes under our observation. This was the amount of his *demonstration*—that is to say, this was the amount of it, according to the conventional cant of the "philosophies." His successors added proof multiplied by proof—such proof as a sound intellect admits—but the *demonstration* of the law itself, persist the metaphysicians, had not been strengthened in any degree.

"*Ocular, physical* proof," however, of attraction, here upon Earth, in accordance with the Newtonian theory, was, at length, much to the satisfaction of some intellectual grovellers, afforded. This proof arose collaterally and incidentally (as nearly all important truths have arisen) out of an attempt to ascertain the mean density of the Earth. In the famous Maskelyne, Cavendish and Bailly experiments for this purpose, the attraction of the mass of a mountain was seen, felt, measured, and found to be mathematically consistent with the immortal theory of the British astronomer.

But in spite of this confirmation of that which needed none—in spite of the so-called corroboration of the "theory" by the so-called "ocular and physical proof"—in spite of the *character* of this corroboration—the ideas which even really philosophical men cannot help imbibing of gravity—and, especially, the ideas of it which ordinary men get and contentedly maintain, are seen to have been derived, for the most part, from a consideration of the principle as they find it developed—*merely in the planet upon which they stand.*

Now, to what does so partial a consideration tend—to what species of error does it give rise? On the Earth we *see* and *feel*, only that gravity impels all bodies towards the *centre* of the Earth. No man in the common walks of life could be *made* to see or feel anything else—could be made to perceive that anything, anywhere, has a perpetual, gravitating tendency in any *other* direction than to the centre of the Earth; yet (with an exception hereafter to be specified) it is a fact that every Earthly thing (not to speak now of every heavenly thing) has a tendency not *only* to the Earth's centre but in every conceivable direction besides.

Now, although the philosophic cannot be said to *err with* the vulgar in this matter, they nevertheless permit themselves to be influenced, without knowing it, by the *sentiment* of the vulgar idea. "Although the Pagan fables are not believed," says Bryant, in his very erudite *Mythology*, "yet we forget ourselves continually and make inferences from them as from existing realities." I mean to assert that the merely *sensitive perception* of gravity as we experience it on Earth, beguiles mankind into the fancy of *concentralisation* or *especiality* respecting it—has been continually biasing towards this fancy even the mightiest intellects—perpetually, although imperceptibly, leading them away from the real characteristics of the principle; thus preventing them, up to this date, from ever getting a glimpse of that vital truth which lies in a diametrically opposite direction—behind the principle's *essential* characteristics—those, *not* of concentralisation or especiality—but of *universality* and *diffusion*. This "vital truth" is *unity* as the *source* of the phenomenon.

Let me now repeat the definition of gravity:—*Every atom, of every body, attracts every other atom, both of its own and of every other body,* with a force which varies inversely as the squares of the distances of the attracting and attracted atom.

Here let the reader pause with me, for a moment, in contemplation of the miraculous—of the ineffable—of the altogether unimaginable complexity of relation involved in the fact that *each atom attracts every other atom*—involved merely in this fact of the attraction, without reference to the law or mode in which the attraction is manifested—involved *merely* in the fact that each atom attracts every other atom *at all*, in a wilderness of atoms so numerous that those which go to the composition of a cannon-ball, exceed, probably, in mere point of number, all the stars which go to the constitution of the Universe.

Had we discovered, simply, that each atom tended to some one favourite point—to some especially attractive atom—we should still have fallen upon a discovery which, in itself, would have sufficed to overwhelm the mind:—but what is it that we are actually called upon to comprehend? That each atom attracts—sympathizes with the most delicate movements of every other atom, and with each and with all at the same time, and forever, and according to a determinate law of which the complexity, even considered by itself solely, is utterly beyond the grasp of the imagination of man. If I propose to ascertain the influence of one mote in a sunbeam upon its neighbouring mote, I cannot accomplish my purpose without first counting and weighing all the atoms in the Universe and defining the precise positions of all at one particular moment.

If I venture to displace, by even the billionth part of an inch, the microscopical speck of dust which lies now upon the point of my finger, what is the character of that act upon which I have adventured? I have done a deed which shakes the Moon in her path, which causes the Sun to be no longer the Sun, and which alters forever the destiny of the multitudinous myriads of stars that roll and glow in the majestic presence of their Creator.

These ideas—conceptions such as *these*—unthought-like thoughts—soul-reveries rather than conclusions or even considerations of the intellect:—ideas, I repeat, such as these, are such as we can alone hope profitably to entertain in any effort at grasping the great principle, *attraction*.

But now,—*with* such ideas—with such a *vision* of the marvellous complexity of attraction fairly in his mind—let any person competent of thought on such topics as these, set himself to the task of imagining a *principle* for the phenomena observed—a condition from which they sprang.

Does not so evident a brotherhood among the atoms point to a common parentage? Does not a sympathy so omni-prevalent, so ineradicable, and so thoroughly irrespective, suggest a common paternity as its source? Does not one extreme impel the reason to the other? Does not the infinitude of division refer to the utterness of individuality? Does not the entireness of the complex hint at the perfection of the simple? It is *not* that the atoms, as we see them, are divided or that they are complex in their relations—but that they are inconceivably divided and unutterably complex:—it is the extremeness of the conditions to which I now allude, rather than to the conditions themselves. In a word, not because the atoms were, at some remote epoch of time, *even more than together*—is it not because originally, and therefore normally, they were *one*—that now, in all circumstances—at all points—in all directions—by all modes of approach—in all relations and through all conditions—they struggle back to this absolutely, this irrelatively, this unconditionally *one?*

Some person may here demand:—"Why—since it is to the *one* that the atoms struggle back—do we not find and define attraction 'a merely general tendency to a centre?'—why, in especial, do not *your* atoms—the atoms which you describe as having been irradiated from a centre—proceed at once, rectilinearly, back to the central point of their origin?"

I reply that *they do*; as will be distinctly shown; but that the cause of their so doing is quite irrespective of the centre *as such.* They all tend rectilinearly towards a centre, because of the sphericity with which they have been irradiated into space. Each atom, forming one of a generally uniform globe of atoms, finds more atoms in the direction of the centre, of course, than in any other, and in that direction, therefore, is impelled—but is *not* thus impelled because the centre is *the point of its origin.* It is not to any *point* that the atoms are allied. It is not any *locality*, either in the concrete or in the abstract, to which I suppose them bound. Nothing like *location* was conceived as their origin.

Their source lies in the principle, *unity. This* is their lost parent. This they seek always—immediately—in all directions—wherever it is even partially to be found; thus appeasing, in some measure, the ineradicable tendency, while on the way to its absolute satisfaction in the end. It follows from all this, that any principle which shall be adequate to account for the *law* or *modus operandi*, of the attractive force in general, will account for this law in particular:—that is to say, any principle which will show why the atoms should tend to their *general centre of irradiation* with forces inversely proportional to the squares of the distances, will be admitted as satisfactorily accounting, at the same time, for the tendency, according to the same law, of these atoms each to each:—*for* the tendency to the centre is merely the tendency each to each, and not any tendency to a centre as such.

Thus it will be seen, also, that the establishment of my propositions would involve no necessity of modification in the terms of the Newtonian definition of Gravity, which declares that each atom attracts each other atom and so forth, and declares this merely; but (always under the supposition that what I propose be, in the end, admitted) it seems clear that some error might occasionally be avoided, in the future processes of science, were a more ample phraseology adopted:—for instance:—"Each atom tends to every other atom &c. with a force &c: *the general result being a tendency of all, with a similar force, to a general centre.*"

The reversal of our processes has thus brought us to an identical result; but, while in the one process *intuition* was the starting-point, in the other it was the goal. In commencing the former journey I could only say that, with an irresistible intuition, I *felt* simplicity to have been the characteristic of the original action of God:—in ending the latter I can only declare that, with an irresistible intuition, I perceive unity to have been the source of the observed phenomena of the Newtonian gravitation. Thus, according to the schools, I prove nothing. So be it:—I design but to suggest—and to convince through the suggestion. I am proudly aware that there exist many of the most profound and cautiously discriminative human intellects which cannot *help* being abundantly content with my—suggestions.

To these intellects—as to my own—there is no mathematical demonstration which could bring the least additional *true proof* of the great *truth* which I have advanced—*the truth of original unity as the source—as the principle of the universal phenomena.* For my part, I am not sure that I speak and see—I am not so sure that my heart beats and that my soul lives:—of the rising of tomorrow's Sun—a probability that as yet lies in the future—I do not pretend to be one thousandth part as sure—as I am of the irretrievably by-gone *fact* that all things and all thoughts of things, with all their ineffable multiplicity of relation, sprang at once into being from the primordial and irrelative *one.*

Referring to the Newtonian Gravity, Dr. Nichol, the eloquent author of *The Architecture of the Heavens,* says:—"In truth we have no reason to suppose this great law, as now revealed, to be the ultimate or simplest, and therefore the universal and all-comprehensive, form of a great ordinance. The mode in which its intensity diminishes with the element of distance, has not the aspect of an ultimate *principle*; which always assumes the simplicity and self-evidence of those axioms which constitute the basis of geometry."

Now, it is quite true that "ultimate principles," in the common understanding of the words, always assume the simplicity of geometrical axioms—(as for "self-evidence," there is no such thing)—but these principles are clearly *not* "ultimate;" in other terms what we are in the habit of calling principles are no principles, properly speaking—since there can be but one *principle*, the Volition of God. We have no right to assume, then, from what we observe in rules that we choose foolishly to name "principles," anything at all in respect to the characteristics of a principle proper. The "ultimate principles" of which Dr. Nichol speaks as having geometrical simplicity, may and do have this geometrical turn, as being part and parcel of a vast geometrical system, and thus a system of simplicity itself—in which, nevertheless, the *truly* ultimate principle is, *as we know*, the consummation of the complex—that is to say, of the unintelligible—for is it not the Spiritual Capacity of God?

I quoted Dr. Nichol's remark, however, not so much to question its philosophy, as by way of calling attention to the fact that, while all men have admitted *some* principle as existing behind the law of gravity, no attempt has been yet made to point out what this principle in particular is:—if we except, perhaps, occasional fantastic efforts at referring it to magnetism, or mesmerism, or Swedenborgianism, or transcendentalism, or some other equally delicious *ism* of the same species, and invariably patronized by one and the same species of people. The great mind of Newton, while boldly grasping the law itself, shrank from the principle of the law. The more fluent and comprehensive at least, if not the more patient and profound, sagacity of Laplace, had not the courage to attack it.

But hesitation on the part of these two astronomers it is, perhaps, not so very difficult to understand. They, as well as all the first class of mathematicians, were mathematicians *solely*:—their intellect, at least, had a firmly-pronounced mathematico-physical tone. What lay not distinctly within the domain of physics, or of mathematics, seemed to them either non-entity or shadow. Nevertheless, we may well wonder that Leibnitz, who was a marked exception to the general rule in these respects, and whose mental temperament was a singular admixture of the mathematical with the physico-metaphysical, did not at once investigate and establish the point at issue.

Either Newton or Laplace, seeking a principle and discovering none *physical*, would have rested contentedly in the conclusion that there was absolutely none; but it is almost impossible to fancy, of Leibnitz, that, having exhausted in his search the physical dominions, he would not have stepped at once, boldly and hopefully, amid his old familiar haunts in the kingdom of Metaphysics. Here, indeed, it is clear that he *must* have adventured in search of the treasure:—that he did not find it after all, was, perhaps, because his fairy guide, Imagination, was not sufficiently well-grown, or well-educated, to direct him aright.

I observed, just now, that, in fact, there had been certain vague attempts at referring gravity to some very uncertain *isms*. These attempts, however, although considered bold and justly so considered, looked no farther than to the generality—the merest generality—of the Newtonian Law. Its modus *operandi* has never, to my knowledge, been approached in the way of an effort at explanation. It is, therefore, with no unwarranted fear of being taken for a madman at the outset, and before I can bring my propositions fairly to the eye of those who alone are competent to decide upon them, that I here declare the *modus operandi* of the law of gravity to be an exceedingly simple and perfectly explicable thing—that is to say, when we make our advances towards it in just gradations and in the true direction—when we regard it from the proper point of view.

Whether we reach the idea of absolute *unity* as the source of all things, from a consideration of simplicity as the most probable characteristic of the original action of God;—whether we arrive at it from an inspection of the universality of relation in the gravitating phenomena;—or whether we attain it as a result of the mutual corroboration afforded by both processes;—still, the idea itself, if entertained at all, is entertained in inseparable connection with another idea—that of the condition of the Universe of stars as we *now* perceive it—that is to say, a condition of immeasurable *diffusion* through space. Now a connection between these two ideas—unity and diffusion—cannot be established unless through the entertainment of a third idea—that of *irradiation*. Absolute Unity being taken as a centre, then the existing Universe of stars is the result of *irradiation* from that centre.

Now, the laws of irradiation are *known*. They are part and parcel of the *sphere*. They belong to the class of *indisputable geometrical properties*. We say of them, "they are true—they are evident." To demand *why* they are true, would be to demand why the *axioms* are true upon which their demonstration is based. *Nothing* is demonstrable, strictly speaking; but *if* anything *be*, then the properties—the laws in question are demonstrated.

But these laws—what do they declare? Irradiation—how—by what steps does it proceed outwardly from a centre?

From a *luminous* centre, *light* issues by irradiation; and the quantities of light received upon any given plane, supposed to be shifting its position so as to be now nearer the centre and now farther from it, will be diminished in the same proportion as the squares of the distances of the plane from the luminous body, are increased; and will be increased in the same proportion as these squares are diminished.

The expression of the law may be thus generalised:—the number of light-particles (or, if the phrase be preferred, the number of light-impressions) received upon the shifting plane, will be *inversely* proportional with the squares of the distances of the plane. Generalising yet again, we may say that the diffusion—the scattering—the irradiation, in a word—is directly proportional with the squares of the distances.

For example: at the distance B, from the luminous centre A, a certain number of particles are so diffused as to occupy the surface B. Then at double the distance—that is to say at C—they will be so much farther diffused as to occupy four such surfaces:—at treble the distance, or at D, they will be so much farther separated as to occupy nine such surfaces:—while, at quadruple the distance, or at E, they will have become so scattered as to spread themselves over sixteen such surfaces—and so on forever.

In saying, generally, that the irradiation proceeds in direct proportion with the squares of the distances, we use the term irradiation to express *the degree of the diffusion* as we proceed

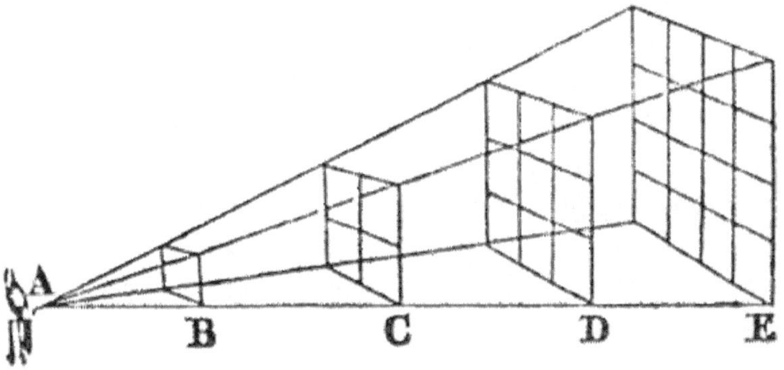

outwardly from the centre. Conversing the idea, and employing the word "concentralisation" to express *the degree of the drawing together* as we come back toward the centre from an outward position, we may say that concentralistion proceeds inversely as the squares of the distances. In other words, we have reached the conclusion that, on the hypothesis that matter was originally irradiated from a centre and is now returning to it, the concentralisation, in the return, proceeds *exactly as we know the force of gravitation to proceed.*

Now here, if we could be permitted to assume that concentralisation exactly represented the *force of the tendency to the centre*—that the one was exactly proportional to the other, and that the two proceeded together—we should have shown all that is required. The sole difficulty existing, then, is to establish a direct proportion between "concentralisation" and the *force* of concentralisation; and this is done, of course, if we establish such proportion between "irradiation" and the force of irradiation.

A very slight inspection of the Heavens assures us that the stars have a certain general uniformity, equability, or equidistance, of distribution through that region of space in which, collectively, and in a roughly globular form, they are situated:—this species of very general, rather than absolute, equability, being in full keeping with my deduction of inequidistance, within certain limits, among the originally diffused atoms, as a corollary from the evident design of infinite complexity of relation out of irrelation. I started, it will be remembered, with the idea of a generally uniform but particularly *un*-uniform distribution of the atoms;—an idea, I repeat, which an inspection of the stars, as they exist, confirms.

But even in the merely general equability of distribution, as regards the atoms, there appears a difficulty which, no doubt, has already suggested itself to those among my readers who have borne in mind that I suppose this equability of distribution effected through *irradiation from a centre*. The very first glance at the idea, irradiation, forces us to the entertainment of the hitherto unseparated and seemingly inseparable idea of agglomeration about a centre, with dispersion as we recede from it—the idea, in a word, of *in*-equability of distribution in respect to the matter irradiated.

Now, I have elsewhere [1] observed that it is by just such difficulties as the one now in question—such roughnesses—such peculiarities—such protuberances above the plane of the ordinary—that reason feels her way, if at all, in her search for the true. By the difficulty—the "peculiarity"—now presented, I leap at once to *the* secret—a secret which I might never have attained but for the peculiarity and the inferences which, in its mere character of peculiarity, it affords me.

The process of thought, at this point, may be thus roughly sketched:—I say to myself—"Unity, as I have explained it, is a truth—I feel it. Diffusion is a truth—I see it. Irradiation, by which alone these two truths are reconciled, is a consequent truth—I perceive it. *Equability* of diffusion, first deduced *à priori* and then corroborated by the inspection of phenomena, is also a truth—I fully admit it. So far all is clear around me:—there are no clouds behind which the secret—the great secret of the gravitating *modus operandi*—can possibly lie hidden;—but this secret lies *hereabouts*, most assuredly; and were there but a cloud in view, I should be driven to suspicion of that cloud."

And now, just as I say this, there actually comes a cloud into view. This cloud is the seeming impossibility of reconciling my truth, *irradiation*, with my truth, *equability of diffusion*. I say now:—

1. *Murders in the Rue Morgue.*

"Behind this *seeming* impossibility is to be found what I desire." I do not say "*real* impossibility;" for invincible faith in my truths assures me that it is a mere difficulty after all—but I go on to say, with unflinching confidence, that, *when* this *difficulty* shall be solved, we shall find, *wrapped up in the recess of solution*, the key to the secret at which we aim. Moreover—I *feel* that we shall discover *but one* possible solution of the difficulty; this for the reason that, were there two, one would be supererogatory—would be fruitless—would be empty—would contain no key—since no duplicate key can be needed to any secret of Nature.

And now, let us see:—Our usual notions of irradiation—in fact *all* our distinct notions of it—are caught merely from the process as we see it exemplified in *light*. Here there is a *continuous* outpouring of *ray-streams*, and *with a force which we have at least no right to suppose varies at all*. Now, in any such irradiation *as this*—continuous and of unvarying force—the regions nearer the centre must *inevitably* be always more crowded with the irradiated matter than the regions more remote. But I have assumed *no* such irradiation *as this*.

I assumed no *continuous* irradiation; and for the simple reason that such an assumption would have involved, first, the necessity of entertaining a conception which I have shown no man *can* entertain, and which (as I will more fully explain hereafter) all observation of the firmament refutes—the conception of the absolute infinity of the Universe of stars—and would have involved, secondly, the impossibility of understanding a reaction—that is, gravitation—as existing now—since, while an act is continued, no reaction, of course, can take place. My assumption, then, or rather my inevitable deduction from just premises—was that of a *determinate* irradiation—one finally discontinued.

Let me now describe the sole possible mode in which it is conceivable that matter could have been diffused through space, so as to fulfil the conditions at once of irradiation and of generally equable distribution.

For convenience of illustration, let us imagine, in the first place, a hollow sphere of glass, or of anything else, occupying the space throughout which the universal matter is to be thus equally diffused, by means of irradiation, from the absolute, irrelative, unconditional particle, placed in the centre of the sphere.

Now, a certain exertion of the diffusive power (presumed to be the Divine Volition)—in other words, a certain *force*—whose measure is the quantity of matter—that is to say, the number of atoms—emitted; emits, by irradiation, this certain number of atoms; forcing them in all directions outwardly from the centre—their proximity to each other diminishing as they proceed—until, finally, they are distributed, loosely, over the interior surface of the sphere.

When these atoms have attained this position, or while proceeding to attain it, a second and inferior exercise of the same force—or a second and inferior force of the same character—emits, in the same manner—that is to say, by irradiation as before—a second *stratum* of atoms which proceeds to deposit itself upon the first; the number of atoms, in this case as in the former, being of course the measure of the force which emitted them; in other words the force being precisely adapted to the purpose it effects—the force and the number of atoms sent out by the force, being *directly proportional.*

When this second *stratum* has reached its destined position—or while approaching it—a third still inferior exertion of the force, or a third inferior force of a similar character—the number of atoms emitted being in *all* cases the measure of the force—proceeds to deposit a third *stratum* upon the second:—and so on, until these concentric *strata*, growing gradually less and less, come down at length to the central point; and the diffusive matter, simultaneously with the diffusive force, is exhausted.

We have now the sphere filled, through means of irradiation, with atoms equably diffused. The two necessary conditions—those of irradiation and of equable diffusion—are satisfied; and by the *sole* process in which the possibility of their simultaneous satisfaction is conceivable. For this reason, I confidently expect to find, lurking in the present condition of the atoms as distributed throughout the sphere, the secret of which I am in search—the all-important principle of the *modus operandi* of the Newtonian law. Let us examine, then, the actual condition of the atoms.

They lie in a series of concentric *strata.* They are equably diffused throughout the sphere. They have been irradiated into these states.

The atoms being *equably* distributed, the greater the superficial extent of any of these concentric *strata*, or spheres, the more atoms will lie upon it. In other words, the number of atoms lying upon the surface of any one of the concentric spheres, is directly proportional with the extent of that surface.

But, in any series of concentric spheres, the surfaces are directly proportional with the squares of the distances from the centre. [2]

Therefore the number of atoms in any *stratum* is directly proportional with the square of that *stratum's* distance from the centre.

But the number of atoms in any *stratum* is the measure of the force which emitted that *stratum*—that is to say, is *directly proportional* with the force.

Therefore the force which irradiated any *stratum* is directly proportional with the square of that *stratum's* distance from the centre:—or, generally:

The force of the irradiation has been directly proportional with the squares of the distances.

Now, reaction, as far as we know any thing of it, is action conversed. The *general* principle of gravity being, in the first place, understood as the reaction of an act—as the expression of a desire on the part of matter, while existing in a state of diffusion, to return into the unity whence it was diffused; and, in the second place, the mind being called upon to determine the *character* of the desire—the manner in which it would, naturally, be manifested; in other words, being called upon to conceive a probable law, or *modus operandi*, for the return; could not well help arriving at the conclusion that this law of return would be precisely the converse of the law of departure. That such would

2. Succinctly—The surfaces of spheres are as the squares of their *radii*.

be the case, an one, at least, would be abundantly justified in taking for granted, until such time as some person should suggest something like a plausible reason why it should *not* be the case—until such a period as a law of return shall be imagined which the intellect can consider as preferable.

Matter, then, irradiated into space with a force varying as the squares of the distances, might, *à priori*, be supposed to return towards its centre of irradiation with a force varying *inversely* as the squares of the distances: and I have already shown that any principle which will explain why the atoms should tend, according to any law, to the general centre, must be admitted as satisfactorily explaining, at the same time, why, according to the same law, they should tend each to each. For, in fact, the tendency to the general centre is not to a centre as such, but because of its being a point in tending towards which each atom tends most directly to its real and essential centre, *unity*—the absolute and final union of all.

The consideration here involved presents to my own mind no embarrassment whatever—but this fact does not blind me to the possibility of its being obscure to those who may have been less in the habit of dealing with abstractions:—and, upon the whole, it may be as well to look at the matter from one or two other points of view.

The absolute, irrelative particle primarily created by the Volition of God, must have been in a condition of positive normality, or rightfulness—for wrongfulness implies *relation*. Right is positive; wrong is negative—is merely the negation of right; as cold is the negation of heat—darkness of light. That a thing may be wrong, it is necessary that there be some other thing in *relation* to which it *is* wrong—some condition which it fails to satisfy; some law which it violates; some being whom it aggrieves. If there be no such being, law, or condition, in respect to which the thing is wrong—and, still more especially, if no beings, laws, or conditions exist at all—then the thing *cannot* be wrong and consequently must be *right*. Any deviation from normality involves a tendency to return to it. A difference from the normal—from the right—from the just—can be understood as effected only by the overcoming a difficulty; and if the force which overcomes the difficulty be not infinitely continued, the ineradicable tendency to return will at length be permitted to act for its own satisfaction.

Upon withdrawal of the force, the tendency acts. This is the principle of reaction as the inevitable consequence of finite action. Employing a phraseology of which the seeming affectation will be pardoned for its expressiveness, we may say that reaction is the return from the condition of *as it is and ought not to be* into the condition of *as it was, originally, and therefore ought to be*:—and let me add here that the *absolute* force of reaction would no doubt be always found in direct proportion with the reality—the truth—the absoluteness—of the *originality*—if ever it were possible to measure this latter:—and, consequently, the greatest of all conceivable reactions must be that produced by the tendency which we now discuss—the tendency to return into the *absolutely original*—into the *supremely* primitive. Gravity, then, *must be the strongest of forces*—an idea reached *à priori* and abundantly confirmed by induction. What use I make of the idea, will be seen in the sequel.

The atoms, now, having been diffused from their normal condition of unity, seek to return to—what? Not to any particular *point*, certainly; for it is clear that if, upon the diffusion, the whole Universe of matter had been projected, collectively, to a distance from the point of irradiation, the atomic tendency to the general centre of the sphere would not have been disturbed in the least:—the atoms would not have sought the point *in absolute space* from which they were originally impelled. It is merely the *condition*, and not the point or locality at which this condition took its rise, that these atoms seek to re-establish;—it is merely *that condition which is their normality*, that they desire. "But they seek a centre," it will be said, "and a centre is a point." True; but they seek this point not in its character of point—(for, were the whole sphere moved from its position, they would seek, equally, the centre; and the centre *then* would be a *new* point)—but because it so happens, on account of the form in which they collectively exist—(that of the sphere)—that only *through* the point in question—the sphere's centre—they can attain their true object, Unity.

In the direction of the centre each atom perceives more atoms than in any other direction. Each atom is impelled towards the centre because along the straight line joining it and the centre and passing on to the circumference beyond, there lie a greater number of atoms than along any other straight line—a greater number of objects that seek it, the individual atom—a greater number of tendencies to unity—a greater number of satisfactions for its own tendency to unity—in a word, because in the direction of the centre lies the utmost possibility of satisfaction, generally, for its own individual appetite.

To be brief, the *condition*, unity, is all that is really sought; and if the atoms *seem* to seek the centre of the sphere, it is only impliedly, through implication—because such centre happens to imply, to include, or to involve, the only essential centre, unity. But *on account* of this implication or involution, there is no possibility of practically separating the tendency to unity in the abstract, from the tendency to the concrete centre. Thus the tendency of the atoms to the general centre *is*, to all practical intents and for all logical purposes, the tendency each to each; and the tendency each to each *is* the tendency to the centre; and the one tendency may be assumed *as* the other; whatever will apply to the one must be thoroughly applicable to the other; and, in conclusion, whatever principle will satisfactorily explain the one, cannot be questioned as an explanation of the other.

In looking carefully around me for rational objection to what I have advanced, I am able to discover *nothing*;—but of that class of objections usually urged by the doubters for doubt's sake, I very readily perceive three; and proceed to dispose of them in order.

It may be said, first: "The proof that the force of irradiation (in the case described) is directly proportional to the squares of the distances, depends upon an unwarranted assumption—that of the number of atoms in each *stratum* being the measure of the force with which they are emitted."

I reply, not only that I am warranted in such assumption, but that I should be utterly *un*-warranted in any other. What I assume is, simply, that an effect is the measure of its cause—that every exercise of the Divine Will will be proportional to that which demands the exertion—that the means of omnipotence, or of omniscience, will be exactly adapted to its purposes. Neither can a deficiency nor an excess of cause bring to pass any effect. Had the force which irradiated any *stratum* to its position, been either more or less than was needed for the purpose—that is to say, not *directly proportional* to the purpose—then to its position that *stratum* could not have been irradiated. Had the force which, with a view to general equability of distribution, emitted the proper number of atoms for each *stratum*, been not *directly proportional* to the number, then the number would *not* have been the number demanded for the equable distribution.

The second supposable objection is somewhat better entitled to an answer.

It is an admitted principle in dynamics that every body, on receiving an impulse, or disposition to move, will move onward in a straight line, in the direction imparted by the impelling force, until deflected, or stopped, by some other force. How then, it may be asked, is my first or external *stratum* of atoms to be understood as discontinuing their movement at the circumference of the imaginary glass sphere, when no second force, of more than an imaginary character, appears, to account for the discontinuance?

I reply that the objection, in this case, actually does arise out of "an unwarranted assumption"—on the part of the objector—the assumption of a principle, in Dynamics, at an epoch when *no* "principles," in *anything*, exist:—I use the word "principle," of course, in the objector's understanding of the word.

"In the beginning" we can admit—indeed we can comprehend—but one *first cause*—the truly ultimate *principle*—the Volition of God. The primary *act*—that of irradiation from unity—

must have been independent of all that which the world now calls "principle"—because all that we so designate is but a consequence of the reaction of that primary act:—I say "*primary*" act; for the creation of the absolute material particle is more properly to be regarded as a *conception* than as an "*act*" in the ordinary meaning of the term. Thus, we must regard the primary act as an act for the establishment of what we now call "principles". But this primary act itself is to be considered as *continuous volition*.

The Thought of God is to be understood as originating the diffusion—as proceeding with it—as regulating it—and, finally, as being withdrawn from it upon its completion. *Then* commences reaction, and through reaction, "principle," as we employ the word. It will be advisable, however, to limit the application of this word to the two *immediate* results of the discontinuance of the divine volition—that is, to the two agents, *attraction* and *repulsion*. Every other natural agent depends, either more or less immediately, upon these two, and therefore would be more conveniently designated as *sub*-principle.

It may be objected, thirdly, that, in general, the peculiar mode of distribution which I have suggested for the atoms, is "an hypothesis and nothing more."

Now, I am aware that the word "hypothesis" is a ponderous sledge-hammer, grasped immediately, if not lifted, by all very diminutive thinkers, upon the first appearance of any proposition wearing, in any particular, the garb of a *theory*. But "hypothesis" cannot be wielded *here* to any good purpose, even by those who succeed in lifting it—little men or great.

I maintain, first, that *only* in the mode described is it conceivable that matter could have been diffused so as to fulfil at once the conditions of irradiation and of generally equable distribution. I maintain, secondly, that these conditions themselves have been imposed upon me, as necessities, in a train of ratiocination *as rigorously logical as that which establishes any demonstration in Euclid*; and I maintain, thirdly, that even if the charge of "hypothesis" were as fully sustained as it is, in fact, unsustained and untenable, still the validity and indisputability of my result would not, even in the slightest particular, be disturbed.

To explain: The Newtonian Gravity—a law of Nature—a law whose existence as such no one out of Bedlam questions—a law whose admission as such enables us to account for nine-tenths of the Universal phenomena—a law which, merely because it does so enable us to account for these phenomena, we are perfectly willing, without reference to any other considerations, to admit, and cannot help admitting, as a law—a law, nevertheless, of which neither the principle nor the *modus operandi* of the principle, has ever yet been traced by the human analysis—a law, in short, which, neither in its detail nor in its generality, has been found susceptible of explanation *at all*—is at length seen to be at every point thoroughly explicable, provided we only yield our assent to—what? To an hypothesis?

Why *if* an hypothesis—if the merest hypothesis—if an hypothesis for whose assumption—as in the case of that *pure* hypothesis the Newtonian law itself—no shadow of *à priori* reason could be assigned—if an hypothesis, even so absolute as all this implies, would enable us to perceive a principle for the Newtonian law—would enable us to understand as satisfied, conditions so miraculously—so ineffably complex and seemingly irreconcilable as those involved in the relations of which gravity tells us,—what rational being *could* so expose his fatuity as to call even this absolute hypothesis an hypothesis any longer—unless, indeed, he were to persist in so calling it, with the understanding that he did so, simply for the sake of consistency *in words*?

But what is the true state of our present case? What is *the fact?* Not only that it is not an hypothesis which we are required to *adopt*, in order to admit the principle at issue explained, but that it is a logical conclusion which we are requested *not* to adopt if we can avoid it—which we are simply invited to *deny if we can:*—a conclusion of so accurate a logicality that to dispute it would be the effort—to doubt its validity beyond our power: —a conclusion from which we see no mode of escape, turn as we will; a result which confronts us either at the end of an *in-*

ductive journey from the phenomena of the very law discussed, or at the close of a *de*-ductive career from the most rigorously simple of all conceivable assumptions—*the assumption, in a word, of simplicity itself.*

And if here, for the mere sake of cavilling, it be urged, that although my starting-point is, as I assert, the assumption of absolute simplicity, yet simplicity, considered merely in itself, is no axiom; and that only deductions from *axioms* are indisputable—it is thus that I reply:—

Every other science than logic is the science of certain concrete relations. Arithmetic, for example, is the science of the relations of number—geometry, of the relations of form—mathematics in general, of the relations of quantity in general—of whatever can be increased or diminished. Logic, however, is the science of relation in the abstract—of absolute relation—of relation considered solely in itself. An *axiom* in any particular science other than logic is, thus, merely a proposition announcing certain concrete relations which seem to be too obvious for dispute—as when we say, for instance, that the whole is greater than its part:—and, thus again, the principle of the *logical* axiom—in other words, of an *axiom* in the abstract—is, simply, *obviousness of relation.*

Now, it is clear, not only that what is obvious to one mind may not be obvious to another, but that what is obvious to one mind at one epoch, may be anything but obvious, at another epoch, to the same mind. It is clear, moreover, that what, today, is obvious even to the majority of mankind, or to the majority of the best intellects of mankind, may tomorrow be, to either majority, more or less obvious, or in no respect obvious at all. It is seen, then, that the *axiomatic principle* itself is susceptible of variation, and of course that *axioms* are susceptible of similar change. Being mutable, the "truths" which grow out of them are necessarily mutable too; or, in other words, are never to be positively depended upon as truths at all—since truth and immutability are one.

It will now be readily understood that no *axiomatic* idea—no idea founded in the fluctuating principle, obviousness of relation—can possibly be so secure—so reliable a basis for any structure erected by the reason, *as that* idea—(whatever it is, wherever we can find it, or *if* it be practicable to find it anywhere)—which is *ir*-relative altogether—which not only presents to the understanding *no obviousness* of relation, either greater or less, to be considered, but subjects the intellect, not in the slightest degree, to the necessity of even looking at any relation at all.

If such an idea be not what we too heedlessly term "an *axiom*," it is at least preferable, as a logical basis, to any axiom ever propounded, or to all imaginable axioms combined:—and such, precisely, is the idea with which my deductive process, so thoroughly corroborated by induction, commences. My *particle proper* is but *absolute irrelation*. To sum up what has been advanced:—As a starting point I have taken it for granted, simply, that the beginning had nothing behind it or before it—that it was a beginning in fact—that it was a beginning and nothing different from a beginning—in short, that this beginning was—*that which it was.* If this be a "mere assumption" then a "mere assumption" let it be.

To conclude this branch of the subject:—I am fully warranted in announcing that *the law which we have been in the habit of calling gravity exists on account of matter's having been irradiated, at its origin, atomically, into a limited* [3] *sphere of space, from one, individual, unconditional, irrelative, and absolute particle proper, by the sole process in which it was possible to satisfy, at the same time, the two conditions, irradiation, and generally-equable distribution throughout the sphere—that is to say, by a force varying in direct proportion with the squares of the distances between the irradiated atoms, respectively, and the particular centre of irradiation.*

I have already given my reasons for presuming matter to have been diffused by a determinate rather than by a continuous or infinitely continued force. Supposing a continuous force, we should be unable, in the first place, to comprehend a reaction

3. "Limited sphere"—A sphere is necessarily limited. I prefer tautology to a chance of misconception.

at all; and we should be required, in the second place, to entertain the impossible conception of an infinite extension of matter. Not to dwell upon the impossibility of the conception, the infinite extension of matter is an idea which, if not positively disproved, is at least not in any respect warranted by telescopic observation of the stars—a point to be explained more fully hereafter; and this empirical reason for believing in the original finity of matter is unempirically confirmed.

For example:—Admitting, for the moment, the possibility of understanding space as *filled* with the irradiated atoms—that is to say, admitting, as well as we can, for argument's sake, that the succession of the irradiated atoms had absolutely *no end*—then it is abundantly clear that, even when the Volition of God had been withdrawn from them, and thus the tendency to return into unity permitted (abstractly) to be satisfied, this permission would have been nugatory and invalid—practically valueless and of no effect whatever. No reaction could have taken place; no movement toward unity could have been made; no law of gravity could have obtained.

To explain:—Grant the *abstract* tendency of any one atom to any one other as the inevitable result of diffusion from the normal unity:—or, what is the same thing, admit any given atom as *proposing* to move in any given direction—it is clear that, since there is an *infinity* of atoms on all sides of the atom proposing to move, it never can actually move toward the satisfaction of its tendency in the direction given, on account of a precisely equal and counter-balancing tendency in the direction diametrically opposite.

In other words, exactly as many tendencies to Unity are behind the hesitating atom as before it; for it is a mere sotticism to say that one infinite line is longer or shorter than another infinite line, or that one infinite number is greater or less than another number that is infinite. Thus the atom in question must remain stationary forever. Under the impossible circumstances which we have been merely endeavouring to conceive for argument's sake, there could have been no aggregation of matter—

no stars—no worlds—nothing but a perpetually atomic and inconsequential Universe. In fact, view it as we will, the whole idea of unlimited matter is not only untenable, but impossible and preposterous.

With the understanding of a *sphere* of atoms, however, we perceive, at once, a *satisfiable* tendency to union. The general result of the tendency each to each, being a tendency of all to the centre, the *general* process of condensation, or approximation, commences immediately, by a common and simultaneous movement, on withdrawal of the Divine Volition; the *individual* approximations, or coalescences—*not* coalitions—of atom with atom, being subject to almost infinite variations of time, degree, and condition, on account of the excessive multiplicity of relation, arising from the differences of form assumed as characterizing the atoms at the moment of their quitting the particle proper; as well as from the subsequent particular in equidistance, each from each.

What I wish to impress upon the reader is the certainty of there arising, at once, (on withdrawal of the diffusive force, or Divine Volition,) out of the condition of the atoms as described, at innumerable points throughout the universal sphere, innumerable agglomerations, characterized by innumerable specific differences of form, size, essential nature, and distance each from each. The development of repulsion (electricity) must have commenced, of course, with the very earliest particular efforts at unity, and must have proceeded constantly in the ratio of coalescence—that is to say, in *that of condensation*, or, again, of heterogeneity.

Thus the two principles proper, *attraction* and *repulsion*—the material and the spiritual—accompany each other, in the strictest fellowship, forever. Thus *the body* and *the soul* walk hand in hand.

If now, in fancy, we select any one of the agglomerations considered as in their primary stages throughout the universal sphere, and suppose this incipient agglomeration to be taking place at that point where the centre of our Sun exists—or rather where it *did* exist originally; for the Sun is perpetually shifting his position—we shall find ourselves met, and borne onward for a time at least, by the most magnificent of theories—by the nebular cosmogony of Laplace:—although "cosmogony" is far too comprehensive a term for what he really discusses—which is the constitution of our solar system alone—of one among the myriad of similar systems which make up the Universe Proper—that Universal sphere—that all-inclusive and absolute *Cosmos* which forms the subject of my present discourse.

Confining himself to an *obviously limited* region—that of our solar system with its comparatively immediate vicinity—and *merely* assuming—that is to say, assuming without any basis whatever, either deductive or inductive—*much* of what I have been just endeavouring to place upon a more stable basis than assumption; assuming, for example, matter as diffused (without pretending to account for the diffusion) throughout, and somewhat beyond, the space occupied by our system—diffused in a state of heterogeneous nebulosity and obedient to that omniprevalent law of gravity at whose principle he ventured to make no guess;—assuming all this (which is quite true, although he had no logical right to its assumption) Laplace has shown, dynamically and mathematically, that the results in such case necessarily ensuing, are those and those alone which we find manifested in the actually existing condition of the system itself.

To explain:—Let us conceive *that* particular agglomeration of which we have just spoken—the one at the point designated by our Sun's centre—to have so far proceeded that a vast quantity of nebulous matter has here assumed a roughly globular form; its centre being, of course, coincident with what is now, or rather was originally, the centre of our Sun; and its periphery extending out beyond the orbit of Neptune, the most remote of our planets:—in other words, let us suppose the diameter of this rough sphere to be some 6000 millions of miles. For ages, this mass of matter has been undergoing condensation, until at length it has become reduced into the bulk we imagine; having proceeded gradually, of course, from its atomic and imperceptible state, into what we understand of visible, palpable, or otherwise appreciable nebulosity.

Now, the condition of this mass implies a rotation about an imaginary axis—a rotation which, commencing with the absolute incipiency of the aggregation, has been ever since acquiring velocity. The very first two atoms which met, approaching each other from points not diametrically opposite, would, in rushing partially past each other, form a nucleus for the rotary movement described. How this would increase in velocity, is readily seen. The two atoms are joined by others:—an aggregation is formed. The mass continues to rotate while condensing. But any atom at the circumference has, of course, a more rapid motion than one nearer the centre. The outer atom, however, with its superior velocity, approaches the centre; carrying this superior velocity with it as it goes. Thus every atom, proceeding inwardly, and finally attaching itself to the condensed centre, adds something to the original velocity of that centre—that is to say, increases the rotary movement of the mass.

Let us now suppose this mass so far condensed that it occupies *precisely* the space circumscribed by the orbit of Neptune, and that the velocity with which the surface of the mass moves, in the general rotation, is precisely that velocity with which Neptune now revolves about the Sun. At this epoch, then, we are to understand that the constantly increasing centrifugal force, having gotten the better of the non-increasing centripetal, loosened and separated the exterior and least condensed *stratum*, or a few of the exterior and least condensed strata, at the equator of the sphere, where the tangential velocity predominated; so that these *strata* formed about the main body an independent ring encircling the equatorial regions:—just as the exterior portion thrown off, by excessive velocity of rotation, from a grindstone, would form a ring about the grindstone, but for the solidity of the superficial material: were this *caoutchouc*, or anything similar in consistency, precisely the phenomenon I describe would be presented.

The ring thus whirled from the nebulous mass, *revolved*, of course, *as* a separate ring, with just that velocity with which, while the surface of the mass, it *rotated*. In the meantime, condensation still proceeding, the interval between the discharged ring and the main body continued to increase, until the former was left at a vast distance from the latter.

Now, admitting the ring to have possessed, by some seemingly accidental arrangement of its heterogeneous materials, a constitution nearly uniform, then this ring, as such, would never have ceased revolving about its primary; but, as might have been anticipated, there appears to have been enough irregularity in the disposition of the materials, to make them cluster about centres of superior solidity; and thus the annular form was destroyed.[4] No doubt, the band was soon broken up into several portions, and one of these portions, predominating in mass, absorbed the others into itself; the whole settling, spherically, into a planet.

That this latter, *as* a planet, continued the revolutionary movement which characterized it while a ring, is sufficiently clear; and that it took upon itself, also, an additional movement in its new condition of sphere, is readily explained. The ring being understood as yet unbroken, we see that its exterior, while the whole revolves about the parent body, moves more rapidly than its interior. When the rupture occurred, then, some portion in each fragment must have been moving with greater velocity than the others. The superior movement prevailing, must have whirled each fragment round—that is to say, have caused it to rotate; and the direction of the rotation must, of course, have been the direction of the revolution whence it arose. *All* the fragments having become subject to the rotation described, must, in coalescing, have imparted it to the one planet constituted by their coalescence.

This planet was Neptune. Its material continuing to undergo condensation, and the centrifugal force generated in its rotation

4. Laplace assumed his nebulosity heterogeneous, merely that he might be thus enabled to account for the breaking up of the rings; for had the nebulosity been homogeneous, they would not have broken. I reach the same result—heterogeneity of the secondary masses immediately resulting from the atoms—purely from an *à priori* consideration of their general design—relation.

getting, at length, the better of the centripetal, as before in the case of the parent orb, a ring was whirled also from the equatorial surface of this planet: this ring, having been uniform in its constitution, was broken up, and its several fragments, being absorbed by the most massive, were collectively spherified into a moon. Subsequently, the operation was repeated, and a second moon was the result. We thus account for the planet Neptune, with the two satellites which accompany him.

In throwing of a ring from its equator, the Sun re-established that equilibrium between its centripetal and centrifugal forces which had been disturbed in the process of condensation; but, as this condensation still proceeded, the equilibrium was again immediately disturbed, through the increase of rotation. By the time the mass had so far shrunk that it occupied a spherical space just that circumscribed by the orbit of Uranus, we are to understand that the centrifugal force had so far obtained the ascendency that new relief was needed: a second equatorial band was, consequently, thrown off, which, proving ununiform, was broken up, as before in the case of Neptune; the fragments settling into the planet Uranus; the velocity of whose actual revolution about the Sun indicates, of course, the rotary speed of that Sun's equatorial surface at the moment of the separation. Uranus, adopting a rotation from the collective rotations of the fragments composing it, as previously explained, now threw off ring after ring; each of which, becoming broken up, settled into a moon:—three moons, at different epochs, having been formed, in this manner, by the rupture and general spherification of as many distinct ununiform rings.

By the time the Sun had shrunk until it occupied a space just that circumscribed by the orbit of Saturn, the balance, we are to suppose, between its centripetal and centrifugal forces had again become so far disturbed, through increase of rotary velocity, the result of condensation, that a third effort at equilibrium became necessary; and an annular band was therefore whirled off, as twice before; which, on rupture through ununiformity, became consolidated into the planet Saturn. This latter threw off, in the first place, seven uniform (ununiform?) bands, which, on rupture, were spherified respectively into as many moons; but, subsequently, it appears to have discharged, at three distinct but not very distant epochs, three rings whose equability of constitution was, by apparent accident, so considerable as to present no occasion for their rupture; thus they continue to revolve as rings. I use the phrase "*apparent* accident;" for of accident in the ordinary sense there was, of course, nothing:—the term is properly applied only to the result of indistinguishable or not immediately traceable *law*.

Shrinking still farther, until it occupied just the space circumscribed by the orbit of Jupiter, the Sun now found need of farther effort to restore the counterbalance of its two forces, continually disarranged in the still continued increase of rotation. Jupiter, accordingly, was now thrown off; passing from the annular to the planetary condition; and, on attaining this latter, threw off in its turn, at four different epochs, four rings, which finally resolved themselves into so many Moons.

Still shrinking, until its sphere occupied just the space defined by the orbit of the asteroids, the Sun now discarded a ring which appears to have had *eight* centres of superior solidity, and, on breaking up, to have separated into *eight* fragments no one of which so far predominated in mass as to absorb the others. All therefore, as distinct although comparatively small planets, proceeded to revolve in orbits whose distances, each from each, may be considered as in some degree the measure of the force which drove them asunder:—all the orbits, nevertheless, being so closely coincident as to admit of our calling them *one*, in view of the other planetary orbits.

Continuing to shrink, the Sun, on becoming so small as just to fill the orbit of Mars, now discharged this planet—of course by the process repeatedly described. Having no Moon, however, Mars could have thrown off no ring. In fact, an epoch had now arrived in the career of the parent body, the centre of the system. The *de*-crease of its nebulosity, which is the *in*-crease of its density, and which again is the *de*-crease of its condensation, out of which latter arose the constant disturbance of equilibrium—must, by this period, have attained a point at which the efforts for restoration would have been more and more ineffectual just in proportion as they were less frequently needed. Thus the processes of which we have been speaking would everywhere show signs of exhaustion—in the planets, first, and secondly, in the original mass.

We must not fall into the error of supposing the decrease of interval observed among the planets as we approach the Sun, to be in any respect indicative of an increase of frequency in the periods at which they were discarded. Exactly the converse is to be understood. The longest interval of time must have occurred between the discharges of the two interior; the shortest, between those of the two exterior, planets. The decrease of the interval of space is, nevertheless, the measure of the density, and thus inversely of the condensation, of the Sun, throughout the processes detailed.

Having shrunk, however, so far as to fill only the orbit of our Earth, the parent sphere whirled from itself still one other body—the Earth—in a condition so nebulous as to admit of this body's discarding, in its turn, yet another, which is our Moon;—but here terminated the lunar formations.

Finally, subsiding to the orbits first of Venus and then of Mercury, the Sun discarded these two interior planets; neither of which has given birth to any moon.

Thus from his original bulk—or, to speak more accurately, from the condition in which we first considered him—from a partially spherified nebular mass, *certainly* much more than 5,600 millions of miles in diameter—the great central orb and origin of our solar-planetary-lunar system, has gradually descended, by condensation, in obedience to the law of gravity, to a globe only 882,000 miles in diameter; but it by no means follows, either that its condensation is yet complete, or that it may not still possess the capacity of whirling from itself another planet.

I have here given—in outline of course, but still with all the detail necessary for distinctness—a view of the Nebular Theory as its author himself conceived it. From whatever point we regard it, we shall find it *beautifully true*. It is by far too beautiful, indeed, *not* to possess truth as its essentiality—and here I am very profoundly serious in what I say. In the revolution of the satellites of Uranus, there does appear something seemingly inconsistent with the assumptions of Laplace; but that one inconsistency can invalidate a theory constructed from a million of intricate consistencies, is a fancy fit only for the fantastic. In prophesying, confidently, that the apparent anomaly to which I refer, will, sooner or later, be found one of the strongest possible corroborations of the general hypothesis, I pretend to no especial spirit of divination. It is a matter which the only difficulty seems *not* to foresee. [5]

The bodies whirled off in the processes described, would exchange, it has been seen, the superficial *rotation* of the orbs whence they originated, for a *revolution* of equal velocity about these orbs as distant centres; and the revolution thus engendered must proceed, so long as the centripetal force, or that with which the discarded body gravitates toward its parent, is neither greater nor less than that by which it was discarded; that is, than the centrifugal, or, far more properly, than the tangential, velocity. From the unity, however, of the origin of these two forces, we might have expected to find them as they are found—the one accurately counterbalancing the other. It has been shown, indeed, that the act of whirling-off is, in every case, merely an act for the preservation of the counterbalance.

After referring, however, the centripetal force to the omniprevalent law of gravity, it has been the fashion with astronomical treatises, to seek beyond the limits of mere Nature—that is to say, of *secondary* cause—a solution of the phenomenon of tangential velocity. This latter they attribute directly to a first cause—to God. The force which carries a stellar body around its primary they assert to have originated in an impulse given immediately by the finger—this is the childish phraseology employed—by

5. I am prepared to show that the anomalous revolution of the satellites of Uranus is a simply perspective anomaly arising from the inclination of the axis of the planet.

the finger of Deity itself. In this view, the planets, fully formed, are conceived to have been hurled from the Divine hand, to a position in the vicinity of the suns, with an impetus mathematically adapted to the masses, or attractive capacities, of the suns themselves.

An idea so grossly unphilosophical, although so supinely adopted, could have arisen only from the difficulty of otherwise accounting for the absolutely accurate adaptation, each to each, of two forces so seemingly independent, one of the other, as are the gravitating and tangential. But it should be remembered that, for a long time, the coincidence between the Moon's rotation and her sidereal revolution—two matters seemingly far more independent than those now considered—was looked upon as positively miraculous; and there was a strong disposition, even among astronomers, to attribute the marvel to the direct and continual agency of God—who, in this case, it was said, had found it necessary to interpose, specially, among his general laws, a set of subsidiary regulations, for the purpose of forever concealing from mortal eyes the glories, or perhaps the horrors, of the other side of the Moon—of that mysterious hemisphere which has always avoided, and must perpetually avoid, the telescopic scrutiny of mankind. The advance of science, however, soon demonstrated—what to the philosophical instinct needed no demonstration—that the one movement is but a portion—something more, even, than a consequence—of the other.

For my part, I have no patience with fantasies at once so timorous, so idle, and so awkward. They belong to the veriest *cowardice* of thought. That Nature and the God of Nature are distinct, no thinking being can long doubt. By the former we imply merely the laws of the latter. But with the very idea of God, omnipotent, omniscient, we entertain, also, the idea of *the infallibility* of his laws. With Him there being neither Past nor Future—with Him all being *Now*—do we not insult him in supposing his laws so contrived as not to provide for every possible contingency?—or, rather, what idea *can* we have of *any* possible contingency, except that it is at once a result and a manifestation of his laws? He who, divesting himself of prejudice, shall have the rare courage to think absolutely for himself, cannot fail to arrive, in the end, at the condensation of *laws* into *law*—cannot fail of reaching the conclusion that *each law of Nature is dependent at all points upon all other laws,* and that all are but consequences of one primary exercise of the Divine Volition. Such is the principle of the cosmogony which, with all necessary deference, I here venture to suggest and to maintain.

In this view, it will be seen that, dismissing as frivolous, and even impious, the fancy of the tangential force having been imparted to the planets immediately, by "the finger of God," I consider this force as originating in the rotation of the stars:—this rotation as brought about by the in-rushing of the primary atoms, towards their respective centres of aggregation:—this in-rushing as the consequence of the law of gravity:—this law as but the mode in which is necessarily manifested the tendency of the atoms to return into imparticularity:—this tendency to return as but the inevitable reaction of the first and most sublime of acts—that act by which a God, self-existing and alone existing, became all things at once, through dint of his volition, while all things were thus constituted a portion of God.

The radical assumptions of this discourse suggest to me, and in fact imply, certain important *modifications* of the Nebular Theory as given by Laplace. The efforts of the repulsive power I have considered as made for the purpose of preventing contact among the atoms, and thus as made in the ratio of the approach to contact—that is to say, in the ratio of condensation. In other words, *electricity*, with its involute phenomena, heat, light and magnetism, is to be understood as proceeding as condensation proceeds, and, of course, inversely as density proceeds, or the *cessation to condense*. Thus the Sun, in the process of its aggregation, must soon, in developing repulsion, have become excessively heated—perhaps incandescent: and we can perceive how the operation of discarding its rings must have been materially assisted by the slight incrustation of its surface consequent on cooling.

Any common experiment shows us how readily a crust of the character suggested, is separated, through heterogeneity, from the interior mass. But, on every successive rejection of the crust, the new surface would appear incandescent as before; and the period at which it would again become so far encrusted as to be readily loosened and discharged, may well be imagined as exactly coincident with that at which a new effort would be needed, by the whole mass, to restore the equilibrium of its two forces, disarranged through condensation. In other words:—by the time the electric influence (Repulsion) has prepared the surface for rejection, we are to understand that the gravitating influence (Attraction) is precisely ready to reject it. Here, then, as everywhere, *the body and the soul walk hand in hand.*

These ideas are empirically confirmed at all points. Since condensation can never, in any body, be considered as absolutely at an end, we are warranted in anticipating that, whenever we have an opportunity of testing the matter, we shall find indications of resident luminosity in *all* the stellar bodies—moons and planets as well as suns. That our Moon is strongly self-luminous, we see at her every total eclipse, when, if not so, she would disappear. On the dark part of the satellite, too, during her phases, we often observe flashes like our own *Auroras*; and that these latter, with our various other so-called electrical phenomena, without reference to any more steady radiance, must give our Earth a certain appearance of luminosity to an inhabitant of the Moon, is quite evident. In fact, we should regard all the phenomena referred to, as mere manifestations, in different moods and degrees, of the Earth's feebly-continued condensation.

If my views are tenable, we should be prepared to find the newer planets—that is to say, those nearer the Sun—more luminous than those older and more remote:—and the extreme brilliancy of Venus (on whose dark portions, during her phases, the *Auroras* are frequently visible) does not seem to be altogether accounted for by her mere proximity to the central orb. She is no doubt vividly self-luminous, although less so than Mercury: while the luminosity of Neptune may be comparatively nothing.

Admitting what I have urged, it is clear that, from the moment of the Sun's discarding a ring, there must be a continuous diminution both of his heat and light, on account of the continuous encrustation of his surface; and that a period would arrive—the period immediately previous to a new discharge—when a *very material* decrease of both light and heat, must become apparent. Now, we know that tokens of such changes are distinctly recognisable. On the Melville islands—to adduce merely one out of a hundred examples—we find traces of *ultra-tropical* vegetation—of plants that never could have flourished without immensely more light and heat than are at present afforded by our Sun to any portion of the surface of the Earth. Is such vegetation referable to an epoch immediately subsequent to the whirling-off of Venus? At this epoch must have occurred to us our greatest access of solar influence; and, in fact, this influence must then have attained its maximum:—leaving out of view, of course, the period when the Earth itself was discarded—the period of its mere organisation.

Again:—we know that there exist *non-luminous suns*—that is to say, suns whose existence we determine through the movements of others, but whose luminosity is not sufficient to impress us. Are these suns invisible merely on account of the length of time elapsed since their discharge of a planet? And yet again:—may we not—at least in certain cases—account for the sudden appearances of suns where none had been previously suspected, by the hypothesis that, having rolled with encrusted surfaces throughout the few thousand years of our astronomical history, each of these suns, in whirling off a new secondary, has at length been enabled to display the glories of its still incandescent interior?—To the well-ascertained fact of the proportional increase of heat as we descend into the Earth, I need of course, do nothing more than refer:—it comes in the strongest possible corroboration of all that I have said on the topic now at issue.

In speaking, not long ago, of the repulsive or electrical influence, I remarked that "the important phenomena of vitality, consciousness, and thought, whether we observe them generally or in detail, seem to proceed *at least in the ratio of the heterogeneous*." I mentioned, too, that I would recur to the suggestion:—and this is the proper point at which to do so. Looking at the matter, first, in detail, we perceive that not merely the *manifestation* of vitality, but its importance, consequences, and elevation of character, keep pace, very closely, with the heterogeneity, or complexity, of the animal structure. Looking at the question, now, in its generality, and referring to the first movements of the atoms towards mass-constitution, we find that heterogeneousness, brought about directly through condensation, is proportional with it forever. We thus reach the proposition that *the importance of the development of the terrestrial vitality proceeds equably with the terrestrial condensation.*

Now this is in precise accordance with what we know of the succession of animals on the Earth. As it has proceeded in its condensation, superior and still superior races have appeared. Is it impossible that the successive geological revolutions which have attended, at least, if not immediately caused, these successive elevations of vitalic character—is it improbable that these revolutions have themselves been produced by the successive planetary discharges from the Sun—in other words, by the successive variations in the solar influence on the Earth? Were this idea tenable, we should not be unwarranted in the fancy that the discharge of yet a new planet, interior to Mercury, may give rise to yet a new modification of the terrestrial surface—a modification from which may spring a race both materially and spiritually superior to man. These thoughts impress me with all the force of truth—but I throw them out, of course, merely in their obvious character of suggestion.

The Nebular Theory of Laplace has lately received far more confirmation than it needed, at the hands of the philosopher, Comte. These two have thus together shown—*not*, to be sure, that matter at any period actually existed as described, in a state of nebular diffusion, but that, admitting it so to have existed throughout the space and much beyond the space now occupied by our solar system, *and to have commenced a movement to-*

wards a centre—it must gradually have assumed the various forms and motions which are now seen, in that system, to obtain. A demonstration such as this—a dynamical and mathematical demonstration, as far as demonstration can be—unquestionable and unquestioned—unless, indeed, by that unprofitable and disreputable tribe, the professional questioners—the mere madmen who deny the Newtonian law of gravity on which the results of the French mathematicians are based—a demonstration, I say, such as this, would to most intellects be conclusive—and I confess that it is so to mine—of the validity of the nebular hypothesis upon which the demonstration depends.

That the demonstration does not *prove* the hypothesis, according to the common understanding of the word "proof," I admit, of course. To show that certain existing results—that certain established facts—may be, even mathematically, accounted for by the assumption of a certain hypothesis, is by no means to establish the hypothesis itself. In other words:—to show that, certain data being given, a certain existing result might, or even must, have ensued, will fail to prove that this result *did* ensue, *from the data*, until such time as it shall be also shown that there are, *and can be*, no other data from which the result in question might *equally* have ensued. But, in the case now discussed, although all must admit the deficiency of what we are in the habit of terming "proof," still there are many intellects, and those of the loftiest order to which *no* proof could bring one iota of additional *conviction*.

Without going into details which might impinge upon the Cloud Land of Metaphysics, I may as well here observe that the force of conviction, in cases such as this, will always, with the right-thinking, be proportional to the amount of *complexity* intervening between the hypothesis and the result. To be less abstract:—The greatness of the complexity found existing among cosmical conditions, by rendering great in the same proportion the difficulty of accounting for all these conditions *at once*, strengthens, also in the same proportion, our faith in that hypothesis which does, in such manner, satisfactorily account for them:—and as *no* complexity can well be conceived greater than that of the astronomical conditions, so no conviction can be stronger—to my mind at least—than that with which I am impressed by an hypothesis that not only reconciles these conditions, with mathematical accuracy, and reduces them into a consistent and intelligible whole, but is, at the same time, the *sole* hypothesis by means of which the human intellect has been ever enabled to account for them *at all.*

A most unfounded opinion has been latterly current and even in scientific circles—the opinion that the so-called Nebular Cosmogony has been overthrown. This fancy has arisen from the report of late observations made, among what hitherto have been termed the "nebulae," through the large telescope of Cincinnati, and the world-renowned instrument of Lord Rosse. Certain spots in the firmament which presented, even to the most powerful of the old telescopes, the appearance of nebulosity, or haze, had been regarded for a long time as confirming the theory of Laplace. They were looked upon as stars in that very process of condensation which I have been attempting to describe.

Thus it was supposed that we "had ocular evidence"—an evidence, by the way, which has always been found very questionable—of the truth of the hypothesis; and, although certain telescopic improvements, every now and then, enabled us to perceive that a spot, here and there, which we had been classing among the nebulae, was, in fact, but a cluster of stars deriving its nebular character only from its immensity of distance—still it was thought that no doubt could exist as to the actual nebulosity of numerous other masses, the strong-holds of the nebulists, bidding defiance to every effort at segregation.

Of these latter the most interesting was the great "nebulae" in the constellation Orion:—but this, with innumerable other miscalled "nebulae," when viewed through the magnificent modern telescopes, has become resolved into a simple collection of stars. Now this fact has been very generally understood as conclusive against the Nebular Hypothesis of Laplace; and, on announcement of the discoveries in question, the most enthusiastic defender and most eloquent populariser of the theory, Dr. Nichol, went so far as to "admit the necessity of abandoning" an idea which had formed the material of his most praiseworthy book. [6]

Many of my readers will no doubt be inclined to say that the result of these new investigations *has* at least a strong *tendency* to overthrow the hypothesis; while some of them, more thoughtful, will suggest that, although the theory is by no means disproved through the segregation of the particular "nebulae" alluded to, still a *failure* to segregate them, with such telescopes, might well have been understood as a triumphant *corroboration* of the theory:—and this latter class will be surprised, perhaps, to hear me say that even with *them* I disagree. If the propositions of this discourse have been comprehended, it will be seen that, in my view, a failure to segregate the "nebulae" would have tended to the refutation, rather than to the confirmation, of the Nebular Hypothesis.

Let me explain:—The Newtonian Law of Gravity we may, of course, assume as demonstrated. This law, it will be remembered, I have referred to the reaction of the first Divine Act—to the reaction of an exercise of the Divine Volition temporarily overcoming a difficulty. This difficulty is that of forcing the normal into the abnormal—of impelling that whose originality, and therefore whose rightful condition, was *one*, to take upon itself the wrongful condition of *many*. It is only by conceiving this difficulty as *temporarily* overcome, that we can comprehend a reaction. There could have been no reaction had the act been infinitely continued. So long as the act *lasted* no reaction, of course, could commence; in other words, no *gravitation* could take place—for we have considered the one as but the manifestation of the other. But gravitation *has* taken place; therefore the act of creation has ceased: and gravitation has long ago taken

6. *Views of the Architecture of the Heavens.* A letter, purporting to be from Dr. Nichol to a friend in America, went the rounds of our newspapers, about two years ago, I think, admitting "the necessity" to which I refer. In a subsequent lecture, however, Dr. N. appears in some manner to have gotten the better of the necessity, and does not quite *renounce* the theory, although he seems to wish that he could sneer at it as "a purely hypothetical one." What else was the Law of Gravity before the Maskelyne experiments? and who questioned the Law of Gravity, even then?

place; therefore the act of creation has long ago ceased. We can no more expect, then, to observe the *primary processes* of creation; and to these primary processes the condition of nebulosity has already been explained to belong.

Through what we know of the propagation of light, we have direct proof that the more remote of the stars have existed, under the forms in which we now see them, for an inconceivable number of years. So far back *at least*, then, as the period when these stars underwent condensation, must have been the epoch at which the mass-constitutive processes began. That we may conceive these processes, then, as still going on in the case of certain "nebulae," while in all other cases we find them thoroughly at an end, we are forced into assumptions for which we have really no basis whatever—we have to thrust in, again, upon the revolting reason, the blasphemous idea of special interposition—we have to suppose that, in the particular instances of these "nebulae," an unerring God found it necessary to introduce certain supplementary regulations—certain improvements of the general law—certain retouchings and emendations, in a word, which had the effect of deferring the completion of these individual stars for centuries of centuries beyond the aera during which all the other stellar bodies had time, not only to be fully constituted, but to grow hoary with an unspeakable old age.

Of course, it will be immediately objected that since the light by which we recognise the nebulae now, must be merely that which left their surfaces a vast number of years ago, the processes at present observed, or supposed to be observed, are, in fact, *not* processes now actually going on, but the phantoms of processes completed long in the past—just as I maintain all these mass-constitutive processes *must* have been.

To this I reply that neither is the now-observed condition of the condensed stars their actual condition, but a condition completed long in the past; so that my argument drawn from the *relative* condition of the stars and the "nebulae," is in no manner disturbed. Moreover, those who maintain the existence of nebulae, do *not* refer the nebulosity to extreme distance; they declare it a real and not merely a perspective nebulosity. That we may conceive, indeed, a nebular mass as visible at all, we must conceive it as *very near us* in comparison with the condensed stars brought into view by the modern telescopes.

In maintaining the appearances in question, then, to be really nebulous, we maintain their comparative vicinity to our point of view. Thus, their condition, as we see them now, must be referred to an epoch *far less remote* than that to which we may refer the now-observed condition of at least the majority of the stars.—In a word, should astronomy ever demonstrate a "nebula," in the sense at present intended, I should consider the Nebular Cosmogony—*not*, indeed, as corroborated by the demonstration—but as thereby irretrievably overthrown.

By way, however, of rendering unto Caesar *no more* than the things that are Caesar's, let me here remark that the assumption of the hypothesis which led him to so glorious a result, seems to have been suggested to Laplace in great measure by a misconception—by the very misconception of which we have just been speaking—by the generally prevalent misunderstanding of the character of the nebulae, so misnamed. These he supposed to be, in reality, what their designation implies. The fact is, this great man had, very properly, an inferior faith in his own merely perceptive powers. In respect, therefore, to the actual existence of nebulae—an existence so confidently maintained by his telescopic contemporaries—he depended less upon what he saw than upon what he heard.

It will be seen that the only valid objections to his theory, are those made to its hypothesis *as* such—to what suggested it—not to what it suggests; to its propositions rather than to its results. His most unwarranted assumption was that of giving the atoms a movement towards a centre, in the very face of his evident understanding that these atoms, in unlimited succession, extended throughout the Universal space. I have already shown that, under such circumstances, there could have occurred no movement at all; and Laplace, consequently, assumed one on no more philosophical ground than that something of the kind was necessary for the establishment of what he intended to establish.

His original idea seems to have been a compound of the true Epicurean atoms with the false nebulae of his contemporaries; and thus his theory presents us with the singular anomaly of absolute truth deduced, as a mathematical result, from a hybrid *datum* of ancient imagination intertangled with modern inacumen. Laplace's real strength lay, in fact, in an almost miraculous mathematical instinct:—on this he relied; and in no instance did it fail or deceive him:—in the case of the Nebular Cosmogony, it led him, blindfolded, through a labyrinth of Error, into one of the most luminous and stupendous temples of Truth.

Let us now fancy, for the moment, that the ring first thrown off by the Sun—that is to say, the ring whose breaking-up constituted Neptune—did not, in fact, break up until the throwing-off of the ring out of which Uranus arose; that this latter ring, again, remained perfect until the discharge of that out of which sprang Saturn; that this latter, again, remained entire until the discharge of that from which originated Jupiter—and so on. Let us imagine, in a word, that no dissolution occurred among the rings until the final rejection of that which gave birth to Mercury.

We thus paint to the eye of the mind a series of coexistent concentric circles; and looking as well at *them* as at the processes by which, according to Laplace's hypothesis, they were constructed, we perceive at once a very singular analogy with the atomic *strata* and the process of the original irradiation as I have described it. Is it impossible that, on measuring the *forces*, respectively, by which each successive planetary circle was thrown off—that is to say, on measuring the successive excesses of rotation over gravitation which occasioned the successive discharges—we should find the analogy in question more decidedly confirmed? *Is it improbable that we should discover these forces to have varied—as in the original irradiation—proportional to the squares of the distances?*

Our solar system, consisting, in chief, of one Sun, with sixteen planets certainly, and possibly a few more, revolving about it at various distances, and attended by seventeen Moons assuredly, but very probably by several others—is now to be considered as *an example* of the innumerable agglomerations which proceeded to take place throughout the Universal Sphere of atoms on withdrawal of the Divine Volition. I mean to say that our solar system is to be understood as affording a generic instance of these agglomerations, or, more correctly, of the ulterior conditions at which they arrived. If we keep our attention fixed on the idea of the *utmost possible relation* as the omnipotent design, and on the precautions taken to accomplish it through difference of form, among the original atoms, and particular in equidistance, we shall find it impossible to suppose for a moment that even any two of the incipient agglomerations reached precisely the same result in the end.

We shall rather be inclined to think that *no two* stellar bodies in the Universe—whether suns, planets or Moons—are particularly, while *all* are generally, similar. Still less, then, can we imagine any two *assemblages* of such bodies—any two "systems"—as having more than a general resemblance.[7] Our telescopes, at this point, thoroughly confirm our deductions. Taking our own solar system, then, as merely a loose or general type of all, we have so far proceeded in our subject as to survey the Universe under the aspect of a spherical space, throughout which, dispersed with merely general equability, exist a number of but generally similar *systems*.

Let us now, expanding our conceptions, look upon each of these system as in itself an atom; which in fact it is, when we consider it as but one of the countless myriads of systems which constitute the Universe. Regarding all, then, as but colossal atoms, each with the same ineradicable tendency to Unity which characterizes the actual atoms of which it consists—we enter at once upon a new order of aggregations. The smaller systems,

7. It is not *impossible* that some unlooked-for optical improvement may disclose to us, among innumerable varieties of systems, a luminous Sun, encircled by luminous and non-luminous rings, within and without and between which, revolve luminous and non-luminous planets, attended by moons having moons—and even these latter again having moons.

in the vicinity of a larger one, would, inevitably, be drawn into still closer vicinity. A thousand would assemble here; a million there—perhaps here, again, even a billion—leaving, thus, immeasurable vacancies in space.

And if, now, it be demanded why, in the case of these systems—of these merely Titanic atoms—I speak, simply, of an "assemblage," and not, as in the case of the actual atoms, of a more or less consolidated agglomeration:—if it be asked, for instance, why I do not carry what I suggest to its legitimate conclusion, and describe, at once, these assemblages of system-atoms as rushing to consolidation in spheres—as each becoming condensed into one magnificent Sun—my reply is that μελλοντα ταυτα-—I am but pausing, for a moment, on the awful threshold of *the future*. For the present, calling these assemblages "clusters," we see them in the incipient stages of their consolidation. Their *absolute* consolidation is *to come.*

We have now reached a point from which we behold the Universe as a spherical space, interspersed, *unequably*, with *clusters*. It will be noticed that I here prefer the adverb "unequably" to the phrase "with a merely general equability," employed before. It is evident, in fact, that the equability of distribution will diminish in the ratio of the agglomerative processes—that is to say, as the things distributed diminish in number. Thus the increase of in equability—an increase which must continue until, sooner or later an epoch will arrive at which the largest agglomeration will absorb all the others—should be viewed as, simply, a corroborative indication of the *tendency to one.*

And here, at length, it seems proper to inquire whether the ascertained *facts* of astronomy confirm the general arrangement which I have thus, deductively, assigned to the Heavens. Thoroughly, they do. Telescopic observation, guided by the laws of perspective, enables us to understand that the perceptible Universe exists as *a cluster of clusters, irregularly disposed.*

The "clusters" of which this Universal "*cluster of clusters*" consists, are merely what we have been in the practice of designating "nebulae"—and, of these "nebulae," *one* is of paramount interest to mankind. I allude to the Galaxy, or Milky Way. This interests us, first and most obviously, on account of its great superiority in apparent size, not only to any one other cluster in the firmament, but to all the other clusters taken together. The largest of these latter occupies a mere point, comparatively, and is distinctly seen only with the aid of a telescope. The Galaxy sweeps throughout the Heaven and is brilliantly visible to the naked eye. But it interests man chiefly, although less immediately, on account of its being his home; the home of the Earth on which he exists; the home of the Sun about which this Earth revolves; the home of that "system" of orbs of which the Sun is the centre and primary—the Earth one of sixteen secondaries, or planets—the Moon one of seventeen *tertiaries*, or satellites.

The Galaxy, let me repeat, is but one of the *clusters* which I have been describing—but one of the miscalled "nebulae" revealed to us—by the telescope alone, sometimes—as faint hazy spots in various quarters of the sky. We have no reason to suppose the Milky Way *really* more extensive than the least of these "nebulae". Its vast superiority in size is but an apparent superiority arising from our position in regard to it—that is to say, from our position in its midst. However strange the assertion may at first appear to those unversed in astronomy, still the astronomer himself has no hesitation in asserting that we are *in the midst* of that inconceivable host of stars—of suns—of systems—which constitute the Galaxy. Moreover, not only have *we*—not only has *our* Sun a right to claim the Galaxy as its own especial cluster, but, with slight reservation, it may be said that all the distinctly visible stars of the firmament—all the stars visible to the naked eye—have equally a right to claim it as *their* own.

There has been a great deal of misconception in respect to the *shape* of the Galaxy; which, in nearly all our astronomical treatises, is said to resemble that of a capital Y. The cluster in question has, in reality, a certain general—*very* general resemblance to the planet Saturn, with its encompassing triple ring. Instead of the solid orb of that planet, however, we must picture to ourselves a lenticular star-island, or collection of stars; our

Sun lying eccentrically—near the shore of the island—on that side of it which is nearest the constellation of the Cross and farthest from that of Cassiopeia. The surrounding ring, where it approaches our position, has in it a longitudinal *gash*, which does in fact, cause *the ring, in our vicinity*, to assume, loosely, the appearance of a capital Y.

We must not fall into the error, however, of conceiving the somewhat indefinite girdle as at all *remote*, comparatively speaking, from the also indefinite lenticular cluster which it surrounds; and thus, for mere purpose of explanation, we may speak of our Sun as actually situated at that point of the Y where its three component lines unite; and, conceiving this letter to be of a certain solidity—of a certain thickness, very trivial in comparison with its length—we may even speak of our position as *in the middle* of this thickness.

Fancying ourselves thus placed, we shall no longer find difficulty in accounting for the phaenomena presented—which are perspective altogether. When we look upward or downward—that is to say, when we cast our eyes in the direction of the letter's *thickness*—we look through fewer stars than when we cast them in the direction of its *length*, or *along* either of the three component lines.

Of course, in the former case, the stars appear scattered—in the latter, crowded.—To reverse this explanation:—An inhabitant of the Earth, when looking, as we commonly express ourselves, at the Galaxy, is then beholding it in some of the directions of its length—is looking the *along* the lines of the Y—but when, looking out into the general Heaven, he turns his eyes *from* the Galaxy, he is then surveying it in the direction of the letter's thickness; and on this account the stars seem to him scattered; while, in fact, they are as close together, on an average, as in the mass of the cluster. *No* consideration could be better adapted to convey an idea of this cluster's stupendous extent.

If, with a telescope of high space-penetrating power, we carefully inspect the firmament, we shall become aware of a *belt of clusters*—of what we have hitherto called "nebulae"—a *band*, of varying breadth, stretching from horizon to horizon, at right angles to the general course of the Milky Way. This band is the ultimate *cluster of clusters*. This belt is *The Universe*. Our Galaxy is but one, and perhaps one of the most inconsiderable, of the clusters which go to the constitution of this ultimate, Universal *belt* or *band*. The appearance of this cluster of clusters, to our eyes, as a belt or band, is altogether a perspective phenomenon of the same character as that which causes us to behold our own individual and roughly-spherical cluster, the Galaxy, under guise also of a belt, traversing the Heavens at right angles to the Universal one.

The shape of the all-inclusive cluster is, of course *generally*, that of each individual cluster which it includes. Just as the scattered stars which, on looking *from* the Galaxy, we see in the general sky, are, in fact, but a portion of that Galaxy itself, and as closely intermingled with it as any of the telescopic points in what seems the densest portion of its mass—so are the scattered "nebulae" which, on casting our eyes *from* the Universal *belt*, we perceive at all points of the firmament—so, I say, are these scattered "nebulae" to be understood as only perspectively scattered, and as part and parcel of the one supreme and Universal *sphere*.

No astronomical fallacy is more untenable, and none has been more pertinaciously adhered to, than that of the absolute *illimitation* of the Universe of Stars. The reasons for limitation, as I have already assigned them, *à priori*, seem to me unanswerable; but, not to speak of these, observation assures us that there is, in numerous directions around us, certainly, if not in all, a positive limit—or, at the very least, affords us no basis whatever for thinking otherwise. Were the succession of stars endless, then the background of the sky would present us an uniform luminosity, like that displayed by the Galaxy—*since there could be absolutely no point, in all that background, at which would not exist a star.* The only mode, therefore, in which, under such a state of affairs, we could comprehend the voids which our telescopes find in innumerable directions, would be by supposing the distance of the invisible background so immense that no ray from it has yet been able to reach us at all. That this may be so, who shall venture to deny? I maintain, simply, that we have not even the shadow of a reason for believing that it *is* so.

When speaking of the vulgar propensity to regard all bodies on the Earth as tending merely to the Earth's centre, I observed that, "with certain exceptions to be specified hereafter, every body on the Earth tended not only to the Earth's centre, but in every conceivable direction besides." The "exceptions" refer to those frequent gaps in the Heavens, where our utmost scrutiny can detect not only no stellar bodies, but no indications of their existence:—where yawning chasms, blacker than Erebus, seem to afford us glimpses, through the boundary walls of the Universe of Stars, into the illimitable Universe of Vacancy, beyond. Now as any body, existing on the Earth, chances to pass, either through its own movement or the Earth's, into a line with any one of these voids, or cosmical abysses, it clearly is no longer attracted *in the direction of that void*, and for the moment, consequently, is "heavier" than at any period, either after or before. Independently of the consideration of these voids however, and looking only at the generally unequable distribution of the stars, we see that the absolute tendency of bodies on the Earth to the Earth's centre, is in a state of perpetual variation.

We comprehend, then, the insulation of our Universe. We perceive the isolation of *that*—of *all* that which we grasp with the senses. We know that there exists one *cluster of clusters*—a collection around which, on all sides, extend the immeasurable wildernesses of a space to all *human perception* untenanted. But *because* upon the confines of this Universe of Stars we are compelled to pause, through want of farther evidence from the senses, is it right to conclude that, in fact, there *is* no material point beyond that which we have thus been permitted to attain?

Have we, or have we not, an analogical right to the inference that this perceptible Universe—that this cluster of clusters—is but one of a *series* of clusters of clusters, the rest of which are invisible through distance—through the diffusion of their light being so excessive, ere it reaches us, as not to produce upon our retinas a light-impression—or from there being no such emanation as light at all, in these unspeakably distant worlds—or, lastly, from the mere interval being so vast, that the electric tidings of their presence in space, have not yet—through the lapsing myriads of years—been enabled to traverse that interval?

Have we any right to inferences—have we any ground whatever for visions such as these? If we have a right to them in *any* degree, we have a right to their infinite extension.

The human brain has obviously a leaning to the "*Infinite*," and fondles the phantom of the idea. It seems to long with a passionate fervour for this impossible conception, with the hope of intellectually believing it when conceived. What is general among the whole race of man, of course no individual of that race can be warranted in considering abnormal; nevertheless, there *may* be a class of superior intelligences, to whom the human bias alluded to may wear all the character of monomania.

My question, however, remains unanswered:—Have we any right to infer—let us say, rather, to imagine—an interminable succession of the "clusters of clusters," or of "Universes" more or less similar?

I reply that the "right," in a case such as this, depends absolutely upon the hardihood of that imagination which ventures to claim the right. Let me declare, only, that, as an individual, I myself feel impelled to the fancy—without daring to call it more—that there *does* exist a *limitless* succession of Universes, more or less similar to that of which we have cognisance—to that of which *alone* we shall ever have cognisance—at the very least until the return of our own particular Universe into unity. *If* such clusters of clusters exist, however—*and they do*—it is abundantly clear that, having had no part in our origin, they have no portion in our laws. They neither attract us, nor we them. Their material—their spirit is not ours—is not that which obtains in any part of our Universe. They could not impress our senses or our souls. Among them and us—considering all, for the moment, collectively—there are no influences in common. Each exists, apart and independently, *in the bosom of its proper and particular God.*

In the conduct of this discourse, I am aiming less at physical than at metaphysical order. The clearness with which even material phenomena are presented to the understanding, depends very little, I have long since learned to perceive, upon a merely natural, and almost altogether upon a moral, arrangement. If then I seem to step somewhat too discursively from point to point of my topic, let me suggest that I do so in the hope of thus the better keeping unbroken that chain of *graduated impression* by which alone the intellect of man can expect to encompass the grandeurs of which I speak, and, in their majestic totality, to comprehend them.

So far, our attention has been directed, almost exclusively, to a general and relative grouping of the stellar bodies in space. Of specification there has been little and whatever ideas of *quantity* have been conveyed—that is to say, of number, magnitude, and distance—have been conveyed incidentally and by way of preparation for more definitive conceptions. These latter let us now attempt to entertain.

Our solar system, as has been already mentioned, consists, in chief, of one Sun and sixteen planets certainly, but in all probability a few others, revolving around it as a centre, and attended by seventeen moons of which we know, with possibly several more of which as yet we know nothing. These various bodies are not true spheres, but oblate spheroids—spheres flattened at the poles of the imaginary axes about which they rotate:—the flattening being a consequence of the rotation. Neither is the Sun absolutely the centre of the system; for this Sun itself, with all the planets, revolves about a perpetually shifting point of space, which is the system's general centre of gravity.

Neither are we to consider the paths through which these different spheroids move—the Moons about the planets, the planets about the Sun, or the Sun about the common centre—as circles in an accurate sense. They are, in fact, *ellipses—one of the foci being the point about which the revolution is made.* An ellipse is a curve, returning into itself, one of whose diameters is longer than the other. In the longer diameter are two points, equidistant from the middle of the line, and so situated otherwise that if, from each of them a straight line be drawn to any one point of the curve, the two lines, taken together, will, be equal to the longer diameter itself. Now let us conceive such an ellipse. At one of the points mentioned, which are the *foci*, let us fasten an orange. By an elastic thread let us connect this orange with a pea; and let us place this latter on the circumference of the ellipse. Let us now move the pea continuously around the orange—keeping always on the circumference of the ellipse.

The elastic thread, which, of course, varies in length as we move the pea, will form what in geometry is called a *radius vector.* Now, if the orange be understood as the Sun, and the pea as a planet revolving about it, then the revolution should be made at such a rate—with a velocity so varying—that the radius vector may pass over *equal areas of space in equal times.* The progress of the pea *should be*—in other words, the progress of the planet *is,* of course,—slow in proportion to its distance from the Sun—swift in proportion to its proximity. Those planets, moreover, move the more slowly which are the farther from the Sun; *the squares of their periods of revolution having the same proportion to each other, as have to each other the cubes of their mean distances from the Sun.*

The wonderfully complex laws of revolution here described, however, are not to be understood as obtaining in our system alone. They *everywhere* prevail where attraction prevails. They control *the Universe.* Every shining speck in the firmament is, no doubt, a luminous Sun, resembling our own, at least in its general features, and having in attendance upon it a greater or less number of planets, greater or less, whose still lingering luminosity is not sufficient to render them visible to us at so vast a distance, but which, nevertheless, revolve, Moon-attended, about their starry centres, in obedience to the principles just detailed—in obedience to the three omniprevalent laws of revolution the three immortal laws *guessed* by the imaginative Kepler, and but subsequently demonstrated and accounted for by the patient and mathematical Newton.

Among a tribe of philosophers who pride themselves excessively upon matter-of-fact, it is far too fashionable to sneer at all speculation under the comprehensive *sobriquet*, "guess-work." The point to be considered is, *who* guesses. In guessing with Plato, we spend our time to better purpose, now and then, than in hearkening to a demonstration by Alcmaeon.

In many works on astronomy I find it distinctly stated that the laws of Kepler are *the basis* of the great principle, gravitation. This idea must have arisen from the fact that the suggestion of these laws by Kepler, and his proving them *à posteriori* to have an actual existence, led Newton to account for them by the hypothesis of gravitation, and, finally, to demonstrate them a priori, as necessary consequences of the hypothetical principle. Thus so far from the laws of Kepler being the basis of gravity, gravity is the basis of these laws—as it is, indeed, of all the laws of the material Universe which are not referable to repulsion alone.

The mean distance of the Earth from the Moon—that is to say, from the heavenly body in our closest vicinity—is 237,000 miles. Mercury, the planet nearest the Sun, is distant from him 37 millions of miles. Venus, the next, revolves at a distance of 68 millions:—the Earth, which comes next, at a distance of 95 millions:—Mars, then, at a distance of 144 millions. Now come the eight Asteroids (Ceres, Juno, Vesta, Pallas, Astraea, Flora, Iris, and Hebe) at an average distance of about 250 millions. Then we have Jupiter, distant 490 millions; then Saturn, 900 millions; then Uranus, 19 hundred millions; finally Neptune, lately discovered, and revolving at a distance, say of 28 hundred millions.

Leaving Neptune out of the account—of which as yet we know little accurately and which is, possibly, one of a system of Asteroids—it will be seen that, within certain limits, there exists an *order of interval* among the planets. Speaking loosely, we may say that each outer planet is twice as far from the Sun as is the next inner one. May not the order here mentioned—*may not the law of Bode—be deduced from consideration of the analogy suggested by me as having place between the solar discharge of rings and the mode of the atomic irradiation?*

The numbers hurriedly mentioned in this summary of distance, it is folly to attempt comprehending, unless in the light of abstract arithmetical facts. They are not practically tangible ones. They convey no precise ideas. I have stated that Neptune, the planet farthest from the Sun, revolves about him at a distance of 28 hundred millions of miles. So far good:—I have stated a mathematical fact; and, without comprehending it in the least, we may put it to use—mathematically. But in mentioning, even, that the Moon revolves about the Earth at the comparatively trifling distance of 237,000 miles, I entertained no expectation of giving any one to understand—to know—to feel—how far from the Earth the Moon actually is. 237,*000 miles!*

There are, perhaps, few of my readers who have not crossed the Atlantic ocean; yet how many of them have a distinct idea of even the 3,000 miles intervening between shore and shore? I doubt, indeed, whether the man lives who can force into his brain the most remote conception of the interval between one milestone and its next neighbour upon the turnpike. We are in some measure aided, however, in our consideration of distance, by combining this consideration with the kindred one of velocity. Sound passes through 1100 feet of space in a second of time. Now were it possible for an inhabitant of the Earth to see the flash of a cannon discharged in the Moon, and to hear the report, he would have to wait, after perceiving the former, more than 13 entire days and nights before getting any intimation of the latter.

However feeble be the impression, even thus conveyed, of the Moon's real distance from the Earth, it will, nevertheless, effect a good object in enabling us more clearly to see the futility of attempting to grasp such intervals as that of the 28 hundred millions of miles between our Sun and Neptune; or even that of the 95 millions between the Sun and the Earth we inhabit. A cannon-ball, flying at the greatest velocity with which a ball has ever been known to fly, could not traverse the latter interval in less than 20 years; while for the former it would require 590.

Our Moon's real diameter is 2160 miles; yet she is comparatively so trifling an object that it would take nearly 50 such orbs to compose one as great as the Earth.

The diameter of our own globe is 7912 miles—but from the enunciation of these numbers what positive idea do we derive?

If we ascend an ordinary mountain and look around us from its summit, we behold a landscape stretching, say 40 miles, in every direction; forming a circle 250 miles in circumference; and including an area of 5000 square miles. The extent of such a prospect, on account of the *successiveness* with which its portions necessarily present themselves to view, can be only very feebly and very partially appreciated:—yet the entire panorama would comprehend no more than one 40,000th part of the mere *surface* of our globe. Were this panorama, then, to be succeeded, after the lapse of an hour, by another of equal extent; this again by a third, after the lapse of another hour; this again by a fourth after lapse of another hour—and so on, until the scenery of the whole Earth were exhausted; and were we to be engaged in examining these various panoramas for twelve hours of every day; we should nevertheless, be 9 years and 48 days in completing the general survey.

But if the mere surface of the Earth eludes the grasp of the imagination, what are we to think of its cubical contents? It embraces a mass of matter equal in weight to at least 2 sextillions, 200 quintillions of tons. Let us suppose it in a state of quiescence; and now let us endeavour to conceive a mechanical force sufficient to set it in motion! Not the strength of all the myriads of beings whom we may conclude to inhabit the planetary worlds of our system—not the combined physical strength of *all* these beings—even admitting all to be more powerful than man—would avail to stir the ponderous mass a *single inch* from its position.

What are we to understand, then, of the force, which under similar circumstances, would be required to move the *largest* of our planets, Jupiter? This is 86,000 miles in diameter, and would include within its periphery more than a thousand orbs of the magnitude of our own. Yet this stupendous body is actually flying around the Sun at the rate of 29,000 miles an hour—that is to say, with a velocity 40 times greater than that of a cannon-ball! The thought of such a phenomenon cannot well be said to *startle* the mind:—it palsies and appals it. Not unfrequently we task our imagination in picturing the capacities of an angel. Let us fancy such a being at a distance of some hundred miles from Jupiter—a close eye-witness of this planet as it speeds on its annual revolution. Now *can* we, I demand, fashion for ourselves any conception so distinct of this ideal being's spiritual exaltation, as *that* involved in the supposition that, even by this immeasurable mass of matter, whirled immediately before his eyes, with a velocity so unutterable, he—an angel—angelic though he be—is not at once struck into nothingness and overwhelmed?

At this point, however, it seems proper to suggest that, in fact, we have been speaking of comparative trifles. Our Sun—the central and controlling orb of the system to which Jupiter belongs, is not only greater than Jupiter, but greater by far than all the planets of the system taken together. This fact is an essential condition, indeed, of the stability of the system itself. The diameter of Jupiter has been mentioned:—it is 86,000 miles:—that of the Sun is 882,000 miles. An inhabitant of the latter, travelling 90 miles a day, would be more than 80 years in going round a great circle of its circumference. It occupies a cubical space of 681 quadrillions, 472 trillions of miles. The Moon, as has been stated, revolves about the Earth at a distance of 237,000 miles—in an orbit, consequently, of nearly a million and a half. Now, were the Sun placed upon the Earth, centre over centre, the body of the former would extend, in every direction, not only to the line of the Moon's orbit, but beyond it, a distance of 200,000 miles.

And here, once again, let me suggest that, in fact, we have *still* been speaking of comparative trifles. The distance of the planet Neptune from the Sun has been stated:—it is 28 hundred millions of miles; the circumference of its orbit, therefore, is about 17 billions. Let this be borne in mind while we glance at some of the brightest stars. Between this and the star of *our* system, (the Sun,) there is a gulf of space, to convey any idea of which we should need the tongue of an archangel.

From *our* system, then, and from *our* Sun, or star, the star at which we suppose ourselves glancing is a thing altogether apart:—still, for the moment, let us imagine it placed upon our Sun, centre over centre, as we just now imagined this Sun itself placed upon the Earth. Let us now conceive the particular star we have in mind, extending, in every direction, beyond the orbit of Mercury—of Venus—of the Earth:—still *on*, beyond the orbit of Mars—of Jupiter—of Uranus—until, finally, we fancy it filling the circle—*17 billions of miles in circumference*—which is described by the revolution of Leverrier's planet. When we have conceived all this, we shall have entertained no extravagant conception. There is the very best reason for believing that many of the stars are even far larger than the one we have imagined. I mean to say that we have the very best *empirical* basis for such belief:—and, in looking back at the original, atomic arrangements for *diversity*, which have been assumed as a part of the divine plan in the constitution of the Universe, we shall be enabled easily to understand, and to credit, the existence of even far vaster disproportions in stellar size than any to which I have hitherto alluded. The largest orbs, of course, we must expect to find rolling through the widest vacancies of space.

I remarked, just now, that to convey an idea of the interval between our Sun and any one of the other stars, we should require the eloquence of an archangel. In so saying, I should not be accused of exaggeration; for, in simple truth, these are topics on which it is scarcely possible to exaggerate. But let us bring the matter more distinctly before the eye of the mind.

In the first place, we may get a general, *relative* conception of the interval referred to, by comparing it with the inter-planetary spaces. If, for example, we suppose the Earth, which is, in reality, 95 millions of miles from the Sun, to be only *one foot* from that luminary; then Neptune would be 40 feet distant; *and the star Alpha Lyrae, at the very least, 159.*

Now I presume that, in the termination of my last sentence, few of my readers have noticed anything especially objectionable—particularly wrong. I said that the distance of the Earth from the Sun being taken at *one foot,* the distance of Neptune would be 40 feet, and that of Alpha Lyrae, 159. The proportion between one foot and 159, has appeared, perhaps, to convey a sufficiently definite impression of the proportion between the two intervals—that of the Earth from the Sun and that of Alpha Lyrae from the same luminary. But my account of the matter should, in reality, have run thus:—The distance of the Earth from the Sun being taken at one foot, the distance of Neptune would be 40 feet, and that of Alpha Lyrae, 159—*miles*:—that is to say, I had assigned to Alpha Lyrae, in my first statement of the case, only the *5280th part* of that distance which is the *least distance possible* at which it can actually lie.

To proceed: However distant a mere *planet* is, yet when we look at it through a telescope, we see it under a certain form—of a certain appreciable size. Now I have already hinted at the probable bulk of many of the stars; nevertheless, when we view any one of them, even through the most powerful telescope, it is found to present us with *no form*, and consequently with *no magni*tude whatever. We see it as a point and nothing more.

Again;—Let us suppose ourselves walking, at night, on a highway. In a field on one side of the road, is a line of tall objects, say trees, the figures of which are distinctly defined against the background of the sky. This line of objects extends at right angles to the road, and from the road to the horizon. Now, as we proceed along the road, we see these objects changing their positions, respectively, in relation to a certain fixed point in that portion of the firmament which forms the background of the view. Let us suppose this fixed point—sufficiently fixed for our purpose—to be the rising Moon. We become aware, at once, that while the tree nearest us so far alters its position in respect to the Moon, as to seem flying behind us, the tree in the extreme distance has scarcely changed at all its relative position with the satellite. We then go on to perceive that the farther the objects are from us, the less they alter their positions; and the converse.

Then we begin, unwittingly, to estimate the distances of individual trees by the degrees in which they evince the relative alteration. Finally, we come to understand how it might be possible to ascertain the actual distance of any given tree in the line, by using the amount of relative alteration as a basis in a simple geometrical problem. Now this relative alteration is what we call "parallax;" and by parallax we calculate the distances of the heavenly bodies. Applying the principle to the trees in question, we should, of course, be very much at a loss to comprehend the distance of *that* tree, which, however far we proceeded along the road, should evince *no* parallax at all. This, in the case described, is a thing impossible; but impossible only because all distances on our Earth are trivial indeed:—in comparison with the vast cosmical quantities, we may speak of them as absolutely nothing.

Now, let us suppose the star Alpha Lyrae directly overhead; and let us imagine that, instead of standing on the Earth, we stand at one end of a straight road stretching through space to a distance equalling the diameter of the Earth's orbit—that is to say, to a distance of 190 *millions of miles*. Having observed, by means of the most delicate micrometrical instruments, the exact position of the star, let us now pass along this inconceivable road, until we reach its other extremity. Now, once again, let us look at the star. It is precisely where we left it. Our instruments, however delicate, assure us that its relative position is absolutely—is identically the same as at the commencement of our unutterable journey. *No* parallax—none whatever—has been found.

The fact is, that, in regard to the distance of the fixed stars—of any one of the myriads of suns glistening on the farther side of that awful chasm which separates our system from its brothers in the cluster to which it belongs—astronomical science, until very lately, could speak only with a negative certainty. Assuming the brightest as the nearest, we could say, even of *them*, only that there is a certain incomprehensible distance on the *hither* side of which they cannot be:—how far they are beyond it we had in no case been able to ascertain. We perceived, for example, that Alpha Lyrae cannot be nearer to us than 19 trillions, 200 billions of miles; but, for all we knew, and indeed for all we now know, it may be distant from us the square, or the cube, or any other power of the number mentioned.

By dint, however, of wonderfully minute and cautious observations, continued, with novel instruments, for many laborious years, Bessel, not long ago deceased, has lately succeeded in determining the distance of six or seven stars; among others, that of the star numbered 61 in the constellation of the Swan. The distance in this latter instance ascertained, is 670,000 times that of the Sun; which last it will be remembered, is 95 millions of miles. The star 61 Cygni, then, is nearly 64 trillions of miles from us—or more than three times the distance assigned, *as the least possible*, for Alpha Lyrae.

In attempting to appreciate this interval by the aid of any considerations of *velocity*, as we did in endeavouring to estimate the distance of the Moon, we must leave out of sight, altogether, such nothings as the speed of a cannon ball, or of sound. Light, however, according to the latest calculations of Struve, proceeds at the rate of 167,000 miles in a second. Thought itself cannot pass through this interval more speedily—if, indeed, thought can traverse it at all. Yet, in coming from 61 Cygni to us, even at this inconceivable rate, light occupies more than *ten years*; and, consequently, were the star this moment blotted out from the Universe, still, for *ten years*, would it continue to sparkle on, undimmed in its paradoxical glory.

Keeping now in mind whatever feeble conception we may have attained of the interval between our Sun and 61 Cygni, let us remember that this interval, however unutterably vast, we are permitted to consider as but the *average* interval among the countless host of stars composing that cluster, or "nebula," to which our system, as well as that of 61 Cygni, belongs. I have, in fact, stated the case with great moderation we have excellent reason for believing 61 Cygni to be one of the *nearest* stars, and thus for concluding, at least for the present, that its distance from us is *less* than the average distance between star and star in the magnificent cluster of the Milky Way.

And here, once again and finally, it seems proper to suggest that even as yet we have been speaking of trifles. Ceasing to wonder at the space between star and star in our own or in any particular cluster, let us rather turn our thoughts to the intervals between cluster and cluster, in the all comprehensive cluster of the Universe.

I have already said that light proceeds at the rate of 167,000 miles in a second—that is, about 10 millions of miles in a minute, or about 600 millions of miles in an hour:—yet so far removed from us are some of the "nebulae" that even light, speeding with this velocity, could not and does not reach us, from those mysterious regions, in less than 3 *millions of years.* This calculation, moreover, is made by the elder Herschel, and in reference merely to those comparatively proximate clusters within the scope of his own telescope. There *are* "nebulae," however, which, through the magical tube of Lord Rosse, are this instant whispering in our ears the secrets of *a million of ages* by-gone. In a word, the events which we behold now—at this moment—in those worlds—are the identical events which interested their inhabitants *ten hundred thousand centuries ago*. In intervals—in distances such as this suggestion forces upon the soul—rather than upon the mind—we find, at length, a fitting climax to all hitherto frivolous considerations of *quantity*.

Our fancies thus occupied with the cosmical distances, let us take the opportunity of referring to the difficulty which we have so often experienced, while pursuing *the beaten path* of astronomical reflection, *in accounting* for the immeasurable voids alluded to—in comprehending why chasms so totally unoccupied and therefore apparently so needless, have been made to intervene between star and star—between cluster and cluster—in understanding, to be brief, a sufficient reason for the Titanic scale, in respect of mere *Space*, on which the Universe is seen to be constructed. A rational cause for the phenomenon, I maintain that astronomy has palpably failed to assign:—but the considerations through which, in this essay, we have proceeded step by step, enable us clearly and immediately to perceive that *space and duration are one.*

That the Universe might *endure* throughout an aera at all commensurate with the grandeur of its component material portions and with the high majesty of its spiritual purposes, it was necessary that the original atomic diffusion be made to so inconceivable an extent as to be only not infinite. It was required, in a word, that the stars should be gathered into visibility from invisible nebulosity—proceed from nebulosity to consolidation—and so grow grey in giving birth and death to unspeakably numerous and complex variations of vitalic development it was required that the stars should do all this—should have time thoroughly to accomplish all these divine purposes—*during the period* in which all things were effecting their return into unity with a velocity accumulating in the inverse proportion of the squares of the distances at which lay the inevitable end.

Throughout all this we have no difficulty in understanding the absolute accuracy of the divine *adaptation.*The density of the stars, respectively, proceeds, of course, as their condensation diminishes; condensation and heterogeneity keep pace with each other; through the latter, which is the index of the former, we estimate the vitalic and spiritual development. Thus, in the density of the globes, we have the measure in which their purposes are fulfilled. *As* density proceeds—as the divine intentions *are* accomplished—*as* less and still less remains *to be* accomplished—so—in the same ratio—should we expect to find an acceleration of *the end*:—and thus the philosophical mind will easily comprehend that the divine designs in constituting the stars, advance *mathematically* to their fulfilment:—and more; it will readily give the advance a mathematical expression; it will decide that this advance is inversely proportional with the squares of the distances of all created things from the starting-point and goal of their creation.

Not only is this divine adaptation, however, mathematically accurate, but there is that about it which stamps it *as divine*, in distinction from that which is merely the work of human constructiveness. I allude to the complete *mutuality* of adaptation. For example; in human constructions a particular cause has a particular effect; a particular intention brings to pass a particular object; but this is all; we see no reciprocity. The effect does not react upon the cause; the intention does not change relations with the object. In divine constructions the object is either design or object as we choose to regard it—and we may take at any time a cause for an effect, or the converse—so that we can never absolutely decide which is which.

To give an instance:—In polar climates the human frame, to maintain its animal heat, requires, for combustion in the capillary system, an abundant supply of highly azotized food, such as train-oil. But again:—in polar climates nearly the sole food afforded man is the oil of abundant seals and whales. Now, whether is oil at hand because imperatively demanded, or the only thing demanded because the only thing to be obtained? It is impossible to decide. There is an absolute *reciprocity of adaptation.*

The pleasure which we derive from any display of human ingenuity is in the ratio of *the approach* to this species of reciprocity. In the construction of *plot*, for example, in fictitious literature, we should aim at so arranging the incidents that we shall not be able to determine, of any one of them, whether it depends from any one other or upholds it. In this sense, of course, *perfection* of *plot*, is really, or practically, unattainable—but only because it is a finite intelligence that constructs. The plots of God are perfect. The Universe is a plot of God.

And now we have reached a point at which the intellect is forced, again, to struggle against its propensity for analogical inference—against its monomaniac grasping at the infinite. Moons have been seen *revolving* about planets; planets about stars; and the poetical instinct of humanity—its instinct of the symmetrical, if the symmetry be but a symmetry of surface:—this *instinct*, which the Soul, not only of Man but of all created beings, took up, in the beginning, from the geometrical basis of the Universal irradiation—impels us to the fancy of an endless extension of this system of *cycles*. Closing our eyes equally to *de*-duction and *in*-

duction, we insist upon imagining a *revolution* of all the orbs of the Galaxy about some gigantic globe which we take to be the central pivot of the whole. Each cluster in the great cluster of clusters is imagined, of course, to be similarly supplied and constructed; while, that the "analogy" may be wanting at no point, we go on to conceive these clusters themselves, again, as *revolving* about some still more august sphere;—this latter, still again, *with* its encircling clusters, as but one of a yet more magnificent series of agglomerations, gyrating about yet another orb central *to them*—some orb still more unspeakably sublime—some orb, let us rather say, of infinite sublimity endlessly multiplied by the infinitely sublime.

Such are the conditions, continued in perpetuity, which the voice of what some people term "analogy" calls upon the fancy to depict and the reason to contemplate, if possible, without becoming dissatisfied with the picture. Such, *in general*, are the interminable gyrations beyond gyration which we have been instructed by Philosophy to comprehend and to account for, at least in the best manner we can. Now and then, however, a philosopher proper—one whose frenzy takes a very determinate turn—whose genius, to speak more reverentially, has a strongly-pronounced washer-womanish bias, doing every thing up by the dozen—enables us to see *precisely* that point out of sight, at which the revolutionary processes in question do, and of right ought to, come to an end.

It is hardly worth while, perhaps, even to sneer at the reveries of Fourier—but much has been said, latterly, of the hypothesis of Mädler—that there exists, in the centre of the Galaxy, a stupendous globe about which all the systems of the cluster revolve. The *period* of our own, indeed, has been stated—117 millions of years.

That our Sun has a motion in space, independently of its rotation, and revolution about the system's centre of gravity, has long been suspected. This motion, granting it to exist, would be manifested perspectively. The stars in that firmamental region which we were leaving behind us, would, in a very long series of years, become crowded; those in the opposite quarter, scattered. Now, by means of astronomical History, we ascertain, cloudily, that some such phenomena have occurred. On this ground it has been declared that our system is moving to a point in the heavens diametrically opposite the star Zeta Herculis:—but this inference is, perhaps, the maximum to which we have any logical right. Mädler, however, has gone so far as to designate a particular star, Alcyone in the Pleiades, as being at or about the very spot around which a general *revolution* is performed.

Now, since by "analogy" we are led, in the first instance, to these dreams, it is no more than proper that we should abide by analogy, at least in some measure, during their development; and that analogy which suggests the revolution, suggests at the same time a central orb about which it should be performed—so far the astronomer was consistent. This central orb, however, should, dynamically, be greater than all the orbs, taken together, which surround it. Of these there are about 100 millions. "Why, then," it was of course demanded, "do we not *see* this vast central Sun—*at least equal* in mass to 100 millions of such suns as ours—why do we not *see* it—*we*, especially, who occupy the mid region of the cluster—the very locality *near* which, at all events, must be situated this incomparable star?"

The reply was ready—"It must be non-luminous, as are our planets." Here, then, to suit a purpose, analogy is suddenly let fall. "Not so," it may be said—"we know that non-luminous suns actually exist." It is true that we have reason at least for supposing so; but we have certainly no reason whatever for supposing that the non-luminous suns in question are encircled by *luminous* suns, while these again are surrounded by non-luminous planets and it is precisely all this with which Mädler is called upon to find any thing analogous in the heavens—for it is precisely all this which he imagines in the case of the Galaxy. Admitting the thing to be so, we cannot help here picturing to ourselves how sad a puzzle the *why is it so* must prove to all *à priori* philosophers.

But granting, in the very teeth of analogy and of every thing else, the non-luminosity of the vast central orb, we may still inquire how this orb, so enormous, could fail of being rendered visible by the flood of light thrown upon it from the 100 millions of glorious suns glaring in all directions about it. Upon the urging of this question, the idea of an actually solid central Sun appears, in some measure, to have been abandoned; and speculation proceeded to assert that the systems of the cluster perform their revolutions merely about an immaterial centre of gravity common to all. Here again then, to suit a purpose, analogy is let fall. The planets of our system revolve, it is true, about a common centre of gravity; but they do this in connexion with, and in consequence of, a material Sun whose mass more than counterbalances the rest of the system.

The mathematical circle is a curve composed of an infinity of straight lines. But this idea of the circle—an idea which in view of all ordinary geometry, is merely the mathematical, as contradistinguished from the practical, idea—is, in sober fact, the *practical* conception which alone we have any right to entertain in regard to the majestic circle with which we have to deal, at least in fancy, when we suppose our system revolving about a point in the centre of the Galaxy. Let the most vigorous of human imaginations attempt but to take a single step towards the comprehension of a sweep so ineffable!

It would scarcely be paradoxical to say that a flash of lightning itself, travelling *forever* upon the circumference of this unutterable circle, would still, *forever*, be travelling in a straight line. That the path of our Sun in such an orbit would, to any human perception, deviate in the slightest degree from a straight line, even in a million of years, is a proposition not to be entertained:—yet we are required to believe that a curvature has become apparent during the brief period of our astronomical history—during a mere point—during the utter nothingness of two or three thousand years.

It may be said that Mädler has really ascertained a curvature in the direction of our system's now well-established progress through Space. Admitting, if necessary, this fact to be in reality such, I maintain that nothing is thereby shown except the reality of this fact the fact of a curvature. For its *thorough* determination, ages will be required; and, when determined, it will be found indicative of some binary or other multiple relation between our Sun and some one or more of the proximate stars. I hazard nothing, however, in predicting, that, after the lapse of many centuries, all efforts at determining the path of our Sun through Space, will be abandoned as fruitless. This is easily conceivable when we look at the infinity of perturbation it must experience, from its perpetually-shifting relations with other orbs, in the common approach of all to the nucleus of the Galaxy.

But in examining other "nebulae" than that of the Milky Way—in surveying, generally, the clusters which overspread the heavens—do we or do we not find confirmation of Mädler's hypothesis? We do *not*. The forms of the clusters are exceedingly diverse when casually viewed; but on close inspection, through powerful telescopes, we recognize the sphere, very distinctly, as at least the proximate form of all:—their constitution, in general, being at variance with the idea of revolution about a common centre.

"It is difficult," says Sir John Herschel, "to form any conception of the dynamical state of such systems. On one hand, without a rotary motion and a centrifugal force, it is hardly possible not to regard them as in a state of *progressive collapse*. On the other, granting such a motion and such a force, we find it no less difficult to reconcile their forms with the rotation of the whole system (meaning cluster) around any single axis, without which internal collision would appear to be inevitable."

Some remarks lately made about the "nebulae" by Dr. Nichol, in taking quite a different view of the cosmical conditions from any taken in this discourse—have a very peculiar applicability to the point now at issue. He says:—

"When our greatest telescopes are brought to bear upon them, we find that those which were thought to be irregular, are not so; they approach nearer to a globe. Here is one that looked oval; but Lord Rosse's telescope brought it into a circle. Now there occurs a very remarkable circumstance in reference to these comparatively sweeping circular masses of nebulae. We find they are not entirely circular, but the reverse; and that all around them, on every side, there are volumes of stars, *stretching out apparently as if they were rushing towards a great central mass in consequence of the action of some great power*." [9]

Were I to describe, in my own words, what must necessarily be the existing condition of each nebula on the hypothesis that all matter is, as I suggest, now returning to its original Unity, I should simply be going over, nearly verbatim, the language here employed by Dr. Nichol, without the faintest suspicion of that stupendous truth which is the key to these nebular phenomena.

And here let me fortify my position still farther, by the voice of a greater than Mädler—of one, moreover, to whom all the data of Mädler have long been familiar things, carefully and thoroughly considered. Referring to the elaborate calculations of Argelander—the very researches which form Mädler's basis—*Humboldt*, whose generalising powers have never, perhaps been equalled, has the following observation:—

"When we regard the real, proper, or non-perspective motions of the stars, we find many *groups of them moving in opposite directions*; and the data as yet in hand render it not necessary, at least, to conceive that the systems composing the Milky Way, or the clusters, generally, composing the Universe, are revolving about any particular centre unknown, whether luminous or non-luminous. It is but Man's longing for a fundamental First Cause, that impels both his intellect and fancy to the adoption of such an hypothesis."[10]

The phenomenon here alluded to—that of "many groups moving in opposite directions"—is quite inexplicable by Mä-

9. I must be understood as denying, *especially*, only the *revolutionary* portion of Mädler's hypothesis. Of course, if no great central orb exists *now* in our cluster, such will exist hereafter. Whenever existing, it will be merely the *nucleus* of the consolidation.

10. *Betrachtet man die nicht perspectivischen eigenen Bewegungen der Sterne, so scheinen viele gruppenweise in ihrer Richtung entgegengesetzt; und die bisher gesammelten Thatsachen machen es auf s wenigste nicht nothwendig, anzunehmen, dass alle Theile unserer Sternenschicht oder gar der gesammten Sterneninseln, welche den Weltraum fullen, sich um einen grossen, unbekannten, leuchtenden oder dunkeln Centralkörper bewegen. Das Streben nach den letzten und hochsten Grundursachen macht freilich die reflectirende Thätigkeit des Menschen, wie seine Phantasie, zu einer solchen Annahme geneigt.*

dler's idea; but arises, as a necessary consequence, from that which forms the basis of this Discourse. While the *merely general direction* of each atom—of each Moon, planet, star, or cluster—would, on my hypothesis, be, of course, absolutely rectilinear; while the *general* path of all bodies would be a right line leading to the centre of all; it is clear, nevertheless, that this general rectilinearity would be compounded of what, with scarcely any exaggeration, we may term an infinity of particular curves—an infinity of local deviations from rectilinearity—the result of continuous differences of relative position among the multitudinous masses as each proceeded on its own proper journey to the end.

I quoted, just now, from Sir John Herschel, the following words, used in reference to the clusters:—"On one hand, without a rotary motion and a centrifugal force, it is hardly possible not to regard them as in a state of *progressive collapse*." The fact is, that, in surveying the "nebulae" with a telescope of high power, we shall find it quite impossible, having once conceived this idea of "collapse," not to gather, at all points, corroboration of the idea. A nucleus is always apparent, in the direction of which the stars seem to be precipitating themselves; nor can these nuclei be mistaken for merely perspective phenomena:—the clusters are *really* denser near the centre—sparser in the regions more remote from it. In a word, we see every thing as we *should* see it were a collapse taking place; but, in general, it may be said of these clusters, that we can fairly entertain, while looking at them, the idea of *orbitual movement about a centre*, only by admitting the *possible* existence, in the distant domains of space, of dynamical laws with which *we* are unacquainted.

On the part of Herschel, however, there is evidently *a reluctance* to regard the nebulae as in "a state of progressive collapse." But if facts—if even appearances justify the supposition of their being in this state, *why*, it may well be demanded, is he disinclined to admit it? Simply on account of a prejudice;—merely because the supposition is at war with a preconceived and utterly baseless notion—that of the endlessness—that of the eternal stability of the Universe.

If the propositions of this discourse are tenable, the "state of progressive collapse" is *precisely* that state in which alone we are warranted in considering all things; and, with due humility, let me here confess that, for my part, I am at a loss to conceive how any *other* understanding of the existing condition of affairs, could ever have made its way into the human brain. "The tendency to collapse" and "the attraction of gravitation" are convertible phrases. In using either, we speak of the reaction of the First Act. Never was necessity less obvious than that of supposing matter imbued with an ineradicable *quality* forming part of its material nature—a quality, or instinct, *forever* inseparable from it, and by dint of which inalienable principle every atom is *perpetually* impelled to seek its fellow-atom.

Never was necessity less obvious than that of entertaining this unphilosophical idea. Going boldly behind the vulgar thought, we have to conceive, metaphysically, that the gravitating principle appertains to matter *temporarily*—only while diffused—only while existing as many instead of as one—appertains to it by virtue of its state of irradiation alone—appertains, in a word, altogether to its *condition*, and not in the slightest degree to *itself*. In this view, when the irradiation shall have returned into its source—when the reaction shall be completed—the gravitating principle will no longer exist. And, in fact, astronomers, without at any time reaching the idea here suggested, seem to have been approximating it, in the assertion that "if there were but one body in the Universe, it would be impossible to understand how the principle, gravity, could obtain":—that is to say, from a consideration of matter as they find it, they reach a conclusion at which I deductively arrive. That so pregnant a suggestion as the one quoted should have been permitted to remain so long unfruitful, is, nevertheless, a mystery which I find it difficult to fathom.

It is, perhaps, in no little degree, however, our propensity for the continuous—for the analogical—in the present case more particularly for the symmetrical which has been leading us astray. And, in fact, the sense of the symmetrical is an instinct which may be depended upon with an almost blindfold reliance. It is the poetical essence of the Universe—*of the Universe* which, in the supremeness of its symmetry, is but the most sublime of poems. Now symmetry and consistency are convertible terms:—thus poetry and truth are one.

A thing is consistent in the ratio of its truth—true in the ratio of its consistency. *A perfect consistency, I repeat, can be nothing but a absolute truth.* We may take it for granted, then, that man cannot long or widely err, if he suffer himself to be guided by his poetical, which I have maintained to be his truthful, in being his symmetrical, instinct. He must have a care, however, lest, in pursuing too heedlessly the superficial symmetry of forms and motions, he leave out of sight the really essential symmetry of the principles which determine and control them.

That the stellar bodies would finally be merged in one—that, at last, all would be drawn into the substance of *one stupendous central orb already existing*—is an idea which, for some time past, seems, vaguely and indeterminately, to have held possession of the fancy of mankind. It is an idea, in fact, which belongs to the class of the *excessively obvious*. It springs, instantly, from a superficial observation of the cyclic and seemingly *gyrating*, or *vorticial* movements of those individual portions of the Universe which come most immediately and most closely under our observation.

There is not, perhaps, a human being, of ordinary education and of average reflective capacity, to whom, at some period, the fancy in question has not occurred, as if spontaneously, or intuitively, and wearing all the character of a very profound and very original conception. This conception, however, so commonly entertained, has never, within my knowledge, arisen out of any abstract considerations. Being, on the contrary, always suggested, as I say, by the vorticial movements about centres, a reason for it, also,—a *cause* for the ingathering of all the orbs into one, *imagined to be already existing,* was naturally sought in the same direction—among these cyclic movements themselves.

Thus it happened that, on announcement of the gradual and

perfectly regular decrease observed in the orbit of Encke's comet, at every successive revolution about our Sun, astronomers were nearly unanimous in the opinion that the cause in question was found—that a principle was discovered sufficient to account, physically, for that final, universal agglomeration which, I repeat, the analogical, symmetrical or poetical instinct of Man had predetermined to understand as something more than a simple hypothesis.

This cause—this sufficient reason for the final ingathering—was declared to exist in an exceedingly rare but still material medium pervading space; which medium, by retarding, in some degree, the progress of the comet, perpetually weakened its tangential force; thus giving a predominance to the centripetal; which, of course, drew the comet nearer and nearer at each revolution, and would eventually precipitate it upon the Sun.

All this was strictly logical—admitting the medium or ether; but this ether was assumed, most illogically, on the ground that no *other* mode than the one spoken of could be discovered, of accounting for the observed decrease in the orbit of the comet:—as if from the fact that we could *discover* no other mode of accounting for it, it followed, in any respect, that no other mode of accounting for it existed. It is clear that innumerable causes might operate, in combination, to diminish the orbit, without even a possibility of our ever becoming acquainted with one of them. In the meantime, it has never been fairly shown, perhaps, why the retardation occasioned by the skirts of the Sun's atmosphere, through which the comet passes at perihelion, is not enough to account for the phenomenon.

That Encke's comet will be absorbed into the Sun, is probable; that all the comets of the system will be absorbed, is more than merely possible; but, in such case, the principle of absorption must be referred to eccentricity of orbit—to the close approximation to the Sun, of the comets at their perihelia; and is a principle not affecting, in any degree, the ponderous *spheres*, which are to be regarded as the true material constituents of the Universe.—Touching comets, in general, let me here suggest, in passing, that we cannot be far wrong in looking upon them as the *lightning-flashes of the cosmical Heaven*.

The idea of a retarding ether and, through it, of a final agglomeration of all things, seemed at one time, however, to be confirmed by the observation of a positive decrease in the orbit of the solid Moon. By reference to eclipses recorded 2500 years ago, it was found that the velocity of the satellite's revolution *then* was considerably less than it is *now*; that on the hypothesis that its motions in its orbit is uniformly in accordance with Kepler's law, and was accurately determined *then*—2500 years ago—it is now in advance of the position it *should* occupy, by nearly 9000 miles. The increase of velocity proved, of course, a diminution of orbit; and astronomers were fast yielding to a belief in an ether, as the sole mode of accounting for the phenomenon, when Lagrange came to the rescue.

He showed that, owing to the configurations of the spheroids, the shorter axes of their ellipses are subject to variation in length; the longer axes being permanent; and that this variation is continuous and vibratory—so that every orbit is in a state of transition, either from circle to ellipse, or from ellipse to circle. In the case of the Moon, where the shorter axis is *de*-creasing, the orbit is passing from circle to ellipse, and, consequently, is *de*-creasing too; but, after a long series of ages, the ultimate eccentricity will be attained; then the shorter axis will proceed to *in*-crease, until the orbit becomes a circle; when the process of shortening will again take place;—and so on forever. In the case of the Earth, the orbit is passing from ellipse to circle. The facts thus demonstrated do away, of course, with all necessity for supposing an ether, and with all apprehension of the system's instability—on the ether's account.

It will be remembered that I have myself assumed what we may term *an ether*. I have spoken of a subtle *influence* which we know to be ever in attendance upon matter, although becoming manifest only through matter's heterogeneity. To this *influence*—without daring to touch it at all in any effort at explaining its awful *nature*—I have referred the various phenomena of electricity, heat, light, magnetism; and more—of vitality, consciousness, and thought—in a word, of spirituality. It will be seen, at once, then, that the ether thus conceived is radically distinct from the ether of the astronomers; inasmuch as theirs is *matter* and mine *not*.

With the idea of material ether, seems, thus, to have departed altogether the thought of that universal agglomeration so long predetermined by the poetical fancy of mankind:—an agglomeration in which a sound philosophy might have been warranted in putting faith, at least to a certain extent, if for no other reason than that by this poetical fancy it *had* been so predetermined. But so far as astronomy—so far as mere physics have yet spoken, the cycles of the Universe are perpetual—the Universe has no conceivable end. Had an end been demonstrated, however, from so purely collateral a cause as an ether, man's instinct of the divine *capacity to adapt*, would have rebelled against the demonstration.

We should have been forced to regard the Universe with some such sense of dissatisfaction as we experience in contemplating an unnecessarily complex work of human art. Creation would have affected us as an imperfect *plot* in a romance, where the *dénouement* is awkwardly brought about by interposed incidents external and foreign to the main subject; instead of springing out of the bosom of the thesis—out of the heart of the ruling idea—instead of arising as a result of the primary proposition—as inseparable and inevitable part and parcel of the fundamental conception of the book.

What I mean by the symmetry of mere surface—will now be more clearly understood. It is simply by the blandishment of this symmetry that we have been beguiled into the general idea of which Mädler's hypothesis is but a part—the idea of the vorticial indrawing of the orbs. Dismissing this nakedly physical conception, the symmetry of principle sees the end of all things metaphysically involved in the thought of a beginning; seeks and finds in this origin of all things the *rudiment* of this end; and perceives the impiety of supposing this end likely to be brought about less simply—less directly—less obviously—less artistically—than through *the reaction of the originating act.*

Recurring, then, to a previous suggestion, let us understand the systems—let us understand each star, with its attendant planets—as but a Titanic atom existing in space with precisely the same inclination for Unity which characterized, in the beginning, the actual atoms after their irradiation throughout the Universal sphere. As these original atoms rushed towards each other in generally straight lines, so let us conceive as at least generally rectilinear, the paths of the system-atoms towards their respective centres of aggregation:—and in this direct drawing together of the systems into clusters, with a similar and simultaneous drawing together of the clusters themselves while undergoing consolidation, we have at length attained the great *now*—the awful *present*—the *existing condition of the Universe.*

Of the still more awful *future* a not irrational analogy may guide us in framing an hypothesis. The equilibrium between the centripetal and centrifugal forces of each system, being necessarily destroyed upon attainment of a certain proximity to the nucleus of the cluster to which it belongs, there must occur, at once, a chaotic or seemingly chaotic precipitation, of the moons upon the planets, of the planets upon the suns, and of the suns upon the nuclei; and the general result of this precipitation must be the gathering of the myriad now-existing stars of the firmament into an almost infinitely less number of almost infinitely superior spheres. In being immeasurably fewer, the worlds of that day will be immeasurably greater than our own. Then, indeed, amid unfathomable abysses, will be glaring unimaginable suns. But all this will be merely a climacic magnificence foreboding the great end.

Of this end the new genesis described, can be but a very partial postponement. While undergoing consolidation, the clusters themselves, with a speed prodigiously accumulative, have been rushing towards their own general centre—and now, with a thousand-fold electric velocity, commensurate only with their material grandeur and with the spiritual passion of their appetite for oneness, the majestic remnants of the tribe of stars flash, at length, into a common embrace. The inevitable catastrophe is at hand.

But this catastrophe—what is it? We have seen accomplished the ingathering of the orbs. Henceforward, are we not to understand *one material globe of globes* as constituting and comprehending the Universe? Such a fancy would be altogether at war with every assumption and consideration of this discourse.

I have already alluded to that absolute *reciprocity of adaptation* which is the idiosyncrasy of the divine art—stamping it divine. Up to this point of our reflections, we have been regarding the electrical influence as a something by dint of whose repulsion alone matter is enabled to exist in that state of diffusion demanded for the fulfilment of its purposes:—so far, in a word, we have been considering the influence in question as ordained for matter's sake—to subserve the objects of matter. With a perfectly legitimate reciprocity, we are now permitted to look at matter, as created *solely for the sake of this influence*—solely to serve the objects of this spiritual ether. Through the aid—by the means—through the agency of matter, and by dint of its heterogeneity—is this ether manifested—is *spirit individualized*. It is merely in the development of this ether, through heterogeneity, that particular masses of matter become animate—sensitive—and in the ratio of their heterogeneity;—some reaching a degree of sensitiveness involving what we call *thought* and thus attaining conscious intelligence.

In this view, we are enabled to perceive matter as a means—not as an end. Its purposes are thus seen to have been comprehended in its diffusion; and with the return into unity these purposes cease. The absolutely consolidated globe of globes would be *objectless*:—therefore not for a moment could it continue to exist. Matter, created for an end, would unquestionably, on fulfilment of that end, be matter no longer. Let us endeavour to understand that it would disappear, and that God would remain all in all.

That every work of Divine conception must coexist and co-expire with its particular design, seems to me especially obvious; and I make no doubt that, on perceiving the final globe of globes to be *objectless*, the majority of my readers will be satisfied with my "*therefore* it cannot continue to exist." Nevertheless, as the startling thought of its instantaneous disappearance is one which the most powerful intellect cannot be expected readily to entertain on grounds so decidedly abstract, let us endeavour to look at the idea from some other and more ordinary point of view:—let us see how thoroughly and beautifully it is corroborated in an *à posteriori* consideration of matter as we actually find it.

I have before said that "attraction and repulsion being undeniably the sole properties by which matter is manifested to mind, we are justified in assuming that matter *exists* only as attraction and repulsion—in other words that attraction and repulsion are matter; there being no conceivable case in which we may not employ the term 'matter' and the terms 'attraction' and 'repulsion' taken together, as equivalent, and therefore convertible, expressions of logic."

Now the very definition of attraction implies particularity—the existence of parts, particles, or atoms; for we define it as the tendency of "each atom &c. to every other atom," &c. according to a certain law. Of course where there are *no* parts—where there is absolute unity—where the tendency to oneness is satisfied—there can be no attraction:—this has been fully shown, and all philosophy admits it. When, on fulfilment of its purposes, then, matter shall have returned into its original condition of one—a condition which presupposes the expulsion of the separative ether, whose province and whose capacity are limited to keeping the atoms apart until that great day when, this ether being no longer needed, the overwhelming pressure of the finally collective attraction shall at length just sufficiently predominate and expel it:—when, I say, matter, finally, expelling the ether, shall have returned into absolute unity,—it will then (to speak paradoxically for the moment) be matter without attraction and without repulsion—in other words, matter without matter—in other words, again, *matter no more*. In sinking into unity, it will sink at once into that nothingness which, to all finite perception, unity must be—into that material nihility from which alone we can conceive it to have been evoked—to have been *created* by the Volition of God.

I repeat then—Let us endeavour to comprehend that the final globe of globes will instantaneously disappear, and that God will remain all in all.

But are we here to pause? Not so. On the Universal agglomeration and dissolution, we can readily conceive that a new and perhaps totally different series of conditions may ensue—another creation and irradiation, returning into itself—another action and reaction of the Divine Will. Guiding our imaginations by that omniprevalent law of laws, the law of periodicity, are we not, indeed, more than justified in entertaining a belief—let us say, rather, in indulging a hope—that the processes we have here ventured to contemplate will be renewed forever, and forever, and forever; a novel Universe swelling into existence, and then subsiding into nothingness, at every throb of the Heart Divine?

And now—this Heart Divine—what is it? *It is our own.*

Let not the merely seeming irreverence of this idea frighten our souls from that cool exercise of consciousness—from that deep tranquillity of self-inspection—through which alone we can hope to attain the presence of this, the most sublime of truths, and look it leisurely in the face.

The phenomena on which our conclusions must at this point depend, are merely spiritual shadows, but not the less thoroughly substantial.

We walk about, amid the destinies of our world-existence, encompassed by dim but ever present memories of a destiny more vast—very distant in the bygone time, and infinitely awful.

We live out a youth peculiarly haunted by such dreams; yet never mistaking them for dreams. As memories we *know* them. *During our youth* the distinction is too clear to deceive us even for a moment.

So long as this youth endures, the feeling *that we exist,* is the most natural of all feelings. We understand it *thoroughly.* That there was a period at which we did *not* exist—or, that it might so have happened that we never had existed at all—are the considerations, indeed, which *during this youth,* we find difficulty in understanding. Why we should *not* exist, is, *up to the epoch of manhood,* of all queries the most unanswerable. Existence—self-existence—existence from all time and to all eternity—seems, up to the epoch of manhood, a normal and unquestionable condition:—*seems, because it is.*

But now comes the period at which a conventional world-reason awakens us from the truth of our dream. Doubt, surprise and incomprehensibility arrive at the same moment. They say:—"You live and the time was when you lived not. You have been created. An intelligence exists greater than your own; and it is only through this intelligence you live at all." These things we struggle to comprehend and cannot:—*cannot,* because these things, being untrue, are thus, of necessity, incomprehensible.

No thinking being lives who, at some luminous point of his life of thought, has not felt himself lost amid the surges of futile efforts at understanding, or believing, that anything exists *greater than his own soul.* The utter impossibility of any one's soul feeling itself inferior to another; the intense, overwhelming dissatisfaction and rebellion at the thought;—these, with the omniprevalent aspirations at perfection, are but the spiritual, coincident with the material, struggles towards the original unity—are, to my mind at least, a species of proof far surpassing what man terms demonstration, that no one soul *is* inferior to another—that nothing is, or can be, superior to any one soul—that each soul is, in part, its own God—its own Creator:—in a word, that God—the material *and* spiritual God—*now* exists solely in the diffused matter and spirit of the Universe; and that the regathering of this diffused matter and spirit will be but the re-constitution of the *purely* Spiritual and Individual God.

In this view, and in this view alone, we comprehend the riddles of divine injustice—of inexorable fate. In this view alone the existence of evil becomes intelligible; but in this view it becomes more—it becomes endurable. Our souls no longer rebel at a *sorrow* which we ourselves have imposed upon ourselves, in furtherance of our own purposes—with a view—if even with a futile view—to the extension of our own *joy*.

I have spoken of *memories* that haunt us during our youth. They sometimes pursue us even in our manhood:—assume gradually less and less indefinite shapes:—now and then speak to us with low voices, saying:

"There was an epoch in the night of time, when a still-existent Being existed—one of an absolutely infinite number of similar beings that people the absolutely infinite domains of the absolutely infinite space. It was not and is not in the power of this Being—any more than it is in your own—to extend, by actual increase, the joy of his existence; but just as it *is* in your power to expand or to concentrate your pleasures (the absolute amount of happiness remaining always the same) so did and does a similar capability appertain to this Divine Being, who thus passes his Eternity in perpetual variation of concentrated self and almost infinite self-diffusion.

What you call The Universe is but his present expansive existence. He now feels his life through an infinity of imperfect pleasures—the partial and pain-intertangled pleasures of those inconceivably numerous things which you designate as his creatures, but which are really but infinite individualisations of Himself. All these creatures—those which you term animate, as well as those to whom you deny life for no better reason than that you do not behold it in operation—these creatures have, in a greater or less degree, a capacity for pleasure and for pain:—*but the general sum of their sensations is precisely that amount of happiness which appertains by right to the Divine Being when concentrated within Himself.*

These creatures are all too, more or less conscious intelligences; conscious, first, of a proper identity; conscious, secondly and by faint indeterminate glimpses, of an identity with the Divine Being of whom we speak—of an identity with God. Of the two classes of consciousness, fancy that the former will grow weaker, the latter stronger, during the long succession of ages which must elapse before these myriads of individual intelligences become blended—when the bright stars become blended—into one. Think that the sense of individual identity will be gradually merged in the general consciousness—that man, for example, ceasing imperceptibly to feel himself man, will at length attain that awfully triumphant epoch when he shall recognise his existence as that of Jehovah. In the meantime bear in mind that all is life—life—life within life—the less within the greater, and all within the *Spirit Divine.*

The Raven

Once upon a midnight dreary, while I pondered, weak and weary.
Over many a quaint and curious volume of forgotten lore—
While I nodded, nearly napping, suddenly there came a tapping.
As of some one gently rapping, rapping at my chamber door.
"'Tis some visiter," I muttered, "tapping at my chamber door—
Only this and nothing more."

Ah, distinctly I remember it was in the bleak December;
And each separate dying ember wrought its ghost upon the floor.
Eagerly I wished the morrow;—vainly I had sought to borrow
From my books surcease of sorrow—sorrow for the lost Lenore—
For the rare and radiant maiden whom the angels name Lenore—
Nameless *here* for evermore.

And the silken, sad, uncertain rustling of each purple curtain
Thrilled me—filled me with fantastic terrors never felt before;
So that now, to still the beating of my heart, I stood re-

peating
"'Tis some visiter entreating entrance at my chamber door—
Some late visiter entreating entrance at my chamber door;—
This it is and nothing more."

Presently my soul grew stronger; hesitating then no longer,
"Sir," said I, "or Madam, truly your forgiveness I implore;
But the fact is I was napping, and so gently you came rapping.
And so faintly you came tapping, tapping at my chamber door.
That I scarce was sure I heard you"—here I opened wide the door;—
Darkness there and nothing more.

Deep into that darkness peering, long I stood there wondering, fearing.
Doubting, dreaming dreams no mortal ever dared to dream before;
But the silence was unbroken, and the stillness gave no token.
And the only word there spoken was the whispered word, "Lenore?"
This I whispered, and an echo murmured back the word, "Lenore!"—
Merely this and nothing more.

Back into the chamber turning, all my soul within me burning.
Soon again I heard a tapping somewhat louder than before.
"Surely," said I, "surely that is something at my window lattice;
Let me see, then, what thereat is, and this mystery explore—

Let my heart be still a moment and this mystery explore;—
'Tis the wind and nothing more!"

Open here I flung the shutter, when, with many a flirt and flutter.
In there stepped a stately Raven of the saintly days of yore;
Not the least obeisance made he; not a minute stopped or stayed he;
But, with mien of lord or lady, perched above my chamber door—
Perched upon a bust of Pallas just above my chamber door—
Perched, and sat, and nothing more.

Then this ebony bird beguiling my sad fancy into smiling,
By the grave and stern decorum of the countenance it wore,
"Though thy crest be shorn and shaven, thou," I said, "art sure no craven.
Ghastly grim and ancient Raven wandering from the Nightly shore—
Tell me what thy lordly name is on the Night's Plutonian shore!"
Quoth the Raven "Nevermore."

Much I marvelled this ungainly fowl to hear discourse so plainly.
Though its answer little meaning—little relevancy bore;
For we cannot help agreeing that no living human being
Ever yet was blessed with seeing bird above his chamber door—
Bird or beast upon the sculptured bust above his chamber door.
With such name as "Nevermore."

But the Raven, sitting lonely on the placid bust, spoke

only
That one word, as if his soul in that one word he did outpour.
Nothing farther then he uttered—not a feather then he fluttered—
Till I scarcely more than muttered "Other friends have flown before—
On the morrow *he* will leave me, as my Hopes have flown before."
Then the bird said "Nevermore."

Startled at the stillness broken by reply so aptly spoken,
"Doubtless," said I, "what it utters is its only stock and store
Caught from some unhappy master whom unmerciful Disaster
Followed fast and followed faster till his songs one burden bore—
Till the dirges of his Hope that melancholy burden bore
Of 'Never—nevermore'."

But the Raven still beguiling my sad fancy into smiling.
Straight I wheeled a cushioned seat in front of bird, and bust and door;
Then, upon the velvet sinking, I betook myself to linking
Fancy unto fancy, thinking what this ominous bird of yore—
What this grim, ungainly, ghastly, gaunt, and ominous bird of yore
Meant in croaking "Nevermore."

This I sat engaged in guessing, but no syllable expressing
To the fowl whose fiery eyes now burned into my bosom's core;
This and more I sat divining, with my head at ease reclining
On the cushion's velvet lining that the lamp-light gloated o'er.

But whose velvet-violet lining with the lamp-light gloating o'er.
She shall press, ah, nevermore!

Then, methought, the air grew denser, perfumed from an unseen censer
Swung by seraphim whose foot-falls tinkled on the tufted floor.
"Wretch," I cried, "thy God hath lent thee—by these angels he hath sent thee
Respite—respite and nepenthe, from thy memories of Lenore;
Quaff, oh quaff this kind nepenthe and forget this lost Lenore!"
Quoth the Raven "Nevermore."

"Prophet!" said I, "thing of evil!—prophet still, if bird or devil!—
Whether Tempter sent, or whether tempest tossed thee here ashore.
Desolate yet all undaunted, on this desert land enchanted—
On this home by Horror haunted—tell me truly, I implore—
Is there—*is* there balm in Gilead?—tell me—tell me, I implore!"
Quoth the Raven "Nevermore."

"Prophet!" said I, "thing of evil!—prophet still, if bird or devil!
By that Heaven that bends above us—by that God we both adore—
Tell this soul with sorrow laden if, within the distant Aidenn,
It shall clasp a sainted maiden whom the angels name Lenore—
Clasp a rare and radiant maiden whom the angels name Lenore."

Quoth the Raven "Nevermore."

"Be that word our sign of parting, bird or fiend!" I shrieked, upstarting—
"Get thee back into the tempest and the Night's Plutonian shore!
Leave no black plume as a token of that lie thy soul hath spoken!
Leave my loneliness unbroken!—quit the bust above my door!
Take thy beak from out my heart, and take thy form from off my door!"
Quoth the Raven "Nevermore."

And the Raven, never flitting, *still* is sitting, still is sitting
On the pallid bust of Pallas just above my chamber door;
And his eyes have all the seeming of a demon's that is dreaming.
And the lamplight o'er him streaming throws his shadow on the floor;
And my soul from out that shadow that lies floating on the floor
Shall be lifted—nevermore!

Al Aaraaf

PART 1

O! Nothing earthly save the ray
(Thrown back from flowers) of Beauty's eye,
As in those gardens where the day
Springs from the gems of Circassy—
O! nothing earthly save the thrill
Of melody in woodland rill—
Or (music of the passion-hearted)
Joy's voice so peacefully departed
That like the murmur in the shell,
Its echo dwelleth and will dwell—
Oh, nothing of the dross of ours—
Yet all the beauty—all the flowers
That list our Love, and deck our bowers—
Adorn yon world afar, afar—
The wandering star.

'Twas a sweet time for Nesace—for there
Her world lay lolling on the golden air,
Near four bright suns—a temporary rest—
An oasis in desert of the blest.
Away—away—'mid seas of rays that roll
Empyrean splendour o'er th' unchained soul—
The soul that scarce (the billows are so dense)
Can struggle to its destin'd eminence—
To distant spheres, from time to time, she rode,
And late to ours, the favour'd one of God—

But, now, the ruler of an anchor'd realm.
She throws aside the sceptre—leaves the helm,
And, amid incense and high spiritual hymns,
Laves in quadruple light her angel limbs.

Now happiest, loveliest in yon lovely Earth,
Whence sprang the "Idea of Beauty" into birth,
(Falling in wreaths thro' many a startled star,
Like woman's hair 'mid pearls, until, afar,
It lit on hills Achaian, and there dwelt)
She look'd into Infinity—and knelt.
Rich clouds, for canopies, about her curled—
Fit emblems of the model of her world—
Seen but in beauty—not impeding sight
Of other beauty glittering thro' the light—
A wreath that twined each starry form around.
And all the opal'd air in colour bound.

All hurriedly she knelt upon a bed
Of flowers: of lilies such as rear'd the head
On the fair Capo Deucato, and sprang
So eagerly around about to hang
Upon the flying footsteps of deep pride—
Of her who lov'd a mortal—and so died.
The Sephalica, budding with young bees,
Uprear'd its purple stem around her knees:
And gemmy flower, of Trebizond misnam'd—
Inmate of highest stars, where erst it sham'd
All other loveliness: its honied dew
(The fabled nectar that the heathen knew)
Deliriously sweet, was dropp'd from Heaven,
And fell on gardens of the unforgiven
In Trebizond—and on a sunny flower
So like its own above that, to this hour,
It still remaineth, torturing the bee
With madness, and unwonted reverie:
In Heaven, and all its environs, the leaf
And blossom of the fairy plant, in grief

Disconsolate linger—grief that hangs her head,
Repenting follies that full long have fled,
Heaving her white breast to the balmy air.
Like guilty beauty, chasten'd, and more fair:
Nyctanthes too, as sacred as the light
She fears to perfume, perfuming the night:
And Clytia pondering between many a sun,
While pettish tears adown her petals run :
And that aspiring flower that sprang on earth—
And died, ere scarce exalted into birth.
Bursting its odorous heart in spirit to wing
Its way to Heaven, from garden of a king:
And Valisnerian lotus thither flown
From struggling with the waters of the Rhone:
And thy most lovely purple perfume, Zante!
Isola d'oro!—Fior di Levante!
And the Nelumbo bud that floats for ever
With Indian Cupid down the holy river—
Fair flowers, and fairy! to whose care is given
To bear the Goddess' song, in odours, up to Heaven:

"Spirit! that dwellest where,
In the deep sky,
The terrible and fair.
In beauty vie!
Beyond the line of blue—
The boundary of the star
Which turneth at the view
Of thy barrier and thy bar—
Of the barrier overgone
By the comets who were cast
From their pride, and from their throne
To be drudges till the last—
To be carriers of fire
(The red fire of their heart)
With speed that may not tire
And with pain that shall not part—

Who livest—*that* we know—
In Eternity—we feel—
But the shadow of whose brow
What spirit shall reveal?
Tho' the beings whom thy Nesace,
Thy messenger hath known
Have dream'd for thy Infinity
A model of their own—
Thy will is done, Oh, God!
The star hath ridden high
Thro' many a tempest, but she rode
Beneath thy burning eye;
And here, in thought, to thee—
In thought that can alone
Ascend thy empire and so be
A partner of thy throne—
By winged Fantasy,
My embassy is given,
Till secrecy shall knowledge be
In the environs of Heaven."

She ceas'd—and buried then her burning cheek
Abash'd, amid the lilies there, to seek
A shelter from the fervour of His eye;
For the stars trembled at the Deity.
She stir'd not—breath'd not—for a voice was there
How solemnly pervading the calm air!
A sound of silence on the startled ear
Which dreamy poets name "the music of the sphere."
Ours is a world of words: Quiet we call
"Silence"—which is the merest word of all.
All Nature speaks, and ev'n ideal things
Flap shadowy sounds from visionary wings—
But ah! not so when, thus, in realms on high
The eternal voice of God is passing by.
And the red winds are withering in the sky!

"What tho' in worlds which sightless cycles run,

Link'd to a little system, and one sun—
Where all my love is folly and the crowd
Still think my terrors but the thunder cloud.
The storm, the earthquake, and the ocean-wrath—
(Ah! will they cross me in my angrier path?)
What tho' in worlds which own a single sun
The sands of Time grow dimmer as they run,
Yet thine is my resplendency, so given
To bear my secrets thro' the upper Heaven.
Leave tenantless thy crystal home, and fly.
With all thy train, athwart the moony sky—
Apart—like fire-flies in Sicilian night,
And wing to other worlds another light!
Divulge the secrets of thy embassy
To the proud orbs that twinkle—and so be
To ev'ry heart a barrier and a ban
Lest the stars totter in the guilt of man!"
Up rose the maiden in the yellow night,
The single-moonèd eve!—on Earth we plight
Our faith to one love—and one moon adore—
The birth-place of young Beauty had no more.
As sprang that yellow star from downy hours
Up rose the maiden from her shrine of flowers,
And bent o'er sheeny mountain and dim plain
Her way—but left not yet her Therasaean reign.

Part 2

High on a mountain of enamell'd head—
Such as the drowsy shepherd on his bed
Of giant pasturage lying at his ease,
Raising his heavy eyelid, starts and sees
With many a mutter'd "hope to be forgiven"
What time the moon is quadrated in Heaven—
Of rosy head, that towering far away
Into the sunlit ether, caught the ray
Of sunken suns at eve—at noon of night.

While the moon danc'd with the fair stranger light—
Uprear'd upon such height arose a pile
Of gorgeous columns on th' unburthen'd air.
Flashing from Parian marble that twin smile
Far down upon the wave that sparkled there.
And nursled the young mountain in its lair.
Of molten stars their pavement, such as fall
Thro' the ebon air, besilvering the pall
Of their own dissolution, while they die—
Adorning then the dwellings of the sky.
A dome, by linked light from Heaven let down,
Sat gently on these columns as a crown—
A window of one circular diamond, there,
Look'd out above into the purple air,
And rays from God shot down that meteor chain
And hallow'd all the beauty twice again.
Save when, between th' Empyrean and that ring,
Some eager spirit flapp'd his dusky wing.
But on the pillars Seraph eyes have seen
The dimness of this world: that greyish green
That Nature loves the best for Beauty's grave
Lurk'd in each cornice, round each architrave—
And every sculptur'd cherub thereabout
That from his marble dwelling peered out,
Seem'd earthly in the shadow of his niche—
Achaian statues in a world so rich.
Friezes from Tadmor and Persepolis—
From Balbec, and the stilly, dear abyss
Of beautiful Gomorrah! O, the wave
Is now upon thee—but too late to save!

Sound loves to revel in a summer night:
Witness the murmur of the grey twilight
That stole upon the ear, in Eyraco,
Of many a wild star-gazer long ago—
That stealeth ever on the ear of him
Who, musing, gazeth on the distance dim,

And sees the darkness coming as a cloud—
Is not its form—its voice—most palpable and loud ?

But what is this?—it cometh—and it brings
A music with it—'tis the rush of wings—
A pause—and then a sweeping, falling strain
And Nesace is in her halls again.
From the wild energy of wanton haste
Her cheeks were flushing, and her lips apart;
And zone that clung around her gentle waist
Had burst beneath the heaving of her heart.
Within the centre of that hall to breathe
She paus'd and panted, Zanthe! all beneath.
The fairy light that kiss'd her golden hair
And long'd to rest, yet could but sparkle there!

Young flowers were whispering in melody
To happy flowers that night—and tree to tree;
Fountains were gushing music as they fell
In many a star-lit grove, or moon-lit dell;
Yet silence came upon material things—
Fair flowers, bright waterfalls and angel wings—
And sound alone that from the spirit sprang
Bore burthen to the charm the maiden sang:

"Neath blue-bell or streamer—
Or tufted wild spray
That keeps, from the dreamer,
The moonbeam away—
Bright beings! that ponder,
With half closing eyes,
On the stars which your wonder
Hath drawn from the skies,
'Till they glance thro' the shade, and
Come down to your brow
Like eyes of the maiden
Who calls on you now—
Arise! from your dreaming

In violet bowers.
To duty beseeming
These star-litten hours—
And shake from your tresses
Encumber'd with dew
The breath of those kisses
That cumber them too—
(O! how, without you, Love!
Could angels be blest?)
Those kisses of true love
That lull'd ye to rest!
Up !—shake from your wing
Each hindering thing:
The dew of the night—
It would weigh down your flight;
And true love caresses—
O! leave them apart!
They are light on the tresses,
But lead on the heart.

Ligeia! Ligeia!
My beautiful one!
Whose harshest idea
Will to melody run,
O! is it thy will
On the breezes to toss?
Or, capriciously still,
Like the lone Albatross,
Incumbent on night
(As she on the air)
To keep watch with delight
On the harmony there?
Ligeia! wherever
Thy image may be,
No magic shall sever
Thy music from thee.
Thou hast bound many eyes

In a dreamy sleep—
But the strains still arise
Which *thy* vigilance keep—
The sound of the rain
Which leaps down to the flower,
And dances again
In the rhythm of the shower—
The murmur that springs
From the growing of grass
Are the music of things—
But are modell'd, alas!—
Away, then my dearest,
O! hie thee away
To springs that lie clearest
Beneath the moon-ray—
To lone lake that smiles.
In its dream of deep rest,
At the many star-isles
That enjewel its breast—
Where wild flowers, creeping,
Have mingled their shade,
On its margin is sleeping
Full many a maid—
Some have left the cool glade, and
Have slept with the bee—
Arouse then my maiden.
On moorland and lea—
Go! breathe on their slumber,
All softly in ear.
The musical number
They slumber'd to hear—
For what can awaken
An angel so soon
Whose sleep hath been taken
Beneath the cold moon,
As the spell which no slumber

Of witchery may test.
The rhythmical number
Which lull'd him to rest?"

Spirits in wing, and angels to the view,
A thousand seraphs burst th' Empyrean thro',
Young dreams still hovering on their drowsy flight—
Seraphs in all but "Knowledge," the keen light
That fell, refracted, thro' thy bounds, afar
O Death! from eye of God upon that star:
Sweet was that error—sweeter still that death—
Sweet was that error—ev'n with *us* the breath
Of Science dims the mirror of our joy—
To them 'twere the Simoom, and would destroy—
For what (to them) availeth it to know
That Truth is Falsehood—or that Bliss is Woe?
Sweet was their death—with them to die was rife
With the last ecstasy of satiate life—
Beyond that death no immortality—
But sleep that pondereth and is not "to be"—
And there—oh! may my weary spirit dwell—
Apart from Heaven's Eternity—and yet how far from Hell!
What guilty spirit, in what shrubbery dim,
Heard not the stirring summons of that hymn?
But two: they fell: for Heaven no grace imparts
To those who hear not for their beating hearts.
A maiden-angel and her seraph-lover—
O! where (and ye may seek the wide skies over)
Was Love, the blind, near sober Duty known?
Unguided Love hath fallen—'mid "tears of perfect moan."
He was a goodly spirit—he who fell:
A wanderer by moss-y-mantled well—
A gazer on the lights that shine above—
A dreamer in the moonbeam by his love:
What wonder? for each star is eye-like there,

And looks so sweetly down on Beauty's hair—
And they, and ev'ry mossy spring were holy
To his love-haunted heart and melancholy.
The night had found (to him a night of woe)
Upon a mountain crag, young Angelo—
Beetling it bends athwart the solemn sky,
And scowls on starry worlds that down beneath it lie.
Here sate he with his love—his dark eye bent
With eagle gaze along the firmament:
Now turn'd it upon her—but ever then
It trembled to the orb of Earth again.

"Ianthe, dearest, see! how dim that ray!
How lovely 'tis to look so far away!
She seem'd not thus upon that autumn eve
I left her gorgeous halls—nor mourn'd to leave.
That eve—that eve—I should remember well—
The sun-ray dropp'd, in Lemnos, with a spell
On th' Arabesque carving of a gilded hall
Wherein I sate, and on the draperied wall—
And on my eye-lids—O the heavy light!
How drowsily it weigh'd them into night!
On flowers, before, and mist, and love they ran
With Persian Saadi in his Gulistan:
But O that light!—I slumber'd—Death, the while,
Stole o'er my senses in that lovely isle
So softly that no single silken hair
Awoke that slept—or knew that he was there.
The last spot of Earth's orb I trod upon
Was a proud temple call'd the Parthenon—
More beauty clung around her column'd wall
Than ev'n thy glowing bosom beats withal,
And when old Time my wing did disenthral
Thence sprang I—as the eagle from his tower,
And years I left behind me in an hour.
What time upon her airy bounds I hung
One half the garden of her globe was flung

Unrolling as a chart unto my view—
Tenantless cities of the desert too!
Ianthe, beauty crowded on me then.
And half I wish'd to be again of men."
"My Angelo! and why of them to be?
A brighter dwelling-place is there for thee—
And greener fields than in yon world above.
And woman's loveliness—and passionate love."

"But, list, Ianthe! when the air so soft
Fail'd, as my pennon'd spirit leapt aloft.
Perhaps my brain grew dizzy—but the world
I left so late was into chaos hurl'd—
Sprang from her station, on the winds apart,
And roll'd, a flame, the fiery Heaven athwart.
Methought, my sweet one, then I ceased to soar
And fell—not swiftly as I rose before,
But with a downward, tremulous motion thro'
Light, brazen rays, this golden star unto!
Nor long the measure of my falling hours,
For nearest of all stars was thine to ours—
Dread star! that came, amid a night of mirth,
A red Dædalion on the timid Earth.

"We came—and to thy Earth—but not to us
Be given our lady's bidding to discuss:
We came, my love; around, above, below,
Gay fire-fly of the night we come and go.
Nor ask a reason save the angel-nod
She grants to us, as granted by her God—
But, Angelo, than thine grey Time unfurl'd
Never his fairy wing o'er fairier world!
Dim was its little disk, and angel eyes
Alone could see the phantom in the skies.
When first Al Aaraaf knew her course to be
Headlong thitherward o'er the starry sea—
But when its glory swell'd upon the sky,
As glowing Beauty's bust beneath man's eye,

We paus'd before the heritage of men,
And thy star trembled—as doth Beauty then!"

Thus, in discourse, the lovers whiled away
The night that waned and waned and brought no day.
They fell: for Heaven to them no hope imparts
Who hear not for the beating of their hearts.

Tamerlane

Kind solace in a dying hour!
Such, father, is not (now) my theme—
I will not madly deem that power
Of Earth may shrive me of the sin
Unearthly pride hath revell'd in—
I have no time to dote or dream:
You call it hope—that fire of fire!
It is but agony of desire:
If I *can* hope—Oh God! I can—
Its fount is holier—more divine—
I would not call thee fool, old man,
But such is not a gift of thine.

Know thou the secret of a spirit
Bow'd from its wild pride into shame.
O yearning heart! I did inherit
Thy withering portion with the fame,
The searing glory which hath shone
Amid the Jewels of my throne,
Halo of Hell! and with a pain
Not hell shall make me fear again—

O craving heart, for the lost flowers
And sunshine of my summer hours!
The undying voice of that dead time,
With its interminable chime.
Rings, in the spirit of a spell,

Upon thy emptiness—a knell.

I have not always been as now:
The fever'd diadem on my brow
I claim'd and won usurpingly—
Hath not the same fierce heirdom given
Rome to the Caesar—this to me?
The heritage of a kingly mind,
And a proud spirit which hath striven
Triumphantly with human kind.

On mountain soil I first drew life:
The mists of the Taglay have shed
Nightly their dews upon my head,
And, I believe, the wingèd strife
And tumult of the headlong air
Have nestled in my very hair.

So late from Heaven—that dew—it fell
('Mid dreams of an unholy night)
Upon me with the touch of Hell,
While the red flashing of the light
From clouds that hung, like banners, o'er,
Appeared to my half-closing eye
The pageantry of monarchy.
And the deep trumpet-thunder's roar
Came hurriedly upon me, telling
Of human battle, where my voice,
My own voice, silly child!—was swelling
(O! how my spirit would rejoice,
And leap within me at the cry)
The battle-cry of Victory!

The rain came down upon my head
Unshelter'd—and the heavy wind
Rendered me mad and deaf and blind.
It was but man, I thought, who shed
Laurels upon me: and the rush—
The torrent of the chilly air

Gurgled within my ear the crush
Of empires—with the captive's prayer—
The hum of suitors—and the tone
Of flattery 'round a sovereign's throne.

My passions, from that hapless hour,
Usurp'd a tyranny which men
Have deem'd, since I have reach'd to power,
My innate nature—be it so:
But, father, there liv'd one who, then,
Then—in my boyhood—when their fire
Burn'd with a still intenser glow
(For passion must, with youth, expire)
E'en *then* who knew this iron heart
In woman's weakness had a part.

I have no words—alas!—to tell
The loveliness of loving well!
Nor would I now attempt to trace
The more than beauty of a face
Whose lineaments, upon my mind.
Are shadows on th' unstable wind:
Thus I remember having dwelt
Some page of early lore upon.
With loitering eye, till I have felt
The letters—with their meaning—melt
To fantasies—with none.

O, she was worthy of all love!
Love—as in infancy was mine—
'Twas such as angel minds above
Might envy; her young heart the shrine
On which my every hope and thought
Were incense—then a goodly gift,
For they were childish and upright—
Pure as her young example taught:
Why did I leave it, and, adrift,
Trust to the fire within, for light?

We grew in age—and love—together—
Roaming the forest, and the wild;
My breast her shield in wintry weather—
And, when the friendly sunshine smil'd,
And she would mark the opening skies,
I saw no Heaven—but in her eyes.

Young Love's first lesson is—the heart:
For 'mid that sunshine, and those smiles,
When, from our little cares apart.
And laughing at her girlish wiles,
I'd throw me on her throbbing breast,
And pour my spirit out in tears—
There was no need to speak the rest—
No need to quiet any fears
Of her—who ask'd no reason why,
But turn'd on me her quiet eye!

Yet *more* than worthy of the love
My spirit struggle'd with, and strove,
When, on the mountain peak, alone.
Ambition lent it a new tone—
I had no being—but in thee:
The world, and all it did contain
In the earth—the air—the sea—
Its joy—its little lot of pain
That was new pleasure the ideal,
Dim, vanities of dreams by night—
And dimmer nothings which were real—
(Shadows—and a more shadowy light!)
Parted upon their misty wings,
And, so, confusedly, became
Thine image and—a name—a name!
Two separate—yet most intimate things.

I was ambitious—have you known
The passion, father? You have not:
A cottager, I mark'd a throne

Of half the world as all my own.
And murmur'd at such lowly lot—
But, just like any other dream.
Upon the vapour of the dew
My own had past, did not the beam
Of beauty which did while it thro'
The minute—the hour—the day—oppress
My mind with double loveliness.

We walk'd together on the crown
Of a high mountain which look'd down
Afar from its proud natural towers
Of rock and forest, on the hills—
The dwindled hills! begirt with bowers
And shouting with a thousand rills.

I spoke to her of power and pride,
But mystically—in such guise
That she might deem it nought beside
The moment's converse; in her eyes
I read, perhaps too carelessly—
A mingled feeling with my own—
The flush on her bright cheek, to me
Seem'd to become a queenly throne
Too well that I should let it be
Light in the wilderness alone.

I wrapp'd myself in grandeur then
And donn'd a visionary crown
Yet it was not that Fantasy
Had thrown her mantle over me—
But that, among the rabble—men,
Lion ambition is chain'd down—
And crouches to a keeper's hand—
Not so in deserts where the grand—
The wild—the terrible conspire
With their own breath to fan his fire.
Look 'round thee now on Samarcand!—

Is she not queen of Earth? her pride
Above all cities? in her hand
Their destinies? in all beside
Of glory which the world hath known
Stands she not nobly and alone?
Falling—her veriest stepping-stone
Shall form the pedestal of a throne—
And who her sovereign? Timour—he
Whom the astonished people saw
Striding o'er empires haughtily
A diadem'd outlaw!

O, human love! thou spirit given,
On Earth, of all we hope in Heaven!
Which fall'st into the soul like rain
Upon the Siroc-wither'd plain,
And, failing in thy power to bless.
But leav'st the heart a wilderness!
Idea! which bindest life around
With music of so strange a sound
And beauty of so wild a birth—
Farewell! for I have won the Earth.

When Hope, the eagle that tower'd, could see
No cliff beyond him in the sky.
His pinions were bent droopingly—
And homeward turn'd his soften'd eye.
'Twas sunset: when the sun will part
There comes a sullenness of heart
To him who still would look upon
The glory of the summer sun.
That soul will hate the ev'ning mist
So often lovely, and will list
To the sound of the coming darkness (known
To those whose spirits harken) as one
Who, in a dream of night, *would* fly
But *cannot* from a danger nigh.

What tho' the moon—the white moon
Shed all the splendour of her noon.
Her smile is chilly—and *her* beam.
In that time of dreariness, will seem
(So like you gather in your breath)
A portrait taken after death.

And boyhood is a summer sun
Whose waning is the dreariest one—
For all we live to know is known
And all we seek to keep hath flown—
Let life, then, as the day-flower, fall
With the noon-day beauty—which is all.

I reach'd my home—my home no more—
For all had flown who made it so.
I pass'd from out its mossy door.
And, tho' my tread was soft and low,
A voice came from the threshold stone
Of one whom I had earlier known—
O, I defy thee. Hell, to show
On beds of fire that burn below,
An humbler heart—a deeper woe.

Father, I firmly do believe—
I *know*—for Death who comes for me
From regions of the blest afar,
Where there is nothing to deceive.
Hath left his iron gate ajar.
And rays of truth you cannot see
Are flashing thro' Eternity—
I do believe that Eblis hath
A snare in every human path—
Else how, when in the holy grove
I wandered of the idol. Love,
Who daily scents his snowy wings
With incense of burnt offerings
From the most unpolluted things,

Whose pleasant bowers are yet so riven
Above with trellis'd rays from Heaven
No mote may shun—no tiniest fly—
The light'ning of his eagle eye—
How was it that Ambition crept,
Unseen, amid the revels there.
Till growing bold, he laughed and leapt
In the tangles of Love's very hair?

Annabel Lee

It was many and many a year ago,
In a kingdom by the sea,
That a maiden there lived whom you may know
By the name of Annabel Lee;—
And this maiden she lived with no other thought
Than to love and be loved by me.

She was a child and *I* was a child.
In this kingdom by the sea,
But we loved with a love that was more than love—
I and my Annabel Lee—
With a love that the wingèd seraphs of Heaven
Coveted her and me.

And this was the reason that, long ago.
In this kingdom by the sea,
A wind blew out of a cloud,' by night
Chilling my Annabel Lee; .
So that her high-born kinsmen came
And bore her away from me,
To shut her up in a sepulchre
In this kingdom by the sea.

The angels, not half so happy in Heaven,
Went envying her and me:—
Yes! that was the reason (as all men know,
In this kingdom by the sea)
That the wind came out of the cloud, chilling
And killing my Annabel Lee.

But our love it was stronger by far than the love
Of those who were older than we—
Of many far wiser than we—
And neither the angels in Heaven above,
Nor the demons down under the sea,
Can ever dissever my soul from the soul
Of the beautiful Annabel Lee:—

For the moon never beams without bringing me dreams
Of the beautiful Annabel Lee;
And the stars never rise but I see the bright eyes
Of the beautiful Annabel Lee;
And so, all the night-tide, I lie down by the side
Of my darling, my darling, *my life* and my bride
In her sepulchre there by the sea—
In her tomb by the sounding sea.

For Annie

Thank Heaven! the crisis—
The danger is past,
And the lingering illness
Is over at last—
And the fever called "Living"
Is conquered at last.

Sadly, I know
I am shorn of my strength.
And no muscle I move
As I lie at full length—
But no matter!—I feel
I am better at length.

And I rest so composedly
Now, in my bed,
That any beholder
Might fancy me dead—
Might start at beholding me.
Thinking me dead.

The moaning and groaning,
The sighing and sobbing.
Are quieted now,
With that horrible throbbing
At heart:—Ah that horrible,
Horrible throbbing!

The sickness—the nausea—
The pitiless pain—

Have ceased with the fever
That maddened my brain—
With the fever called "Living"
That burned in my brain.

And oh! of all tortures
That torture the worst
Has abated—the terrible
Torture of thirst
For the napthaline river
Of Passion accurst:—
I have drank of a water
That quenches all thirst:—

Of a water that flows,
With a lullaby sound,
From a spring but a very few
Feet under ground—
From a cavern not very far
Down under ground.

But ah! let it never
Be foolishly said
That my room it is gloomy
And narrow my bed;
For man never slept
In a different bed—
And, to *sleep*, you must slumber
In just such a bed.

My tantalised spirit
Here blandly reposes,
Forgetting, or never
Regretting, its roses—
Its old agitations
Of myrtles and roses:

For now, while so quietly
Lying, it fancies
A holier odour

About it, of pansies—
A rosemary odour,
Commingled with pansies—
With rue and the beautiful
Puritan pansies.

And so it lies happily,
Bathing in many
A dream of the truth
And the beauty of Annie—
Drowned in a bath
Of the tresses of Annie.
She tenderly kissed me,
She fondly caressed.
And then I fell gently
To sleep on her breast—
Deeply to sleep
From the heaven of her breast.

When the light was extinguished.
She covered me warm,
And she prayed to the angels
To keep me from harm—
To the queen of the angels
To shield me from harm.

And I lie so composedly,
Now, in my bed,
(Knowing her love)
That you fancy me dead—
And I rest so contentedly.
Now, in my bed,
(With her love at my breast)
That you fancy me dead—
That you shudder to look at me.
Thinking me dead:—

But my heart it is brighter
Than all of the many

Stars in the sky.
For it sparkles with Annie—
It glows with the light
Of the love of my Annie—
With the thought of the light
Of the eyes of my Annie.

Spirits of the Dead

1

Thy soul shall find itself alone
'Mid dark thoughts of the gray tombstone—
Not one, of all the crowd, to pry
Into thine hour of secrecy:

2

Be silent in that solitude,
Which is not loneliness—for then
The spirits of the dead who stood
In life before thee are again
In death around thee—and their will
Shall overshadow thee: be still.

3

The night—tho' clear—shall frown—,
And the stars shall look not down.
From their high thrones in the heaven,
With light like Hope to mortals given—
But their red orbs, without beam,
To thy weariness shall seem
As a burning and a fever
Which would cling to thee for ever.

4

Now are thoughts thou shalt not banish—
Now are visions ne'er to vanish—
From thy spirit shall they pass
No more—like dew-drops from the grass.

5

The breeze—the breath of God—is still—
And the mist upon the hill
Shadowy—shadowy—yet unbroken,
Is a symbol and a token—
How it hangs upon the trees,
A mystery of mysteries!

The Haunted Palace

In the greenest of our valleys
By good angels tenanted,
Once a fair and stately palace—
Radiant palace—reared its head.
In the monarch Thought's dominion—
It stood there!
Never seraph spread a pinion,
Over fabric half so fair!

Banners yellow, glorious, golden.
On its roof did float and flow,
(This—all this—was in the olden
Time long ago,)
And every gentle air that dallied,
In that sweet day,
Along the ramparts plumed and pallid,
A wingèd odour went away.

Wanderers in that happy valley.
Through two luminous windows, saw
Spirits moving musically.
To a lute's well-tunèd law.
Round about a throne where, sitting,
Porphyrogene,
In state his glory well befitting.
The ruler of the realm was seen.

And all with pearl and ruby glowing
Was the fair palace door,

Through which came flowing, flowing, flowing
And sparkling evermore,
A troop of Echoes, whose sweet duty
Was but to sing,
In voices of surpassing beauty.
The wit and wisdom of their king.

But evil things, in robes of sorrow,
Assailed the monarch's high estate.
(Ah, let us mourn!—for never morrow
Shall dawn upon him, desolate!)
And round about his home the glory
That blushed and bloomed
Is but a dim-remembered story
Of the old-time entombed.

And travellers, now, within that valley.
Through the encrimson'd windows see
Vast forms that move fantastically
To a discordant melody.
While, like a ghastly rapid river,
Through the pale door
A hideous throng rush out forever
And laugh—but smile no more.

The Conqueror Worm

Lo! 'tis a gala night
Within the lonesome latter years!
An angel throng, bewinged, bedight
In veils, and drowned in tears,
Sit in a theatre, to see
A play of hopes and fears.
While the orchestra breathes fitfully
The music of the spheres.

Mimes, in the form of God on high.
Mutter and mumble low.
And hither and thither fly—
Mere puppets they, who come and go
At bidding of vast formless things
That shift the scenery to and fro.
Flapping from out their Condor wings
Invisible woe!

That motley drama—oh, be sure
It shall not be forgot!
With its phantom chased for evermore,
By a crowd that seize it not.
Through a circle that ever returneth in
To the self-same spot.
And much of Madness, and more of Sin,
And Horror the soul of the plot.

But see, amid the mimic rout
A crawling shape intrude!

A blood-red thing that writhes from out
The scenic solitude!
It writhes!—it writhes!—with mortal pangs
The mimes become its food,
And seraphs sob at vermin fangs
In human gore imbued.

Out—out are the lights—out all!
And, over each quivering form,
The curtain, a funeral pall.
Comes down with the rush of a storm,
While the angels, all pallid and wan.
Uprising, unveiling, affirm
That the play is the tragedy, "*Man*,"
And its hero the Conqueror Worm.

The Skeleton-Hand

(Attributed to Poe-from *The Yankee*, August, 1829)

Lo! one is on the mountain side,
While the clouds are passing by—
With their black wings flapping heavily,
Like eagles in the sky;
Or lying up in the forest trees,
And waiting there for the mountain-breeze.

And now he passes through the clouds—
And up to the mountain-top.
Nor yet to look for the joyous sun
Does the hasty traveller stop.

But he leapeth down in the broken path
With a step as light and free—
As ever in his days of mirth,
In the dance and revelry.

Why endeth he his hasty speed?
Why stoppeth on his way?
In truth it is a fearful thing.
For human tongue to say.

He fears that toward him pointeth there,
A fleshless human hand;
Where the mountain rains have swept away.
Its covering of sand;
That hand his very soul doth stir,
For it proveth him a murderer.

Ay long ago on the mountain side,

The fearful deed was done;
And the murderer thought him safe, that none
Could see, save the broad bright sun,
As he rolled in the heavens the dead above,
And flooded the earth with his rays of love.

Now lifted he his clouded eye,
To the mountain crests behind;
And o'er them came the broad black clouds,
Upheaving with the wind;
And on them their thick darkness spread—
A crown upon the mountain's head.

And then shone out the flaming sun,
From the waters of the sea;
And God's own bow came in the clouds.
And looked out gloriously;
But its colours were of woe and wrath,.
That threw their light o'er the murderer's path.

And now God's chariots—the clouds,
Came rolling down with might;
Their wheels like many horsemen were,
In battle or in flight.
And yet no power to move hath *he*,
His soul is in an agony.

Over the murderer and dead
They rolled their mighty host;
Old ocean's waves come not so thick,
By northern tempests tost.

Forth from their mighty bosom came,
A flash of heaven's wrath.
And away the heavy clouds—and sun.
Rolled from the murder-path.
And the sun shone out where the murderer lay,
Before the dead in the narrow way—
With his hand all seared, and his breast torn bare—
God's vengeance had been working there.

Ulalume—A Ballad

The skies they were ashen and sober;
The leaves they were crisped and sere—
The leaves they were withering and sere:
It was night, in the lonesome October
Of my most immemorial year:
It was hard by the dim lake of Auber,
In the misty mid region of Weir—
It was down by the dank tarn of Auber,
In the ghoul-haunted woodland of Weir.

Here once, through an alley Titanic,
Of cypress, I roamed with my Soul—
Of cypress, with Psyche, my Soul.
These were days when my heart was volcanic
As the scoriac rivers that roll—
As the lavas that restlessly roll
Their sulphurous currents down Yaanek
In the ultimate climes of the Pole—
That groan as they roll down Mount Yaanek
In the realms of the Boreal Pole.

Our talk had been serious and sober.
But our thoughts they were palsied and sere—
Our memories were treacherous and sere;
For we knew not the month was October,
And we marked not the night of the year—
(Ah, night of all nights in the year!)
We noted not the dim lake of Auber,

(Though once we had journeyed down here)
We remembered not the dank tarn of Auber,
Nor the ghoul-haunted woodland of Weir. ,

And now, as the night was senescent
And star-dials pointed to morn—
As the star-dials hinted of morn—
At the end of our path a liquescent
And nebulous lustre was born,
Out of which a miraculous crescent
Arose with a duplicate horn—
Astarte's bediamonded crescent
Distinct with its duplicate horn.

And I said—"She is warmer than Dian;
She rolls through an ether of sighs—
She revels in a region of sighs—
She has seen that the tears are not dry on
These cheeks, where the worm never dies,
And has come past the stars of the Lion
To point us the path to the skies—
To the Lethean peace of the skies—
Come up, in despite of the Lion,
To shine on us with her bright eyes—
Come up through the lair of the Lion,
With love in her luminous eyes."

But Psyche, uplifting her finger,
Said—"Sadly this star I mistrust—,
Her pallor I strangely mistrust—
Ah, hasten!—Ah, let us not linger!
Ah, fly!—let us fly!—for we must."
In terror she spoke, letting sink her
Wings till they trailed in the dust—
In agony sobbed; letting sink her
Plumes till they trailed in the dust—
Till they sorrowfully trailed in the dust.

I replied—"This is nothing but dreaming:

Let us on by this tremulous light!
Let us bathe in this crystalline light!
Its Sybillic splendour is beaming
With Hope and in Beauty tonight:—
See! it flickers up the sky through the night!
Ah, we safely may trust to its gleaming,
And be sure it will lead us aright—
We surely may trust to a gleaming,
That cannot but guide us aright.
Since it flickers up to Heaven through the night."

Thus I pacified Psyche and kissed her.
And tempted her out of her gloom—
And conquered her scruples and gloom;
And we passed to the end of a *vista*.
But were stopped by the door of a tomb—
By the door of a legended tomb;
And I said—"What is written, sweet sister,
On the door of this legended tomb?"
She replied—"Ulalume—Ulalume!—
'Tis the vault of thy lost Ulalume!"

Then my heart it grew ashen and sober
As the leaves that were crispèd and sere—
As the leaves that were withering and sere;
And I cried—"It was surely October
On *this* very night of last year
That I journeyed—I journeyed down here!—
That I brought a dread burden down here—
On this night of all nights in the year,
Ah! what demon hath tempted me here?
Well I know, now, this dim lake of Auber—
This misty mid region of Weir—
Well I know, now, this dank tarn of Auber—
This ghoul-haunted woodland of Weir."

Said *we*, then—the two, then—"Ah, can it
Have been that the woodlandish ghouls—

The pitiful, the Merciful ghouls—
To bar up our way and to ban it
From the secret that lies in these wolds—
From the thing that lies hidden in these wolds—
Have drawn up the spectre of a planet
From the limbo of lunary souls,
This sinfully scintillant planet
From the Hell of the planetary souls?"

The Magician

(Attributed to Poe-from *The Yankee*, December, 1829.)

Thou dark, sea-stirring storm,
Whence comest thou in thy might—
Nay—wait, thou dim and dreamy form—
Storm spirit, I call thee—'tis mine of right—
Arrest thee in thy troubled flight.

STORM SPIRIT

Thou askest me whence I came—
I came o'er the sleeping sea,
It roused at my torrent of storm and flame,
And it howled aloud in its agony.
And swelled to the sky—that sleeping sea.

Thou askest me what I met—
A ship from the Indian shore,
A tall proud ship with her sails all set—
Far down in the sea that ship I bore.
My storms wild rushing wings before.

And her men will forever lie.
Below the unquiet sea;
And tears will dim full many an eye,
Of those who shall widows and orphans be,
And their days be years—for their misery.

A boat with a starving crew—
For hunger they howled and swore;
While the blood from a fellow's veins they drew

I came upon them with rush and roar—
Far under the waves that boat I bore.

Two ships in a fearful fight—
When a hundred guns did flash
I came upon them—no time for flight—
But under the sea their timbers crash
And over their guns the wild waters dash

A wretch on a single plank—
And I tossed him on the shore—
A night and a day of the sea he drank,
But the wearied wretch to the land I bore—
And now he walketh the earth once more—

MAGICIAN

Storm spirit—go on thy path—
The spirit has spread his wings—
And comes on the sea with a rush of wrath,
As a war horse when he springs—
And over the earth his winds he flings—
And over the earth—nor stop nor stay—
The winds of the storm king go out on their way.

www.ingramcontent.com/pod-product-compliance
Lightning Source LLC
Chambersburg PA
CBHW030922020726
47498CB00001B/70

* 9 7 8 1 7 8 2 8 2 1 8 1 6 *